The Sundered Isle

BOOKS BY ELDON THOMPSON

THE LEGEND OF ASAHIEL
The Crimson Sword
The Obsidian Key
The Divine Talisman

WARDER
The Ukinhan Wilds
The Blackmoon Shards
The Sundered Isle

WARDER
III
THE SUNDERED ISLE

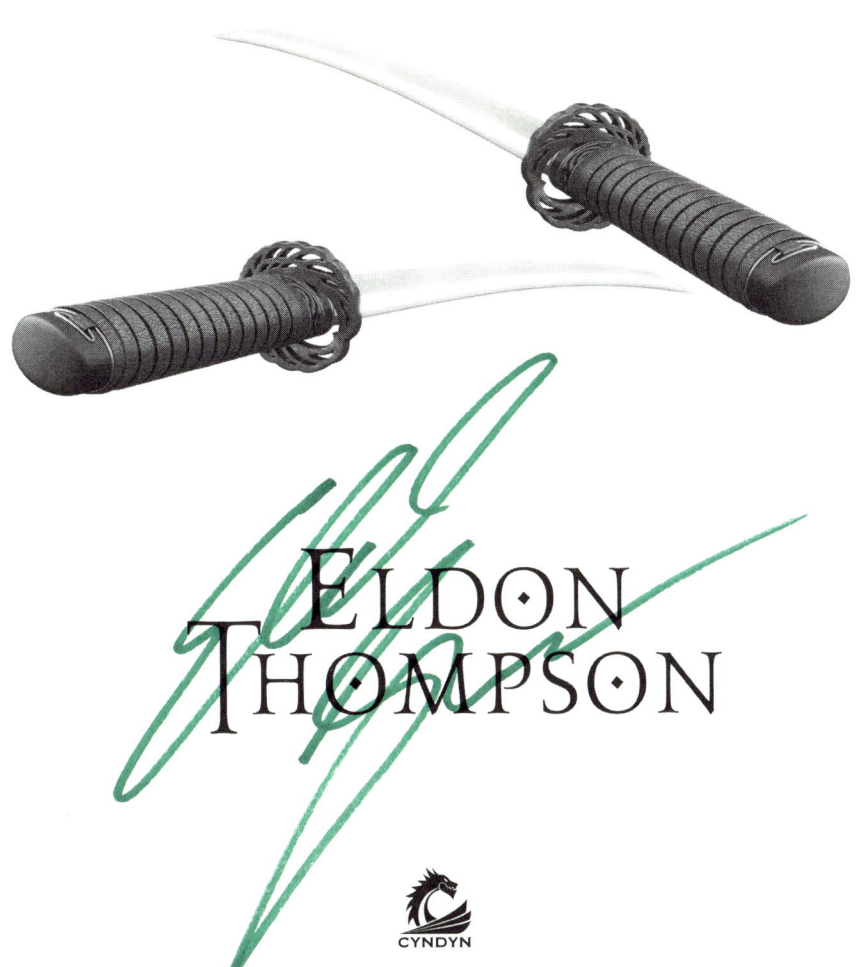

ELDON THOMPSON

CYNDYN

THE SUNDERED ISLE
Copyright © 2018 by Eldon Thompson
All rights reserved

This book is a work of fiction. All characters, events, and dialogue depicted herein are derived from the author's imagination. Any resemblance to actual persons or events, whether living or dead, present or past, is entirely coincidental.

Cover illustration by Daren Horley
Addaranth map by Maxime Plasse

Library of Congress Control Number: 2018903353

ISBN 978-1-948825-02-3
Trade Hardcover – Limited Edition

Published by Cyndyn; Irvine, California
Printed in the United States of America

Prologue

THE SCREAMS INTENSIFIED as she descended along the scabrous corridor. A chorus of agony and desperation. Of mewling pleas punctuated by shrill howls and spine-rattling shrieks. Echoes clawed at the tunnel walls as they scrabbled past. Flush with despair. Urgent with need. Seeking escape, only to wither in the coring void.

A song of torment.

Succulent to the ear.

She turned the corner at the base of a crude stair. Dathus and Horvus, together serving sentry, stiffened as she entered their view, sable faces gleaming in the torchlight like burnished blackwood. Horvus moved to open the ironbound door they warded. Dathus flattened himself to one side. Both clapped fist to heart and dipped chin to chest as she brushed by, her brisk passage stirring the flames ensconced along the walls.

Through the door, a stench assailed her. Of burning hair and seared flesh. Of sweat and blood and entrails. Of rancid hopes and festering fears. Deeply, she inhaled.

The aroma of conquest.

As she neared the bank of cells, the song reached its crescendo. Wails and bellows underscored now by plaintive moans and pitiful whimpers. Amid these chords of frailty and cowardice, the means of their suffering. The snap of bone. The hiss of hot iron. The clangor of spikes and chains. The wrench and squeak of rope and pulley. Harsh, discordant, yet all part of the same tune. Strains of a melody that hailed her triumph, that sent chills of victory worming through her flesh.

In a cavernous chamber to her right, Baccus and Pirrus were tending their garden of human wreaths—Addaran landsnakes lashed naked to spinning wheels, struck by hammer until their broken limbs were mashed and twisted in grotesque angles amid the spokes, then left to writhe and moan in a withering torment meant to endure for days.

At this particular moment, Baccus carried the hammer, while Pirrus inspected the wilted victims. Watering those in need. Sussing out the dead by slapping at mangled appendages or tugging at their hair. Few resembled human form.

"This one's dead," he announced, when a senseless wretch, unspeakably gnarled and knotted, failed to respond.

"Ivory fist says he's breath in there yet," Baccus argued.

"Wagered."

She paused, observing as Pirrus withdrew from the tangled ruin, and Baccus hefted his hammer. The strike splintered an already pulverized forearm—and raised a ragged yowl from the victim.

Baccus grinned fiercely, while Pirrus frowned and shook his head. In doing so, he caught sight of her—quickly nodding and thumping a sharp salute. Baccus rounded and did the same.

"You owe him a fist," she said.

Pirrus bowed again. "Yes, my kiros."

"Half pay for dead wreathes," she reminded them, and left them to their work.

"Overlord," they replied in unison, offering a parting salute.

Venturing forward along the central hall, she found more of the same. Chambers to either side filled with Addarans put to various forms of torture. Some were being actively tended with saws, peelers, screws, or vices. Others had been abandoned to cradles or collars, some of which teased the victim with survival so long as their own stamina held. Still others had been encased with insects, crabs, or agitated vermin, to be slowly stung, torn, or gnawed to death.

Several were being actively interrogated. Others lay beyond questioning, their horror persisting merely to be witnessed by others. Regardless, each treatment seemed crueler than the last, the agony of each victim more severe. As she had commanded. A menagerie of pain. One to fill this hole with every conceivable stench and ear-splitting cry. Burns, bruises, lacerations. Shattered bones and severed appendages. Men awash in one another's blood, bowels, and vomit, or slathered in their own.

But it was their gazes she sought, from which she derived a richer pleasure. Red-veined eyes shuttered by bruising or swollen with tears. Where she could peer past the carnage and into that purer well of raw anguish. Where their prayers for death burned with increasing fervor.

And went unanswered.

Deeper within the den, she found at last her chief inquisitor, overseeing Samrus's application of a knee splitter. The landsnake strapped to the chair dared look to her arrival in hope.

"Thrassus," she said. "I would see the general."

"Overlord," he acknowledged, and rose to lead the way.

"Proceed," she bade Samrus, and smiled as the pathetic hope curdled upon the snake's pale face.

Overwrought. Petty. Unnecessary. She cared not how others might describe this effort. A long time had she and her people sought retribution against their Addaran betrayers. Generation after generation, over the course of one hundred and ninety-two years. Here at last, victory. The annals would record that it was she, Sabrynne Stormweaver, Great Grendavan the Eighth, who had finally restored the Grenarr to their ancestral homeland. How she had conceived and then executed a daring, multifaceted plan that had repaid the landsnakes' treachery and seen them driven from their stolen nest. The city of Avenell was now hers, and with it, the heart of the isle of Grenah.

As such, she had no intention of repeating the mistake the Addarans had made by merely driving her people from the isle's shores. Her forces had held the city for more than two weeks now. But not two hours had marked its fall before she had turned eye to those who might later rally against her.

Determined not merely to supplant her hated enemies, but to eradicate them.

"Have we gleaned nothing of value?" she asked of Thrassus, as he plucked a lantern from the wall and led her even deeper into the torture grounds.

"Only chaff," her hulking inquisitor huffed. "Kernels aplenty, but naught more than empty husks."

Sabrynne nodded, seeing no reason to question his assessment. She hadn't charged him with oversight of this task for either his stomach or imagination—formidable as they were—but for his uncanny ability to measure and sift truth from lie. His previous reports had established already the relative ease with which these landsnake tongues were loosened. But the whole of their hissing and wagging had thus far proved contradictory and disjointed. Most of these rags and wretches simply lacked the information she required, and so offered up tales in the desperate hope of appeasing their tormentors.

"Word from Grenathrok?" Thrassus asked.

"East of rudder. Barkavius and the fleet are en route." *Having overcome some minor complications,* she might have added, as detailed in the steward's message. Regrettable, in some respects. But the overall gains would seem to far outstrip their losses. Either way, her faithful inquisitor need not be troubled, for all the bearing such dealings had upon his task.

Thrassus swelled with the news, turning his head—spattered in Addaran blood—to offer her a grateful smile. His wives and children would be among the arriving colonists. To be reunited after nearly a year's separation. Because of *her* foresight and tenacity.

Their stroll through the blood-soaked warren ended at another ironbound door. The rusty latch bolt shrieked a lament as Thrassus wrenched it free of its housing. The door squealed a similar protest, but relented to his powerful shove.

His lantern pushed back the veil of shadows to reveal the lone figure housed within. The figure stirred. General Ohrma. A man for whom her father had borne a grudging respect. A once-worthy adversary who had repelled countless Grenarr landing attempts over his decades of service to the Addaran crown—including the ill-fated spring invasion hailed as the Blood Tide, now more than twenty years past, in the One Hundred Sixty-Seventh Year of Exile.

Of stark humiliation to her proud people, as most of the blood that season had been their own.

It had culminated not long after in her father being deposed by the Clamcrusher, Uruthus, who had seen his great vessel burned to cinders, her elder siblings butchered, and herself, a mere waif, escaped with her infant brother to become outcasts. The tribulations that had followed . . .

To think on them now caused her to smile. So long ago.

She admired her father to this day through the foolish eyes of a devoted young daughter. Nonetheless, she found it difficult to reconcile his description of the Addaran general with the decaying remnant of a man before her. Immersed in a tub to his shoulders. Force-fed milk and honey, until steeped in a stagnant stew of his own liquid excrement. His face lathered with the excess, to draw the mask of flies he now wore—a nest to maggots and their larvae. A breeding ground he was, for filth and disease, taking root in every orifice. Another rag who prayed vainly for death.

"Raise him," she commanded.

Hanging his lantern on a hook, Thrassus circuited the tub, loosing the cords whose cinched lengths—attached to a neck collar—anchored the former general in place. The inquisitor then worked his way to a whim at the back of the chamber and wound it in a steady circle, reeling in a length of chain looped through an overhead ring, which in turn drew Ohrma skyward by a set of cuffs binding his wrists.

Sabrynne snorted at the putrid stench given rein as the general was hefted from the foul soup. Clouds of flies, disturbed by the unfamiliar tremors, flew free, buzzing their distress. A handful found their way to her. Brushing them aside, she stepped closer, defying her own disgust.

Ohrma scarcely stirred. Stripped and pale. Riddled with worms and rot. Seeming more than half dead, if not completely so.

"Softened, was my command," she said, filling her voice with irritation.

With all but the general's feet pulled from the tub, Thrassus latched the whim and took a nearby spear in hand. Exuding a cheerless confidence, he raked the spearhead against the top of Ohrma's shins, just below the knee. Sagging skin tore away in strips under its own swollen weight, sloughing from the exposed meat and bone. The general twitched. Then coughed. Then roused, bucking and kicking as if his legs had been set afire.

"Feeble will, overlord," Thrassus muttered, his own tone lacking apology.

The general opened his eyes, blinking against the sweet paste that had soured there, and against the maggots clinging to it. His kicking steadied. Not for lack of pain, given the rictus of his face, but for a lack of sustainable strength. Beneath leathery skin that had taken on the shriveled texture of rotting plums, the fruit of aged muscles had gone slack.

Sabrynne smirked. "He fought lustily enough when seeking to repel our incursion." She titled her head, angling her gaze to meet his. "Or is it that he overtaxed himself, having expended so much strength already in the course of his own revolt?"

She had triggered her long-brewing assault with a fleet of her warships, sent south through the Gorrethrian Sound. A retaliatory strike, it had seemed, for the Addarans' murder of a decoy they had believed to be the Grenarr overlord, Great Grendavan. In truth, a feint that had served to lure the bulk of King Kendarrion's forces north to reinforce the city of Indranell—thereby depleting those forces dedicated to defending the home city of Avenell.

Those who remained? Divided from within. Portraying herself as the Grenarr emissary assigned to oversee Kendarrion's adherence to the accord that would see his abducted heir returned unharmed, she had won open admission to the Pretender's court. A lamb among wolves, it would seem, were *she* not the one stalking *them*. Teasing, taunting, and otherwise flaunting herself among them, she had plowed a field of disgust and opposition in which to sow the seeds of civil discord. While the king himself protected her from those dissidents who would sooner see her killed or used for sport, her seeds had taken root, casting irrefutable light upon Kendarrion's incapacity to lead during this personal crisis involving his royal children.

Spurring his critics toward insurrection.

Once Avenell had been weakened by the deployment of the bulk of its military, an uprising was sprung by the opposing "Loyalists"—those who would see a stronger leader raised in Kendarrion's stead. A leader who would refuse the Grenarrian accord, built as it was upon an act of ransom. Who would sacrifice Prince Dethaniel and whomever else if it would deny the loathsome tar-skins so much as a toehold upon Addaran shores.

Ohrma, the retired general retained as Kendarrion's chief advisor, had served as that leader.

"Are you savoring your treatment?" she asked him, coaxing in her tone.

The faithless general fought to raise his head. A loll, he managed, as he swayed there in his shackles. Twice his mouth twitched as if to speak before words finally worked themselves free. "It is . . . no more . . . than I deserve."

Sabrynne scowled. For his sorrow and self-loathing, she brooked no sympathy. This, they had discussed already. "I asked you not to weep at me over the injustice wrought by your own hand. You might have quashed any attempt to betray your king, yet chose to spearhead the rebellion against him instead. That much was not my doing. Nor is it why you are here."

He tensed, shifted. An understanding, stripped from something she had said, emboldened him, lending him a spark of will. It glinted in his eyes and caused his lips to tighten with the barest hint of a mad smile. "My lord . . . is yet . . . beyond your reach."

"Nothing is beyond my reach. Time is all I require. The only thing your stubbornness serves is to prolong this ordeal." She flicked a knife from the sheath at her wrist, and used it to remove a leech from his thigh. "Where is Darr?"

Ohrma blinked, then looked away, clinging to his silence.

"You should know I've received word that your Princess Denariel is en route." The general's gaze lifted again, reflexive concern shaded by suspicion. "Captured by my chief steward," she explained. "If you will but inform me of your king's whereabouts, I will not only end your suffering, but I will spare her—his daughter and only surviving child—a torture less pleasant than your own."

"His Highness . . . Prince Dethaniel—"

"Dead. Slain upon my order, given wing the moment the city fell."

A penetrating sorrow crept across the general's brow, even as he strained to ward it off with desperate denial. A vein emerged along his reddening temple. His lower lip quivered.

"If you have any love for your king or his bloodline, you will do this."

She believed that love genuine, inasmuch as a treacherous landsnake was capable of it. By all accounts, Ohrma—keenly aware of the internal outcry to which his king was unwilling to listen—had been opposed to her people's ransom proposal from the outset, and advised Darr against it. Yet his personal loyalty had led him to stubbornly resist the notion of taking the crown by force, even as those within his city's hierarchy increasingly demanded it. It had taken considerable goading to realign his thinking, as she'd heard it. And *that* bolstered in no small measure by a professed belief that he might at some point restore power to Darr once the conflict had settled.

While this last may have been but a lie to assuage his guilty conscience, she believed—from his lips and others—that it was only with a heavy heart that he had, in the end, succumbed to their mounting pressure. His justification for personally advising Kendarrion to send the bulk of Avenell's garrison north? Not only to defend against the Grenarr landing at Indranell, but to execute his own takeover with minimal struggle and loss of life.

Convinced he was acting in his people's best interests.

She could see him struggling with a similar decision now. If her claims were true, did he owe it to his ruler and longtime friend to do what he could to spare the last of Darr's royal progeny some measure of pain? Surely, his confusion was bolstered by the effects of his own torment. As glimpsed in the gazes of his abused countrymen, she sensed the weaker part of him grasping at any thread of hope for ending his present anguish.

After a long moment of teary-eyed distress, his expression smoothed, a sheen of clarity overcoming his addled senses. "What drop of venom . . . from your tarred lips . . . can I take as truth?" He managed at last to heft his chin from his chest. "I will be no pawn . . . in your games. The best I can serve . . . is to die in His Majesty's stead . . . and greet my grave . . . knowing my people . . . still had a chance."

Vexing, truthful as it was. The Loyalist uprising had served well its primary purpose. During the mass confusion of the revolt, the city effectively torn in two, Sabrynne had sent a small, secret force to infiltrate and sabotage the Seagate. A battery of Grenarr ships, standing by and teeming with warriors, had thus been able to enter the bay and assault Avenell from within. Making possible her victory, where so many other forays by her people had failed.

But the attack had foundered in its secondary objective: to capture Kendarrion himself. Upon recognizing the Grenarr sneak attack through the bay, Ohrma had released the freshly deposed king with his deepest apologies, and mobilized instead a rearguard defense while Darr and a sizable contingent of city soldiers fled north. The fickle general's feeble rally had scarcely slowed the Grenarr invasion, but had succeeded in buying the Pretender's escape.

Scouts sent to track them had returned in failure or not at all. While fighting to secure the city, she had lacked numbers sufficient to the task. Bolstering those numbers in the days since had made no difference. Hers were warriors of the sea. Masters of wind and swell. Men and women who speared fish and wrestled sharks. Yet ill-equipped to scale mountain, meander through canyon, or slog through jungle while seeking sign of cowering landsnakes.

She had patrols scouring the main roads, of course, but had fully expected Darr to avoid those—to slink instead along some series of back trails like a harried animal. Well known as an enthusiastic explorer in his youth, he would seek in this hour of defeat to grasp at every perceived advantage, his knowledge of the surrounding landscape being chief among them.

Even now, with reinforcements pouring in, she was loath to spend Grenarr lives by sending them thrashing into the wilderness in vain pursuit. Like casting seeds into the wind and expecting them to take root. She had other tasks for which her warriors would be needed, and so had focused from the outset on a more targeted approach. With Ohrma and a host of fellow captives delivered to Thrassus and his inquisitors, she had expected to mine the information necessary to locate Darr and his flock. To pinpoint the royal rebel before he could reunite with his northern army at Indranell. To decapitate the most likely source of resistance and thereby strengthen her as-yet tenuous hold upon these shores.

Unable to sustain its weight, the general lowered his head. A crawling maggot fell from his matted white hair, only to join those infesting his beard. Sabrynne eyed its wriggling struggle, and considered. By now, she might be too late. It might be that the Pretender had already slipped through her loose net and found his way to that bastion of his in the north. And once empowered with his reserve army . . . A pitiless ruler. An aggrieved parent. Army? Were Darr more a man, a stick in hand would be sufficient with which to seek his revenge.

Her armada in the sound would continue to demand their attention, of course. Should the bulk remain at Indranell, she was inclined to let them rot, rather than waste lives trying to flush them out. But she harbored little doubt that they would mount a return. She knew too well what a dispossessed people, driven by a sense of vengeance, was capable of. Whomever their leader, they would at some point rally southward in an attempt to retake the capital. She could press to take some of the land between them now, but those who resisted would be experienced ground fighters who outnumbered her, knew the terrain better than she, and who would fight her every step of the way. Better to let them come to her so that she could ambush them at a time and place of her choosing.

To that end, the more she could learn about their movements and intent, the better prepared she would be to receive them. Unfortunately, her few spies amid that army were all but useless, with no easy means of contacting her from the field—and, more critically, no way to receive payment. For this and other reasons, she had placed the bulk of her confidence in Ohrma.

Quickly proving a wasted effort.

Sabrynne tapped her blade, still in hand, against her lip. Perhaps mistaking it as a sign of hostility, the general summoned another defiant breath.

"My pain . . . is well earned," he rasped. "Your torments . . . just punishment . . . for my foolish treachery."

A muted whisper of the same, tired refrain. As irksome as the persistent buzzing of flies or the pervasive stench of his bowels. Sabrynne had scoffed at his attempt at nobility in the beginning, and was unimpressed by it now. "An honorable man does not absolve himself. Nor laden his deeds with justification as you have."

"Honor . . . or not . . . you will kill me . . . before I betray my king . . . a second time."

Sabrynne eyed him dispassionately, as again his momentary strength failed. How much more could his wasted form tolerate? What chance that he might be swayed?

She glanced at Thrassus. Sensing her question, he shook his head.

It chafed her, the thought of his suffering gone numb. She had half a mind to have him hauled fully from that tub and nursed back to health, that she might begin again. But that could take weeks, time better spent devising a new plan. There were others she might use to track the craven king and his rebels. Others of a heartier constitution and more willing persuasion. None as well trusted by Darr, perhaps. But with Denariel set to be delivered . . . that would seem to open any number of possibilities. And Kronus . . . Kronus had proven malleable, and would be put to use, one way or another.

If her thickening patrols hunting along the northern road could continue to wall the Pretender off from his army, she might yet achieve her aims sooner rather than later, the fleshy pustule before her be damned.

She marked the blood dripping down his shins, as distant screams raked at the wells of her ears. A rivulet tracing a ridge of exposed bone spurred her decision.

"Thrassus. Deliver this festering sack to Baccus and Pirrus. Let us weave another wreath with which to welcome the princess's return."

With the day bending toward dusk, she returned to her royal quarters. Wending from dungeon bowels toward the palace's hilltop pinnacle. Ascending through cramped, windless tunnels rank with squalor; through broad, windowed halls stark in function; and finally through expansive, cushioned corridors perfumed and appointed for royal comfort. Arriving ultimately at a suite of chambers occupied just over a fortnight ago by the Pretender, but belonging now—like the rest of his stolen possessions—to her.

Along the way, she sent for Trathem.

She did not find him waiting, and so poured herself a wine to soften her thirst. Cup in hand, she retreated to a balcony to escape the mild din of craftsmen at work—chamberlain and stewards attended by draftsmen, stonemasons, carpenters, weavers, sculptors, jewelers, and other artisans, all laboring in some fashion to remove the stain of Darr's presence and remake the space more to her liking.

Facing south, she gazed down along the city's terraced hillsides and twisting roadways. Quiet, with a fair size of its former populace fled. The rest of the cornered landsnakes hunkered indoors, else risked the wrathful whims of her warriors. Only a handful of fires burned. Buildings wherein her forces had trapped rebel elements, or heaps of bodies caught out and slaughtered for their resistance. Fewer than the day before, she observed. Among the conquered civilians, grim acceptance was taking root.

Farther south, the descending sun cast a shimmering layer of molten gold upon the inner bay. So long closed to her, its inner shores were now being traced in slow, steady circuit by a handful of Grenarr Prowlers. At dock were four Marauders and a dozen Reavers. A meager fleet of Addaran ships had been completely destroyed—six in battle, and numerous others razed in their berths. Large craft and small. Royal and private. Too feeble to be of any meritable use, the vessels had served better as another sign of her superiority and will.

Another four Marauders, along with ten more Reavers and nearly a score of Prowlers, sailed the ocean waters nearby, most within a day's reach. Some had deposited a portion of their crews before taking up patrol routes along the lands beyond the Seagate. Others were still en route, not yet arrived. The latter included her colony ships, of course, along with the warships serving escort. Still two weeks out, or more, depending on the winds—and on how long it took for them to gather the Grenarr populations of the various atolls dotting the seas between Grenathrok, to the east, and Grenah, here in the west.

A voyage long-awaited. And, for all her eagerness, worth savoring. As, for many of her people, she intended it to be their last.

With the thought came a strange ache. An underlying pang reminding her that, triumphant as it might be, this momentous event marked a shift in the Grenarr way of life. After nearly two centuries of hard-fought lessons, the last thing she wanted was for her people to relinquish their dominion over the seas. Now that they had reclaimed their homeland, would they become complacent? Would they begin to neglect or forsake the skills that had made them who they were today?

Not under my rule, she determined, and cast the thought like an oath into the wind. The world she had won for them would bolster them, empower them. She would *not* let it consume them. If it meant bringing down a mountain or capturing a thunderbolt, she would—

"Overlord," Tonlynne announced at her back, "the snake you summoned has arrived."

"Have Wrakus send him in. See the others out."

"As commanded, my kiros."

The distaste was thick in her chamberlain's voice, but Sabrynne chose not to address it. Truth unleashed, her expectation of what must likely follow made her queasy in a way she had never felt at sea. Before, the necessity had been clear. Now . . .

She had hoped for another way.

Draining the last of her wine, she turned and refilled her cup. By then, the sitting room had nearly emptied, laborers funneling dutifully toward the door, leaving behind their tools and materials. A few turned to bow and salute in departure, only to sneer or grimace on their way out at the pale-faced Addaran stopped just beyond the portal by Wrakus's halberd.

Like any good shepherd, Tonlynne made certain the flock had cleared before taking her own leave. She regarded the visitor with a critical gaze of revulsion as Wrakus—with a threatening expression—let him enter.

"The door," Sabrynne said.

Glaring from beneath her brow, the chamberlain obeyed.

"I daresay your watchdogs would sooner gut me than admit me,"

Trathem groused.

Sabrynne poured a second cup. "Fret not, my sweet. They'd not dare upset me so." She extended his drink. "Not for the influence I hold with our overlord."

He did not yet know that *she* was Grendavan. Nor would he discover it, she had determined, until she no longer had need of him. The truth might make her too inviting a target.

Not that she couldn't defend herself. But he was of no potential use to her dead.

And useful he had proven. A highly regarded sergeant of the Stonewatch—Kendarrion's land-based military force. Ranking high enough to be of influence, but not so high as to merit constant suspicion or accusation from political rivals. A man who'd been serving capably as an informant for her people for more than a year now—ever since his precious young daughter had been abducted in a Grenarr raid on the eastern shores of the Gorrethrian Sound.

Upon coming as an emissary to the Addaran court, hated and alone, she had sought him out and threatened to expose him to his superiors. A ransom of information had he paid already, to keep his stolen daughter safe. How merciful might his king be to learn of this?

Fear, for himself and his daughter, had made him impressionable and compliant from the outset. To serving as her eyes and ears within the palace. To listening in on Darr and his counselors as they debated their response to the accord proposed by her kind. To helping her determine whether they meant to follow through with their side of the forced arrangement as they professed to her.

Then the princess Denariel had gone missing, and everything was thrown into doubt. Doubt as to whether the king was being truthful with her. Doubt as to whether Trathem was. Desperate to prove his loyalty, the sergeant had worked that much harder to uncover and persuade her of the truth of things. That Nara had slipped away of her own volition. That she refused to abide by the terms of the accord to which her father cowed, and had sailed off to seek reinforcement from cousins occupying some distant land. That Darr, furious, had set a sizable contingent of Shadowguard to retrieve her . . .

All just so much distraction, welcomed by Sabrynne as a suitable diversion to her greater purpose. Amid the turmoil, she had found Trathem willing to take on additional responsibilities. To stir the pot and season the brew. To campaign among favorable ears—however quietly, at first—for Darr's incapacitation and removal from office. Should he have been caught or reprimanded, no terrible loss to her. But he hadn't. He had again served admirably, doing much to spark the flames of civil unrest by expressing his disgust toward her. Admitting that, after a lifetime of battling their dark kind, her mere presence served as an affront to his senses. As it should to theirs. How they should consider killing her. Against His Majesty's wishes? To the swells with His Majesty's wishes. Was His Majesty even fit to rule when he placed his son's welfare above that of the Addaran people?

The sentiment had quickly gained favor and acceptance. A groundswell rising like a king's tide. From Trathem, Sabrynne had learned who was most likely to revolt—those unafraid to match deeds to words—and worked in her own ways to fluster and frustrate them in passing. All while coaching her pet sergeant on how to bring them to action.

It was also around this time that she had begun to ply him with other forms of persuasion. With prompts and challenges of a more enticing nature. Raising possibilities that stoked a man's deeper yearning for acceptance and fulfillment. However the Addaran power struggle played out, how high could he hope to rise under Darr? How high under a Loyalist regime led by General Ohrma? The Great Grendavan was pleased with his work. In addition to reuniting him with his daughter, her overlord could raise him to a station of wealth and comfort unlike anything an Addaran soldier could hope to earn.

Why would he do this? Trathem had naturally wondered. To which she had confessed her attraction to him. A forbidden fantasy, he had become to her. Could she ever be the same to him? The world she envisioned denied no man his desires simply because others said it could not be. She could take him as her lover, her husband even. When the Grenarr were restored to power, his would be a position of great esteem—of both honor and envy.

A song of temptation, sung with the perfect blend of earnestness and vulnerability. An ageless seduction, but one to which she had found him susceptible. Serving to strengthen her influence upon him. To deepen his belief in her and what she hoped to achieve. To make her more intimate plans known to him. To make them *his*.

And himself a willing instrument in bringing them about.

But as she watched him now, she saw an old uncertainty resurfaced in his eyes. A deep mistrust held at bay only by foolish hope. She forced herself to smile sweetly, and again lifted his cup to him.

"Come," she beckoned, and drank from her own.

Trathem hesitated, then crept forward and accepted her offering. Timid. As he had been in the beginning of their acquaintance. "I've asked for you."

Sabrynne added a tinge of weariness to her smile. "Your pardon, my sweet. I've been otherwise engaged."

Slowly, so as not to startle him, she raised her empty hand to cup his bearded cheek. He was not an ugly man, by Addaran standards, yet small and weak compared to her own. Wrapped in that damnably pale skin—tanned and freckled, but otherwise unfinished by the sun.

He warmed a measure at her touch. Self-consciously, he looked to his wine, and drank.

"Any word as to your lord's arrival?" he asked.

"On schedule. It will please me for you to meet him at last."

"Should I survive that long," Trathem scoffed. He did so with a lighthearted tone, but his genuine concern was palpable. Doubtless, her fellow Grenarr had done all they could over the past couple weeks to make him feel unwelcome—short of stripping him from his skin. Permitted to bark and growl, but ordered not to bite. She felt no pity for him. For how long had she tolerated similar conditions?

But she could tell they had taken a toll on him. His eyes moved quickly, warily, almost feral in their gleam. For more than a week had she separated herself from him. Long enough to stir his suspicion. Now that her kind had taken the city, what place did he have in their world? Did she mean to cast him aside? Just how much sway did she truly have with the unknown master who would ultimately determine his fate?

The questions went unasked. He understood them to be irrelevant. He had cast his lot already, risking everything for the promise of his daughter's return. Much as Darr had for *his* child.

The royal fool.

She itched to tell him as much. To see his expression crumble and his trusting hopes dashed.

Instead, she slid close, and pressed her mouth against his, kissing him hard. Reminding herself that he had earned better. For his efforts in spurring the Loyalist opposition. For sheltering her after she had fled the wedding massacre—when she had reassured him that the slain Grendavan was an imposter, and that her real master would yet deliver all that she had promised. For leading the pack of soldiers that had sabotaged the Seagate once Ohrma's uprising had been triggered, allowing her ships to enter the bay.

But acknowledging the extent to which she owed him only kindled her disgust. That she might in any way be beholden to a landsnake . . .

She broke the kiss, smiling sweetly and offering her hand. He took it, seeming mildly assuaged. She looked to the nearest furnishings, covered in the detritus of unfinished labors, and drew him instead toward her bedchamber.

A potpourri of flowers and spices couldn't quite drive out the stale mustiness of castle stone, or the strong hint of smoke carried by the breeze. It made her yearn for the deck of her ship—or even one of her balconies. Yet she hesitated to share with him the views from her quarters, where he might be reminded of the destructive chaos by which his countrymen had so recently been consumed.

She seated herself at the foot of her bed, and peered up at him imploringly. "I trust our time apart has not weakened your devotion to me."

"No."

A lie. He merely feared to speak the truth.

She pulled at his hand, until he sat down beside her.

"My sweet pearl. You've done all that I begged, and more. Kept me from assassination. Furthered my lord's aims. But when I lie awake, alone, I cannot fool myself that any of it was truly done for me."

She turned her head, as if dreading his lack of denial.

"Not so," he insisted, and squeezed her hand in emphasis. "I . . . I worry for Kesha, yes. I long to see her again. As I long to see you when forced to endure such absence."

She declined to meet his gaze. "You have plotted against and betrayed your people. Shed their blood. Listened to their screams. Heavy must be your regret."

"What you told me in the beginning was true. My people would have abandoned my baby girl, imprisoned me on the mere suspicion of conspiracy, had they believed her taken and not killed in that raid." He nudged her chin toward him. "What we have done here, we have done together. For our future."

She hid her laughter with a hopeful smile. Why seek to reassure him, when it was so easy to spin the blade and force *him* to reassure *her*?

She eyed him gratefully, then pressed her head to his shoulder in a gesture of intimacy. After a moment of silence, she stiffened and withdrew. Sighing. Wearing a pained expression.

"You're troubled," he observed.

"My sweet. There's something else I must ask of you."

Again the flicker of doubt, fueled by a sense of self-preservation he was too deaf to listen to.

"A task unfinished. The one to ensure our peace is a lasting one."

"Darr. You've found him?"

"No. But I believe I know how we might do so."

She told him, then, of Denariel's anticipated arrival. Of her plan to imprison the princess with some of the other Addaran captives—only to let this brood of prisoners escape.

"That they might find their way to Darr," Trathem surmised.

"And with Nara among them, be welcomed into his midst." She paused. "I would have you join them."

Her pet snake scowled. "Why not simply hold her hostage?"

"For what? Your king's surrender? He has already shown a willingness to spend her as currency."

"He might feel differently, if your lord means to kill Thane as you've indicated."

One of the half-truths she had confided in him, as a means of furthering his trust. Admitting that Grendavan did not intend to let Thane live. "See?" she said, seeing no reason to inform him that the sentence had already been carried out. "The treachery has gone too far for there to be any faithful bartering. And there is too much dissent within Darr's camp—as already proven—to trust that his objectors would allow him to make any foolish pacts."

She rubbed the side of his face, inwardly cringing at the scratch of his close-cropped beard against her palm. "I need someone I can trust to infiltrate their ranks. A reliable agent within their camp to apprise me of their movements. Nara will get you there. She has proven already to be a fighter. The rebels will trust her."

"And me? My countrymen may be suspicious of my late entry to the prisons, given their fear of spies."

"So we spin a tale by which you eluded us thus far, spearheading an underground resistance only recently rooted out."

"My word alone, as there are none to back the claim."

She envisioned her nails digging like talons into his ear, and ripping it from his head. "Suspicion is easily deflected," she assured him. "If they wish to see shadows? We'll give them one."

Already, she had the man in mind. A captain of the Pretender's so-called Shadowguard, taken captive by her warriors when discovered bound by his own people. Rendered useless to her, it had seemed, by his disgraced status. Easily bought, perhaps, but clearly unreliable, likely to switch sides or desert at the first sign of trouble. But as a diversion . . .

"What is the name of that greasy wretch who failed to ward your king? The flamebeard."

"Ruhklyn."

"Ruhklyn, yes." Offer him the chance to prove himself valuable by informing against his own. Reposition him within the dungeons in a manner in which he might do so. A man such as him would be agreeable to this—to whatever he must say or do to gain favor. Dependable in his unreliability. Set *him* to play mole in order to draw attention from her real one.

Deceit within layers, using false aims nonetheless believable in order to mask her true intentions. Thus had her kingdom been won.

She smiled as his confusion smoothed with a rough understanding. Not entirely daft, this pawn of hers. At times, when not blinded by need, he could be downright clever.

"We've still no evidence of my own defense," he said.

Again she kissed him, warm and deep. Imagined tearing off his tongue and swallowing it. Replacing the void in his mouth with another piece of his body, pared from his trunk with a rusty blade.

She settled for biting his lip, sharply enough to draw blood. Off his pained grunt, she withdrew, and slapped him. Hard.

"A few bruises should help tell the tale," she said, and smiled seductively. "I can make sure you enjoy them."

Eyes glittering with hunger, he did not protest.

1

The shriek and squall of distant gulls ushered Kylac from the shadowed recesses of the ship's hold.

That, and his captors' spears.

A dozen jailor escorts in all. Four to each flank, with a pair fore and another pair aft. Towering frames laden with lean muscle beneath their raven skin. Together, they marched him through the cavernous cargo space toward a harshly lit gangplank ahead, where a general furor underscored the strident birdsong. Their pace was eager, expectant. Difficult to match, given his own shorter stride, the burden of his shackles, and the inactivity his legs had known for the better portion of a month now. But the occasional prod made it clear they would brook no hesitation.

Anxious to attend their homecoming.

As was Kylac, for reasons of his own. Else, he'd not be suffering their fetters.

He squinted as he crossed into the flood of sunlight pooled at the hold's mouth. An inferno when measured against the meager lamplight with which his eyes had grown accustomed. Searing in its brightness. He shied, angling his neck to better shield his face, only to draw another piercing nudge from one of the warders at his back.

Mayhap he'd suffered long enough.

He tamped down the reflexive urge to show them how helpless he truly was, focusing on his feet as they cleared the lip of the junction between ship and gangplank. He'd come too far to give rein to petulance now. Returned from the distant atoll of Grenathrok, amid the archipelago of Haverstromme, all the way back . . .

As expected, to the docks at Avenell. Even half-blinded by the sun, he recognized them at once. Their structure and layout, edging the city's bayside shore like the threads of a fraying garment. Their din, a raucous murmur of shouts and thuds and clanks and clattering. Their blended scent, both fresh and foul, as ocean breezes stirred a thousand and more odors of fish and brine, of pickled foods and fermented drink, of sweaty men and lathered beasts, of mold and rot and deep-seated filth.

But the setting had *changed*, also. Swarmed over with Grenarr, unmistakable with their resonant voices, their towering frames, the oily gleam of their half-clothed, sable-skinned bodies. The din? Not the hawkish, combative commerce of a people preying upon or defending against its own, but the tingling exuberance of joyful cooperation. And the smells. As before, but seasoned now by the stench of damp ashes and acrid smoke—the remnants of fires that had feasted on more than just logs and kindling, but on pitch and plaster, paints and lacquers, leathers and fabrics . . .

Bones and flesh.

His eyes followed his nose. All along the wharf, and stretching inland to the north, lay further evidence of destruction. Buildings reduced to scorched mounds of rubble, their faces collapsed to cinders, their skeletons a wreckage of blackened beams. Sooty swaths tracked upward through the city, like poisoned veins carrying their venom toward her heart. Weeks old, most of it. The scars of a battle long since decided. The fires that burned now suggested a cleansing effort. The toppling of safehouses. The disposal of human refuse. Smoky plumes huffed skyward before spreading into veils that hung overhead in wispy layers. A shroud unmoved by the sun.

Avenell is fallen . . . As he'd been told. As he'd believed. The frail hope that he might be mistaken, that it might have all been a lie, withered now, consumed by a gnawing tension in his gut.

Again the savage shrieking of gulls. It drew his gaze to a thick, grounded cloud of the gray-and-white birds. Beneath their flapping, pecking forms, Kylac recognized the tangled shapes of loose-limbed bodies, bloated and gathered in soiled heaps. Here were the inhabitants he'd known. The ones left behind. Pale-faced Addarans supplanted by those with whom they'd once shared this land. Reaping the treachery sown by their forebears.

He cast about nearer at hand, in semi-anxious search as he descended the ramp at his feet. A drawbridge, given the enormous hull looming behind him like a city's curtain wall. Peering forward, he watched Grenarr colonists stream outward from other planks and bridges in her side, welcomed by packs and individuals of countrymen already put ashore. His vessel had made multiple stops during the course of her voyage, replenishing supplies and gathering up civilians from other atolls. He had to presume the other colony ships had done the same. And here, the result of that collective effort. Scores. Hundreds. Thousands in all.

Among them, he searched for sign of his fellow prisoners. Of Ledron, of Taeg, of Talon. Of any of the Whitefists or Redfists who'd accompanied them in their ill-fated search for the crown prince, Dethaniel. He looked for Aythef, who'd betrayed them, and Ithrimir, the half-mad Elementer, who in joining them had been betrayed.

Above all, he sought Her Highness, Denariel. The redoubtable princess. His onetime charge. The one he'd agreed to defend when setting forth from Kuuria, but whose misery in the weeks and months since he'd only managed to compound. He believed her safe, but was anxious to know for certain. He'd not seen her since embarking from Grenathrok, isolated as he'd been to his own prison hold. One of a private bank of supply closets beneath the captain's quarters. Close enough to overhear the scuffle between the Great Grendavan and Temerius when the latter had come to kill the former . . .

Or so he'd understood it at the time. He'd later been told that the murdered overlord's real name was Yultus, whose privilege it had been to serve as a decoy while the true Grendavan was back on Addaranth—or Grenah, rather—seeing to the assassination of King Kendarrion and an overthrow of his island nation's principal city.

Believable enough, save that the claim had been made by a dying Temerius, who'd become obsessed with making Kylac suffer. The vengeful Grenarrian had rebelled against his own kind to make an attempt on Kylac's life. So it had to be believed that, defiant to the end, he might spend his final breaths crafting whatever tale would instill in Kylac the slightest doubt or concern, thereby sapping a measure of triumph from the detested outlander's perceived victory.

Clearly, the claim had been more truth than lie.

Seeing nothing of a familiar face among the masses from his own ship, Kylac braved the afternoon glare to peer further westward, into the teeth of the radiant sun. Another colony ship had moored ahead of his, to spill masses of her own. He knew not which vessel his former companions might have been consigned to. He'd been warned by his captors that they were scattered amid the convoy, and would be summarily executed should he attempt escape. They might have disembarked already, or still be waiting for their turn to dock.

They might have all been butchered.

The distances were too great, the day's light too piercing, the throngs too thick and boisterous. Kylac turned his eye aft, out past his ship's keel and the next ship astern—and the next beyond that—to the mouth of the bay. A pair of links of the mighty Seagate hung slack from the north tower. Stained with salt, encrusted with barnacles and algae. The rest of the great chain was submerged, plunging toward the bay floor. Lowered to permit their passage. Another symbol of the Addarans' defeat. Having thwarted Grenarr attacks both direct and indirect for generations, something had shifted the tide and paved the way for an enemy landing.

How had it happened?

But then, that was why he was here, in this shackled condition. He'd come for answers. Weary of lies and misdirection, he hoped to learn the precise nature of the snare he'd stepped into nearly six months ago now, upon joining Ledron's company as one of Denariel's warders. As much as he craved his freedom, he'd recognized upon the ambush resulting in his company's surrender off the shores of Grenathrok that his best hope of returning to this ground was by the will of their captors. It was this, more than the threats to his fellow slaves, that had persuaded him to remain compliant and docile throughout the voyage.

The itch remained—the temptation to free himself and retrieve his stolen blades flaring now that his feet were within reach of soil. Yet, having endured captivity this far, he might as well endure it awhile longer. To examine at long last the underlying strands of the web in which he'd become entangled. In hopes of extricating himself without making matters worse.

A withering hush welcomed his descent at the base of the gangplank. Until now, he'd been but one more piece of cargo being offloaded. Now that the greater masses waiting to receive him could see clearly what it was being delivered, they seemed momentarily taken aback. Gazes hardened. Expressions soured. Labors ceased. A chilling silence radiated outward through the throng.

Another prod from behind. Black smiles broke free among the observers, and the jeers began to rain. Pale-faced he might be. A presumed Addaran, most likely. But a prisoner. An enemy vanquished. Nothing to be feared. Merely a target of ridicule and amusement.

A tunnel opened through the crowd as his handlers pressed him forward. On level ground, all at least a head taller than himself, they obscured much of his view. Just as well. His answers weren't likely to come until he met with someone in command. With the steward Barkavius, mayhap, or Grendavan herself.

Her.

Until then, better that he remain largely concealed within that ring of iron and steel. The bulk of the throng might be content to mock and deride him, but he could feel the darker sentiments of those among them clinging to his flesh like barbs. Probing. Tearing. Here, a foreman manning the hook of a loading arm. There, a wagonmaster adjusting the halter of a mule. Grenarr who for whatever reason eyed him with predatory hunger, reeking of revulsion and vengeance unsated. Should one or more be moved to lay hands on him and incite a larger reaction . . . well, a dozen spearmen would be hard-pressed to deny such a mob.

Even if inclined to do so.

Most however, continued to forget him almost as quickly as he passed. Too involved with their endeavors. Preoccupied with the greeting of family and friends. Rushing to meet fresh arrivals with warm embraces, hearty arm clasps, or merely a hand extended in neighborly assistance. Kylac watched parcels in every form—sacks, bundles, barrels, sheaves—being piled into carts and wagons or loaded onto pack animals. He saw husbands and wives, children and siblings, grip each other while weeping tears of joy. In all, a heartfelt display of love and pride and community, stirring to behold.

In stark counter to the lingering taste of massacre and devastation lying thick on the wind.

However impeded his sight, he continued to search for Denariel. Seeking disturbance amid the friendly tumult, some eddy amid the flow, that might indicate her presence. Unable to help himself. His jailors had made it clear she wasn't to be harmed or violated during their voyage. By order of Grendavan—which Kylac had come to believe referred to the real Grendavan, and not any decoy. The same set of instructions had kept Kylac alive. Uncomfortable, malnourished, but unmolested. Wherever the order had stemmed from, Barkavius held it inviolable, else he'd have killed Kylac as a matter of practicality long before.

But how much of that was truth, and how much a rationalization on Kylac's part? Had he believed her to be imperiled, he'd have had to put a stop to it, which would have complicated any hope for a return voyage. However faithful his intuition, which continued to reassure him of her well-being, there were any number of ways an individual might be made to suffer without leaving lasting sign of physical harm . . .

Not that he believed Denariel incapable of bearing torment. Since he'd known her, there wasn't a single moment in which she hadn't been subjected to oppression, indignity, or outright threat in some form. Much of which he'd been blinded against, or chosen not to see. No more. He'd played too large a role in this, at this juncture, to possibly walk away without doing what he could to see her affairs safely settled.

An arrogant proposition, some might say, for one in his present standing.

It wouldn't be the first time he'd been so accused.

The murmur spawned by his appearance continued to mark his passage through the multitude. A ripple of momentary silence, followed by a swell of scorn that receded again into cheerful clamor—with a few hateful stares lingering at his back. He couldn't yet determine where his escorts were taking him. An inland course, but a worming one, as they skirted work crews, dodged loading arms, rounded supply lines, threaded aisles of crates, or paused to wait for carts, wagons, and other wheeled platforms. A creaking, barking, maddening tumult of close, fast-moving bodies that almost made him miss the shipboard hole in which he'd been chained the past three weeks. Where at least he'd been able to hear his own thoughts.

For all the good they'd done him of late.

When his forward escorts again drew up short, Kylac did the same. A spearhead nicked his ribs in response. Gavrus, of course. Among the more spiteful of Kylac's jailors over the past few weeks. "Scales," Kylac had dubbed him, when first they'd met. So named for a nasty burn scarring his forearm. An ill-tempered brute who had yet to decline an opportunity to taunt Kylac or elsewise ply him with petty torments. Among the first to die, he'd decided, once he'd shed these chains.

For now, he matched the Grenarrian's snide grimace with a teasing smirk. His enemy lacked the boldness to do anything more than goad and threaten. While he might strain at his collar, Scales had proven well leashed.

As Kylac turned forward again, his leading escorts split to either flank, revealing a small gap in the crowd. Within that gap, his carriage awaited. A barred cell on the back of a wagon bed. A stern-faced Grenarr pikeman stood alongside, holding the rear-facing gate ajar.

Scales loosed a hissing chuckle. "Into your cage, rat."

Kylac saw little reason to resist. Though his stomach knotted at the thought of willfully committing himself to such confinement, he couldn't have expected much better. They might have forced him to shuffle through the city in ankle irons, else seen him dragged along his belly.

He'd have felt safer were Barkavius there to oversee his transport personally. Though harsh and taciturn, the leader of the Grenarr colonists had proven starkly loyal to the mysterious Grendavan's desires. Kylac had much less faith in the present crew of underlings to deliver him as commanded, rather than staging an accident along the way. A loose harness, mayhap. A wheeled prison barreling downhill, hurtling toward ocean or bay . . .

But he'd spied no trace of the absent steward. Well ahead of him, mayhap. Else occupied with obligations behind. Small matter. It seemed unlikely, at this juncture, that his assigned handlers would dare let him come to harm before their overlord had ruled upon his fate. Grendavan had clearly taken an interest in him, and if she proved to be whom he suspected, it was easy enough to comprehend why. He'd taken countless risks thus far in trusting to his enemies' restraint. What was one more?

He sidled forward, keenly aware of the edged weapons poised to cut him down should he bolt or falter. Attended by a chorus of hecklings and insults from the growing circle of onlookers. Biting down against his innate fear of captivity, he climbed the wooden step and into the barred cabin. There, he seated himself on a sideboard and calmly waited while his jailors secured his manacles—both ankles and wrists—to iron rings hammered into the floor and ceiling.

The latter required a moment's focus and tenacity, as the key his captors employed was ill-fitting. To be expected of a crude replacement. The primary key had at some point gone missing. Kylac waited patiently, comforted by the raw irritation of its small iron form, nestled like a fishbone in the pouch of his lower cheek. A gift, put once already to good use. Concealed all this time. Ready to serve again.

When confident he'd been secured, a pair of jailors took turns verifying their companions' work. They did the same with the door, after bolting it closed. Armed escorts took up positions on the wagon's running boards. Eight to a side, not counting the pair up front and a pair standing at the back. Fresh ones, specifically assigned to the next stretch of his transfer. Scales appeared disappointed, almost sullen, when realizing he was to be left behind. With Kylac having provided him no reason to quench his pike's insatiable thirst.

"Mayhap we'll cross paths again," Kylac offered in consolation.

His adversary sneered. "Best pray we don't."

Kylac chuckled at the banality of the threat, then looked away dismissively. Peering through the narrow window of his bars, beyond the bodies of his handlers, he caught sight of a Grenarr youth at the edge of those gathered. Not more than six years in age, frowning curiously, clinging with one hand to a woman's forearm. His mother, mayhap. Kylac acknowledged the child's fascination with a slight nod, wiggling his fingers in a shackled wave.

To his surprise, the youth mimicked his expression, all ten fingers wagging. To which his mother reacted promptly by slapping his hands and drawing his head tight against her waist. Angrily, she muttered, shaking him in reprimand. Though her words were lost, their meaning rang clear. Fury. Loathing. Vengeance. Dutifully ensuring—despite the reclamation of these lands—that the next generation of Grenarr did not soon forget the grievances of the past.

Kylac pitied the boy his lesson, before supposing it inevitable enough. Then his driver cracked a whip, horses neighed, and his wheeled prison lurched forward, iron rims crunching against hardpacked gravel. Drawing him on to whatever destination his enemies had in mind.

Leaving the lad to his teachings, Kylac set his gaze to roving anew. Searching the shifting slivers of scenery left to him for Denariel, Ledron, or any others he might know.

Wondering as to their fates, while rolling inexorably toward his.

2

The setting sun formed a bloody pool on the tiled floor. A series of pools, actually, spilled through the arched, open-air windows of the solar's outer wall. But Kylac's gaze was fixed on the one at his own feet, as it spread slowly, almost imperceptibly, across the polished marble flagstones, inching toward his naked toes . . .

His handlers had stripped him—boots, stockings, and all—before leading him inside. He wore now only his manacles, cuffed around his ankles, wrists, and neck. Attached at the far end to prod poles held by his captors. As if he were some ravening beast on the verge of rampage.

Never mind that he hadn't so much as twitched in the past quarter-mark since being delivered to this chamber. His handlers weren't about to lapse in their duty. He felt their hard, unblinking stares, some wary, others almost daring him to test his restraints. Disappointed they'd be, if believing he couldn't outlast them. Thirsty, weary, deprived, he'd not deny. But if it was his stamina they meant to gauge, they'd not yet taken his measure by half.

In truth, he was encouraged to be in this condition, in this location. They might as easily have dumped him into some depthless cell, there to fester until such time as they desired to call upon him. To have brought him instead to this, the king's solar, nestled amid the highest reaches of the palace, bespoke the importance of that eventual caller. As did the unyielding position of his handlers and the theft of his garments. Judging by their actions, no risks were being taken, and nothing left to chance.

Unnecessary precautions, were anyone other than Grendavan intending to see him.

Of course, he'd been introduced to two overlords already, both slain and said later to be imposters. By that, it might be wiser to question whether this Grendavan truly existed.

He imagined he'd learn soon enough, and so remained patient. Retreating inward, insofar as his guards could tell. Giving them nothing to study save his motionless stance and downcast gaze. An occasional blink, for those paying close attention. He suspected few were. Oh, they continued to stare hard enough, ignoring all else while clinging dutifully to their weapons and poles. But their staunch fixation on his unmoving form was rendering them increasingly numb, their intense vigilance eroding as he lulled them into an unwitting stupor.

To avoid the same, Kylac's less obvious attentions were everywhere, flitting constantly so as to keep himself alert. On the faded echoes of gullsong, their volume diminished by distance, but their intensity undulled. On the lingering smell of scorched homes and charred bodies, befouling the winds that blew even here, near the peak of the highest tower planted at the city's summit. On the sights glimpsed during his most recent journey, while rolling through eerily empty streets or marching through strangely hollow halls. He'd managed more than once to look back on the collection of quays and piers to the south, still teeming with newly arrived colonists. He'd seen Grenarr warships swimming the bay like sharks in a pond. Here and there, he'd heard wailings of grief and protest, followed often by pitiless growls or harsh laughter. Or the whimper of Addarans being herded like sheep, goaded by spear and whip.

Nearer at hand, he marked the darkening of the light that bled through the windows, the rustle of breezes among potted flower stems and sun-bleached tapestries, the loosening tension of the poleman holding fast to the cuff at his left wrist, the faintest murmur of voices approaching from outside . . .

A scratch and rattle, and the solar's double doors swung open. Kylac's handlers stiffened abruptly, startled from the slackness that had crept over them. Kylac declined at first to uproot his gaze, listening instead to the slap of approaching footfalls. A cadre of ten—no, twelve—Grenarr warriors. Fanning wide to permit the advance of a mere pair. Another dozen warriors following on their heels.

As the attending warriors filed toward posts to either side, arcing along the chamber's circular walls, Kylac narrowed his focus to the central pair. To the length, weight, and pace of their strides. An uncertain venture. But if he wasn't mistaken, he'd identified already both individuals. Mayhap only because he'd been expecting them all along. Either way, he cast silent wager with himself before turning his head.

To let his eyes confirm what he already knew.

Sabrynne.

Precisely as he remembered her, or near enough. The unwelcome Grenarr emissary met in Kendarrion's court. Sent by her people to deliver their terms of ransom, and to oversee thereafter the Addarans' willingness—or lack thereof—to conform to the so-called accord. A forced agreement that would grant the seabound Grenarr a parcel of wild Addaran shoreline to the north in exchange for the life of Prince Dethaniel, the king's only son.

A multilayered falsehood.

She swept toward him now with the same proud grace shown before. Presenting the same jutting curves and sleek, bald head. The same broad shoulders and stiffly arched back. Lithe. Fearless. The presence of her guard ring, Kylac suspected, was less for her protection and more as a gleeful display of power. For he sensed the exultation radiating from her. An aura of supremacy and confidence impossible to contain as she looked upon him. He, a lordless, aimless stripling who'd twice dared to threaten her life. Who'd slain her countrymen and stolen their property. Now just another rival brought to heel. A creature to be broken and reshaped to her purposes.

Else a trophy for her amusement.

Still ten paces away, she could deny it no longer. A fierce grin broke free, revealing polished teeth gritted in fiendish delight. All the whiter against the blackness of her skin.

"My eyes must deceive," she practically crowed, in that smooth, resonant timbre he remembered. "To see again before me the Pretender's hatchling."

Barkavius, who'd entered at her shoulder, betrayed no such pleasure. The chief steward of Grenathrok grunted a word in a language unknown to Kylac. His handlers responded, driving him with their poles and polearms toward the floor. Kylac obliged them by bending to his knees. An unfamiliar and innately uncomfortable position. But then, he supposed he'd earned it.

Sabrynne feigned a gasp. "No, no," she said, arms lifting from her revealing tabard in a gesture of dismay. "What need is there to treat him so?"

The gesture was as false as her sympathetic tone. Though her cheeks frowned sullenly, her eyes glinted like a knife's edge, reflecting the bloody sunlight. Barkavius was nonetheless moved to overtake her with a single long stride. He put forth a warding hand, arresting her approach.

"We know his work, my kiros. None better than you."

Sabrynne paused, playing along, though it was clear to Kylac she was alone in her game. Barkavius held firm and uncompromising as seemed to be his way, cheerless in his stance. Withholding her while making certain all attending warriors had gained their proper positions. Likely it was he who'd insisted upon their presence. He glared suspiciously at Kylac—even naked, bound, and on his knees—the entire time.

Mayhap because Kylac's gaze had slipped toward the bundle tucked under the steward's left arm. A bundle consisting of several sheathed blades. A slender longsword, edged on one side. Two shortswords, shaped and styled the same. A clutch of matching knives, six in all, of varying length.

Kylac knew because they were his.

"Kiros," he acknowledged, his own tone laced with black mirth. "Shall I calls ya Sabrynne, then? Or Grendavan?"

"You'll address her not at all," Barkavius snapped from his wary distance. "Until she demands otherwise."

A driving prod from the pole attached to his neck collar forced Kylac lower, nearly face-first to the tiles. Just within the sunset pool, so that he felt its bleeding warmth on his cheek. The handlers at his wrists pulled apart, holding his arms high and wide. Flexible enough to tolerate the stretched position, he offered no resistance. Save to peer up past his own brow from the angle of a cringing dog. That he might meet Sabrynne's gaze with a wry smirk, and let her see that his eyes held anything but defeat.

Their overlord she was. Or at least the person currently pretending to be so. Confirming a fear—a knotting certainty—held these past three weeks. Ever since Temerius's taunt in that closet hold. *On Grenah, executing her assault.* Her. From that very moment, Kylac had suspected Sabrynne might be the elusive enemy leader. A far-reaching assumption, mayhap. Yet he hadn't forgotten the relief displayed months ago, shortly after setting out in search of Prince Dethaniel, by the imprisoned Yultus—posing at the time as Tormitius, prior to his turn as Grendavan—upon learning that Sabrynne still lived. How the impersonator's glowering demeanor had altered, grown more smug and confident, after that particular revelation.

This would explain why.

Still, a measure of Kylac had resisted the notion, knowing that twice he'd let her escape. On each occasion, he'd had his reasons. The emissary had done everything he'd asked of her. And it had seemed almost irrelevant that she be allowed to go free. Even if she managed to evade capture at the hands of the Addarans, what harm could she do?

Amid the culture of informants and mistrust and divided loyalties that prevailed among the Addaran populace, word of the cathedral massacre initiated by Kylac's hand was going to emerge regardless— faster than anyone could chase it. *Her* account, at least, would be more quickly accepted by the Grenarr, cresting the flood of rumor to establish Kylac's blame over that of Kendarrion. In his ignorance, Kylac had further believed that the reported death of their overlord might actually benefit his quest to retrieve Dethaniel, triggering a confusion that would allow him to embark on his rescue attempt before the Grenarr filled their leadership void and sorted out their response.

But all of those considerations pertained to his search for the crown prince. In hindsight, his meddlesome conscience with regard to Sabrynne had steered him wrong. How much death could have been avoided with one more thrust of his blade?

He watched her now place a calming hand on her steward's thickly muscled shoulder. Though his brutish expression failed to soften, Barkavius relented as she brushed past, continuing toward her captured foe.

"Address me as you will," she teased, her gaze gripping him like a raptor's talons. "I've no concern for titles. Great Grendavan the Eighth. Sabrynne Stormweaver. Overlord, kiros, emissary, tar-skin. Your life I hold, at the end of a spear. And that makes you mine."

She took her pause at two paces, Barkavius clinging like a barnacle to her side. The steward's meaty black fingers stroked the hilt of Kylac's longsword, as if itching to draw it. Kylac allowed himself to be distracted by the motion. How many would call it justice, should he end up impaled by his own blade?

Sabrynne marked his wayward glance. Her smile grew. "You wish now you'd killed me when you had the chance. I suppose you might have, had you not been so swollen with false confidence. Thinking you had surprised me. That you held the upper hand."

She snapped her fingers. Without a word, Barkavius drew the longsword from its sheathe and bent it smoothly back against his forearm, extending it to her hilt first. Sabrynne accepted it without taking her eyes from Kylac. Only when she raised the weapon before her did she look to it, as if to admire its unique form.

"The blood this blade has tasted," she cooed. "Honorable beyond your understanding." Her gaze caressed its length, its pearlescent sheen, as she twisted it in the evening twilight. The fingers of her free hand traced the weapon's side without quite touching it. Like a child mesmerized by the candle's dance, yet wary of its heat. Kylac watched her, waiting, trusting to inner senses that assured him he wasn't in any true peril.

Not yet.

Her attention slipped back to him, gleaming eyes separated by the narrow line of the blade between them. "Your murderous act in Darr's cathedral did not catch me off guard, you see. I had anticipated already some form of treachery. I permitted it only because it served my people's endgame."

Executing her assault, he heard Temerius echo again, *while all of this . . . posturing unfurled.*

"Indeed, it was your betrayal that gave me believable cause to send an armada through the sound. A seemingly foolish attack, given the fortified nature of its southern shore. But none of Darr's commanders could be sure it was a ruse, given our perceived hunger for retribution—and without knowing the nature of whomever my people might have raised to their command."

"A fair piece o' cunning," Kylac admitted, recalling a starkly similar conversation he'd had with Dethaniel while imprisoned on Grenathrok. While she might not care what he called her, Sabrynne was here in part to be congratulated for her achievements, no mistake. Much as Thane had been then. "If'n begging leave to ask, to what end?"

Her cruel grin felt both icy and warm. "To draw the bulk of Avenell's forces north to repel the attempted landing. Comfortable in their remaining strength, given the impenetrability of the Seagate. Darr's own chief military advisor, made leader of a landsnake faction looking to depose him, supported this shipment of troops, so as to weaken the city's defenses. The resultant infighting opened the door for my own, secret assault." Her smile broadened, even as her lips pressed tight. "And here we are."

Her strategy all along. Kylac recalled an earlier interrogation, in which their roles had been reversed. In which he'd openly questioned how deep a man's machinations could go. No deeper than a woman's, it seemed. From the moment she'd accepted an idealistic Dethaniel's proposed accord, she'd viewed it as an opportunity to gain admittance, under the guise of a disposable emissary, to the palace at Avenell. Where she might manipulate its defenders to allow for whatever portion of her army had infiltrated the city.

"A rare boldness," he granted, "to stroll so naked into your enemy's lair."

Sabrynne beamed at the compliment. Else merely wished to acknowledge the playful arrogance of his words. "My lieutenants urged me to send one of them in my stead," she admitted. A bend of her slender neck indicated the still-frowning Barkavius. "Or to utilize one of our many spies embedded already within the city. But I can trust the latter only so far. And I'll not ask of my own anything I myself am not willing to give."

"And had I slit your throat in that guest tower? Or later in the cathedral?"

Her smile remained bright, calm. *Fearless.* "My people would have found a way to ensure it wasn't in vain."

Then her captains had been aware of her plans. Enough of them, at least, as needed to help her carry it out. Of note only because he'd wondered what specifics the rebellious Temerius had been privy to. Or his more faithful father, Tormitius. Or Tormitius's impersonator, Yultus. Or any of those surrounding him now. How secret did she keep her secrets?

Sabrynne's focus turned back to his blade. "What your actions before *did* accomplish was to rouse my interest. We Grenarr would not have survived even our first decade of ocean exile had we not learned to harvest what resources were available to us. Yours has proven to be a unique set of skills." Again she angled and twisted his sword in appreciative study, peering along its unmarred length. "Unrivaled, even." She nestled the weapon against her shoulder, and eyed him anew. "I decided soon after witnessing them that I would possess them."

Kylac glanced at the dour Barkavius before loosing a chuckle. "I's been known to serve where I may. But seldom would I be accused o' being so fickle in my causes."

"Nor did I imagine you would be. Hence why I so willingly surrendered name of the Blackmoon Shards. To send you scudding across the ocean, far removed from the heart of my plan. Had I the excess time and resources to track you down, I might have been tempted to do so. But why, when all I had to do was send word that you were to be secured alive once you presented yourself?"

"I suppose all it cost ya was your flagship."

"So I've been told. A cost I intend to recoup. As you must suppose, it held certain . . . *sentimental* value."

The way in which she fumbled the word made it clear she put little stock in such impractical notions.

"Is that also why ya had Dethaniel killed?" Kylac asked. "For sentiment?"

The Stormweaver sneered. "After a fashion. A loose thread, Thane became, with the city in my clutches. And of little value. The rebel landsnakes who managed to flee have no love for him. And Darr is no longer in a position to be manipulated by threat of harm to his prized seed."

"Dead, ya mean."

"Would it please you to learn otherwise?" She took a moment to entertain his dubious expression. "He lives, insofar as I know. But as a powerless wretch, no longer of consequence. Thane's life was taken in payment of Tormitius Shorecleaver's and those others who were slaughtered by your hand. In essence, for no better reason than to make certain *you* failed in your professed pursuit."

That he had. But the same could have been said even before Dethaniel's execution. As soon as Kylac had learned that Thane had been complicit in his own abduction. That the whole of the accord had been none other than the prince's well-intentioned, yet ill-fated idea to bring about a lasting peace between age-old enemies.

With all of this, Kylac had come to terms already. So he indeed found Sabrynne's admission encouraging. If what she said was true, if Temerius had lied about Kendarrion's fate, then he still had a chance to mitigate his failure. He might yet reunite Denariel with her father, return the pair to power, and send the Grenarr scuttling from these ill-begotten—or at least ill-retaken—lands.

Mayhap even win Denariel's forgiveness in the process.

"And now as I's learned my place, ya'd has me . . . what? Profess my undying fealty?"

"A wild horse must be broken before it's ridden," Sabrynne agreed. "But I would sooner tempt you than tame you, for fear of dulling your natural edge." She lowered herself into a crouch, narrowing the gap between them. Placing her own life within his reach. As if sensing his thoughts, his handlers leaned on him in unmistakable warning. "Outlander, you are. With no allegiance to any but yourself. So put aside this undue loyalty to these false landsnakes. Mine are the people native to these lands. Serve *our* rightful interests, and you shall have all the wealth and freedom you require."

A sound argument, it would seem, if he was to believe—as he did—that the Grenarr had a legitimate ancestral claim to this island. That the cruelty being inflicted now upon the Addarans was but a reflection of that shown *by* them at an earlier point in history.

Trouble was, Kylac hadn't known these ancestors—on either side. Nor did he believe that slaying someone's scions served just punishment to some ancient forebear long since rotted in his grave. Seldom as it might actually occur, he believed people should reap the rewards of their own actions. By that measure, he couldn't begin to support Sabrynne's grievance against Denariel and expect not to be flayed for it by his own burdensome conscience. Not when one of them was stealing and murdering *today*, while the other was merely seeking to defend the rights to which she'd been born.

Quite certain he knew the answer already, Kylac asked, "By what word or deed would ya has me prove myself?"

Sabrynne's walnut eyes gleamed wolfishly. "Your part in this began with the harboring of a certain princess. Or so you believed. Put aside that self-assumed duty," she urged, glancing meaningfully at the blade in her hand, "and I'll no longer hold you aligned against me."

As he'd presumed. It was the same offer Yultus—Grendavan, at the time—had made him, back before they'd embarked from Grenathrok. An extension of the true Grendavan's wishes from across the seas.

Kylac shook his head.

"One small life," the Stormweaver pressed, before he could refuse her, "and ally shall I name you to our long-awaited homecoming. A handsome payment shall you then receive for each task benefiting our reclamation of these shores. The hunting of mutants along our inner borders. The rooting out of insurgents beneath our feet. The infiltration of their northern holdfast. The tracking of the escaped Pretender. Wherever you feel your talents would be best plied."

Though she spoke of it casually enough, her mention of Kendarrion made Kylac wonder if the king was truly as powerless as she'd suggested moments earlier, or if she feared that he might yet muster some greater resurgence. Regardless, it would seem easy enough to agree. Capitulate now and decide later as to what *tasks* he might see through. Only, he wasn't willing to purchase his own freedom at the cost of Denariel's life. One more murder might scarcely register in the ledger of his misdeeds as tallied by others. But he knew unquestionably that such a concession would haunt him for the remainder of his days.

"By your own reckoning," he determined, "the mutants has stronger claim to these shores than even you, predating your kind as they do."

Sabrynne's encouraging smile faltered. "You would take the part of wild beasts over men?"

Kylac smirked. "In my experience, the difference is slight. Add to that, we's spoken thus far only o' *me* winning *your* trust. What o' *you* winning *mine*?"

Indeed, for all her gloating confessions, there was a depth to her words even now that she wasn't sharing. A void that hinted of further deception. Mayhap he was being unduly cynical, but he didn't believe for a moment that any agreement they entered into wouldn't end in an attempt on his life. Likely culminating in *him* taking *hers*. Alas, such partnerships might too often be unavoidable. But he didn't care to enter into one knowingly from the start.

"And what is it you do not trust?" she asked.

Kylac glanced at the shark's fin tattoo that adorned the left side of her throat. That adorned *all* Grenarr throats. "For one, how can I knows you're truly the Great Grendavan? Ya claimed to be but an emissary when last we met. And I has twice already been duped."

"You doubt my command," she echoed flatly. She stood abruptly, rising from her crouch. "Barkavius," she snapped.

"Overlord."

"Take this blade," she said, reaching its hilt toward him. As when accepting it, she kept her gaze locked on Kylac. No sooner had the steward's hand touched hers upon the haft than she released her own grip. "Slay me with it."

Barkavius stiffened.

"Did you not hear me?"

"My kiros, I would sooner sever my own sword hand than raise it against you."

"Would you?"

Kylac felt the tension of every Grenarrian in the chamber. Their rigid postures. Their disbelieving stares. Their tightly held breath.

Barkavius scowled at him, then stepped toward a marble plinth. One of several posted round the solar floor. To one side of its flat surface, he deposited the bundle of Kylac's blades. Atop the pile, he set the naked longsword.

No one spoke, no one moved, as the steward shrugged loose of a leather strap and cinched it tight around his right forearm. All the while, he glared murderously at Kylac. Kylac looked to Sabrynne, but she only stared back at him, her grim features set. Cold, resolute, implacable.

Kylac turned back to Barkavius, who now took up the longsword with his left hand and raised it slowly, to hover high over his right. There he hesitated, as if awaiting reprieve.

When it didn't come, he gritted his teeth, fired daggers at Kylac with his gaze, and growled.

Before bringing the sword down in a hacking arc.

Whatever examination of the blades he may have made before, he certainly wasn't accustomed to their deceptive strength. The force with which he struck himself not only severed his hand at the wrist, but embedded the sword's edge in the marble below.

Still no one responded, until Sabrynne herself swept fluidly to his side. A kerchief appeared from within her tabard. She wrapped the cloth immediately over and around the end of the steward's bleeding stump, tying it off with a leather thong. She hushed him as she worked, though he had yet to cry out. Barkavius trembled, but said nothing, continuing only to glare at Kylac through red, watery eyes.

When finished with the makeshift dressing, Sabrynne clutched her steward's shoulder, gripping him until his gaze met hers. Peering deep into those suddenly ravaged wells, she said, "For your loyalty, I thank you. It would please me now to see that wound properly tended."

Barkavius grunted, taking a moment to find his voice. "If I may,

I would see the prisoner caged, first."

Sabrynne cupped his cheek, bending her head to his chin as if to beg his forgiveness. She then rounded upon Kylac, still pressed to the floor.

"Does this not convince you?"

While duly impressed, Kylac saw nothing to gain in admitting as much. "I witnessed not so long ago an entire Marauder full o' Grenarr renegades kill themselves when their captain was slain." His eyes grazed the ring of warriors positioned throughout the chamber. "Mayhap, if'n I was to see a few dozen o' yours do the same . . ."

The Stormweaver's eyes glinted dangerously. Her tight smile lacked any hint of its prior mirth. "The next I have maimed or killed will not be my own, but one of yours. Captain Ledron, perhaps. Or that thorny Elementer. Beginning at dawn," she promised, "with another to follow for each arc of the sun. Should you force me to torture and kill Nara herself before your eyes, you will have lost any chance to persuade me of your allegiance."

She held his gaze for a moment, as if to make certain he understood. Then she turned and plucked his longsword from its shallow marble groove. "An impossibly fine weapon, I was told. And so it seems." She made brief study of its flawless edge, unnotched, unscratched, then sheathed it alongside the others. "But even iron and steel can be softened. Made malleable. With sufficient heat, sufficient pressure."

She retrieved his bundle of blades as she spoke, lifted the seat from a box bench beside her, and deposited the weapons inside the storage hollow.

"So it shall be with you."

Again she snapped her fingers. "Up," Barkavius snarled. Sweating fiercely now as he clutched his wounded arm. Grimacing savagely as Kylac was yanked, stretched and choking, to his feet. There they held him, while the steward looked to the Great Grendavan.

She nodded. He bowed in turn.

"Consider my offer," she urged. A veil of deepening shadow fell across the chamber, as the setting sun dipped below the threshold of the solar's windows. "We'll speak again at dawn."

Kylac glanced at the bloody pools from before, only to find them dried up. When he looked back, Sabrynne was exiting through the double doors, attended by a quartet of Grenarr warriors, having drawn the nearest pair to either flank.

Barkavius stepped close, to block his view. A slight tremor shook his towering frame. In the steward's red-rimmed eyes, Kylac glimpsed the all-too-familiar threat of reprisal. "Softened," he rumbled, before beckoning his men.

3

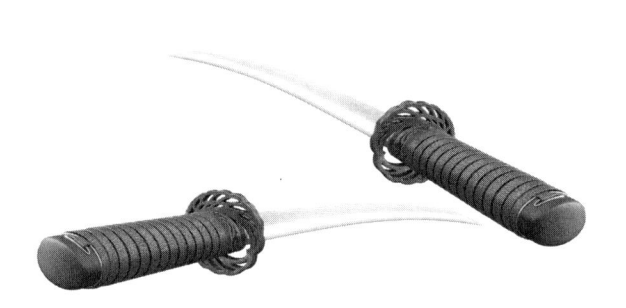

He was delivered first to a knuckle-faced brute who answered to the name of Thrassus. The Grenarrian was in the midst of his evening meal—hunched over a platter of squash and potatoes, his greasy fists engaged in tearing apart a half-roasted chicken—when Kylac's party came upon him. Alone, he sat, in the stark, dimly lit room. A receiving chamber, of some fashion, its stone walls cluttered with various pegs, cubbies, racks, and crates, all filled with crudely sorted personal items—cloaks and tunics, belts and pouches, weapons and armor, boots, buckles, and other trinkets and sundries less easy to discern.

Given the Grenarrian's blood-spattered smock, charnel-house smell, and the chorus of screams echoing from a deep-throated tunnel beyond, Kylac quickly gathered this Thrassus more torturer than jailor. If troubled by the interruption, however, or keen to take up his butcher's skills on a fresh victim, the brute didn't show it. He simply dropped the carcass of his bird, listened without interest to Barkavius's brief instructions for Kylac's confinement, then pushed to his feet, a blunt expression on his grizzled black face.

"With me, then," he grunted.

Forsaking his half-eaten meal, the torturer-jailor crossed the chamber and set down the tunnel. Not one word for Barkavius's blood-soaked stump, Kylac noted. Nor even a fleeting expression of curiosity or concern. Just an ear for his orders, and his subsequent obedience.

Kylac's handlers started after, the poleman at his neck dragging him forward, the others prodding from behind. He cast a backward glance at Barkavius when he realized the steward wasn't moving to follow. Anticipating murder in the Grenarrian's eyes, Kylac was surprised to find something nearer to . . . regret?

A trick of shadow, mayhap. Else a sign of distress settling in from the fresh amputation. He was given no time to puzzle on it, as the tunnel walls closed around. Chill and clammy. Formed by a singular stretch of naked bedrock, amid arching ribs of roughhewn blocks crudely stacked and mortared. Smelling of limestone and brine beneath the thick, festering tang of blood and bowels that hung stagnant in the windless air. Even his fierce handlers, Kylac observed, were coughing and choking on the rank brew. Kylac himself inhaled only shallowly, and that through his mouth.

Thrassus pressed ahead, seemingly unaffected. Inured, mayhap, or dull-sensed to begin with. His eyesight seemed sharp enough, for he carried no torch, and those they passed, ensconced in iron brackets along the walls, were only sparsely spaced, leaving them to traverse rugged lengths steeped almost entirely in darkness. The temptation arose in Kylac to free himself then and there. Use the shadows as his allies. Shed his escorts and seek his own path amid the coring dank.

But that was sure to set off a string of alarms that would only make his task more difficult. Were escape his only aim, he wouldn't hesitate.

Were escape his only aim, he wouldn't be here now.

Denariel. Ledron. Ithrimir. He'd intended to free them all, and still did. *After* he'd learned all he needed to. Once he could reasonably assure himself that his next step, if successful, wouldn't prove yet another mistake.

Sabrynne would seem to have dispelled any fears over the latter. Confirming his suspicions, revealing her methods, even surprising him with word that Kendarrion still lived. But there remained something oddly discomfiting about their brief reunion. She'd clearly refused his prior demand for truthfulness, disregarding a warning made evident months ago when he'd proclaimed his intolerance at being played false. While he had yet to identify a specific lie spilled from her lips, her overarching pretense had shaded all else in a deceptive light. Making it impossible now for him to see her in any other.

Or mayhap he was merely suffering the pangs of guilt. At setting her free to wreak her havoc. At failing to recognize the strands of her web, so intricately laid. His life's course was forever one of action. He had no interest in intrigue, and no eye for it. Yet, had he bothered to look . . .

Was it possible the indignation he felt toward her was better pointed at himself?

Whichever, he was left now with only his determination to set matters aright. And leaving a lone party of Grenarr to rot amid this putrid, earthen corridor would bring him no closer, on that count, than he would have been had he freed himself at sea. For his restraint thus far to be rewarded, he would have to endure it awhile longer.

Patience.

The resonating screams trapped within the tunnel were underscored now by moans and pleas and other plaintive calls of despair. Those whom Kylac was too late to aid. *Their suffering cannot be undone,* he told himself. A justification that rang hollow in the noisome chambers of his nagging conscience.

Ahead, the tunnel mouth glowed with muted firelight. Kylac sensed the void beyond, a yawning emptiness that suggested a larger cavern. A relief, however meager, from the suffocating closeness of this oppressive tube. Its promise tugged at Kylac like that of a desert mirage.

The cavern proved less spacious than Kylac had imagined. No bigger than the hold of a midsized carrack, with shallow floor and a sagging ceiling. Well lit, though, with brightly burning fires and a thick, smoke-filled air. A hub, of sorts, Kylac quickly realized, as he spied two more cave mouths piercing its rim—one from which echoed the cacophony of tormented cries, the other spewing only ominous silence.

A score of Grenarr were clustered here. Some labored—feeding coal to the fires, lugging or coiling chains, heating or hammering iron, oiling implements of torture, stirring vats of gruel. The remainder were engaged, as Thrassus had been, with their evening meal. Their rumbles of conversation and hoarse laughter curbed quickly upon sighting the new arrivals. One among them stood and saluted, and the others swiftly followed. Several wore scowls of curiosity at the sight of so many handlers for a single prisoner.

"The Kronus," Thrassus grunted in response to their unspoken question.

The announcement drew growls, exclamations, and muttered oaths.

"Bugger me. This minnow?" said one. Tall and thickly muscled like most Grenarr, but with flat gray eyes rather than the rich brown typical of his kind.

"He's the one'll be buggered," snarled another, slivers of bemusement rooted still amid the disdainful furrows of his ebony brow. His broad, knobby nose sat scrunched on his face as if repulsed by Kylac's scent. "Just fetch me the blade that felled the Shorecleaver."

"Scrubbed and shackled just now," Thrassus corrected, mimicking Barkavius's orders.

Amid the resulting grumbles and jeers, the phrase echoed in Kylac's mind, mocking in its tone, as if possessed of some hidden meaning.

"There's a disappointment," said Stone-eyes. "Then he's to stew with the others?"

"The Red," Thrassus replied. Another echo of Barkavius's instruction. As if the jailor had no thoughts or words of his own. *Put him with the Red.* A phrase of indecipherable meaning.

Another round of snorts and snarls, while the more threatening Knob-nose looked Kylac up and down and said, "To it, then, shall we?"

With a lusty zeal, the additional jailors and torturers, if that's what they were, abandoned their food and rest and rushed to take part in Kylac's processing. Coming at him like a pack of rabid dogs. Making him wonder if they intended only to tear him apart.

But Barkavius hadn't sacrificed his hand only to defy his overlord's wishes the moment she turned her back, Kylac assured himself. And Sabrynne's confessed goals made too much sense to draw doubt at this initial stage of his confinement. His skills were far too valuable to discard while there remained even the slightest hope of harnessing them. If he believed nothing else, he believed she wanted him whole and hale until such time as he proved unbreakable.

And she'd already amply demonstrated *her* patience.

Or could it all be but a ruse to forestall resistance?

A hand or two should have been sufficient, given the work involved. Yet it was fully sixteen jailors, in addition to his twelve base handlers, who clustered round as he was drawn toward a mineral pool at the cavern's far edge, and submerged in its chill, milky waters. As he was scoured with coarse-haired brushes until it felt as though they meant to strip him of his skin. As they scraped a dull-edged blade across the patchy scruff of a beard he'd been compelled to grow over the past few weeks. As they produced for him a baggy, roughspun tunic and leggings and lashed them to his waist with thin ropes—twine, really—tearing away the excess fabric at the elbows and knees.

All the while, Kylac listened to their snickers and sneers and thinly veiled promises of future suffering. But Thrassus supervised the entire procedure, and there was nothing feigned about the deference commanded by the terse torturer. Which made Kylac all but chortle at the idle threats. That, and knowing here they were, more than a score of prideful warriors doing a chambermaid's work, for no reason other than to see him cowed by their numbers.

Not enough by half.

Still, he held his tongue and did nothing to antagonize them. Not because he feared a fight, but because the sooner he finished with all of these needless preliminaries, the sooner he could take steps toward the real challenges ahead.

The discomforts of their brutish handling aside, Kylac felt reasonably refreshed by the time they'd finished with his cleansing and set off with him down the quieter of the two tunnels—treading *away* from the caterwaul of torment. As the volume of cries diminished, the subterranean track grew more rugged, bending and cutting at random intervals, the depressions in its pocked and pitted walls deepening into caves and side tunnels. Kylac couldn't determine how far these branches ran, as Thrassus bypassed them all without interest, clinging doggedly to the only corridor lit by the intermittent string of torches. Dead-end stubs, the others might have been, else a honeycomb of natural tubes twisting and coring through the mountain's belly. Whichever, Kylac's winding passage among those dark, gaping mouths evoked memories of past adventures in similar environs, and none of them pleasant.

Upon the walls, he came to notice the shelled imprints of ancient sea creatures etched into the bedrock. The observation startled him, at first, triggering his fear of confinement, causing him to feel light-headed. As if he'd been turned upside-down, the markers by which he measured his place in the world rendered invalid.

He closed his eyes. The sensation passed.

They'd covered more than two hundred paces before they came upon a gateway spanning the tunnel mouth—a mesh of iron bars attended by a pair of Grenarr sentries. Kylac recognized neither of them, and their slack expressions betrayed no great desire to introduce themselves. While they seemed to share the same curiosity exhibited by those earlier at the sight of a lone, unarmed youth commanding such a guard contingent, neither was moved to give it voice.

Nor did Thrassus address it as he nudged forward between them, wrenching at a crude linchpin in order to free the door's latch-bolt mechanism. Kylac watched him work, already determining how he might do the same if coming at it from the other side.

The bolt shrieked from its latch housing. The gate itself swung inward with a whine. Thrassus ambled through, holding the door as Kylac's handlers prodded him after.

It was there that those from the cavern who'd attached themselves in escort finally let him go.

"He'll see to your comfort," Knob-nose promised. "We'll see it's undisturbed."

Kylac ignored the meager jape and the gruff snickers that trailed after him. Down the throat of the tunnel he padded, the craggy floor pricking at the soles of his naked feet, the cuffs of his manacles chafing his skin. A thick, oppressive silence filled the earthen corridor. Little more than the crackle of torchlight, the clink of his chains, the squeak of his handlers' leathers, the shuffle and slap of their footfalls. The occasional grunt or wheeze, particularly from the handler at his left wrist, breathing heavier than the others. Beyond that, they might have been alone, a clutch of spirits lost in the halls of the Abyss.

Kylac knew elsewise. He smelled others up ahead. Their filth. Their sweat. Stronger yet, the scent of their defeat. Of curdled hopes and hollowing despair. Vanquished Addarans, or some small measure of them. Whose own ears would have warned them by now of the enemy's approach. Not yet victims of torture, but dreading their turn. Worried it had come.

He came upon their cages—barred hollows inlaid to either side of the scabrous corridor. Some elevated upon the walls, some half-buried along the floor. For the most part, the figures within were scarcely visible, retreated to the deepest recesses in an attempt to go unnoticed by the lumbering torturer or those who followed him. Kylac nonetheless felt their trepidation, followed by curiosity as their furtive gazes fell upon him. Others sat pressed up against their cage doors, a scant few tinged with defiance, the rest confined to enclosures that were little more than crevices in the tunnel's broken skin, affording them no retreat. Even these seemed to hold their breath, regarding the new arrival with varying amounts of grim pity and anxious pleading.

Kylac searched the grimy faces and desperate visages, but none struck familiar. Nor did any regard him with recognition, be it fair or foul. Whomever they might have assumed him to be—however many Grenarr it had taken to reel him in—he was but another captive now. Of no benefit to their own, bleak prospects.

The passageway beyond these cages remained empty, untraveled, until a pair of Grenarr—ever by two, it seemed, save for Thrassus—emerged from its gullet. Each carried a shoulder basket full of burned-out torch stubs. These, too, betrayed interest at the company's approach. But they, like the sentries without, held silent as Thrassus shambled past them without a word, only scarcely acknowledging their humble salutes. And they stepped aside when the handlers reached them, pressing flat against the tunnel walls so as not to impede the party's progress.

For several moments, Kylac delved through those earthen depths, carved once by natural forces, bent now toward cold human purpose. Twice, he was diverted along intersecting side tunnels, to find only more of the same—niches and furrows and empty buds covered with rusted iron grates, serving to cage the haggard, pale-faced forms harbored within. So many cells. Dozens had he glimpsed, of the scores, mayhap even hundreds, that might well fill the complex. What need for so many? Was it Addarans who'd built this, falling victim now to their own designs? Or had they usurped it from earlier generations of Grenarr? Or might it go back even further, to the days of the ancient Gorrethrehn, the so-called Breeders who'd ruled this isle back before the Mage Wars?

The possibilities were dizzying . . . and ultimately meaningless. It was now a dungeon compound housing Addarans taken from the homes and streets above and crammed into these harsh, immutable depths. For what eventual purpose, Sabrynne herself might not yet know. Mayhap she sought to make use of them. Mayhap they'd been locked away only to rot. Whatever her eventual intentions, Kylac meant to make sure they didn't go to plan.

He'd all but stopped peering into the various cells, his focus more on memorizing his path through the increasingly intersected passageways, when he caught wind of a distinctly briny musk both familiar and misplaced. He'd no sooner traced it to a grate on his right than a body thrust up against the bars, gripping the rusted iron in withered, vein-striped fists. A sharp nose sniffed through the opening, set between a pair of mismatched eyes. The left a bright cobalt, striking in its almost iridescent intensity. The right, an inhuman orb more like a shark's, dull and implacable, with a hint of cloudiness suggesting near or total blindness.

"I told them I smelled you."

Kylac felt a spike of relief. Ithrimir. The Sea Scribe. The mysterious Elementer from the isle of Mistwall who'd forsaken that home, which he held as doomed, to take up with Kylac's crew aboard the stolen *Vengeance*. Who'd served as their guide to the archipelago of Haverstromme, where it was believed they would find Prince Dethaniel. A rather hideous creature, with his sallow, rash-spotted flesh, his hunched, knotted right shoulder, his savage, piercing expression and spiked, coral-shaped hair.

Kylac had rarely seen anyone more beautiful.

Nonetheless, remembering his company, he spat at the Scribe's filthy robes. "Fine guidance, ya odious crustacean."

The Scribe scowled, but Kylac would make no apology. Not among Thrassus's brood, who might use even the slightest sense of camaraderie against him. Sabrynne had already plainly threatened as much.

"Move, whelp," the poleman at his waist demanded with a shove.

Kylac's gaze had already searched the Scribe's enclosure. Caged with the old Elementer were none other than Taeg, promoted to first mate before their voyage had concluded, alongside fellow Whitefists Jaleth, Rehm, and Stannon. Kylac saw also the glimmer of recognition that flashed across their faces—the unmistakable gleam of sudden hope—before he was dragged past.

Fleeting as it was, their spark of excitement lit in him a surge of confidence. Accompanied by guilt, yes, that they'd been left to suffer this long. Yet, he was no longer being deposited merely alongside throngs of faceless strangers, but his former shipmates. Alive, they were, at least in part. They'd survived the journey home. Spared, as he'd been. Now reunited. Whatever the circumstances, however dire, it was the first real step toward Kylac's aim of deliverance.

For it meant he wasn't yet too late.

The corridor closed off ahead, only to branch into shoots diverging left *and* right. To the left, at what appeared another dead end some forty paces on, stood a wall of bars larger than any Kylac had yet seen, shaped like a toppled egg, the ground fronting it awash in torchlight. Small figures stirred amid the darkness beyond. Before Kylac could determine anything of their nature, Thrassus led him right, past yet another pair of roving sentries—these unencumbered save for their spears, headed in the other direction.

There appeared nothing special about the door of his own cell, when finally they came to it, near the tip of another dead-end tunnel branch. Out came the pin, the bolt giving only a feeble yelp as Thrassus yanked it clear of the catch. As before, the lead jailor held the grate open while motioning the others inside.

A small cavern, it turned out to be, its floor sloping sharply up to a shelf on the right. Despite its wedge shape, a sizable space, given what he'd seen of the others. A half dozen shackles lay like snakes upon the ground, their tails linked to rings in the high wall, their empty mouths agape. All save one, which was fastened securely around the neck of a man who sat slumped upon the angled floor. A barrel-chested wretch in the garb of a Blackfist, filthy and torn as it might be. His bowed head revealed a horseshoe hairline, skin and hair alike painted in grime and caked with dried blood.

Then the face came up, revealing more grime, more blood, but also a forked red beard amid the filth and bruises. And Kylac realized with a stab of distaste that he knew this man.

4

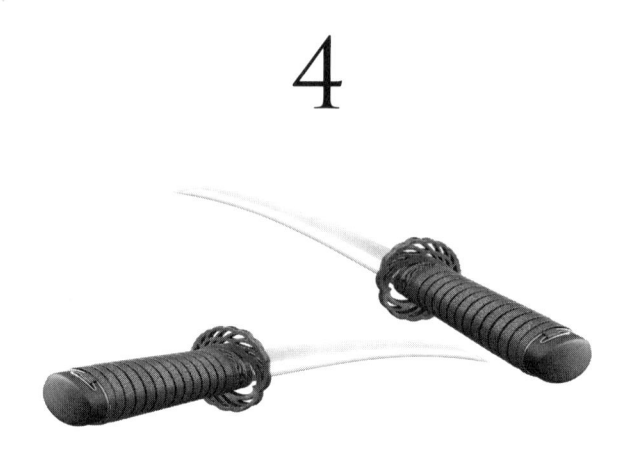

*P*ut *him with the Red.*

Had Kylac been given to name a hundred or more he might be pleased to see again, Ruhklyn would have fallen far short of his list. Not for any particular quality, save that the Blackfist had been too smug, too overbearing, and unduly critical when first they'd met. Captain of King Kendarrion's personal Shadowguard regiment, he'd been, having usurped the role in Ledron's absence—and not ashamed to trumpet Ledron's failings in an attempt to keep it.

It hadn't helped that Ledron had promptly voiced his own, unfavorable opinion of the man, and this just days after having made a concerted effort to save Kylac's life. Shading Kylac's own judgment, mayhap. Making him susceptible to the other's grudges.

But even if he'd been so swayed, and Ledron's rancor nothing more than jealousy toward a longstanding rival, there was something about Ruhklyn's boorish mien and belligerent behavior that chafed at Kylac like wet leathers. The sooner shed, the better.

Countering that, the king's warder he was, barring demotion since last they'd met. Positioned to know much about the Grenarr assault, Avenell's fall, mayhap even Kendarrion's flight and subsequent whereabouts. Kylac was allowing himself to be incarcerated in order to learn the condition and viewpoints of the other Addarans imprisoned or fled. As a potential witness and spokesman for those left behind during his search for Dethaniel, who better?

So Kylac swallowed the bile risen from his gorge at the sight of the guardian soldier, and held his tongue as his handlers shoved him into position alongside.

Ruhklyn proved unwilling to do the same. "You would put this filth beneath my nose?" he croaked, retreating as far as his chains would allow. "Just take my head and be done with it."

Thrassus, a step back of the others, took one long stride toward the shackled Blackfist and dropped him a heavy blow across the face. A strong, meaty backhand that seemed to nearly grant Ruhklyn his request. Given the resounding crack, Kylac half expected the fool's head to remain hanging over the rim of his iron collar like a broken cornstalk.

But the Shadowguard captain managed to collect himself, peering up at his assailant with glazed eyes and a petulant scowl. He looked as if he might actually have more to say, but a flinch of Thrassus's hand set him to cringing lower upon the floor, licking fresh blood from the corner of his broken mouth.

"Collar," Thrassus grunted.

A prompt for the distracted handlers. They remembered themselves quickly, the point man bending to gather one of the empty wall manacles while the others returned their gazes to Kylac, dark visages etched with warning. Kylac himself put forth an air of only partially feigned disinterest. Tiring of the tedium, yet careful not to raise challenge where it would serve no purpose.

His roving eye marked the iron ring as it was raised to his neck. Half-bands joined by a central hinge, with a self-latching mechanism that clicked greedily as the pronged end slid into a gullet of interlocking teeth. Clapped round his throat and there to stay, barring the intervention of a small, peg-shaped key.

No great difficulty there.

His handlers tugged at the collar, testing it, before Thrassus drew his eye from the glowering Ruhklyn and turned to inspect it for himself. A cursory effort, he gave, as if the shackling band was of no great consequence. He made a quick slicing gesture, one hand flat against the other, upon which the handlers began releasing their other restraints. Cuffs and chains and poles fell away. For Kylac, a liberating sensation, though he remained anything but free.

When they'd finished, Thrassus stepped close, brushing them aside like flies. Placing his face mere inches from Kylac's, the jailor sniffed as if at week-old mutton. A scent with which he must have been familiar, smelling himself like rancid meat. His scarred lip curled up in a half-snarl. Satisfaction? Disgust?

The jailor's grunt was equally indiscernible. Whatever his intent, he withdrew without comment, gesturing his brood on ahead before he lumbered toward the cavern's mouth. A few regarded Kylac with expressions of lingering threat. Others eyed him or Ruhklyn with scorn. The remainder simply filed out and vanished into the corridor, content to be on their way.

Thrassus counted among the latter, his broad back eclipsing the tunnel's torchlight as he exited, but only briefly, for he scarcely paused to secure the gate before drawing his hulking shadow back down the tunnel beyond.

Kylac waited for the echoing rasp of his footfalls to fade, then asked of Ruhklyn, "Has they served ya supper?"

His cellmate stiffened, frowning indignation. "Supper?"

"Evening meal. Typically follows dinner? Given the smell o' that corner over there, I assume they's been making *some* effort to feed ya."

Ruhklyn turned reflexively toward his small cesspit. When he looked back, angled brows canted sharply with his deepening scowl. "Gruel, I tasted, much too long ago."

His tone was that of an overindulged child. While leaner in the face than before, the captain was still well short of starvation. "Can we expect supper soon, then?"

"Is it the hour you're looking for?" the Blackfist scoffed, still massaging his bloody lip. "Night and day have been much the same of late, on account of you."

"Me?"

"It was you who spared that black bitch. Warded her retreat. Remember?"

Sabrynne. Then the captain hadn't been kept completely in the dark. "What do ya know o' her?"

"Grendavan, she calls herself now. Says the one you slew was a decoy. Truth or lie, I've seen others cow to her wishes."

"As has I," Kylac admitted. Looking duly abashed, he folded at the knees to sit cross-legged upon the floor. Ruhklyn needed someone to blame? So be it. Whatever kept the other's tongue wagging. "But why would she tell ya this?"

"She'd have me serve her," the Blackfist claimed, and not without a puff of pride. "Says she'll spare me, should I sell her my loyalty."

The notion caught like a burr in Kylac's ears, triggering suspicion. "Did she, now? To what end?"

"She'd have me track down our forces escaped with His Majesty. This after I sacrificed my own freedom to shield my lord's retreat."

Or did they simply outrun ya? Either way, a sensible aim on Sabrynne's part, consistent with what she'd expressed to Kylac. But Ruhklyn? King's guardian or no, Kylac had difficulty envisioning the Stormweaver putting her faith in such. "So ya refused."

The Blackfist bristled. "Would I be found here if I hadn't?"

Kylac couldn't say. The shackles and bruises did lend credence to Ruhklyn's claim that he'd thus far spurned Sabrynne's entreaties. Or might they be evidence of beatings used to sway him to the enemy's cause?

As soundly as the story struck, its reverberations rang hollow.

"That's why you're here," Ruhklyn guessed suddenly. His features soured with the realization, as if it carried a tart taste. "She made you similar offer."

Kylac withheld response. Why should he engage with someone Sabrynne had intentionally paired him with—placed here in a position of sole confidence? Could she be using the Blackfist to suss out Kylac's intentions? Mayhap she was relying on the captain's prominent rank, along with sheer desperation, to elicit trust. She'd have seen from before that the two were far from friends. But without knowing the instinctive nature of Kylac's aversion . . .

Or was this bevy of recent scheming merely causing him to see ghosts in the alcoves?

"She feels I's no particular allegiance in this fight," he admitted.

Useless it would be to claim elsewise. Nor would he do so if these words were meant for Sabrynne. "But she asks a steep price."

"Price?"

"She'd have me slay Her Highness."

"Nara lives?" The Blackfist didn't truly seem surprised. Nor particularly relieved. "Why hesitate? If you let her be captured, you've as good as killed her already."

"I'm considering it."

Ruhklyn snorted, and looked away.

"And what price did she set for you?"

"His Majesty's head. Short of that, I'll never truly be rid of her fetters."

And dead thereafter, I'll wager. Kylac supposed their situations weren't entirely similar, as the Addaran was far more easily leashed than he. Should Ruhklyn be freed to lead a Grenarr contingent in search of Kendarrion, there was much less risk of escape or damage should he betray them. But if Kylac were loosed . . . well, he understood why Sabrynne should require of him a prior act of good faith.

He abandoned the thread and reached for another. "How came they to occupy the city?"

Ruhklyn grimaced. "An armada in the sound drew half our army north to reinforce Indranell. Fool traitors here at home saw an opportunity to overthrow His Majesty. Next we know, we've got tar-skins crawling up our cracks. Time we recognized it, we were too late."

Effectively the same account relayed by Sabrynne. Whether that could be counted upon as a legitimate corroboration was less certain.

To that, he was largely wasting his time here. Well and good it was to hear the tale from all angles, but if he couldn't bring himself to accept the man's word as full and true, he'd be better served seeking another.

"What's your plan, then?" Kylac asked.

"Plan?"

The man might have been a parrot, for all his echoing responses. "Does festering in this cell further your king's aims?"

"I protect him with my silence."

"And perish most gruesomely, I'll wager, when they tire of it."

"If that is my fate."

Kylac chuckled. "Ya's no thought of escape?"

"Would you have me gnaw through these irons?"

"Your irons, I can see to. My question is when. Must I ask again about supper?"

The Blackfist's face remained taut with confusion. When finally smoothed by understanding, mockery took its place. "You believe you can get us out of here?"

"To no great avail, if'n they discover us missing moments later."

Ruhklyn nodded, finally seeming to consider Kylac's request. "I've had my meal this day. I don't anticipate another."

"Patrols?"

"They saunter past here and again. Just often enough to keep a torch or two burning."

And those in the hall had been fresh upon Kylac's incarceration. "You're certain?"

"I'm beaten and starved and half blind for all the endless sitting in the dark. I know not if it's weeks I've been caged, or months. Have it as certain as I can be that I'm speaking to you now."

Kylac nodded. Ruhklyn was worse for the wear, no doubt. Sustained by nothing so much as his unassailable pride, it seemed. Alive, alert, but how much so without the fire sparked by Kylac's arrival?

Now then, Kylac determined. Neither Sabrynne nor Barkavius had said anything about feeding him. He might wait for an hour in which his jailors and the city above slept, but couldn't know that they slept at all. Nor did he feel like waiting around for days in which to determine for himself their routine. Not with the Stormweaver's promise to start killing his shipmates with the coming of dawn.

If he was to do this blind, he might as well get started. Sooner, mayhap, than they could possibly expect.

He reached into his mouth, deep into the pocket of his left cheek, down to where the key smuggled him by Aythef had resided for three weeks now. Plucking it free caused him to feel as though a tooth were being ripped from his mouth. No matter the soreness caused, it belonged there now. A part of him.

"What's that?" Ruhklyn asked, his bitter tone rife with suspicion.

Kylac only tongued the void in his mouth, massaging the ulcer that had formed there, while rotating the clasp of his neck collar forward. His left hand found and gripped the latch. His right twirled the key and inserted it into the lock. Too small for a proper fit, but small was better than too big. The key was sturdy enough, unlikely to bend or break as he probed and twisted, hefting the lone pin above the shear line . . .

The lock surrendered with scarcely any resistance. While disengaged, Kylac withdrew the pronged end of his manacle free of the catch, and dropped the gaping collar to the ground.

"What . . . how did you . . . ?"

He didn't care to explain what little magic there was to it, or how he'd tripped his first such lock at the age of four. Latch, really. Any lock that didn't require at least a pick and a tension wrench wasn't deserving of the name.

"A token o' subjugation," he said, gesturing absently at the empty manacles as he approached his cellmate. "Meant merely for our discomfort. I'll need your belt."

"My belt?"

"The leather strap round your waist. Quickly, now."

Ruhklyn squinted sharply, his mistrust evident. But when Kylac reached for the item, the Blackfist evidently decided he'd sooner remove it himself. His fingers were slow, fumbling things, clearly hampered by the weeks of deprivation. Kylac chose to be patient.

No sooner was the belt in hand than he slung it over his shoulder and turned away.

"Wait," his companion hissed, and climbed painfully to his feet. He thumbed his own collar. "What of mine?"

Kylac raised a finger to his lips before slipping down to the door of their dungeon cage. There he paused, exploring the limited field of view, reaching out with his other senses. Only faint whispers disturbed the silence. The crackle of torches, the skittering of insects, a slow drip of water. Various, indistinct echoes that struck Kylac as nothing so much as the soft breath of a slumbering beast. The stone beneath his fingers, his toes, was silent. A thick, solid flesh undisturbed by thrum or vibration, it muted the rhythm of energies at play in the world above, causing him to feel uncomfortably disconnected. The cave's musty breath, a blend of molds and minerals seasoned with smoke, permeated the tunnel's throat. A pleasing aroma compared to the rank stench of his own cavern and cellmate. If Grenarr sentries had been posted anywhere near, their own odor was well masked.

It troubled him, momentarily, that his cell had been left unguarded. Unnecessary as it might have seemed, they had before now taken every precaution. Did they not fear he might seek to escape? Did they not imagine him capable? The itch of invisible eyes niggled the nape of his neck. Might it be this was some kind of test?

If so, he meant to exceed any expectations his jailors might have, to stretch whatever boundaries they might have set. Too often, he watched men be paralyzed by little more than their own perception. Ruhklyn and his collar, for instance. It might be he hadn't even tried to slip it, for fear of the next obstacle, or the next. But if Kylac's father had taught him nothing else, it was to express his own will, and never submit to another's.

One challenge at a time. And if Sabrynne was still playing games with him, she would come to regret it.

"Masterful," Ruhklyn muttered dryly, "to have ventured so far."

Kylac didn't bother signaling again for silence. He merely listened for any potential response to the Blackfist's words while loosing the twine his captors had cinched around his waist. The near-perfect instrument for his next task. The more cautious voice within him questioned if it could have been provided with that very intent.

After tying his key to the center of the twine for added heft, he fashioned an open clasp-hitch and reached through the bars to toss it at the door's linchpin. He lassoed the pin on the second try, then tugged both ends of the twine to draw the loop taut. The combined bite of the metal key and slender twine provided a grip that a thicker rope might have lacked. With tension from both ends of the hitch, and a firm upward yank, the pin slid free.

From there, it was a small matter to catch the bolt with Ruhklyn's belt and draw it toward him, free of the latch keep. A reverse bolt would have proven more challenging, though not impossible, even with his limited tools. At worst, he might have had to wait for a guard to enter the cell—whose later absence might have drawn notice, limiting his time for subsequent exploration. Then again, it would have provided him with a weapon or two . . .

Whatever. There were enough variables before him without worrying over what *might* have been. Any situation presented advantages and drawbacks. Assess and adapt and strike with confidence.

After stowing his key and twine, Kylac shouldered his leather strap and pushed against the door. It opened with a gentle creak.

"Hisk!" Ruhklyn called, and rattled his chain. "What of me, now?"

"I need to has a look around, first. See how many there are, and in what state."

"Fester that. Safer with me to watch your back."

Kylac did his best not to scoff. Having the Blackfist on his heels would only strip his blanket of stealth. "They catch ya outside your cage, they're liable to gut ya for it."

"And just as likely to gut me for not heralding your escape. Better, perhaps, that I cry it now."

"Do so, and I'll crush your windpipe with your own belt." Off Ruhklyn's glowering expression, he added, "You're safer here until I's a plan for springing us from the dungeons."

"And if you don't return?"

"Then I's gone somewhere ya don't wants to follow." Kylac donned his most earnest expression. "Save your strength. You're going to need it."

The Blackfist's countenance grew sullen, but he held his tongue as Kylac slipped from the cage, closing and latching the door behind him.

"Grant me an hour or so," Kylac said. "After that, be ready to move."

Trusting the Red to silence, he put his back to the grate and set off down the tunnel.

5

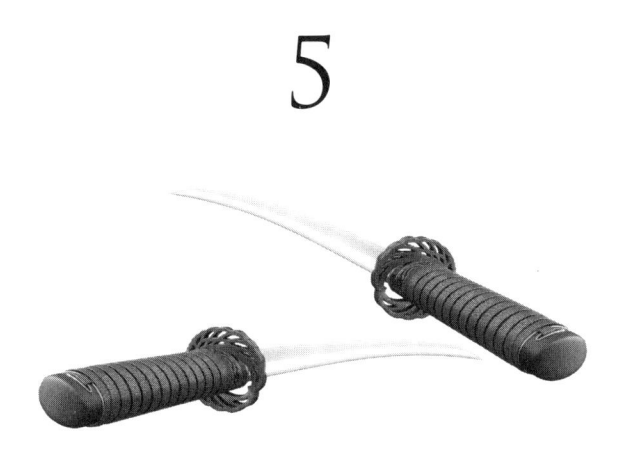

K<small>YLAC PADDED DOWN</small> the earthen corridor, skirting halos of torchlight. Though tempted to return to the cell in which he'd seen Ithrimir, he found himself drawn to the larger, egg-shaped cage glimpsed nearer his own. The one fronted by what seemed an excessive number of torches. He couldn't have described his attraction. The extra lighting? Its size? Proximity? Whatever, its allure was strong, and, while prone to inconvenient gaps, his instincts seldom served him wrong.

He passed only a handful of cells en route, and paid them but fleeting notice. Men dozed or sulked within, some shackled, others loose, most withdrawn from view and steeped in darkness. With heads lowered or faces turned, none were immediately recognizable. A few resembled the forms of men he knew. Men with whom he'd sailed upon the *Vengeance* and, later, *Denariel's Wail*. Else it may have been only that he saw what he wished. Truth unfettered, they could have been anyone. And he wasn't going to begin his explorations by calling out to every mysterious figure encountered in these depths.

Upon nearing his target, he crouched low to one side, no more than a jag of stone protruding from the wall. The torchlight fronting the cell pooled before him, precious little spilling past the bars. Human shapes skulked amid the writhing shadows, shifting or shuffling in discomfort. Amid the rustle of clothes and the clink of chains, Kylac heard their coughs, their grunts, their restless breathing.

He waited for his eyes to adjust, but the garish globe of light between himself and the cell served to screen the black hollow beyond. He might move closer, of course, but would risk making himself visible. Without knowing the cell's layout, the orientation of the prisoners, or the identities of those housed within, it would seem foolish to saunter in blind—no matter what his intuition suggested.

Better, mayhap, that he go back and consult with Ithrimir after all.

He'd just about persuaded himself of this when a muffled thump—a punch or a kick—triggered an abrupt rattling of chains.

"Touch me again and I'll have you flogged with your own arm," a voice growled.

A female voice. A *familiar* voice. Kylac's heart bucked against the wall of his chest. It couldn't be. He'd imagined someone of import housed within, but Denariel herself? Surely Sabrynne would have lodged the princess somewhere in the palace above, not here among the near-useless fodder comprised of the other Addaran captives.

In the same breath, Kylac was forced to remind himself that the Stormweaver's purposes could be but assumed, and only imprecisely. How, then, could he know the value of any particular member of their imprisoned brood?

"Beg pardon, Highness," someone growled. Aramis. The pock-faced porter who'd journeyed with them to the Shards. Among those chosen by fortune to survive the voyage, there and back.

Kylac found himself stealing forward, creeping swiftly, soundlessly, along the edge of the near wall. The voices hailed from the far end, but elation overruled caution. His arrival wouldn't long remain kept from the others, once revealed to a few.

He reached the bars unnoticed, and there recognized the hunched form of burly Havrig. The Redfist was wedged back into a shallow corner between stone wall and bars, peering out into the tunnel as if set there as a lookout. Were it anyone but himself who'd approached, Kylac would have found it difficult to forgive the soldier the oversight.

A pace away, he announced his arrival with a soft, warbling whistle.

"Shards!" Havrig huffed in startled response.

"Calm, friend. Ya'll rouse the entire coop."

From the sound of it, he already had. A murmur swept through the darkness. Chains clanked as bodies shifted—rising from restive slumber, scrabbling back from the bars, repositioning themselves for what was surely an unwelcome visitation.

A few pressed forward. Protective of those behind them, or mayhap merely drawn by curiosity. Nearer the cell door, another familiar face appeared in profile, features taut, radiating concern as its owner cast about in grim search.

"It's only me, Captain," Kylac ventured with a reflexive smile.

He slipped out along the face of the bars, exposing himself in the light. The murmurs increased, tinged with exclamation, yet were wisely kept muted, quiet. Ledron turned toward him, eyes seeking. Bearded now, and bruised, with a half-ring of gray-blond stubble beneath his bald pate. Aged suddenly beyond his years, the worry and defeat of the past few weeks having exacted more than their fair toll.

When his gaze found Kylac's, he squinted uncertainly before blanching with recognition. "Mother's mercy." Whatever his surprise or relief, they were quickly smothered by a cascade of accusation and disapproval. "Been wondering when you might turn up."

Another crowded forward, squirming past Ledron in obvious irritation at his efforts to shield her. Her face thrust into view at the end of her neck chain.

Denariel.

Kylac grinned, but her ever-present scowl only deepened at the sight of him. Deeper than Ledron's. Deeper than Ruhklyn's. Forced to admit it, Sabrynne appeared to be the only one pleased to see him.

"Sold your services and come to gloat?" the princess asked.

"Beg pardon?"

"Where are your shackles?"

"I found them . . . cumbersome."

He tried another smile. A wasted effort.

"You're a prisoner?" Ledron asked pointedly.

Kylac glanced at the captain—noting the array of soiled, beady-eyed faces gathering behind him—before turning back to Denariel. Her dark skin was made darker by the cave's shadows and a coating of grime. Evidently, Kylac was the only one to have received the courtesy of a bath. His new garments, coarse as they were, and clean face, though nicked and burned from his rough shave, must have seemed royal treatment to the ragged souls now peering out at him.

"Caged down yonder," he assured them, gesturing vaguely over his shoulder. "Did ya not see our little band pass through a spell ago?"

"Pack of tar-skins come through," Havrig agreed, off to Kylac's left now. His words were for Ledron. "Couldn't much see who they was herding."

"Come to free us?" Denariel pressed. "Or merely taunt us on your way out?"

Kylac cast a quick look back down the corridor. "A plan, we'll need. Might I joins ya?"

Taking their silence for an answer, he pulled the linchpin and released the bolt. After slipping through the door and drawing it closed behind him, he pressed deeper into the shadowy hollow. A relatively short depression, no more than six paces deep, but sloping down somewhat into a shallow trench. He took stock of those around him. Thirteen in all, splayed side-by-side, each wearing a neck collar chained to the rear wall. In addition to Aramis, he saw and acknowledged Whitefists Hessel, Stannon, Vosh. Moh, Hamal, and Kahrem were among the Redfists he recognized, apart from Havrig. Not one of them could he rightfully call friend. Yet, clustered there with so many familiar faces, it seemed among the happier reunions he could remember.

"Our quarters are rather cramped," Denariel groused, as the group did its best to gather round. In his eagerness, Aramis brushed against her. "What did I just tell you?" she shouted, slapping at the unfortunate porter.

"Quiet!" Ledron hissed at her, before lashing at Aramis a withering scowl. An almost pleading expression that suggested, however inadvertent his offense, the Whitefist should know better.

With Aramis carefully withdrawing as best as his shackles would allow, Denariel, Ledron, Stannon, and the snakelike Kahrem closed round, crouching as Kylac did.

"Pleased I am to find ya alive," Kylac confessed. "Unharmed." He searched their faces—Denariel's, especially—to be sure of the latter. However convinced he'd been of their relative safety, he couldn't have known—not truly—until this very moment.

"No debt to you," Kahrem muttered. Reptilian eyes glittered as he searched the corridor at Kylac's back, as if expecting betrayal.

Denariel waved dismissively. "We've endured worse."

Indeed ya has, Kylac thought—she and Ledron in particular—even if based solely on his own travels with them. First through the Ukinhan Wilds, and then again upon their quest to find the Blackmoon Shards.

"Has ya met with Grendavan?" he asked.

Ledron's gaze narrowed with suspicion. "Have you?"

Kylac would have preferred an answer to an echo. A chance to compare what *he'd* learned to what *they* had. Time being short, he decided to show his hand first, rather than wrestle with the Head's mistrust.

"Yes. If'n truth she tells."

"She?"

They didn't know. "The emissary. Sabrynne."

A flush rose along Ledron's neck. Simmering anger fueled by sorrow. "The one *you* spared."

"And the one who killed Thane?" Denariel prompted, more skeptical than confused.

"Some Lieutenant. Yultus, by name, if'n it bears any meaning for ya."

Her icy glare suggested it didn't. Only that he, Kylac, her self-professed warder, had again found means to fail her.

"Dead now," he added, "should it soothe ya to know."

"Why would it?" Denariel snapped, "if his deeds were but the will of another?"

"One who *might* have been denied chance to give the order," Ledron snarled.

The Head hadn't seemed to care before that Sabrynne had been allowed to live. Nonetheless, a meaningless contention. Kylac would sooner shoulder the blame than engage just now in a game of conjecture over opportunities missed.

"If'n we're to give time to regret, we's much more to lament. I'd sooner focus on the path yet before us."

"A short one, it would seem," Kahrem groused, gesturing at the cell's bars.

"Your father lives," Kylac told Denariel, and watched her brighten reflexively. "Or so our enemy professes. It's why she looks to make use o' me."

Her brightness dimmed, yet continued to flicker. Hers and Ledron's. Hope warring with doubt and ever-present suspicion.

"And what course do you suggest?" the captain asked.

Kylac shrugged. "As it was when springing His Highness Dethaniel. Seek an escape route and make use of it, while I serves up a diversion to cover your retreat."

"To it, then," Kahrem agreed.

Denariel differed. "Retreat? Why not retake the city?"

A harsh and heavy silence ensued. Kylac sensed that each man within hearing was waiting on another to refute her.

It was Ledron who finally did so. "That would seem foolhardy, Highness."

"Foolhardy?"

"Even if we can surprise them in the night and somehow wrest control, how long could we possibly maintain it?"

If called upon, Kylac was well and ready for a fight. A good part of him ached for it. But Ledron's view seemed the more sensible. Whatever its total numbers, theirs would be a skeletal force of deprived soldiers, unlikely to withstand a marshaled response.

"A cowardly view," Denariel stated flatly.

"Practical," Ledron argued. "At present, I'm compelled to worry first and foremost for your safety. Once away—"

"Hah! My safety? You've proven time and again that you care nothing for me except as it pertains to my father's orders. His mindless lapdog."

The accusation struck a resounding chord, drawing from Kylac's memory a forgotten claim—made weeks earlier by the hostage Grenarrian ultimately named Yultus—regarding Prince Dethaniel's abduction. The charge being that the prince couldn't have fallen victim without betrayal from someone within. A Shadowguard captain such as Ledron, perchance?

Kylac had believed it then to be a false implication, meant only to drive a wedge between him and his acting captain. But after learning that Thane had in fact masterminded his own capture, might it bear now further consideration? Did the staunchly loyal Blackfist truly serve Kendarrion as faithfully as Denariel suggested? Or might he have served her brother and what was perceived a greater good, supporting the prince's designs for a more peaceful, prosperous future?

Moot questions, likely as not. Even if Ledron had in fact contributed to Thane's scheme, matters had since changed drastically, and there appeared to be no motive now for the Blackfist to serve anyone but his king.

And himself, of course. Here, however, those objectives appeared one and the same.

"Disparage me as you will, *Highness*," the Head answered finally. "But my oath is to safeguard your royal person, not to suffer your madness as others may have."

An allusion to Ulflund, mayhap. The Shadowguard captain who'd joined the princess in her ill-advised and ultimately ill-fated voyage to Kuuria. In search of a military response to Thane's abduction that her own father had refused to mount.

"I'm better suited to safeguarding myself, *Captain*. And *my* oath is to the welfare of my countrymen, poorly honored by fleeing like a rat from a foundering vessel."

Stubbornness, most might call it. Kylac was more charitable. Her resilience amazed him, though by now he knew it shouldn't. He recalled how she'd come to join them. Lasting for days as a stowaway upon the stolen *Vengeance*. Determined to remain hidden long enough to ensure that they didn't simply put round to return her to her father. She'd had a secret ally in this, but the major discomforts had been hers to endure alone. Shivering in dank confines, steeped at times in her own vomit and other bodily filth, subsisting on insects and rodents to supplement her minimal use of stores that, on a ship, were closely inventoried . . .

All so as to oversee her brother's rescue personally. Never mind the patent refusal put forth by her father and everyone else, the perils posed by the elements and her enemies, or the prejudices and superstitions of her own shipmates. Because she felt it best, and wouldn't hear elsewise.

Could any of it seem now worthwhile? For all her toughness, the voyage had ended in failure. Dethaniel was dead, a victim of his own misguided ideals. Her city had been taken, her people slaughtered and scattered. Such immeasurable losses. Unbearable. Yet still she clung to this rawhide exterior, seemingly impervious to grief.

Unless, of course, it was grief alone that fueled her now, prompting her to lash out in a desperate cry for blood. While understandable, the latter struck Kylac as a shortsighted aim. He decided to find out.

"I'm happy to see to Grendavan's death," he offered, "if'n it's vengeance alone Your Highness desires."

Ledron's jaw clenched. "The death of a single tar-skin, whatever her rank or station, cannot outweigh the survival of our people."

Kylac ignored the outburst, matching stares with Denariel until she bucked beneath his gaze. "Thane's rescue was never my ultimate goal," she declared. "I'd have seen him safely returned, yes. But chiefly to weaken our enemies' influence over my father."

As Kylac would have wagered. The life of her brother had been of secondary import—justifiably so, now that they knew he'd willfully sacrificed her own happiness by using her as a pawn in his games.

"Given that, if'n your aim now is to retake the city, we might do better to heed the captain."

"We're going to need an army," Ledron added, casting a glare at Kylac that dared rebuttal, "assuming His Majesty still has one."

"Though it would mean allowing the tar-skins to further entrench themselves?" Denariel challenged. "We'll not as easily gain access to the inner city later."

Ledron shook his head, unmoved. "No matter the walls or hills we might claim, until we can drive them from the harbor, they're here to stay."

Kylac declined this time to intercede. Whatever grudging respect either might have for him, he sensed it best if they resolved the question without his interference. Force a decision—either way—and they'd all be much less likely to follow him. Were it elsewise, he needn't be sparing them so much time for debate.

"Regardless, we magnify our strength if rallying from within," Denariel maintained, intractable as the stone around them. After a moment in which she smoldered at those whose silence seemed to scream their support for Ledron, she added, "If you're too afraid to fight, we could wait to release ourselves upon my father's return. Forming a second battlefront."

"Without hint as to when that might be," Ledron pointed out. "We might none of us be left alive by the time His Majesty returns. And any who *are* will be further weakened from prolonged captivity." Surrounding heads nodded in the darkness. "We must act now, while we know we still can."

A handful of the nearer soldiers and sailors—Redfist and Whitefist alike—murmured this time a rough consent. Denariel regarded them as if bearers of plague. Her lips pursed as if to speak again, but her chin hefted as if she wouldn't deign to waste her breath.

"We'll not have great opportunity to persuade the others," Kylac observed gently. "Which plan is apt to win support among those jailed throughout?"

Retreat and regroup, as Ledron proposed? Or Denariel's daring revolt, whether now or delayed? Kylac didn't have to articulate it. All understood where the lines had been drawn. And all understood, as he did, that it was the masses, whatever their number and condition, who held the loudest voice.

Denariel's face soured. She misliked the answer, yet couldn't deny it. "They'll follow *you*," she spat at Ledron, with a gesture of contempt.

Kylac gave her a moment to change her mind. When she didn't, he asked of Ledron, "I presume there are bolt-holes from the palace? A path or two ya mights make use of?"

The Head frowned, nodded. "Several. Suitably marked, for those given to know the signs. Assuming the Grenarr haven't managed to find and seal them off."

"So be it." His pause met with silence. "If'n that's our course, we'd best be about it." *Before any o' you are tortured or killed,* he could have added, but realized there was no need.

6

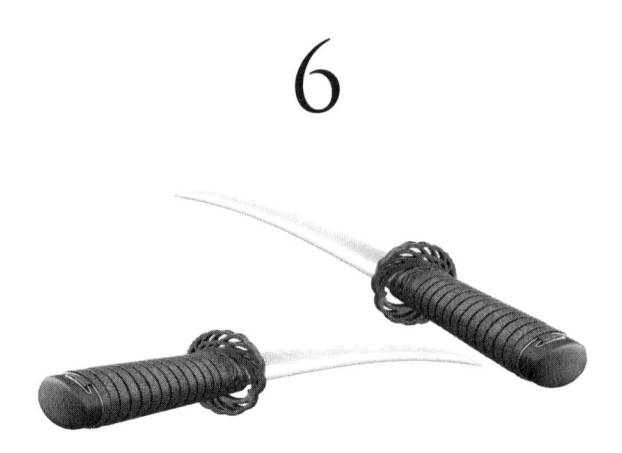

A punch to the throat kept the first Grenarrian gasping while Kylac stole his dagger and plunged it into his companion's kidney. A twist was all it took to send the second man arching in breathless agony, at which point Kylac plucked the dagger free and jabbed it into the first's already damaged windpipe. Before Kidney could muster a scream, a kick to the knee caused him to buckle, allowing Kylac to catch him in a chokehold from behind.

Together, they watched Throat gurgle and sputter. Enflamed eyes viewed Kylac with shock and rage. Hands came up and jerked the blade free. But the breath he drew to cry an alarm only filled his lungs with a drowning gulp of blood.

As the would-be crier toppled, his comrade in Kylac's arms grew slack. Just a pair of roving sentries caught making their rounds through the dungeons. Kylac had been left with little choice. Proceed any deeper, and they'd have discovered the string of emptied cells leading back toward Ledron's. An alert would have been sounded, and the jailbreak would have been thwarted before it had truly begun.

Pity, death as a matter of timing. But then, which man's wasn't?

He waited for the involuntary twitches of forced sleep to give way to the spasms of suffocation, then laid the limp Grenarrian on the tunnel floor beside his sightless companion. As he often did in such circumstances, Kylac wondered if he might have made their passings any gentler. Just now, his options were limited. And, likely as not, these men had enacted greater cruelties in their own lives.

He swept up a knife in each hand and crouched low for a moment, waiting to see if the killings had drawn further attention. But the tunnel's throaty silence held deep and undisturbed. Regardless, his time now had been shortened—limited to whatever duration remained in the dead pair's rotation. When they failed to report . . .

Kylac gave a low whistle. No more than five paces behind him, a cell door—already unbolted—eased open. The Redfist Sethric peered out into the corridor. Kylac motioned an all-clear. The door swung wide with a shrill squeak, and the pack of prisoners clustered within filed out—some tentative, others eager. More than one paused to regard Kylac and the fallen bodies with something like awe, fear, or dark satisfaction. Their precise emotions at this juncture were difficult to read if limited to an individual, put aside the group.

Though some started to press forward, the sandy-haired Sethric was quick to usher them back the other way—deeper into the dungeons, along a path marked by various Addaran lookouts to where the other escapees were gathered with Denariel and Ledron. Unless Kylac had missed a passage somewhere, the tunnels at his back were clear of enemies. Small measure of good that would do them if their movements were discovered by a fresh shift of jailors and the lone exit ahead barricaded against their departure.

He was still weighing the risks when Sethric shuffled forward to crouch beside him.

"Next?" the Redfist prompted, fingering the key with which the various prisoners were being relieved of their shackles.

"I'm thinking not," Kylac lamented. He hadn't gotten as far as he would have liked. By his estimation, they'd sprung barely more than half of those held. But the farther they advanced, the sooner their efforts here would be discovered by the next group sent to look in on them.

"We'll spring the rest on the fly," he determined, growing more certain of the decision. "Let's go see what our good captain has come up with."

They took an extra moment to drag the bodies of the Grenarr sentries back to the nearest cell and shackle them inside. As a ruse, it might buy them only a few extra heartbeats. But a few heartbeats in this endeavor might mean an extra heart or two continuing to beat thereafter. Kylac still carried with him a gnawing discomfort. Natural it might seem, in an undertaking such as this. But Kylac had been in worse predicaments with less anxiety. It felt now as if his movements were being watched, and therefore didn't matter. He had to keep assuring himself elsewise.

With the cage bolted, they scurried back down the tunnel, stolen spears, swords, and daggers in hand.

"I'll stand watch here," Sethric offered at a crook in the corridor. He hefted his Grenarr spear, turning the remainder of his weapons over to Kylac.

Kylac nodded in wordless affirmation, then hastened his pace. Empty cells and branching tunnels filled with more of the same fell past as he trotted soundlessly through the maze. When he slowed now and again, it was only to reassure the posted lookouts that all was well, but that he was on his way to verify the next phase of their escape. Most of these were Redfists with whom he'd sailed. The notch-eared "Quill," the leather-skinned Hamal, and the prideful "Crawfoot," whose sour smell hadn't been helped by his weeks in captivity. He passed Moh and then Ysander, a pair of Denariel's assigned warders once her presence aboard the *Vengeance* had been revealed. The Whitefist Hessel had a place in line, as did two faces with which Kylac was unfamiliar—Shadowguard, by their garb. Captured, it would seem, when Avenell had been overrun.

By then, Kylac had overtaken the last batch of prisoners freed before his encounter with the sentries. So he slowed his pace again—to forestall any panic and additional noise their own running was sure to breed—and crept instead with sure, swift strides down the final stretch of tunnel with their numbers at his heels.

"What is it?" Ledron asked, as Kylac approached the brood mustered before the captain's former cell. "Are we discovered?"

After sighting Denariel, Kylac waved off the Head's rising urgency, and that of those around him. Dozens now, in all. As many as a hundred, swelling restlessly amid the walls like ocean waves caught in a cove. His comrades, such as they were. Those he'd fought alongside before, and others he'd likely be fighting alongside in the days ahead.

"Matter o' time now," he admitted. He extended the small cache of weapons and watched them be snatched up like scraps of fish by hungry gulls. A spear went to the hairy-armed Olekk. The swords, suitably, to Havrig and Jorrand. The first dagger, he was pleased to see, made it into Talon's hand, while Kahrem darted in to take the other so quickly that he nearly severed Wooton's fingers in the bargain. "What has we decided?"

Ledron scowled at the momentary furor, but stopped short of asking any to relinquish their blades. If the bulk of them were forced to fight, then this night had gone horribly awry.

"We'll be dividing into smaller packs as soon as we exit the dungeons," the Head replied, "so as to better mask our flight. Aim is to rendezvous again at Tetherend. Deep in the Bonewood, roughly nine leagues north-northwest of the city's west gate. Was once a borderland outpost along the southern edge of the Reach. Abandoned decades ago when persistent flooding turned that area into a marshland and the road rerouted more than a league eastward." The captain hesitated. "It may be we find reinforcement there."

The king, thought Kylac. But if Ledron had stopped short of saying as much, Kylac wasn't going to give it voice. Even if most of the others assembled were already thinking the same.

"Anything else?" he asked.

"We were predetermining our paths through the city," Ledron admitted. "So that all are not funneling along the same course."

Sensible enough, as a single stampede would be easier to detect and corral. He searched the gathering, trying to gain a sense of its dynamic. Were they united in this, or were they yet hampered by dissent? None had yet uttered challenge, to either the plan or the captain's authority. That would seem auspicious. Countering that, few struck him as pleased or ardent. Only desperate and fretful.

He sought out others he knew. There was Ithrimir, huddled against a distant nook as if none of this pertained to him. Near him was Taeg, looking oddly confused and out of place—like a landed fish.

First mate he may have been, but they were no longer aboard ship, diminishing his influence. Aythef was removed further still, wedged into a far corner as if it might become his burial niche. The prince's secret consort. Hampered by injuries suffered at the hands of some brutish Grenarr, he'd be lucky to reach the surface, let alone trek leagues-deep into wilderness. Worse, the forlorn air about him suggested he didn't care.

"Not all will be able to travel swiftly," Kylac observed.

"Then they'll creep and hobble as best they can," Ledron replied flatly. "Else wait here for our eventual return."

Kahrem had finally realized that his blade was bloodied. While wiping his hands, he looked at Kylac as if he'd somehow been cheated.

"If I may," a new voice interjected.

Unfamiliar, it took Kylac a moment to pinpoint it amid the assembly. It belonged to a Redfist who nudged forward now from the rear. Of the meaty, handsome variety known to weaken maidens' knees. His black hair and beard had gone weeks untrimmed, and his tanned flesh was marred with cuts and bruises of similar age. Elsewise, he appeared hale and energetic, spurred by a barely bridled aggression. One of Avenell's defenders, Kylac presumed, apprehended more recently than the others. Motivated now by some unspeakable loss.

"I fear I must question the wisdom of flowing forth in random streams, allowing fate to determine which might be dammed up again."

Ledron's gaze narrowed, brow pinching around the bridge of his nose. "What is your concern, Sergeant . . . ?"

"Trathem," the newcomer answered. "Here to warn, sir, that the tar-skins have been out scouring and setting traps for us since bespoiling our fair city. Movement, even concealment, has become ever more difficult, as my own presence here can attest."

"You eluded the initial wave."

"And several sweeps thereafter. Only to end up shackled all the same."

"To what point?" Ledron asked.

"To suggest it unlikely we all slip through unnoticed. And to recommend, therefore, that some of us draw the enemy's eye intentionally, that Her Highness should stand a better chance of escaping it."

"We have Kronus here to serve diversion."

Trathem gave Kylac an appraising look. "With respect, Captain, he won't be enough."

Ledron gritted his teeth. "And who would you charge with this assignment?"

"I can but speak for myself," the sergeant announced bravely. "Though I'd invite others to join me."

A soft murmur broke out, as the other captives regarded one another uncomfortably.

"No," said Denariel.

"Your Highness," Trathem began, "I would implore you—"

"Do not. If we are to bolt like rabbits, I'll take my chances the same as the rest of you."

"The more of us the tar-skins must round up, the more time we purchase for those who might—"

"And those being recaptured may simply be killed instead." Denariel shook her head in flat refusal. "No man here willfully trades his life for mine."

"We need every man we can muster," Ledron reminded them all. "The longer they believe the bulk of us caged, the better."

The steadfast sergeant seemed so earnest, so determined in his perceived duty, that Kylac very nearly invited the soldier to join him.

"I'm capable o' rousing quite a stir," he offered instead. "Find Her Highness a path through their snares, if'n ya would, and don't look back." He could see that his words had all the soothing comfort of a tourniquet cinched round a freshly severed stump. But soothing had never been his strength. "Just determine your paths quickly," he added, "because I dare not tarry much longer."

He looked around, nodding an assurance or farewell here or there to those he knew, silently assessing the measure of their strength, and willing upon them what he could of his. Knowing as he did so that he'd not likely see all of them—if any—again.

"Off to free the rest, then?" Ledron asked, when Kylac had begun to back away.

"I leave that to *you* now, while I clear our path out o' here," he replied. He thumbed his borrowed leather belt, envisioning already how he meant to use it, when he recalled its original owner. "Let's not forget my cellmate down yonder," he bade them, nodding down the other arm of the split corridor. "One Captain Ruhklyn."

Predictably, Ledron frowned his distaste. A few others groaned or murmured at the name, further suggesting an unfortunate reputation.

Trathem was more vocal yet. "Ruhklyn? Might be better we left that one to rot."

A handful of non-shipmates muttered their assent. Kylac paused. "Ya say?"

"Man's a worm," claimed another city defender. A salt-stubbled Blackfist perched on the edge of Ledron's inner circle.

"Thought we needed every man we can muster." Sure, some made less ideal companions than others. He considered Kahrem, Hamal, Olekk, and a few others who'd chafed at him in the course of their travels. Truth unfettered, he wasn't certain he could trust a man among them to so much as shout a warning should an enemy raise a spear to his back. But that didn't mean necessarily that any of them deserved to be left behind.

"His Majesty's own shadow," Trathem answered, looking to Ledron as if the Head, among all of them, should understand. "But when the insurgents launched their revolt, Ruhklyn couldn't surrender his sword fast enough. Not for taking their side, mind you, but for recognizing their numbers and position and fearing for his own life. It was *his* cowardice that caused the king's loyal defenders to wilt, and for His Majesty to be apprehended."

As others familiar with events nodded their confirmation, Ledron shook his head and spat.

"Ya witnessed this?" Kylac asked.

"No," Trathem confessed. "But the tale is consistent among those who did."

"When the tar-skins invaded"—it was the unnamed Blackfist near Ledron who spoke now, taking up the fallen thread—"and our own coup put aside, General Ohrma left Ruhklyn trussed, deciding he couldn't be trusted with the king's retreat. I was there," he added solemnly. "On the wrong side, perhaps, but like the general, steadfast in my convictions. His Majesty forgave Ohrma, pardoned me and those with him, but left Ruhklyn bound. Worm tried to argue that he'd merely been reluctant to shed the blood of his compatriots, but His Majesty had seen for himself—as we all did—the captain's true shame."

In the uncomfortable silence, Kylac's gaze sought out Warmund, a Whitefist whose comrades had nicknamed him Worm—for none of the same reasons referenced here. The term now was being used as an epithet. A reminder that their own assembly was not a brotherhood, but a citizenry shattered by civil unrest. Decayed and weakened from within. Riddled with strife and opposition. Even when marshaled as they were now against their common enemy, theirs was a pieced-together assortment of shards. For all they knew, there remained Grenarr agents among them—spies purchased with coin or with hostages claimed over the years during any of the countless raids against their people. In that context, it must have been sobering indeed to speak of one in such a prominent position who'd betrayed their trust. For he was but one of many who, whatever their reasons, might yet do so.

"Ever the opportunist," Ledron snarled. "Man has always said or done whatever it takes to gain favor."

Refocusing the collective mistrust on the individual, rather than allow it to encompass them all. Kylac couldn't have said for certain, but believed the captain had done so with that express purpose. Whatever his resentment toward Ruhklyn, the Head Kylac knew was not so prideful as to openly denigrate a fellow soldier purely as a matter of spite.

Unless it was really that simple. If Ruhklyn had managed to climb the ranks not through skill or effort so much as his obsequious nature, his appointment to captain of the king's Shadowguard might genuinely strike Ledron as an affront. A judgment borne out, it would seem, by Ruhklyn's self-serving survivalist actions when counted upon the most.

Still, there was a difference between a man breakable, and a man already broken. With Ruhklyn's capture, much might have been compromised, seeming to support Trathem's fear that they could be captured again before escaping the city.

"Would Ruhklyn know the routes ya mean to take?" Off Ledron's scowl, he added, "Might be he's alive only for having revealed verifiable knowledge o' use to our captors."

"Some," the Head admitted. "But each Shadowguard captain is called upon to design his own route of retreat, shared with and approved by His Majesty alone." He gritted his teeth. "I've reason to hope mine is still clear."

A hope that would have to suffice, Kylac supposed. Because there would seem few means of testing it in advance, and no time to do so.

Still, the revelation wasn't all bad. "Strikes me, a man who can be counted on to serve only himself can still be counted on," he mused.

"Meaning what, eh?" demanded the salty Blackfist-turned-traitor-and-back-again.

"Meaning, if'n it's further diversion ya seek, our friend may yet have his uses." Kylac searched the gathered faces for a smirk to match his own, but found himself wading a sea of soiled frowns. "Ruhklyn goes with me," he stated more plainly. "And let us bid the rest o' ya silent steps and favorable winds."

7

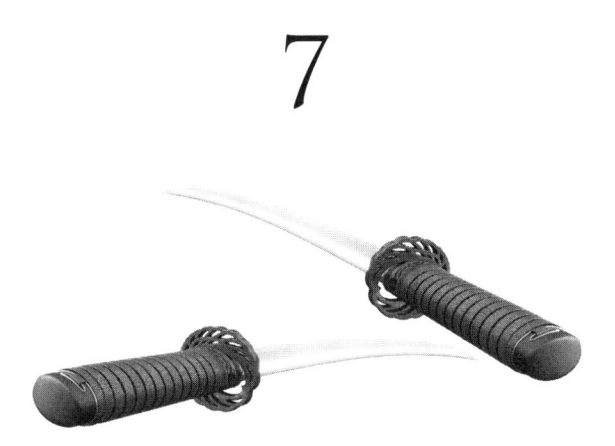

"What now?" Ruhklyn hissed at Kylac's shoulder.

I empty your lungs, Kylac could have said, *should ya speak again.* Instead, he motioned for silence and dropped a restraining arm. Signaling the Blackfist to remain where they crouched at a crook in the tunnel.

Ruhklyn leaned back, his sneering expression twisting with doubt. Smug in his certainty that their proposed escape had come already to an end.

Kylac peered down the length of corridor separating them from the gated entrance to the dungeons. Or *egress*, as he would have it. More than a dozen paces distant, the ground between well-lit by ensconced torches. With their backs to the bars were the pair of sentries encountered more than an hour earlier. Still at attention. Staving off boredom, at this point, more likely than anything else.

Still, he could see where it might seem foolish, to imagine he could so brazenly steal upon them. Unarmed. Locked on the wrong side of the portal.

His father would have demanded he do it blindfolded.

He started forward. He could feel Ruhklyn grasping after him—not physically, but with an air of panicked incredulity. It lasted no more than a heartbeat before the Blackfist fell back, recoiling from view, as if to distance himself from Kylac's madness. Mayhap he'd scurry clear back to his cell. If so, Kylac might just leave him there.

But that, too, proved a fleeting instinct, as he felt Ruhklyn freeze in place. Crouched down. Unable to watch, yet unable to turn away. Transfixed by whatever Kylac intended.

The entire reaction unfolded in the span of three swift strides. By his fourth, his companion was all but forgotten, as Kylac drew focus on his targets ahead. Not reaching out to them so much as attuning his senses to the energy streams flowing *from*. It often happened that way, like giving ear to the wail or thrum of a particular instrument amid a symphony, and allowing all others to fall aside. Not straining, but relaxing. Allowing instinct to take rein. Relinquishing any vision of what he *expected* to happen, and trusting instead that the mechanics of motion—muscle and bone, limb and joint—would respond as needed, when called upon.

At six paces, he removed the borrowed leather belt tied loosely around his waist. At ten, he raised it before him, folding it in half. An icy surge of anticipation climbed his spine, spilling over his shoulders. As familiar and comfortable as a well-worn cloak. His steps were weightless, his presence no more than a breath. The larger sentry, to his left, smelled chiefly of barrowleaf. The smaller, to his right, of vinegar. He marked the gentle pulse of a vein in the side of Barrowleaf's neck . . .

He pressed the looped end of the belt through the bars and around the unsuspecting Grenarrian's throat. A yank drew the startled sentry back against the grate, gasping. Kylac twisted the straps and put both in his left hand. His right went to the warrior's waist, snatching a sheathed dagger.

Vinegar turned. A wiser reaction would have been to withdraw and sound an alarm, assuming there was anyone near enough to relay it. But the Grenarrian made the instinctive decision to aid his companion, lowering his spear and taking aim at Kylac through the bars.

Kylac side-stepped the hasty thrust while tossing his stolen dagger in a small arc, testing its heft and balance. As it struck his palm again, he flung it underhand through the narrow opening. Three quick rotations, and the spinning blade split the peak in the spearman's throat.

Vinegar fell back, choking and sputtering, dropping his spear to clutch at the dagger's hilt. Kylac caught the discarded polearm in his right hand, and yanked it toward him, letting the shaft slide through his fingers. Halfway down, he tightened his grip and twirled its head skyward, released it in order to reverse his grip, caught it again, and jammed its head into the base of Barrowleaf's skull.

The sentry stiffened, no longer resisting the pull of the belt at his throat. Kylac withdrew the spear, slipped the belt free, and let the twitching warrior fall.

Vinegar glared at him with wide eyes, red veins forming cracks amid the white. But for all his spluttered objections, his protest ended as they all did, with his legs buckling beneath him, a final breath rattling from his lungs, and his sightless gaze set to chasing ghosts.

With belt and spear as his tools, Kylac reached through the bars and forced the gate's pin and bolt. As the portal swung open, he peered back down the corridor to where Ruhklyn stood gaping, body still sheltered by the tunnel's bend.

A sharp, shrill whistle seemed to wake the Blackfist from his stupor. Remembering himself, Ruhklyn turned and echoed the signal farther down the tunnel. Kylac bent to the bodies, doing them the courtesy of closing their eyelids before seating them against the wall to either side of the dungeon entrance. By the time Ruhklyn reached him, trailed by Ledron, Denariel, and a small contingent serving vanguard to the herd of fellow prisoners, he'd stripped the sentries of their remaining weapons.

"Grant me five minutes to clear the cavern ahead," he bade the Head and those with him. Clanging reverberations amid the rasp and rustle of approaching captives told him that the remaining cages were still being opened. But, with the door opened, the escapees could handle themselves from here. "Journey safe. I'll find ya at the rendezvous."

Not all of them, of course. But as to who might make it, he had no suitable means of guessing. Nor was there time to bid proper farewell, even had he known which of them would be recaptured, killed, or lost along the way. So he simply looked them over—those he knew, among those he didn't—and nodded. Trusting Ledron to do everything within his power to see to Denariel's safety. Leaving fortune's whims to sort out the rest.

He turned to Ruhklyn to remind the reluctant Blackfist of *his* place. "On my hip, Captain."

Ruhklyn, caught studying the slain Barrowleaf, nodded dumbly before puffing his chest in a show of confidence. In truth, he'd wanted no part of the role offered him. But Kylac hadn't truly given him a choice. As a condition of release, the Blackfist was to join him in setting a diversion for the princess's escape. It was what His Majesty would request of him, was it not? Chafe and stammer as he had, Ruhklyn had been unable to refuse.

This because the witnesses' account of Ruhklyn's behavior during the coup had sealed Kylac's suspicions that the Blackfist had been set to spy on him—or elsewise betray him at the first opportunity. Either way, he fully expected the former captain to play him false, and therefore wanted Ruhklyn under thumb—as far as possible from Denariel and the others.

While freeing him from his collar and cell, Kylac had gone on to feed him misinformation about the planned escape—the wrong route, the wrong destination. Further diminishing any harm he might do. Should the Blackfist acquit himself in their efforts, Kylac would decide whether to guide him out safely. If not, well, his would be a fate of his own making.

Most men could only wish for the same.

Striking an urgent pace, he led his reluctant companion down the tunnel, over ground that lay quieter than before. Some two hundred steps later, he motioned for the Blackfist to hold back. Just ahead lay the cavern in which he'd been bathed. Alone, he ventured to its threshold. A swift survey revealed just ten Grenarr jailors—half the number present earlier, discounting the two roving sentries already killed. He wondered briefly what might have happened to the other eight.

Before setting about his business.

He'd slain four along the fringe, including Stone-eyes, before the other six, clustered closer together, realized he was there. By then, he had a collection of borrowed knives in hand. One of his remaining victims mustered a shout. Another, Knob-nose, managed a garbled cry. Neither much distinguished itself from the agonized moans emanating from the unexplored cave mouth opposite the one he'd returned from.

As soon as he'd finished, Kylac contemplated further the enemy's reduced number, and where the others might have gone. Haunted by the restless sensation that he may have missed something. An oversight to which Denariel and the other escapees might prove vulnerable.

If so, he could only hope that he'd be the first to confront it.

He considered delving into the corridor of tortured screams, to follow the echoing cries to their source and see how many might yet be in a condition to flee. But that would be up to the Addarans trailing him, if they so chose, using their numbers to spread out and eliminate any handlers or lookouts that Kylac might be bypassing. If he was to distance himself sufficiently so that the response to his and Ruhklyn's emergence didn't endanger that of the others, he needed to press ahead as he'd said he would.

He whistled for Ruhklyn, who slunk from the shadows to join him. The Blackfist softened, somewhat, upon sighting the corpses cooling upon the cavern floor. Sullen bitterness making way for cruel satisfaction.

"Leave 'em," Kylac said, when Ruhklyn reached for a dead Grenarrian's weapons. "Our friends need 'em worse than we."

The Blackfist frowned petulantly. "Am I to remain weaponless?"

Even had they blades to spare, Kylac was in no rush to see one in Ruhklyn's hand. The longer his companion remained unarmed, the safer his own back would likely be. "Soon enough."

Ruhklyn glowered, but ceased his looting. However fierce his pride, he'd seen enough of Kylac's work to know better than to challenge him directly.

Back through the final stretch of tunnels, they crept. Where, at one point, a chill gust grazed Kylac's cheek, out of place in the windless dark. The fleeting brush of a lost soul, mayhap. Some poor wretch he'd failed to save, set now to wander the labyrinthine depths. The nicks on his roughly shaven face itched, reflecting a deeper irritation. *Can't help 'em all,* he told himself, and wondered why that should trouble him. He'd committed already to this cause more than his share.

He told himself this again as he led Ruhklyn up through the charnel house smells clogging the upper corridors. Nearing Thrassus's domain. He half hoped Thrassus himself would be found in his receiving chamber. He wasn't. Another had taken his chair, scratching notations onto some ledger. Kylac did him the courtesy of killing him before he knew he was beset.

Again, Ruhklyn sought to claim a weapon. Again, Kylac denied him.

Their path from there continued to unfold as it had below, a forked and twisted climb along the route of Kylac's original descent. A maze it was, but one he'd walked already, and thus committed unerringly to memory. Earthen tunnels gave way to corridors built from blocks of carved stone. Locked grates surrendered to open archways and banks of wooden doors. Most of the halls and chambers and stairwells were dimly lit, empty save for the occasional watchman or servant making his or her rounds. Kylac left most untouched, seeking to avoid any perceptible disruption to the palace's normal functions. Trusting those who by now would be venturing forth along the paths of their own escape to do the same.

Only when he'd reached ground levels did he begin to leave evidence of his passing. A slain watchman dragged clumsily into an alcove here, a short-lived trail of bloody footprints there. When he crossed paths with a startled chambermaid bearing a platter of fruit from the kitchens, he locked her in a candle closet and warned her to keep silent. Ruhklyn, armed by then with a sword and dagger, had urged him to slit her black throat. Kylac, while binding and gagging her only loosely amid the racks of wax and tallow, had calmly suggested there was no need.

Remarkably, the Blackfist swallowed this and other protests and kept dutifully to Kylac's side. It wasn't until they bypassed a garden exit, turning instead toward a stair leading up into the royal wing, that Ruhklyn balked.

"We can slip out right here," he urged, gesturing with his stolen sword. "The stables lie west, just beyond the orchard."

"Not without my blades," said Kylac.

The Blackfist frowned. "You can't make do with those?"

The Grenarr swords tucked into his borrowed belt were comfortable enough. Like sabers in their styling, with a pair of throwing knives to complement them. Reasonably sharp and strong, though notched and scratched with use, with acceptable balance and heft. But cudgels they were, when compared to his own blades, serving replacement in the way that a mule might function as a charger, or a lizard might mimic a dragon. Ruhklyn may as well have asked him to sever his own hands and sew hooves in their stead.

"I'll *make do* with any weapon or none at all," he replied. "But there aren't gems enough in your king's treasury to buy my own weapons from me. I's no intention of abandoning 'em."

Moreover, he suspected Sabrynne knew it. Which was what made his effort at their retrieval such a natural, believable distraction.

Ruhklyn looked again to the nearby exit, his craving plain. "If we lose our chance at the horses—"

"Enter those gardens and ya'll bed among them. As compost."

The Blackfist glared. By his expression and stance, tempted to make a break for it. Wisely, he surrendered the notion and approached instead.

"Cling to me, and I'll sees us through this," Kylac promised him.

Ruhklyn only smoldered.

Up the winding stairs they crept, Kylac no louder than a passing shadow, his cautious companion huffing and plodding by comparison. Three flights up, they crossed a hall, slaying a pair of sentries set to bar another stairwell. He left them where they fell, his focus shifting from stealth to speed. It couldn't be long now before one or more of his earlier victims was discovered. He was a little surprised that his ascent wasn't spurred by shouts and screams already.

Atop two more flights, another pair of sentries fell. Slipping down the next corridor, he encountered and slew one more. From there, he shortened his path by accessing a balcony overlooking an entertainment hall, cut across an empty corridor, dipped through a foyer, an antechamber, and entered the solar.

It appeared much the same as he'd left it hours earlier, with its grand statuary, opulent flowers, and intricate tapestries. The shadows they cast around the central pool were deeper and cooler now, bred by moon and stars rather than a bleeding sun. The pool itself was placid, its waters stirred only by a gentle breeze.

Kylac knew at once that something was amiss.

He darted ahead regardless, taking aim at the storage bench in which he'd seen Sabrynne stash his blades. His sense was of a snare tightening around him. Should it close, better that it find him more suitably armed.

Upon reaching the bench, he paused in reflexive examination. Seeing no traps, scenting no poisons, he lifted the seat.

To find the hollow within empty.

His heart withered. All along, he'd acknowledged the fell possibility. Ever since the ambush off Grenathrok, where he'd yielded them in the first place, he'd understood the risk he was undertaking. The chance that he might not lay hand on them again. But the likelihood had seemed so small, his unflappable confidence had almost dared him to do it. If he couldn't let them go, then he'd become too reliant on them. If he feared the challenge, then it was one he needed to conquer. Should he fail somehow to retrieve them . . . well, then he didn't deserve to keep them.

Peering now into that bare box, staring at the vacant space as if his treasured weapons might magically reappear, he couldn't help but curse himself for a fool.

A heartbeat later, he felt the weight of their encircling advance. The sounds and smells came next, rasps and jangles accompanied by the oils and leather and sweat stirred by a sudden breeze. Kylac smirked, his momentary distress falling away, his fighter's spirit kindled. Folding his arms across his chest, he rounded to meet them.

"Well?" Ruhklyn hissed in question.

Then he, too, heard them . . . and saw them, as they appeared in the doorways, the alcoves, even filed in from an outer balcony. The Blackfist froze, a skittish stag paralyzed by the hunting party's approach, unsure which way to bolt. By the time it occurred to him to look, every possible egress was covered, clogged with towering, black-skinned bodies rippling with muscle and brandishing an array of spears and swords and arrows.

Kylac remained still, as well. Held not by fear or uncertainty, but patience, anticipation. If they knew he'd be coming, and prepared for it with a force this sizable, then this wasn't a killing ambush, but another play in some kind of game.

As the noose tightened, Ruhklyn began backing away, retreating toward Kylac. He halted again when Sabrynne herself entered, pushing though the forward wall of her personal guard ring to leer down at him from the north end of the chamber.

Kylac only tipped his brow in greeting.

The overlord flashed him a toothy smile. "Again, your prowess fulfills its promise. Do you ever disappoint?"

A test, then. A simple exercise in the form of catch-the-mouse. Toying with him as a means of further demonstrating her control.

But could she truly believe that? She'd been there, in the cathedral, when her first decoy had fallen. She'd witnessed his *prowess* firsthand. Granted, she'd taken precautions here. Deprived him of his deadlier instruments. Hemmed him in with a complement of some threescore fully armed warriors—at least a score more than had been present to bear witness to their false lord's wedding. His only potential ally was Ruhklyn, where before there'd been more than a hundred Addaran soldiers and citizens spoiling for an altercation. Her own position was elevated, and distant. Mayhap she thought it enough.

That, even without his restraints, she had him trapped.

One or the other, a spike of apprehension lanced through him. A chilling concern for Denariel and the others left behind. If Sabrynne had anticipated *this*, what safeguards might she have put in place to forestall *their* escape?

But he bridled the thought, refusing to guess at the myriad possibilities. He couldn't help them now, except mayhap by engaging her here for as long as possible. Hadn't that been his aim from the start?

"No clever retort?" she asked. "No sally of insult?"

Kylac shrugged, arms still folded across his chest. "I'm not one for spitting from the gallows."

"Admitting defeat?" The starlit gleam of her smile vanished. "Perhaps you *do* disappoint."

He saw no need to respond. While waiting for her to realize it, the reverberations of a distant outcry filtered in from the outer corridors. One of his victims had finally been discovered, spawning an overdue alarm.

He marked Sabrynne's reaction. Having permitted this, she was no more surprised than he. Though she did exude a mild dissatisfaction.

"Clumsy, to let your trail be so soon discovered. Owing to your haste, I presume?"

Let her presume as she wished. Kylac held himself guarded, impassive, declining to—

"The prisoners!" Ruhklyn blurted, and Kylac felt the thread-thin tether of his protectiveness toward the Blackfist unravel. "He freed them all."

"Did he now?" Her tone was again flat, unsurprised. "And by which gate do they foolishly think themselves capable of leaving this city?"

"No gate," Ruhklyn replied. With a glance at Kylac, he lowered his stolen swords and stepped slowly, imploringly, toward Sabrynne. "They mean to steal down to the river, creep north by barge."

"Asp!" Kylac snarled.

He felt the weight of Sabrynne's scowl, even if he couldn't quite mark its lines in the moonlit dark. Whether her irritation stemmed from Ruhklyn's news, the traitorous man himself, or Kylac's unusual outburst, was even harder to discern.

After a momentary deliberation, she signaled to one of her lieutenants. An intricate motion, bespeaking some message likely known only to the Grenarr. With a sharp, Grenarr salute, the hound-faced lieutenant peeled away from the group, striding briskly back through the nearest entrance.

"Have you anything further to report?" Sabrynne asked of Ruhklyn.

The Blackfist seemed at a loss. "I . . ." he groped. He glanced back at Kylac before turning quickly away again.

"If you've nothing more to report, what value do you offer me?"

"I would pledge you my sword."

"In earnest?"

"I would . . . my lady."

"Then turn it on him," she said, thrusting her chin toward Kylac.

A spike of panic. "My . . . my lady?"

"Show me what your sword is worth. Disarm your companion there, and we'll discuss what further role you may serve among us."

Ruhklyn scoffed with forced mirth, as if seeking to expose a jape. None so much as faked a smile to match. At a gesture from Sabrynne, a pair of bowmen flanking her raised their ready arrows, taking aim at the reluctant Blackfist.

Arms still crossed, Kylac waited. Rank with desperation, Ruhklyn actually rounded on him. Amid the filthy nest of his once-red beard, the craven's expression was part terror, part pleading. Kylac could almost pity him.

The traitorous Blackfist took only a single step before twin arrows punched into his back, the heads emerging from his chest—smeared with the juices of his black heart. Kylac watched his eyes widen. He gasped for breath, only to spit it up in a cough of blood. His face contorted, grappling with denial. Anger bloomed, but failed to take root before the sword slipped from his grasp and he pitched forward, slapping face-first on the marble tiles at the edge of the pool, there to twitch like a landed fish.

"A kinder end than he earned," Sabrynne said.

Kylac couldn't tell if it was the man's inconstant nature that displeased her, or his failure to serve. If placed in those dungeons as her agent, surely she'd hoped for more from him than this.

"As it will be for you," she added, "should you force me to have you dropped beside him. So tell me, where do *your* swords lie?"

The furor within the palace was growing. Marshalling in response to his activities. And to those of the other companies? If they hadn't yet been discovered, they soon would be. The time had come to draw the enemy to him—and more than the mere handful in this chamber.

"Would that I knew," he said, allowing a wistful tone to betray his meaning.

"Should the princess manage to escape, you'll have lost the opportunity to win them back."

He could agree to head their pursuit, he supposed, using that pretense to string them along awhile. But it would likely mean returning to his restraints, and he'd had quite enough of those. It would also be an outright lie, which he preferred to live his life without.

"So be it," he said.

Something in Sabrynne's mien sharpened. "I'll grant you a tally of five to alter your stance. One."

He lowered his gaze, letting his shoulders slowly droop.

"Two."

The very portrait of reluctant submission, as best as he could portray it.

"Three."

All while giving feel to the energies eddying throughout the solar.

"Four."

And the icy tingle crested his spine.

When Sabrynne signaled, he dropped low, hands falling to his sides and drawing his borrowed sabers. A pair of arrows whizzed overhead. A wave of spearmen descended from all sides. Kylac slid behind a plinth for a moment's cover, and gave ear to the satisfying clatter of arrowheads chipping at chiseled stone.

Another set of bowmen took aim at his back. He waited for the telltale twang of release before leaning sharply left to avoid the first, then rolling right to elude the rest. By then, the spearmen were on him, shafts reaching . . .

Up came his swords in a whirling flourish. They felt at first like cleavers, heavy and awkward. But he'd spent years using such—and every other variety of blade—before. His body remembered. He knocked the stabbing spears aside, dodging and deflecting at the same time. He then countered with thrusts and swipes of his own. Iron tasted flesh, nipping and slashing, spitting strings of blood into the air. His victims grunted and hissed, their cries tempered. These were not the type to yowl or wail.

Not yet.

They pressed him from all sides. As he would have it. Clearing a flank would only expose him again to their range weapons. Better that he let them crowd round, walling him off from those lancing barbs. Leaving him an enemy more predictable to contend with.

Their effort wasn't feigned. Each seemed desperate to be the one to present him to their overlord skewered on the end of a shaft or blade. Even the mortally wounded seemed loath to withdraw. For a few moments, he let them tighten their ranks. Alive, he felt, at the heart of their swarm. After the weeks of inactivity, he wondered now how he'd managed to restrain himself for so long.

Only when wounds overcame fervor did they begin to fall aside, succumbing to blood loss, to punctured lungs, to severed muscles and tendons that no longer functioned as they should. As the sphere of slaughter expanded, their brethren and comrades found it harder to engage him, for wading through the mass of lurching, tumbling, writhing bodies. A widening no-man's-land that would, be it late or soon, invite the bowmen to try their hand at him, no matter who stood gathered in backdrop.

He considered permitting just that. To see what frustration he might breed by letting them unleash their fire at him in a close-knit circle. But he saw no need to tempt fate in such a manner. In such conditions, even an errant shot might prove to him unfavorable. Apart from that, he needed a lot more than those in this chamber to be taking shots at him, if he was to give Denariel her best chance at stealing away.

So he set finally to carving an escape path of his own. Still engaging or evading those at his flanks, spinning and ducking and leaping and rolling, but proceeding east, back the way he'd come, drawing after any who could follow. Most seemed more than inclined to do so, huffing and growling with enraged exertion.

Calls went out to block his exit, once his goal became apparent. But it mattered little. Already, they were slowing, their motions growing leaden and weary. Kylac was just now finding his stride, settling into a sustainable rhythm. In their crush to thwart his departure, they really only hampered their own movements.

Kylac felt no real hesitation at taking advantage.

As he neared the open archway to the adjacent antechamber, where Grenarr were crying madly for external reinforcements, he did catch a glimpse of Sabrynne at the north end of the solar. Nestled in moonlit shadow, surrounded by her guard ring. On seeing her, Kylac had a fleeting impulse to reverse direction. If he truly meant to disturb this nest of hornets, what better way than to slay their queen?

Yet something cautioned him against it. The fact that she remained present at all, mayhap, almost as if baiting him. Or the reminder that his mission of the moment was better served on the move, now that he had their attentions. No matter how loud and sharp the cries, they could echo only so effectively from this solitary location.

Or mayhap he only wanted her to tell him yet where his blades could be found. A question she was unlikely to answer unless he could catch her in a quieter moment—*before* being forced to drain her throat. Here, he might not get that chance.

So he flicked her a mock salute with the tip of a bloodied saber upon reaching his archway, then took a bow as he took his leave.

8

A knot of snarling Grenarr spilled through the archway on his heels, gnashing and sputtering invectives. Kylac felt a twinge of regret. That they should make themselves his enemies. That they should have to die for no better reason than the will of an unyielding master with an aim contrary to his.

All else burned with exhilaration.

Whatever the cause or ethical implications, a challenge had been extended and accepted. It was their skill now against his. A contest of desire and determination. Those clever enough to fall back or maintain distance—with or without wounds to show for their effort—might well glimpse another sunrise. The more stubborn or witless . . . well, at least their lives would no longer be hampered by it.

He cared little for the numbers, one or the other. Needless as killing had always seemed to him, he wasn't troubled by it—not against willing combatants, anyway. He'd stopped counting years ago those he'd slain. Often, it was difficult to know. Where one man might survive a seemingly catastrophic injury, another might succumb to even a minor wound given later to rot. Having not always been on hand to see the final results of his work, he could offer but rough estimates.

Measured at this point in hundreds, more easily than scores.

Mayhap even thousands, if numbering creatures alongside men—however marginal the difference.

So it mattered not to him whether the night's tally proved akin to a company or legion. All that mattered, on this occasion, was that the conflict be sustained. Long enough for Denariel and the others to make their way.

Spinning back now and again to engage those flowing after him, Kylac danced across the squat tables and cushions furnishing the antechamber and on through a doorway to the foyer beyond. He was met by streams of shouts approaching now from multiple directions. Reinforcements. Good. They were still a mite distant, though, so he held up in the foyer, waiting for them as he waited for those giving chase from the solar. He made a momentary play at bottling the latter up in the doorway to slow them down. Though unafraid of being surrounded, he didn't necessarily want them to know that, for the sense of powerlessness it might breed. As long as he wished for them to maintain their fight, better to grant them little victories along the way. Just enough to foster in them a false hope.

As the swell of cries strengthened from corridors north and south, he made pretense at being forced back from the doorway by the thrusting spears and the occasional lancing arrow. Withdrawing toward the foyer's heart and allowing those from the solar to spill out along his flanks. Seeing the sparks of grim triumph that flared within the corners of their eyes.

Their numbers overtook the north-south archways, then fought to pinch around to the east portal at his back, amid ringing shouts of, "Sever his retreat!" While most remained focused directly on him, others moved to close the door itself. Kylac feigned a measure of desperation in forestalling that effort, withdrawing quickly before dropping and rolling through the exit.

He came to his feet upon the entertainment hall balcony. A surge of Grenarr joined him, their numbers bolstered by those flooding the foyer now from three directions, their confidence buoyed by the impression that they had him on the run.

Kylac offered further encouragement by retreating steadily along the balcony. Pouncing from bench to balustrade to bench again.

Darting in and out of heavy curtains. Slowing only for the time required to draw another optimistic opponent after him—then countering with a prick or scratch that forced them back or lured them on with a yelp of frustration.

His random, unpredictable movements had comrades stumbling over and against one another, their numbers a hindrance as much as an advantage. Amid the fray, commanders barked orders and elsewise tried to coordinate strikes, but Kylac gave them no real chance to do so. He could see before they did what they might do to rein him in. He recognized before they how they must respond. He didn't have to know their thoughts. The physical laws of their weapons and their stature, shaped by a communal mindset and its overall objective, provided all the clues he needed. By the time they thought to shift a formation or raise a defense or execute an advance, Kylac was already reacting to it. Disrupting it, if need be, or allowing them to carry it out and learn too late what little it had won them.

That, in a way, he actually *could* sense their thoughts—the ambitions and fears and indignation and bloodlust of nearly each man who came before him—only made the task of thwarting them that much easier.

It wasn't something he'd ever undertaken with conscious effort. It had always simply *been*, an innate ability to discern the emotional energies of those around him. Too often, it was all just so much noise. Love and hate and joy and sorrow and faith and bitterness and myriad others, awhirl like a shrieking funnel cloud. Further muddled by delusion and dishonesty and the occasional voids generated by those who either lacked feelings or were simply better at guarding them.

In battle, though, those sensations had always crystalized for him. No matter how swift, or how numerous. No matter the attempts at deception. For whatever reason, when a man or beast confronted him with harmful intent, Kylac could see with distinct clarity just how they would go about it, and how to prevent it. Not in any thoughtful, tactical way, but in a more natural, instinctive one.

Like a heart knowing when to flex, and when to relax.

He'd learned long ago to stop questioning it. If his father, master of so many martial arts, had been unable to explain or even comprehend the experience, then it was quite possible no one could. Mayhap, if Kylac were to ever encounter his equal, he'd have someone to converse with about it.

Until then, he simply relied on his inimitable blend of intuition and abilities and stamina and training, and plied them to his advantage. He certainly didn't expect to encounter anyone who could match him here. If the Grenarrian existed who could, Sabrynne wouldn't have seen any need to recruit a pale, smooth-cheeked, mercenary outlander to her cause.

When he'd reached the balcony's midsection, a fresh wave of Grenarr came howling in through the opposite entrance. An eastern front to mirror the west. Kylac very nearly smirked at their arrival. At last, his little disturbance was making something of itself. Like a pebble triggering a rockslide.

He let the two sides close like a pair of shears, thinking they had him, before springing to the balustrade and toeing nimbly along its length. Blades hacked and stabbed at him, in a manner not at all dissimilar to the threshing chamber back at Talonar. Leaping, halting, twisting, or leaning as needed, he left them cleaving only air. Until finally he dropped off the far side, angling back so as to catch a supporting pillar with his feet and the pommels of his sabers. Half sliding, half grinding, in a descent that carried him to the floor of the entertainment hall below.

Predictably, his surprised, frustrated enemies railed at him from above. A few leaned out as if considering the leap, before wisely thinking better of it. Bowmen were ushered forward, and a rain of arrows unleashed. Kylac heard the missiles thunk and clatter around him as he sped across the floor, climbed and traversed a central platform, and leapt from the far side. A ramp ahead climbed past an array of bench seats toward an arched exit. Amid the roaring echoes, he darted up the slope, pausing at the threshold to make sure they intended to follow. With a furor of shouts coming not just from the balcony, but from various portals at ground level, Kylac ducked from the hall, trusting he'd not long find himself alone on the other side.

A curving promenade awaited him, in which more angry shouts converged from either flank. He started left, eschewing a shorter path to the outer grounds by way of the west wing, thinking to head deeper into the palace proper. For all the warriors Sabrynne had summoned, and all the notice his actions had drawn since, there were still far more whose presence was unaccounted for. He didn't dare believe that all of the alarms resounding throughout the palace were for him. Surely some would be responding by now to word of the larger jailbreak, seeking to cut off whatever secret and not-so-secret pathways Ledron intended to make use of. While Kylac couldn't possibly attract them all, he intended to try.

Faces poked out at him from various alcoves and intersecting corridors. Servants, heralds, watchmen. Most who spied him fell back into shadow or darted quickly away again. Others, generally catching sight of him from the perceived safety of an encircling overlook, were more likely to point and add their own voices to the escalating outcry. Their efforts were well suited to his. Seen, but not stopped. A shadow fleeting hither and yon among them. Sowing outrage and confusion with every stride.

He left the promenade behind to make his way along a series of inner passages. Wending toward the palace's main entrance hall along an indirect route. At last, the scattering of individuals gave way to a cluster here or a pack there. Warriors marshaling, but not entirely certain as to where. This was not yet their home. Not truly. They might have laid claim. They might have secured its walls and wormed their way through the majority of its halls. But they couldn't possibly have devised yet any clear protocols for defending it. They were but scattered patrols assigned to one area or another. Well versed, mayhap, in hunting stray Addarans, but hardly equipped to muster a sustained engagement against an unwelcome intruder. After weeks of unbroken success against their enemies, how many even contemplated the possibility?

He could have slaughtered any number of them while scarcely breaking stride. Instead, he turned and ran from this clutch and then that, allowing them to give word on his position and gather their strength. To close off pathways and narrow the ground available to him. Let them suppose him a rat trapped in a maze. Not quite realizing—or refusing to accept—which of them was predator, and which was prey.

When he broke at last into the central foyer, he found no fewer than a hundred Grenarr assembled, divided into regiments, awaiting further command. The sight of him, along with the furious echoes traveling in his wake, was enough to determine their response. With the barking of a couple commanders, they surged toward him like a breaking wave, crested by a foam of iron and steel.

Kylac shot forward to meet them, sabers leading, aching again for the feather-light heft, the incomparable strength and sharpness, of his own blades. The entry doors stood shut and barred. He wouldn't be escaping that way. Not unless he slew every man in the room—and those coming after—for the time it would take him to wrest aside the heavy beam and free the array of bolts and latches. But this seemed as suitable a space as any in which to make a prolonged stand, given its central, obvious location. It remained only to determine for how long.

He tore into the very center of their throng, carving his initial path along a seam between squads, then selecting one with a loud-barking commander and gashing toward its heart. Deep within, he opted to trade blades, sheathing his dulled, dented saber in the noisome commander's shark-fin-tattooed throat, and taking the Grenarrian's own, fresher sword in hand.

His other saber was also well spent, so he found a replacement for that one shortly thereafter. And then again, just moments later, when the new blade broke beneath the weight and angle of a descending pole-axe. A shrewder adversary, less incensed, might have stopped supplying him weapons at that point. Sought to turn this into a battle of hand strikes, and thereby mitigate the damage he could inflict. Alas, they were long past such logic or reason, carrying forward now with the sheer momentum of their bloodlust.

He labored ceaselessly amid the ebbs and flows of that momentum, fueled by his own. Part of him had worried he might tire. Not since striking forth from Talonar nearly four years ago now—and only once that he could recall before then—had he been compelled to endure a period of inactivity such as that by which he'd returned to Avenell. In the back of his mind had lingered that whisper of concern. How might that forced dormancy, that near-utter stagnation, have sapped his strength and endurance?

If anything, however, it had served to rejuvenate him. As if all that latent energy had simply been bottled up, preserved until the moment it would be required. For he felt no signs of fatigue—no worrisome weight upon his limbs or undue pressure against his lungs. His heart beat steadily; his skin sweated comfortably. Even as those around him sucked for breath, dripped rivers from their brows, or edged back—enraged hunger notwithstanding—to let their comrades have a go.

He consigned himself for a time to the foyer floor, elusive as a rainbow, while his enemies gave chase. Like a great vat of milk, and he the stick churning them into butter. He maimed and killed, but no more than necessary. None of these did he recognize. None had wronged him, by any specific means. And, tactically, it made more sense to continually goad and exhaust those with whom he'd already engaged than to kill them and make room for the fresher incoming waves.

And they *had* come. He felt the increasing weight of their press, even those who couldn't yet make their way forward. Those who'd chased him from the west. Those drawn to this clangor from the east. There were mobs upon the twin stairs curling up to a first-level landing above. And pushing in from the north corridor between their crests. A chamber packed with squirming, grunting, growling bodies, all clamoring for a piece of him.

He decided to give these others their chance, and so moved toward the east stair. Those left behind scrambled after. Those ahead surged eagerly to meet him. As always, that eagerness soon curdled, become fury and confusion, as he tore through them. There one instant and gone the next. Never far. Just a lean or shift, duck or twist, lunge or spin, or some seamless combination thereof. Enough to evade their strikes or deflect them with his own.

Like shards amid a hurricane, he must have seemed, slicing and piercing from every conceivable angle. A raking flurry that took no pause, except to reverse direction or veer along some new path. Random or deliberate, few would be able to say. Unstoppable regardless.

Or so he always felt, in the throes of combat's dance. Driven by invisible currents he couldn't quite understand, but relenting to their influence. If puppet he was, his unknown masters had yet to cause him harm. And as long as they guided him unerringly in accordance with *his* will, he had no cause to chafe at their perceived control.

He continued to change weapons as he went, refreshing them as needed. Shards, but he missed his own blades. A fitting exercise this was, then. And encouraging, to know for certain that his ever-increasing prowess over the past few years wasn't solely due to his enhanced weaponry. He'd clearly been spoiled by their attributes, but his reliance went only so far.

Indebted, yes. Bound, no.

Knives, flails, even a spear haft chopped into a pair of staves served him for a time. Even those fleeting moments in which he'd surrendered all weapons—usually leaving them buried in one or more opponents—were but misleading invitations to test his rawer defenses. In those instances, he simply relied on an assortment of punches, kicks, locks, and twists to inhibit breathing, snap bones, tear joints, or elsewise stun an adversary into momentary submission. One roaring brute dove at him halfway up the stairs, only to find his momentum doubled uncontrollably, sending him pinwheeling over the handrail. Another lunged from above into a body throw that sent him crashing into a clutch of warriors clambering up from below. The resulting collapse and tumble of bodies down the steps resembled nothing so much as a small avalanche.

It wasn't but moments thereafter that he'd reached the upper landing, twin sabers from two different dead men in hand.

And everything began to change.

It happened gradually, at first. A stream of shouts relayed from the north and east, followed by a slackening pressure from those directions. A summons, drawing Grenarr out from the slaughterhouse the grand foyer had become. The newest arrivals being the first to turn back, but not the last, as those packed deeper within detached and rerouted. Not all, of course. Some wouldn't. Others couldn't. But, wave after retreating wave, Kylac found himself increasingly forsaken by those who'd been striving so fixedly to reach him mere moments before.

A thief's tide, ripping the sharks back out to sea. Kylac saw it not as a victory, but the first strides toward defeat. The enemy wasn't rerouting out of fear or capitulation. It had simply caught another scent. A scent worthy of abandoning him in order to take up a more likely or meaningful pursuit.

Kylac tried not to consider too closely the implications. It needn't mean that Denariel herself had been discovered. It might have been any of the parties organized by Ledron and sent forth in a desperate race for freedom.

But if all were at risk, why not her?

He hesitated, caught still among a raging mesh of blades and spearheads, uncertain of his next move. Did he give chase to those departing, seeking to join and affect whatever conflict they were rushing off to? Dragging along another throng of enemies in the bargain? Or would it be more fitting to his aims now to make his own exit and see how many of these potential reinforcements he could lead astray?

He struck east across the landing, hacking clear of those yet committed to him, seeking to force as many of the would-be departees as possible to come about and reengage him. It worked, but only so well. Theirs was clearly a rearguard action, meant only to slow him as they fell back so that the bulk of their number could race on ahead unharried. And he still had a swarm behind him, preventing him from pursuing with adequate haste. Whatever the forward action, he wasn't likely to reach it with the speed and focus needed to alter its outcome. Nor, again, without ushering in a fresh wave of Grenarr for his embattled companions to contend with. They'd all pretty well agreed, back in the dungeons, that any party caught out was on its own. To either die fighting or to yield and hope for recapture. Kylac found himself gritting his teeth now in a very Ledron-like manner at the truth of it.

So he turned mind to the more likely course available to him, and set after it with a flourish. East, still, down the corridor, but only as far as the next hall. A receiving hall, lushly appointed, its furnishings remarkably unscathed by all of the conflict in recent weeks. It included an outer terrace with a view of the southeast gardens. A bank of floor-length windows were latched and curtained just now, but Kylac backed toward them all the same. A slow, steady drift amid the unrelenting vortex of his movements. Nipping and slashing at his pursuers, pressing them so as to draw as many as were still willing after him.

The others would be all right, he assured himself. The false information relayed by Ruhklyn to Sabrynne would have bought them some extra time. For all Kylac knew, this fresh uproar was but in reaction to the realization that the prisoners had in fact gone missing. Not necessarily that any of them had been discovered.

So intent was his focus on luring those with whom he was still engaged, and so nagging his reflections concerning his comrades, that he very nearly stepped into the awaiting trap.

The curtains at his back parted, and a wall of netting appeared, held together by a string of warriors. As one, they hastened to encircle him, their nets stretched high and wide. A finely honed movement by men who'd been fishermen since birth, practicing such maneuvers likely as soon as they'd learned to stand.

Kylac plowed forward, seeking refuge amid the storm of the pursuing bladefront, so as to evade the would-be captors behind him. A spike of alarm jolted through him, telling him that, were he brought to heel now, his stay would be far less pleasant than before.

The frigid certainty dissipated, however, as the possibility melted, burned away by the fire of his counterassault. Bodies fell around him, blood blooming from countless gashes. Then he reversed and attacked the netting. Not the strands themselves—not with *these* blades—but their human seams. A moment's exhilaration, and it was done, the wall collapsed, the trap broken.

He veered past it before it could reform. Scampering south, toward the terrace. This couldn't be their only snare. Pushing deeper into the palace at this point would surely trigger more. The battle's flow had shifted, its tide turned. Sabrynne's forces had overcome his momentary advantage. While expecting him, his reaction and its severity had caught them off guard. But they were no longer staggering about, unprepared. The more coordinated their own responses, the less he stood to gain, and at increasing risk. He wasn't certain how many Grenarr actually occupied the palace, but he saw scant reason to find out simply for the challenge of escaping them.

Wan moonlight exposed the terrace window-doors where the curtains had been thrust aside. When Kylac reached one, he didn't trouble to trip the latch, but rather shattered the glass with a saber's pommel strike. A salty breeze gusted through as the shards settled. Kylac winced when they bit at his bare feet. He'd have acquired a pair of sandals by now, if only he'd come across a pair amid these giants small enough to fit his feet. Alas, it had seemed better that he remain nimble—and this but the first cause he'd had to regret it.

So he weathered the pain and pressed on, through the portal and out to the terrace. Breaking from his pursuers, he needed but three bounding strides to reach the balustrade. There he held while the Grenarr punched after, some on his heels, the rest smashing through glass doors of their own.

He let them advance—the first wave, anyway—while making cursory examination of the palace courtyard and gardens below. The yard was astir with enemies milling about the barred entry doors, several of whom were pointing and shouting now in his direction and shifting eastward. The gardens themselves were empty. Inviting.

Kylac hopped onto the stone rail. As the enemy's spears reached for him, he somersaulted backward, and fell.

He cushioned his landing with an impact-absorbing roll. The grasses that caught him were soft and spongy enough that he needn't have bothered. A thrown spear pierced the earth near his shoulder. And then another. He rolled again, scuttled left, scampered right, and then dashed off, past a hedgerow and into a veritable forest of shade trees.

He could have vanished at that point, but worried his pursuers might surrender the hunt. So he continued to reveal himself in occasional flashes, enough to tempt them on. To the river, they intended to flee, he'd told Ruhklyn. In keeping with that lie, he angled east as he scurried southward. A lengthy stretch of misdirection. Well over a league to where the nearest barge could be found tethered to the river docks. So be it. The farther he could lead them, the longer it would take them to retrace their missteps.

Nightbirds shrieked and squalled at the disturbance. Wild dogs barked and bayed. For all the furor within the palace, the city without was largely quiet, serene. Kylac tried not to think too closely on the chief cause being that most of its former residents were enslaved, dead, or driven already into the wilderness.

With any fair measure of fortune, he'd increased this night the number of the latter, without adding too much to the tallies of the former. It might be a day or more before he knew. The Owl's Hour had flown, with the Raven now winging toward midnight. But it'd likely be daybreak or beyond before any of those fleeing the dungeons would know themselves to be safe.

Even then, there was sure to be a multipronged pursuit. While Sabrynne struck him as too wise to scatter her limited forces in desperate search across unfamiliar earth, she was all but certain to employ scouts and patrols to mark the trails by which her prisoners had fled. Hoping to run down even one or two whose retrieval might ease the sting of those lost.

Or mayhap she and hers would be too busy sitting back, licking their wounds. Kylac mustered a smile at the thought. It troubled him more than he cared to admit, fleeing like this. Leaving behind his blades, his garments, his shoes. Not knowing whom he might be abandoning in the process. But such was the incomplete, unreliable nature of plans. He'd chosen his course of action, and would see it through. Should he learn within the next few days that the results were unacceptable, he would simply choose another.

Taking solace for now in freedom won and enemy plans foiled. Convinced that ample opportunities for more of each yet lay ahead.

Upon reaching a stretch of the wall encircling the palace grounds, Kylac tucked his bloodied sabers into his belt and shimmied up its near-bare face. At its top, he lingered again, allowing himself to be seen. Only then did he drop to the other side, taking aim at the river upstream from where it emptied into the bay.

With a song of pursuit in his ears and a determined grimace drawn across his face, he sped gamely into the waning night.

9

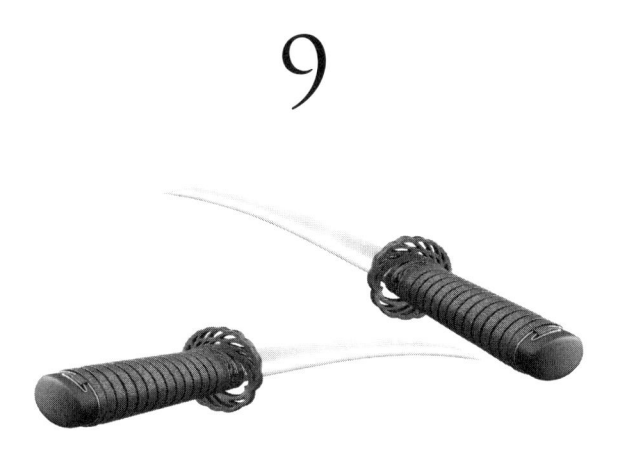

They crept through the brush in an effort at stealth, single file along the narrow animal track. What they actually achieved could better be described as a mild ruckus—and that if Kylac was being charitable. Still, he'd circled their column twice already, sweeping the surrounding area, and found it to be clear of enemies. A stray hunting cat, on two separate occasions. And the small pack of skin-bellied wolves whose hungry curiosity had keyed him to their position in the first place. But no Grenarr lying in ambush, stalking either flank, or trailing on their heels.

So it would seem that, for now, they were safe.

He announced his presence with a low whistle. Simalen, serving point, started nonetheless when he saw Kylac standing there, in the center of their thread-thin trail, more than half screened by the protrusion of wild foliage. Outfitted no longer in his prisoner's roughspun, but green woolen breeches, gray linen tunic, and assorted leathers discovered in an abandoned tailor's workshop during his flight from Avenell. Loose-fitting, as he preferred, so as not to restrict his motions. Sim, a seasoned Redfist, had fallen back on his heels, a longknife in hand, before recognition eased his troubled features.

Havrig and Jorrand thrashed forward to join him. Ledron, scarcely more than a shadow among those farther back, motioned Moh and

Ysander to oversee the formation of a shield around Denariel before skirting on ahead.

Kylac greeted them with a lazy wave. "Calm, friends."

He sensed little enough of friendship from them, but watched them lower their stolen blades with evident relief. All save Ledron.

"I trust you weren't followed," he snapped, eyeing the surrounding brush with suspicion.

"For a time," Kylac admitted. "None managed to keep pace."

"How did you find us?"

Kylac might have laughed, had he thought he could do so without raising Ledron's ire. Provided their heading, a scything search pattern had quickly revealed the webwork of likely trails—some more recently traveled than others. It had taken him nearly two full days to track them down not for lack of signs, but because he'd discovered and followed more than one party on the run from Avenell's dungeons.

But Ledron's concern was not so much his methods of search as it was whether the Grenarr might duplicate them.

"I know a game trail when I sees it. Not like them raised upon the waves."

"You think them unable to follow?"

"Lacking desire more'n ability. It's our return they'll be guarding against."

Ledron seemed to search for another argument, but that well had run dry. His expression soured as Denariel shoved forward, grunting and cursing amid those seeking still to encircle her.

"Are we calling a halt, then?" she asked.

"Merely ensuring he's alone," Ledron grumbled, still searching the jungle growth.

"Reckless, he's proven, not clumsy."

"I didn't mean to suggest elsewise."

"Then it's his loyalties you doubt."

Ledron gritted his teeth, bypassing his chance to deny it.

"Is that it, mercenary?" Denariel demanded, turning her dust-streaked face upon Kylac. "Have you sold us out?"

"I didn't see Your Highness freed only to lead her into ambush."

"Perhaps not," she agreed, brushing angrily at a fly buzzing round her ear. "But it may be I'm not your intended prize. Could be my father's head you've been tasked to collect, and us just the bait used to lure him."

Kylac bit back a reflexive denial. "Could be. Or could be I'd have run him aground on my own in the time it's taken to see to the rest o' ya."

"Enough," Ledron snarled, betraying his frustration with the topic. And why not? The same accusation might be made of most any man among them. "If we're to peck and squabble, I'd sooner do it on the march."

Denariel sneered. "A remarkable notion, Captain. Shall I take the point?"

Ledron fumed, but gestured at Sim to resume, with Havrig and Jorrand taking to the Redfist's heels. The captain went next, beckoning Kylac alongside him. Denariel took it upon herself to thrust after them, her shield dissolving to fall closely behind her.

"Any trouble making your escape?" Kylac asked Ledron. While he hadn't observed any fresh wounds among their company, they numbered a mere score, leaving many a familiar face unaccounted for.

"The Fair Mother seems to have smiled upon us," the Head replied. "At last."

"What o' Taeg? Aythef? Ithrimir?"

"Taeg stole off with a separate party. As did Aythef, as I would not abide that traitor in Her Highness's midst."

"Would that you'd been so discerning before," Denariel interjected, overlooking their close-pressed shoulders.

"Would that I had," Ledron agreed.

Unless Kylac was mistaken, her rebuke was more for herself than for the captain. As mayhap was warranted. Denariel had known the royal cook and eventual traitor better than anyone aboard. She alone had known the true nature of his relationship with Thane. She alone had consorted with him to smuggle herself aboard—as Kylac had heard it from Aythef, anyway. If anyone, *she* should have been the one to expose him for his true intent.

All apparently lost on Ledron, given the way he'd just swallowed her reprimand. Suggesting to Kylac that Denariel hadn't troubled to confess anything beyond the obvious betrayal already revealed by the cook himself.

Her scowl as Kylac glanced back at her seemed to dare him to voice his thoughts.

Except it seemed not to matter now. Only that, in Kylac's mind, the cook had suffered aplenty, and in no small measure absolved himself, earning better than to be cast off like chum.

"And the Scribe?" he asked instead.

"Chose to remain," said Ledron, "rather than chase about the island."

The words pinched Kylac's stomach. He should have known. Or at least suspected. Too many other, more pressing concerns. But the end result left the Elementer who'd more than once saved his life at the mercy of Sabrynne and her minions.

"Have you not encountered any others?" Ledron asked him, before he could dwell too deeply upon it.

"I did. Companies led by Olekk and Rehm. Engaged them long enough to inquire as to whether ya'd escaped. Neither knew, so I kept searching."

"And now?"

"Would ya has me search for more? Or remain to ensure Her Highness's safekeeping?"

Denariel snorted. "Else I may simply wither and die."

Ledron cast her an irritated glance over his shoulder. "For all that it grieves her, I've none better suited to defend her." Looking back to Kylac, he added, "If that is truly your aim."

"As pledged from our very beginning, Captain."

A lifetime ago, it seemed to him now, though it had been less than six months. Their ill-fated and mayhap ill-conceived bargain, struck there upon Kuurian shores. Shadowed by deceit on Ledron's part, and by blithe ignorance on his own. But they were each of them too far committed now. Whatever failures suffered along the way—and whatever tragedies ahead—their paths at this juncture appeared hopelessly entwined.

Ledron only gritted his teeth. A sign, mayhap, of having drawn similar conclusion.

"A joyful reunion, then," said Denariel, her tone thick with derision.

"I dare not beg of the Fair Eriyah anything more."

She fell quiet after that. When it became clear she'd be missing out on no further conversation from Ledron, either, she fell back a pace. Kylac chose to respect the captain's silence. Questions wormed through his mind, but he supposed the answers could wait. Assuming the Head had any to give.

So he concentrated his attentions on the dry, enveloping jungle as they tread the narrow, knotted, overgrown path through its thorny heart. Curious birds marked their passage, along with scavenging rodents and hovering clouds of insects. But the only threats he sensed were those of the weariness, dejection, and general trepidation borne upon the shoulders of his companions. Whatever joy or relief they may have felt upon their safe departure from Avenell had clearly eroded over the past couple days, worn away by thirst, hunger—or any number of the harsh realities that lay yet before them. Theirs was a ragged, patchwork crew. Lightly armed, sparsely provisioned. Evicted from their home city. Worried for their families and friends. Wondering if and when they might ever be reunited. Untrusting of those among them. Skeptical of what blessings the future could possibly bring.

Kylac was more hopeful. Granted, he'd lost less than they had—largely because he lived his life with little to lose. But he need look no further than his own feet to be reminded of his failings. Shod now in soft leather boots taken from a cordwainer's workshop downroad from the tailor who'd unknowingly provided him his clothes. Boots and clothes that weren't his. Weapons no better than those he might craft himself. Were he to escape this isle now, in his present condition, it would have to be counted among his young life's most devastating setbacks.

But that didn't mean he would allow it to ruin him. This fight wasn't yet ended, its stages and trials still unfolding. What the others saw as obstacles and defeats, he would greet as skill-honing challenges and victories in progress.

Death itself would have to prove him wrong.

His confidence intact, he was all too willing to wait until nightfall to raise those questions that needed to be asked. In the few intervening hours, he remained at Ledron's side. While he would have preferred to take a turn scouting on ahead or falling back to learn whether they were being followed, he'd stirred the captain's suspicions merely by proposing as much. *Have you somewhere else to be?* Ledron had openly wondered. As if leaving their company, even for a time, might suggest a relaying of messages to some other faction. Conceding the responsibility to Ledron's more trusted companions, Kylac had held his place in line, where the Head could keep watch of him. Vaguely regretting revealing his presence when he had.

Given the tangled roof of the Bonewood's canopy, dusk arrived early, and sunset swift upon. Ledron shared a muttered disappointment at failing to reach their destination before the day's close, but insisted it unwise to go stumbling about these reaches in the dark. Kylac offered again to slip ahead, to discern whether this outpost—Tetherend—was inhabited by Addaran refugees as the captain believed. But the Head promptly scowled and determined that they would learn together sometime on the morrow.

"How certain are we His Majesty is there?" Kylac ventured later, when huddled alone with Ledron and Denariel at the hub of their makeshift camp. No fires for food or warmth. No shelter save that offered by hastily pilfered travel cloaks and the span of boughs overhead. Just a loose ring of their company some fifty paces out in every direction from where the captain had staked himself and the princess among a thicket of grandenfoot.

Ledron, chewing on a gnarled length of sallowroot, took a long time before responding. "With the likes of General Ohrma and Ruhklyn left behind, His Majesty will have sought a secondary safehold. One that few—if any—of even his most trusted advisors would know."

"How is it *you* know of it?"

Again the Head hesitated. Then looked to Denariel.

"He doesn't," she answered primly. "I do."

Ah. A place of refuge known only to members of the royal family. Which meant Ledron was taking Denariel's word in this. Another reason, mayhap, for the Head's overarching dissatisfaction with the entire venture.

It also meant . . . "Did His Highness Dethaniel know of it, as well?" Kylac asked. "Could it be something he might have revealed to the Grenarr?"

"I see not why," Denariel snapped. A raw wound, the subject of her royal brother. "He cannot have suspected we would have need of it."

The implication being that he'd never have gone through with his conspiracy against his own people had he known they might be chased from their home city like this. A fair assumption, from all that Kylac knew.

"If able," Ledron interjected, "His Majesty will not have lingered long, but will have struck north for Indranell. Only there will he find strength enough to repel a concentrated tar-skin assault. Or to muster a force large enough to retake Avenell."

"If so, he'll have left clues for us to find," Denariel maintained. "A course we can follow without resorting to the Karamoor."

Kylac found the name unfamiliar. "Karamoor?"

"The principal highway between Indranell north and Avenell south," Ledron grunted.

"Patrolled now by Grenarr," Kylac surmised.

Princess and captain nodded almost in unison.

"Fair enough," Kylac allowed, knowing full well that neither had requested his appraisal. "Then your earlier suspicion bears further consideration."

"Which suspicion was that?" Ledron asked.

"As to how wary we should be o' leading this entire company into the king's midst."

"Where else would you have us lead them?" asked Denariel.

"I only mean, this strikes me as a critical time. Straight off, might be there's wolves among us wearing lambskin."

"And it might be His Majesty is plagued by spies already," Ledron countered gruffly. "Safer to presume that his every move is known to our enemy, with or without our arrival."

"Making it more important to rally swiftly," Denariel agreed.

"Swiftly," Kylac echoed. "If'n we's guessed correctly as to the location o' your father's refuge."

"We've seen signs suggesting a sizable company may have beaten its way through this brush," Ledron claimed.

"My second point o' caution, Captain. Even if'n clear o' enemy moles, a larger group'll be easier to track, should the Grenarr choose to pursue us."

"You'd have us remain scattered until . . . when? We've regrouped at Indranell?"

"Ya divided us in our escape. Yet would bring us together now at a place ya claim may not be suitably defensible?"

Ledron shook his head. "If by chance His Majesty is still at Tetherend, he'll need our numbers as reinforcement. The trek north will not be an easy one if the Karamoor is closed to us."

"With me, he'd be safe enough. Mayhap safer, as I, unencumbered, could escort him nearly undetected."

Denariel chuffed a bitter laugh. "Forsaking the rest of us in the bargain. A fine notion nonetheless, save my father trusts you no more than we do. *Less*, in truth."

Ledron's glare seemed to mirror the princess's assessment. "Keen you appear, again, to find yourself in His Majesty's company. I thought we'd spoken of this already."

Of the Head's mistrust. Of the false assumption that Kylac's motives could only be nefarious in their purpose. "I needn't shed the rest o' ya to harm the king," he said, "if'n harming him was my goal." In an effort to appear less threatening, he crossed his arms and leaned back against a fallen log. "Would ya not have me lead him clear, should we encounter any trouble?"

"As a last, desperate resort, perchance," the Head admitted with a pained grimace. "Until then, I would perform the duty to which I'm sworn."

Meaning the king's welfare was the commission of the Shadowguard, not that of a rogue outlander. "We wait, it might be too late," Kylac pointed out. He straightened his back, dropping his hands to his knees. "But if'n that's your choice—"

"It is," Ledron insisted, just barely outpacing a similar retort from Denariel.

And respect it, he would. He'd had no intention of abandoning *all* of them, as the princess assumed. He certainly wouldn't have forsaken her defense for defense of her father—even if Ledron had begged him to do so. He'd merely wanted to ensure their decisions here had been measured against the full range of possibilities. Or at least as many as he'd troubled to guess at.

For guesses were nearly all they had. Denariel's play at confidence was as thin as wet parchment, while Ledron's dogged attempt to wrangle the situation had all the earmarks of a one-legged swineherd chasing after a squealing, mud-slicked sow. While it did appear to Kylac that a company might have made use of this trail in recent weeks, it remained to be determined whether Kendarrion had been among them. Whether he'd reached Tetherend by this or some other path. Whether the Grenarr had flushed him from the suspected safehold already.

Whether anything they did or didn't do now would have any sway whatsoever on the outcome of this conflict.

"If'n that's your stance, I'd best be about my rounds," Kylac said, rolling forward to his feet. "Ensure our lads out there stay safe through the night."

Neither captain nor princess voiced objection. Content, it would seem, with having him patrol the perimeter of their company's circle. Ledron did flash him a parting scowl. One that warned him to confine his path accordingly, or to not bother returning. In terms of their reaction, the best he might have hoped for. For he imagined it too much to expect a word of gratitude.

On either count, their bitter silence didn't disappoint.

They resumed their trek at the first blush of dawn.

Most had merely to rise from where they lay or crouched amid the brush the moment Ledron's whistled summons went out. Those still hunkered in some semblance of sleep were woken roughly by their nearest comrades. Kylac encountered an array of cramped limbs, stiff joints, and deeply shadowed eyes as he rejoined their gathering. Their apparent misery made him grateful for his youth—or whatever factors prevented him from experiencing such common discomforts.

He'd dozed in but a few brief snatches himself, a quarter-mark for every hour since midnight. All the rest he required in order to welcome the new day.

They trudged slowly at first, in deference more to the faint sunrise than to any of the company's aches or exhaustion. The brume-slicked jungle woods were filled now with sharp birdcalls, the chitter and croak of rodents and reptiles, and the ceaseless hum of insects. Each darting shape, each fleeting shadow, seemed to set any number of his companions on edge. As Kylac understood it, centuries had passed since this area had been reclaimed from the wilderness region known as the Harrows. A territory lorded over by the mutant Ukinha and other creations of the ancient Breeders. But the trepidation with which they traveled led Kylac to wonder if they suspected one of the so-called grolls to be stalking them even now.

Mayhap it was merely the Grenarr they feared. Or ambush from any of the wild creatures who'd made these woods their home. While far from the poisoned lands of the Ukinhan Wilds, it was clearly an untamed region, and thus something most Addarans had been raised to avoid. Even the land-based soldiers of the Stonewatch, Kylac had learned, were stationed chiefly along travel routes and the edges of established settlements. Those who dared to hunt, forage, or travel stretches like this disappeared far too often for those with good sense to follow in their footsteps.

By all appearances, Denariel was untouched by their wariness. Bitter, frustrated, yet unafraid. But then, her royal father had roamed these woods and others in his thirst for adventure, exploring much of the Addaran borderlands—the so-called Reach—with his royal family alongside. Not even the dreaded Harrows had been entirely off-limits, given that he'd had Denariel and surely Dethaniel partake of the rare sageryst mineral said to defend a man against ingested groll venom. Moreover, the Ukinha were widely held as the most fearsome creatures upon these island shores. Not only did the princess not loathe them as others did, she'd gone on to develop a relationship with one. If unmoved by sharks, one wasn't likely to start at minnows.

To what degree her bravery benefitted her remained a fair question. Lesser perils could still be lethal perils, and a certain amount of fear kept a man sharp. Kylac might have felt better had she exhibited at least a healthy respect for the potential dangers around them.

Not that it greatly mattered while he was here to protect her.

As the sun strengthened, so too did their collective stride. Muscles warmed, and the jungle's darker shadows dispersed. An eagerness took hold, fueled by the promise that, whatever awaited, their destination was within reach.

That burgeoning optimism began to wane when the firmer ground gave way to marsh. Brackish waters rose around them at first in stagnant pools separated by muddy fingers of earth. Then those trails thinned, and all that remained were the waters themselves. Reeds and rushes and mangroves grew in increasing clumps, while the trees thinned, growing gnarled and twisted and wreathed with moss. The number of rodents and other small mammals decreased, replaced by snakes and salamanders and ever-thickening insect swarms.

A smattering of murmurs couched in jest were swiftly quashed by the uncompromising Ledron. Comfort be damned, they'd known they would have to navigate these salty wetlands. That they were finally being called upon to do so only meant they were drawing close. Time didn't permit them to scout about for a drier, easier track through the swamp. They would slog, wade—swim if they had to—in order to reach the other side.

So they slogged, waded, and at one point even swam through the murky, rust-tinged waters that rose before them. Keeping their complaints to themselves while trusting in Ledron's lead. Kylac recognized well enough by their discontent the three, mayhap four men among them who might choose elsewise. But a minority, they were, among those committed to captain and king. And wise enough to know that, as long as Kylac obeyed Ledron, they would be ill-advised to cross him.

Else mayhap they only lacked inspiration as to where they might tread on their own.

Midmorning surrendered to midday before they came at last upon the outskirts of Tetherend. Just the remnants of outbuildings, at first, their crumbled walls protruding from the marsh like poorly tended gravestones. The roofs had collapsed, the rotten, mulch-like remains serving now as nesting material for the breeding of water-born insects. The stench thickened, built on a foundation of moldering decay.

Ledron signaled for silence. Unnecessary, Kylac would have thought, given that the Head had been threatening to sever loose tongues throughout almost the whole of their journey. After motioning Havrig and Jorrand to extend along their left flank, and Moh and Ysander to reach out along the right, the Blackfist captain gestured Sim carefully on ahead.

The dutiful Redfist had waded all of three strides, sending light ripples through the mud-thickened waters around him, when Denariel's booming call shattered the ghostly quiet.

"Father!"

Kylac smirked as Ledron and those around him crouched abruptly. Birds took to the air, startled by the invasive echoes that swept through the trees. Lizards and other creatures scurried or scampered for deeper shelter.

The Head whirled on her, his face flushed.

"Father, are you here?"

For half a heartbeat, it appeared Ledron might muzzle her with his own hand. Instead, he bridled his rage and faced forward again, waiting to see what further disturbance her outburst might have raised.

As the echoes faded, the land reclaimed its quiet. Birds continued to squawk their disapproval, but from distant reaches. Many of the other animal sounds had given way to eerie stillness. Insects hummed with their incessant movements, unfazed.

"I should've had you gagged," Ledron growled.

"A mite late now," said Kylac. "Would ya has us proceed? Or set root here?"

If able, Ledron might have drowned him right there in the knee-deep muck. As it was, the Head could only grit his teeth until it seemed they must break. When they didn't, he drew his longsword. An Addaran blade pilfered from a reserve armory during his escape from Avenell's dungeons.

Through clenched jaw, he hissed, "Quietly, should it please you."

He waited for the surrounding Redfists to draw their weapons. Like Kylac, Denariel left hers sheathed. Ignoring what he must have viewed as an act of insolence, the Head started forward again, casting about for sign of peril. The swampland ahead was a latticework of dark growth backlit by shards of brilliant daylight. Difficult to penetrate with vision alone. Kylac wondered again why he wasn't simply allowed to run point in order to suss out any threat. Alas, he knew better than to ask.

On the uncertain horizon, the earth appeared to rise, though the squishy ground remained flat beneath Kylac's feet. Twenty paces farther in, the humped earth resolved itself as a bulwark. A wall of stone, rising from the marsh. A curtain wall, he realized, or what remained of it. Great cracks ran through its seams, forming crumbled rifts here and there—some large enough to permit a man's passage. Vines and buttonwood and other upshoots of swamp growth probed these breaches or crept along the wall's face—thick, hungry tendrils resembling nothing so much as the tentacles of a kraken, sent by the marsh to drag the tumbledown fortification into its depths.

Defensible, mayhap. But hardly siegeworthy. At a glance, it was clear to Kylac why Ledron had claimed His Majesty Kendarrion unlikely to remain here any longer than necessary.

Assuming he'd visited at all.

Beyond the wall rose a pair of square towers, twin horns comprising Tetherend's inner keep. Impressive for a frontier outpost. Less so if become a seat of royal power.

"Father!" Denariel shouted again.

"Curse you!" Ledron snarled.

Kylac, beside the princess on the captain's heels, took a half step forward, holding back an arm to arrest her. Not because he feared her call, but because it had already done its work. From atop the wall, he felt the telltale itch of gazes, followed by the more pointed sensation of arrows trained in his direction.

"Hold, Captain," he advised. "They's eyes upon us. And more."

Ledron halted. His nervous gaze probed the crumbled battlement, still some thirty paces distant. "You're certain?"

Kylac couldn't see the figures amid the crenellations and arrow loops, but sensed their intent like the stinging of bees. "We're not yet welcome here."

The Head glared at Denariel, then turned back to the wall. "I am Captain Ledron of His Majesty's Shadowguard! Who commands here?"

For a moment, nothing. Then a quiet jostling, preceding the wary emergence of a shadow from behind the edge of a guard tower. "Come forward," the figure barked in return.

"And be feathered for my trouble? You have my name and rank. What's yours?"

"Mother's mercy!" Denariel hollered, and plowed forward until Kylac restrained her. She thrashed momentarily against his hold, then backed away as if blighted by his touch. "I am the Princess Denariel. Is my father within? Father!"

"Ho!" the voice on the wall shouted back. "Sergeant Penryn of the Stonewatch. Cease her bloody crowing, Captain, I beg you. Lest I be forced to put an arrow in her throat."

10

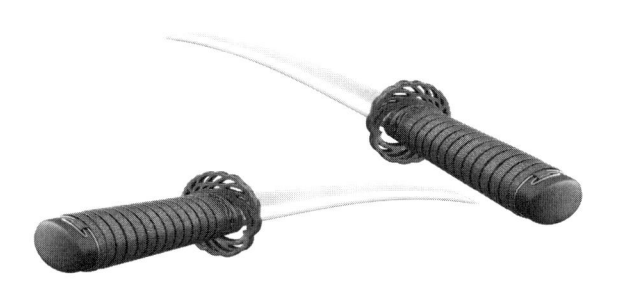

They were admitted through a sally port, the base of its thick, banded oak rotted away where engulfed by the marsh. Ledron led their column, his sword now sheathed. Havrig and Jorrand, the largest members of their company, shadowed him, their own blades still drawn. Kylac entered behind them, keenly aware of the sharp-eyed bowmen marking his stride from above.

Denariel tread on his heels. He sensed her chafing aggravation, but Ledron had insisted she remain there—with Sim, Moh, and Ysander to ward her back. Threatening elsewise to lash her to a tree and leave her behind until he'd made certain it was safe for her to enter.

A clutch of halberdiers stood ready to greet them, their half-moon formation preventing deeper entry into the flooded bailey. Ledron paused, clenching his jaw. Clearly insulted, but seemingly resigned to submit to whatever precautions were being imposed. Mayhap taking them as a sign—as Kylac did—that Kendarrion himself could indeed be housed within.

When the whole of their party had been corralled in that small area just inside the curtain wall, a soldier descended from the rampart along a worn flight of steps, trailed by two others carrying bare swords and shields. His tunic was ragged and filthy, his armored accouterments soiled and scratched. His face looked much the same, smudged with grime and weathered beyond its age. When he doffed his helmet, he appeared scarcely more than a boy, albeit one long shed of any innocence.

"Captain Ledron," he hailed. He stopped on the last step just above the waterline, and offered a salute that seemed laden with apology. "Sergeant Penryn. Begging pardon for any ill-mannered treatment."

His armed attendants still bristled at his back. As did those upon the wall above, with bows drawn and arrows trained.

"An arrow in my throat?" Denariel asked.

Penryn granted her a curt bow. "If need be, Your Highness, to stopper that cry of yours. As I am sworn to the defense of those within."

"My father, you mean."

"His Majesty?" Ledron questioned. An official tone, yet Kylac discerned the note of long-bridled anxiety.

A short, shrill whistle came from above. Penryn looked to a watchman atop the wall behind him, who appeared to be relaying signal from a herald or watchman atop one of the inner towers—the east one.

Penryn gestured to his man above, then looked the new arrivals over again before nodding. "Should you wish it, I'll take you to him."

It took them several moments to negotiate the logistics, which began with Penryn wishing to escort Her Highness and Ledron alone. The Head flatly refused, insisting on taking a detachment of his own. The level of mistrust among them boded ill, Kylac thought, but at this point couldn't be judged wholly unnecessary. Penryn relented to the addition of fellow Redfists Havrig and Jorrand, to which Ledron consented, provided Kylac was also permitted to join them. The request surprised Kylac, who'd assumed he'd have to fight for his own inclusion. It also told him just how desperate the captain was to avoid any possible ambush within the keep.

"You would vouch for him?" Penryn asked, his expression dubious.

While the Head considered, Denariel huffed impatiently. "What further harm can he do?"

An ominous question, under the circumstances. Even Kylac recognized it as a clumsy tact. "Ya can have my sabers, should it ease your concern," he offered Penryn. With a knowing glance meant to reassure Ledron, he added, "I won't be needing them."

That seemed to balance the scales. After turning his blades over to one of Penryn's Redfists, Kylac joined Ledron, Denariel, Havrig, and Jorrand in following the sergeant, his two attendants, and a small flock of Stonewatch who closed round their heels. The remainder of their company was left behind with a thin-limbed lieutenant charged with seeing to their accommodations.

"I should inform you, Sergeant, there may be others arriving," Ledron said, as they sloshed across the yard toward the keep's entrance. "Fellow escapees of Avenell's dungeons."

"Arrived," Penryn confessed. "Late last night. A party led by Kahrem of the Stonewatch."

"Kahrem? What happened to Wooton?"

"Taken by wolves, I'm told."

Ledron winced. "Then you must have anticipated our coming."

"We did. But I was commanded to maintain alert and hold fast against any potential intruder, on the chance Kahrem's tale was a Grenarr ruse."

"Commanded by whom?"

Ahead, a portcullis marking the mouth of the keep began to rise, reeled skyward by rusted chains. The doors fronting it were already ajar, bowed to either side on ruined hinges.

"Colonel Fayne," Penryn answered, "who helped guide His Majesty's escape."

"Is my father injured?" Denariel asked. "Unwell?"

Penryn squirmed. "Feverish, my lady, from all I hear."

"*My lady* now, is it?"

The Redfist seemed eager now to pacify her. "He fell from his horse while fleeing a band of tar-skins that chased us from the city. He rode ably enough, upon reclaiming his saddle, and marched on his own strength thereafter. But he took ill upon arrival. I . . . I fear I cannot speak to the severity."

A cadre of soldiers greeted them within the keep's foyer, but spread to either side at a signal from Penryn. Like all else at ground level, the foyer was flooded. Filled with brackish waters, home to rushes and sickly mangroves, nest to insects and tiny marsh creatures that skipped or swam above or below the rippling surface. The sun's rays streamed through empty windows in the high walls, forming beacons amid the banks of shadow hunkered between.

"Who tends him?" Denariel demanded.

Penryn turned right, toward a broad flight of lichen-covered steps climbing to the east wing. "Chamberlain Hahneth and Seneschal Egrund," he replied. "Echoes have it that neither will leave his side."

The princess seemed to relax a measure at that. Evidently, this Hahneth and Egrund were individuals meriting her trust. Nonetheless, Kylac observed the fresh tension that gripped her ever-scowling features, and felt the increasing weight of concern that pressed like a yoke upon her shoulders.

"Take care with your footing," Penryn advised as they stepped clear of the foul waters.

The stones beyond were slick with slimy growth, their grip uncertain. Regardless, a relief it was to be rid of the marsh's grasp.

Atop the stairs, the sergeant turned them down an east-running corridor filled with ghostly, torchlit shadows. "You must understand what a miracle it is to see you again—any of you—after all these weeks. Perhaps you of all, my lady."

Kylac would grant them that. The last Penryn or his countrymen could have known, Ledron's crew had set sail in a stolen Grenarr warship—by command of His Majesty—on a mission so fraught with peril that it had to have been assumed by most that they'd never be heard from again. Unless she'd left some kind of message behind of which she'd made no mention, Denariel would have appeared to simply vanish. Presumed to have stolen after them, mayhap, when her absence was discovered. But with one royal child abducted already by the hated Grenarr, how could Kendarrion or anyone else have known for certain?

Ledron scoffed. "Presumed slain, were we?"

"A common wager," Penryn admitted, as he entered a tight stairwell winding skyward. "Else captured and enslaved. After the tar-skin invasion, and the uprising that preceded it . . . I know of none who dared hope elsewise."

"Distracted by your own concerns," Ledron allowed, though the words rang with accusation. "And tell me, Sergeant, who did *you* stand with in the attempted overthrow of our king's rule?"

"I reported even then to Colonel Fayne," Penryn replied crisply. "Who, I'm proud to say, ordered us to resist the insurgency. Though I fear we were too far removed to affect its outcome."

Denariel's harsh laugh echoed within the narrow confines. "Fortunate for you, to not have to truly pick a side."

An uncomfortable silence lingered in the wake of her comment, until Penryn shifted the tide back toward Ledron. "I trust the tale of your adventures will match Kahrem's?"

"If truth he tells," Ledron grumbled, his breathing become labored now as they continued to climb the wedge-shaped steps. "How much of it did you hear?"

"Whispers only. Though enough to be glad I took no part in it."

A jape, it might have been, given the sergeant's rueful smile. When none among them returned it, he cleared his throat and returned focus to the spiraling course they tread. Atop a fourth-floor landing, he took them from the stairwell and down another torchlit hall. Sentries lined its length. Word of Denariel's coming must have already been relayed, however, because none moved to halt or question their arrival. Reinforcements, Kylac realized. On hand should they need be called upon.

At the end of the hall, they cut left down another corridor, this one more densely populated with Addaran soldiers than the last. All were armed and armored, including several in Shadowguard attire. The bulk were clustered before a closed door at the far end, giving ear to the hushed instructions of a fine-cloaked soldier stooped centrally among them, his back to the new arrivals.

Off the reactions of his listeners, the cloaked soldier straightened, squaring his shoulders and hefting his jaw as he turned. A tall, dashing sort with an air of natural command. Clean-shaven cheeks, unruly blond hair, piercing blue eyes at the heart of a captivating gaze. Broad lips parted in a tight, welcoming smile at the newcomers' approach.

Kylac misliked him at once.

"Sergeant Penryn," the leader greeted in a firm, smooth voice. "Is it the whole of their party you bring to us, then?"

"These five, sir. I'm afraid Captain Ledron insisted."

"Colonel," Ledron acknowledged tersely. Fayne, then, unless there were other colonels stashed about the keep. The Head looked over those assembled, and seemed not to like what he saw. But then, when did the suspicious captain, trained to see an assassin's blade in every nook and shadow, ever like the look of anyone? "His Majesty is within?"

"Sleeping just now, I'm told," Fayne replied. "But I hear he left standing order, upon your departure, to inform him immediately should you return." The colonel's calculating gaze studied each of the visitors in turn, its chill belying the warmth of his smile. "To my knowledge, that order has yet to be rescinded."

"No, sir," a man before the door in Blackfist garb agreed. His head was shorn like Ledron's, but his face and torso were much more bulbous. Without the uniform, Kylac might have guessed him a baker or a butcher, rather than a royal guardian.

"And Your Highness," Fayne addressed the princess finally, with the barest dip of his brow. "Feared lost. Again. Yet here before us, to bring us hope."

"Spew your mockery, Colonel, but step aside that I may see my father."

Fayne's eyes glittered. "Of a certain, Your Highness. Now that you've arrived, let us call upon him."

He nodded at the baker-Blackfist, who rapped on the closed door. They waited. The rasp of slippered feet approached. A viewing slat scraped open, revealing a pair of rheumy brown eyes. "Yes?"

"We've visitors for His Majesty," said Fayne. "If he should wish to receive them?"

The eyes searched, widening at the sight of Denariel, standing out among the others with her dark skin and diminutive frame. And the fierceness of her scowl, mayhap, which conveyed her impatience. Kylac wouldn't fault her for it. He could have done with far less formality himself.

"Highness," the disembodied voice managed to wheeze. "A moment, I beg."

He turned and skittered off, leaving the viewing slat open. Fayne rounded back to the rest of them. "Shall we determine who may be admitted?"

This again? But then, it made sense, as the armed guard deemed necessary to escort Denariel into this unknown stronghold was unlikely required for a private consult with her royal father. Already, Kylac could sense Ledron relenting.

"Unless His Majesty objects," the Head determined, "I'll accompany Her Highness."

"The pair of us, then," Fayne agreed.

Ledron eyed him in challenge. "And for what purpose is the colonel's presence necessary?"

"For the purpose of His Majesty's continued security."

"From his daughter?" the Head balked. "The captain of his sworn Shadowguard?"

"Oaths and allegiances have been tested of late. If my own company displeases you, I'm certain Captain Jyserra would be willing to attend in my stead."

The bulbous Jyserra nodded smartly. Clearly a puppet to Fayne, his *willingness* seemed of scant consolation.

"Discuss as you will, I prefer to go alone," Denariel said.

"Once I's seen what awaits inside," Kylac agreed.

All three glared at him.

"Her Highness can have her privacy, insofar as I'm convinced o' *her* security. Should any attend her, I'll be among them."

Ledron gritted his teeth. "I don't feel—"

"No more secrets, Captain, if'n I'm to play part in this. And begging pardon, I'll take the life of any man seeks to deny me. After which I may just take your king's head, if'n that's what ya fear. As a trophy to lay beside that o' the false Grendavan's."

The gathered soldiers gawked. None seemed to know how else to respond. Penryn looked to Fayne, awaiting the colonel's command, though seeming also afraid of it.

"A feisty boast," Fayne decided, "from a runt who isn't even armed."

"I can kill ya with your own blade, Colonel, as easily as any o' mine."

He knew not whether Fayne had attended Denariel's infamous wedding ceremony, but was certain the colonel had at least heard account of it. Elsewise, the indignation flashing in the soldier's eyes would have overcome already the false smile still set upon his lips.

Before the posturing commander could react further, the slippered feet and rheumy brown eyes returned. "His Majesty will see them," the voice said. Already, his unseen hands worked the door's locks, freeing pins and bolts from their respective housings.

The door opened, revealing the attending steward in full form. A squat man with fleshy, beardless cheeks and cropped, graying hair. His velvet trousers were wrinkled and torn, his linen shirt soiled with mud and sweat. Flecks and splotches of blood stained both, none of which appeared to be his own.

"A glimpse, then," Fayne determined, as if it was *his* say that still mattered. "Then Her Highness visits alone."

The chamberlain or seneschal—Kylac didn't yet know which—blinked in momentary confusion. "Begging pardon, Colonel, His Majesty wishes to see Captain Ledron and the bold outlander alongside."

Fayne's smile finally slipped, broad lips compressing into a tight frown. "The outlander, too? I'm not sure I can allow—"

"By specific request, Colonel. You may ask him yourself if you like."

"I believe I shall," said Fayne, ducking through the portal and marching past the steward with an imperious stride.

Ledron and Denariel strode swift upon his heels, veering left into the heart of the room. With none moving to stop him, Kylac followed softly upon theirs.

"Your Majesty," Fayne hailed, while yet halfway across the cavernous bedchamber. "Pleased I am to proclaim your daughter's return. But to the presence of the others . . . at this time, I must protest."

As forewarned, they found Kendarrion abed at the far edge of the room. The other aforementioned steward—chamberlain or seneschal—was at his side, leaning over him, helping to prop the king upright against a mound of pillows. Though the empty windows were unshuttered, allowing for a breeze, the smell of mold was thick in the air.

The king coughed fluid from his lungs as he fought to speak. "Your protest is noted. Are they . . . ? Where are they?" he asked, seeking to look past the colonel's form where it blocked his line of sight.

"They're here, my lord," the bedside steward assured him, straightening into better view. At which point, Kylac recalled meeting this one before, during his first visit to the palace at Avenell, upon reuniting Denariel with her royal father. A tall skeleton of a man compared to the steward at the door. Head and face fully shaved, he was gaunt and sickly looking himself, as if all that held his features in place was a thin sheet of pale skin. His sleeves were rolled up to the knots of his elbows, his slender forearms as wrinkled and blood-spattered as his attire. "The princess, the captain, and . . . the other."

Clearly, the bony steward hadn't forgotten *him*, either.

Ledron held up beside Fayne, permitting Denariel to move alone to the foot of her father's bed. Kylac claimed a position of his own two paces removed to the left.

The king looked them over, each in turn, as if facing a gathering of ghosts. While he did so, the steward from the door, having shut and locked them in, hastened to the side of his lord's bed opposite his skeletal companion.

None seemed to know how to break the silence. Else feared to do so. Kylac wished to be respectful, given the weight of the moment, but had just about determined to trigger matters himself when Kendarrion spoke.

"Where is my son?"

He could have been speaking to any of them. The brash rogue who'd first volunteered to retrieve Dethaniel from enemy clutches. The stalwart captain who'd been tasked with making certain the endeavor met with success. The rebellious daughter who'd stolen after them, against her father's wishes, thinking herself better suited to the task. All culpable, in some measure, for the unspeakable truth.

But it was Fayne who answered. "My lord, we've heard already—"

"I would hear it from them!" Kendarrion barked, his voice ringing like a hammer fall. The sudden intensity left him coughing. Skeleton bent quickly with a rag to wipe up the blood that spattered forth.

The king pushed him away, feeble as he seemed. His reddened gaze fixed upon Denariel. "Answer me, child, since it is you who feels she knows best. Or you, Captain, who swore to return with my royal heir or not at all. Or *you*," he snarled, turning his livid stare at last upon Kylac. "The whelp who foiled our accord, and in doing so cost us everything. Tell me, any of you, why it is you stand before me, when my son does not."

His voice cracked, there at the end, before his expression eroded into tearless sobs. He slumped toward the doorman—Hahneth, Kylac decided, for all the difference it made, whom was which. While the deposed ruler and grieving father shook with unabashed sorrow, Kylac noted the bloody water bowls, bloody rags, and bloody coverlet, chiefly around the king's chest and stomach. A fall from his horse, Penryn had said. Breaking a rib or two in the process, Kylac would have wagered. A dangerous proposition for one of Kendarrion's age.

As if offended by his gaze, the gaunt Egrund drew the heavy blankets covering Kendarrion's legs up to hide the stains, while Hahneth held the king before carefully easing him back against his pillows.

None had any words, until Denariel found her tongue.

"It was Thane who felt he knew best. For all of us. Steep the price," she admitted, her own voice near to cracking before she tightened her resolve. "But here we stand, before you, and so have not yet lost everything."

"No?" the king asked. Mites and fleas danced around his moldering bedding, black specks stark against his sallow skin. "My city. My people. My bloodline."

Denariel's jaw clenched. "Cities can be recaptured, rebuilt, settled anew. And to them, a people restored." She hesitated, then squared her shoulders. "And while I cannot replace your son, I would see that your name lives on."

"Name?" Kendarrion echoed with a cough. "Bloodline, I say. How will you preserve *that*, when you are not of my loins?"

A spear to her heart would have been kinder. Denariel stiffened, her royal father's words all the harsher for the truth they carried. His wife's child, she'd been. But not his. Not in the way he needed her to be now. Mayhap not in *any* way. Denariel quivered with the unspoken fear of it. That she was a monster in his eyes. An abomination. Never loved so much as tolerated—for her mother's sake. A vile seed, conceived not in love, but an enemy's act of conquest. A living, breathing curse that he should have stamped out ere he let it ruin him.

If Kendarrion realized the pain he'd caused, he refused to apologize for it. "My name can live now only in ignominy. Better that it should be forgotten. Better that *all of you* be forgotten. Consumed by the plague loosed by your arrogance and your failings."

Another wracking fit had the king spitting blood, but he thrashed and flapped his strengthless arms to keep his stewards at bay.

"To my grave I go," he added when able. He clutched his blankets with bone-white fists, his body seized by pain, his face a rictus of hate. "With a prayer that the Fair Mother speed you swiftly to yours."

11

They exchanged no further words with the grieving king. Following his denouncement, Denariel stormed from the chamber. Kylac slid after her, maintaining a cautious distance. Ledron came after him. By the time Fayne finished bowing and begging His Majesty's pardon, Denariel had wrenched the door's locks from their housings and flung the portal wide, to excuse herself down the hall.

Her brisk, heavy strides carried her past the string of Blackfists and Redfists filling the outer corridor, then through an alcove that couched an ascending stair. Her deliberate route was marked by a decided lack of hesitation, suggesting she knew her way around the keep. That, or she simply cared not where her steps led, so long as they led *away*.

She didn't pause until she'd punched through a door and out onto a private section of battlement atop the keep's eastern tower. Its view opened to the south, over the tangled roof of the marshland through which they'd so recently slogged. The afternoon sun was cloud-choked, giving the already dismal setting an even drearier cast.

Denariel moved at once to the parapet, slapping at a pair of weathered merlons flanking the nearest crenel. She seemed half inclined to hurl herself through the gap. Kylac might have moved to arrest her, but knew her will to be stronger than that.

"Coward," she growled to the wind. Its swirling grip bore the rank smells of the bog's breath. "Feeble, aging coward."

Kylac eased aside as Ledron shoved up through the portal to join them. The Head spared him a sour glance before closing the distance at the princess's back.

"If he's lost everything, it's only because he was too craven to fight for it," she sniped, rounding at the captain's approach.

Ledron halted. To Kylac's surprise, his stony features softened, giving way to a mask of what might have been sympathy. He wore the unfamiliar expression with evident discomfort. "His Majesty is unwell," he tendered. "His anger will pass."

"I would sooner he use it. Were he willing to lash at our enemies as he does us, we'd not now find ourselves on such desperate footing."

Kylac sensed the strain in her voice, its strident tones thick with bridled anguish. But her reddened eyes held no tears. Wounded as she might appear, she'd not let it hamper her resolve.

If given to guess, Kylac would have echoed Ledron's assessment. Already distraught at being betrayed by his own, and then driven from his city, Kendarrion would have been understandably heartbroken by their failure to prevent Dethaniel's death—word of which a churl like Kahrem would not have shared gracefully, even if there'd been a graceful way to tell it. The king's fury just now, so raw and scathing, didn't have to mean that he cared nothing for his daughter's return, or for their chances at a reclamation of their lands.

Denariel's gaze shifted to the portal as Colonel Fayne climbed into view, trailed by a pair of Shadowguard. Her lips twisted into a snarl. "But let him choke on it, if that is his wish."

Fayne looked them over before nodding to the rearmost Blackfist, who shut the portal behind him and there held position within the stairwell. The other shadow clung to the colonel's heels as he joined the trio atop the battlement. "I suppose, then, it is time *we* speak."

"Of?" Denariel challenged.

"Our course," the colonel replied. He glanced warily at Kylac while plying the princess with that fetching smile of his.

Denariel crossed her arms. Ledron's familiar scowl returned.

"I've consulted with my lieutenants. Twice daily, since our arrival.

They grow increasingly anxious to move on from this outpost."

"They?" Ledron asked archly, with a sour look for the attending Blackfist.

"It is but a matter of time before the prowling tar-skins discover us," Fayne proclaimed bluntly. "The longer we wait, the thicker their numbers."

Denariel huffed. "And my father issues no order to depart."

"No, Your Highness. Nor do we dare wait for it much longer. We are less than four hundred, here within these ruined walls."

"With more on the way," Ledron reminded him.

"From what Kahrem says, if all of yours reach us, we shall crest five, yet fall well short of six."

"Enough to hold against all but a full-scale siege."

"Enough to draw further attention," Fayne amended, twisting the captain's argument, "all but guaranteeing the assault you mention."

Betraying the colonel's fear. Where one might have seen the arrival of Ledron and the other escapees as reinforcement, Fayne and those with him looked only to what foul threat might be trailing in their wake.

"And you propose what, Colonel?" Denariel demanded.

"A swift departure. No later than dawn tomorrow."

Despite their ready suspicion, both captain and princess appeared taken aback.

"His Majesty is clearly unfit for travel," Ledron observed.

Fayne nodded. "The only cause we've had to linger this long. But his condition has worsened since our arrival. And I daresay Her Highness's coming may not gladden his heart the way we'd all hoped."

Kylac watched the daggers that formed in Denariel's narrowed gaze, and sensed the heat of Ledron's rising indignation.

"You would abandon him?" the captain asked through clenched teeth.

"Wiser to bring him, I think. But there is risk either way. If he wishes to remain, I'll not be so arrogant as to advise elsewise."

Denariel spat. "Just arrogant enough to strip him of those who would defend him."

"Any who wish to defend him are free to do so," Fayne corrected, his voice rising clear and sharp against the aged stones of the battlement. "En route to Indranell, or by hunkering here. This wind blows not of my will, Your Highness. I merely apprise you of its coming."

Kylac let his eye shift to Fayne's attending Blackfists. Drawn here for the colonel's defense, else merely to bear witness. The nearer eyed him darkly, gloved hand wringing the pommel of his sword. The other, back at the door, declined to meet his gaze. Whatever their prior oaths, these were Fayne's men now. And why not? In the face of dire uncertainty, men were prone to heed voices of strength.

"Is that what we've come to?" Ledron asked. "Disdaining all leadership? Leaving men scrambling every which way of their own accord?"

Fayne glanced again at Kylac, but held himself unabashed. "Those among us are not all soldiers."

"Yet owe fealty to their king, nonetheless."

"Their king has failed them. Are the rest of us to succumb solely because he seeks to do so?"

The colonel's flinty gaze met Denariel's, daring her to contradict him. An untenable argument for her, given her own rant only moments before.

"I'll not forsake him," she insisted. "The fight is yet unfinished, even if he cannot see it. I mean to prove it to him. And if he commands you to stay—"

"We can but hope that command holds sway," Fayne agreed, adding an impolite bow. No matter his words or posture, there was no submission in his tone. "Perhaps Her Highness will be able to persuade her countrymen where I have not."

At that, the colonel straightened, and retreated toward the portal. His shadows followed, the nearer eyeing Kylac with an attempt at warning.

As a mouse might warn a hawk.

Behind them, Ledron's jaw clenched, while Denariel's dusky cheeks darkened in fury. But neither called after the departing soldier. Content to be rid of him. Wondering, mayhap, if he was entirely wrong. Kylac himself couldn't say, save that he was glad it wasn't his decision to make.

"My place is with my king," Ledron growled against the growing silence.

Denariel scoffed. "Because your ever-wavering commitment held us in such doubt." Though she spat it as an insult, it was likely the nearest Kylac had ever heard her come to complimenting the faithful captain.

The silence resumed, pressing as it settled about them. For several moments, they remained there atop the secluded stretch of rampart, permitting the princess the turmoil of her thoughts and emotions as she peered out over the desolate landscape. Kylac knew already that he would follow her lead. But he found himself unable to guess as to which course she was more likely to choose. Would she cleave to her word to remain at her father's side? Or would she come to recognize the danger and potential futility in attaching herself and her people's future to one who seemed more comfortable in welcoming death's embrace?

"I'll beg of His Majesty another audience," Ledron announced finally. "And warn him of this brewing treachery."

"Of which he is doubtless already aware," said Denariel. "If somehow blind to it, I see not how it might kindle his recovery."

"What then do you propose?" the Head grumbled, forsaking any honorific.

The princess turned from the parapet, regarding Kylac—as she often did—as if he were some insect or rodent, at the heart of all her ills. But there was something else there, too. A quality tingeing toward respect. Almost as if she were acknowledging their kindred nature when it came to abiding by the established rules. An ally, loathsome as he might be, if only she could determine how best to put him to use.

"We change the wind."

THE STORM had brewed slowly, at first. Darkening skies. Roiling clouds. A damp chill forming in the air, while the limbs of trees swayed and shook, bent by a strengthening breeze.

That was *outside* the keep.

Inside, the gusts had blown swift and loud, as Denariel marched through the halls and corridors, demanding the names and ranks of those most prominent among them. Tetherend's common areas, astir already with word of the princess's arrival, were set to buzzing like the chambers of a hornet's nest. In a training hall, the commotion had drawn the attention of a Redfist lieutenant. When he and his detachment of watchmen sought to forcibly escort Her Highness to more comfortable quarters, Kylac had promptly laid them out in a sprawling tangle of bruised limbs, scattered weapons, and shattered pride.

"Enough!" Ledron had roared at that point. "We've not the strength to waste, fighting among ourselves."

The others, mayhap marking Kylac's ready willingness to treat them as he had their comrades, had quickly agreed, lowering their weapons and begging Her Highness's intent.

"To have your measure," she'd said. "To know where our allegiances lie."

By then, Colonel Fayne had arrived, upon a mezzanine overlook, conveniently emerging from that position of authority with a disgruntled air. Feigning surprise to find them at such odds, and with an affected tone of conciliation, he'd urged his men to call a gathering at once, and to heed whatever request the princess might have in the interim.

"Food for her belly," he'd suggested. "And drink, perhaps, to cool her burning thirst."

Denariel had denied any such need, initially. But when informed by the colonel that his two highest-ranking lieutenants had struck forth that morning with scouting parties sent to welcome her and any other friendly arrivals, and that they must need await their return for any full reckoning to be had, Ledron had quietly urged the princess to put aside her request for council until as many as possible could attend.

Surprisingly, Denariel had agreed.

So they'd retired to the chambers appointed her, and partaken of pickled rations dredged up from some larder. Kylac had learned that while Denariel hadn't visited Tetherend herself in some years, her father had ever been diligent about ensuring it was kept suitably stocked. In the event of unforeseen crisis, she'd explained tersely, though Kylac was given to sense that none of those involved had envisioned circumstances as tragic as these.

Then they'd waited.

And waited, as the storm beyond the keep's walls had gained in intensity. Kylac had largely kept to himself as Denariel and Ledron debated how best to present their argument. Their location was remote. If they'd been followed, their precise footsteps would be difficult to track, given the nature of the surrounding swamp. If discovered, it would take a sizable enemy force to overrun the keep—especially with Kylac on hand to deter them. They could weather this storm, they convinced themselves. For however long it might take for the king to recover—his health *and* his will.

In the hours that had passed thereafter, he'd watched captain and princess take turns pacing anxiously, settling down for short snatches of restless sleep, and venturing forth to demand word as to whether the absent lieutenants had yet seen fit to return. They hadn't. Not in the third hour, or the fourth, or the fifth.

In that same interim, however, three parties of escapees were permitted inside Tetherend's walls. None arrived whole. The first had lost a man to a sinkhole. The second had seen a member's throat flayed by the claws of a hunting cat. The third had unraveled into a string of stragglers come upon the keep over more than an hour's time. Several among each company had been wounded. All had been starved and haggard. But Ledron and Denariel had received them all, with Kylac alongside, and seemed buoyed by their arrival. Voices that would count in their favor, they presumed, with a measure of guarded optimism. Supporters against Fayne and those who would give rein to fear.

Kylac had been less sure, even as it pleased him to greet Taeg and Rehm, Talon and Sethric, Hessel and Irryn, Stannon and Vosh, Jaleth and Nadrum and Warmund. So many with whom he'd voyaged, among the lesser known faces of those they'd briefly been jailed alongside. It had even warmed his heart to see Aythef, who'd betrayed them, shuffle in among the trailing dregs of the third company. A man battered, but unbroken. Of the sort whose spirit they would need.

He recalled the afternoon's events now for the peaceful lull they'd served when compared to the storm that had arisen in their wake. Peals of thunder and the ceaseless roar of torrential rains without were but a backdrop to the incessant squabbling of those who'd been summoned at last into Tetherend's great hall. Some three hundred souls, at least. Their constant jockeying and jostling, with men coming and going in fits and huffs, made their precise number difficult to count. More than half the garrison's total strength, it was clear. And all with an opinion more passionate and vociferous than the next. Tales of loss, of personal strife, of what they'd individually sacrificed to get to this point resounded within the walls, given in evidence as to why they shouldn't be asked to sacrifice anything more. After nearly an hour of their bellowing and bickering, Kylac's ears and head had come to ache, and he wondered now if Fayne's goal from the outset—his forewarning—had been but to spare them all this crude and ultimately senseless furor.

Senseless because the outcome had never truly come to doubt. For all the shifting tides of emotion, one way or the other, as this frayed collection of countrymen traded grievances and insults and threats, assaulting one another's honor as if aligned with the common enemy, the pervasive thread woven throughout was that which Fayne had already revealed to them atop the battlement of the east tower. For all of Ledron's and Denariel's carefully crafted arguments, Fayne's lieutenants had a ready rebuttal. There was too little to cling to here. Only broken walls to repel the enemy, an empty armory beyond blades and arrows already in hand, and a decaying marsh from which to forage for provisions in the event of siege. The only true, sustainable defensive ground was to the north at Indranell. And with each passing day, their chances of reaching that northern bastion diminished. While they rotted here, the tar-skins entrenched their position at Avenell, and spread north in a stranglehold upon the Karamoor. Already, the northbound highway was likely closed to them, forcing them through a flanking wilderness riddled with perils. The longer they hesitated, the farther and deeper they would be compelled to tread that course.

And the grimmer their prospects grew.

Kylac hadn't forgotten that Denariel and Ledron had until recently championed several of these arguments themselves. And might eagerly do so again, were it not for the failing monarch who lay abed several stories above their heads. But that single loyalty had clearly worked to undo all other beliefs they might hold, rendering moot any option they might elsewise pursue.

"Put it to a vote!" someone cried.

A fresh call of a tired refrain. A swell of angry voices surged in support, drowning out the roars of denial. Fayne stood at the heart of those cries, positioned to one side at the head of the hall. He'd not spoken in some time, choosing instead to let his men speak for him. Kylac wouldn't have been surprised were he to learn that the colonel had been prepping and bolstering *his* arguments throughout the same long afternoon hours in which Ledron and Denariel had been considering theirs. Kylac hadn't yet determined whether the bulk of those gathered had reached this consensus on their own, or if it was Fayne's charisma that had worked to convince them of it, up to and beyond the moment of Denariel's arrival. All he knew was that his companions were fighting a losing battle, if trying to deter this mob from a course they had in their own minds already decided.

"I await the command of my king!" shouted one of the few dissenters. Sergeant Trathem, as Kylac recalled. The earnest Redfist encountered in Avenell's dungeons. He stood nearby, hovering near Denariel—also at the head of the hall, albeit to the side that represented only a thin sliver of those present. The soldier had stood among the princess's more staunch supporters from the onset of this tedium. A voice that many who'd gathered seemed to respect, encouraging them to seek backing from those around them before crying out against him.

"I would obey His Majesty, if only he would speak his will!"

"He abandons us!"

"—sold all when agreeing to their cursed accord!"

"We've waited too long already!"

"—cost me my wife and daughters!"

"I'll not risk my sons' lives on his account—"

"What power has he to see us through this?"

And on and on the hurricane blew, while thunder and rain rattled the shuttered windows, and flashes of lightning peeked between their seams. Kylac imagined a strike destroying the roof over their heads, and smiled inwardly at the fantasy of it bringing all of this to an end. Elsewise, it seemed to him they might remain here throughout the night, and still come no closer to reconciling the division that separated them.

Another quarter-mark had passed before Fayne raised his arms. A purposeless gesture, it would seem, as Ledron and others had struck a similar pose several times, only to be shouted down all the louder. This time, however, the furor abated. Kylac took note of the lieutenants positioned strategically throughout the hall, who worked to quiet their respective regiments. Not by mistake, he'd have wagered, and felt again a grudging respect for the clever colonel, conniving as he seemed.

"My countrymen! We are refugees here. Spared, by the Fair Mother's mercy. I, too, await command of my lord." A swell of groans from his own side of the hall threatened to curtail his speech, but his flock of lieutenants moved swiftly to curb it. "But. But! I would honor my oath, to defend my nation and its people, to the utmost of my knowledge and will. We journeyed here, at His Majesty's behest. But His Majesty refuses now to lead us. And in the absence of that leadership—" A few shouts from Denariel's side sought to cut him off, but he forged through them. "In the absence of that leadership, I seek command from my lone remaining superior officer, General Bahsk, of the northern front at Indranell."

Jeers rose, and cheers to drown them out. Kylac observed Denariel's stiff-necked fury and Ledron's stone-faced resignation. Had Fayne resolved to this farce of an outcome an hour ago, Kylac might have thanked him for it. Now, it would have pleased him more to see the colonel's head on a pike.

Notwithstanding the soldier's prior attempt to warn them.

"I see no cause to call a vote!" Fayne shouted above the din. "We will, each of us, weather the storm this night beneath these rafters, and give rein to our deepest hearts. In the morning, I strike north in pursuit of my oath, imploring His Majesty to accompany me, or to command me elsewise. Should he refuse, I'll cast no judgment upon him. Nor shall I judge any man a traitor—should he choose to lie down here, beside our fragile king, or join me in search of the next fight."

The cheers, louder than before, swiftly overwhelmed the strengthless outcry of those still opposed.

"I can only beg similar clemency of Her Highness's judgment," the colonel added, turning to gaze upon her with an air of exaggerated regret, "and pray she marks me an ally, should again we meet."

12

True to his proclamation, Fayne and his followers departed at daybreak.

The storm had blown over during the night, clawing northward through the Bonewood. And while another looked to be brewing in its wake, there was no debate about awaiting its passing. Though the world had become gray and dismal and more sodden than before, the colonel and his renegade refugees wouldn't be dissuaded.

"Even the winds flee north," Fayne had observed, in answer to those few who'd sought one final time to shame him from his chosen course. "We do but heed Eriyah's breath."

False piety aside, the colonel's arguments had gone at that point largely unchallenged. Denariel, who'd fueled the dissent, elected not to appear at the morning muster. Deigning not so much as to peek from the tower window of the quarters set aside for her. Condemning with her absence the entire proceedings. She'd staked her position already, planting her standard, as it were. Those who would not rally to it were men she was better rid of.

Ledron had disagreed.

The captain had waited until morning, giving to hope that Fayne might see cause to change his mind. The weather, the arrival of more reinforcements, a command from the king. The first two had made manifest. But the seasonal storms, common in late spring, weren't likely to afford better opportunity. And three more companies of escapees from Avenell's dungeons, informed of the situation upon their arrival during the night, had promptly pledged to join ranks with the would-be departees. When the colonel's intent to follow through had become clear, Ledron had gone to him and made private plea of his own.

To no avail.

The Head had gone then to see the king. To beg of His Majesty a ruling to truly test Fayne's allegiance. The colonel's strongest argument for leaving rested on the king's silence. Were Kendarrion to demand they stay, the colonel and any with him would have to become outright traitors to disobey. Cause even half of them to reconsider, and the rest, for fear of their depleted numbers, might do the same.

He'd brought Kylac with him, as an unspoken warning against Fayne, Jyserra, or any of their lieutenants seeking to forestall him. Doing so had brought them untroubled to the king's door. But the portly steward who'd answered their call—the chamberlain Hahneth, as Kylac had correctly guessed—had refused their request for admittance.

"His Majesty is unwell."

"And stands soon to be even less well, if deprived of his garrison," Ledron had snarled.

"His Majesty desires them gone, those who would depart."

As petulant as the daughter he disavows, Kylac had thought.

"Colonel Fayne claims he'll remain, if His Majesty will but ask him to do so," Ledron had implored.

"The colonel stood with General Bahsk in urging the attempt to unseat His Majesty," Hahneth had hissed haughtily through the viewing slat.

"We were told he ordered *against* the insurgency."

"Positioned at what distance?" The chamberlain's voice had been thick with contempt. "He is no friend to us, Captain. We are well deprived of his company."

"We need his swords."

"His Majesty has spoken. A favorable day to you."

With a snap of the viewing slat, they'd been dismissed.

"Shall I open the door from within?" Kylac had offered. "Or do ya mean to simply ram it down?"

Despite his furious expression, the Head had desired neither. "Let the blight remove itself," he'd determined through painfully clenched teeth. "Perhaps the sound of his cowardly thrashing will serve to draw the tar-skins from us."

So it was that, with neither Ledron's nor Denariel's voice to succor them, the few who'd sought to dissuade or censure those seeking exodus did so with quiet, hollow voices. A whisper meant to calm a rockslide. As the slide's rumble grew, the whisper ceased to be heard at all.

From a position atop the curtain wall overlooking the postern through which the departing columns filed, Kylac had briefly entertained notion of serving up a more emphatic deterrence. But few were likely to thank him for keeping any here against their will. Nor would he have truly considered doing so, unless Denariel had beseeched him elsewise. Better a dozen swords pledged to the king's defense of their own accord than a hundred or more coerced into such service. An opinion to which he'd have readily confessed, had any bothered to ask. To secure their most fervent effort, let each man be permitted to combat this ordeal in what manner he desired.

Even so, it had admittedly pained him to see so many pass beneath his gaze. The brawny Jorrand, who'd served at Havrig's hip since Kylac had known him. The veteran Simalen, who'd seemed so steadfast in his commitment to Ledron's command. Ysander and Moh, oft-assigned as Denariel's warders, marching forth side by side. Mutton and Graves. Hamal and Kahrem and Yoden and Quill, following Olekk like a brood of hatchlings. Jaleth and Nadrum, among the crew who'd borne him and Ithrimir from the shores of Mistwall. Rehm, who'd taken the role of second mate before their voyage's completion. And Taeg. Helmsman and later first mate.

"Got me a sister up at Indranell," he'd divulged to Kylac while offering the courtesy of a farewell. "And Brenham's widow alongside. Four whelps between them, and none now with a father to look to. Seems I ought to . . ."

The Whitefist had trailed off, seeming to acknowledge his own helplessness in this affair. With a tight nod, he'd added, "Fair skies and favorable winds, eh?"

Kylac had only dipped his brow in silent parting, then watched his former shipmate take a place in line, gray mane twisted by the blustering wind.

His disappointment had admittedly been assuaged by the surprising handful of those who'd elected to remain. Aythef, for one. Though shunned still by the bitter Ledron, the cook and secret consort to Prince Dethaniel was one of those whose knowledge of royal affairs might prove valuable to them. If nothing else, he stood among the few whom Kylac held no doubt would wholeheartedly wring the neck of Grendavan herself, if given the chance.

Of the Redfists with whom he'd sailed, there was burly Havrig, quiet and undeterred by the loss of Jorrand; Talon, who'd proven himself on more than one occasion already; the congenial Sethric, whose arm still bore the enflamed scar of a wound inflicted by the savage Ladrakari; and the sour-smelling Crawfoot, whose real name turned out to be Laritanis. Sergeant Trathem, from Avenell's dungeons, had also aligned with them, and been unafraid to chastise those lacking the courage and commitment, as he saw it, to do the same.

Of the Whitefists, there had been only one. "Worm" Warmund, who'd at first sought to slink out alongside Jaleth and Nadrum, had caught Kylac's eye and hesitated at the moment of departure. After bidding farewell to his companions and declining their entreaties, he'd found his way to stand beside the rogue outlander, mumbling, "Always assumed I'd die at sea."

The largest surprise of all had been Fayne's own Sergeant Penryn. The youthful soldier who'd first ushered them into the outpost's walls had suffered no shortage of taunts and barbs from his fellow Redfists, and had weathered a heated glare from Fayne himself upon apprising the colonel of his decision. Insubordination, it may have been called, had Kylac not been looking on, compelling Fayne to maintain his stance that each man was to choose his own path. Even so, the unspoken threat in the colonel's eyes upon parting had suggested that Penryn would do better not to fall under Fayne's direct command again.

Theirs had been among the final notable exchanges. After them, the last of the servants and pack animals comprising the meager supply train had filed out, and the rearguard had formed up at its back. Within moments, the final pikeman had passed through the outer wall, and the ripples in the floodwaters filling the bailey had belonged only to the handful of soldiers and attendants loyal to the king. Most looked on with a forlorn cast, as if wondering whether they'd made a mistake.

Well, Kylac thought to himself, while turning to watch Fayne's regiments slog northward into the mired tangle of the Bonewood. *This promises to be fun.*

"This vigil grows tiresome," Trathem confessed.

Kylac eyed the sergeant and said nothing, content to let the soldier's own words echo an agreement. The larder was small, and near to barren. Little more than a congregation of stark hooks and empty shelves that served to amplify even the thinnest voice. Kylac had chanced upon the Redfist scouring the dank vault in hunger, while delivering a satchel full of sour berries and withered roots foraged during his morning's explorations. His deposit of rations was only slightly more bountiful than his other findings, which had revealed nothing of the companies of escaped prisoners still missing, and nothing of the enemy believed to be scouting for them. Fair news, the latter had seemed, for those here with suitable cause to fear for their lives. But Trathem's mien had only darkened upon hearing it.

"No change in His Majesty's condition?" Kylac presumed finally.

"None finding its way to *my* ears," came the soldier's glum reply.

Kylac thought momentarily to suggest the Redfist sally forth in exploration of his own, if feeling so ensnared by the outpost's walls. But it was his own voice that had initially discouraged any others from doing so. If it was signs of passage the Grenarr might be seeking, why provide any more than they already had? Let them chase after

Fayne's, should those tracks be discovered. In the meantime, Kylac would scout the surrounding area without leaving mark or print that might alert anyone to their continued presence here.

Ledron had agreed, and none had fought him on it. Willing enough to hunker down, peering out guardedly from the crumbled towers and ramparts, clinging to their stillness and silence. Kylac had therefore ranged unencumbered throughout each of the past four days, and again on this one. Sparing himself the same slow, stale stagnation endured by the others. Yet he imagined it easily enough. Just the twelve of them, discounting himself and the king. A number small enough to make even this tumbledown keep seem vast. Their only hope being . . . what? That Kendarrion would regain his strength. That he might remember his will to fight, likely agreeing at that point that they should trek north to rejoin the rest of their countrymen. A destination they might soon be reaching, had they joined with Fayne. For what possible reward, then, had they stayed behind?

But it seemed clear enough that none of those who'd remained had done so with thought of gain. They lingered solely for love of their king—or some sense of devotion to what he represented. Which was likely what truly pained them. For Kendarrion continued to shut them out. Save for his personal attendants, Hahneth and Egrund, he refused to acknowledge their effort, their sacrifice, their very existence. None were permitted to see him, except to deliver food, drink, medicinal herbs, dressings, and the like. Even these, Kylac had been told, had largely been seen to by Hahneth personally. Anyone else who dared poke head or toe through the door did so unbidden, only to be summarily cursed and ridiculed by Kendarrion in such a manner that the entrant feared he might be the one to push the fragile king over death's threshold.

So most had simply stayed away, Denariel included. She'd demanded that Hahneth or Egrund make report to her the moment either of them chanced to step from her father's chambers, but elsewise had resolved to honor the king's wishes. Rather than seeking excuse to intrude, she'd spent her time, Kylac had been told, pacing her own quarters, else roving the battlements, the halls, the yards of the keep. Seeking some purpose, some solace, or some encouragement yet to be found.

"Regretting a path untaken?" Kylac asked.

"A choice cannot be unmade," the sergeant from Avenell's dungeons huffed. "Only buried under other choices."

"Strikes as wisdom to me. Or near enough. Thinking time has come to choose again?"

"I just . . ." The soldier frowned. His hands twitched with nervousness, balling rhythmically into fists that refused to stay closed. Clearly agitated, though his mind and gaze seemed far removed from the vault in which they stood. "How long will the war wait on us?"

Eager to return to the fray, then. Kylac couldn't fault him that. "I doubt it waits at all. But I daresay it won't end without word from us."

Mayhap Sabrynne would march on Indranell. Mayhap this General Bahsk would march south against *her*. Overlords and generals might fall, with others climbing to power atop their bones. But Kendarrion's voice would have to be heard, even if it rang too late.

"If His Majesty dies . . ." Again the Redfist trailed off, a haunted expression grappling with a combative wringing of his features. "I'm not sure where that leaves us."

Nor was Kylac, though of course he'd given the matter some thought. With her elder brother slain, Denariel would be queen. But in whose eyes? A bastard daughter who owed half her blood heritage to the enemy. Bartered and then disavowed by her own father, who'd already lost her kingdom's capitol. Unloved, as best as Kylac had seen, by those who would become her subjects. To say nothing of those who commanded what was left of her kingdom's swords.

If matters could be deemed now a fractured mess, Kylac hesitated to consider what might happen should he be denied opportunity to restore Kendarrion to Addaranth's throne.

So he reached instead into his pouch of foodstuffs, and offered the famished Redfist a sprig of bitter dammenroot. "Shall we pray to your Fair Mother it doesn't come to that?"

The king died at dusk.

They'd been gathered in the common dining hall, the eight of them, when Hahneth had come in search of the princess. Ledron of the Shadowguard. Penryn, Trathem, Havrig, and Sethric of the Stonewatch. And Warmund of the Seawatch. Talon and Crawfoot had been standing their turn as lookouts upon the keep's twin towers. Aythef had seen fit to take his supper alone in the kitchens, keeping himself from Ledron's sight. But the latter three—aside from the king and his stewards—had been the only absentees. For, despite Kylac's own well-despised presence, Denariel had indeed joined them. Descended from her chambers to partake of a bread and stew fashioned by Aythef from moldy, rancid, infested ingredients into something more than merely palatable.

She'd even been polite in their company, uttering nary a word, but ready enough with a *please* or *thank you* where civility would seem to warrant it. Suspicious of this rare temperament, Kylac had been half tempted to test it by drawing nearer, but had chosen instead to remain far across the hall, positioned in a stone window seat affording him an east-facing view of the Bonewood where it lay steeped in settling darkness. The others had seemed not to know what to make of the princess's attendance any more than he had, and so declined to comment on it, except to bow in due deference and extend an acknowledging *Your Highness* where dictated by royal decorum.

Mayhap she had something to ask of them, but knew not how to phrase her request. Mayhap she wished to thank them, in her own way, for remaining with her. Mayhap she merely required companionship, proving human after all.

Whichever, it was but an awkward silence Hahneth had disturbed when his slippered feet had come rasping down an elevated corridor, bringing him into view atop a balcony. His haste had been such that he'd doubled over the rail upon reaching it, forced to grope for breath before begging, "Your Highness . . . Your father . . . I fear you must come at once."

A visage of dread had frozen Denariel's features before she'd shot like an arrow from her bench seat. Those seated with her scrambled to stand, but there paused in shock or uncertainty. Kylac had looked on, a touch more discerning than the princess, and a mite less concerned than the others, before rising from his windowed nook and darting soundlessly after her.

Up through the keep they'd raced, dashing through halls and corridors, angling up stairs and around corners, plunging through alcoves and open portals. Kylac could have beat both steward and princess to the king's door, had that been his aim. But he'd understood this to be a private moment, and meant not to usurp it. Merely to observe, should some other, more sinister purpose reveal itself.

Despite his ample lead, Hahneth had only scarcely managed to arrive at the royal bedchamber before Denariel brushed past him, frantic. The chamberlain had moved then to shut the door against Kylac's entry, but Kylac blocked the effort with a stiff arm and an expression to brook no argument. With a reassuring clap of the steward's shoulder, Kylac had left him there to catch his wind while gliding within.

Egrund had been sitting at the king's side in a wooden chair, his skeletal form hunched forward with his face in his hands. Upon Denariel's advance, he'd looked up, to reveal reddened eyes swollen with tears. The princess had scarcely glanced at him before finding her place on the opposing bedside.

At first, Kendarrion appeared to have expired already. He'd lain still, quiet. His cheeks were sallow, and his eyes closed. Pale hands lay folded upon his breast, over covers smoothed and crisply arranged. But no sooner had Denariel knelt upon the floor, her feather weight and sharp elbows falling heavily upon the mattress's edge, than the king had stirred.

"Erial?" he'd rasped, eyes fluttering sightlessly. "My Erial . . . sweet Erial."

Without warning, Denariel had broken then into tears of her own. One hand went to her father's forehead. The other clasped his weakly outstretched fingers. "Shh. No, Father. We need you. We need you here."

"Lyther—" The name had caught in the king's throat as his gaze fell upon her and his eyes drew focus. "Nara," he'd hissed, and even in his frailty, it sounded a curse. "Plague me no more, child."

With a terrible effort, he'd wrested his hand from hers, and rolled his head away, returning his gaze to the rafters. "Your mother . . . she beckons me."

"Then go not in shame," Denariel had urged. Part rebuke, part plea. "She knew you to be strong. Courageous. When the time comes to reunite, you should meet her as such."

From his position near the doorway, Kylac had felt the wringing contrast of emotion. Denariel's like a forge, burning deep and bright. Kendarrion's more like an empty bowstring drawn taut. Full of tension and rage begging release, but without clear target, and powerless to cause harm. Just searching . . . straining . . .

"My Lytherial. Ever I loved you. Even unto succoring this . . . spawn. Ask no more of me, my love, my jewel. But let us commence our eternal voyages at last."

Denariel's expression had faltered, her shoulders tightening, her weeping slowed. But she didn't speak, didn't interrupt. She'd simply knelt there, at the side of her father's bed, arms extended against his pillow, his blankets. Positioned to embrace him, but frightened by then to do so. Waiting . . .

For the king to shy from death's door, it had seemed. For her people's precious Eriyah to instill in him the miracle that would keep him with her awhile longer. Or for the spirit of her dead mother, Lytherial, to turn him away, to refuse him until his worldly tasks were done.

Or mayhap simply for the man she held as her father to acknowledge her once more, on the chance that he might find a word of kindness for her before his passing.

She'd waited, but all the man had mustered in the bloody half-light of sunset was a final, rattling breath. With it, Kendarrion, deposed ruler of the Sundered Isle, set foot on his ultimate journey beyond memory.

For long moments thereafter, Kylac stood silent witness. Behind him, Hahneth wept. Beside the fallen king, Egrund buried his face in his hands. Denariel took again her father's hand, and this time gripped it without threat of protest. With her other, she stroked his pale brow, while finding and spilling a fresh well of tears.

When the dying light had given fully to moon and stars, she at last moved to close her father's sightless eyes. Like an apparition, she arose, faltering on unsteady knees. Kylac held himself a shadow in the corner as she approached. Her eyes never turned his way. Without a word, she found the open portal beyond him, and stepped through.

Kylac followed, his strides without weight or sound, his desire only to be present if called upon. Not because she might ask. Merely should the need arise.

He sensed her surprise when she came to realize that the others had gathered in the outer corridor. All save Talon and Crawfoot, still at watch for what their eyes might detect in the darkness. Even Aythef had come, though he hunkered like a thief at the far edge of the corridor.

Ledron awaited her front and center. "Your Highness. How fares His Majesty?"

Denariel sought and eventually found her voice. She spoke as if testing the words. "Our lord and king has departed us. He resides now with the Fair Mother Eriyah."

None gasped or buckled or wailed. Ledron looked as if he might. The Shadowguard captain's lip quivered, while his eyes came to gleam. Kylac looked to the rest. Amid the terrible, engulfing silence, the torches in the corridor crackled and danced.

Then the Head replied, his voice choked at first, but strengthening with each new word. "To you I am bound. To heed neither threat of pain, nor promise of death. To your service, I impart my life's meaning, pledging every breath I draw, until you or I should draw our last. With this oath, I am yours to command. To you I am bound."

The Blackfist fell to a knee, and bowed his head. "Hail Her Majesty, Queen Denariel, ruler of Addaranth."

He held there for but a moment, while holding his new liege speechless. He then stood, turning briskly to one side, aligned as if awaiting upon her command. His gaze shot down the corridor, piercing the others. Kylac, still aback of Denariel's shoulder, watched them put aside their own hesitation, their own reservations, scrambling to be the first to fall.

"Hail Her Majesty," they echoed together in near unison, *"Queen Denariel, ruler of Addaranth!"*

13

P ENRYN, ADVANCING FROM his rearguard position, coughed as he drew up alongside the others just below the ridge crest.

The echoes chased a sparrow from a poplar stretched raggedly overhead. Denariel cast the sergeant a cutting glance, bristling at his clumsiness. Ledron hissed, an irritable demand for silence. Others who crouched or lay in the needle-filled dirt along the lip of the ridge tensed or cringed or shook their heads, then resumed focus on the scene below, straining for some glimpse of the danger of which they'd been warned.

Kylac ignored their noisome fidgeting, his own eyes trained on the array of structures rooted within the dagger-shaped vale beyond. No movement or sound indicated awareness of his party's approach. At this distance, those he'd detected below were unlikely to hear them unless they were to start shouting at one another. Not over the murmuring of the stream that cleaved the vale along its length, flowing and splashing in its rocky bed toward the cliffs that marked the hamlet's western edge.

Not over the dull roar of those same waters as they plummeted into the gorge below.

The others seemed to realize this, even as the chagrinned Penryn settled down among them, his expression now worried.

"Ambush," Havrig explained, his voice a soft rumble.

The others continued to search the vale, gazes piercing the hamlet's heart and roving along its narrow borders, formed north and south by the squat ridges that paralleled the stream knifing across their path.

"I see nothing," Sethric admitted.

"She looks abandoned to me," Ledron agreed. "What makes you so certain?"

Kylac had smelled the Grenarr before he'd seen them, their scent carried to his approaching position on a southerly wind. Back when he'd been serving point for their loosely scattered company. So it was that he'd slowed his advance and that of his companions, bringing them to the crest of the ridge in a careful crawl. Though the musk of his comrades had soon overpowered the telltale scents of the distant Grenarr, he'd spotted his enemies from that vantage point quickly enough.

"They've a lookout in that pine, beyond the smithy, three-quarters high," Kylac said. "Another just outside the bulwarks east, near that crook in the road where it bends north. Among that trio of cedars."

Further search on the part of his companions spawned only rising frustration.

"Say there is," Ledron allowed, squinting and clenching his jaw. "I see none to respond to their call."

"I'll wager twoscore," Kylac corrected, "clustered within those huts and cottages throughout."

He expected the Head to question how it was he could count those he couldn't see. Instead, "A paltry number, by your standards. Is it not?"

Kylac shrugged. "Should they stand their ground, I could slay them all. But what o' those sniffing along the Karamoor?"

They'd glimpsed the massing enemy patrols more than once over the past five days, as their thirteen-member company had stolen northward along the western outskirts of the perilous highway. More than once, they'd been forced deeper into the jungles to evade Grenarr scouting parties sent to probe the wooded depths. Commanded by Ledron to remain together, they could but hazard a guess as to how many had come to infest the Karamoor. But Kylac had crept out alone from time to time under night's cover to have himself a more definitive look. From what he'd gathered, Sabrynne had a thousand warriors or more crawling along the highway in staggered companies two- and threescore strong—with none more than a league apart.

"Might be we can move on before any reinforcements are summoned," Ledron posed stubbornly.

"And it might be we wiggle this strand, the spiders come swarming. Would ya stake Her Majesty's life on it?"

Ledron huffed. Kylac would have thought the captain pleased by his rare concession to caution. Alas, the Head seemed as disgruntled as ever. Encumbered by oaths, mayhap, that he now realized he never should have made. In addition to upholding Denariel as his queen, the fiercely devoted Blackfist had vowed to see her father avenged and herself seated upon the throne of Addaranth. Bold claims they'd have been in far better circumstances than these.

"We're within a half day's march of the city," the captain grumbled finally.

Ah. Then it was anxiousness setting in. The kind that drove a mouse to dash for its hole, when sometimes the cat was waiting to pounce. "All the more reason for them to tighten the noose."

It was a snare that lay before them. Of that, Kylac harbored no doubt. They'd encountered others like it during the course of their northward trek. A couple had been old snares, already triggered, but successful in claiming the lives of those foolish enough to wander into them—including one of the missing companies of fellow escapees from Avenell's dungeons.

A relief it had been to find no indication, as of yet, that Fayne's company from Tetherend had been beset. But then, their own path had diverged from the colonel's on day one, and hadn't crossed the other since. From all he'd seen, Kylac put the odds at a little worse than even that the colonel's force might have slipped on ahead of the web the Grenarr had since laid across the Karamoor and its flanks.

"Do we but root here, then," Ledron groused, "and wait for the tar-skins to find us?"

"Safer to venture round," Kylac suggested. That was how they'd responded to other such snares or blockades. Simply creep westward, deeper into the untamed wilds, beyond the enemy's penetrating reach.

Denariel snickered. "That gorge to the west? Dendaginor's Breach. The Silver Schism. Stretches for some thirty leagues, growing only wider and deeper as she goes."

A circuitous trek time wouldn't allow for, even if the terrain eventually did. Something she might have mentioned before, Kylac thought to remark. But he'd learned it wiser to regard any words offered up by the land's new queen as only bait for an argument. Easier to accept and absorb her petty jabs than be drawn into a more spirited altercation.

His eyes tracked westward again, this time drawing a mental boundary along the crest of the falls. Chasm's End, they'd dubbed this village, when alerting him to it as they'd drawn near. Or Riverfell, to those stalwart few who called it home. Some five hundred friendly souls, they'd hoped to find, though none had been surprised to discover it abandoned like so many other outposts and settlements along their way, its citizenry fled north. *Safely*, it would appear, which was more than could be said for others farther south that had been ransacked or razed before warning could be sent—or at least believed.

In none of his companions' reports, however, had they made it known there would be no circumnavigating this particular ground. Alone, he might simply descend the near wall of the gorge and scale the opposite face. But without ropes and climbing gear, there was no chance Denariel or her ragtag band would be able to follow alongside. They were to cut across the narrow valley, else veer east, back toward the Karamoor. A foolish proposition, barely a league removed from its swarming edges.

The snare it was. "We'll wants to wait until nightfall."

"And squander the entire afternoon?" Ledron balked. Other heads turned, a reflex of their tacit agreement. Though he spoke for the group, the captain wasn't alone in his anxiety.

"If'n one o' ya is sighted, they'll have our trail, even should we slip through."

Ledron gritted his teeth.

"What difference, should they discover us sitting here?" Penryn asked.

"Might be we've others on our trail already," Havrig added.

"Or is that why we wait?" Ledron asked, brow pinched in suspicion.

Kylac might have been annoyed, had he not found the Head's incessant mistrust so comfortably reliable. "Truth'll bare itself quickly enough, Captain, should ya choose to venture on down this slope."

Denariel scoffed. "I doubt the rogue has guided us this far only to betray us now."

"As a clever traitor might have us believe."

The queen's mirthless chuckle was quick and harsh. "We've enough obstacles before us, Captain, without deliberating the absurd."

Kylac considered thanking her for her faith, but imagined easily enough the angry tone of whatever retort she might summon. "Respecting our need for haste," he said, "a gallows wager it'd be to traverse that hollow in this daylight."

"Would that I were trekking alone," Denariel muttered.

Kylac felt the stirrings of a frown. Offended not for himself, but for those who'd courageously remained by the young queen's side when there'd been little reason to do so. Was she truly so thankless? Less likely she might be to draw attention on her own, now, yes. But what caused her to believe she'd have made it even this far?

With a sidelong glare to proclaim his lingering doubts, Ledron let the matter of Kylac's dubious loyalties lie. "Remove the lookouts, and there'll be none to spy us," the Head pressed bluntly.

"Done quietly," Kylac agreed. "And how long before their absence is discovered?"

"Upon the next guard rotation. Which might be hours away."

"Those lookouts have signal mirrors," Kylac corrected, having seen them flash once already. "Might be we'll have bought ourselves minutes only."

The Head scowled, squinting again in the direction of the lookouts he had yet to spy. "Then we fell both at once, together."

Kylac suppressed a smirk. Alongside another of his father's pupils, the notion might have been tantalizingly sound. But he'd traveled enough with these men to know that none were adequate to the task.

A feeling like resignation stole over him, followed by the stirrings of a familiar tingle. It was, after all, the sort of challenge he relished.

"All respect, Captain, better that I alone venture so near." Off the Head's deepening frown, he added, "Thereafter, I'll have to range untethered. And we'll be no slower than a trot the rest of the way. Is that something we can manage?"

Ledron grunted. Denariel hefted her chin against any implication to the contrary. Kylac considered the others. The soldiers, he didn't doubt, deprived and exhausted as they were. Even Warmund, the lone sailor, seemed hale and determined enough. It was the stewards—Hahneth, Egrund, and Aythef, the latter still recovering from injuries inflicted upon him prior to setting sail from Grenathrok—who most concerned him. For the faithfulness and tenacity they'd offered up already, it'd gnaw at him were he forced to leave any of them behind.

"By your command, then," Kylac resolved. After a final survey of the enemy-infested hamlet and its borders, he detached himself from the ridge crest, withdrawing and motioning for his comrades to follow. When all had huddled round amid a small copse of withered birch and dry undergrowth, he leaned in centrally among them. "This is what I suggest."

THE SPICY FRAGRANCE of needles and bark enveloped Kylac as he descended along the bole of the towering pine. He moved steadily, neither fast nor slow in the shifting of hands and feet from one branch to the next. Soundless, weightless as a breeze, he crept, giving feel to the great tree's gentle sway, the stir of wind filtered through its boughs, the coarse texture of its scabrous, sap-sticky skin.

From the Grenarrian lookout still far below him, he smelled only boredom and discomfort and irritation. They'd been at this waiting game for some time, Kylac supposed. Long enough that any thrill they might have initially enjoyed at the anticipation of catching their quarry unawares had been eroded and engulfed by the tedium that must have played out since. These were warriors of the seas, where all was shifting, heaving, churning movement. To trade that for the intractable stillness of dead, motionless earth . . . well, he suspected it must only add to the inherent monotony of their present task.

He estimated the gap between them at sixty heads . . . fifty-five . . . fifty. The lookout shifted in his perch, but only to arch his back. His face remained directed to the south, toward the tuft of jungle beyond the abandoned vale. On the stretch of wild growth from which they'd imagined their quarry might choose to emerge. A fine wager. For what little it would win them.

Forty . . . thirty-five . . . thirty . . .

A startled squirrel darted aside, racing out to the limb's end before rounding to chitter a rebuke. Kylac wordlessly begged the animal's pardon. He might have made his climb from below. Despite the daylight, the uncertain number of enemy eyes, and the fact that a man in a perch was far more likely to glance down than up, he was confident he'd have found the means to scale undetected, had circumstances demanded he do so. But when Ledron had balked, he'd agreed to forgo those risks and make his way among the interwoven treetops instead, to attack from above.

Admittedly, a safer route.

Twenty-five . . . twenty . . .

He could smell now the lookout himself—a tang of sweat and leather and the oils used to preserve his blades. That, and the sharp flavor of the barrowleaf on which he gnawed, reminding Kylac of another stolen upon not so long ago.

Fifteen . . . ten . . .

Just five heads removed, Kylac eased to a stop. Near enough to identify the shark's fin tattooed on the Grenarrian's throat. To watch the pulse of inner bloodflow at his neck. Among the last few beats his heart would ever know. Alas that he must die, here and now, for scarcely more than the whim of chance. A cruelty. But chance carried the scars of choice, Kylac's father had liked to insist. And life was nothing if not cruel. Why should death be any different?

There he lingered, for but brief moments. He'd timed his approach so that his wait would be short. The lookout reached for his belt. From a pouch came the small signal mirror. The Grenarrian found the sun, then angled his mirror toward his fellow lookout, concealed among the cedars near the mouth of the vale. Twice it flashed, and twice the cedars reflected a spark of sunlight in return.

As the Grenarrian sheathed his mirror, Kylac closed. Not hurried, like a viper, but calmly, like a constrictor. He clamped a hand over his victim's mouth as his dagger bit into the back of the man's neck at the base of the skull. The blade required more thrust than one of his own, and grated home as if among gravel rather than sliding through sand. But the dead man crumpled all the same, with no thrashing, and very little twitching. Nerve tether severed, he failed to muster objection as Kylac slit his throat and freed his life's blood in a crimson wash over his chest.

Leaving the lookout draped facedown over his chosen branch, Kylac resumed his descent, shimmying quickly now down the trunk. By his observations, he had less than a quarter-mark before the dead lookout missed his signal. He'd considered using that very distraction to draw the other Grenarr from hiding, but decided that the longer he concealed his own presence, the better. Remove *both* lookouts, and he would give Denariel and company whatever additional time might remain before the next rotation, as Ledron had suggested.

Provided he could successfully do so.

Given time to explore and observe more thoroughly, he'd have harbored no doubts. But Ledron's demand for haste had permitted him only limited understanding of the enemy snare he was attempting to disable. Were there additional watchmen concealed beyond his view? What *were* the patterns and timing of their rotation? How far away were the nearest reserves, or the scouts and runners connecting them?

Granted, such investigations weren't always possible. And, in truth, he was generally more comfortable engaging in such activities without the constraints of a predetermined path. But then, he typically had only his own skin to concern himself with, and not an entire party to defend.

A change, of late. Hardly pleasing.

But his obligations couldn't be unmade. Short of severing them, his course was set.

He dropped to the earth from a branch about twenty heads high, keeping to a fold in the north side of the thick trunk so that it might shield him from those within the hamlet. The forest floor was thick with undergrowth and snaking groundcover. In a crouch, he raced through the concealing brush, steering himself along the tracks and trails formed by man and animal alike. He kept his senses alert for additional watchmen, suspecting the Grenarr might have posted their lookouts in part as decoys. An unnecessary layer of subterfuge, it might seem. But one he refused to fall prey to.

He encountered naught but rodents and birds and insects, however, as he dashed and wound eastward. Their incessant stirrings served to mask his own motions, their calls to draw roving eyes. More cover than he required, but welcome all the same.

Closing upon the clutch of cedars, he took to the branches of a sentinel spruce that overshadowed them all. Halfway up, he encountered a sizable hornet's nest nestled in the hollow of a broken limb. He'd already rerouted to give the swarm suitable berth when he felt the tug of intuition. His plan was to signal Ledron when the second lookout was disabled. But what if there were other straying eyes as the captain's company made its crossing of the narrow vale? Using himself as a distraction had been overruled, for fear of the resultant alarms. But here before him lay the promise of a disturbance every bit as striking, yet far less likely to draw suspicion.

He deliberated for mere heartbeats before removing his shirt and using it to seize and bag the hornet's nest. Ledron would be caught off guard, initially, but would discern what had happened quickly enough.

Or so Kylac reassured himself.

After tying and hooking the makeshift sack around a dagger hilt, Kylac left behind the thin cloud of hornets buzzing in confusion around the area of their former nest, and resumed his climb. The hornets carried with him hummed in growing irritation. Good.

As before, he chose a height well above the position of his target before leaping to the tree in which the lookout was nestled. He then descended several rungs, winding down until he found an ideal opening amid the spiral of branches. As he unhooked his shirt from his hilt and prepared to loose the treasure within on his unsuspecting victim, he reflected upon the quirk of chance that had spared the blood of the man below him.

Life was nothing if not rife with fortune.

The nest crumbled as it struck the lookout's branch, unleashing its swarm. Predictably, a startled grunt gave way to yelps and curses before resolving into a string of garbled cries. The response from the hamlet was almost immediate. From cottages near and far, Grenarr warriors streamed in a rush, clutching at weapons and turning east toward the commotion. Kylac crouched within the cedar, donning his shirt while marking their movements. He then peered farther west, his gaze searching the lip of the falls at the mouth of the gorge.

For a moment, nothing. The moment lengthened.

The scrabbling lookout toppled from his perch, skidding and clawing and careening off branches as he fell. While Grenarr barked and bayed and hastened toward his position, Kylac caught the flicker of motion near the falls. A thin line of shapes, hunched and staggered, creeping from their positions amid the southern ridge and darting down into the fast-emptying vale.

Kylac grinned. Like the squirrel he'd so recently offended, he darted from his own perch, retracing his path through the trees. The furor carried on beneath him, the lookout's howling spawning a chorus to match—fueled in part by dismay, and in part by harsh laughter. Kylac gave ear to its echoing tenor as he sprinted back through the forest, attuned to any significant change that might dictate a shift in his strategy.

But the hornets had served their purpose even better than he might have hoped. The uproar was only barely settling by the time he reclaimed his position beside the slain lookout in the pine tree. Propping the corpse as if it were a puppet, he returned signal with his mirror when, several moments later, a furious Grenarr commander finally sought report. His presence merited no greater attention than that as the others in the enemy company—some twoscore, as believed—collected themselves from the brush and the stream. A pair of runners were dispatched to the east, likely to deliver some explanation of the disturbance to allies stationed beyond. The remainder, many still cursing and flinching and swatting defensively at the surrounding air, returned to their prior places of concealment, amid much anger and black amusement.

It took some time for all to settle back into position. None seemed in any hurry. Clearly, they understood that the tumult had been enough to betray their presence and warn off any nearby quarry. And it soon became clear to Kylac by the tone of their voices, if not the precise words, that most had lost patience with this business of sitting ambush, and were in no great rush to resume it.

With the hornets dispersed, a fresh lookout climbed into one of the adjacent cedars. Once more, Kylac signaled an all's-well at his end. He then abandoned his puppet of blood and barrowleaf, and shimmied down again, wondering idly if the second victim—though stung and scratched and hobbled from his fall—might feel better about his condition when his comrade was discovered.

Aiming north, Kylac slipped into the trees in pursuit of his own companions, trying not to think too closely on the vagaries of chance.

14

"Rather noisier . . . than we discussed," Ledron managed between breaths as Kylac caught up to him.

It had taken more than half an hour and nearly a full league to do so. A positive sign, were the captain and his companions not so lathered and red-faced less than a third of the way to their goal.

"Rare's the plan that unfurls precisely as intended," Kylac replied. He stopped short of reminding Ledron of their encounter with Vorathus Shrikeskinner and his so-called Banshees in their flight from Mistwall. When the Head had left him to fend for himself—contrary to their agreed-upon strategy.

"I recall also . . . you wished to range . . . untethered."

"Just came to measure your progress, Captain. And reassure you o' mine."

The Head glowered, but opted to save his breath. Kylac looked round at the others, loping or laboring along in their staggered lines. Denariel, setting the pace alongside Ledron, had refused to acknowledge his arrival with anything more than a scowl, making a concerted effort to stare forward. Havrig and Sethric had their backs, the former huffing like a bellows. Trathem was flanked out left with Crawfoot, and Talon to the right with Warmund. Penryn trailed by a good forty paces, dutifully shepherding stewards Hahneth and Egrund while keeping eye on Aythef, who pursued doggedly with the assistance of a crude walking stick. A miracle they'd not fallen farther aback, as there seemed little concern from anyone else as to whether they kept up.

"No sign o' friend or enemy?"

"If any stalk us . . . they do so . . . *silently*."

The emphasis in the captain's words might have been merely an artifact of his breathlessness. But it struck Kylac as a thinly veiled suggestion that *he* be silent, as well. One or the other, he chose to ignore it. "Begging pardon, Captain, the lot o' ya look a mite ragged. Might be time to snatch a breath."

"Too much ground . . . yet to cover."

"O' which at least some o' ya will fall short, should ya insist at this pace."

The Head looked set to carry on the argument, then appeared to reconsider. Surely, he understood the danger in trying to push too hard, too fast. Mayhap he simply hadn't wanted to be the one to suggest a respite, with the infamously stubborn Denariel pressing so relentlessly beside him. Now that the notion had been tendered, he seemed almost relieved as he presented it to his queen.

"We were never . . . going to finish this course . . . in a single bite."

"We?" Denariel echoed archly.

"Would ya drive your horse without water or rest?" Kylac asked her.

A bit of a gamble, as he'd never actually glimpsed her astride a horse. And he'd seen little indication the animals were widely used on this island. It might be she had no experience with them.

But the queen, after gritting her teeth for a moment, eased her weary trot and brought herself to a halt with a sigh of aggravation.

"Take your rest, then," she said, fighting to control the heaving of her own lungs. "But do not get comfortable."

Ledron stopped beside her, signaling to those around him to circle in close. He then followed her as she strode slightly off the trail toward a small clearing amid the mismatched forest brush. There she leaned against a moss-laden deadfall, and proceeded to drink deeply from her waterskin, spilling a trickle down her throat.

"Ten minutes," Ledron informed the others when the last of them had arrived.

"Five should do," said Denariel.

Kylac suspected she was less concerned with the extra time than she was with enforcing her will. Unnecessary as that would seem here, among those who'd sworn themselves to her, he saw no reason to challenge her. "I'd spend it stretching," he advised.

He set an example of doing so, though his own muscles scarcely needed it. Within moments, all twelve of his companions—even Denariel—were following his lead, though the queen made sure that not one of her movements precisely mirrored his.

They'd barely managed to settle their breathing and dispel some of the redness from their faces when she put forth the call to resume. None complained. Kylac couldn't have said what drove them. Fear, he presumed, in one form or another. Of the enemy, of their queen, of being the first to falter and thus losing standing in their comrades' eyes.

Whatever, they gathered themselves and resumed their arduous jaunt for another half hour, and, after another brief rest, another half-mark beyond that. At that point, they paused at a freshwater stream to hurriedly wash themselves, and to refill their skins. They were still in the midst of enjoying its cooling embrace when the shrill, whistling moan of a seashell horn peaked above the stream's chattering and echoed on through the woods.

"From the south," Ledron observed.

"They's found our trail," said Kylac. Stiff with tension, the others looked at one another, and then to him. "We's time yet. Fret not."

Yet fret they did, in varying measure. Kylac did his best to ensure they adhered to their rest routine, but most seemed to prefer to remain on the move. Twice, Egrund fell. Once, he took Hahneth with him. Thereafter, the pair struggled to maintain pace with even Aythef, as one suffered a twisted ankle, and the other a swollen knee. Penryn persisted in hanging back with them, even when they insisted he run on ahead and concern himself with the queen. "His Majesty would not have abandoned you," the sergeant argued bravely. But Kylac read the concern at the edges of his stubble-faced smile.

Periodically, the seashell's throaty call came again. Louder and nearer it sounded, each time. When it came within a mile, it was answered by another to the east, at perhaps a league's distance.

Ledron gave Kylac a pointed look. "They seek to entrap us."

"Carry on," Kylac urged. "I'll sees to it."

South he dashed, sprinting through the gnarled, half-dead foliage. Darting past trunks and branches, dancing over rocks and stumps and deadfall, skirting pitfalls and quagmires. Only moments later, he came upon them, the twoscore from Chasm's End, thrashing northward at a reckless pace. As he drew his borrowed blades, Kylac felt the creeping threat of exhilaration, which he fended off with a sneer of self-reproach. Amid this plethora of cover, his adversaries stood no chance.

A quarter-mark later, he was sprinting north again, the scent of Grenarr blood thick in his nostrils. He'd slain eight of them before they'd realized they were under attack, and another dozen while they'd tried frantically to determine the nature of the pack of wild beasts that so stealthily hunted them from all angles. Less than a score remained when they'd come to understand they were fighting against men, and only six when he revealed himself to be assailing them singlehandedly. Amid the desperate bellows of their shell horns, he'd scattered their screams to the winds.

He'd permitted them their noise in hopes of luring other enemy parties away from Denariel's company. Certain enough, as he veered east, he encountered a patrol racing south. He dispatched them much as he had the last, though he broke one of his sabers in the process. While he had no shortage of replacement weapons to choose from, none were truly to his liking, leading him to lament again the loss of his own blades—a loss he could only hope wouldn't prove permanent.

The next pack of Grenarr he encountered numbered only a score. He dispatched them quickly, though not before observing a difference in the tone and pattern of the blasts from their shell horns. Those who echoed a reply did so from farther north—and farther still when next they sent relay. No longer distress calls, but warnings. His enemies were not merely trumpeting alarms to one another, but communicating, coordinating, plotting. This near to the northern holdfast, they understood well enough the direction in which any refugees were fleeing.

They needed but marshal accordingly.

So Kylac spent another hour and a half weaving northward, generally clinging near enough to his companions to ensure their safety, but venturing on ahead or out wide as needed in order to forestall those in a position to intercept or ambush them. As various packs of Grenarr drew near, Kylac darted off time and again to sow death and confusion—reducing their numbers, redirecting their attentions. Like damming up streams, seeking to alter their convergence.

In truth, he was but forming eddies in a river's current—disruptive, but not enough to divert its flow. Amid the raspy wails of the horns by which his adversaries conferred, one group with another, Kylac sensed an overall massing to the northeast. He was therefore unsurprised when he tracked back to his companions and found them within a hundred paces of the forest's fringe, hunkered behind a wild bramble wall, peering desperately ahead at a blockade of Grenarr warriors just barely visible through a mesh of jungle woodland—the whole of the scene cloaked in the shroud of evening twilight.

"Trail's end," Ledron muttered as Kylac sidled in among them.

Kylac withheld comment as his gaze pierced the tangle ahead, conducting his own survey. Beyond the blockade at the forest's edge loomed the bulk of a curtain wall, its toothy parapets limned in starlight and the glare of torches. Well over two hundred paces distant, and likely closer to three. All over open ground, the surrounding jungle long since hacked into retreat by the city's defenders so as to prevent any unexpected approach.

"Looks like a cordon, alright," Kylac allowed. The Grenarr were arrayed only single-file, but none more than a man's length apart. Hundreds in all, primed in readiness, set to converge at a moment's notice.

"Cordon? A wall, I'd say."

"So we carves a doorway."

"To merely reach the no-man's-land beyond," Denariel reminded him. "So that we can outrace scores of tar-skins to the edge of a stake moat. Where we'll . . . what? Howl at the ramparts and beg them open a portal for us?"

"Have ya means to send signal?" Kylac asked. "To let them know their queen is trapped without?"

"What signal," Ledron groused, "that won't also draw the enemy?"

"Tunnels, then. A bolt-hole, mayhap, we might trigger and follow in reverse."

The captain shook his head. "The city is fortified principally to the north, to shield against invasion by sea. It has ever been assumed that any retreat would be through the south gates."

Or north via boat through the Gorrethrian Sound, Kylac supposed, in the far less likely event of a land invasion. No city worth its foundations left itself only one point of egress. But there would be no slipping around to the sound's heart. Not without overcoming terrain and fortifications shaped or erected against precisely that.

As with the hamlet of Chasm's End, their fastest and most tenable route was *through* this blockade, not around it.

"Your commanders within," Kylac mused. "How long will they tolerate this congregation?"

Denariel snorted. Ledron gritted his teeth before mustering reply. "Difficult to say. General Bahsk will be spoiling for a fight, to see this many tar-skins so brazenly strutting before his gates. But we know not what Grenarr pressures may lie to the north. He'll suspect a trap, and may therefore refuse the bait."

The more indignant attitude might have made Kylac's task here easier. The more cautious one wouldn't. "Then we need that signal," he determined. "I could penetrate the city, deliver word myself. But I can't say as to how long ya might remain naked out here." He left the rest unspoken. *Should the Grenarr begin sweeping the forest . . .*

"Or?" Ledron prompted, seeking alternative.

"Or I seeks to draw 'em off and let ya send signal yourself."

"What about Ruhmheld's Barrow?" asked Penryn.

Kylac expressed his interest with a raised brow.

"A derelict watchtower some half mile southwest of here," Trathem answered, when no one else did. "Served as an overseer's keep centuries ago, during Indranell's quarry and construction. With Ruhmheld nearing his deathbed as the city was nearing completion, he sought and was granted to be entombed beneath its stones."

"Flame atop that tower would be seen from the battlements," Havrig agreed in his flat, rumbling tone.

"I can borrow one o' their horns while I'm at it," Kylac offered, "if'n there's a call that would identify us."

"Anyone lighting torch or trumpeting atop that tower would soon be surrounded and trapped," Ledron argued. "With or without luring a host of tar-skins over this very ground."

"Let him bear signal," Denariel decided.

"Your Majesty—"

"It's as suitable a position as any other, and better than most."

"When that blockade comes crawling—"

"It won't. Not all of it. Else it would already be thrashing about in search of us. It's a net cast against anyone slipping through." Her heavy brow furrowed with focus. "So we find ourselves some thicker shelter and burrow deep. When the general responds, brushes this rabble aside, we'll have our escort into the city."

Ledron appeared unconvinced. "And how do we ensure the general responds?"

Denariel's gaze shifted to Kylac, dark eyes gleaming with purpose. "We send signal he cannot refuse."

THE AGED TOWER STONES flaked into sand beneath his feet. A larger man, with heavier tread, might not have been able to climb them at all. But then, the overseer's keep hadn't been raised to be a permanent structure, and had been abandoned the moment its purpose had been served. To be devoured and reclaimed by the jungle from which it had been born.

The half-mile distance Trathem had estimated proved closer to three-quarters before Kylac had located the stony mound at the ancient quarry's edge and the remnants of the tower atop it. A pile of crumbled stones that might better be described as a cairn, given its condition and the bones rumored to lie beneath it. Centuries of neglect had seen it eroded by weather and swarmed over with strangling jungle growth. Only the north wall remained intact, thrusting skyward like a jagged tusk. A mulch of mud and moss and rotten leaves plugged its broken seams.

Kylac had set to scaling it without hesitation, undeterred by its ravaged appearance, or by its treacherous skin. Every heartbeat he spent here was one in which he'd not be there to shield his charges should they be discovered. He'd traveled too far, overcome too many obstacles, to let Denariel be captured or killed now.

Mites and spiders and centipedes danced and skittered and wormed before him, unaccustomed to the intrusion. He paid them scant attention, though some wore the bright markings or serrated patterns by which Trajan, his guide through the Ukinhan Wilds all those weeks ago, would have identified them as venomous. The threat of bite or sting wasn't going to slow him. For someone rumored to have felled a dragon, death by insect might actually serve a poetically fitting end.

Upon reaching the ruined battlement, he pressed to the parapet to find a view of Indranell's walls largely unobstructed by the intervening forest. A number of trees clawed skyward, as if to extend or escape the jungle canopy, but not so many as to impair his line of sight. So he harvested a dead branch, soaked the tapered end in stolen oil, and lit it with stolen flint, producing the necessary firebrand. Hefting it high overhead with his left hand, he produced his borrowed seashell with his right.

His first attempts to use it as a horn produced little more than sputtering rasps that made him lightheaded and caused his lips to ache. But he persisted in the effort, experimenting with positioning and pressure until finally a long, mournful bellow emerged. By then, his flame was already drawing notice, given the shuffle of torches along the Grenarr line—and higher up, atop Indranell's walls, if the shadowy movement of figures there amid their own, stationary torches could be interpreted as a response.

Unquestionably, he'd captured the field's attention, for good or ill. So he began trumpeting the series of notes Denariel had given him. Hummed herself, in fact, upon deciding that Ledron's attempt at the melody was lacking. A refrain, they'd told Kylac, used to pronounce the king's return from a royal hunt.

He followed that up with a series of blasts denoting the trajectory of his party's intended approach, expressed in the number of paces west of the city's south gate. A means of telling their rescuers where they might be found. If rescuers there were, and an approach made.

He'd repeated the entire call twice before a detachment of Grenarr mobilized and made for his position. In this, Denariel proved correct, as most of the line held its ground. Just a score of the enemy peeled off from the western flank to thread south, with another score dispatched from the east. The remainder—some four hundred, by Kylac's estimate—clung to their defensive positions, maintaining their cordon.

So he continued signaling, waving his torch and blowing his horn, seeking to draw some manner of reply from the city battlements. His eyes scanned her parapets for return signal. Anything that might indicate an acknowledgment or reaction. Alas, whatever concern or deliberations his efforts may have triggered was taking place beyond his sight and hearing.

When the advancing patrols of Grenarr had drawn to within fifty paces, converging upon either flank, he jammed the butt of his torch into a crevice in the parapet and made his descent along the southwestern face of the ruins. His shell he deposited into its carrying pouch, on the chance it might be of later use. Leaping out through a fissure in the crumbling tower wall, he melted into the trees, leaving the shouts of his enthusiastic attackers behind him.

Weaving a long, switchback course against possible pursuit, he returned to where he'd left his companions. To his relief, they remained crouched in the same muddy ravine, beneath a thick cover of vines and brambles and nocturnal shadows. Their filthy faces regarded him with a shared sense of nervous expectation.

"Our friends are astir," he reassured them, certain they'd heard as much already. "But their net holds."

"What of the city watch?" Ledron asked. "Did they send answer?"

"None I recognized as such."

The captain's frown seemed to speak for them all. "Then here we wait."

And wait they did, listening to the occasional shouts and whistles and horn blasts with which their enemies communicated, but hearing nothing that might indicate a rescue attempt was being mustered. Worse, Kylac's signal seemed to have incited the Grenarr—as Ledron had feared—to explore the nearby woods. While the blockade held its overall lines, the men forming its links were taking turns probing south, into the jungle. The entire net dipping deeper, in search of its prey.

Nearly an hour had passed since Kylac's return when hollered reports and a thrashing through the brush indicated approach. Just a handful of men, advancing on their sheltered position. But all knew how quickly the reporting of that probe—or the lack of reporting—would bring the entire line knotting around them.

Kylac watched his companions crouch deeper amid the muddy ravine, breathlessly hoping the searchers might pass them by. His own instincts canted in the other direction. He could still slip out and initiate an attack that might lure the enemy elsewhere—back toward the city walls, mayhap. Unleash a slaughter that would leave them no choice but to pursue, onto clear ground that would reveal he fought alone. What commander would be able to resist the temptation to finish him?

Still just a temporary solution. At his best, he'd be hard-pressed to massacre more than four hundred men on his own. Yes, a pack of most any size could be whittled down one at a time, as his father had taught him. But hundreds? Even *his* energy wasn't boundless. And with these inferior weapons . . .

Moreover, he had that infernal seed of a conscience his father lacked. Were he willing to murder every last Grenarrian to obtain his objective, who then was the real villain here?

But his choices in the matter were dwindling. Come to it, a temporary answer might be all he needed. Moments that might serve to coax Indranell's defenders from their shell. In a sally that might scatter these invaders and drive them south again as Denariel had envisioned.

The closing enemy was all but overhead. Kylac smelled the collective fear of his companions. Could almost hear the drumbeat of their hearts. Given the manner in which those with weapons clutched at their hilts, it wasn't difficult to imagine one of them doing something rash.

He was just about to slither forth, before it was too late, when the trumpets blared. Not the wispy song of seashells, but horns hammered from copper and bronze. The enemy's reaction was immediate. A fresh wave of shouts and blasts went out, and those who'd been creeping toward their ravine rushed suddenly to the northeast, tearing through the woods with abandon.

Denariel's fierce grin was triumphant. "They're coming."

Ledron's appraisal was more circumspect. "We should wait to be sure, Your Majesty."

Even he, however, nodded at Kylac. A gesture that fell somewhere between command and permission, as Kylac was at the lip of the ravine already.

A quick survey promptly confirmed the queen's suspicions. Though he could discern little visually across the thickly forested, night-shrouded expanse, the sounds told Kylac all he needed to know. The thunder of horse hooves, dozens strong. The clank and clangor of armored riders, howling with too-long-restrained hostility. The piercing hum of arrows unleashed in a cloud from atop the ramparts, meant at last to chase this vermin from the city's outskirts.

Within moments, he'd determined that the bulk of the action was centered near the south gate, from which Indranell's sortie had been launched. Spilling out onto the muddy fields fronting the city walls, where the Grenarr were mobilizing, refusing yet to give way. Shrieks and battle cries pierced the night as the killing commenced.

"Seems we have our diversion," he hissed back down into the ravine.

"Safer still to remain," Ledron posed. "We've no instructions yet from within. We can't even know this sally is intended for us."

"Then who, pray tell, is it intended for?" Denariel griped.

"We could yet be trampled in the enemy's retreat," the captain cautioned. "It's too soon to risk open approach."

"Assuming the enemy retreats," Kylac observed. "That they's cracked a door for us doesn't mean they intend to leave it open."

The Head scowled at him. He couldn't say if the other's irritation was for his argument, or the fact that he might be correct.

"I'd sooner be on the move," Denariel determined finally, "and decide for myself."

Ledron took the defeat in stride. "Upon your command, Your Majesty."

Kylac watched over them as they filed from their shelter, then assumed a vanguard position. The rest formed a tight ring around Denariel, with Penryn again staking unspoken claim to rearguard. With racing hearts and furtive gazes, they followed dutifully along the course Kylac set for them. Their anxiety weighed on him as if he were dragging stones—and it felt at times as if his passage might have been quieter if he *had* been. But he couldn't well chide them for it, as they were moving as stealthily as they could manage.

Amid their rustlings, he caught ear of another party approaching head-on. So he signaled a halt and motioned his companions down, lower into the brush. Alone, he crept on ahead. The other party continued toward him, oblivious. Just a pair of stragglers, it seemed, easing southward, about ten paces apart. Scouts, given the caution of their movements. Searching, not fleeing.

Kylac drew a dagger.

As the distance between them closed, the wind strengthened. Addarans, Kylac realized abruptly, not Grenarr.

On the narrow chance that he might be wrong, he drew a second dagger to match the first before rising to reveal himself.

"Addarans," he called softly.

The surprise nearly rattled the pair from their boiled leathers. Both were lean and lanky. Neither was heavily armed or armored. Notwithstanding a patchy beard worn by the man to his left, their throats were exposed. Kylac struck a nonthreatening posture, arms crossed casually—daggers ready to fly.

"We received signal from His Majesty," the bearded one managed finally.

"Indeed ya did," Kylac reassured them. "Your orders?"

The pair glanced guardedly at each other. "To lead him to safety."

"Relieved to hear it. Come."

He let them approach, giving feel to their continued wariness and the innocence of their intentions before guiding them back toward Ledron.

"Our escorts," he announced from a distance.

The Head rose, followed quickly by his companions, blades drawn. "This is it?"

"We're sent to guide His Majesty within," said Patchbeard. Clearly their spokesman.

"Sent by whom?" Ledron asked.

"Colonel Fayne, who now leads himself the diversionary attack." The escort's gaze roved their company, his expression tightening with concern. "Where's His Majesty?"

"Where the brave colonel left him," Denariel snapped.

"Your fealty is to Her Majesty, Queen Denariel," Ledron pressed. "Whom you now keep waiting."

The escorts regarded each other with a measure of uncertainty, but raised no argument. Summoning his companion to his side, Patchbeard turned, beckoning the others to follow.

A fog of fear and suspicion lingered among them as they hastened northward. At the forest's edge, they took pause, peering east to where some two hundred Addarans, roughly a third of them mounted, continued to engage more than four hundred Grenarr, who as of yet had refused to flee. No more than a hundred paces lay between their own small party and the melee, with well over two hundred separating them from the city ahead.

"We make for the southwest watchtower," Patchbeard said. "If need be, we'll have cover from above."

"Then we're waiting for what?" Denariel asked crossly.

The escort leveled her a sour glare, but withheld whatever retort bristled upon his tongue. "Proceed with haste," he advised needlessly.

Ahead he dashed, with the others hard upon his heels. Gazes shifted, but fixed chiefly upon the tumult to the east. Kylac positioned himself to that flank, reflexively shielding his charges to the west.

They'd covered some forty paces before they were sighted by the enemy. Almost at once, the nearest fringe of Grenarr peeled clear of the fighting to give chase.

"Run!" Patchbeard urged.

They did. Those who could. Unsurprisingly, Aythef and the stewards soon fell behind, their winded lungs and hobbled strides preventing them from matching pace. Penryn continued to hang back with them. Kylac slowed enough to remain at the company's heart, halfway between its head and its tail. Near enough to respond in either direction, as needed.

As promised, a screen of arrows was laid down from the city battlements, harrying the enemy's attempt to reach them. For all of his companions' apprehension, Kylac quickly perceived that the race wasn't really going to be close.

A narrow drawbridge opened in the tower before them, to span the stake moat. Kylac saw Denariel to the edge of that bridge before turning east, blades raised in warning. A dozen Grenarr were still coming on, howling a lusty cry. Arrows felled three, four, five of them, thinning their ranks. As the bowmen above reloaded, Kylac rushed the remaining seven, cutting them down before another arrow could be loosed.

He returned to the bridge as Penryn ushered Egrund across, then darted himself to the open postern beyond.

He hesitated before entering, drawing a stern look from the Addaran guardsman poised to drop the portcullis. "Captain," Kylac piped, drawing Ledron from conference with another, higher-ranking watchman.

The Head's brow furrowed with concern. "What is it?"

"Her Majesty is secure?"

"So it would seem. You believe elsewise?"

"Just thinking I might put my swords—such as they are—to further use," he said, with a nod toward the fight outside. He'd told the captain before, he wasn't accustomed to letting others battle in his stead.

Concern gave way to annoyance. "Serve as you please," Ledron grunted. "But clear that portal, this side or the other."

The captain returned to his conference. Kylac glanced at Denariel, who withdrew her own gaze with a dismissive toss of her head.

Bowing to her and the others, Kylac took his leave, vaulting across the drawbridge and back onto open ground. Drawn by the clangor of swordplay, and the promise of repaying Fayne and his regiment for their aid this night.

Mayhap even finding a better weapon or two along the way.

15

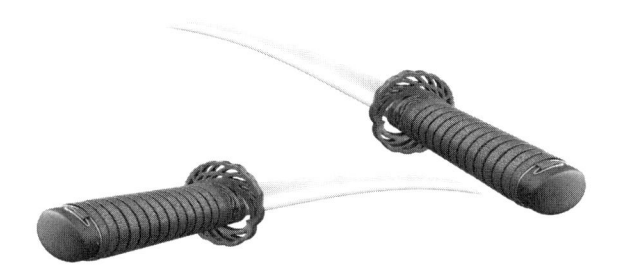

Kylac strode down the castle corridor, ushered by the echoing clatter of hard-heeled footfalls. Colonel Fayne marched beside him, still outfitted in his studded leather riding armor. Painted in sweat and grime and spattered with gore. Flush with that blend of exhaustion and exhilaration particular to battle. A hand-picked retinue of soldiers a dozen strong surrounded the proud commander, their appearance and mood much the same. United in triumph, basking in the afterglow of a hard-fought and long overdue victory.

For what little their efforts had actually won them.

Kylac stopped short of expressing as much. Given the catastrophic defeats this people had suffered of late, he supposed they should be permitted whatever encouragement they might find. That they'd finally driven the Grenarr outside into retreat would seem a fleeting victory, as there was little to prevent the enemy from regrouping. That they'd done so with minimal casualties was preferable to the alternative, but hardly significant, given the meager reward those lives and injuries had purchased. In the end, all they'd really done was welcome a ragtag band of fellow refugees into their midst, venting a measure of frustration in the process.

Of course, he'd withheld *that* thought from his present companions, as well. When he'd approached Fayne following the battle, expressing due gratitude for his soldiers' service that night, the colonel had been understandably nervous—despite a thin attempt to hide it—when inquiring in turn after His Majesty's welfare. Having no desire to engage in a lengthy report on the circumstances of their arrival, Kylac had decided instead to let the colonel squirm a mite longer, replying simply, "Let's go and see, shall we?"

Thereafter, he'd continued to deflect or ignore any questions and comments, making it clear that Fayne's compatriots should be the ones to apprise him of events, and deferring to their discretion in doing so. Suffice to say, they were pleased to count themselves among the colonel's company again.

In fair exchange, he kept his own questions to himself, relying instead on personal observations as he accompanied Fayne and contingent through the city. Along public roads and plazas, their return was hailed with fierce fanfare. But the citizens themselves were unkempt, dispirited, and half-starved, crammed beneath awnings and alcoves and other outdoor housing spaces never intended as such. Tensions ran thick, with an overworked garrison of Redfists set to regulating scuffles and skirmishes unfolding all around them—squelching fires, as it were, before they could spawn a blaze. Near to bursting with Addaran refugees she was ill-equipped to support, Indranell had the feel of a cornered rabbit worrying over her litter of kits, with the hungry fox clawing at the warren entrance . . .

He'd been provided a horse for the trek through the city, so his time among the masses had been brief. Packed and littered as the central thoroughfare had been, it had taken them barely half an hour to carve a path to the foot of the hill on which the governor's citadel was erected. Upon winding their way to the top, Kylac was presented a clear view of the Gorrethrian Sound to the north, where it lay cradled by sheer, rugged cliffs crested by defensive ramparts. A chill wind carried its salty breath upon the muggy air, stirring recollection of sea-based adventures he would sooner forget.

Out upon the night-cloaked surface of the sound itself, pinpricks of firelight helped to reveal a gathering of insect-like forms that looked like nothing so much as a swarm of beetles come to scratch and nibble at the protected shoreline. Dozens in all, extending northward.

Not beetles, Kylac knew, but ships. Grenarr warships. An armada of them. Prowlers, Reavers, and at least two Marauders that he could see, identifiable by their number of masts and their sheer, sleek bulk.

Sabrynne's southbound feint through the sound. A mere feint no longer. Mobilizing for a siege, more like. Giving cause for the heavy concentration of soldiers huddled upon the horseshoe network of northern bulwarks. While it certainly looked as if the enemy was sleeping, Indranell's defenders were maintaining close watch of their activity, assuming nothing.

Of actual battle, he saw few signs. Some ragged gaps in the terraced parapets. Here and there a scorch mark. But of the overwhelming stench of pitch and flame, the moans of wounded, or the presence of aid tents, he found the battlements refreshingly clear. Mayhap the siege had yet to commence. Mayhap he'd arrived just in time.

But he'd cleared his mind of any assumptions. Answers lay near enough—or at least reports providing further evidence of what the Grenarr intended here. No need to draw premature conclusions that might prove unwarranted.

Putting the grim vista to his back, he'd entered a bailey wherein he'd been relieved of his borrowed steed by a young stablehand. Thereafter, he'd entered the citadel itself, relying on Fayne to reassure the watchmen that he should be permitted.

Within, he found himself escorted through halls of limestone and granite with the promise of being reunited with the royal arrivals from Tetherend. Sentries posted at various corners and checkpoints had directed the colonel's party to the corridor they traversed now, a stark passage unsoftened by rugs or tapestry, adorned instead with shallow niches, shields and halberds, and iron sconces bearing the torches that lit their path. Trappings that served only to magnify the clopping echoes of his companion's thick-soled strides.

The corridor branched left and right before ending at a pair of double doors that rose shoulder to shoulder in a high, pointed arc. Armored sentinels warded the closed portal, stiffening somewhat at Fayne's approach.

"I'm told the general is in council within," the colonel said as he halted before them.

"He's expecting you," the sentinel to the left admitted. A slab-jawed beast of a lad with shifty eyes. Like so many others, he seemed unable to quite reconcile Kylac's presence. "But said nothing of these others."

"These others are faithful soldiers, come fresh from a victory outside the city gates."

"He claimed it a *private* council, sir."

"I'm sure he'd not deny me *or* our heroic outlander," Fayne suggested. His expression remained pleasant, but there was now an abrupt edge to his tone. "Our attendants are merely to ensure order and safety."

Despite his reluctance, Slab-jaw seemed to grasp the colonel's meaning. Kylac wasn't to be trusted, but there wouldn't likely be any denying him, either. Where *he* went, the colonel felt it better that a host of loyal swords followed.

"Permit me to bear word of your arrival," the sentinel begged. He motioned to his companion to open the door, then offered a curt nod before slipping within.

With a smile of false apology from Fayne, Kylac set to waiting. He might have hoped that his interactions with this people would have rendered such fears and pretenses unnecessary by now, but supposed he'd do as well wishing to have been born to the throne of Addaranth himself. If Ledron and Denariel—those he knew and had served best—could scarcely tolerate his presence, what chance did he have of winning over those who knew him only by fell rumor?

Slab-jaw's retreating footsteps gave rise to a distant murmur of voices, commencing with the sentinel's announcement. The respondent's indistinct words were couched in gruff tones. A third voice joined the conversation, no less irritable, yet more resigned in its appraisal. Ledron, if Kylac wasn't mistaken.

A brief debate ensued, interrupted by a sharp, scathing retort that could belong only to Denariel. Kylac had hoped to find the queen taking a much-needed rest. He should have known elsewise.

The argument settled, Slab-jaw made his return. "The general will see you, Colonel. The outlander, too, if he insists. I fear your retinue has been asked to remain without."

Fayne scowled, his jaw clenching ever so briefly before a smile and a nod served to mask his discontent. "As the general commands," he said. Turning to Kylac, he extended an arm toward the open door. With practiced civility, he added, "I follow at the pleasure of our guest."

Kylac pressed forward without reply, slipping through the opening into a surprisingly intimate chamber that seemed at once half receiving hall, half indoor garden. Empty windows with open shutters lined the far wall, permitting a wash of muted starlight to join the garish glow of wall-mounted torches. A massive table of burnished walnut dominated the room's heart beneath a central dome, covered curiously enough in dirt and moss and sand. Along the back wall to his left, over a bank of cupboards, hung various gardening implements such as rakes, trowels, and shears. To the right, bins of earthen materials such as soil and seeds and small stones of multiple variety. The only chair was a throne-like monstrosity atop a dais at the windowed end, the only galleries a single, broad step that rimmed the chamber's edges. All sat unoccupied just now. Ledron and Denariel, standing near the table's head, were accompanied by a single man, broad-shouldered and fur-clad, who peered up at Kylac with a discerning eye and all the warmth and welcome of a disgruntled badger.

"What has we missed?" Kylac asked, edging around the table toward his companions—neither in any rush to acknowledge him, he noted.

"A recitation of events," Ledron grumbled finally, "with which you're well enough familiar."

"Wonderful," said Kylac. "Then I's sidestepped the tedious part."

"So this is our infamous outlander," the other—General Bahsk—observed. His skin was seamed and sun-browned, his dark hair flecked with flinty gray. An equally stony visage had taken on that expression of fascination and bemusement with which Kylac was so familiar. As folks who'd heard tell of his exploits fought to attribute those deeds to his slender, boyish frame.

"General," Kylac replied simply. "Indebted to your hospitality."

Bahsk continued to stare at him, his jutting chin made even more imposing by the thicket of a beard sprouting sharply from it. Kylac felt the scouring look as he turned his own gaze back to the unusual tabletop. The isle of Addaranth, he now realized, recreated in miniature scale. Peppered with marbles and stones that would seem to mark cities and holdfasts, with threads of roadway unspooled in between. There were sheets and ribbons of padded velvet denoting lakes and rivers, and various wooden tokens that might suggest troop concentrations, strategic objectives, resource stockpiles, or something else altogether. All amid the cultivated growth denoting fields and forests and marshes—including a broad, empty swath dominating the northwest section of the isle that Kylac took to be the unexplored reaches of the Harrows.

"General," Fayne barked, and gave a sharp salute. As if to remind Kylac of Bahsk's rank and station, for whatever that was supposed to mean to him. "Pleased to confirm that the enemy beyond the south gate is routed."

Bahsk gestured vaguely. "Thank you, Colonel." Word would have been heralded some time ago, and likely required no confirmation. "A measure of fair tidings on this dark night." Or mayhap the general merely understood the limited nature of their victory.

"Captain. Your Highness," Fayne offered, bowing a greeting as Kylac reached Denariel's side—maintaining a respectful distance, of course. "I trust His Majesty is resting?"

"His Majesty is dead," Bahsk declared bluntly. "Or so I'm told."

"Dead?" Fayne echoed. A not-so-secret relief eased whatever sorrow the news bore for him. "Your Highness, I'm grieved to hear it."

"Spare me your sorrows, Colonel," Denariel sniped. "When my father's life yet hung in the balance, you responded with cowardice and insubordination. For which I intend to hold you accountable."

Fayne, taking position at Bahsk's shoulder, struck a pose of wounded astonishment. "Your Highness, I assure you—"

"Your *Majesty*," Ledron corrected.

The colonel raised a lone eyebrow in question. "Queen?" He shared a knowing look with his general. "And here was I, uninvited to the coronation."

"Now here we *all* are," Kylac interjected, discerning easily enough where this debate was headed. "With enemies arrayed south *and* north."

"Meaning any accounts of aggrieved propriety must needs be settled later," Bahsk agreed, glaring from beneath his brow. "Colonel Fayne serves me now in commanding the city's defenses."

"Serves *you*," said Denariel. "What of Governor Merrinem? If we're now to discuss commissions and strategies, where is *his* voice?"

"The governor has abdicated his stewardship to me, given the state of military crisis."

Denariel and Ledron stiffened in reaction. "Abdicated?" the queen echoed. "Or was supplanted?"

"Would you sooner that preening peacock be the one to safeguard what remains of our people?" Bahsk leaned forward, his thickly muscled forearms pressed upon the table's edge as if intent on flipping it over. "If so, give the word, *Highness*, and you may have my resignation to go with his."

Denariel matched his glare, stewing silently.

"Perhaps you should finish delivering your assessment, first, General," Ledron suggested coolly.

The pairs continued to face off across the table—queen and captain, general and colonel—in a clash of iron wills. Kylac measured the sparks, concerned only with flames.

Bahsk seemed to relent. "As I was saying, the tar-skins in the sound have launched only token bombardments thus far. But their very presence demands our attention. Should they unleash a full-scale assault, we'll be hard-pressed to repel them—to say nothing of mustering a force sizable enough to retake Avenell."

"You mean then to wait them out?" Ledron clarified.

Bahsk shook his head. "That's what our governor suggested. But with the number of refugees we've drawn, and without provisions from Avenell, we'll be lucky to survive the spring's ebb. We *must* fight free, one way or another."

"We've not the ships to break past their armada north," Ledron remarked.

"And nothing to claim if we could," Bahsk agreed, "short of a life of piracy at sea."

Kylac studied the map of the isle as they spoke, to better envision the consequences being discussed. The battlements that warded Indranell to the north were flanked by cliffs and offshore rock formations that would appear to make a landing untenable for leagues in either direction. Residents of the few hamlets and villages dotting the sound's unprotected shorelines would have already fled south weeks ago, when the Grenarr warships were first sighted. Beyond lay untamed wilds marked as all but impassable, to which Kylac himself could attest. Essentially eliminating the possibility of any northern assault that wasn't funneled through the sound, and rendering any Grenarr raids or incursions along those stretches largely irrelevant. Any man brave or foolish enough to put aground was welcome to contend with the terrible creatures who hunted the harsh and inhospitable landscape of northern Addaranth.

But the same held true for the Addarans, leaving no escape in that direction. Which left them only a single feasible option.

"So we push south," Ledron determined. "Make for Avenell before their numbers are too great to repel us. And pray that the remaining garrison here can hold."

"Save our enemy knows this," Bahsk warned. "Our web of scouts has reported a massing of tar-skin forces on the march, north from Avenell. Some two thousand, at least."

A number to double Kylac's estimate of those plaguing the Karamoor and surrounding territory thus far. If the reports were true, it would seem Sabrynne had decided not to let the Addarans wither in the north after all, but to press her advantage.

"We cannot stay, but we cannot march," Denariel summarized derisively. "Is that the extent of your appraisal, General?"

"Merely conveying what we've learned," Bahsk replied. "My *appraisal* as it pertains to action would mirror your captain's. I'll not have us wait to be squeezed from both sides. The sooner we drive south, the greater our chances of reclaiming the capital."

"Before they've burrowed in like ticks. Sounds very much like something I suggested before abandoning her at all," Denariel remarked, directing her pointed gaze at Ledron.

The Head frowned, resenting the implication. "Your Majesty," he tried to explain, "we lacked sufficient strength to—"

"As I recall you arguing then," she interrupted with a wave of her hand. Disinterested in traversing old ground. Merely pointing out that they may have done better to listen to her before. When she looked again at Bahsk, her smirk had the air of a taunt. "And this is the only course you can see?"

The general's scowl deepened. "Short of scattering into the wilderness, yes."

"Then permit me *my* assessment," she said. "You claim we've mustered some three thousand Stonewatch of our own, bolstered by less than a thousand Seawatch, yes?"

Numbers relayed before his own arrival, Kylac supposed. Though wary, the general nodded his confirmation.

"With what number needed to defend the sound?"

"I would leave behind no fewer than a thousand," Bahsk admitted.

"Marching forth with three." The queen clicked her tongue in disapproval. "Far too few to go butting heads on open ground, if the tar-skins have already marshaled a near equal number to stand against us."

"On open ground," Bahsk echoed, "a tar-skin is no equal."

"How do we know? When did we last battle them in that manner on a large scale?"

Brow furrowed in confusion, Ledron gave rein to his annoyance. "Your Majesty would now ask that we hold back?"

"I'm but following the course *you* set for us, Captain. To hunker down and weather their siege while reserves are summoned."

"Reserves," Fayne parroted smugly, rejoining the debate while his senior commander smoldered. "Hailing from where, do you suppose?"

"From Kuuria," she answered. "We send missives north, across the sea, beseeching Emperor Derreg his aid."

As she'd intended herself months ago, Kylac recalled, when first learning of her brother's abduction and the predicament it presented her royal father. When realizing that Kendarrion was not going to resist, but rather succumb to the terms of ransom proposed by the Grenarr.

The others were already smirking or scowling or cursing beneath their breath.

"I see," Fayne allowed, only barely troubling to contain his cruel mirth. "Simply slip a ship north through that blockade below. Else trek overland to one of the coastal settlements, if any are yet untouched. And in mere weeks, months, we might hope to receive aid."

Ledron shared the other's pessimism. "Unlikely it would be, Your Majesty, given the many decades of isolation between our people and theirs."

"*Forced* isolation," the queen reminded them. "Imposed by a mutual enemy. The Kuurians are our cousins. They must be made to understand."

"Even should it be so," the Head permitted, "your plea received, any answer would surely come too late."

Bahsk said nothing, having taken to eyeing Kylac in stern contemplation—as if evaluating him for some task. Denariel waited until the protests of the other pair had waned before responding with carefully measured confidence. "It is the best way to even the scales. A fleet of soldiers dispatched by the emperor could be diverted north *and* south. Used to press the backs of our enemies—to fence them in, as we are now. Give *them* two fronts to contend with."

"A pair of tempests steered by the Fair Mother could accomplish the same," Bahsk responded finally. "If it's but prayers we're casting, why not that one?"

"Is it not a prayer to believe you can sweep aside this southern army of theirs like chaff?" Denariel countered, unrelenting. "Without a clear advantage of force, even if we should break through or overwhelm them, how many of ours will be left, and in what condition, to press the assault back to Avenell?"

"We've repelled every large-scale Grenarr landing attempt for nearly two centuries," Bahsk declared proudly.

"*Attempt.* Not an army already entrenched against us. And certainly none of this size."

"The tar-skins cannot withstand us aground," the general maintained, steadfast in his belief. "And I'll not have us cower here like whipped dogs while they seek to solidify their strength."

"Yet that is precisely what you've done, General. The time to act as you suggest would have been the moment Avenell was overrun."

"And prepared was I to do so, if not beholden to those of weaker will."

"I cannot speak for Merrinem or his councilmen," Denariel said. "But I assure you, *my* will is resolute."

"Your will."

"My will, and my command."

"As queen."

"As the daughter and sole surviving heir of Kendarrion, the late king of Addaranth. Yes, as queen."

The general's slow-roiling anger gave vent to a cloud of suspicion. "You bear word of a crown prince murdered, and a royal king laid to rest. But I've recent witness that His Majesty yet lives. And I've seen no evidence of His Highness Dethaniel's demise. Pray tell, are we to receive you at your word, without confirmation of these tidings?"

"You have my testament, as well," Ledron reminded him. "And his," he added, indicating Kylac.

"A disgraced Blackfist. A renegade outlander." Granite eyes regarded each man with disdain before resettling on Denariel. "Standing to gain from a usurper's favor."

The queen's fury was swift, intense. "You accuse me of fratricide? Of regicide?"

"I do not say you've killed anyone. Only that you stake claim to titles that may yet belong to another."

"We've other witnesses," said Ledron.

"As do I," said Fayne. "In greater numbers."

"None who cleaved to His Majesty's side," the Head growled.

"Would that circumstances had permitted he accompany us, that I might have ensured his health."

"Festering filth!" Denariel spat. And lunged. And would have been at the colonel's throat in a matter of strides, Kylac was certain, had Ledron not caught her around the waist. "I'll have you scourged with a flail fashioned from your own tongue!"

"Your Majesty, no," Ledron hissed, pleading as he wrestled with her.

Bahsk's eyes had gone to Kylac, whose fingers itched, but had yet to go for his hilts. Matters appeared to be escalating well enough without his involvement.

"A violent instinct," the general said. "The nature of your blood, perhaps."

Kylac caught the clear reference to her Grenarr heritage, and was quite certain the others had, too. The queen herself acknowledged it by ceasing to struggle, willfully summoning her composure.

"You *will* heed me, General," she warned. "Else burn in the boat set sail with *him*." A toss of her head targeted Fayne.

"I mean not to quarrel," Bahsk assured her, the words belying his stony intent. "With any of you. But you have long shown a rebellious nature, Your Highness. Defied your royal father time and again. Is this not so?"

Denariel seethed through gritted teeth, as if not trusting herself to words.

"I am not deaf to your counsel," the general continued. "But our very existence is at stake. And I'll no longer be run like a blinded horse, made to gallop along a course I sense to be tainted with folly or treachery."

Denariel balked. "Treachery? Like that committed by Ohrma in seeking to overthrow my father to begin with? And who rode him along *that* course, I wonder. Could it have been voices like yours, long opposed to peace with the Grenarr in any form?"

Bahsk was unmoved. "Much like yours, if I'm not gravely mistaken. Which serves my argument. We are too far undone by deceit and betrayal to recklessly commit our faith to any lone individual. Even you, be it Highness or Majesty. Not unless your vision were to spawn a consensus among those of us struggling for survival."

Denariel scoffed. "Should my vision align with yours, you mean."

"Should you wish to present your proposal before a city council—"

"My father never begged approval of a city council."

"To the detriment of all, it might be said."

Fayne grinned. Denariel caught it. "A council cowed by you, no doubt."

"Our people seek leadership. I but answer the call."

"To waste further time we do not have."

"We've preparations yet to make," Bahsk admitted. "Should you wish to plead your case before the council, petition their authority, I shall be pleased to arrange it."

Denariel's eyes narrowed with doubt. "And if they should support me?"

The general's return gaze was piercing. "I fear no dissent. Just know now that I'll not willingly succor further madness."

An open challenge, Kylac determined, that made cooperation unlikely. Whatever the outcome of any council deliberations—be the participants friendly or hostile—this was a man whose mind was set. He would have his way, or he would step aside. The latter a minimal risk, if measured by his confidence.

"Suppose then I have you removed, here and now."

"I'm sure Your Highness will have no difficulty explaining her decision to the council. Or to my loyal lieutenants. Or to theirs, on down to the rank and file."

Denariel fumed. "Or I might simply have Kronus here take your head, and thereby eliminate any uncertain allegiances."

The general flicked a glance at Kylac, as if to discern whether the threat posed genuine possibility. "Less easily explained, perhaps. But who knows? There might be some who admire your boldness."

"I've twenty men just outside who might think elsewise," Fayne advised.

"Who will be hard-pressed to kill Grenarr as corpses," Kylac countered. He had no intention of killing the general, who as of yet had said nothing he deemed entirely unreasonable. But the smug colonel would be better served keeping silent.

"I think we might be done here, Your Majesty," Ledron urged.

The general looked them over, blunt in his consideration. "Better that tempers be allowed to cool," he agreed. "If Your Highness will take her rest, I'll see to it that a council is convened on the morrow."

Denariel clung to her fierce pout. For a long moment, she seemed set to disagree. "I shall take you at your word, General. And hold you to it."

With that, she spun and marched toward the exit. Ledron followed, frowning his stern frown and gritting his teeth. Kylac inserted himself among their shadows, with a tip of his brow toward the queen's headstrong compatriots. Eyeing thereafter the map of the lands at the heart of so much strife and turmoil.

Wondering how, in the end, any of it could prove worthwhile.

16

"Fiends!" Denariel fumed as she paced her balcony. "Oathbreakers! Black as tar-skins themselves!"

Kylac had positioned himself at the east end of the balcony, opposite Ledron at the west. Ceding the queen sufficient ground to vent her frustrations, yet near enough to arrest any rasher impulses she might have, or ill-favored attentions she might draw.

The Head flinched as Denariel turned abruptly and charged the balustrade, betraying his fear that she might simply fling herself over it. Judging solely by the intensity of her movements, Kylac might have feared the same. But he sensed clearly the nature of her livid fury. Breeding hostility, not despair.

Even so, she slapped up against the rail hard enough to break Ledron's stance, drawing him hastily toward her as she leaned out and shrieked a wordless, trumpeting cry at the fire-dotted expanse of the night-cloaked sound.

"Your Majesty, please."

"Unhand me!" Denariel barked, chafing at her captain's touch.

Ledron withdrew, remaining within arm's reach. "Your Majesty—"

"Spare me your devotions, Captain. My need of your support lay in that chamber, against those who would refuse me theirs."

"Your Majesty, I endeavored to—"

"You disrespected me. You disrespected my father's memory. My sworn defender," she added disgustedly, before spinning back to the rail and the congregation of enemies in the black waters far below.

Surely without meaning to, Ledron turned his helpless gaze toward Kylac. But the queen wasn't ready to be coaxed or calmed. Clearly, she wanted to fight.

"Devotions," Kylac echoed, and chuckled. "After Your Majesty strove so fervently to endear herself."

Her head rounded on him like an asp's. "I should not have to *endear* myself. I am their queen."

"By writ. Or decree. Upheld by those with sword and spear."

Denariel's thunderous countenance darkened further, her eyes agleam with venom. "Would you imply again that I submit to the will of a few knuckle-minded soldiers?"

As she had while plotting their course of escape from Avenell's dungeons. Making her loath to do so again. But reluctance in this matter didn't overshadow need.

"We ride still the tide o' revolt unleashed against your father. Your governor is deposed. Your *knuckle-minded* soldiers beyond blind obedience. If'n ya mean for them to follow—"

"They are soldiers. *Bred* to follow."

"Where a sense o' duty or desire takes them. A man coerced is far less reliable than one who fights o' his own will."

The queen shook her head, refusing to be persuaded. "Were I to replace the disloyal commanders—"

"We would find others, Your Majesty," Ledron interjected. "Else those who may not speak for the rank and file."

"And swaying a mere portion o' the swords remaining to ya will only further fragment an already weakened force."

"We're too battered to waste strength against ourselves," the Head agreed. "I beg Your Majesty. Better to appease the general now and look later for an opportunity to prove yourself."

Denariel seethed, burning with contempt. "To the swells with him and his pack of traitors. I *will* find those loyal to me, if I have to swim the seas to do it."

"A lengthy swim that'd be," Kylac observed. "Requiring months ya simply don't has."

"With debt to you," she snarled, coiling dangerously. "Were it not for your interference, this war might be ended already. We might even now be rewarding our allied commanders and sending them home, with gratitude to Emperor Derreg for—"

"Derreg is dead." As the queen's glare soured with skepticism, he added, "The Culmarils rule now over a devastated kingdom. Ravaged by a war o' their own."

"What war?"

"With all respect, one to make ours here seem scarcely a quarrel. Involving creatures I'll not attempt to describe."

"Dragons?" Ledron asked. Familiar with the rumors. Even if, until now, he'd expressed no interest in them.

Denariel snorted. "Absurd."

"More so, were I to share the tale. Ending in victory, amid terrible ruin. I know one young sovereign we *could* turn to," he admitted, "and others who might help. But I'd wager against any Pentanian kingdom having manpower to muster on our behalf."

Their sober silence suggested they might actually believe him. Inasmuch as it concerned the likelihood of reinforcements, at least. Else mayhap they understood already the narrow chances of even *sending* their request, much less receiving answer. Ledron certainly did. Mayhap his stubborn queen was beginning to accept it, as well.

"What chance have we without aid?" she countered, if only to retake the offensive.

The sound responded, offering a dull, discontented roar from where it heaved and slapped against the rocky shoreline far below. A rush of wind caused the flames within nearby stanchions to flicker and crackle. Curtains whispered, billowing lightly within the lavishly appointed chambers from which the balcony emerged. Tickled chimes rang their mischievous laughter. Out amid the starry darkness, a circling spearwing shrieked. Ledron looked to Kylac. Kylac looked back.

Neither had answer she wanted to hear.

Denariel grunted, somehow satisfied, and turned her gaze back to the open night.

"Your Majesty," Ledron tried, "the general needn't be wrong. If we can secure ourselves a tactical advantage—"

"What about the Ukinha?" she asked.

The Head blinked, his expression a slate of confusion. "Your Majesty?"

"If we were to rally the Ukinha . . ." Her features brightened at the thought. "Now *that* would be a force to send the tar-skins screaming."

Ledron looked again to Kylac, who shrugged. "A fearsome sight it would be," the captain allowed. "Though I hardly—"

"You think I raise it as a fancy?" Denariel asked, her visage sharpening.

The Head scowled. "However raised, a fancy it is."

"And why is that, Captain?"

Kylac watched Ledron redden, the Blackfist bridling his tongue while he collected his volatile thoughts. "The mutants serve only themselves. By what means would Your Majesty imagine they might be persuaded to our cause?"

"I've done so before, if you'll recall."

Her Ukinh. The one taken into her company when first fleeing north to Kuuria. Believed left behind in Wingport, only to pursue her doggedly south again, secretly venturing with them across the seas before hunting them across a nightmare stretch of the Harrows. A mutant with which she'd borne some manner of venom-induced infatuation, of which Kylac had learned too late.

Only after—in Denariel's eyes—he'd murdered the creature.

Amid a bothersome twinge of unwarranted guilt, Kylac felt a slow stirring born of intrigue.

"A lone groll," Ledron reminded her, teeth clenched against whatever it was he truly wished to say. "The presence of which only a madman like Ulflund could have abided."

"Ulflund *abided* him easily enough. Far more familiar with their kind than you, Captain."

"Perhaps the only reason *it* abided *him*."

Another guilty pang—this one well deserved. Kylac had encountered Ulflund before knowing him to be Denariel's chosen protector. A Shadowguard captain turned renegade, it was said, after being shunned by Kendarrion as a result of the crown prince Dethaniel's abduction. Traitorous, it had turned out, only insofar as taking up with Denariel's quest to seek military aid against the Grenarr—well short of kidnapping her, as Ledron had claimed. A dutiful guardian who'd served for many years along the edge of the Ukinhan Wilds, during which time he'd come to know and respect the mysterious mutants better than most.

Acting a touch too eagerly upon assumptions that had seemed safe at the time, Kylac had killed *him*, too.

And the remainder of his Shadowguard alongside.

It was that event that had triggered Kylac's involvement in all the rest. The voyage to Addaranth. To Haverstromme and back again. To Tetherend, and now here. Like kicking a pebble down a slope, oblivious to the rockslide that would result.

"Nonetheless," Ledron pressed, "we speak of a single mutant. Not a pack, and certainly not an army. Your Majesty knows well enough there is no unity among the creatures."

To that, Kylac could attest. The two grolls he'd crossed paths with had also crossed paths with each other. Only one had survived the brief, savage interaction.

Denariel, however, grew suddenly still, as if steeling herself with grim resolve. "What if there were one they might serve? One who could compel them toward a common cause?"

The knot of Ledron's visage tightened. "Talathandria?"

Kylac searched his memory for the name, finding it vaguely familiar, yet beyond his mental grasp.

Taking the queen's silence as confirmation, Ledron snorted. "A myth. A fireside fable to unsettle greenhorns at the edge of the Harrows, or frighten willful children to sleep."

The Harrows, Kylac recalled. South of the Cindercrag, they'd passed through Talathandria's Run. Named for an adulterous queen of Addaran legend, said to have escaped her royal husband's bounty hunters by taking refuge with the Ukinha. To consort with them and, eventually, become one of them, drawing on an unnatural vitality by which she survived to this day.

"If real . . ." Denariel teased.

"A ghost," the Head insisted, "if ever she lived."

"Supposing elsewise," Kylac permitted, giving Ledron a chance to calm his roiling exasperation. "What cause would she has to favor your people over the Grenarr?"

The queen didn't immediately respond, seeming taken with her own reflections. "We'd have to *make* her understand."

"There can be no alliance with monsters," Ledron growled emphatically. "Dismiss me from your service if you must, but none will you find who would entertain this madness."

Kylac might have disagreed. Mad as it seemed, he'd not so easily dismiss the idea, if Denariel could provide but some seed of reason by which it might succeed.

Instead, the queen grew silent, surprisingly despondent, beneath the weight of her captain's refusal.

"I should have capitulated from the first," she said finally. "Simply honored my father's decision and surrendered to my brother's scheme."

The sentiment took her listeners aback.

"And gained little for it," Kylac reminded her, "given the Grenarr's treatment of His Highness." The only real difference, insofar as he could see, would have been that *her* life might by now have been forfeit, too. Else leaving her wishing that it had been.

"Save that it may have been my defiance alone that caused them to reconsider the terms. For all that *I've* gained, better perhaps that I'd never resisted to begin with."

"We'll find a way, Your Majesty," Ledron tendered awkwardly. "A surer, safer path."

"More likely with rested minds than those addled for want o' sleep," Kylac suggested.

The Head agreed. "We've journeyed long and hard, Your Majesty. Please, take your rest."

The queen failed to respond, focusing on the ominous northern vista under a disconcerting pall of acceptance and regret. Gods knew she'd suffered. If finally succumbing to weariness and sorrow, the real wonder was that she hadn't done so sooner. And yet it troubled Kylac to see her—ever so strong and willful—relenting in any measure to the notion of defeat.

"As you see it, Captain," she said finally, and turned toward the inner chamber, gaze falling to her feet.

Kylac exchanged a glance with Ledron, whose relief in that moment clearly outweighed his concern. Hanging back, Kylac watched the Blackfist shadow her within, where she shed her filthy tunic and breeches without a trace of modesty before crawling into bed beneath its mound of blankets and furs. She seemed not to care what her warders did with themselves, until Ledron moved to stand post near the entry.

"The sitting room, if you please, Captain," she said, eyes closed as she settled into her pillows. "I suspect you'll sleep yourself, at some point in the night, and I shan't like to be awakened by your snores."

The Head frowned, but gave a bow and beckoned Kylac after him.

"I'll take first watch," the Blackfist determined upon closing the bedchamber door behind them.

"Ya don't mean to leave her unattended," Kylac objected.

"There's no entry from that balcony. She'll be safe. I'll look in on her to be sure."

Kylac withheld further protest, mindful of the fact that the defense of royal persons was Ledron's express duty in life, and that he was not inexperienced at it. "Will Bahsk honor his word?"

"I take no man at his word."

"Strikes me he was overly keen to extend us every comfort."

Ledron snorted. "Small appeasement, given the manner with which he received Her Majesty."

"Appeasement? Or distraction?"

The Head soured, taking Kylac's meaning. "Against what?"

"The general's mind was set. If'n his plans aren't already firmer than revealed, I'll wager he makes haste to solidify 'em."

"That any dissent we might raise will be too late."

Kylac nodded.

"As a course of strategy, I cannot say the general is wrong."

"Nor would I. But I might like to know what tactics he means to employ."

Ledron eyed him sternly, suspiciously. Imagining as always some darker motive behind Kylac's stated intent. "Go then," he agreed at last. "Learn what you can. I'll expect report by the Shrike's Hour."

He found Bahsk and Fayne where he'd thought he might, convened in the map chamber in much the same positions as he'd left them. They were joined now by a coterie of what looked to be battle-seasoned officers—hard-faced soldiers gruff and grizzled, knotted and scarred, each with a younger lieutenant at his shoulder, worn like a token of rank. All huddled around the great map table, some stooped near with urgent interest, others more aloof in their stance, with rigid backs and arms folded across their chests.

None appeared particularly pleased at what they were hearing.

". . . simply surrender the Karamoor?"

". . . a craven's path."

". . . should cut right through them."

". . . trading one bastion for another."

". . . take back the right hand if giving them the left?"

Kylac himself crouched upon a narrow lip on the external face of the windowed wall, perched amid the starlit shadows cast by the stone framing. The shutters remained open, granting him a clear view and unobstructed ear of the proceedings within. As clear and unobstructed as could be, given the cluster of bodies and their assorted rumblings.

His broad, fur-heaped back to the windows, Bahsk let his officers mutter and rail, then raised his arms in a gesture meant to silence them.

"I mean in no way to forsake Indranell," he assured them. "If we do not control our borders north *and* south, we control nothing."

"How then can you deprive us of more than half our current garrison, and do nothing to stem the tide of those flowing against us?"

"Because our numbers are better spent securing Avenell first, while her northern walls are undermanned. Catching the tar-skins in between and forcing *them* to divide their strength north and south. Forcing them to overcome our bulwarks, rather than our naked columns."

"But to bypass the very force we mean to crush—"

"To secure the more favorable ground."

"—when we might simply mow through them?"

"And if we do not?" Bahsk challenged. "The longer we're stalled along the Karamoor, grinding them into the mud, the more of their foul ilk pour in through the bay, reinforcing their thieving hold and further defiling our fair capital."

"I shudder to believe, General, that you of all would shy from a beached shark. What cause have we to fear their so-called infantry?"

A swell of murmurs rose in support of the challenge. The man bearing the flag of dissent looked to be one whose actual fighting days were long behind him. A white-maned giant portly about the belly, who wore a steel fork fitted over his missing left hand. He used it now to scratch at the flesh beneath a patch covering his right eye. Rough as he appeared at a distance, Kylac could only imagine how mangled he might look face-to-face.

"As a matter of practicality," Bahsk answered candidly. "Much as it would satisfy me to butcher them like mongrels on the open road, only a fool would give rein to such base desire at the expense of a more favorable strategy."

Kylac could scarcely believe the general's pragmatic appraisal. Was this the same man who just an hour earlier had scoffed at Denariel's suggestion that they seek reinforcement? Who had proclaimed no tar-skin his equal aground? Yet here he stood, evidently proposing a course that would have his men evading skirmish with Sabrynne's forces until *after* circumventing them somehow to retake the city at their backs. Compelling others to ply him with the same prideful logic—or illogic—that he'd wielded against Her Majesty.

Might Denariel have said something that had swayed his thinking? Or was he merely playing games of deceit and control as he jockeyed for power with the would-be queen? With the throne on such vulnerable footing, there had to be those like Bahsk who would present themselves as would-be claimants, should theirs prove the guiding hand that restored their people to prominence.

Mayhap Fork-hand was another.

"I fail to see the *favor* in bypassing the infestation, leaving the wolves to roam."

"Aimlessly," said Bahsk, hunching forward. "Trapped. Pissing and howling, but with nowhere to go. We retake Avenell behind them, we cut off their retreat. Starve them for a time, if need be. Then bite down like a huntsman's trap and annihilate them."

That argument seemed to win the general some support, judging by the whispers and grunts arising in its wake. Kylac couldn't say yet whether this was to be a voting council, or if Bahsk had summoned them merely to disseminate orders. Either way, a good share of those spoiling for a fight, fearing their commander had somehow softened, seemed to see now the reasoning behind his judgment.

Why drive their enemies back to the sea if they could eradicate such a sizable portion of them utterly?

Fork-hand grew quiet for a moment, thunderous in his silence, while his own supporters grumbled indistinctly, encouraging him to continue the fight. Even if they couldn't offer any specific justification for doing so.

"A blade in the back can be effective, certainly," he allowed, his husky voice thick with disparagement. "But how do you mean to move three thousand of ours past this pack of sea wolves without alerting its scouts?"

"Here," said Bahsk, and Kylac thought he detected a note of victory in the general's tone. "At Praxu. Where we might follow the river canyon into the heart of the Strebolen. The defiles will hide our movements from any tar-skin not traveling by wing. After navigating Ollerman's Pass, we emerge here, to the south of Dormund. Within a day's trek of Northgate."

Kylac had no view of the path being drawn. But he saw clearly enough the press of bodies leaning in to trace it with their eyes upon the table, and who proceeded thereafter to nod and straighten with evident satisfaction. Again, the swell of murmurs bore a note of approval, despite the sour expressions and snide comments that sought to dismiss it as folly.

"A remote stretch of broken earth," Fork-hand complained. "Marked by chokehold paths. Where our numbers would count for naught."

"Only if they should find us," Bahsk contested calmly. "Even if they were to detect our diversion into the canyon, they'll know not where we intend to emerge."

"And the stepstone terrain? *Should* they anticipate our course, and gain any of these ridges ahead of us, they might rain pummeling fire from the heights, while we stew and roil in our self-made cauldron."

"A risk," the general permitted. "But our own scouts would alert us to any such ambush."

"There might be no going back," Fork-hand warned.

"Retreat is not a choice I intend to consider," the general admitted, steely in his resolve. "Nor should any who accompany me."

A challenge, it seemed. Reversing the course of the debate so that it was now Fork-hand and his dissenters on the defensive.

"Given choice, I go where I can collect trophies of my victims," Fork-hand snarled. His head turned toward Fayne, shadowed expression twisting with contempt. "Let others harry from the heights of tower and battlement."

"I serve as called upon," Fayne replied. "Asked by my general to weather siege here with a skeletal garrison, that is what *I* intend."

Fork-hand snorted. "A soldier too pretty to part with his limbs. May as well have been a bowman."

A few snickered at the jape. Fayne waited them out before tendering reply. "If it's ugliness you favor, let us pray no more of you is whittled away."

An abrupt silence took hold. Then Fork-hand bellowed a mirthless laugh. "Agreed we are, then. My company marches, General. Under protest of this cowardly digression of yours. Staking claim to the front line should the Fair Mother grant us a more direct confrontation."

"So noted, Colonel," Bahsk agreed. "And the rest of you? Any man here who would chafe at his assignment, I'll have it be known now."

A stir of grumblings filled the chamber, though clearly diminished in strength. Whatever the lingering dissatisfaction, it lacked a clear voice, now that the primary challenge had seemingly been quashed. Kylac tarried a few moments longer, clinging to the tower wall against the cries of invisible seabirds and the occasional gust of midnight breezes. But as conversation turned to matters of logistics—preparation, provisioning, and the positioning of specific companies and commanders—he grew bored and decided it best to begin his way back. He hadn't yet heard anything on the matter of schedule, but had taken sufficient measure of Bahsk's plans to know whether anything the general revealed later to Ledron or Denariel was a lie.

He hoped not. Unlike Ledron, life struck him a great deal simpler in those rare instances where a man's word could be taken for truth.

He took his time in returning to the queen's quarters. Ledron had given him until the Shrike's Hour, granting him opportunity to venture further throughout the citadel. To explore its various levels and wings, while seeing what else he might learn. Even at this late hour, there would be watchmen on patrol, and servants going about their nightly duties. Men and women with busy hands and idle tongues. And while a thread of chatter here or there might tell him nothing, myriad strands woven together could reveal an entire tapestry.

On this night, most of the active whispers regarded the arrival of Princess Denariel—notably unattended by the king. This word had sparked all manner of rumor concerning His Majesty's health and condition, the nature of Her Highness's long, unexplained absence, and what either might mean for the ongoing Grenarr siege. While some grieved to presume the king dead, others shrugged or bid welcome riddance, regretting only that his headstrong daughter hadn't been felled alongside.

Naturally, some had it the other way around, insisting it was His Majesty who'd arrived. Her Highness had long since been abducted as her brother had, in retribution for the murder of the Grenarr overlord on Addaran soil. Others had it that her royal father had sold her to the enemy in secret as an attempt at appeasement, only to be betrayed. Still others had it that Kendarrion had betrayed his own by conspiring himself with the Grenarr to open the Seagate, so desperate was he to win the return of his son.

Such conspiracies better explained the chiefly dull sentiment with which the evening's victory had been received. Kendarrion or Denariel, it scarcely mattered. Neither carried much in the way of hope or expectation that the city's fortunes might turn. Trapped here at Indranell, with the enemy at their gates north and south, the people of Addaranth were living out the most dire hour in their isle's history. The return of a failed king or half-breed princess hardly constituted the miracle for which they prayed.

He did discover that the other members of his party from Tetherend had been made safe and comfortable, granted quarters here within the citadel as promised, as members of Denariel's retinue. He also confirmed, gleaning from multiple accounts, that the city governor, Merrinem, had indeed willingly surrendered his authority to General Bahsk in this hour of martial need. Merely a recounting of events as the general wished for them to be perceived, mayhap. But Kylac chose to take it as evidence that Bahsk's domineering leadership was in service more to his beleaguered countrymen than to a personal quest for power.

Beyond that, what he heard most were private laments over horrors and indignities suffered, and fears of how much worse conditions might become. Suppositions were bandied about regarding how long the siege might last, whether they'd be better treated were they to surrender now, and what chance they might have if they were to scatter instead into the wilderness. Few seemed to carry with them any semblance of hope. Several cautioned that only the Fair Mother could save them—and *that* in accordance with their faith. Some spoke of those who'd taken their own lives already, due to the loss of cherished ones—a husband, a wife, a child—they couldn't persevere without. In one dark corner of the lower citadel, he came across a cook and a scullery maid shirking their chores to steal a moment of intimacy. Mismatched by age and appearance, yet uncertain how many opportunities might be left to them in this world to seek a measure of warmth and tenderness.

By the time the Woodcock's Hour neared its tail, Kylac had partaken more than his fill of mourning and melancholy. He almost regretted now having escorted Denariel and company here at all. Their last haven, it might have seemed. But the sense of sorrow and defeat that choked its halls formed a morass as thick and suffocating as the flooded grounds of Tetherend, and made the very air seem difficult to breathe.

So he climbed swiftly, at that point, to the keep's higher reaches, intending to enter the antechamber to the queen's quarters through the same window from which he'd departed. Easy as it would have been to disable the sentries posted outside Her Majesty's suite, he hadn't wished to explain later why he'd done so. Simpler by far to use another point of egress and avoid the guards altogether.

As he rounded a turret near his entry point, however, he sighted a thick rope of curtains and bed linens dangling from a baluster of Denariel's balcony. The lower end of the twisted, knotted strand hung more than two dozen heads above a paved courtyard—dominated by a large, inset pond. Even in the dim starlight, Kylac could make out the dark trail of half-dried footprints leading away from the pond's edge, out onto a terraced garden hillside.

He considered pursuing those prints directly, but decided to first make sure. With a muttered curse, he completed his climb, scrambling up into the nearest window of the sitting chamber.

To find Ledron sprawled in a padded divan, fast asleep.

He flew to the bedchamber door. Finding it barred, he kicked it open, shattering the latch housing. The sound roused Ledron, to whom Kylac turned after confirming that the queen's chambers were empty.

"What . . ." the Head tried groggily. "Her Maj . . . Majesty is—"

"Gone," Kylac finished for him, and cursed again.

17

"Gone?" ledron asked, blinking his bleary eyes.

Kylac gave rein to his amusement, so as to stave off anger. "Look about, Captain. Tell me I'm wrong."

The Head stumbled as he rose from the divan, struggling to find his feet. In observing the Blackfist's difficulty, Kylac noted a silver platter atop a nearby sideboard, bearing flagon and goblet.

"Send for a drink, did ya?"

"For the queen," Ledron replied. "She complained of wakefulness . . ."

He was moving now, brushing past, staggering toward the open portal to the queen's bedchamber. Kylac let him go, moving to a second cup, spilled on the floor beside the captain's divan. He picked it up, smelling only water. But when he ran a finger along its inner bowl, he felt a sandy residue.

"An herbal brew," he guessed. "Something to soothe."

"Vallurynth," Ledron confirmed, growing frantic now as he witnessed for himself the rumpled ruin of his queen's bed. "Ground, per request."

Kylac followed him now, still holding the empty water cup. "And none for yourself?"

The Head paused in his search long enough to cast a glare of indignation.

"Your cup," said Kylac, extending it to him.

Ledron frowned fiercely, wary of deception. But he took the vessel, and tested it as Kylac had. Red eyes widened with understanding. "Her Majesty. She must have . . . While I dismissed the server . . ."

The captain looked back to the outer door, as if recalling the events in his mind. A moment's distraction would have been sufficient. With her warder focused on ensuring the visiting servant's departure, Denariel could have deposited the granular blend of herbs in Ledron's water pitcher, rather than her own flagon. An honest misstep on the Blackfist's part, if a clumsy one, given all he knew of Her Majesty's intractable nature and troublesome past.

"When?" Kylac asked.

"Not a half-mark after you'd gone. Nearing midnight."

"The balcony," Kylac urged.

Furious now with himself, the Head cast the cup aside and stormed out as directed. A moment later, he was inspecting the knotted strand by which the queen had descended, and the watery drop at its end, stewing in wonder and frustration.

"Dawning winds," he growled. "What does she intend now?"

"Seems her lament, there at the end, was a front."

As should have been obvious to them the moment the despairing sentiments had escaped her lips. Regretting resistance? At this stage? She'd sought to put them off their guard, was all. And it had worked. Familiar as they were with all her volatile history, they'd swallowed her ruse and lapsed in their vigilance.

"But that would mean . . ." Ledron gripped the stone rail as he continued to corral his muddled thoughts. "You don't think . . ."

Kylac climbed over the balustrade, putting his feet near the makeshift rope. "None would she find to entertain her madness. Was that not your claim, Captain?"

The Head fought to restrain the horror spilling now along the lines of his face. "Surely she cannot believe . . . The Harrows? Alone?"

"Pray we're wrong, while I sees about running her down."

"Wait!" Ledron barked, as Kylac dropped down to grasp the knotted line. "We should marshal a search party."

"Then do so. Quietly, I'd suggest. But it might be I can still catch her before she escapes the city."

"Kronus!" the Head barked again, when Kylac had scurried halfway down. "The city walls. Give no pursuit beyond them without me."

Kylac hesitated. "Doubling back without her would only extend her lead."

"Promise me," Ledron demanded. "You find sign she's left the city, you return, that we might track her together."

"As ya wish," Kylac agreed. Hoping it wouldn't come to that. Knowing that the longer he dangled here, bartering, the more likely he was to fail.

With a final nod, he scrambled down to about three-quarters of the line's reach before releasing his hold, straightening his body as he plunged feetfirst into the pond below. The waters weren't deep. His legs folded beneath him as he struck the mud-softened bottom. But he gathered himself quickly, pressing hard against the slimy sediment to launch himself to the surface, where he swam to the nearest edge and pulled himself free.

Ledron's timeline granted the queen about a two-hour advance. But the trails of her dripping emergence were wetter than that. Meaning the captain could be wrong, and her lead shorter than estimated. A reasonable expectation, as she'd likely have waited to make certain the vallurynth had done its task, her warder fallen asleep, before fashioning her rope and initiating her escape.

Or it might simply mean that here, at the edge of the sound, on this dark and sultry night, the moist air had little interest in lapping up her tracks.

His own spattered along next to hers as he dashed to the edge of the patio and through the wall of shrubbery at its fringe. Down along the hillside gardens he proceeded, dropping from terraced retaining walls made from stone and tarred timbers, descending slopes covered with deep-rooted groundcover meant to resist erosion and mudslide. Denariel hadn't bothered with the various switchbacks laid down as service trails, so neither did he, forgoing safety in favor of speed. In more than one area, torn plants and scraped soils suggested she'd lost her footing and gone skidding for a stretch. He found himself hoping she hadn't suffered serious injury.

An ache or strain to slow her progress, now . . .

The hillside ran for a little more than a hundred paces, ending in another squat retaining wall and a graveled access path that ran along its base. A wrought-iron fence marked a clear boundary from the sheerer cliffs beyond, its crowning spikes curled outward to defend against unauthorized entry to the citadel grounds.

Kylac checked east and west, and quickly turned west after Denariel's continuing tracks. The path was an uneven one as it traced the terrain, dipping and climbing, widening and narrowing, the cause of its patterns known only to whatever combination of forces had shaped it. Though fairly well tended, he did come across sections in disrepair—the gravel eclipsed by hillside overgrowth, bars bent by veins of landslide, or erosive cutaways leaving small sections of fence hanging out over open air. It was at one of the latter where signs suggested Denariel had passed through. A clay escarpment lay beneath, with a steeply sloping drop of some sixty paces or more to a briar-ridden ridge of wild grass below. But the angle was just gentle enough that a desperate woman might think to slide and tumble without breaking her neck or splintering any bones in the process.

Mayhap.

He scouted around for other signs to be sure. The queen was crafty enough to lay a false trail—and this an ideal place to do so. Because a man who made the drop wasn't going to be able to scale his way back.

Most men, anyway. And even he, allowing exception, didn't want to waste the time climbing back if the drop was a deceit to begin with.

But he found no trace to suggest she'd dropped some stone or log before continuing on through the groundcover to mask her passage. Her trail along the fence ended here. All other signs—from the rough edge of the bluff where she'd chipped away to widen the gap, to her dirty finger marks where she'd gripped the base of the iron rail before dropping through—clearly indicated descent.

So he made his own, worming through the breach with his sheathed weapons drawn close, letting his weight and the ground's insatiable pull do the rest. Down he slid, skidding over bumps in the bluff's face, scraping free a fresh layer of silt and pebbles. The ridge below seemed to rise up, its thorny grasses anxious to receive him. As he grated in among them, the slope flattened, with a berm of gathered soils to further arrest and cushion his momentum. That and the clawing brush swiftly brought him to a halt.

He arose carefully, not wishing to smother any of Denariel's tracks with his own. As before, it appeared she'd turned west, beating a path through the taller grasses. Thinking, mayhap, that they might help hide her movements from any watchmen perched atop tower or battlement, above or below.

Unlikely. The steep, inaccessible terrain made this a remote stretch along the city north-facing heights. A no-man's-land between the citadel defenses above, and those erected upon the bluffs overlooking the sound below. Lookouts stationed upon the one or the other had no known cause to search this forsaken stretch. Particularly with the flock of enemy ships at the mouth of the city's waterside threshold demanding every available eye.

The dim starlight offered only muted clarity to the path he followed. But his eyes were strong, and his instincts stronger. Even so, he proceeded with due caution, determined not to over-pursue along any dead ends. As of yet, he'd discovered no attempts on the queen's part to bait him. But that didn't mean she wouldn't.

As he wove westward through the grasses and clumps of stronger, spinier growth, he couldn't help but wonder at her intent. Did she truly mean to brave the Harrows on her own? She wasn't carrying any weapons that he knew of. Forget the outlandish notion of persuading the reclusive Ukinha to band together around a ghost and join her in a struggle that would seem not to concern them. What made her think she could stroll into their treacherous wilderness and survive?

But then, she knew their territory better than he. Between her past excursions and the fact that she'd lived upon this isle her entire life, it was entirely conceivable—even likely—that she had some secret cause to believe in her chosen venture. Cause that he, as an outlander, couldn't yet grasp.

Of course, Ledron hadn't found it feasible, either. Were the Blackfist here, he'd doubtless be railing openly against her folly. How could she possibly think she might succeed in this? Of all her mad, reckless choices, this had to be the most foolhardy yet.

Against that imagined voice, something in Kylac wasn't so certain. Not only because of her prior experience, but because of her exceptional perseverance. Bartered for the sake of her brother. A daring flight across strange seas, and the betrayal that had culminated in her retrieval. The return voyage, made under duress. Their trek through the Harrows. Her broken thumb. Her near marriage to the presumed leader of her hated enemy. Her stowaway effort to gain berth aboard the stolen *Vengeance* . . . Outrageous as it might seem, this rogue act of hers was just one more instance in which she'd chosen to demonstrate her headstrong independence. Acting as she believed she must, regardless of what anyone else might have to say on the matter. Never once doubting her own capabilities.

He'd witnessed in his life more than once the great lengths to which sheer determination could carry a person. And, truth unfettered, he had yet to meet anyone more determined than the Princess Denariel.

Or queen, if queen she might be. Try as he might, he found it difficult to imagine Bahsk, Fayne, and others like them bending knee. Notwithstanding the stirring pledges and declarations of a handful of dispossessed soldiers, would there ever be a true coronation?

Distant challenges, to be dealt with later. The slope along which he ran steepened as it curled westward, buckling at the same time. Clefts and fissures crossed his path, as did slab-shaped boulders of granite and limestone tumbled down from ancient heights. Ahead, a stone wall arose, climbing north along the rugged rise. Its crest was a plumage of iron spikes, curled outward like those along the fence above. A wall to mark the western border of the citadel grounds, separating it from the outer city.

Kylac hastened his pace.

Eighteen heads tall, he determined, when stood at the wall's base. Built with stones sanded for a smooth, snug fit amid hairline mortar seams. Denariel couldn't have climbed this, he decided, even with her thumb now fully mended. So he reconsidered her tracks, which had appeared to end at the wall, and found that she'd back-stepped over the same footprints into a weed-choked ravine running a jagged course farther down the hillside.

Following its splintered path brought him to a streambed used to collect and redirect runoff. Empty just now, it meandered westward again, some dozen paces up from the ledge of another bluff. Overturned stones betrayed Denariel's hasty passage, bringing him back toward the wall—

And a drainage culvert at its base. Barred, but with a hinged grate, latched from the inside to prevent intrusion.

But not escape.

Kylac shook his head as he inspected the bolt, hanging loose from its housing. Cursing his misfortune that she should have found this access point so quickly. Except *found* wasn't right. She'd known it was here. While Avenell may have been her primary home, as a member of the royal family, she'd have spent ample time in residence at Indranell, as well. And been shown bolt-holes from this city just as she had from the deepest reaches of the capital.

Not only did she have an hour or more on his position, she knew precisely where she was going.

With a pang of renewed urgency, Kylac pushed through the grate, not bothering to close it. He was beyond the citadel grounds now, which likely meant a greater string of wide-open routes for his quarry to choose from. If he was to find her before having to decide whether to honor his promise to Ledron, he had no time to waste.

The slope outside the wall looked much the same as it had within, ragged and fissured and peppered with rocks. A hundred paces farther on, however, the hillside flattened, giving way to orchards of nuts and fruits. These surrendered to fields of berries and vegetables, the plots quickly growing smaller as an array of manses and cottages sprouted up among them. Fine homes, depicting wealth and status, with manicured grounds and broad terraces granting panoramic views of the sound below. Steeped in shadow, save for the occasional cresset or lantern kept fueled through the night, illuminating key pathways or entrances gated and barred. Pools of flickering fire, set to ward off whatever the darkness might bring.

Denariel's trail wove along the borders of these grand properties, finding the seams between them. Following hedges and tree lines planted as demarcation barriers. Her overall course had begun to veer south, spilling finally onto a switchback trail snaking down toward a cove at the foot of the sound. A cove in which private boats and pleasure barges had been shoved aside, to make room for the enemy warships anchored now among them.

A fresh concern sprouted in Kylac's mind. Had the queen sought the Grenarr, instead? He couldn't envision what her purpose might be in doing so, but he'd already decided that, with her, it didn't have to make sense. Her motives and rationale were her own.

To his relief, her trail deviated from the waterside path about halfway down the bluff, still well above many of the fortifications and checkpoints dotting the cliffs. West, she'd turned again, rounding a crag by way of a narrow lip at its base. Far below, dark waves surged against a cluster of glistening rocks. Had she fallen . . .

But her trail resumed on the other side, slanting down along a rocky pathway into a pitted cave mouth. Nests of seabirds filled nooks and ledges overhead, many of the birds squawking in irritation. Kylac ignored them as he ventured into the cave, soon finding himself beset by blackness. His footing was rugged and slick and treacherous, and again he wondered how Denariel had managed. Determination was well and good, but a broken neck could steal one's fortitude right quick.

Concerned as he continued to be that he might stumble across her corpse, he felt his way along without incident until emerging from another cave mouth on the opposite side of the jutting, seaside bluff. A tunnel. Natural or manmade, she'd known where to find it, and how to use it.

He passed through other tunnels as he proceeded, though none as long as the first. Mostly just cracks and holes—slender breaches worn by wind and rain in the mountain's ageless skin. Pathways came and went. A descending array unnavigable in reverse. Clearly, the queen had intended hers to be a one-way trek.

For the better part of an hour, Kylac traced her path, undaunted, refusing to lose hope. In addition to the chiefly remote reaches, he navigated small stretches populated by citizens and townsfolk. Most were at slumber, and he left them undisturbed. Nor did he speak with those few, furtive souls who crossed his path, reluctant to spend time questioning them when he had her trail fresh before him. From the bluffs, she'd wound westward—and south, and west—curving around the sound and toward the open highlands north. She'd skirted or traversed parks and plazas, homes and workshops, farm and foundries—even ventured down an abandoned mineshaft, to tunnel out through a shuttered entrance several hundred heads below another towering bluff. She'd outfitted herself along the way, thieving salted meats and dried fruits, vegetables pickled and raw, a loaf of flatbread and a wedge of cheese. She'd acquired a brace of knives, along with skins of water and wine. Clearly embarking on a journey of some distance.

Her passage hadn't gone completely unnoticed. A troop of miners was astir over a missing packhorse. Farther on, following hooves now instead of feet, Kylac encountered a rancher who'd seen the animal at a pained gallop across his south ridge. At a lakeside fishery, a gray-haired woman, hunched and knotted, was berating a stout, bearded lad as he rowed up to the dock, towing an empty boat behind him.

" . . . near useless as your father!"

"Simmer, Mah. I got the boat back."

"And its thief drowned, I said. You ain't got the stones, you could've dragged him back here, so's I could show you how."

"How'm I dragging anyone back?" the son asked as he tethered his small craft and drew in the next. "I told you, they was already gone."

"Then it's just free passage we're giving out now. Mark me. Word among these vermin gets out, and its like flies to the carcass. You don't set example, and they . . ."

The old woman trailed off as Kylac made visible his approach. After a moment's gaping, she asked, "You lost, boy?"

"Matter o' truth, I am. Looking for someone stole through here 'bout an hour ago."

"Stole is right," the woman spat. "You ain't seen that chain you crossed over to get down to my dock?"

"Just looking for my friend," he repeated.

"Well your friend owes me an ivory finger." The woman gave her brutish son a meaningful look. "You here to settle his debt?"

"Wish I could. 'Fraid I lost my purse when fleeing Avenell."

"Damned refugee. You see?" she barked at her son. He'd finished mooring the boats, and approached now with a thick wooden handstave in his meaty grip. Both he and his weapon stank of old fish guts.

"Don't suppose ya might tell me where ya found that boat," Kylac tried.

The lad's slack jaw tightened. "'Cross the—"

"For a silver knuckle, he'll show you," the woman interrupted, glaring at her son. The hulking lad halted beside her, shoulders bunched, handstave slapping rhythmically against his free palm in open threat.

But his heart wasn't in it, his entire posture irritable for want of sleep. He'd as soon turn that stave against his mother, Kylac suspected, as some strange boy half his size and weight.

Kylac considered his options. He had nothing of value to barter with the fisherwoman. He could disable both her and her son, and borrow a boat himself, but how long might it take him to discern where Denariel had made her landing along the far shore? Disable just the mother, he might persuade the son to aid him, but at what cost to their already rancorous relationship?

"Lessin' you're wanting my boy here to shake you down for any gold in them pretty young teeth, I suggest you turn about the way you come. Tellin' all you other war urchins to aim wide of old Urseth's marina on out. Hear me?"

His only other option would seem to be to reveal the identity of his "friend." Peering into the woman's eyes, he somehow doubted she'd believe him—or care.

"Urseth's marina," Kylac echoed, eyeing her small fleet of boats and barges before looking upshore to the next such collection of vessels, more than a mile distant.

"Scurry back to your walls, city rat. 'Fore I change my mind."

Kylac perked. "Back?" Across the lake's league-wide expanse, he saw clearly enough the squat, merlon-crowned profile of a stone wall, which he'd presumed to mark the city's border.

"Don't even know where he is," the woman scoffed. "City line is that bluff behind you, fool. Perridon's Crest."

Kylac looked. Tracing the ridgeline to the north, he could just make out where the corner of a battlement abutted its heights. A battlement that wasn't needed atop the bluff, which served naturally as an impregnable barrier.

The mine, Kylac realized. He'd descended and departed Indranell without even realizing it.

"This here's the foothill town of Severstone," the woman pressed. "And we ain't catering to homeless rabble."

"Ya do know the Grenarr muster for siege."

"Bah! Tar-skins ain't coming through this way lessin' they sack Indranell first. That happens, they'll have to strip me of my skin 'fore I leave the banks my great-grandsire settled."

Kylac accepted the claim as truth, for all the impact her choice might have on his own plans. The temptation resurfaced to enforce his will in this matter. Having already violated his promise to Ledron, what harm in pressing further? Especially when compared to the harm Denariel might do herself, given to range unchecked.

But she still had her hour's lead or more. Unless she'd stopped somewhere ahead, he gave himself no chance of catching her before dawn. Ledron would be livid at that point, and probably embarked on his own search. What slender thread of trust Kylac had worked so hard to weave between them would be severed for good and all. And, as matters stood, he suspected he might need that trust before these trials were ended.

All else aside, there was a significant difference between disregarding one's oath by accident, and then again willfully. Without the integrity of his word to define him, what was he?

"Begging pardon for disturbing ya, madam," he said, pulling his gaze from the distant lakeshore. A yoke of frustration settled over him, which he fended off with the knowledge that he'd likely be back here before the sunrise, this time with Ledron's search party in tow. Let her try to dismiss the disgruntled captain as she had him.

Under a cloud-filtered gleam of starlight, and with the fisherwoman and her son glaring after him, Kylac dashed toward the nearest road, his eye on the city heights.

18

"She eluded you, then?"

Kylac saw the desperation in Ledron's eyes. Beneath a blunt countenance, the captain's disposition was a brew of fear and fury.

"Crossed a sprawl of a lake at Severstone," Kylac admitted.

The Blackfist's gaze narrowed. A rebuke formed on his lips, but failed to escape his clenched teeth. "Right, then," he growled with evident restraint. He shouldered a leather satchel lying limp on the trestle table before him. With a sweeping glance at his assembled companions, he added, "On my heels."

The others gathered up their weapons and pouches and satchels, as well, the stiffness of their movements betraying their aches and exhaustion as they rose from their bench seats. Six there were, at the captain's behest. Penryn, Trathem, Havrig, Talon, Laritanis, and Warmund. All who'd traveled with him from Tetherend save for Sethric and the stewards Hahneth, Egrund, and Aythef. Summoned to a secluded, candlelit corner of a garrison mess hall. Fed a brief meal of porridge, given the scraped pot and bowls before them, but clearly unrested. Haggard from their recent journey. In no rush to begin the next.

But the Blackfist captain had given them no choice. Or so Aythef had told it. Upon reentering the citadel, Kylac had found the queen's sitting room empty, and so had ventured down to the chambers given over to Denariel's makeshift retinue. Therein, he'd found the trio of stewards alone, sitting up and worrying together over what they might do to help. From them, Kylac had learned that Ledron had come calling a couple hours earlier, to inform them of Her Majesty's disappearance. After demanding all swords accompany him to the mess hall to prepare for pursuit—and flatly refusing that any of the slow-footed stewards should do so—he'd ordered the three of them back to their beds, to inform Bahsk of events only if the general should make inquiry come dawn, *after* their anticipated departure.

The stewards had confessed their hope that Kylac would have returned with Her Majesty alongside. Having learned elsewise, the rising soldiers shared now a similar dismay. Kylac knew not which details Ledron may have shared with or kept from them. But he felt the weight of their resentment, in varying degrees, as they squared their shoulders for the task at hand, and fell into step behind their captain.

"I still feel it wiser that we inform the general now," Penryn admitted, clinging to Ledron's ear. "We don't know that—"

"I'll not take the risk," the Head snapped irritably. "Must I echo my reasons as to why, Sergeant?"

"No, sir," Penryn replied, and fell back, glancing warily at Kylac.

Kylac caught and considered the conflicted expression. He hadn't been there for whatever reception the sergeant may have received from his former commander, Colonel Fayne. He couldn't say whether they'd met yet at all, following the soldier's decision to align with his dying king rather than his superior officer. But it wasn't difficult to imagine the potentially awkward position in which Penryn now found himself. Having cast his lot, was he committed henceforth to captain and queen? Or might he have sensed already the untenable nature of Denariel's influence, and be seeking a way to return to his prior commander's good graces?

As they moved from the empty mess hall to a thickly shadowed corridor beyond, Kylac sidled near to Ledron. "What excuse did ya give Her Majesty's sentries?"

Jailors, more likely. Despite their claim to have been posted outside Denariel's quarters for her protection.

"That Her Majesty couldn't abide my snoring," the Head answered gruffly. "I left warning that you were with her, and commanded that she not be disturbed."

"Sethric?" Kylac asked, noting the Redfist's absence.

"I sent him to secure mounts. Knowing that if you returned empty-handed, we'd have ground to make up."

A sensible notion, though the plan would seem to present other difficulties. "Her Majesty's path from the citadel isn't one a steed could follow. How do ya mean that we ride out o' here without notice?"

Drawing their small troop into a soldiers' mess hall for an early breakfast might have been simple enough. Even mustering a few provisions, as they clearly had, needn't have proven terribly daunting for a captain of the Shadowguard. But departing a barricaded city without authorization promised to pose an altogether different challenge, if the Head hoped to do so in secret.

"The mounts I mean to secure lie beyond the citadel," Ledron replied. "And their proprietor has means of getting us outside the city walls."

A tinge of disdain in the captain's voice triggered suspicion. "Smuggler?"

"He's been called worse."

"Yet a Blackfist worth his gloves must stockpile all manner o' contingencies," Kylac guessed, "to ward against calamity." As the revolt against Kendarrion had demonstrated, a royal guardian would be ill-advised to rely solely on crown-sanctioned resources. "Though it must pain the noble captain to consort with such."

Ledron gave him a sour look. "More so, knowing the fiend is my cousin."

Kylac suppressed a smirk, expecting the Head was all too serious. He opted to shift topic. "Name o' Urseth familiar to ya?"

"Should it be?"

"Charming woman. Runs the marina Her Majesty used to cross the lake."

"Has she a barge that'll convey our horses?"

"I spied one or more should manage the task," Kylac replied. Already he was feeling better about this venture. Ledron would have his own bolt-hole or two by which to escape the citadel. From there, assuming they did manage to secure mounts and steal outside the city, they ought to be able to run Denariel down in relatively short order. "We'll have Her Majesty in hand before noon."

The captain grunted. Less certain, mayhap. Certainly less enthused. A needless diversion, whatever the outcome. But Kylac wasn't exactly keen to begin sitting around the keep, an unwelcome visitor, while the eventual siege unfolded. Or in suffering through whatever series of council meetings might be required for Denariel to plead an alternate course of action. Whatever else this day's effort entailed, it promised to be more interesting than initially expected.

Deferring to Ledron's lead, he fell back among the loose clutch formed by the others, quietly taking their measure. Havrig and Talon struck him as being among the more willing and able on this particular excursion, though Havrig's shoulders had taken on a weary slump, and Talon limped slightly upon an ankle injured weeks earlier, during a race from the Grenarr across Grenathrok. Laritanis's odor had gone from sour to rancid, but the man dubbed Crawfoot by his closer companions was beholden to a fierce pride, and not likely to be among the first to falter.

Penryn, Trathem, and Warmund seemed the more nervous among them. To be expected of the latter, who'd displayed an uneasy temperament for as long as Kylac had known him, but had yet to prove unreliable. The source of Penryn's anxiety seemed clear and reasonable enough, and bore the potential for concern. Yet the man had stood with them when he'd had every reason not to, and done nothing since to warrant significant doubt.

And Trathem . . . Admittedly, the sergeant from Avenell's dungeons remained a bit of a mystery. Dutiful and determined, yes. But guarded, secretive. Bent by some private burden of the heart. Mistrusting, to a great degree, of those around him, while simultaneously striving to win theirs. Given the tumultuous nature of everything he'd endured, however, with everything and everyone he'd likely lost along the way, was it not to be expected that he should display signs of cynicism?

Were he placing his life into these men's hands, Kylac might have explored more fully their condition and motives. But for all that their dependability truly mattered to his own fate—or to Denariel's, once they found her—he could muster only so much interest. Whatever their individual strengths and weaknesses, he would deal with their impact as the need arose.

He wondered briefly if Ledron meant to send word back to the stewards confirming their departure, but realized it unlikely. A mere courtesy it would be, for their peace of mind. Far from the forefront of the captain's concerns.

They encountered a mere handful of souls as they made their way. Sunrise remained more than an hour distant, putting most of the keep's occupants still deep within their dreams. Among the others, Ledron moved with purpose and authority, frowning sternly and giving none the chance to question him. He seemed also to know what halls and entrances to avoid, where sentries might feel duty-bound to stall him. Instead, he snaked along a string of descending passageways, past old armories and neglected storage vaults, forsaken libraries and abandoned interrogation chambers, each stretch more empty and isolated than the last.

Before long, they were pressing by handheld torchlight through gloom and shadow, brushing aside cobwebs and stirring carpets of dust gathered at their feet. Stone gave way to hard-packed dirt, and hard-packed dirt to mountain bedrock. Corridors thinned, the air becoming stale and oppressive. *More tunnels,* Kylac lamented privately. The only means by which it seemed most men could manage to travel in secret.

They came at last to an iron door that appeared rusted in place. Except that it stood slightly ajar, as if grown too large for its frame. Kylac recognized the fresh footsteps before it—a trail they'd been following for some time—and presumed them to be Sethric's. The heavy portal gave a shrill squeak of protest as Ledron hauled it open, and a more satisfied groan as it closed behind them.

Beyond lay a cavern filled with forges long since gone cold. Feeding the cavern was a wide, squat tunnel vanishing into deeper darkness. An underground vein for delivering wood and ore and other materials to the citadel depths, Kylac guessed, for whatever purposes they were once used.

Into the tunnel he and his companions delved, trotting now to match Ledron's pace, still following the trail of retreating footprints set down in a thin layer of rocky soil. Rutted lines scarred that same ground, furrows that betrayed the ceaseless passage of heavy-laden carts and barrows over the course of years some decades past. Some of these carriages still sat parked to either side, collapsed beneath their own weight, rotting wood and rusting iron laid to rest beneath shrouds of dust.

For a little more than a mile their company ran, ignoring several smaller branches in the coring earth, before coming finally to a rusted iron mesh that would seem to wall off their exit. A closer inspection revealed a shallow trough hewn in the earth at the base of the bars to one side, which enabled them to slide upon their backs or bellies, one by one, to pass underneath.

Beyond the gated opening, they found themselves in a bowl-shaped gully overgrown with knee-deep scrub and waist-high grasses. Steep walls arose to either side, shepherding any further progress directly ahead along a somewhat gentler incline.

Kylac misliked the setting at once.

"Keep close now," Ledron cautioned. "Low and fast and silent. We follow the ravine, skirting Hendrian's Tower and the northwest rampart. Unseen, we'll reach the banks of the Gallowyn, which we'll follow down to the Daybreak Quarter."

A breeze had gathered as the Head spoke, swirling down from the gully's rim. Bearing scents that raised the hairs on the back of Kylac's neck, and set his fighter's nerves to tingling.

"Might be too late for that, Captain."

Even as the Head looked to him for clarification, the slow tamp of hooves, accompanied by the creak and jangle of saddle and traces, announced the arrival of a ring of mounted soldiers. They closed round from above, atop gully walls north and south, with loaded crossbows at the ready. A score to either side, aligned tightly in their formation, with no more than an arm's length between riders.

Bahsk himself rode among them, at the far end of the north troop. Armored in light mail and partial plate, head covered by a chain hauberk so that his face appeared to be all beard. Across from him, at the far end of the south troop, rode Colonel Fayne, whose eyes shone as bold and bright as his mocking smile.

"Captain Ledron," the colonel greeted, loosely gripping his reins. Across from him, Bahsk surveyed the party below with an intense, calculating eye. "Pray tell, what draws you out here at this unsavory hour?"

"The want of fresh air," the Head growled. "And you?"

Scenarios flashed through Kylac's mind, as he was certain they did through the minds of his companions. Hemmed in by the gully walls, it would seem their only choices were retreat—squirming prone beneath the gate at their backs—or plunging ahead down the gully's throat. Neither seemed tenable, given their adversary's numbers and position. Even if they were to break free in a mad dash, they'd not outrun the steeds of Bahsk's company, or the riders' quarrels.

"We received word of an infestation," the colonel teased. "Rats in our sewers." He peered at his general across the ravine, and to the rider on Bahsk's left flank. Where a nasal helmet did little to mask the soldier's lean jaw and copper-green eyes.

Sethric.

"Our sewers empty to the southeast," Ledron replied, carrying on the game. The grating fury in his voice told Kylac that he'd recognized the traitor, too. "Though I see some filth has indeed found its way here."

"Startled I'd be to learn you've deprived Her Highness of your protection. Save, I hear she has relieved you of that particular duty."

"Her *Majesty* has a way of indulging her whims. It affects not my duty, except to hone my patience."

Kylac sensed the heightened anxiety of his more nervous comrades. Penryn, who should have acted sooner to realign himself as Sethric evidently had. Trathem, who seethed as if regarding this delay as a needless and small-minded obstacle to more meaningful endeavors. Warmund, who hunched in upon himself, sensing his death and happier to meet it with eyes closed. The more stalwart trio—Havrig, Talon, and Laritanis—glared balefully, eyeing the flock of soldiers as if selecting which man they would try to fell before meeting their own end.

"Only, it would seem the princess has abandoned us," Bahsk interjected finally, his beard thrusting as he spoke. "Aligning instead with her darker ilk."

"Preposterous," Ledron snapped, though his tongue-tied reaction allowed that mayhap he hadn't yet considered the possibility. Kylac recalled having faced the notion earlier, and been unable to immediately dismiss it. He wondered if the Head was having the same trouble. "She seeks the aid for our people that you refused her."

"The Kuurians? A misguided fancy, as you yourself attested."

"Nonetheless, I'm sworn to her defense. And our banter now delays me in that course."

"And *I'm* sworn to the defense of an entire nation," Bahsk reminded him, leaning upon his saddlehorn as his powerful courser fidgeted beneath him. "One that can no longer succor the impulses of a lone citizen—whatever the measure of her worthy blood—at the cost of swords as skilled as yours."

There it was, uttered in words clear and bold. The assessment they'd feared and thus sought to circumvent. That Bahsk would never sanction their effort to retrieve Denariel, made once more a renegade of her own volition. An appraisal become an open threat, given the general's plainly hostile response.

"Our swords are not yours to command," Ledron countered darkly.

"I count three, four, five Stonewatch among you," Fayne replied at once, making an exaggerated show of tallying heads. "Forsworn, should they renounce their general's command."

Ledron smoldered. "So be it. But the three of us have other allegiances."

"Admiral Vohrst defers to me, and the Seawatch with him," Bahsk corrected. "As for yourself, Captain, in the absence of a royal charge, yours is to report to the nearest provincial authority—Governor Merrinem, in this instance. Who, as we've discussed, has also named me commander in his stead."

Kylac felt the explosive rage building in the Blackfist beside him, as surely as if stood before an active forge. "I'll sees to Her Majesty," he proposed, frustrated now that he'd set himself back another couple hours in that very pursuit.

"It is *my* duty," the Head insisted, hissing through gritted teeth.

"Her Highness's swords belong to the crown," Bahsk declared flatly. "Loathsome and inadequate as you may find me, I stand now as its steward. Until that should change, you will serve as *I* deem, else stand accused of treason."

"I'm subject to no crown," Kylac asserted, "no steward."

"You'll fight for us nonetheless, or I'll have you feathered where you now root."

Some twoscore crossbows shifted slightly, their wielders adjusting aim to center him as their target.

"More easily imagined than carried out," Kylac advised.

"You suppose I jest? Given your position, no man could evade them all."

Kylac had half a mind to accept the challenge, but feared for what might happen to Ledron and his other companions should the missiles start flying. And he believed they would. For all the general's reasoning that their swords were too critical to the war effort to be permitted free range, the soldier was clearly more concerned with establishing his own unassailable dominance, for good and all.

"A man cannot be forced to fight," Kylac observed instead.

"No," Bahsk agreed. "But placed in a situation dire enough, he will *choose* to do so, as a matter of preservation."

"And if such situation fails to present itself?" Ledron demanded, wedging his voice back into the confrontation.

"So much the better, as it means your services were not vital after all. But this I promise," the general added, his volume rising to address all present. "When this war is over, loyalty, disloyalty, will each be paid in kind."

He half turned toward Sethric, as if to present the Redfist as a standard for the ideal.

Beside Kylac, Ledron scoffed. "Loyalty? A strange notion, presented by you."

A man who would plot against his liege, forsake his queen, and silence or shackle his perceived rivals. It went unsaid, but Kylac knew Ledron well enough in this matter to finish for himself the Head's thought.

Beyond those tacit accusations, however, the Blackfist could offer scant resistance. Refusal meant death, for him and his men. Clearly, he believed as Kylac did that the general's advantage wouldn't be permanent. That there would come a time, be it late or soon, when they would exert their own will, make their own way, exact their own justice.

Provided they survived long enough to see it.

At a nod from Bahsk, Fayne gave a signal. A near rider from either side of the gully lowered his crossbow and descended the slopes, each digging warily into a saddlebag full of manacles. Understanding what was intended, Kylac gave another moment's consideration to testing the general's resolve.

Thinking better of it, he decided to grant warning instead. "With respect, General, ya'd best be certain." When convinced he had the other's full attention, he added, "Do this, and I'll be taking your life when I takes my leave."

Amid his bristle of a beard, Bahsk gave a mirthless, tight-lipped smile. "You'll do as you must. As I have done here."

19

The creak and clatter of his prison wagon over rocky terrain filled Kylac's head like a helmet full of gravel. A dull roar of hooves and boots, of tramping and snorting and shuffling, echoed in backdrop like the stir of a restless ocean. But it was the cacophonous song of his own, grinding advance that most assailed him. The rasp and scrape of iron-rimmed wheels against earth and stone. The squeak of iron bars and groan of wooden boards, bending and flexing. The scratch of thorns, the rustle of dead grasses, the pop of pebbles sent flying.

A lament to mark his captivity.

But Kylac had made his choice, and resolved not to regret it. Even as he endured the clink and rattle of the chains by which he was bound. Or suffered the sharp screech of the left rear hub, in need of grease, that cried out with every rotation, resonating like a knife along his spine. The planks beneath him were hard and coarse and full of splinters, providing no comfort as he jolted and jounced along. His throat was raw with thirst, and a choking dust filled the air.

Suffer the weak, and you will suffer their weakness . . .

He opened his eyes to help chase away his father's ghostly admonition. Ledron sat across from him, shackled like himself, features locked in a sullen grimace. They'd shared no words on this, their third day out, for there was nothing more that needed to be said. Nothing that would serve to alter the course they'd agreed to upon their capture.

"Do it, then," Ledron had muttered, while they were being led in shackles from the gully, back toward the citadel. "If you can, see to Her Majesty."

Kylac had considered the armed soldiers serving escort to their return. "And leave the rest o' ya to die?"

"As is my oath."

"But not theirs," Kylac had observed, indicating their companions.

"Betrayers all," the Head had fumed. "If not now, then when it better serves them."

Vilifying Sethric, given the direction of the captain's glare. But Kylac hadn't believed that to be entirely fair. "Murky waters for the judging of oaths." Off Ledron's scowl, he'd added, "He misled us, yes. But for himself? Or in honor o' his soldier's vow?"

Ledron had shrugged the question aside. "Her Majesty is not safe alone."

"Yet that was clearly her wish. What o' *your* oath, should ya defy her?"

"We agreed—"

"You're the one set leash upon me. Regret as we might, the queen is on her own for now. I'll not draw her back here to a pile o' your corpses."

By then, Colonel Fayne had ridden near, drawn by their argument. Incensed by the colonel's amiable grin, Ledron had frowned fiercely and distanced himself from Kylac, jaw clenched in tooth-grinding frustration.

They'd completed their predawn march in silence—a trek that had ended with Ledron and Kylac locked in stocks at the edge of a garrison training yard. With an additional audience of soldiers arriving for the day's sunrise muster, General Bahsk had invited the rest of their companions to join them in the stocks, or to take their place among the army's ranks. Most had looked to either Ledron or Kylac as if seeking permission. While the Head had met their gazes with only stony silence, Kylac had offered encouraging nods and suggested that they were all fighting toward the same end. Better with blades in hand than heads ensnared.

In the end, all six had succumbed. Penryn, Talon, and Warmund had been sullen, Trathem and Havrig angry, Laritanis indignant. But none had resisted as they were dispersed and led away, still in their chains, each man with his own trio of Bahsk's soldiers in escort. Assigned to separate companies, that any further defiance they might foolishly consider would be isolated, scattered about the army's ranks.

Kylac had caught only stray glimpses of any of them since.

He and Ledron, of course, had been given no such option. Because of his unremitting allegiance to Denariel, the captain could offer no capitulation that would be trusted—even had he deigned to do so. And Kylac . . . Simply too dangerous.

So there they'd festered throughout the day, while a steady rotation of crossbowmen stood watch, with orders to kill both men should either attempt to liberate so much as a finger. Around them, the army had made preparations to depart, with officers streaming in and out of a nearby barracks command structure, armorers and quartermasters and wranglers barking various needs, and runners dispatched in every direction on all manner of assignment. From their limited vantage, he and Ledron had witnessed but a fraction of the undertaking. But they saw enough to grasp its scope and magnitude.

An offensive to ensure reclamation of the Addaran capital.

Else the annihilation of its people.

With Ledron brooding silently beside him, Kylac had retreated inward, bearing his public imprisonment with mute dignity. If the treatment had been meant in any way to shame him, the general had miscalculated. Most passersby were too busy to consider him at all. Those who did were burdened too heavily with uncertainty and curiosity to mete out ridicule or scorn. Opinions to which Kylac was immune, regardless. Had they been friends and kin, rather than strangers, he'd have felt no different. He knew well his own triumphs, his own failings. The judgments of others had and would forever be wasted on him.

They'd been watered and fed at midday, again in the afternoon, and once more as the sun had descended. A warning they'd served, to any soldier or servant contemplating insubordination. But it had seemed Bahsk wished that they remain hale enough. Intending, mayhap, to test his conviction that they might yet serve in battle, should circumstances demand it.

An hour after nightfall, they'd been pulled from the stocks and transported to a holding cell, where they were instructed to lie down and sleep. Fayne oversaw the transfer, informing them that the army would depart at daybreak, and they with it.

"Unless, of course, Captain Jyserra finds cause to have you put down during the night," the colonel had added, smiling broadly at the threat.

"Does the general have a strategy in mind?" Ledron had demanded in turn. "Or does his pride dictate we simply ram heads with our enemy and hope ours proves the harder?"

"He means to navigate the Strebolen. Entering at Praxu, emerging south of Dormund."

As Kylac had shared with the captain earlier that day, when their time in the stocks had finally offered suitable occasion—following Denariel's unexpected departure and their subsequent pursuit—in which to relay what he'd overheard in Bahsk's clandestine strategy session the night before. Seeming to confirm that plans hadn't been altered in the interim. Unless, of course, Fayne had seen cause to lie to them.

"While you hold Indranell with a skeletal garrison," Ledron had mused. "A dire risk, on multiple fronts."

Fayne had shrugged. "No more than any other course of action. Or inaction, for that matter. Regardless, it is the general's decision to make, no?"

The Head had only scowled deeper and clenched his teeth. Lacking disagreement or the desire to voice it. Kylac had wondered briefly at Fayne's motives. Clearly, the colonel was being placed in a position to assume command should Bahsk fail or be killed. Might that justify his apparent lack of concern? Shortsighted he'd have to be to desire such an outcome, as it would merely put him next in line to fall under Sabrynne's bootheels. But then, it had obviously become harder and harder to know where any man's loyalties lay, to say nothing as to why.

Fighting to clear his thoughts of the weblike strands of deceit and intrigue woven by those around him, Kylac had clung to the shelter of silence before and after he'd been deposited in his night's cell. Under the vigilant eye of Jyserra's crossbowmen, he'd stretched and rested his body from the awkward position it had been forced to tolerate throughout the day.

But sleep itself had eluded him. Captivity made him restless—particularly in confined spaces. Between those irritations, his hours-long immobilization, and his concern for Denariel and those others he'd taken under wing, he'd found himself lying in place, edgy and agitated, unable to let the night simply pass him by.

"Tell me about Her Majesty," he'd whispered to Ledron, upon deciding that the Head's restive tossing and squirming revealed a similar suffering.

"What?"

"Seems the time has long since passed that I learned more about her. To better fathom her thinking."

"A road to madness," the Blackfist had snorted.

"O' potential aid, nonetheless, should I find occasion to seek her trail."

Ledron had glanced warily at their alert guard contingent. A second shift of four crossbowmen, arrived an hour earlier in relief of the first. Positioned just beyond the cell's bars, they'd seen that the prisoners were conversing, even if they couldn't quite make out the hushed exchanges. To that moment, however, they'd done nothing to express concern. Reluctant to intercede, mayhap, given their instructions not to engage the prisoners unless lethal force should be required.

"What would you know?" the captain had whispered finally.

Who could say? Formative moments. Life-altering events and decisions. Anything that might have had hand in shaping her attitudes and beliefs—particularly toward those involved in the present crisis.

"Her conception," Kylac had decided. "I's gathered it wasn't entirely agreeable."

Ledron's expression had soured—to the point in which he'd seemed to reconsider granting Kylac's request. "Her royal mother, Queen Lytherial, was ravished by a Grenarr slave," he answered at last. "Beast served the royal household faithfully for many years, and was well treated in turn. Then, one day, for no discernible cause beyond sheer animal lust . . ."

No cause the captain was aware of, Kylac had quickly determined. But the question of motive could have easily sparked a debate to jeopardize the entire conversation, so he'd kept it to himself.

"While the queen lay for weeks unconscious, adrift between life and death, His Majesty had the brute gelded and killed. Then he set about purchasing and executing all other tar-skins kept throughout the city. No longer would they live among us, even as slaves. Rabid dogs, he decreed them. And he refused that another should be permitted opportunity to bite."

A barbaric response, however impassioned. "Doing nothing to soothe the enmity between your people and theirs, I'll wager."

"No. The Grenarr raids were fierce that season, and for the pair to follow, exacting a heavy toll on our shoreline borders. But their true revenge manifested when Lytherial gave birth to a seed not of His Majesty's loins, but of theirs."

The guards beyond their cell had straightened attentively, scowling at their inability to discern what the prisoners were plotting. But they'd remained silent, suspecting some manner of ruse and refusing to be cozened by it.

"The king must have been devastated," Kylac had prompted.

"But the Queen Lytherial—Mother soothe her gracious heart—made plea for her newborn daughter's life. The child being innocent, she would brook no harm to it. Else her own life would be forsaken, and the king left to seek another to bear him any true-blooded male heirs."

Casting Denariel as the elder of the royal siblings. Only in that moment had Kylac realized that he couldn't have said as much prior to the revelation. Prince Dethaniel hadn't been in the fittest of conditions when Kylac had met him, and was near enough his sister's age as to make the order of their births uncertain. Crown prince he'd been, but only by gender and blood.

"For all his pain and rage," Ledron had continued, "His Majesty's love for his wife was stronger. He could deny her nothing, and so granted Denariel his mercy. The queen in turn forgave him his murderous response against the Grenarr, which her tender heart could never condone, and for which His Majesty himself had expressed a measure of remorse. Together, they came to nurse each other's broken hearts. Nineteen months later, His Highness Prince Dethaniel was born."

"To the king's pride. And Denariel's neglect."

"His Highness was *everyone's* pride. The king, the queen—all of Addaranth—rejoiced at his birth. None benefitted from this more than the infant Denariel. Heir to our throne no longer, she was relieved, to great extent, of the loathing and outrage that had attended her like a storm cloud. Now, she was but a beacon for vigilance. A reminder of the horrid and enduring nature of our enemies. A bedtime caution, and better tolerated as such."

"Then she wasn't mistreated in her upbringing?"

"Not in any overt fashion. For to raise even whisper against her was to summon the king's ire. Her childhood was suitably sheltered."

"She and Dethaniel . . . were close?"

"Inseparable. A natural protector, she cherished and defended her royal brother, and he her. As their parents encouraged. A more tightly woven family, you cannot have met." A sudden pall had eclipsed the pleasant memory. "It was not until Her Majesty Lytherial succumbed to illness that the bonds began to fray."

"About ten years ago." Or so he'd learned from the Blackfist Trajan, back at the onset of this adventure.

The Head had nodded. "A blow to them all, from which none fully recovered. As if she'd been the mortar, all along, that held them together. Fifteen, Her Highness was."

Two years younger than Kylac now. His own mother had been lost much, much earlier. But then, he'd never known the woman at all, and thus never come to rely on her.

Sifting through the details of the account, he'd found plenty to support what he'd already gathered or presumed about Denariel's nature, and nothing to refute it. A strained relationship with father and brother, following the premature loss of a devoted mother. An outcast, in many ways, among her own kind. Fires to forge the strict, hardheaded mannerisms and principles by which she'd learned to carry herself. Yet nothing that would seem to indicate hidden aims against family or people—to undermine or elsewise cast doubt on objectives plainly stated and thus far supported by consistent action since the time he'd known her.

"What about the Ukinha?"

The captain's sour expression had turned rancid. "There was a known encounter, years ago. Shortly before I'd earned my gloves. A retreat by the royal family on the shores of the sound. Her Highness Denariel was eight at the time, His Highness Dethaniel six. Caught unawares by a Grenarr Prowler. Their defenders were overrun. The entire family would have been butchered, save for the timely intervention of a groll. The mutant slaughtered more than half the Prowler's crew, driving off the rest, before taking its leave."

Kylac had found his interest piqued. Reluctant to interrupt, he'd silently willed the captain to proceed.

"Survivor accounts had it that the prince was terrified, plagued by recurring nightmares long thereafter. But Denariel . . . young Denariel was said to be fascinated. Whispers among the Shadowguard abounded, years later, that she'd had further contact with the creatures. During frontier excursions. Visitations within the palace, even. Or so it was feared, though never to my knowledge proven. That she was attended by one in her voyage to Kuuria would seem to support the possibility. I'd assumed it was Ulflund who recruited the beast, yet . . ."

Yet Denariel herself had suggested elsewise, hadn't she?

Whether a stubborn denial or genuine uncertainty, Ledron's words had been left to twist in the stale, chill air between them. Given to wager, Kylac would have sided with those suspecting Denariel of further engagements. Her brother had claimed as much, back on Grenathrok, when attempting to justify the scheme he'd hatched against his own people, his own family. Beyond that, Kylac could point to the tenacity of the Ukinh that had hunted them . . . the intensity of her feelings toward it . . .

Ulflund's pet or hers, the tale had again reinforced a number of understandings, without violating anything Kylac had yet heard from other sources. A seamless twining of threads that lent credence to the resulting tapestry. That Kendarrion had cause to tolerate the mutants better than he had the Grenarr. That his son, Dethaniel, should demonstrate the opposite aversion, holding the Ukinha as monsters. That Denariel may have gone so far as to have romantic interaction with at least one mutant, and so might believe—rightfully or elsewise—that they could be reasoned with, enlisted to a particular cause.

It all seemed to resonate truth, or some tone near enough to it.

"I doubt not that she believes the Ukinha might aid her," Ledron had allowed after a reflective moment. "But she's foolish to do so. If she's not dead already."

They'd let the silence rule after that, each man giving over to his own considerations. Eventually, the night had passed, hours grinding by in slow progression. An hour before dawn, Fayne had returned, to oversee their transfer into the wheeled cage in which they rode now. To take their unceremonious place among the departing ranks of Bahsk's army. Once again, Kylac had been tempted with escape. But his reasons for allowing himself to be captured to begin with hadn't changed. As such, he'd continued to honor them.

As he did now. Despite the tedium. Despite the skull-splitting noises. Despite the chafing, scraping, jarring discomfort. Conceding that his jailors had taken every conceivable precaution. Even shackled and caged, he and Ledron were escorted at all times by a ring of armed riders. Soldiers charged with marking the prisoners' every shift or twitch. Additional lookouts were positioned farther out, to relay word of any struggle. This amid the center of the armored host, requiring them to burrow from its very heart, should they dare, through wave after wave of angry Addaran ranks.

Alone, he might have chanced it. But he gauged it unlikely that he'd be able to slip free without harm to Ledron or those other companions left behind.

Moreover, it might have been that Bahsk was right, that this was where he and Ledron could be of greater service to Denariel's cause. From all he'd been able to discern, the army was marching according to plan. After striking southward on day one, they'd abandoned the Karamoor at midday and traveled eastward along the winding path forged by a river. Presumptuous of their commander, Kylac had thought, to believe they could do so without drawing enemy notice. But he supposed an advance sweep might have been used to brush back or elsewise distract any Grenarr still lingering to the north. And the general's strategy, as he recalled, had put greater faith in the terrain itself to mask their eventual progress.

With ample cause. Before dusk of that first day, the canyon walls he'd seen mapped out at Indranell had sprouted up around them in stark reality. Great, multilayered beds of ancient sediment and long-forgotten history. Soon thereafter, those walls had revealed fissures and crevasses along splintering streambeds and fracturing defiles. Forming a labyrinth of natural passages in which to hide their movements. Easy to pursue, given their obvious tracks. But difficult to anticipate, for anyone seeking to head off their advance.

By sunset, they'd found themselves encamped at the mouth of a pass. Well concealed by jagged, towering bluffs to either side. The desolate landscape was home to only insects, snakes and rodents, and scattered flocks of birds. The second day, they'd veered sharply south again, to find only more of the same. Thus far, the third day had been a repeat of the last. Travel had proven arduous, yet steady. The army's spirits remained remarkably high. For all their present struggle and the dire losses that had led to it, there was a decided sense among them that retribution wasn't far removed.

So Kylac weathered his travails as the Addarans did theirs. In all, his circumstances felt like a sorry echo of his return from Grenathrok, in which he'd been a captive on the high seas, unable to extricate himself until he saw what his destination might bring. Though every moment, every turn of his prison's wheels, carried him farther from Denariel, he reminded himself that she was better equipped for survival than he or Ledron cared to admit.

Should he come to learn elsewise . . .

But any railing along that course would constitute little more than bluster. As of now, he was Bahsk's plaything. What reckonings lay beyond would need follow that one.

Leaving him to watch. And to wait. And to imagine the form his own retribution might take.

20

The blackness churned, gripped with featureless violence. Swirling, clashing, rending, like the waves of a storm-tossed sea. Writhing pain. Twisting hate. A crescendo of screams—

Kylac awoke, jerking upright. Chains clanked, iron cuffs biting at raw, reddened skin. His head spun, reeling with confusion. But a familiar tingling flushed through his veins, setting fire to bewilderment, leaving stark awareness in its wake.

Fueled by warning.

Beyond the bars of his prison wagon, the night lay quiet. Disturbed by the snores of slumbering soldiers, the whicker of restless horses, the windblown flutter of leather and canvas, the crackle of watchfires set to burn amid the encampment. But nothing he heard would seem to warrant alarm. The bulk of the army slept, the dreams of its men warded by sentries stationed along its perimeters. For all the gear and trappings of this assemblage of war, the world seemed at peace.

Trusting to his instincts, Kylac believed elsewise.

He kicked at Ledron, twitching restively across from him. A nudge brought the Shadowguard captain to his senses, to grope instinctively for a weapon that wasn't there.

"What?" the Head managed, amid a grunting disorientation. "What have we?"

"A threat before us. To the south."

Ledron blinked furiously, picking at the dirty crust gathered in the corners of his eyes. "I hear nothing. You're certain?"

Their words drew a stern look from one of their jailors, positioned just outside their cage. "Ay. Dim that ruckus."

But the telltale itch refused to subside. "Mobilize our vanguard," Kylac proposed.

"Did you not—"

"Do it," Kylac insisted. "Send word now."

The jailor was still scowling, fidgeting with his spear and his indecision, when a bouquet of lights blossomed amid the black skies to the southwest.

"Hear this, wretch," another jailor interjected. The bowlegged one. Jerumin. "We're not here to relay orders. Least of all from you."

The lights arced, drawing thin streamers of fire across the felt of night.

And the screaming began.

The jailors turned toward the commotion. Within a span of heartbeats, the whole of the army was astir, cries from the south sweeping over them like an incoming wave. The night was alight again with fresh blossoms, while a flaming haze took bloom below, at the mouth of a draw some half mile away. Fires. Dozens, if not scores. Atop the canyon walls to the west. To the east as well, mayhap, though Kylac's view in that direction was obstructed by the forward wall of his prison. A rain of fires, giving life to the one rising from the canyon floor.

Delivering death to those caught by its surge.

The screams were joined now by shouts of outrage, a baying of commands, and the calls of soldiers eager to unleash a battle-lust too long restrained. Chaos took hold, as soldiers were torn from their slumber and sent off to meet the unexpected threat, sleep still dragging at their heels. Kylac could feel the pounding of their hearts, and witnessed the wild-eyed expressions of those who streamed or staggered past. A roiling mix of fervor and fear, united in heedlessness.

His jailors watched alongside, some with relief to have been assigned a duty that kept them rooted, while others were clearly gnawing at the bit to join the response. He saw it in the restless language of their bodies, and in the resentful looks aimed at him and Ledron.

"Festering fiends," the Head muttered, transfixed by the play of flickering lights. "Is it them? Grenarr?"

"Has we some other enemy ya hasn't confessed to me yet?"

Ledron gripped the bars of their cage, betraying his urgent desire for freedom as the southward rush of Addaran soldiers continued. Pikemen and swordsmen and bowmen afoot, ushered and driven by mounted commanders and their lieutenants. Carts and wagons were wheeled forward among them, bearing bundled armaments or litters for hauling the wounded from the front lines.

"If it's an ambush, why are we rushing headlong into it?" the Head asked, of no one in particular.

A reasonable concern. The onslaught was clearly stemming from the canyon heights. A warning given by Fork-hand, as Kylac recalled. The grizzled dissenter, whose real name he'd overheard as Colonel Garnham, had worried that their clandestine path, if discovered, could put them at the mercy of an aerial assault.

It appeared the patch-eyed giant had been right.

"Are there defiles amid those bluffs?" Kylac asked. "Some covered means o' making the climb?"

"Surely. But to scout them in the dark, beset as we are now?" Ledron gnashed his teeth and shook his head. "Better to withdraw, and minimize our losses."

Or barrel through, thought Kylac. Race past the ambush, weathering the strafing fire from above and hoping not to run afoul of any barricades that might stopper their advance. But that didn't appear to be their general's intent. Else their own cage would be wheeling forward by now, along with the fighting force. As of yet, theirs seemed but a reactionary response. Overzealous. Like a dog roused by a passing cat, to give chase before considering potential perils.

"We's men south o' the attack," Kylac observed. Their head, caught in a noose. "We retreat from this snare, might be we sacrifice those caught on the other side."

"A concession the general will be slow to make."

"If'n the general has yet to take measure o' this fight."

Ledron growled some unintelligible curse over the enveloping din. That their scouts hadn't seen this coming, mayhap. That Bahsk had brought them along this course to begin with. That here he sat, trapped in this cage, while his countrymen were perishing so fruitlessly, just beyond his reach.

"Given a mind to escape, now could be our chance," Kylac said.

The captain cast him an incredulous look before eyeing their jailor contingent. "Our keepers remain at full strength."

Kylac shrugged. "Not suggesting it'd be without risk. But we may not find a better distraction."

Ledron seemed to consider, bitter as the offer tasted, before declining with a sour shake of his head. "Caught or fled, we'd be branded traitors," he claimed. "For all it grieves me, I'd sooner bear witness to this debacle, to know where it leaves us."

A sensible decision, if the Head had surrendered hope of finding Denariel and thus turned focus to aiding this retaliatory incursion in whatever way he might. Though they could each do much more beyond this cage than they could inside it, liberating themselves was not likely to win Bahsk's trust—particularly if Kylac was forced to harm or disable those set here to prevent just that. If intending to serve ally now, better that they submit to the general's pleasure.

So Kylac settled back against the cold iron bars, resolving to watch and wait. While it rankled him to support Bahsk's assertion that they could be made to join this fight against their will, he would respect Ledron's choice. At least until a better one presented itself, or circumstances should demand they reconsider.

Quite likely, in a situation as fluid and frenzied as this. Already, the army's initial thrust seemed to have stalled. Unsurprising, given what they were running into. If knowing the Addarans would be coming this way, the Grenarr would likely have chosen their point of ambush at a place where their quarry couldn't reach them. While it was possible that Sabrynne had rerouted the bulk of her force with a bloodthirsty desire to meet Bahsk head-on, her machinations thus far would suggest a craftier approach. Why dull your blade against an opponent's shield if you could as easily slide it into his back?

A presumption, of course, that raised all manner of related questions. *Was* this the whole of the army the Great Grendavan had sent to sack Indranell, or merely a splinter offshoot? How *had* they known to come this way? Or did there remain some small possibility that this might be a chance encounter?

The answer to the latter would seem a resounding no. From what Kylac had gathered, the route Bahsk had chosen through this network of canyons known as the Strebolen was too broken and too far removed from the Karamoor for any Grenarr outriders to have ventured across it by accident. Not in any significant numbers, anyway. And any stray scout would have required time to fetch those numbers and persuade them to redirect this way. The Addarans had left Indranell behind just three days ago. Impossible, Kylac decided, that their enemy's appearance here could be in reaction to those movements.

The Grenarr had *anticipated* this. And not by guesswork, to have pinned them down in such a precise location, along this particular vein. Ollerman's Pass, Ledron had named it, as they'd wheeled to a stop that evening. A name Kylac had recalled overhearing in Bahsk's secret strategy session. Whether by observation or treachery, the enemy's presence here marked a calculated effort, not a random one.

To that end, he found himself searching as best he could the crests of the canyon walls nearer his own position, seeking sign of a second phase of attack. Answers as to *how* the enemy had found them were at this point far less critical than what Sabrynne might mean to achieve as a result of that information. Was the ambush intended merely to slow them? Cause them to reroute? Thin their ranks? Or had she committed herself to crushing them completely, here and now?

But the jagged ridgelines remained quiet, undisturbed. Revealing nothing that might trigger alarm. The same held true of the canyon floor at their backs. If Sabrynne had wished to entrap them, it would seem she'd been unable to do so.

Which didn't mean that she wasn't positioning herself somewhere to the north even now, thinking to cut off any escape.

"General said he wasn't planning on retreat," Kylac recalled. "Seemed determined to carve past any resistance."

Ledron snorted. "While refusing to conceive of any. Could be a different tale now."

Indeed. Kylac found himself oddly detached, one course or the other. What difference to him, shameful withdrawal or stubborn advance? Mayhap because he had no hand in matters. He couldn't quite discern their chances for success here and now, to say nothing of what road might better benefit them in the long run. While concerns for Denariel tugged him northward, the queen's greater longing was for Avenell's reclamation. If freed this very moment, he would be hard-pressed to predict the immediate cause to which he should apply himself.

A relief, in that regard. But it didn't feel that way. It felt stifling, oppressive, to have his own instincts lying dormant. Smothered. As if they understood their uselessness so long as he remained caged. Making it impossible for him to hope, for this outcome or that.

Not that he was prone to hope in any circumstance. He was far more accustomed to acting as he deemed fit. A failing, at times, but he knew no other way.

Making this forced delay all the less tolerable, even when he had no definitive yearning to satisfy.

Peering ahead, he could see lines of torch-bearing Addarans scratching at the bluffs beneath their assailants, seeking to snake or scale their way to the summit. But these beacons just made them easy targets for the enemy above, who continued to rain arrows and stones down upon them. Doubtless, there would be others seeking to make the climb in the moonlit dark, to fare little better. Navigating the unfamiliar terrain would prove challenge enough in daylight, without the opponent's hailstorm. Under these conditions, it could be deemed no better than desperate foolishness.

A black haze had come to choke the head of their company. A veil of acrid smoke raised by the groundfires. A tepid blaze, given the meager growth among the rocks and boulders and shale. What was there had been easily lit, but quickly consumed. Still, the canyon winds gusted northward, driving the flames and smoke toward Kylac's position, making it ever more difficult for those at the front to ply their feeble counterattack.

With every passing moment, what clues Kylac could detect all suggested their retaliation to be a futile effort. If not the whole of their mission, certainly their response this night. The packed litters he'd seen rushed forward earlier had begun to return, filled with bloodied bodies pricked and mashed and burned. The moans of the injured formed a despairing undertone for the screams farther ahead, and for the strident taunts of those visiting this carnage upon them.

"We're being slaughtered," Ledron growled.

A fair assessment. Leading Kylac to wonder how long their commanders intended to sustain this travesty.

As fortune had it, not long.

Just moments later, scarcely a quarter-mark since the attack had begun, the tenor of the shouts and whistles and horns and drumbeats from the front took a decided turn. Soon thereafter, a tide of soldiers began ebbing northward. Amid the black clouds of roiling smoke and swirling ash that choked his lungs and stung his eyes and carried the gruesome smells of charred brush and burning flesh, Kylac watched the army's gradual withdrawal, building wave upon wave. Among the endless orders being shouted and echoed back along the lines, a command was given that had the brake on their prison wagon being released, and the driver urging the tethered draft horses into motion. Around, the wagon wheeled, bumping and stuttering over the rugged terrain, their ring of jailors marking every motion with stern gazes and ready weapons.

Kylac read what he could of their expressions. Frustration, anger, but also a measure of relief. Whatever their resentment and indignation at being turned away, there was satisfaction to be had in surviving the night, regrouping, and seeing how matters might appear come the dawn. The consequences of their failure would be measured and dealt with later, when the threat to their lives wasn't so immediate.

Shortsighted, mayhap, but discretion had its place. While it might be playing into their enemy's hands, spawning greater challenges on the morrow, better that than to overcommit to a lost cause.

The one or the other, Ledron seemed to approve. So Kylac withheld his own, less charitable judgments, reminding himself that few men, if any, viewed conflict with the same unflappable confidence that he did. Bahsk understood his men's limitations better than anyone, else he'd not be serving as their chief commander. And he certainly had a closer view of matters than Kylac, at this juncture.

Assuming, of course, the general was still alive.

That mystery, too, was quickly solved, when Bahsk rode past, bellowing commands astride his charger, shepherding his personal regiment and the fragments of others north amid the flow. Kylac thought to call out, to request report, but resisted the urge. Even if willing to confide in him—or Ledron—the general wouldn't likely do so now, amid the ongoing furor, with so many witnesses within view. The proud soldier would visit with them when believing he had something to gain from them, and not likely a moment sooner.

Though positioned centrally amid troops forward and rear during the calm, southward march, Kylac found himself relegated now closer to the rear. Due to his wagon's slower pace, mayhap, or to his diminished importance given this turn of events. It was almost enough to make him wish he'd come here of his own accord, so as to have the freedom of movement to determine his own fate and better affect that of his companions, such as they were. Alas, he'd made his choice, and this was where it had left him, laboring along like a wounded animal at the tail of a hunted herd.

As of yet, however, he sensed no pursuit. Despite the nervousness of his jailors, the relative quiet building in their wake suggested that their assailants did not, in truth, have any forces on the canyon floor in a position to give chase or elsewise harry their retreat. Flaming missiles continued to arc from the heights, but these were falling into the distance. Finishing off the wounded, most likely. The patchwork rearguard that Kylac could see among the veils of black smoke appeared to be straggling along without challenge.

A source of vexation for those like Garnham, Kylac realized, when he spied the fork-handed colonel railing amid the fiery gloom. Backing away only reluctantly upon his mount. Making sweeping gestures at those Addarans—mostly injured, at this point—who continued to amble after. Spitting curses and provocations into the wind, meant to bait his adversaries into a more direct engagement.

A cascade of voiceless jeers reverberated amid the canyon walls in response, thick with derision and triumph.

"Listen to the beasts," Ledron muttered. "Baying like hounds in heat."

To Kylac's ears, the lustful cries sounded no different than those trumpeted by any conquering host. Not so long ago, he'd heard a ship full of Ledron's own countrymen delighting in the defeat of a multitude of Mookla'ayan elves, and witnessed firsthand the barbaric glee some had taken in harvesting grisly tokens during the aftermath. In that regard, the Grenarr seemed no more savage than any other pack of men consumed by the bloody thrill of victory.

"Let 'em savor it," Kylac proposed. "They's betrayed themselves now. Set fire to any further chance at surprise. For what great gain?"

Ledron gnawed at the thought. The captain could surely gauge, as Kylac had, that their losses had been minimal. One hundred? Two? Unfortunate, yes, given their limited numbers to begin with. But, from a strategic standpoint, a twentieth of their strength wasn't so great a cost compared to what it might have been, had their adversary made better use of its advantage.

Should it prove an underling's independent decision to launch the ambush here and now, Kylac wouldn't be greatly surprised were it to meet ultimately with Sabrynne's displeasure.

"Unless this was but a prod," Ledron countered, "meant to drive us into the true snare."

Unless that. A possibility, if not a likelihood. Given his freedom, Kylac might have offered to go find out. Infiltrate the enemy's camp. Eavesdrop or interrogate as needed. Know by sunrise whether this would prove a luckless brush, or if they could expect to encounter further skirmishes all the way to Avenell.

He almost suggested it. Just slip out now and have themselves a look. But the same reservations that had bound him from the outset still shackled him now. He couldn't guarantee Ledron's safety. He couldn't say as to what reprisals his former travel companions might suffer in his absence. He'd be branding himself an indisputable adversary, hampering any effort to restore Denariel to her rightful station.

Bahsk's force was certain to uncover the obstacles before it anyway, in the natural course of events. But at what price, should they continue blindly in their chosen course?

Shrouded by sooty blackness, mocked by the howls of their enemy, surrounded by the walking wounded and those borne by their companions, Kylac rolled along in the confines of his cage. Strangled by his own indecision. Assailed by the stench of death and defeat. Reduced to *hoping* they might discover the truth before it was too late.

21

Their arduous retreat stretched on for more than an hour, persisting well after the glow of fire had been eclipsed by the folds of the canyon corridor, the smoke had dissipated, and the echoes of battle had been left to ring only in their minds. While Colonel Garnham eagerly maintained his rearguard, there appeared no signs of enemy pursuit. Nor did Kylac hear, see, or elsewise sense any movement to indicate threat to fore or flanks of the fleeing column. A quiet to suggest that the Grenarr were content to let them withdraw unmolested.

For now.

Nearly two leagues of rugged earth had passed beneath the wheels of their prison wagon before Kylac and Ledron found themselves welcomed again into the heart of Bahsk's army, gathered upon an elevated shelf of rock cradled on three sides by curving bluffs thrust skyward. A natural redoubt, should their enemies seek to give chase. As suitable a site as any in which to weather what remained of the night.

Few had yet been given to stand down. Most were at work fortifying their position. A ring of bulwarks was fast rising along the rim of the plateau, mounds erected from scraped earth, piled rocks, and tangles of thorny brush. Others busied themselves taking inventories or lending aid to the wounded, whose brave grunts and tight-lipped moans were nonetheless magnified by stark canyon walls, to raise an ominous lament.

Just three days into their march, and already this, a staggering defeat. Kylac saw it in the slouch of men's shoulders, the suspicion in their eyes, the stiffness and trepidation in their movements. How could this have happened? What would their commanders have them do about it? Had the entire offensive already been thwarted?

Kylac shared their questions, if not their anxiety. Given his limited vantage, however, he had little means of seeking answers. All he could readily discern was that, no matter their escape, the night's ambush had left even the most zealous among them despondent and disgruntled, casting a pall over the encampment that wouldn't easily be shed.

Then Bahsk came to see him.

It happened roughly a quarter-mark after their chief jailor had sent Jerumin to deliver report. Accompanied by a knot of soldiers, the general emerged briskly through the lines, his bruising attendants shoving aside any who didn't make way swiftly enough. Enabling him to weave forward with the single-minded intensity of a shark scenting prey.

Bahsk swept past the ring of jailors to within a pace of the wagon, anger and accusation brewing amid his thunderous countenance.

"You knew," he spat at Kylac. "Before the first bolt flew."

Kylac glanced at his chief jailor, Dramon, and at Jerumin, arriving now in the general's wake like a stray pilot fish. "Not soon enough, I fear."

"How?"

"Did I sense the attack? Or do ya suspect I harbor some insight as to how they came to be there?"

The general bristled. "All of it. The whole of what you know."

"Precious little, confined as I's been. I should think your scouts'd be better positioned to—"

"Useless," Bahsk snapped, "those who've reported back. The rest will bear better word, else prove wise enough to not return at all."

Traitors. Or so the general feared. And why not, with the Grenarr as notorious for their ability to secure Addaran spies as they were for their raids at sea? "Begging pardon, a keen nose is all I can claim. I cannot speak for whatever machinations took place here."

"Machinations. Of which you just claimed ignorance."

"Personally, yes." Mayhap Kylac had misread the man. Did he truly believe his scouts merely incompetent? "But an evident prospect, even from this cage."

"Someone revealed our position," Ledron agreed, his voice raspy from thirst. "Likely before we even set forth."

"Who?" Bahsk demanded.

The Head seemed taken aback. "The general was stationed at Indranell more recently than I."

"Where we routinely rooted out poisoned elements. It was Avenell that was infested. And those rats who served the tar-skins in their recent conquest would have remained to enjoy the spoils of their treachery, don't you think?"

Kylac was unsure what to think. Bahsk couldn't possibly be certain that his city had been free of informants. Especially given the influx of refugees taken in from the southern city and other surrounding settlements. To believe elsewise would be foolishly naive. Short of that, what cause had he to deny the probability?

Ledron seemed equally confused, as he tactfully measured his response. "It would only be prudent to presume our enemy knows more than we wish them to."

"And for that, I look to those yet to win my trust. My men here are loyal," Bahsk insisted, stiffening against any challenge to the contrary.

The manner in which his eyes shifted to those around him proved telling. Suggesting that his refusal to entertain the notion of betrayal wasn't because he didn't fear it, but because he wished to shield his troops from those selfsame doubts. Difficult it was for a soldier to fight forward while wary of those at his back.

"Would that I had some confession to ease your mind," Kylac offered again. "Merely a warrior's instinct."

Bahsk seethed for a moment, eyeing them through the bars. Weighing his urge to probe further against a desire to demonstrate calm and control for the sake of his men. "I come to learn elsewise, your death will not be pleasant."

Threats to cover failings. Kylac could have laughed, but chose not to. Seeing little to be gained from pouring further oil on this particular flame.

The general departed, his armored flock in tow. To continue his consultations elsewhere, no doubt. Kylac hoped they would prove more fruitful than their own brief visitation here.

Still, it left him and Ledron in the dark. Under the watchful scowls of Dramon and Jerumin and the other jailors. Beyond sight or hearing of whatever plans Bahsk and his lieutenants might devise for them moving forward. Spectators to their own fate.

"Loyal," Ledron snorted. "As if the word holds meaning anymore."

"I wonder what alternative he'd choose to believe. That his *lesser* enemies are superior logicians and strategists?"

"For all the show of blaming us, he'd do better to question his own inner circle."

Kylac thought back to Bahsk's midnight strategy session at Indranell, reflecting on those present. A possible point of origin for any leak. But the attendees that night had been almost entirely strangers to him, making it impossible to discern guilt, one from the next. Aside from Bahsk himself, and Colonel Fayne . . .

He let the image of the latter linger, testing it against his instincts. While the ambush here did nothing to implicate the colonel specifically, it surely did nothing to absolve him of Kylac's earlier doubts.

Of course, none of those original attendees need necessarily have been involved. The presumed leak could as easily have sprung following a dissemination of orders to lieutenants and sub-captains—a much larger pool of potential informants to draw from.

"The higher the rank," Kylac mused, "the more careful he'd have to be to keep his own hands clean."

"Meaning?"

"If'n I'm hunting rats out here, I'm looking at those free to roam from the company's heart. An outrider, a watchman, who might send lantern signal or some other clandestine communication in the dark."

Ledron gritted his teeth. "And wring from him the names of any coconspirators."

"Or set snare for his return. Catch him in the midst o' report."

The Head clanked his chains in frustration. "Easy for us to speculate, for all we can do about it. Unless . . ."

Kylac found his fellow captive eyeing him strangely. A look of appraisal, accompanied by an air of grim acceptance. "Yes?" he prompted.

"You still think you could free yourself?"

Kylac shrugged. "Making no assurance that you or the others would remain unharmed."

The Blackfist snorted ruefully. "Loath as I am to condemn them, the value of our skins would seem to be plummeting—mine included. If selling them now would buy you the opportunity to spare my people further calamity, or track down Her Majesty, it's a trade I'd gladly make."

Kylac took a moment to determine whether the captain was serious. But then, when had he been even a sliver less? Had it been merely his own life at stake, the Blackfist would have offered it up for Denariel's sake days ago. As he had upon their initial capture. It was only for those who'd demonstrated faithfulness, to her and to him—once his temper had cooled and Kylac had been able to convince him of it—that he'd opted to bide his time. Hoping against hope that better circumstances would present themselves.

Of course, much the same held true for Kylac. While he wouldn't claim willingness to lay down his life in the manner that Ledron would, he'd certainly be willing to risk it—with what little risk there truly was to himself in doing so. But he wasn't yet ready to sacrifice the one who'd first recruited him to this business. Disingenuous as the Head may have been when first they'd met, he'd later chosen to preserve Kylac's life when he could more easily have left the young mercenary for dead. Whatever the many conflicts and abiding mistrust between them, Kylac wouldn't freely choose to abandon him.

"A fair notion. Save for the damage that might be wrought if'n it's yourself who proves an agent o' the enemy."

Ledron's surprise was matched only by his indignation. The volatile blend left him red-faced, momentarily speechless. "Preposterous," he blurted finally. "I was shackled alongside you before I ever heard of the general's plans."

"So ya claims. But where were ya while I was eavesdropping, or chasing after Her Majesty?"

His smirk must have betrayed the jest, because Ledron bit down on a ready retort, simmering.

"Best, I think, that I keeps ya within sight. Just to be sure."

The captain looked ready to loose his bridled outrage, then seemed to think better of it. With clenched jaw and a shake of his head, he turned his gaze back through the bars, peering past Kylac in a northwesterly direction. Across the still bustling encampment. Past the canyon walls towering over their plateau. Out into the unseeable night, to span some fathomless distance.

"I suppose it's too late to worry for her," the Blackfist lamented quietly.

Kylac didn't have to ask whom this *her* might be. He thought to offer some hopeful consolation, but swiftly realized he had none to give. None based on favorable odds, anyway. Merely a stubborn desire to believe that the young Denariel, as she had so often before, might have found a way to persevere where most others would surely have succumbed.

As the work of securing the camp against attack drew to completion, activities began to slow. After barking out to those assigned first watch, officers issued the order for non-essential personnel to stand down. A long night it had been, with precious few hours remaining before dawn. Kylac wondered how many might actually find sleep, shrouded as they were in such dire uncertainty. Should the morrow come, they likely had only trial and desperation to look forward to. Further march. Further battle. Further treachery. It depended greatly on what answers their commanders might find, and what responses they might conceive.

Regardless, knowing that the Grenarr had their scent, their endeavor would seem now a game of hound and hare. Which meant none could safely predict when they might again be permitted rest. So Kylac determined to take *his* while he could. Though he seemed to require less than others, it might be that he would need every possible reserve in the days ahead. And as long as he was imprisoned, he saw little enough use in fighting to remain alert, on the chance that he might suss out some clue as to what Bahsk might intend.

He would learn it as it happened, and respond as able.

Closing his eyes, against the night and its settling madness, he set off in search of quieter dreams.

He awoke to a river-like sense of movement, and to the churning, gurgling sounds of its flow.

His eyes opened. A hint of predawn suffused the air, dark and chill beyond the scattering of watchfires. The army was moving out. Or a portion of it, anyway. Soldiers streamed past his wheeled cage, their shadowed features etched with determination. But not all were mobilizing behind them. A detachment. Scores strong, and growing, but a splinter force nonetheless.

The general was dividing their strength.

For what purpose remained to be seen. So Kylac watched, taking count, observing the composition and arrangement of those setting forth. Most looked to be lean and lightly armored. Swifter, more mobile fighters, with bows and slings and throwing spears. There were riders among them, but few in number, dispersed throughout the ranks. Chiefly squad commanders, it would appear. Supplies were light. Reserve artillery. Ropes and grapnels and other scaling gear. All trickling down from the plateau, to take aim at the same track of canyon they'd fled just hours before.

"He must mean to clear the pass," Ledron ventured, his voice a soft rumble at Kylac's back.

"Else put forth the appearance," Kylac agreed. "What o' the rest of us?"

The detachment grew into the hundreds. Roughly a quarter of their overall strength, by Kylac's measure. But the departing flow showed sign thereafter of tapering off. Leaving the bulk of the army to do what, precisely?

There was no immediate indication, given the inactivity of those left behind. And if Ledron had any guesses, he kept them to himself. So Kylac was left again to watch, and to wait, and to wonder. He marked the departing column until it was swallowed by a craggy bend. Pressing his cheek against the bars, he peered up at the crack of sky visible above the canyon walls. Another hour before sunrise, he estimated. Longer before it would touch them, given their sheltered location. Could that be what the general was waiting for?

Again he closed his eyes, resolving not to waste his efforts in blind speculation.

The next stir came less than an hour later, judging by the sky's hue. As suspected, little of the dawn's emerging light managed to filter into the canyon's gullet. But the ribbon above raised clear marker that a new day was pressing. And Bahsk was wasting no more time before striking forth in whatever endeavor he'd laid out for them.

Kylac witnessed the general, briefly, among the rustle of rising soldiers. Trotting about on his charger. Barking out in stern encouragement. Enjoining his troops to rise up with stout hearts and faithful minds. His words were mostly lost amid the dull, clanking uproar of armor and weapons being strapped into place. But they sounded to Kylac little more than platitudes, revealing nothing specific about the nature of their new undertaking.

To the soldiers' merit, Kylac saw little in the way of resentment or disconsolation. The troops were irritable, certainly. Given the long night and short hours of fitful slumber, that much would seem unavoidable. But the signs of bitterness and hostility glimpsed upon the settling of camp had found focus, it appeared, in the duty at hand. With slaps and grunts and challenges steeped in camaraderie, they looked to have added the night's defeat to their long list of grievances, for which they would now seek redress.

Some of which was surely feigned. To deceive their commanders, their comrades, mayhap themselves. To convince one and all that they wouldn't so easily be turned from their objective. That their advance, while momentarily blunted, wouldn't be stalled. That their pride, their collective strength, and the justness of their cause, would carry them through.

Kylac found it grating. While commonplace, he'd never known such demonstrations to serve significant purpose. Quite likely, the Grenarr would be rousing themselves now in much the same manner. Logistics would carry the day. Strategy. Tactics. Morale mattered, but was highly fickle, erratic, entirely susceptible to the ebbs and flows of actual conflict. *Every warrior fancies himself invincible,* his father used to tell him, *until he sees himself bleed.*

Making this rally, here and now, little more than posturing.

But there seemed little chance they'd listen should he advise them to conserve their strength, and even less chance they'd thank him for it. So he swallowed his judgments, and searched instead for clues as to what their bloodthirsty enthusiasm might mean.

"Seems we're not turning about, then," Ledron presumed, giving voice to Kylac's own thoughts.

"Few would so freely express their eagerness to do so," Kylac agreed. "Our good general has some other maneuver in mind."

"Anticipating attack this time, I trust."

"I would think so. If'n not seeking it outright."

The Head gritted his teeth.

"Any ideas, were it you commanding this brood?"

"Send a company to engage those in the pass," Ledron replied. "Work the rest of the army south along another route."

"*Is* there another route?"

"Not one I'd prefer to take. But we bypassed preference long ago."

The mobilization soon encompassed their own contingent, with a fresh rotation of jailors replacing those assigned to watch them over the past few hours. A few put forth scowls or sneers upon their departure. A blend of purposeless warning and meaningless derision. A handful of their replacements offered the same in greeting. Ledron met their expressions with his typical, stony glare. Kylac ignored them, save to note their positions, along with any visible signs of weakness. A hitch here to betray injury to ankle or knee. A stretch there to indicate stiffness or strain in neck or back. After the days of march, and of sleeping on hard ground, all suffered affliction or discomfort of some variety. Little need as he had to rely on such for any tactical advantage, Kylac's lifelong training had him taking notice instinctively, with the same amount of thought given to breathing.

Moments later, their prison wagon took its place in the line of departing soldiers, once again near the center of the column. Fresh grease worked its way into the axles, softening the creaks and squeals. But the rattle and groan remained, amid the stamp of booted feet, the clop of hooves, the squeak of leather, the jangle of traces, the clink of chains. Commanders' voices boomed, to which horses whickered and men mustered hearty cheer. The resumption of a song driven like nails into Kylac's head over the past three days, almost as if the prior night's setback had never occurred.

Leaving Kylac to wonder what they may have learned, and what adjustments they may have made.

Or if they would but saunter blithely into yet another snare.

22

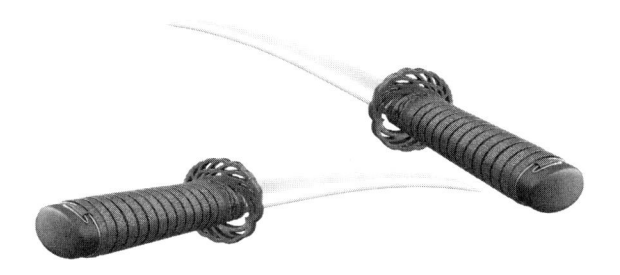

The scout thundered past their cage, urging his lathered mount northward against the army's southerly flow. Barreling at what seemed a perilous pace—for both horse and rider—given the broken track of earth they were attempting to negotiate. Hailing warning, yet scarcely waiting for his countrymen to clear a path. Bearing urgent word, Kylac thought, to proceed with such reckless abandon.

He shared a glance with Ledron before returning eye to the rider, following the scout's weaving progress. A leaning, twisting, leaping display by a skilled horseman and surefooted steed to elude hazards among the staggered lines of soldiers—their formations riven by mounds and shelves, ruts and ravines, thorny brush and calcified deadwood. Hemmed in by the sheer walls of Rendenel Run—the defile they'd entered early that morning, and which had engulfed them now for more than half the day. Plagued by heat and thirst and the uncertain knowledge of whether they might ever march free of its desolate gullet.

Some ninety paces back, Bahsk rode with his command retinue. Marking the scout's approach, the general spurred his own steed ahead to the rim of a small overlook. The scout drew to a dusty halt beneath its rocky horn, and there appeared to deliver his report.

"We've enemies ahead," Ledron determined, as he watched the

rider point and gesture.

Kylac had presumed as much. The entire army had, given the sudden buzz of wary excitement. No conscious man among them could have missed the scout's frantic arrival. What remained to be seen was whether his fervor was a mark of enthusiasm or dread.

"No more than a scouting party," Ledron mused. "Unless the Fair Mother has truly forsaken us."

Meaning only terrible misfortune or the much-feared betrayal from within could damn them this time. For the Head had noted, upon entering this rugged draw, that of all the many splintered paths they could have taken, Bahsk had chosen one of the harshest, least navigable available to them. Suggesting the general was determined to avoid any further ambushes like that encountered the night before. Because the Grenarr couldn't possibly manage to marshal any sizable force ahead of them, along this particular track, save by terrible accident or advance knowledge.

Judging by their guarded optimism, the Blackfist and his fellow soldiers refused to believe their luck could be *that* cursed.

"We've little choice but to press through, either way," Kylac observed.

The Head didn't bother to disagree. Several of the descents they'd dared this day had involved slopes too steep to climb in reverse. Unless the general was willing to abandon his various wagons and supply carts, there would be no retreat as there had been before.

Not that such a turn was utterly beyond question. Kylac was given to wonder, should matters unfold that way, would he and Ledron be left in their cage and abandoned alongside?

The scout finished his report, with Bahsk giving directions now to those around him. Raised flags sent signal forward through the columns. Responding flags went up toward the front, acknowledging the order. A flurry of movement led to the formation of a new vanguard, twoscore in number, composed of mounted soldiers drawn from a pair of forward companies.

"You see?" Ledron remarked with grim satisfaction. "A token force to be run down."

The mounted contingent set heel to flank and bled off to the south, its members falling into a narrow line so as to trace a more favorable path amid the rugged terrain. The soldiers left behind bid silent cheer with fierce smiles and thrusts of their fists. The veiled tension that had gathered in the scout's wake quickly dispersed, giving over to a cruel zeal. The relief of an opponent's arrow missing its mark, making it their turn to strike.

Their own progress continued with renewed vigor and fresh haste. Despite the brutish detour, the general's plan was working. The course he'd drawn, whatever specifics had been left to Ledron and Kylac and others to guess, would yet bring them to their desired destination and a reckoning with their hated enemies. Those usurpers who'd gained advantage only through duplicity and intrigue would taste now the full measure of their blunt fury, and surely wither before it.

That collective outlook, with all of its martial certainty, radiated from the soldiers like the heat from their barren surroundings. Spirits that had been slowly wilting with the day's passage carried them now like a favorable wind at sea. Throughout the Falcon's Hour and the Kingfisher's, morale waxed strong, overwhelming petty difficulties and trite grievances. Enabling them to grind onward, even as the fractured terrain taxed their strength, and a fiendish afternoon sun bore mercilessly down upon them.

As the Kingfisher gave way to the Swallow, they found cause for further celebration, reaching a pitted hollow in which it appeared their mounted vanguard had finally caught up to the Grenarr scouting party. A mere eight strong, the tar-skins had been swiftly and thoroughly slaughtered by the bloodthirsty Addarans. A pair of them were staked out in pools of blood, the flesh of their torsos peeled back and their viscera exposed. Victims of torture, Kylac could see, from a hundred paces out. Whether for information about their cohorts, or merely to slake the thirst of their tormentors, was harder to know.

Bahsk rode ahead at that point, mayhap to ask that very question of the vanguard's commander. Removed as he was, Kylac heard none of their exchange. Nor did those involved exhibit mannerism or gesture telling enough to reveal the commander's explanation, or the general's reaction to it.

The remainder of the army never slowed, flowing sluggishly

onward. Several took delight in trampling the enemy corpses as they marched past, as if to sooner grind the bones to dust. Others satisfied themselves with spitting on their bloody ruin, or in casting snide curses and insults. There were no outright cheers, given that Bahsk wished to suppress any unnecessary noise amid the echoing canyon walls. But Kylac witnessed savage smiles and muted jeers aplenty.

He felt not a seedling of satisfaction himself. Nor did Ledron, judging by the Head's stark, sour-faced demeanor. In truth, the Blackfist appeared discomfited, embarrassed, by the boorish actions of his countrymen. As if surprised—or at least disappointed—to see them demonstrate such animalistic behavior.

To be reminded that, as a people, his were perhaps no better than theirs.

Leaving its victims' remains to the scavengers, the army put the scene of carnage behind it and pressed south in search of greater game. Another hour bled away, marked by the sun's trek across the fissure of sky above the canyon heights. During that time, a sense of unease began blooming in Kylac's gut. A premonition with no apparent source. He'd encountered no further sign of the enemy—no sound or smell to indicate a physical presence beyond those who already accompanied him. But the same instinct that had woken him the night before—the same inner warning that had alerted him of danger countless times in the past—whispered now of impending menace. Darkening his thoughts like a storm brewing on a ship's horizon.

"What is it?" Ledron asked him.

Kylac turned to find his cellmate wearing a mask of grim scrutiny.

"You sense something," the Blackfist insisted.

"Nothing o' which I'm certain."

"Another attack?"

Kylac shrugged. "Could be a rockslide. Rainstorm. A plague o' locusts or a grist o' bees."

"Something unpleasant, regardless."

"A threat," Kylac conceded. "Whatever its form."

Ledron's scowl deepened. A caution too vague to share with Bahsk, even if they could get the general to listen. And to what end? As they'd agreed earlier, there was really no road left to them now save that which would carry them forward.

Soon thereafter, the visible sky began to darken. Somewhere beyond their line of sight, the late afternoon sun was falling into premature shadow. Thunderheads gathered overhead, a dark massing rare to these shores. Ledron's brooding visage skewed hopeful. Could this indeed be the sole source of Kylac's gloomy portent?

Lightning flashed, and thunder boomed in its wake. The soldiers, by and large, paid it no concern. An omen of conquest, befitting their endeavor.

Even when the rains descended, pouring in windblown sheets, the march continued. There was no real refuge out here, save for the handful of tents and pavilions carried with them. Nor did such storms, however violent, typically last long. A half-mark, mayhap, before it blew over. With true dusk still two hours hence, Bahsk wasn't yet ready, it seemed, to consider calling the day's progress. If they couldn't weather this, how would they fare against their enemy in the days ahead?

The squall intensified, its bitter breath howling into their faces along the canyon's gullet, as if bemoaning their advance. While sheltered better than most, Kylac witnessed the struggles of those around him, slipping and sliding along the hard-packed earth, which was suddenly full of flooded gullies, swift-flowing streams, and a treacherous, muddy crust. Horses whinnied objection as they, too, struggled with their footing and balked at the roaring flares that lit the sky. As quickly as that, the threat of rockslide had become all too real, and reflected as such in Ledron's grim countenance.

Nothing like nature's wrath, Kylac supposed, to make even the heartiest of men feel suddenly insignificant.

Abruptly, amid the raging clamor of wind and rain and rushing groundwaters, there arose a telltale whistle and a rising chorus of shouts. Kylac felt it a moment before he heard it, like iron raked against slate. He searched the near-darkness. In the garish glow of a lightning bolt that streaked overhead, he watched a line of soldiers on the western flank crumble—more than a few clutching at the feathered shafts protruding suddenly from their bodies.

"Are ya seeing this, Captain?"

Ledron looked, peering intently through the bars at Kylac's back. "Attack!" he realized, as another wave fell.

The alarms were already being sounded. Though muted by the din of the storm, horns blared and pipes shrilled, seemingly from all directions. Kylac couldn't discern at first if it was the canyon walls and the gusting winds that made it seem so, buffeting them with echoes. But he did feel a suffocating closeness enveloping him like a heavy wool blanket, and understood the sensation to bode ill.

"At your back," he said, upon watching a line of soldiers drop on the *eastern* flank now, as well.

Ledron spun around to his own side of the wagon cell, gripping the bars as he observed the developing conflict. "This is no scouting party," he realized darkly.

Indeed not. With each volley of arrows, a dozen men or more were felled—to either side. Which likely meant at least a score of archers positioned atop each flanking bluff. And that based purely on the slice of battle to which they could readily bear witness. Given the cries farther forward and farther back, Kylac suspected the numbers arrayed here against them to be even greater.

The dire question reflected in Ledron's eyes gnawed at the fore of his own thoughts. Had the Grenarr so divided themselves as to post ambush parties at every possible route through the Strebolen's canyons? An unlikely strategy, if they truly meant to lay siege to Indranell. While it would better let them safeguard Avenell at the same time, there were surely more centralized bottlenecks and bulwarks nearer the capital city designed for that purpose, that Sabrynne's limited forces needn't cast so wide a net.

But that would take him back to the growing likelihood none wanted to accept—that whatever spy or spies might be present among their camp had revealed not only the aim of this offensive, but the precise path along which it was to be carried out. And not just once now, but twice. Informing as to their original course through Ollerman's Pass, and then again here, through Rendenel Run.

Which would seem to absolve Colonel Fayne of suspicion, he noted. For how could a mole left behind at Indranell have foreseen the detour the army had taken upon being repelled the night before?

Countering that, the colonel needn't necessarily be working alone . . .

Kylac severed the mental thread before it could unspool further. More senseless conjecture, at this point. One mole or a hundred, be they here, there, or everywhere, it would seem their work was accomplished. If Bahsk's purpose in sending a company back into Ollerman's Pass was to divert attention from the main force's attempt at circumnavigating that blockade, it would seem to have failed. The army was once again besieged. Ambushed by the enemy. Caught in an even less tenable situation than before.

As obvious as the fear had been, he would have preferred his instincts proven wrong on the matter.

Yet here they were, with nothing to be gained in second-guessing. They would fight forward, withdraw, or perish where they stood. As of yet, it seemed uncertain as to which course of action Bahsk might favor. The soldiers whom Kylac could see were largely milling about in confusion, with some hunkering against the attack while others surged out to meet it. Wordless cries added to the tumult. Organized commands were lost amid the gale. Chaos reigned.

But this was not an untrained force, and its members had in fact anticipated this scenario—particularly after encountering it the night before. Within moments, order took hold, commanders regaining control of their squads as if reining in a startled steed. Where superiors had fallen, lieutenants rose to the challenge. While understandably lacking in cohesion and crispness, the units recalled their training and took to their assignments. Raising shields to deflect incoming arrows. Returning fire between volleys. Continuing to drive forward—for the moment—in relative unison, with each man acting as a link in the same chain.

Their grinding momentum, however, soon stalled. The concentration of attackers seemed thicker ahead, at a point where the defile narrowed. The earth fronting this bottleneck was buckled into a series of broken slabs. A strategic positioning, not likely gained by chance. In addition to navigating the ragged, stormswept terrain, those seeking to advance had to sidestep an increasing number of fallen comrades, while also resisting the press of those being driven back. To maintain formation, the entire column churned to a halt.

"We stop, we die," Ledron fumed, as their prison wagon, too, stuttered to a standstill.

Kylac merely nodded. A death sentence, to remain in that killing cauldron. But there seemed scant alternative. Given the array of ledges and plateaus claimed by their enemy, coupled with the tightness of the corridor they'd chosen, there really was little chance of bringing their full strength to bear against the numbers flanking them.

Only moments old, the battle was heading toward a swift, decisive rout.

In what struck as a desperation maneuver, the stalled squads fanned to either side, raking at the tumbledown slopes in an attempt to engage those above. The struggle met with some success, as the defile walls were neither as sheer, nor as tall as those framing Ollerman's Pass. Formations here were more terraced in nature, filled with crags and boulders behind which to seek cover, and scarred by switchbacks and washouts granting access to higher elevations. A laborious effort, and costly in terms of life. Yet, little by little, the enraged Addarans slowly began clawing their way up the heights, displacing their assailants and laying claim to various veins and tables of broken ground.

Like a slow-coursing venom, penetrating its victim along whatever natural pathways it encountered.

As a result, the enemy tide seemed to recede. There was even forward movement of their cage amid the main column again. A juddering, inconsistent progress, but progress nonetheless. Kylac saw the sliver of wary hope amid the despair in Ledron's eye. Mayhap the day wasn't yet lost.

Then a shearing sensation led to a grating rumble that shook the earth and sent shivers down Kylac's spine. The landslide he'd feared, come to pass. A cascade of rock and mud pouring down from the eastern slope. Hundreds of paces ahead of them, beyond their physical view, but not beyond comprehension. Not amid the earth's ravenous roaring, or the piercing chorus of dismay wrought among those caught in its tumbling sweep.

The latter surged above the tumult once the cracking, clattering echoes had ceased. Ledron strained against the bars on his side of the cage, searching for an angle from which to view the devastation. Kylac relied on more primordial senses. An inner part of him could feel the residue of astonishment, awe, and crushing finality emanating from those buried beneath the slide or serving witness to it. Dozens dead, if he had to guess. Scores. Like some slumbering titan had simply risen up to take a bite out of their flank—to say nothing about what might remain of the path ahead.

The swell of cries from those bearing testament told him soon enough that further advance was unlikely. The army's halt and ensuing press of soldiers battling for retreat confirmed it. When Ledron looked at him, he felt the scathing barbs of disbelief and accusation. As if his predictions had somehow been the cause. Obvious perils, he might have reminded his companion, easy to foresee. And yet, a measure of guilt did indeed weigh upon him. As if giving thought to these hazards, or voice to them, were what had granted them life.

The Blackfist looked away again, searching stubbornly for some new hope, but unlikely to find any. Kylac knew not whether the rockslide had been triggered by their enemy, or represented merely the cruelty of fate. He'd have wagered that not all of the Grenarr had escaped its fury, but had no evidence to support that assertion. All he had were signs of the aftermath, the most meaningful of which was an increasing surge of Addarans returning from the southern front, stumbling north again in what must have appeared in those moments to be the only viable course.

For several moments, he waited alongside Ledron for that course to reverse. For the troops to gird up and defy whatever damage had been inflicted upon them. Rallying cries amid the stormy furor fought to inspire them along that path. But most of those cries rang with desperation, and couldn't match the voices of defeat with which so many others sang. The withdrawal continued unabated—a retreat born not of panic, but of a dreadful understanding of the overwhelming odds now mounted against them.

Soldiers who'd gained foothold upon the slopes began spilling down to join the northward exodus. For every officer who held his ground, urging others to stand fast, Kylac counted a dozen or more leading the reverse charge. Rally they would, but not here, not now.

Like a crumbling dam or a falling tree, Kylac watched the end unfold. Before his eyes, the rush to depart gained speed and mass. Soldiers streamed past his cage, including those bloodied and battered from the front, limping and hobbling alone and in pairs. His jailors had come to look at one another with fretful glances, uncertain as to what they should do. They recognized, Kylac thought, the scant chance of rerouting the wagon and including their charges in the escape. Were they to flee, or stand there and perish alongside?

One by one, more than half of them peeled away, until only three remained. Spurred, mayhap, by their desertion, the wagoner dropped from his perch and worked frantically to unhitch the quartet of horses. No sooner had he accomplished this than he tethered the animals in a line and mounted the lead, riding the pack toward safety.

"Are we to root here, then, until the Grenarr descend upon us?" Ledron asked of the lingering Dramon.

The chief jailor eyed him tersely, but appeared indeed to be wrestling with indecision. He hadn't sought to arrest any of his squad from departing, but neither did he seem comfortable with the idea of abandoning his post. He looked to Jerumin, and Carrick, his lone remaining companions. While stern and stubborn in their expressions, neither man seemed any more decided on the matter than he.

Just when it appeared he might yield and take flight, a booming voice caught and captured his attention. Bahsk, Kylac recognized. The general himself, still shouting orders, closing on their position. Dramon saw it, judging by the manner in which he stiffened in anticipation of his commander's arrival.

It was another moment before the general hove into view astride his charger. There he held, while members of his retinue fought to maintain a defensive ring around him, and soldiers continued to scuttle past. He'd succumbed to the need for retreat, given his gestures and commands, but radiated fury at the notion, at war with his own words and actions.

Sparing a moment from the conflict around him, the defeated Bahsk peered in on them—his captives, still shackled and contained. His helmet was missing. Blood streamed from a head wound, washed by the incessant rains. His eyes smoldered. Kylac couldn't have said in that moment whether the general might free them, or see them set afire in their cage.

"Time to measure your loyalty," he growled at last. "To our cause, and to your own lives."

Ledron just glared in response. Kylac matched his silence. Was the general seeking some form of assurance? Kylac had but one to give—the same promise he'd extended when Bahsk had first seen fit to fetter him.

Fortunately, the general seemed more focused on the attitude of his compatriot, Ledron, than on anything Kylac might say or feel.

"I can do nothing for our people in here," the Head reminded him.

Bahsk took another look around. His left hand gripped his reins. His right, Kylac noted, hung limp, the gloved fingers curled back as if numb or injured. "Turn them loose," he commanded.

Dramon acted swiftly, tossing his spear to Jerumin so as to produce a string of keys from around his neck. After fumbling through them with rain-slicked fingers, he fit a key to the doorlock and pried it open with a click. Bahsk's retinue held a defensive position while Dramon wrested the latchbolt free and swung the door wide.

With another key, he unlocked Ledron's manacles. After which, he hesitated, looking back to his commander as if to verify that Kylac, also, should be released.

Bahsk nodded.

Kylac's chains fell free. Dramon withdrew in a crouch, eyeing him as he might a snake. Kylac simply rubbed his wrists, then gestured an invitation for the jailor to exit.

He emerged on Dramon's heels, into the driving rains. Thunder rattled the murky heavens, as if in echo of the conflict below. Kylac looked skyward and closed his eyes, luxuriating in the weight of his imprisonment falling away. Feeling suddenly as if he could fly.

He followed Ledron around the side of the wagon, aware of the weapons angled warily against any aggressive action he might take, yet pretending to ignore them. With a clearer view, he saw what the others already had—the defile ahead all but buried by the collapse of the canyon's eastern wall. Understandable, now, why even Bahsk had relented to taking flight. Whatever breach might have permitted their passage had been plugged by a mountain of stony earth. Corpses peppered the ruin, Addaran and Grenarr both. But there were many more Grenarr still perched upon the heights—a horde of leather-clad, sable-skinned bodies arranged like a colony of ticks, prepared yet to resist any foolish attempt by their enemies to proceed.

An increasing number of them descending now to give chase.

Colonel Garnham, holding stubbornly at the front, roared amid the tempest. Decrying the cowardice of his fleeing countrymen. Bellowing challenge to the mounting enemy pursuit.

"Sir! Shall I echo signal?" a lieutenant asked.

"The fool's responding," Bahsk replied. "Merely buying us time."

"What would you have of *us*?" Ledron asked, with a nod to indicate Kylac beside him.

Repel the enemy charge? Secure a flank? Safeguard the general's escape? Kylac wasn't waiting for an order he had no intention of obeying. "Begging pardon, Captain, the general and I struck our bargain already."

As Bahsk met his gaze, he launched a spinning kick to Jerumin's midsection. When the jailor doubled over to search for breath at his feet, Kylac stole his spear and, with a precise thrust, drove its tip into the soft underbelly of the general's chin.

"As we must."

Bahsk coughed, spurting blood from his neck and mouth.

For a frozen heartbeat, no one else moved.

Then everyone reacted at once.

"No!" Ledron shouted. Condemning Kylac's action, or the retaliation whipped up in response—a flurry of reprisals brought to bear by the general's personal retinue. Hurled threats, stabbing spears, swinging swords. Kylac had weathered far worse. Executing motions both practiced and instinctive, he dodged or deflected their hasty attacks, disarming, unhorsing, or elsewise disabling his assailants. In doing so, he took care not to cause any lasting injury, to footman or rider or steed. It was only natural of the general's men to seek redress. Kylac saw no reason to punish them for the effort.

For all their hacking, slicing, snarling exertions, it proved no more than a minor eddy amid the river of violence. Within moments, enough Addarans lay sprawled in the muddy earth—stunned, weaponless, powerless—for the remainder to waver and for Ledron to swoop in, arms outstretched, begging for restraint.

"Whoa! Whoa! Whoa!" he barked, coming to stand over Bahsk's sightlessly staring remains. "He means no further harm!" Treating Kylac to an incensed glare, he added, "Tell them!"

"A private dispute," Kylac agreed, a pair of borrowed blades held loosely in his palms, "between the general and I."

The ring of soldiers growled and grumbled, but most had lost their spirit for the fight. Owing in part to what they'd just witnessed from Kylac, but in greater measure to the larger conflict around them. With the bulk of their comrades in full flight and the enemy noose tightening around them, now would seem a poor time to press for any cause beyond that of survival.

Recognizing this, several turned away then and there of their own volition. Others followed, and more with them, blowing away like dandelion spores in a strengthening wind.

Among the stubborn few to remain was a dour-faced lad who, having been toppled from his mount, was gathering himself now to search vainly for his steed. He stopped and sneered, however, as a mounted company approached at Kylac's back. As if relishing a vision of imminent retribution.

"Ho!" a voice boomed. Colonel Garnham, a grizzled mound of bloodied, mud-spattered pelts atop his warhorse, reined in at the head of a pack of others, giving his lone eye to the sight of Bahsk's corpse. "The general is fallen?"

"By my hand, Colonel," Kylac admitted. Garnham may have seen as much, given his urgent arrival. "The rest, I leave to your command. And yours," he added, offering Ledron one of his blades.

"I . . . my duty is to Her Majesty."

"Then dispatch me to find her. Unburdened, the swifter I'll do so."

Garnham glanced round at the Addaran soldiers still hauling themselves from the muck, watching them slink from Kylac and the closing Grenarr with due haste. "What says I don't leave the pair of you to rot alongside him?"

Whether or not the colonel had witnessed Bahsk's murder, Kylac felt certain he'd observed the fight that had ensued. Else he'd have taken sterner action already. "Because your people need every sword and heart they can muster. And the captain here stands among your finest."

Ledron seemed at a rare loss. Ever so staunch and certain in his objectives, he'd come to terms with the likelihood that Denariel was already dead, and his countrymen here in greater, more immediate need of whatever service he might render. It was only his oath as royal guardian, and his intractable dedication to it, that caused him now to consider elsewise.

Garnham spat. "Those who stand with us are on the move," he reminded them, sounding none too pleased by it.

The Head's torment was plain on his face. "You'll return her to me?"

"Or the hide o' the creature that devoured her," Kylac assured him, with all the solemnity he could muster. "At Indranell, if'n ya can rally this brood and keep her walls intact."

Ledron scowled, but finally accepted the offered sword. "I'll leave word, should we find ourselves elsewhere." He extended an arm, which Kylac clasped, even understanding it to be a gesture intended not as friendship, but to hold him to his claims.

"A mount, Colonel, if'n ya can spare it."

Garnham snarled, but signaled to one of his lieutenants, who gripped the lead of a riderless steed. When the horse was brought forward, Kylac motioned for Ledron to take it.

"What of you?" the Blackfist asked.

Kylac nodded toward the canyon's western wall. "I mean to take a more direct route than what brought us here. Mayhap learn a thing or two about our enemy's movements in the process."

Ledron's scowl deepened, but they'd already spent what time there was to waste. Garnham's regiment had formed a defensive wedge around their position, waiting to receive the Grenarr. But the howls of those seeking to test it were fast approaching.

"Farewell, Captain."

Kylac bolted, taking up another discarded sword as he went. Weaving past soldiers fleeing and fallen, skirting boulders and fissures and rain-fed streams, he pressed through the storm, his aim upon the western wall. He didn't look back, trusting Ledron and Garnham and the others to do what was needed for themselves—what was best for their people. They'd have much to sort out later, the army's new leadership. A grievous toll from their defeat here, and the desperate choices it would leave them. But he had his own challenge now ahead of him, and so couldn't be further burdened with theirs.

Ahead, a line of Grenarr awaited him, trickled down from the heights, their weapons gleaming with wetness and a reflected flash of lightning. Kylac felt a familiar tingle rising along his spine, bringing a faint smile to his lips.

Mayhap he could offer his forsaken Addaran comrades some small, final assistance after all.

23

A CLOUD OF BLOOD GNATS took to the air as Kylac pressed through the tall grasses, joining the clinging swarm that had been trailing his progress for the better part of an hour. There was no help for it. He'd discovered that even the slightest brush of the reedy stalks was enough to disturb the insects hidden among them, and that, once uprooted, the gnats seemed to multiply with every step—as if drawn to his pulsing heartbeat. He might have sought to circumvent their domain altogether, but the lowland meadow stretched for miles to either side, with no guarantee that the bothersome insects wouldn't follow him into the jungles beyond.

To say nothing of abandoning the trail he'd labored so diligently to find.

Since abruptly taking his leave of Ledron and the others, he'd been working a jagged course chiefly north and west across the south-central Addaran landscape. From Rendenel Run, he'd angled immediately along that heading, tracing canyon pathways or scaling bluffs—whichever was most direct—until reaching the Karamoor. Skirting the highway, he'd then raced northward until reaching Indranell, completing the return trek in some twenty-four hours—a mere portion of the five days' time it had taken the army to prepare and then stray from her southern gates.

Along the way, he'd found canyons and highway and even the city walls only loosely plagued by Grenarr patrols, suggesting that the bulk of Sabrynne's forces had in fact been diverted through the Strebolen. A welcome reassurance, where reassurances had come to be in short supply. Tempted as he'd been to enter the city to warn Fayne of events to the south—and mayhap question the colonel as to his potential knowledge of enemy troop movements—Kylac had determined to risk no more delays, and thus veered promptly northwest, rounding Indranell along the road to Severstone.

Before dusk, he'd regained the lakeside banks of Urseth's marina, where he skulked about until setting sight upon the same burly son who'd retrieved Denariel's stolen boat on the night of their prior encounter. Conveniently enough, the lad was engaged in boarding an ill-tempered military merchant—along with his armed retainers and their empty wagons—onto a barge. A contingent from Indranell striking forth, it seemed, to retrieve an overdue delivery of weapons from an armorer to the west. So Kylac had taken the opportunity to sneak aboard and cross to the western bank, whereupon, as the merchant soldiers dispersed, Kylac persuaded the youth to show him where Denariel had gone ashore.

Tamping down a useless regret at finally resuming the chase some six days after his initial opportunity to do so, he'd set off in pursuit.

Once upon her trail, he'd had no great difficulty following it. She'd clearly been more concerned with haste, at that juncture, than stealth. Had she shown willingness to venture into more populated areas, along busier roadways, she might have been harder to track. But her footsteps had her keeping clear of any well-worn pathways, and avoiding the mostly abandoned settlements that cropped up now and again along the edges of her course. Here and there, she'd surfaced in search of food stores—invisibly, in most instances. At one point, she'd been identified by a hobbled root-digger as a thieving, half-breed urchin who'd vanished before any could run her down. At another, she'd stolen a mule and ridden the poor beast to an early grave. By and large, however, she'd kept to herself amid the woodland brush, shying from any who might recognize her.

Would that she'd been discovered, captured, delayed, so as to speed resolution to this chase. Alas, an unlikely possibility, as best as Kylac had been able to discern. Even if pinned down, who would believe this vagabond to be the royal princess? And if she *was* found out, who would have cause or the necessary courage to hold her?

The hope had grown only more remote the farther he'd trekked. Villages had given way to hamlets, hamlets to scattered farms and ranches, and farms and ranches to solitary outposts, as Denariel's determined footsteps angled out along the frontier stretches marking the fringes of the Reach.

And finally beyond, into the Harrows themselves.

If there'd been a line to mark the precise boundary or threshold, Kylac had somehow missed it. But he'd not missed the changes that had gradually overtaken the land—the increasingly rugged terrain, the wilder growth, the untamed creatures that inhabited both. He'd sensed their movements, their primal curiosity, their savage, yet wary intentions. By then, he'd ceased to concern himself with the length of her lead. Despite her dogged pace, he'd gained ground swiftly. Refusing to rest but for momentary snatches totaling an hour each day and an hour each night, he'd covered more than seven leagues per arc—seven to her three—since discovering her lakeshore footprints. On his third day out from Severstone, he believed himself to be no more than a day, day and a half, behind her.

What plagued him now was the growing fear that he might stumble across a pile of her bones, scraped and gnawed by the teeth of some wild animal. More and more, he had to steel himself against the mental image, as the land's denizens grew increasingly hostile toward one another. A screech here, a snap or flutter there, to herald the conflict—typically sudden and brief—between predator and prey. While nothing larger than an ant or blood gnat had dared yet to threaten *him*, he could sense a growing menagerie of creatures scenting him, eyeing him, even stalking him now and again before turning away, uncertain what to make of him and thus declining the inherent risk.

It caused him to marvel again at Denariel's fortitude. She'd been right there alongside him, at every step, during his first trek through the Harrows. The one captained by Ledron, and guided by Trajan, in an effort to return her to Avenell from where Kylac had met them, in the city of Wingport on the southern coast of Kuuria. He'd seen evidence then, and understood better now, that she'd viewed some of that death and carnage differently than he had. But she'd witnessed the same horrors, and so understood clearly that the perils she might face would only increase the deeper she delved into this forbidden wilderness.

Yet here she'd been, burrowing onward, into the heart of the most fiendish territory that Kylac, for one, had yet experienced.

Countering that, she'd traveled these lands to a greater extent than most—more, mayhap, than anyone truly knew. And that familiarity did provide her some advantages. That she'd made it even this far demonstrated her recognition of certain hazards, and an understanding of how to avoid them. Which foods to forage, and which to leave untouched. Which game trails to follow, and which to tread clear of. Which streams to drink from, and which to bypass. Had she been oblivious to the land's perils, she'd have fallen ill—or been killed—days earlier.

But did she know where she was going? That she'd become fixated on a particular aim didn't necessarily indicate that she knew where or how to achieve it. Into the Harrows, in search of the infamous Talathandria. One rogue queen seeking another. But, allowing for a moment that the latter even existed, where might this Talathandria be found? Did Denariel have a specific destination in mind, or was her plan to simply wander the Ukinhan Wilds in hopes that the object of her search might find *her*?

Even trusting elsewise, telling himself over and again that the Denariel he knew couldn't be *that* foolhardy, Kylac wasn't quite convinced. And so he continued to be driven by an inescapable sense of urgency. He'd traveled more than sixteen consecutive hours now since his last rest, pausing only to refill his waterskin, scrounge a handful of edible roots, and to more closely inspect the signs of Denariel's passage where the path she may have taken appeared uncertain. While he'd found no recent attempts by her to deceive potential pursuers, he certainly wasn't going to assume that she was finished doing so, should the need or opportunity arise. This lingering suspicion was really the only reason he didn't push himself harder, faster. Wary of making a mistake that would only set him farther back.

The chances for which increased, to some extent, with each stubborn stride. While possessed of an endurance to outstrip that of any other man or woman he'd known, he wasn't entirely immune to exhaustion. He could feel the debilitating effects of his taxing pace—blurring vision, fogging thoughts, to go with the strafing breaths and burning muscles. The toll in terms of recovery was mounting. And yet, content he'd be to pay it, if only for the expression on her face when finally he ran her down.

Hence his determination to push beyond weariness, hunger, pain. Beyond the itch of clutching grasses . . . the choking grit of dust and pollen in his eyes and lungs . . . the growing host of blood gnats. If Denariel had weathered their buzzing, biting presence, so would he. Nettlesome as he found them, they were in no way the most menacing presence to have taken interest in him. There were more dangerous predators out there even now, at the edges of his senses, skittering or slithering or prowling in all their myriad forms. For all Kylac knew, the gnats were what kept them at bay.

The meadow ran west for another league before being intersected by a narrow river. Denariel appeared to have forded at a shallows, so Kylac did the same. On the opposite bank, her trail turned northward, tracing the flow upstream toward a jungle woodland. The ground quickly grew humped and ragged, comprised of sediments pierced here and there by the telltale thrust of ironshore—razored, pitted formations of the limestone that served bedrock to this isle. Having traversed the dreaded Ironshore Wastes, Kylac had navigated more than his share of the treacherous ground already. But if Denariel had seen fit to come this way, so be it.

Fortunately, the ironshore remained mostly buried, its jagged ridges and craggy planes smoothed and softened by hard-packed clays and looser soils. Like a sharp-edged skeleton wrapped in flesh. While carving the earth into misshapen humps, it wasn't the cleaving, shearing obstacle it could have been if fully exposed.

The jungle growth thickened as the afternoon wore on. Kylac welcomed the profusion. Though tangled and thorny, marked by scratching spines and raking nettles, it offered shade from the sun's oppressive heat, and showed more clearly the path Denariel had forged.

It also teemed with wildlife. With birds and rodents and snakes and insects and other clinging, clawing creatures of limitless variety. He heard them more than he saw them, chittering or screeching or wailing or warbling in whatever manner most suited them. He felt as before their collective curiosity, their instinctive wariness measured against a feral hunger. Was he predator, or might he be prey?

He left them to guess, passing through as surreptitiously as he could manage, understanding at the same time that, while he might make himself all but invisible among men, there were surely creatures here who might smell his sweat, sense his body's heat, or feel the vibrations of his movements at a hundred paces or more.

But anything that took note of him maintained a comfortable distance, else settled for some other, more familiar meal upon making approach. Giving Kylac continued hope that they might have regarded Denariel much the same.

As the daylight waned, however, his impressions of the inhabiting brood took on a darkening cast. While it might have been the product of a mind addled for want of sleep, his instincts came to warn him of a growing sense a peril. Of one or more creatures hunting him, and bold enough, this time, to carry through on the threat.

A vague sensation, at first, without focus or direction. But that changed as dusk settled, the ominous feelings growing stronger, more pronounced. The true problem, he decided, was that there were too many of them. Difficult to draw bead on where a particular attack might come from, when there was a plethora of them vying for his attention.

He tried not to be troubled. He'd battled man and beast of every known variety, slain demons and dragonspawn, survived tarrocks and deadskin beetles and a jaggeruunt. Even the dreaded Ukinha he'd encountered had proven less than his equal. What remained on these or any other shores to challenge him?

Of course, he'd been much better armed in most instances, given the blades now lost to him. Nor had he so much *defeated* the deadlier creatures of Addaranth as *escaped* them. His battle-seasoned confidence was well earned. But vain and foolish he'd have to be to believe himself impervious to any number of potential assailants. It needn't be the teeth or claws of some ravening beast to end him. He'd seen firsthand that, in this territory, a single bite, a single sting, a single brush with the wrong vine or leaf, could leave him rotting on the jungle floor as easily as any man.

But if he was vulnerable, Denariel was more so. Warded by her knowledge and experience, but lacking even a sliver of his combat skills. Whatever these promptings of self-concern, his greater worry was for her. For if he were to venture all this way, only to fail . . .

He pushed the thought and others like it from his mind. As often as they struggled to surface, he smothered them, again and again. Taking strength from their warnings, but refusing to submit to fear. At its heart, this excursion represented the very reason he drew breath, to seek and overcome challenges that would either bolster or conclude his life's legacy. Throughout his travels, he'd yet to discover any higher purpose. It was what had carried him from place to place, adventure to adventure, since setting forth on his own.

By that reasoning, what better place to be?

Night fell, and the darkness deepened. But the jungle didn't sleep. If anything, its cacophony grew louder, its activities more frenzied. Amid a rising cadence of chirping and croaking and hissing came the snap, crack, and rustle of heavier movements. Smaller animals shrieked threats, cried out alarms, or trilled laments. But the growls and snarls of larger creatures increased, too, often overlapping in brief flurries of furious struggle—unseen save for the thrashing of the surrounding vegetation. The daylight aromas, so sickly sweet, grew somehow more pungent, more invasive. Kylac thought he smelled blood on the breeze.

If likened to a river, he'd come upon a rapids. Whether stirred by the moonlight, or simply the nature of this deeper region, he couldn't say. Whichever, his senses thrummed in constant warning. It led him to wonder if mayhap he wouldn't have been wiser to take more rest at some point during the day, when it might have been safer to do so. Instinctively, he brought one of his stolen weapons to hand. A Grenarr sword, with all the style and grace and balance of a cleaver. Heavy and nicked and blunted, it felt like a woodsman's axe compared to his own missing blades. Better suited to felling trees and chopping logs than deterring an assailant.

But it was what he had. A pair of them, along with a small assortment of daggers and throwing knives. If called upon, that was what he would use. Better than rocks and branches or his bare hands.

He trekked for another hour, or near enough, before coming upon a hollow in the stony earth beneath a gnarled tuft of upturned roots at the base of a massive deadfall. A burrow of some kind, its mouth draped in moss and vines and a loose screen of freshly spun spiderwebs. Worms and centipedes slithered along its rim, else crawled within the moldering carpet of leaves and needles collected at its threshold—where a line of salt had been laid. Presumably as a deterrent, Kylac had learned, against some of the more venomous insects inhabiting this region.

Intrigued, he ducked through the entrance and down into the chamber beyond. It smelled of mold and fungus and bowels. The bloody remains of what might have passed as a squirrel, along with a dried stain of vomitus, suggested that Denariel had tried—and at least partially failed—to partake of its raw flesh. Indicating in all likelihood that she'd run out of her stolen food stores.

Additional marks confirmed his further suspicion. The young queen had slept here, taking refuge against whatever denizens prowled these jungle woods. It might have been the previous night, or midday before. But she'd resided here for a time, resting safely, before venturing out again to resume her journey.

The temptation overcame him to do the same. But that was the voice of weariness, to which he refused to listen. Resourceful as she continued to prove, there was nothing here to suggest that Denariel was enjoying similar shelter now. Why should he?

Distracted by his concern for her as he emerged from the burrow, Kylac had only a heartbeat's warning of the whiplike motion that coiled round his neck.

The stinging came first, like a collar full of needles, followed by a strangling crush, like a thick cord. An ensuing yank felt as though it might tear his head from his shoulders. But Kylac sprang with the sudden momentum, rather than resist it, bringing his sword up at the same time. A sense of force and angle told him where to aim the tip of his blade, and he did so as calmly and as certainly as he could manage.

The stabbing counter met with a meaty bite, accompanied by an agonized squeal. He gave the weapon a twist. The pressure around his neck slackened slightly. As he withdrew the blade, he selected a new angle and drew down in a slicing motion. Warm juices spurted, the creature shrieked again, and the choking pressure subsided further. Emboldened, Kylac followed with a sawing motion—and abruptly fell.

He landed on his knees, his back remaining to his attacker. But he spun and regained his feet in a single, fluid motion. He still wore the severed length of cord around his neck. A tail, he realized, as he watched the catlike creature at the other end of it flop and thrash atop the fallen tree. Kylac lunged, a sword in each hand now, with which he skewered the beast's neck and belly, putting a swift end to its suffering.

When certain it lacked the strength to retaliate, Kylac sheathed one of his blades and set about shedding the length of tail wrapped around his throat. A painful endeavor, given the barbed spines peppering its rodent-like skin. But better a dozen small rents in his own skin and rid of the thing quickly than to absorb whatever venom those barbs might contain.

Even before he'd tossed the appendage aside, he recognized the creature. He'd seen one before, though stripped of its furry hide. A strangletail, according to Trajan, his then-guide. A tree-dweller that used its tail as a noose, as Kylac had just learned. Somehow, he'd missed its arrival while inspecting Denariel's burrow.

And paid the price.

With all respect to his assailant—whatever its capacity for stealth—it should never have been able to ambush him like that. He should have heard, smelled, *felt* it approach. A culmination, mayhap, of his strange environs, his growing fatigue, his uncommonly weighty fears for Denariel. Collectively serving to dull, deceive, or elsewise confuse his typically reliable senses.

Or mayhap he merely needed something to eat. To drive himself as he had, as he must, he'd be well advised to feed himself better.

He eyed the twitching carcass of the strangletail, taking note of the flies and other insects flocking eagerly toward it. Trajan had never suggested the animals to be inherently inedible. They'd eschewed the one that they'd happened across only because whatever had slaughtered and skinned it had left it poisoned. Having killed this one himself, Kylac could be reasonably certain its meat was as yet unfouled.

He still had a lot of ground to cover before catching up to Denariel. Here he had an opportunity for food and shelter both. Neither was guaranteed on the road ahead. Mayhap he should reconsider leaving these apparent gifts behind. In hindsight, the temptation to rest may have been his intuition alerting him to precisely what his body required.

If so, he'd been mistaken to ignore it, and would be foolish to do so a second time.

The stinging from the cuts at his throat convinced him. He needed to clean them before moving on, mayhap even dress the wounds or at least mask their scent. He'd become overzealous, given to haste now that he was so close. When patience, he knew, was often the more trustworthy ally.

With an eye to the fluttering rhythms of his savage surroundings, he jabbed his unsheathed sword into the earth, planting it within ready reach.

And set about his tasks.

24

The song of the jungle played ceaselessly in Kylac's ears, just beneath the surface of his consciousness. Its harsh, discordant refrains had nonetheless come to approximate a dull roar, normal in all its wild irregularities. Like the crash and swirl of ocean waves against a rugged shore, or the thrumming rage of a lightning storm. Already, he'd come to discern which sounds and tones belonged, and which might indicate danger. Enabling him to slumber undisturbed amid the cacophonous din.

The weighty huffing sound that jarred him awake was something new, and raised his hackles with immediate alarm. He'd listened to dozens of heavy rustlings *before* settling down to sleep, while atop the ironshore ridge where he'd lit a cookfire to roast his spitted strangletail. His fire's light and the smell of roasted meat—providing the best meal he'd enjoyed in days—had proven an irresistible lure for any number of scavenging animals. He'd glimpsed their shadowy forms, both slender and lithe, hulking and brutish, amid the shadowed foliage at the edges of his flames' aura. Each marked by gleaming eyes or probing appendages that reflected its primal hunger. A parade of predators who'd come no nearer than the base of the ridge, held at bay by the heat or the aroma of seared strangletail or whatever it was they sensed of *him*.

But that had been uphill, some sixty paces northeast, where he'd left the fire burning, along with the remains of the carcass, as a distraction while he slunk back down to the burrow that had housed Denariel and now housed him. The carcass had been snatched away and ripped apart, by the sound of it, almost as soon as he'd abandoned the rocky overlook. But the fire continued to serve as a beacon even now—three, mayhap four hours later. The larger visitors that might elsewise have discovered him had been congregating chiefly up there. This would be the first, insofar as his senses had alerted him, to come sniffing around his hole.

He held his cramped position, stilling his own breathing, attuned now to the creature's slow, lumbering approach.

A guttural snarl sent slivers of ice through his veins. It was the only warning he received before a mad dash, startlingly swift, brought an armored head thrusting through the burrow opening. Kylac recoiled instinctively, as the creature's beaklike mouth open and closed repeatedly, snapping like a giant turtle gone mad. Only the broad contours of its squat, disk-shaped, heavily shelled body—also very turtlelike—prevented it from tearing through and having at him in full force.

Even so, Kylac had withdrawn already as far as he could against the burrow's rear wall, and the great turtle, if the rabid beast could be described as such, continued to scrabble and flail in its effort to break through. Horny protrusions and serrated ridges ringed its armored shell, carving at the burrow mouth with each thrashing motion. All while its clawed feet groped and dug at the earth, and its beak snapped at the end of an elongating neck, issuing a stuttering growl.

Kylac produced one of his daggers and took aim at its reptilian throat. With eyes that appeared to be closed, however, the creature's head whipped and jabbed and elsewise worked to swat the countering thrusts aside. A slavering foam had gathered upon the rims of its beak, flinging about in sticky strings. When a line of it fell across Kylac's hand, his skin flared as if singed.

All at once, he regretted confining himself to this restrictive space. His idea, like Denariel's before him, had been to elude detection, and to safeguard himself from all attack vectors but one. The consequence being that he'd left himself trapped. With the bony monstrosity before him filling the only breach, and fighting so furiously to enter, he appeared to have nowhere to run. Should it manage to force its way fully inside . . .

Lacking the space in which to maneuver a sword, he drew another dagger. Feinting with the first enabled him to land a deep prick with the second. The creature screeched in response, retracting its neck and head into its domed shell.

And kept coming.

Kylac poked and jabbed at the shell itself, but the bony plates repelled his weapons with ease. He wasn't certain that his own would have fared much better. A pointless question, given their unknown whereabouts. Rendering him all but powerless as he watched the creature heave and rip and saw in its frantic attempts to reach him.

He couldn't help but wonder what he might have done to incite the beast. Despite the many predators and scavengers that had marked his presence these past few days, only the strangletail had been so brazen as to launch an attack before now. Ill fortune, he supposed, that the second creature to do so would be possessed of such strength and aggression . . .

He scored a number of hits to its legs and feet, but these proved to be of no real deterrent. The scaly appendages bled but little—like gouging a tree trunk to draw thin lines of sap. There was a measure of pain, given the creature's hacking, throaty whines, but it seemed not to regard the strikes as vitally harmful.

Choking back a rising desperation, Kylac took to digging at the back wall of his burrow, aiming upward at an angle that might permit him egress amid the overarching nest of tree roots. Of all the many ways his life might end, he preferred it not be in a pre-hollowed grave such as this, his flesh ground to pulp in a sunless, worm-infested dark. He'd sooner his last breath be one of air freely drawn, rather than a suffocating inhalation of dirt.

The new effort met with some encouraging success. Not only was the packed soil giving way easily, but a fair portion of it was cascading down upon his assailant, confounding its efforts. The loose sediments would hardly slow the beast, should it manage to tear past the thick roots framing the burrow mouth. But its snorting, squealing reactions suggested that its primary senses, whatever those might be, were distracted, confused, or elsewise irritated by the earthen rain falling upon it.

Of course, were he unable to tunnel into the open, he might succeed merely in burying himself alive.

He was still chiseling away, pondering which fate might be worse, when the creature gave a raspy yowl and abruptly retreated. Kylac froze, giving ear to what might have caused its departure, and what it might mean. A screeching, singsong lament suggested injury of some sort. The stamping, thrashing movements further suggested pain . . . or battle. Listening closely, he detected now a rattle he hadn't heard before, accompanied by an occasional, threatening hiss.

Kylac lingered another moment, reflecting on his options. He could remain here and hope that whatever had drawn his assailant would continue to do so. He could continue digging his alternate escape route, in case the creature—or some other attacker—returned. Or he could bolt now, while it seemed he had the chance, and face any further threats this night head-on.

He pushed toward the entrance almost before he knew he'd decided. Another hesitation as he thrust his head—and daggers—through the breach was short-lived. The dome-shelled turtle creature was six paces away, its massive, flat-bellied body spinning and snapping at a hooded, asplike serpent bearing a rattle-tipped tail. Kylac could tell at a glance, based on the portion held upright when it recoiled, that the serpent was more than twenty feet in length. Locked in mortal challenge, neither combatant had time to spend on him.

Or so he imagined.

Flat on his elbows, he scurried through, out into the blissfully open air. The combatants didn't miss his emergence, given the way each eyed and hissed at him. But neither seemed inclined to break away from the confrontation at hand. The serpent was landing continual strikes to the turtle's meaty tail, which swished overhead with a great bony knob at its end. Fighting to line up a clear strike of its own, if Kylac had to guess.

Curious as he was about the outcome, he wasn't waiting around for it to be finished. Instead, he turned at once and dashed along

Denariel's trail, thinking to be well gone by the time the victor could disentangle itself from the vanquished.

Alas, the pair determined elsewise. Plodding footfalls and the scrape of bone against earth suggested the turtle rounding to give chase. A glance confirmed it, and revealed also the serpent slithering in pursuit.

At a full sprint over even ground, he might have been able to outpace them. Amid the jungle's rutted tangle, in the moonlit dark, it would seem a poor decision. For the chance they might keep pace with him anyway, yes, but also because it would be too easy to misread some critical print or marker and veer from Denariel's path, forcing him to double back at some point to find it again.

He cut right instead, angling uphill along the footpath to his earlier cooking site. The turtle veered after him, the serpent still sniping at its tail and the softer edges of its underbelly. The former scurried and squawked, the latter slithered and rattled. Given the commotion of their passage, and the heat of their bestial ire, he marked their progress without looking back, maintaining much-needed focus on the narrow track ahead. Whatever the ferocity of his pursuers, he wasn't going to be so distracted by them that he neglected the myriad hazards that might yet seek to ambush him.

As he made his ascent, he wondered again as to the turtle-beast's rage—and what he might do to mollify it. However slim the hope, he'd prefer it trundle off and leave him be, rather than force him to kill it. All else aside, he'd hate to repeat his mistake and provoke another one.

Upon clearing the fringe of vegetation that marked the base of the ridge, a swarm of rodentlike creatures dispersed like a school of frightened fish. Ignoring them, Kylac sheathed his daggers and produced his swords. That and the open ground made him feel better about his chances. With a running leap, he hurdled the still-burning flames of his fire pit, hoping that their heat—or brightness—might serve some small dissuasion.

On the other side of the fire, he secured his footing and came about, putting his back to the open ledge and bringing his blades up in a spinning flourish.

With another stuttering cry, the turtle-beast came charging through the fire, scattering brands, throwing embers, and shooting sparks into the sky. The heedless approach caught Kylac by surprise, but suggested immediately what to do. With an encouraging yell, he back-stepped nearer the ledge, until his toes were perched upon its very rim. Trusting in the strength of the ironshore to hold his weight. Squinting and holding his breath against the curtains of smoke, he dropped into a crouch . . .

And somersaulted forward as the turtle reached him. Its face craned upward, hardened beak snapping. Its domed body rounded. But its weight and momentum were too great. For half a heartbeat, it teetered upon the precipice, then toppled over the edge.

He listened to its angry wail as it fell, and the great splash it made when it struck the swampy waters some thirty heads below. Alive, he suspected—and hoped, for all the further harm it might do him from down there. Should it drown . . . well, it hadn't presented him a great deal of choice.

His satisfaction proved brief. Deprived of its quarry, the serpent lashed out at *him*, piercing a veil of smoke with fangs extended. With his former blades, Kylac could have swatted it aside. As matters stood, he dodged, knowing he'd never bring the heavier Grenarr swords up in time. The movement left him stumbling momentarily over a tangle of charred branches, while the serpent coiled and lunged, coiled and lunged, and coiled and lunged again in lightning-swift procession.

By the fourth attempt, Kylac had found his balance and taken measure of its rhythms and strike patterns. He caught its next lunge with his blades crossed. When he sheared them apart, the strange asp's hooded head flew from its retreating body.

Kylac spun as the head struck the ground, swatting it with a blade tip out over the ledge—from where he now heard a mournful bellowing that he attributed to the fallen turtle-beast. He used his other blade to hold the serpent's still-thrashing body at bay. Given its continued coiling and lunging, he might have thought it still alive, only blind and therefore directionless in its attacks. But its motions quickly degraded into flipping and flopping along its coiled length, an almost pitiable dance were it not for the intense rattling of its shivering tail.

When that had ceased, and all that remained was the feeble slap of its final death throes against the limestone earth, Kylac peered through the scattered bits of flame and the lingering curtains of smoke to the surrounding jungle. Its dissonant song persisted, trilling and piercing. He heard shrieks and growls amid the night-cloaked tangle, but sensed no imminent threat. Alas. He was fully awake now, fully focused. Tinged with euphoria at the prospect of further challenge.

Mayhap the jungle's denizens could sense it, for they kept their distance, those who watched him from their shadowy perches, or skulked behind their shadowy cover. Better for them that they did so, he thought. Better for him, of course, too. He hadn't ventured out here to confront and butcher strange animals. His purpose was to track Her Majesty and ensure her safety. To that end, he was now but squandering precious moments. He'd taken all the rest he was liable to find here.

Time to be on his way.

Putting the serpent's twitching corpse and the turtle's lamentations behind him, Kylac picked his way past the coals and brands and smoky curtains strewn about the ridge to reenter the jungle. Moments later, he'd resumed a northwesterly course along Denariel's trail. As a consequence of his chaotic scuffle, he wondered now if the queen might have encountered either of the same creatures—and what she could have done to repel them if she had. More likely, she'd avoided them to begin with. Could she continue to do so? What other creatures lay out there, prowling these jungle woods or the deeper wilds that lay ahead?

The question stirred his earlier anxiety, stoking a twinge of guilt. What might have happened to her while he slept? Had his justifications for doing so truly outweighed the need to reach her as swiftly as possible? How might he feel were he to catch up to her, only to discover that he should have done so just a few hours earlier?

A maddening circle of uncertainty, the likes of which he was quite unaccustomed to. Actions bred consequences. Inaction, the same. A man who worried over the limitless possibilities of one or the other could be driven to paralysis. Kylac's past was marred with sufferings inflicted against those to whom he'd committed himself. Yet he couldn't recall a time in which he'd worried more for the outcome of a particular endeavor, or second-guessed himself to the degree he did now.

Did that imply some deeper level of care or concern for Denariel than what he would readily admit to? He didn't believe so. It seemed more a culpability he'd assumed upon involving himself in her affairs without ensuring first a fuller understanding of the forces at play. But then, how many times did he have to risk his life in her defense before that perceived debt was paid? Did she not bear enough responsibility of her own, at this point, to overshadow whatever obligation he might have owed her?

More unanswerable questions. All he knew was that he felt compelled to see the matter through. To what end remained somewhat murky. What if the Grenarr couldn't be repelled? What if Denariel and her people were destined to be slaughtered or driven into the wilds? Would he stand to fight for them? Suffer their fate alongside? Should Denariel fall, would the compulsion to serve her wishes persist?

Easier not think about it. To put the matter aside, insistent as those thoughts were proving to be, and focus instead upon the more immediate task. Survive what remained of the night, and see what the morrow might bring.

He'd soon settled into a comfortable pace, balanced between speed and caution. The eyes of the jungle's denizens marked his progress—amid the gnarled trees, the walls of brush, the tangled ground cover. Cooling breezes were no match for the sultry air, which left him sweaty and chafing in his borrowed tunic. He missed his customary, lightweight garb almost as much as he missed his blades. He wondered when he might lay claim again to either.

A swamp shrike flew overhead, shrieking at him before diving like an arrow into the trees. A little farther on, a flock of winged rodents trimmed with hooks and spines came swirling around him like a small, black funnel cloud. These disappeared once he'd plucked a pair of them out of the air, skewering them with the tips of his swords. He spied weasels of uncertain variety, what might have been a breed of fox, a pack of three-legged boars with spiny plates cresting their backs, and a furred monstrosity that reminded him of the fearsome ta'aktra inhabiting the gulf island of Nivvia, off the Pentanian coast of Vosges. Most were simply on about their own business, moving quickly across or away from his path. Others appeared to have sniffed him out specifically, proceeding to size him up as a potential meal before slinking off elsewhere—often driven by something deadlier. Still others stalked him intently for various stretches of time, darting, hopping, crawling, slinking, or shuffling as suited their various forms.

As always, he gave feel to the rhythms of life around him, exotic and eerie as so much of it seemed. Gaining as before a fundamental sense of what might be deemed normal activities in this region, and what disturbances his presence might cause. Searching for ripples amid the flow like eddies in a river's current. Mindful at the same time of the many hazards that lurked in relative stillness. Creatures, yes, but also vegetation. Plants that Trajan had cautioned him about, some of which he'd seen firsthand. He wasn't likely to forget the great banethistle, stricthyus krahl, that could pull and constrict a man into so many broken pieces, or melt his flesh with the acids that ran through its stalks. Colors and sheens, though muted at night, served warning as to other growth possessed of natural poisons that could irritate or incapacitate. Some rare, some prevalent. All to be avoided.

He could still but guess as to what extent Denariel had spared him by carving this particular track. Surely he'd have found passage more difficult, the dangers greater, had he been following another. A land didn't go untamed for the centuries that this one had were its perils not real and formidable.

Another presented itself as he descended a rugged slope toward a narrow vale. A breed of beechwood grew thickly here, broad-leaved, with stout trunks for all their twisted frames. Amid the network of branches came a chittering that seemed at first almost friendly in tone. The fist-sized faces of the animals responsible for the noise, wizened and leathery and ringed in fur, spoke of innocent curiosity. Their lithe little bodies, no larger than a human infant's, only leaner and hook-tailed, bore none of the scales or claws or spiny ridges that might indicate obvious threat.

But the farther he delved, the more of the creatures he spied, leaping from branch to branch in a thickening swarm. Keeping pace. Calling out to others. Before long, the tenor of their song darkened, becoming more raucous, more mocking, more cruel. At much the same time, Kylac observed that the jungle elsewise had grown increasingly quiet, the great bulk of its inhabitants remaining behind on the slopes above. Whatever lived in these trees, this was their domain, and oddities like himself weren't welcome.

But this was the path Denariel had taken, and so Kylac cleaved to it stubbornly. Even when the clinging, treebound creatures began dropping from their perches, taking up their pursuit of him from all angles. Screeching in anticipation. Revealing now the long fangs hidden behind their false smiles. Bounding and leaping and chittering to one another and to him with maddened glee.

When they dropped before him, too, dozens strong and with a force of hundreds backing them, Kylac paused and drew his swords. He eyed their benign little faces, but sensed their fiendish intent, as their teeming numbers gradually closed round. Watching them bounce and clamber, each over the other, in their eagerness, he wondered how many of their flock he might have to kill before the rest would let him pass.

All at once, they surged at him like a cresting wave, and he set about finding out.

25

The sun's dawning rays cast a crimson sheen over the stream's waters, all but indistinguishable from the russet clouds of blood and dirt scrubbed from Kylac's hands.

And face, and neck, and arms, and torso, once he'd shed his tattered tunic and had a closer look at the many tiny lacerations that raked his skin. The blood in the stream thickened. There was no knowing how much of it was his, and how much his assailants', save that there was more of the latter. For all the scratches and scrapes he'd suffered, he'd wounded or killed at least ten times that number of the savage little tree-clingers—more than seven hundred in all—before leaving them behind in a shrieking chorus of rage and indignity.

Guilty they'd made him feel for it, too, with their mourning outcry, though they'd been the ones to initiate and sustain the attack. Had he been able, he'd have gladly explained to them that he sought only to pass through, intending no harm. Somehow, he doubted it would have made any difference. The viciousness with which the insatiable little creatures had clutched and torn at him had made bloodletting inevitable. In that regard, the burden of their terrible losses was theirs to bear.

Grateful he was that their teeth and claws hadn't been envenomed. Or so he presumed, having carried his injuries with him for hours now without ill effect. For all he truly knew, he was dead already and just waiting for his body to realize it. But he'd opted not to sit around, supposing that might happen. He'd pressed on, through the latter portion of the night and early hours of predawn, determined that the next day should mark his long-sought reunion with Denariel.

The tree-clingers hadn't been the last creature to test him. There'd been the wolfish animal with its quill-like hackles, an acid-spewing worm as thick as his arms, and a pack of rodents armored like beetles who'd sniffed him out when he'd found himself waylaid by a hidden quagmire. None of these, however, had shown the same voraciousness, the sheer tenacity, that the tree-clingers had. Enabling him to dispatch or deter them without strenuous effort.

Still, a relief it had been when he'd come upon the stream, too brackish in taste to refill his waterskin, but clear enough to merit a cleansing of the filth accumulated over the recent course of his journey. Had he more time, he might have followed it for a stretch, seeking a deeper pool in which to immerse himself fully—tarrocks and other hazards permitting. Alas, he dared not stray at this juncture from Denariel's trail. The waters he could capture and direct with cupped hands would have to prove refreshment enough.

When satisfied his stinging injuries were as clean as he might make them, he wrung his tunic and donned it anew. Gathering his few possessions, he crossed the narrow streambed and headed westward, into another meadow of towering grasses. The dry, reedy stalks were thin and willowy, but densely rooted, all but blinding him to his surroundings. Gusty breezes stirred the tips, masking the rustlings of any creatures lurking among them. Kylac was given instead to listen to the chitterings and snortings and raspings of the meadow's many invisible inhabitants, or marking their presence and their intentions by less physical means.

The field enveloped him for more than an hour, shimmering golden as the morning sun climbed higher at his back, a great ocean of windswept shoots and leaves. The trail he followed was little more than a narrow thread, weaving from side to side with the rugged contours of the earth. He came across no campsites, no signs suggesting Denariel had paused to rest. So neither did he.

At last, the grasses tapered off, spilling into a narrow glen wedged between twin hills of pitted ironshore. Kylac kept to the glen as Her Majesty had, eyeing the slopes to either side and the blocks of razor-edged shale piled amid the scrub and brush grown upon them. Angry echoes called down to him, howls and wails and other shrieking calls from creatures beyond the reaches of his vision. Given the dearth of vegetation, it wasn't clear as to where they hid. Amid crags and caves in the hills themselves, he supposed.

The glen gave way to a bog, the bog to a squat range of mountains, and the mountains to what might have been a prairie were it not for the sharp hummocks of ironshore that gave it the look of a frozen sea. The land of the Harrows was proving remarkably diverse. Amid elevations both high and low, he crossed ground that was either smooth or buckled, arid or wet, glaringly desolate or stunningly fertile. He estimated that, by now, he was somewhere amid the heart of the Sundered Isle, as far as he was likely to range from any of her broken shorelines. Still trekking north and west as the terrain permitted.

Into or away from danger, he couldn't have said. Only that, much as he tried, he failed to travel unmolested. Attacks such as those weathered during the night harried him throughout the day. Creatures both solitary and in packs. Some blatant and ferocious, others more subtle and tentative. All seeming desperate and determined to prey upon him—at least until he'd proven himself a more difficult target than what he appeared.

Mayhap it was some scent he carried—or one he didn't. By his observations, the musk that would seem to repel one breed of animal served only to attract or incite another. And while each attack taught him that much more about the nature of the land's denizens, bolstering his already abundant confidence in his ability to survive among them, it stirred also his worries for Denariel, causing him to question anew whether she could have truly managed to progress so far without bodily harm. It wasn't that she'd avoided all conflicts. In several instances, he'd found evidence of struggle between her and the native wildlife. That he'd seen no sign of significant injury, as of yet, didn't necessarily mean she'd passed unscathed.

But her trail stretched on, and so he clung to it, without deviation, carving his way past the various predators rather than seeking to avoid them, fearing that, at any moment, he might happen across the grisly evidence of Her Impetuous Majesty having succumbed to one or more of the land's perils.

For all his misgivings, however, she continued to surprise, defying the odds that would have had her perishing days ago. It wasn't until midafternoon, as the Kingfisher's Hour gave way to the Swallow's, that he found just cause for real concern. For it was then that he spied the tracks that overlapped hers—not in passing, but in pursuit. The large, padded feet resembled a man's, only broader, and much heavier, with splayed toes trimmed in claws. An animal that shed both fur and scales, it trundled at times on four legs, and at others shuffled along upright. Given the length of its strides, it didn't appear to be in any tremendous hurry, giving Kylac hope that Denariel might continue to outpace it. And yet, the mangled condition of the animal carcasses left in its path suggested a remarkably efficient killing capacity that had less to do with hunger, and more with an innate, ravenous cruelty.

For some reason, it caused him to recall the creature that had hunted him and Allion during their trek to Mount Krakken. A bloodless, pitiless, relentlessly savage beast that had followed them without a heartbeat's hesitation into the lair of Killangrathor himself. Though he'd not readily admit it, the memory still haunted his dreams on occasion. And the very thought that such a creature could have set itself in pursuit of Denariel sent a raw chill through his bones.

But that had been a minion of the so-called Demon Queen, Spithaera. A demon hailing originally from some alternate plane of existence, if the Entients were to be believed. Kylac wasn't entirely convinced that they were. For all their knowledge and mysticism, theirs was a secretive, self-serving agenda that merited mistrust. Regardless, he'd encountered no creature before or since characteristic of Spithaera's demons or Killangrathor's dragonspawn. The nearest to their ilk would have to be the mutant groll, universally held as the deadliest creation on these unnatural shores. By that measure, his fears were overwrought.

Were they not?

They nagged at him nonetheless as the Swallow was chased by the

Wren and the Wren by the Eagle. It troubled Kylac that he hadn't caught up to Denariel by then. Another dusk was only an hour away. She'd been traveling more swiftly that day than she had at any point since her initial departure. Did that signify alarm? Desperation? Could she have somehow learned what followed her? Glimpsed it from some stony overlook, mayhap? Might her sudden haste lead her to make some critical mistake?

The possibility gnawed at him until he began questioning his own efforts. Was he still on the correct path, or had a misstep caused him to stray somewhere along the way? Could it be that the trail he now followed belonged to another? How far might Denariel have gone in disguising her movements? Might her tracks, fresh as they now seemed, be but part of some greater ruse?

The echo of a roar served to scatter those doubts like the flocks of riventails sent screeching from the surrounding trees. His senses had carried him this far. If they'd taken to betraying him, losing Denariel would mark but the onset of a new rash of problems. If not, then the animal he followed was no more than a league ahead, and mayhap as little as a mile. Beyond the ridge of the deceptively steep slope he now climbed, certainly. But waiting, mayhap, on just the other side.

Willing it to be so, he broke into a dash along the gully by which Denariel and her stalker had navigated the sparsely wooded slope. Forty-eight bounding, leg-burning strides carried him to the ridge crest, which revealed to him a thorn-shaped valley tufted with jungle growth. Very much like the one at his back. Pausing in survey, his eyes were drawn almost at once to a pinnacle of rock near the valley's heart, mayhap a mile and a half in. Roughly three-quarters up the formation's southern face, a fire was growing, flickering dimly against the waning daylight and the backdrop of a shallow cave mouth. A dark form busied itself beside the flames, flitting here and there like a moth around a candle.

Almost directly beneath the flame-lit ledge, at least a hundred heads below, a great, apelike creature scrabbled against the bluff, seeking purchase with which to drag itself to higher elevations. Rocks and small, flaming projectiles rained upon it—cast down by the figure above, who he told himself could only be Denariel. As Kylac observed its struggle, the ape-thing roared, a huffing bellow rife with frustration and sharp with menace.

Kylac took but a moment to gauge from his perch the rugged features of the slope at his feet and the gnarled tangle of jungle at its base. Then he was running, sliding, skidding down its ravaged face, no longer greatly concerned with Denariel's trail—though it may have been the surest, safest descent—and focused instead on what appeared to be the faster, more direct route. He cringed instinctively at the need to forgo patience, knowing he stood to suffer for it. Yet, another inner voice insisted that the alternative would be the harder to live with.

Branches and brambles swiped and clawed at him in passing. Blind drops and hidden fissures yawned abruptly beneath him, as if to devour or ensnare. He sprang or tumbled past the cracked, rotted bones of creatures that had been so captured, their flesh and marrow consumed. He saw or elsewise sensed serpents, spiders, and crablike creatures lurking amid those darkened seams and hollows, eagerly awaiting his fall.

But Kylac had spent countless hours of his youth dancing upon the shifting beams and unstable pilings of his father's infamous tangleweb, and so proved nimble enough to escape the many potential pitfalls here. The hazardous descent deposited him finally upon the jungle floor, where an ironshore bedrock provided firm, if treacherous footing. Mindful of sinkholes and quagmires such as the one that had claimed him the night before, he dashed and threaded his way through the layers of growth, ducking or hurdling or sidestepping obstacles with every stride. When need be, he brought blades to bear, hacking at or swatting aside invasive strands of brush. Slashing and sawing at curtains of moss and ivy. Tunneling through the jungle's thorny, vine-ridden mesh.

All the while, he listened for indicators as to Denariel's effort to repel the scaling ape-creature. His last glimpse of them had come before reaching the base of the slope, revealing a climbing advance of about fifteen heads on the part of the ape. Enveloped now by the vegetation of the valley floor, he had only that prior pace and the echoes of the creature's continuing roars to go by. By now, he imagined the gap between ape and queen trimmed by half. And himself, too much ground yet to cover by far.

In his heedless haste, he very nearly ran headlong into a banethistle, alerted only heartbeats before by the pained yelp of some weasellike animal caught slinking around the plant's lethal vine tendrils—to be wrung and twisted like a sodden rag. Veering left to avoid near-certain death carried him past a hive of wasps. He felt fortunate to suffer only a half dozen stings in retribution, given the furious cloud that kept pace with him for a time. He felt more fortunate still when a pair of brightly plumed birds flew shrieking across his path, snapping up mouthfuls of the winged insects with their beaks and chasing the rest back toward their nest.

He weathered close encounters and narrow misses with venomous toads, a family of lava lizards feasting upon a hill of storm ants, and a startled strangletail. In each circumstance, however, he leapt or dodged or angled past, caring less for the nearness of his brush with each peril than he did for the ground gained as a result. As if he were running one of his father's dreaded gauntlets back at Talonar—only without the man's disapproving glare in observance. Envisioning it now almost caused Kylac to smile.

At last the brush receded around him, falling back like hungry waves denied by a craggy shore. Only, the shore ran for but a dozen paces before sloping sharply skyward. The base of the monolith, upthrust from the clutching jungle. The ape was more than two-thirds of its way to reaching the ledge inhabited—he was certain—by Denariel. From his present angle, he couldn't see the ledge itself, merely the underbelly of its protruding lip. That, and the glow of the unseen fire, brighter now as evening shadows worked to stake their claim upon the valley.

A flaming projectile like seen from afar dropped and bounced past his position, clattering off the rocks before settling amid the blanket of scree skirting the pinnacle's base. A seed cone, he realized. He wondered how many Denariel might have at her disposal, or how many armaments like it. If they hadn't dislodged or dissuaded the ape by now, what chance remained that they might?

With a cursory assessment of the pinnacle's bluff, he hastened forward to begin his climb. Would that he'd secured himself a bow, that he might loose a barrage of quarrels at the ape from below. But he'd always found bows relatively clumsy to wield and to carry, particularly when considering portage of the arrows themselves. Besides, while Allion's fascinating level of proficiency with the weapons had garnered his respect and piqued his interest for a time, the truth remained that, if inclined to take a life—be it man or beast—he felt he should be able to look his victim in the eye while doing so.

The rock's hide was strong and scabrous, riddled with protrusions and shot through with fissures. Handholds aplenty, most of which felt secure enough beneath his grasping hands and feet. He soon learned to avoid those covered in patches of red lichen, which tore away at the slightest brush. Elsewise, the stony face held few surprises. A scorpion here or there, tucked away in a crack or crevice, but these were generally withdrawn into the deeper, darker recesses, safely clear of his probing fingers. In all, a more efficient ascent than troubling with the shallow, broken switchbacks that crisscrossed the pinnacle's flesh like the scars of a flogging.

The greater dangers were those that continued to fall like hail around him—rocks and flaming seed cones and the broken limbs of dead trees. He didn't suspect that any were actually aimed at him, but that hardly seemed to matter once the missiles began deflecting off crags and ledges to be sent spinning and careening his way. Still, he made for a relatively small target upon so broad a cliff face, and had always boasted a strong sense when it came to separating near-dangers from actual ones. Dodging those projectiles that would have struck him, and ignoring those that only threatened to do so, he continued to focus chiefly on furthering his ascent.

His effort had him gaining swiftly upon the ape above him, which appeared to be neither a natural climber, nor overly anxious, even now, in its pursuit. Now and again, it bellowed needfully, but everything else about the creature screamed of patience, calm. Implacable and unrelenting, yes, but in no tremendous hurry, as if the inevitable end would do nothing to truly satisfy it.

Unfortunately, its lead proved too great to overcome. Kylac was still a good thirty heads below the point of any engagement when the ape reached the ledge and began clambering over its lip.

Its arrival was met by a savage howl. *Denariel!* Or so he imagined. The wordless, feral tone made it uncertain. Regardless, the ape recoiled as if speared, its roar resonating now a timbre of pain. The creature freed a hand to swipe at its assailant, seeming to unbalance it and nearly cost it its perch. For a heartbeat, Kylac had a vision of being forced to skitter out of the way as the ape plummeted directly past him to its death.

But the combined grip of the animal's remaining three limbs carried the day, holding it fast. And while clearly vexed by the flurry of flaming strikes that jabbed at it, they seemed ultimately only to provoke it. Roaring and swatting, it drew itself higher, crossing the ledge and disappearing from view.

Kylac had closed to within twenty heads by then, and labored desperately to overcome the remaining distance. Remarkable, that he should arrive at this moment, just in time to spare Denariel a gruesome death—or to bear personal witness to it. The sort of happenstance that others might attribute to the favor or cruelty of gods or destiny. For all he'd seen, Kylac found it difficult to believe in either, and so determined as always to accept the moment for what it was, and to shape it in what way he could.

The echoes of bestial roar and human shout drew him on, taunting in their nearness. Retreating now, suggesting that Denariel was falling back, the animal pressing her into her cave. How far that cave might delve, and whether it bore any nooks or alcoves that might offer her even momentary shelter, were details he had no means of discerning. Best that he presume elsewise. That her life, however well defended to this point, lay now in his hands.

Hands that clutched and pulled and hauled him continually upward. Though raw and scraped and burning, he refused them a moment's rest. Keenly aware as to what the cost might be.

And then the ledge was in hand, caught firmly within his grasp. His legs pushed, his arms pulled, and he heaved himself over its lip, where he rolled swiftly to his feet.

His swords came to hand as he propelled himself forward, toward the cave mouth. The ape was there, beyond the fire, its thickly muscled arms pawing almost lazily at its quarry. He couldn't yet see its target, obscured by its bulk. He saw only the shifting flare of what must have been a flaming brand or spear tip prodding defensively against the animal's inexorable approach.

Kylac let loose a howl of his own as he skirted the fire and swept in at the ape's back. The creature turned its head, revealing a dull, sharp-toothed expression. The lack of intelligence in its eyes nearly gave him pause. But witless didn't make an animal harmless. He'd seen enough of this one's deeds to be assured of that. So he suffered only a twinge of regret as he rolled forward and drove a sword tip through the small of its back.

The ape-thing barely grunted as it rounded—swiftly enough that Kylac was forced to abandon the buried blade—flinging a heavy paw that might have staved in his face had it landed. But Kylac was rolling already beneath the windmill strike, to rise before the beast and slash at its throat. Assuming that this, too, would scarcely slow it, he drew a dagger and buried it in the side of its waist, where a man's kidney would have been, while scrambling back around behind it.

The ape roared and whined as Kylac darted round it in circles, spinning it one way before drawing it the other, causing it to pivot and twist around itself like a braided length of cord. He glimpsed Denariel's form, hunkered at the edges of his vision, as he hacked and jabbed and slashed, but paid her no notice except to revel in finding her before it was too late. His full attention was elsewise on his adversary, as slow and stubborn in its dying as it had been in tracking her to this ledge.

At last, its movements began to lose strength, its counters to slow. Roars gave way to yelps and growls, pitiable in tone were it not for its callous, destructive nature. What mercy had it offered its many victims throughout its life? What mercy might it have offered Denariel—or him, for that matter?

Or so Kylac asked himself as the ape finally staggered and fell, moaning wretchedly. At which point, he did what he could to pierce its brain and end its lengthy suffering.

Only when its dying cries abruptly ceased, its final breath rattling from its lungs and the madness slipping from its enflamed eyes, did

Kylac withdraw his sword and turn from the furry, scaly, bloody heap.
To discover Denariel missing.

26

He found her majesty swiftly, backed into a corner of her cave, squatting low in inspection of her right forearm.

"Are ya hurt?" Kylac asked.

Denariel raised her crude spear reflexively. Just a branch, really, its sharpened, smoking tip little more than a charred ember. "Come no closer."

"As always, a pleasure it is to serve Your Majesty."

"Then it would please the both of us if you'd hurl yourself from that ledge, that I might see your skull dashed upon the rocks."

Her forearm was neither bleeding, nor broken. A strain, then, and not *too* severe, else she'd not have been able to maintain her grip upon her weapon.

"Alas, I fear such a fantasy to be a luxury Your Majesty cannot presently afford." He took another step toward her. Again Denariel brandished her spear, causing him to hesitate. "If'n she means to survive this journey, that is."

"I seem to have fared better than you." Delighting in his own collection of cuts and scrapes, given her savage grimace.

"'Til now, mayhap." Kylac prodded the ape carcass, which twitched in response.

"Well enough in hand," Denariel claimed. "It clearly wasn't trying to kill me."

Yet he heard the doubt buried in her voice, and saw the exhaustion in her angry posture. *It didn't intend to sing ya ballads, either,* he thought. Her skin was soiled and bruised, riddled with welts and swollen with insect bites. As far as she'd come, it hadn't been without cost. Leading him to wonder how much farther they still had to go.

"I see," he said, and lowered himself into a kneeling crouch. Seeking to assuage her hostility. "Fair to say I acted in haste."

"You typically do, from all I've seen."

"As I might suggest Your Majesty did, in venturing out here alone." Even sitting there, speaking with her, he could scarcely believe that he'd finally run her down. That she still had breath in her lungs, and blood in her veins. Were they to run this course a dozen more times, or even a hundred, it seemed unlikely they could reach such a favorable end.

Denariel was massaging her forearm now, her spear still angled against him. "I told you what was necessary. Both you and Ledron. I cannot help that you refused to listen."

"Your Majesty will forgive the captain, I'm sure, for declining to jeopardize your royal life in such a fashion."

"I'll forgive no one who believes a single life can weigh more than the fate of an entire nation," Denariel snapped. "Not my father, when we believed Thane captive, and not that bull-headed Blackfist, now that he looks to preserve mine."

"I'd not think to argue elsewise," said Kylac. He looked to the bloodied sword still in hand, then up again to seek and hold her gaze. "I bring no argument at all. Only apologies."

Denariel stiffened, scowling with suspicion. "Apologies?"

"For His Highness's loss. For your father's. For all o' my failings to this point on our road together."

The queen seemed taken aback. Confusion settled upon her brow, a fleeting calm amid the storm of her countenance. "Your apologies," she echoed.

"If'n I may, I would set matters right between us."

Her scowl sharpened, and her lips peeled back in a contemptuous sneer. "So you've professed, in one fashion or another. I suppose you feel that sparing me a measure of suffering—or even death—on one occasion or another, should clear the slate of my grievances against you." She reared back and spat. Kylac held his ground, allowing it to strike his knee. "It was *your* actions from the first that waylaid my own plans. *Your* interference that killed Ulflund, Grathe, Torman, and set in motion all the rest. It was you who slew—"

She stopped, catching herself mid-lunge, unable or unwilling to speak its name. Her precious Ukinh. The death above all others for which she held him accountable.

"Your apologies are wind," she continued finally. With a nod toward the slain ape, she added, "Like the grackal's breath. Odious. Repugnant. Should you seek to utter them again, I'll empty your lungs if it costs me my life."

Kylac was quite certain she'd have attempted as much already, had she believed for a moment that she could manage such a trade. Making it an idle threat. Nonetheless, he appreciated the blunt sentiment, as it let him know precisely where he ranked in her esteem.

Lest he'd forgotten.

"On the matter o' grackals, may not be safe to remain where this one raised such a row."

"For all their lumbering, grackals have but one natural predator amid the wilds."

"Ukinha." Kylac glanced at the remains of the fire, then out toward the ledge and the expanse of the valley beyond. Amid the deepening dusk, a realization dawned. "That's why you're here. Ya aim to draw one of 'em to ya." Far more sensible, he had to admit, than crisscrossing the Harrows in aimless hope of finding one.

"And you'll see me leap from this perch before you drag me from it," Denariel huffed. "So you'll keep your distance while I tend to my signal fire."

"Permit me," he said. Rising slowly, non-threateningly, he withdrew toward one of the dry, stunted trees peppering the broad ledge. Feigning a lack of concern for what she might do, he put his weapon to hacking at its slender branches. "What makes Your Majesty believe I'd seek to drag her anywhere?"

Denariel eyed him with evident mistrust. "Are you not here at

Ledron's behest? Because, what, he couldn't make the climb himself?" She angled her neck as if to search the monolith's base, suspicion etched in her brow.

"I left the captain back among the canyons o' the Strebolen," he admitted, "following setback at the hands o' the Grenarr. Rendenel Run is where we parted."

Her reaction was one of surprise and concern, quickly veiled by her usual petulance. "Bahsk marched to retake Avenell."

"Toting us in the bargain. To witness the resulting calamity firsthand." Hauling a pair of freshly hewn branches to the fire, he added, "Captain Ledron remained, in an effort to marshal the survivors and lead them north again."

"I told them we required reinforcement," she hissed. A moment later, she added, "And I'm to believe that the captain sanctioned your pursuit without accompanying you personally?"

"He understood, I think, that he wasn't going to match my pace. I did promise to return ya to Indranell, but gave no oath as to when."

The queen snorted and hefted her chin. "I'll return at the head of an army, or not at all."

"So I's gathered," said Kylac, brushing the grit from his hands and peering out over the ledge. "Ya's picked a defensible spot, at least. I only wish I understood better how ya mean for the Ukinha to ally with us."

"I care nothing for your wishes, as you have shown to care nothing for mine."

Kylac might have reminded her of numerous events bearing evidence to the contrary. But Denariel wasn't one to be persuaded by argument. "I'll submit to them now," he offered instead, "insofar as your attempt to treat with the mutants. But I aim not to leave your side before delivering ya safely as promised—whatever this Talathandria's response."

"Is it a bargain you seek of me?" Denariel asked, eyes narrowing in challenge.

"A *truce*, should that resonate any softer in your fine ears. Tolerating my presence just long enough for me to see ya past the perils o' these wilds."

The queen scoffed. "Of which you know nothing."

"No? Ya'll recall this is not my first excursion."

"The only reason you survived the first was because Abi—" She stopped, glowering. "Because my Ukinh warder was shadowing us. It was *his* presence that kept the countless terrors of the region at bay."

She was curious, Kylac suspected, as to how much he might have been told regarding the nature of her relationship with the groll. Not curious enough to ask, of course. But the question was there, at the edge of her thoughts.

Kylac stoked the fire, repositioning the branches to help the flames rise. "Nonetheless," he said, with another purposeful glance at the slain grackal, "I'm learning as I go."

Denariel rose from her crouch. While it might have been a trick of the firelight, a cruel grin appeared to flash across her face. "With death but a single lesson learned too late."

Giving him due cause to press for answers as to her intended parley with the Ukinha and their supposed queen. How might that work? What gave her reason to believe she might succeed? Was it not far more likely that any groll who happened upon them would simply try to kill them? For his sake, she might intend precisely that. But what of her own? What of her people's?

Yet he decided not to test her on that front. Let her cling to her mysteries, should she feel they empowered her. He didn't have to know what might happen in order to be prepared for it. Better in many circumstances that he didn't. Observe and react, as his father had taught him. Do so swiftly enough, and there was little he couldn't overcome.

He continued to stoke the flames, observing—while pretending not to—as Denariel flexed and stretched her arm and decided it must be sound enough, given the way she ceased regarding it. Or mayhap she only intended that *he* believe her fit, to therefore mask and deny any weakness. As if her ragged condition wasn't plainly evident. As if it might have mattered were she fully hale and healthy. They both understood that it wasn't her spear or her threats that kept him at arm's length. As with the grackal, which had been more curious than enraged, Kylac could have torn through her defenses, had that been his aim, without so much as a heavy breath.

Instead, he watched her retreat into her cave and root through a meager stash of provisions for a waterskin. Though it appeared near to empty, she drank deeply, divulging a thirst she was sure to deny were he to inquire about it.

"What are your food stores?" he asked instead.

"Roots. Mushrooms. Too sparse to share, if that's what you're hoping."

On the contrary, it was *her* hunger that concerned him. The gauntness of her cheeks, the leanness of her frame—readily revealed by a tattered tunic and breeches—told him she hadn't been eating well. As her attempt at the raw rodent back in that burrow had seemed to suggest.

"I brought my own supper," he replied, gesturing at the fallen grackal. "Care to partake?"

She fought to conceal her initial eagerness. "Grackal meat is terribly tough, and terribly bland."

"And yet, I daresay I'll be unable to eat it all. So you're welcome to whatever portion ya may desire."

Her eyes continued to betray a hunger she refused to confess. "I should think so, given that I was the one who trapped the beast."

Attracted might have been the more honest claim, given the lack of any discernible trap or snare. But Kylac wasn't about to discourage her. All he cared was that the creature was edible, and that she should consume some measure of it. "Will your water last the night?"

"Will you go and fetch me some elsewise?"

"I's a skin against the small o' my back, if'n ya need some." The last freshwater pool he'd encountered was more than a mile back. And he wasn't about to let her out of his sight for the time it would take him to draw from it. While confident he could run her down in short order should she flee again, he'd done so far too narrowly the first time to risk another predator's untimely intervention.

"I'd sooner drink the tears of a bristlesnail," she informed him. "Concern yourself with your own provisions, and I'll concern myself with mine."

Kylac suppressed a smile. Her predictable thanklessness and lack of trust had come to be the most reliable forces in his recently unstable life. For all her barbs, he found her loathing remarkably reassuring.

"Can you manage a spit?" she asked tersely, advancing now with a longknife in hand.

Kylac nodded. As he moved to harvest another bit of growth measuring somewhere between a shrub and a tree, she bent to the grackal carcass and began sawing at its fleshy hide. When he saw her wince, he had to resist the urge to offer undertaking *that*, as well. That she was doing it meant she'd already decided she was better suited to the task. And as much as he preferred she rest, it seemed unlikely she would agree to sit idle under *his* care.

Particularly were it *his* suggestion.

He worked in silence for a time, conceding Denariel hers. Her brooding anger surrounded her like a storm cloud, chill and churning with bridled thunder. The skies beyond were much more peaceful, the daylight all but vanquished now by an emergent moon and stars. Though the jungle chirped and howled and carried on with its dissonant chorus, the heights provided a blessed sense of solitude, a welcome removal from the unseen turmoil persisting unabated below.

It wasn't until the grackal had been gutted and dressed, a slab of its thigh set to roasting over the fire, that Kylac dared renew their conversation.

"Should it matter, I'm not so blind and fearful as others."

"Which is to say what?" she responded, in a truculent tone meant to tell him she was unafraid to engage with him. This after sitting across the fire from him for nearly a quarter-mark, observing their surroundings guardedly while making every effort not to catch his eye.

"On Grenathrok, your royal brother, he described your Ukinha as abominations."

Denariel tensed, bristling with reflexive anger. But she declined to respond, shifting her attentions back out into the night.

Kylac turned the spit. "Struck me as narrow-minded. A child's view. But then, Ledron has it that His Highness saw one on the attack, back when he was but a child himself."

"He *defended* us," Denariel corrected. "It was Grenarr raiders who attacked. Our entire family. The Ukinh, he intervened against the tar-skins and in so doing saved us all."

He, Kylac noted as he had before, not *it*. "But a boy of six . . . I can see where he might recall only the mutant's bestial fury."

The queen seethed, letting her scowl and the popping of the flames speak for her. Juices sizzled from the cooking meat, hissing as they dripped upon the coals.

"So you've more courage than Thane. Is that what you'd have me know?"

"I's known other wild peoples. The elves o' Mistwall, who ravaged our borrowed ship. On Pentanian shores, they call themselves Mookla'ayans. Others call them savages, cannibals, inhuman."

Denariel looked away again, tossing her head in a show of rapidly dwindling interest.

"But I sought 'em out," Kylac pressed. "Studied 'em. Lived among 'em for a time, and found 'em to be far less monstrous than the fireside tales would suggest."

"And you expect *what* from me in reward? When I'd sooner curse them for not eating you?"

"When you informed us before, Ledron and me, o' your aim to seek the Ukinha . . . My hesitation spoke only to the captain's concern for your safety, not to any prejudice or intolerance toward the mutants." As she looked to summon another scathing retort, he added, "I should have known by then there'd be no denying your will."

Denariel's unformed response lodged in her mouth. For the second time that night, she seemed taken aback, as if momentarily uncertain how to reconcile his words with her harsh opinions of him. Had she chinks in her armor after all?

As before, she hid it quickly. "You wish to know my plans. You think to goad or distract or lure me into revealing my mind."

"I say merely that I look forward to the adventure. Your Ukinha are undeniably fascinating creatures. And if'n ya says they're the key to this war, to freeing your people, then the key they are."

Despite her ever-present scowl, he felt again as if he might finally be reaching her. Like the first faint brush of a fly's leg against a spider's web, mayhap, but a connection nonetheless.

"Then I would remind *you* that I care nothing for your motivations—professed or elsewise—save that they do not interfere again with mine. Follow me, if you'll not be dismissed, since I cannot forcibly banish you. But we are not companions in this. You are a blister on my heel that I must tolerate if I am to continue pressing forward. A pus-spewing boil best ignored. You are my enemy until the end of our time together, which cannot come too soon."

He should have taken offense, of course. Recalled for her, mayhap, the many risks he'd taken on her behalf without any profit to himself. But he didn't necessarily need her to think better of him in order to keep her safe in her chosen course. And altering her views of him, were it even possible, would do little or less to dull the pain that had spawned those feelings to begin with. In all his travels, he'd discovered no salve for wounds of an emotional nature.

Making the most severe scars often the least visible.

Since he could think of nothing to say that might soothe her deeply rooted anguish, or that couldn't be twisted somehow to sound self-fulfilling, he broke from her challenging gaze, holding his tongue and letting the matter lie. He'd informed her that he wasn't opposed to her reasoning in coming here, whatever that might entail going forward. Whether she chose to accept it, or to decide she could trust him in this endeavor, was on her.

In the interim, he wasn't about to fault her for her honesty.

With the quiet between them resettling thick and heavy, the fire's crackle and the jungle's song grew sharper in their refrains. Kylac busied himself turning the spit, while Denariel stared now into the flames, a fierce grimace chiseled onto her brow. If perceiving herself victorious in another discussion provided her the slightest satisfaction, she did nothing to reveal it.

When he sensed her hunger overcoming her patience, Kylac drew the half-cooked grackal meat from the fire and extended it to her on the spit. She accepted it wordlessly and proceeded to carve a chunk from the still-sizzling slab, burning her fingers in her haste to collect it. Thinking it wiser not to fuss over so minor an injury, Kylac watched her wince and flap her hand and said nothing, knowing she'd endured far, far worse.

She flung the remainder of the skewered meat back to him with a halfhearted toss. Kylac bent forward, reaching out and snatching it up before it could hit the dirt. Denariel frowned at his serpentine reflexes, even as she pretended not to notice.

They worked thereafter at consuming their meal in silence—a deafening ocean to fill the gulf between them. Kylac thought the meat juicy enough, if indeed bland and tough to tear. He stopped himself from asking the queen's opinion. She'd all but finished hers by the time he'd taken his fourth bite. If not the best meal she'd ever tasted, it was clearly far from the worst.

He was watching her lick her fingers, and about to ask her if she might care for more, when he detected the ragged echoes of a terrible, multi-voiced wailing. His ears pricked immediately at the unfamiliar sound, which struck him as harsh and vengeful. Whatever wretched creature had drawn the ire of these ones had his pity.

"Another bite?" he went ahead and asked his companion.

"That you might watch me vomit it up with the last?" she demanded tersely. "Grackal settles poorly. But you have my leave to gorge yourself."

She stood with a haughty air that followed her back to the cave, where she produced and uncorked another waterskin. Kylac watched her drink and thought nothing more of the distant wailing, even as it increased in volume and intensity. It wasn't until Denariel returned to the fire with a mud-smeared, rank-smelling travel cloak around her shoulders that he took pause, noting the fretful expression that seized her features.

"Your Majesty?"

"Silence!" she hissed. Listening intently, it seemed she heard the wailing now, too. Her walnut-hued skin seemed to lose a measure of its color. "No," she said. "No, no."

She rushed toward the southeast rim of the ledge, in the direction from which Kylac had arrived. Marking her alarm, he rushed to join her, carrying his half-eaten dinner with him. At the edge of the precipice, they stopped together, to peer out over the jungle choking the pinnacle's base. Its night-cloaked fringe whipped and swayed, in part from the wind, but in greater part from something more tangible, more threatening, that swept like a dark ripple through the boughs of the trees.

Crested by that dreadful wailing.

"Mother's mercy," Denariel whispered, a genuine terror gathering about her in a chilling cloud. The cloud darkened with a sudden suspicion. "You," she snarled in accusation. "*You* did this."

Kylac, as yet unfazed, kept his gaze upon the jungle. Around a half-chewed mouthful of grackal, he asked, "What? What did I do?"

Then the jungle seemed to rupture, bursting up against the stony foundation of their perch.

And he saw.

27

As he stood there upon the rocky precipice, watching the flood of keening, dark-bodied forms gush from the jungle wall, the taste of grackal soured in Kylac's mouth.

"What are they?" he asked.

"Orngarath," Denariel replied, spitting the name like a curse. "Shadow-weepers. Twice-dead. The Darkfather's heralds."

"They do raise quite the caterwaul." The weepers, or whatever name best suited them, swelled like a tide to swirl and roil at the pinnacle's base. "Are they coming for us?"

"For *you*," his resentful companion corrected. "Though they'll not satisfy themselves with your flesh with mine so near."

"Would that I knew how I offended them."

"Do you not recognize them?" Denariel asked, her tone still rife with accusation.

Their forward numbers appeared to slosh and spray now like foam astride a cresting breaker, buoyed by those still pouring in behind them. Rangy little creatures, all flailing limbs and tiny, toothy heads. And tails, he saw, long and arcing. Save for their furless flesh, sable skins, and savage song, they might have been kin to the tree-clingers that had scratched him up in the waning hours of the previous night.

"Might be I killed some o' their fairer cousins," Kylac realized.

"No. You killed *them*. These are their corpses, risen to seek vengeance."

The selfsame creatures he'd felled before? "How is that possible?"

But he knew the answer to that already. Gorrethrehn. The so-called Breeders who'd once lorded over this isle. That sect of ancient magi whose special interest and talent lay in manipulating nature's handiwork, so as to give birth to new—and typically deadlier—creations that might better carry out . . . whatever their masters' desired purpose.

"How many did you slay?" Denariel asked.

"Some dozen or so notches past seven hundred."

The queen blanched, inasmuch as the hue of her skin would allow it. "Seven *hundred*?"

At least half that many had emerged from the jungle already, to screech and wail as they circled the base of the monolith, swatting and snapping at one another. Scratching around its stony roots like a weasel scouring for grubs—if that weasel were thrashing about in a rabid frenzy and numbered in the hundreds.

"So, what happens? We kill them again?" Kylac asked.

"No simple matter, once morphed into an orngarath. Better by far not to harm an ornga from the first."

More easily spoken than done, had she been there when the little tree-clingers had set themselves upon him. He wondered how she'd passed through their domain without antagonizing them. In the present moment, however, it scarcely seemed the most relevant question.

"But they still bleed, yes?"

Denariel cast him a scornful glance. "Doubtless, *you* might kill dozens of them. Scores, even. But hundreds?" She returned her gaze earthward and shook her head, undeniably awestruck.

"Mayhap we can wait them out." Though the weepers had encircled the monolith's base, they'd made no effort yet to scale the sheer slopes. Should they prove unable to do so, might they lose interest?

"And perhaps we'll sprout feathers and wings and ride the winds from this valley."

He took that as an expression of doubt. And indeed, even as she uttered it, the beasties appeared to finish sniffing about the base of the rock, and began to clamber over one another in a maddened attempt to claw their way skyward. "I see," he said.

He wondered briefly if it might be better to descend now, to carve past them and seek to outpace the inevitable pursuit. But that was only his instinctive fear of confinement demanding to be heard. Should he and the queen attempt to repel now, they'd be swarmed over in the attempt. Uncomfortable as it made him to accept it, they were already trapped.

By that reckoning, a boon that the weepers looked to attack. Because they could as easily have waited, holding him and Denariel captive there atop the ledge while the numbers of their pack grew. Or while the pair starved to death—or at least grew so weak from thirst and hunger that they could no longer summon the strength to defend themselves.

If they were to perish now, at least it would be while fighting.

He stopped short of voicing this sentiment, suspecting it unlikely the queen would share his enthusiasm. Whether or not she truly believed she could have fended off the grackal alone, it seemed indeed that he may have personally ushered this latest challenge to her threshold. Better, in her mind, that he'd not come at all.

Whichever, she'd turned already to make for the cave, and so he turned with her. Listening to the swell of shrieking that marked the rising threat from below. Swallowing a final bite of grackal and tossing aside the rest. It occurred to him that they might heave the remainder of the carcass over the edge in hope of satisfying the creatures, but dismissed the thought at once. According to Denariel, they'd come not for food, but revenge. He and his unwilling charge, on the other hand, might well require further nourishment if they were to sustain themselves atop this ledge for any appreciable length of time.

Presuming they survived the night.

He watched Denariel retrieve her makeshift spear. Rather than build another flamehead, however, she drew one of her knives and set to notching the spear's butt.

"No fire this time?" Kylac asked.

"Flame will not deter them. Nor will wounds have much effect. Our best chance is to maim those we can, while sweeping the rest from the cliff."

Kylac strayed across the ledge, wishing now that it were smaller. Even with the two of them, they couldn't possibly defend the whole of the rim if the weepers were to crest its full length at once. "We'll have to sweep quickly. And be swift afoot."

"That we will," Denariel growled. Shimming her blade's haft into the notch, she produced a length of twine and began lashing it in place. "Again and again, as those who fall climb back."

Not without their limbs, thought Kylac. But then, the tree-clingers' feet and tails had served as well as their hands, and, by all appearances, death had taken none of that dexterity from these weepers—plenty of whom would already be missing an arm or two, should Denariel's accusations prove out. Difficult to discern, as of yet, amid the writhing tangle of bodies scaling the bluffs. But until he learned elsewise, safer to assume that the dread little beasties would require the loss of four of their five appendages before being truly disabled.

That, or their heads.

They'd ceased gushing from the jungle, at least. Causing it to appear, then, that the whole of their multitude was that which ringed the base of the monolith or clung to its sides like a swarm of bees. Whatever else, their numbers were not unending.

He patrolled the ledge's perimeter, noting the weepers' progress along the various slopes and folds. Though cloaked in shadow, their eyes beamed with reflected moonlight, and their frenetic motions became almost as noisome and grating as their ceaseless keening. The currents of energy unleashed by their furious need rose ahead of them, surging and slapping at Kylac like the shoreline waves of a tumultuous sea.

In response, his veins tingled with that familiar blaze, like streams of lightning sent coursing through his body in search of release. His hands itched. His arms and legs thrummed. *Soon,* he promised himself, as if soothing an anxious steed.

He took a moment to add fuel to their campfire, not knowing when he might next be able to do so. Sparks shot skyward as he poked the burning branches and livid embers with fresh shoots of dead brush. Denariel glanced up from her lashing effort, but said nothing.

Checking again on the weepers' progress, he found them scaling the south face the fastest, and the eastern flank faster than the west. He didn't concern himself as much with the north, which was largely hidden from view, serving backbone to ledge and cave and overshadowing their position by another eighty heads. Any orngarath keeping to that course would be of small consequence unless veering southward along the ledge's flanks or spilling over the top of the pinnacle's peak. A chilling image, should they indeed pour down like an avalanche from overhead. But as there was nothing he could envision doing to prevent it, he resolved not to fret over the possibility.

Of a certain, he was going to miss his blades, though.

While Denariel cinched and tied off her freshly lashed spearhead, he continued to pace the ledge, memorizing its rugged features with his eyes and his feet. Here and there, he plucked a rock from the ground, the shape or size or position of which he misliked. These, he cast earthward, looking after to see if he might dislodge any of the nearest climbers. Twice, he found stones large enough to do so, with all the effect of a lone teardrop washing a muddy cheek.

Then the time for anticipation and preparation was ended, and the true fight upon them. Denariel was still testing her new spear tip when the first of the weepers crested the southern lip, leaping up onto the ledge in almost the exact same spot that Kylac had just a couple hours earlier. Presenting themselves in a sudden, squealing flourish. Clambering over one another in their vicious haste. Kylac awaited them, Grenarr swords in hand. As akin to bills as sabers, yet better suited to his preferred fighting style than the Addaran longswords and broadswords he might have acquired in their stead. Twirling them in his palms, he stepped forward and met his fiendishly gleeful assailants. Biting into the neck of the first to reach him. Finding it to be like hacking at a fresh bramble stalk—heartier than its thickness gave it any right to be. Tough and sinuous and resisting of his weapons' edges. The weeper screeched, its head only partially severed, and continued to scrabble toward him, hissing, from where it fell to the ground.

Kylac kicked it clear of the ledge, his swords already engaged with the next pair. One, he backhanded into the air with the flat of his blade. The other swiped at him, and so he met its arm with a blade's edge. He'd shed dozens of ornga limbs in similar fashion, directing his weapon through the softer gristle between bones. In this instance, however, the blade failed to bite through, thwarted by the orngarath's shriveled, corded flesh. Where he'd imagined severing his first arm of the night, he'd but opened a near-bloodless gash. It took him two more strikes, in rapid succession, to send the creature pinwheeling back, to fall shrieking after the others.

He laid hacking and swatting and swirling into those gushing up after, who were clearly undaunted by the cries of those gone before. If anything, the pain of their kin fueled their bloodlust, filling them with rage and defiance and exhilaration to have their enemy finally at hand. Kylac, in turn, could but marvel at the metamorphosis of these creatures, their flesh transformed from that of, say, a furry, fleshy peach to something nearer that of the wrinkled pit inside. His swords, nicked and dulled from so many recent conflicts, would be sore-pressed indeed to inflict the degree of damage he was accustomed to. The degree of damage he would *need* in order to give himself and Denariel a fighting chance.

Laments aside, he was emboldened by the challenge. An almost childish zeal overcame him, as it so often did in such moments. A test worthy of his inimitable talents. A trial to determine if his skills were as matchless as he'd come to believe. Similar to other situations he'd overcome, and yet undeniably unique when all factors were weighed and measured. Permitting a sliver of doubt amid his ironclad confidence. Might this, then, be where he met his end?

Rather than shy from the possibility, he confronted it headlong. Applying all of his finely honed knowledge and training. Plunging into the ocean of life's energies and giving himself over to its currents. Riding its swells, rather than seeking to dictate them. Giving rein to instincts that, in a sense, rendered him puppet to a power beyond comprehension, but had yet to betray his trust.

When Denariel arrived beside him, he shifted to his left, toward a fresh spring of enemies upon the eastern lip. Like defending a castle parapet from scaling ladders, though he'd never actually stood against such a siege, and lacked here any sort of bulwark to shelter behind. No matter. The lack of shield worked as much or more in his favor as it did his attackers, for it gave him clear access with his whirring blades, and the weepers no place to hide.

He worried for Denariel, initially, but found her remarkably adept with her spear. As she must have been, in order to ward off the curious grackal long enough for him to arrive. True to her suggestion, she made no real effort to harm the orngarath, only to poke and prod and fling them clear as they sought to gain purchase upon the ledge. To that end, her weapon was really better suited than his, as it provided her a longer reach against the weepers' flailing limbs and gnashing teeth.

From side to side he danced, sweeping as much of the southern and eastern ledge as he could. To let Denariel focus on just a narrow patch to the southwest. Knowing that exhaustion was likely to affect her long before it affected him or their assailants. And that, given the speed and relentlessness of the orngarath press, a single slip or miss could allow a trickle that might quickly spawn an unstoppable rush.

It felt refreshing, invigorating, to have her fighting beside him, their weapons joined in common cause. Mayhap because he sensed that, even now, she'd enjoy nothing so much as to plunge that freshly lashed spearhead of hers into his back. Comrades due to dire necessity, and nothing more. But it gave him a sort of dark satisfaction nonetheless, to see the spiteful young queen compelled to admit—in deed if never in word—that she required assistance, and his in particular.

So he lent it with a grim smile upon his face, his legs lunging and sidestepping, his blades thrusting and arcing, his little flat-faced enemies squalling as they were pricked and sliced and swatted aside. Their hardened flesh continued to repel strikes that would have killed or maimed them in their prior form less than a day ago, but he couldn't let that trouble him. If wishing for matters to be other than what they were, he may as well have wished the orngarath to be a flock of butterflies, or for Denariel to be tucked safely away in her home castle, feasting on roasted duck and fresh applesauce.

Fortunately, the ledge was thus far serving his desires, the pits and protuberances of the bluff beneath limiting ascent to a select few navigable pathways. Rather than seeking to resist a uniform tide, he and his comrade-in-arms had but to repel a handful of gushing streams. He could feel the swell of excess weepers that clutched and clawed for additional veins of access, but in doing so, they did as much or more to disrupt the efforts of their fellows amid the surer cuts and grooves. Better they might do, at this juncture, to bank their passions and commit themselves to a more orderly approach.

There seemed as much chance of that as of their brood transforming into his imagined flock of butterflies. A small boon, then, amid the litany of factors working against him. Leaving him to find an almost comfortable rhythm of whirring and slashing against those who wrestled one another for the pleasure of rending his flesh with their curved claws and spiny teeth.

Yet here they were in a contest only moments old, the night still in its infancy. As he listened to Denariel grunt and snarl, he had to wonder, how long might he and the young queen maintain their effort? A half-mark? A full hour? Whatever the limit of their stamina, could it match that of the orngarath? If not, it seemed plain enough that they would perish. If so, and the weepers retreated, how long before they gathered themselves and came again?

While all looked more or less identical to him, he'd encountered several now sporting stunted or missing limbs. The evidence he'd been waiting for to support Denariel's assessment. That this tide was likely a direct consequence, however unintended, of his earlier slayings. Leading him to wonder how many other times in life he might have turned to his weapons too soon, choosing action over deliberation. Was it not such a choice that had spurred him on this adventure from the first?

He'd been accused by Denariel and others of being rash or even negligent in his judgment, and he wasn't about to claim elsewise. Was that something for which he need apologize? A flaw of character he should seek to address?

Would that moon or stars or midday sun could guide him in such matters. Alas, he thought, as he gave another wailing weeper a taste of his weaponry, all he knew of fairness or injustice were the instincts with which he'd been born, and the lessons imparted by his father. Steering himself in a direction that he believed would displease the man was about as reliable a compass as he'd heretofore been able to find.

Whatever failings were left to him, he would carry.

A new stream opened farther to the east, forcing him to widen his range of defense. Faster his legs moved in response, and faster his blades, adjusting to the quickening rhythm. The weepers left behind as he dashed from one breach to the next seemed to sense an opportunity, thinking their pathway open in his absence. Again and again, he was pleased to disappoint them, racing back to slash and scythe into their flailing forms, casting them back to begin their effort anew.

He knew not how many he and Denariel had faced by now. More than three hundred, but less than four. Roughly half the number they could expect to repel if each came at them only once. Unlikely, according to the queen, and he had yet to see anything with which to refute her. A daunting prospect, as he listened to her struggles and noted her flagging efforts. Barely perceptible, but she was surely tiring. Not that she'd ever admit as much. And, as of yet, her growing weariness hadn't hampered the effectiveness of her labors. Nonetheless, an unfortunate sign if weighing their long-term prospects.

Farther out, the jungle chittered and screeched and clamored, brimming with orngarath echoes, but seeming also to resonate excitement. As if itself a living creature delighting in the chaos and bloodshed wreaked by its minions.

Were it so, Kylac would be only too willing to slake its thirst.

Minutes churned past, casualties of the slaughter. A sweat gathered upon Kylac's brow, pooled beneath his arms, streamed down his chest and spine. Unusual for him. But then, this was a humid land, even at night. And seldom were his fighting efforts so sustained. Most who presented themselves as adversaries would by now be vanquished, either killed or elsewise persuaded of the futility of their efforts.

But the weepers kept coming, hissing and keening in approach, yelping and squealing in departure. Relentless. Determined. Seemingly unconcerned with their failure thus far to overwhelm their quarry. Confident in the inevitability of their hunt.

And correct they might be. But Kylac cared only for the moment, for executing each thrust and swipe with speed and precision. Never hesitating, bent on maintaining his own offensive. Permit them a toehold upon this ledge, and the dynamics of this conflict would be altered appreciably—and not in his or the queen's favor. So he could ill afford to lose focus, except where given to instinct and reflex. To give attention here to what *might* be was more likely to open a door to fouler possibilities.

Mayhap some cruel god could hear his thoughts, and decided to make them manifest. Else his mind was simply that well attuned to the world's machinations. Whatever, it wasn't but a moment later that a new stream of weepers came trickling up from the farthest northeast corner of the ledge. A previously untapped vein of access to the far rear of Kylac's flank. A point as distant as any his attackers could have hoped to discover. The orngarath seemed to sense it, given the exultation that preceded their bounding rush. A spear of perceived triumph sent hurtling at his exposed back.

Kylac let them advance, at first, untroubled by their scant numbers, aimed solely at him. Only at the last possible—and first necessary—instant did he spin to intercept them, hacking and whirring and adding them to those he flung back into the empty night air. Their fury was matched only by their surprise, heightened by their prior certainty of success.

When the taste of defeat was at its most bitter.

Now that the path had been forged, however, more and more orngarath saw fit to follow it. The trickle gave way to another spring, and the spring to a torrent. At which point, he made the decision to reach out and confront it.

An overextension, mayhap. But he felt the effort within the bounds of the battle's patterns. A note delayed, yet falling still within the overall rhythm.

And it was, he realized, permitting himself a moment's elation upon proving—to himself and his enemies—that he could indeed make the stretch, sweeping the ledge's eastern rim from face to spine and back again. Repelling all orngarath risen before him, or those thinking to scramble up at his back. Extending the limits of what even *he* might have guessed was possible.

As he so often did.

Unfortunately, his companion didn't share his confidence. Before he could complete his daring sweep and return to the center of the ledge's face, where a pack of orngarath had bubbled up in his absence, Denariel panicked and sought to deal with them herself.

"No!" he barked, foreseeing the inevitable result.

But Denariel only cast him an angry glance before putting her spear to work. By the time he reached her, she'd already prodded the stubborn weepers from the ledge.

The problem lay in those now at *her* back, on the western flank. The ones she'd so dutifully resisted since the battle's inception. Untended, their numbers now were beyond her control. He sensed it, even if she, as yet, did not.

So he wheeled around her to meet them, carving into their surging press without hesitation or mercy. Dispatching those whose angle and velocity of attack would have overwhelmed her a moment later. Casting them aside like chaff.

Even so, the song had changed. Denariel held the ledge face, but the eastern rim was already overflowing. As abruptly as that, their perimeter defense was breached.

"Back!" he yelled. "To the cave!"

"We cannot relinquish the—"

"The edge is lost! Go!"

Knowing she wasn't likely to listen to him, he allowed a cluster of orngarath to convince her. Once they'd forced her into retreat, he laid into them just enough to stall their rush. By then, she recognized what he had—that the weepers, overrunning the ledge in half a dozen scattered places, were pooling swiftly, to surround them like a rising storm tide.

Still radiating protest, she half turned and shuffled toward the cave mouth. Her steps were slow and staggered, and her spear sagging in her weary arms. Kylac withdrew with her, dashing out now and then to dissuade probing waves of gleeful orngarath. Left, right, forward, back, and again, while the weeper waves thickened, surged in height, and roiled nearer, from all directions.

They reached the cave, if barely. Kylac had to sweep aside a pack swarming in from that troublesome northeast corner. Denariel backed safely inside, spear thrusting at those orngarath flailing at her upon the western flank. Kylac concentrated on the rest of the opening, blades working a ceaseless flurry against those who sought to intrude. The fight was more vicious than before. He couldn't simply swat a weeper from its perch and draw a breath while the next clambered up in its stead. He faced now a tidal wave of closely knit weeper bodies, cresting upon itself as creatures from the rear bounded atop the backs of those come before, spitting and lunging and lashing out in their attempt to reach him. Sensing the imminent end.

Fortunately, that desperate haste continued to work against them, to some extent. With all of their heaving and yanking and tussling, they trampled and blinded and impeded one another to the point of hindering the collective effort. Though dozens strong, with scores and eventually hundreds drawing up behind them, Kylac need only concern himself with the rolling press of those at the front lines.

For all that had changed, then, his fight remained much the same. His goal not necessarily to kill, merely to resist, to batter his enemies back until they returned again—hopefully weaker and wearier and less dangerous than before.

In other respects, the revised conflict actually shifted in his favor. For, the longer he fought, the better he came to understand his enemies—their strengths and weaknesses and passions and instincts—enabling him to better anticipate their movements. Their cinching noose also left him with much less ground to cover. So while an enemy denied was swifter to return, there were, again, only so many who could engage him at once.

Still, they did so relentlessly, scarcely slowed by the injuries inflicted upon them. He stabbed eyes and slit throats and severed fingers. He hacked into limbs and tails until these, too, had been removed from their bodies or rendered useless, left hanging by strands of sinew. As he'd feared, however, those left with any two of their five appendages simply kept coming, crawling or squirming or writhing amid their more able-bodied kin with feral madness and fiendish persistence.

When Denariel twisted an ankle and stumbled back in search of balance, Kylac widened his shifting stance, spreading his blade-work across the whole of the cave mouth and allowing her no room to return to the fray. For once, she uttered no objection, wearied beyond protest. She simply crouched there in the shadowed darkness, massaging her leg and heaving breathlessly.

Out upon the ledge, their fire disintegrated, scattered into sparks and embers overrun by thrashing orngarath. Without its light, the darkness deepened. Smoke filled the air. Kylac felt the night pressing closer, drawing around them like a shroud.

Could this indeed be his final test? He lashed out in defiance, exhilarated by the prospect. Should this pack of beasties prove superior to his skills, so be it. But if these were his ultimate moments, he was determined to enjoy them.

Behind him, he could feel Denariel's despair, tempered by her usual fury, and seasoned by an undeniable awe. At the press of their assailants. At his ability to hold them off. He could feel himself moving as fast as he ever had, whirling and ducking and lunging and leaning with every variety of maneuver in between. What that dance must look like to an observer, he could only imagine. If trusting the words and expressions of others, something to behold.

He took his damage in turn. Cuts and scrapes like those he'd suffered the last time he'd faced these creatures—as ornga. Such was necessary, if he was to stave off graver injury. The test was in knowing which attacks he could absorb with minimal consequence, versus those—more harmful—that had to be dodged or deflected. But he'd always had a strong sense as to the severity of a particular danger, steeped more in instinct than in training. Whichever, it continued to serve him here.

He felt Denariel stirring behind him, itching to rejoin the fight. She could scarcely stand. So he held her back by virtue of his movements, giving her no opening beside him. A warm flush at his back warned of a new, potential threat. The frustrated queen, it seemed, had half a mind to spear *him* instead.

Near to drowning already beneath the churning crush, he was considering rendering her unconscious when the keening of the more distant weepers—those still skirting the sides of the cliffs—struck a discordant refrain. The strange chord sent a ripple through their ranks, reaching all the way to the front lines. All at once, the orngarath seemed to panic. While dozens of those nearest continued to hiss and swipe and lunge at Kylac, the bulk of their multitude seemed to fracture, its members turning upon each other and tearing in all directions at once, as if in frantic search of escape.

"What's this?" he called back to Denariel.

The queen failed to respond. Given her bewilderment, she wasn't certain. But the fresh spikes of dread concern rising from her did little to inspire optimism.

The weepers continued to withdraw, scrabbling and swarming in mad confusion. An ebbing wave, receding not a moment too soon. Kylac found his blades slowing, along with his frenetic footwork, as the orngarath abandoned their quest for vengeance and scrambled for the nearest precipice, repelling or simply leaping from the edge.

He was still searching for a reason as to why when he sensed it, his flesh tingling with a warning he knew better than to ignore. A sensation he'd first felt months ago, in that stub of an alley back in Wingport. Upon rescuing Sallun from Ulflund and his Shadowguard—at the very inception of this misadventure. The unique feeling of being observed by a creature the likes of which he hadn't encountered before.

Groll.

"Stay back," he cautioned.

It appeared a moment later at the center of the ledge face, springing atop the rim. A presence blacker than the surrounding night. Humanoid in form and size. Crouched low on a pair of spindly legs that somehow supported its impossibly top-heavy, hunch-shouldered bulk.

Kylac felt its gaze sweeping the ledge, piercing as it found him.

Abruptly, its legs swelled and its shoulders shrank, and the mutant strode forward. Advancing steadily, with a prowling gait. Neither rushed nor hesitant. Wading through the retreating waves of orngarath, which screeched and wailed and recoiled from it, fleeing like roaches from a flame.

Mostly, the groll let them, seeming disinterested, its attentions fixed upon the cave mouth. When one of the jostling weepers was knocked into its knee, however, it caught the unfortunate beastie by the neck and pierced its throat with its claws. The weeper's thrashings did nothing to weaken the groll's iron hold. Nor did it inhibit the poisons that coursed through its veins, forging bubbling trails through its flesh. Bucking and convulsing with strangled voice, foul fluids oozing from its mouth, it died within a span of heartbeats.

After which, the groll flung it aside.

The remaining orngarath withdrew from the defiled carcass as if fearful of contracting its taint. By now, there were but a few dozen scattered across the ledge, each departing faster than the others. The final streams of an ant colony abandoning a spoiled nest.

The groll continued to ignore them, clearly targeting Kylac, crouched there at the mouth of the shallow cave. Stalking nearer. Radiating malevolence. And Kylac knew, as *it* did, that there would be no escape without confrontation.

Sliding his blades' edges against each other, scraping away droplets of orngarath blood, he readied himself to receive it.

28

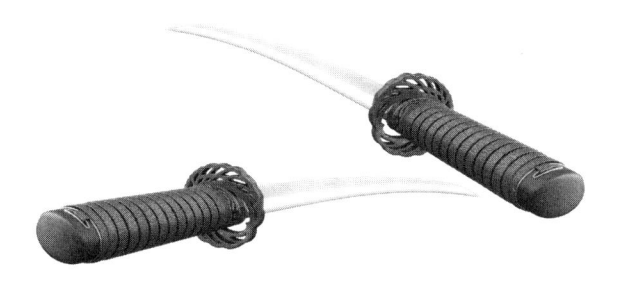

Kylac felt the tear of indecision as he marked the mutant's approach. Its arrival would seem to have saved them. Were he to kill it, would he not simply be inviting the orngarath to return in its stead?

Countering that, he couldn't well stand idle and let it ravage them.

Mayhap sensing his hesitation—else burdened by questions of its own—the groll paused, halting at a distance of three paces. Kylac kept his blades at the ready, knowing it could cover the span with scarcely a twitch. Bathed in moonlight, its mottled flesh shimmered through a range of dark colors. Ridged hackles rose and fell along the crest of its shoulders, betraying the rhythm of its pulse. Gleaming eyes reflected both feral savagery and profound intelligence.

The keening of the weepers continued to recede with their departure. A terrible lament of failed retribution. In the relative silence gathering in its wake, high above the jungle's ceaseless cacophony, Kylac heard the groll's ragged breathing and the soft snarl issuing from its lips.

Leaving him to wonder, what was it waiting for?

Its gaze shifted slightly, the nostrils beneath its blunt nose hissing as they flared. Sniffing. At Denariel, Kylac realized, who hunkered on her heels a pace back of his right shoulder.

"Seems your summons was received," he observed, drawing the

mutant's livid gaze back to him. "What now?"

"Lower your weapons," the queen suggested.

Kylac scoffed. "Do ya mean to lower yours?"

He felt Denariel's frown, followed by her slow rise. Her spear fell from her hand, to kiss the stony ground. "He won't kill us, provided you do nothing to provoke him."

Kylac wished he could believe that. "Ya know this one, then?"

"I know his kind," she boasted bravely. Braver than she felt, given the tremor in her voice. "*Torna sunga Ukinha,*" she called to the Ukinh. "Denariel."

A spark of recognition, given the manner in which the groll cocked its head. Kylac half expected the creature to speak. But it only stared in response, its baleful eyes unblinking. Its flesh continued to worm and ripple with subtle movements, the flowing patches hard and scaly and riddled with bony spurs one moment, soft and smooth and devoid of texture the next. Muscles swelled or shrank, thinning or thickening the creature's limbs and torso by turns, making its precise form indistinct. Ukinha could become as hulking as bears, or as lithe as panthers, within the span of a heartbeat.

As he knew all too well.

"Mayhap it didn't hear ya."

"He heard," Denariel insisted. "And he understands. Sheathe your swords."

"And what's to keep *him* from ripping our throats out?"

"Were that his intent, we'd not be having this discussion."

That much, at least, aligned with Kylac's instincts. Still, he couldn't quite convince himself that the creature's interest in them was purely benign. Ukinha, as he'd heard them described, were fiercely territorial. This was *its* domain, and themselves trespassers within it. "And his intent is what, then?"

"To discern ours. He serves as my guardian," she said to the groll, pressing forward to Kylac's side. "Uncommissioned and uninvited, but he means no further harm. *Sheathe . . . your . . . swords,*" she demanded again.

Had this not been Denariel's hope in setting her blaze atop this rock? To attract a Ukinh to her side? Despite what little he knew about her aims, she'd done well enough in making it this far. Mayhap it was time to extend her a measure of trust.

He decided to risk it. It wasn't as if he wouldn't be able to draw the weapons again. Whatever disadvantage might result, he'd have to trust *himself* to overcome.

"Just going to tuck them away here," Kylac assured the groll, easing his blades slowly toward the throats of his scabbards.

The Ukinh bristled nonetheless, watching him the entire time. Eyeing the blades as if they might be flaming torches, and itself standing in a vat of oil.

"He knew nothing of the ornga," Denariel added apologetically. "I would have warned him, stopped him, had he found me sooner."

Had the groll favored the creatures in their erstwhile form? Such would provide natural cause for its hostile arrival. Kylac hadn't just ventured into its territory uninvited, but had slain the ornga and unleashed a swarm of orngarath in their place. Mayhap the Ukinh found this displeasing.

Begging the question, was it merely curious as to those who'd caused such a stir? Or was a punishment in order?

When crossguards struck lockets, Kylac released his hilts. "I mean only to keep her safe."

The Ukinh hissed and snorted, still bristling in its posture, seeming offended by Kylac's very breath.

"*Empedes morta*," Denariel declared fiercely, before touching a splayed hand over her breast and repeating from earlier, "*Torna sunga Ukinha. Abinama.*"

Whatever the language, Kylac found it unfamiliar. Tempted as he was to ask, he held his questions as to her meaning and purpose. He keyed instead on the groll's movements, for the slightest shift or lean that might signal attack. As he'd been given nothing to go on here, this was clearly Denariel's parley. Let her make it, while he did his best to ensure it didn't cost her her life.

"*Etretay nooranga, bine* Addaran," she pressed. Struggling with the words, but doing her best to utter them respectfully. "*Gulgari*. Audience, I seek. And gift I bear. *Handradus . . . demuun . . . Talathandria.*"

The last, Kylac recognized well enough. So too did the groll, given its narrowing gaze and the heat of its contorting visage. While no expert—or even novice—in Ukinhan expressions, he sensed a sharp skepticism and palpable warning that required no translation.

"*Hik thur guul*," the mutant growled in reply.

Unless they were but meaningless, guttural noises dredged from its throat or coughed up from the depths of its lungs. Again, Kylac clung to his own silence, waiting for something more. Beside him, Denariel held her breath. For all her bluster, she was no more certain of the outcome here than he. From the groll, he interpreted only roiling anger and venomous mistrust. Slaver dripped from the corners of its mouth as it studied them, seething, determining their fates.

Then it crouched low, snarling as it shrank on its haunches all the way down to its heels. At the same time, its torso flared like the hood of an asp. Bony protrusions sprouted as plates upon its shoulders and as a string of knobbed horns that formed a crest from the base of its spine to the ridge of its brow. The claws of its right hand scratched at the earth. Once, twice. Believing it meant to pounce, Kylac nonetheless remained steady, hands motionless above his hilts, revealing nothing of his own, willing anxiety.

Finally, the Ukinh dipped its head and abruptly put its back to them, making for the ledge face.

"Come," Denariel said, exhaling in relief. She turned at once to gather her meager provisions, slinging sacks and skins across her back.

"Where?"

"Where I'd hoped. Would that I could leave you here to settle matters with the orngarath, but I have spoken for you, and will not therefore leave you to roam untended."

"We're to follow it?" Off her glare, he added, "*Him*, I mean. To this Talathandria?"

"As asked, so agreed."

Mayhap. Kylac had no evidence to dispute her. Only a hollow sense that they might be making a mistake. He looked to the groll, which had paused again, this time at the ledge's rim, to glance back over the knotted hunch of its shoulder. Waiting on them, it would appear.

Only for a moment. In the next, it had clambered spiderlike from view, slipping over the precipice.

"Come," Denariel repeated, plucking her spear from the ground before hustling after.

Kylac kept pace alongside, still dogged by a nagging uncertainty. This way lay new adventure. Something that should have thrilled him. Instead, his stomach churned with misgiving. Like the first brewing of an illness, portending tribulation and suffering.

But what exactly awaited them here? Or back at Indranell, should they strike course instead toward the city?

So he told himself that it was only the many unanswered questions that disturbed him. That and his concern for Denariel, whose life would be so much harder to safeguard than his own. Acknowledging that there was nothing he might say or do to dissuade her, it would seem he had little choice but to follow.

Their descent unfolded along a different path than the mutant's—different also from the one Kylac had negotiated in his climb. A longer, more meandering path that relied upon grades and cuts and switchbacks that Denariel could manage. Kylac did nothing to hurry her, even though the groll had already reached the pinnacle's base. It crouched there like a pool of shadow, all but invisible in the lee of a boulder sheared at some point in history from the cliff face. Though he couldn't see its eyes, he sensed its gaze upon them.

It met them a half-mark later, emerging soundlessly from the shadows as they tread down a final, buttress slope amid the sprinkle of shattered blocks and blankets of scree skirting the monolith's foundation. An eerie quiet had settled over the area, the surrounding jungle less boisterous than Kylac remembered. A handful of orngarath peppered the moonlit ground, those who'd been swept from the heights and landed awkwardly enough to break their spines, bend rib bones into their hearts, or dash the brains from their small skulls. No more than a score, out of the hundreds he'd fought. Yet the groll's gimlet gaze brimmed with accusation, drawing from him a pang of remorse.

Of the rest, there remained no sign, save for the trails carved by their frantic departure. Trails leading east, back into the tangled reaches of the night-cloaked jungle.

The Ukinh turned west, descending the hump of the monolith's roots before plunging into a narrow rift in the jungle wall. Denariel hastened after, her prior nervousness consumed by the fire of her more customary determination. Kylac settled in at her heels, warding her back while marking the groll's slithering progress through the labyrinth of trees and vines and brush. An acceptable arrangement, as the mutant maintained a lead of twenty paces or more. A distance suited more to its own desires, surely, than in consideration of Kylac's comfort. Either way, it gave him plenty of time to intercept it, should it decide to turn on her.

They trekked for more than an hour in silence. Only Denariel made any sound with her movements, and that but a whisper amid the rustlings of the jungle—themselves diminished from what he'd heard and seen earlier. Out at the farthest edges of the surrounding darkness, he still sensed perils lurking. But there was a wariness to them now, keener and more profound than any felt before. A fearful respect for their Ukinh guide, if Denariel was to be believed. Making them doubly indebted. For if chasing off the orngarath weren't gift enough, the mutant would unquestionably earn Kylac's appreciation if enabling them to travel through the Harrows unmolested.

But travel to where? The question pressed him relentlessly, weighing heavier with every stride. Which in itself continued to irk him. For seldom was he given to anxiety as to where his next step might lead. His had often been a path dictated by happenstance or curiosity. An urge here, an opportunity there. Yet he felt now like a man blithely toting a noose to his own hanging.

And the only way to make sense of matters, he finally decided, was to know better what he might be heading into.

"That language ya spoke earlier," he hazarded. "It wasn't Entien, Old *or* New."

"What?" Denariel replied tersely.

"Or Illian. Or even Gohran. Was it *theirs*?"

The queen eyed him crossly, her expression a blend of stark irritation and smug authority. "It was the tongue of their former masters."

"The Breeders?" Kylac made no effort to bridle his surprise. He caught their guide glancing back at them from the point. But if their words troubled it, the groll gave no further indication. "One might guess that tongue would rile, rather than soothe."

"And why is that?"

"The language o' one's slavers?"

"*Masters*, I said."

"Did the Ukinha not revolt against them? Eradicating them?" He seemed to recall hearing as much from the lips of Brenth, in the company of Ledron's Shadowguard at the edge of the Gorrethrian Sound, none of whom had disputed the account.

Denariel looked set to do so now, though he couldn't tell if she was more angry or amused. "A common reckoning, bred in ignorance. The Ukinha revered their Gorrethrehn creators, serving and defending them with staunch devotion."

"How, then, did the Breeders fall?"

"A pestilence, albeit one of their own making. A parasitic contagion invisible to the unaided eye. Developed as a weapon against their enemies, it was unleashed in the cataclysm of the Sundering, to claim *them* instead."

So they *had* fallen victim to their own creations, just not the ones he'd been led to believe. Assuming, of course, that Denariel had the truth of it. Given the intervening centuries, who could truly know?

"Is that why ya believe he won't harm ya?" Kylac asked. "Or lead us astray?"

Judging by her visage, a part of her wished to continue shutting him out, to refuse him the answers for which he was groping. But a greater part, it seemed, was ready to revel in the success stemming from her superior knowledge.

"He won't harm me because I'm a woman," she gloated finally.

Kylac blinked. "Is that so?"

"Ukinha are male. All of them. They instinctively honor and defend women of any breed."

Could it be that simple? "Which is why ya felt it safe enough to traverse the wilds alone."

"No Ukinh I could find or draw would permit me to suffer. Which is more than I can say for you."

"While believing yourself experienced enough to evade or bypass other threats."

"Did I not?"

He supposed she had. Mostly. "And you're convinced this Talathandria is real."

"From the lips of one who would know."

The Ukinh. *Her* Ukinh. He moved quickly to skirt that particular subject. "So, if'n our friend here has come to revere her in some fashion, why would he lead ya—a stranger with male in tow—to her?"

"Because I told him who I am, and of a proposition I might make."

"A gift, ya mentioned." Himself, he might have thought, had he believed he could hold any value to these creatures.

"To end the pioneering efforts of my people," she declared, ducking a gnarled branch and pushing through a curtain of vines. "And thereby forestall our encroachment upon her territories."

Then *that* was how she meant to persuade the erstwhile Addaran queen—now queen of the Ukinha, by the sound of it—to give ear. And why she thought she could elicit a favorable response. "In exchange for her aid in driving off the Grenarr."

Denariel's tart silence was his only confirmation.

"And ya believe that to be gift enough? Presuming Your Majesty could impose such an edict."

"It's the real reason Ukinha prowl and sometimes hunt along our borders. As a matter of dissuasion and self-defense."

"I mean, if'n your people are such thorns to her, why not let the Grenarr wipe you out?"

"Because the tar-skins will offer no such peace."

A rationale it was. However frail and presumptuous, at least the plan that had brought them here wasn't entirely devoid of reasoning.

If only Kylac felt better about it. He *should* have, having unearthed at least a kernel of her logic. Yet, while peering ahead at the creature they now followed, he couldn't make himself believe it would be that easy. Barter as she might, what would be the true cost of this desperate foray?

"I'll confess, I's wondered at times what gives your people any greater claim to these lands than the Grenarr."

Denariel's eyes ignited like coals blown to life. "Claims aside, my father only ever dealt openly with Grendavan's brood. He didn't backstab and deceive, as they did him. And though I may bear none of his blood, I'll give my dying breath, if need be, to prevent *their* ideals from trampling his."

Kylac felt himself nodding inwardly. Save for casting all Grenarr in their overlord's light, he'd long viewed the situation much the same. Hostility and conflict were cornerstones of the natural world. Prevarication, deception, and needless cruelty were not. Or at least, not part of any nature he intended to condone.

"I must say, Majesty—"

"Nothing," she snapped, drawing another glance from their Ukinh guide. "You're alive now at my mercy alone. That means your tongue, also, belongs to me. And I'll have him remove it, if I must, that I might focus on my path."

With that, she stormed ahead, swatting irritably at the protruding brush, nearly tripping over an exposed root in her haste. Kylac let her be. She hadn't for a moment convinced him it was her *mercy* that had spared him confrontation with the groll. More likely, she was as yet unsure of his potential use, as her confidence in all of this continued to be, in some measure, an affectation. Nonetheless, she'd shared with him already more than he'd expected, and he, too, wanted her to focus chiefly on whatever hazards might lurk at her feet.

For now, he would satisfy himself with respecting her wishes, resolving to learn more at some future juncture.

As he watched her stomp and thrash ahead of him, he felt a twinge of guilt at having aggravated her. A pity that his mere presence continued to so offend, because that hadn't in any way been his aim. Given her ragged condition, he marveled that she was able to keep moving, and wondered at her motivation. But then, he already knew. Her yearning for vengeance. Her hunger to set matters right.

Of which he was no small part. In that regard, if hating him fueled her strength, then mayhap he had no cause to feel guilty after all.

As always, even the specter of that emotion sparked recollection of Briallen. His onetime friend, never far from his thoughts, whose name he'd long since felt unworthy to mention. In some respects, Denariel's frustration and tenacity reminded him of hers. Pairing the two, how much of his presence here, he wondered, constituted an effort to atone for that earlier failing?

Like most of his endeavors since, more than he cared to admit—even if only to himself. So he nudged her ghost back in his mind, both relieved and saddened by her willingness to depart, and re-attuned himself to the road ahead, imagining better choices and nobler deeds by which he might hope one day to win her forgiveness.

Such reflection stirred images of others he'd tried to assist, too many of whom, of late, could scarcely claim to have benefitted from the interaction. How might Ledron be faring, back at Indranell? Had he reached the northern city safely? Had he found and freed Talon, Warmund, Havrig, and the rest of their captured company from whatever assignments Bahsk had forced them into? How might he be dealing with Colonel Fayne and other Addaran leaders, to say nothing of the ongoing conflict with Sabrynne's cunning siege force?

And what of Ithrimir, left even farther behind at Avenell? What had Sabrynne decided to do with him, once it was discovered that the rest of her prisoners had escaped? It rankled Kylac to think of the Elementer or any others suffering the overlord's wrath on his behalf. He never should have permitted it. He should have gone back and seen to the Scribe's deliverance. One more coin laid upon the scales against him. Scales he meant to balance before taking final leave of the Stormweaver and her bloody machinations.

Before that, it had been Sallun, and Trajan, and all of those with whom he'd first trekked across the Harrows. To recall their fates didn't bear thinking on, except to imagine that they would all have been a good deal better off had they never set sail from Kuurian shores.

There, at least, his brooding memories came upon a ray of light amid the darkness. For that was where he'd battled alongside Torin, Allion, Corathel, and their allies, aiding them in their war against Spithaera, Killangrathor, and the countless minions of demon and dragonspawn. A conflict that required no embellishment from those recounting the tale. A present-day legend that would likely come to stand among those by which mankind measured the history of this world. Or not. But hundreds of thousands of lives had been at stake, and he'd helped to preserve them. To save the peoples of an entire island continent from annihilation.

He could take some small pride in that, could he not?

Then again, he knew nothing of what had transpired since. The tedious process of rebuilding a clutch of shattered realms, he suspected. That was what had prompted him to seek further adventure elsewhere, anyway. Now, given his recent string of miscalculations, he had to wonder what may have befallen his former friends. For their sakes, he hoped their road had been smoother than his.

Westward, he delved, shadowing Denariel in pursuit of the groll, through the deepening night. Resolving not to succumb to this plague of unusually black thoughts. By and large, the path he and the queen followed had proven reasonably easy on them. The jungle growth thickened at times, clutching at them or seeking to trip them up, but inflicted only minor welts and scratches. The stony ground, while rugged and uneven, seemed flatter and less treacherous than before. Mires and sinkholes and cliffs and briar walls marred the savage landscape, but never severed their path directly, sparing them from having to reroute. Clearly, their Ukinh guide knew well this stretch of wilderness, to chart them such a favorable course. Protecting them, as it did from the menagerie of fearsome denizens that Kylac could feel marking their progress. Keeping them safe.

Or was it all part of some larger trap?

Denariel expressed no concerns, so neither did he. She did, however, begin to stumble, and drag, and falter, more and more, as the passing hours weighed heavier upon them. Any attempt by Kylac to lend support was summarily rejected, and seemed to spur her on for a time. But it became clear to him, as the Nightingale of midnight flew past with the Woodcock and then the Shrike on its tail feathers, that the queen was taxing herself beyond any strength she might soon recover.

He was considering how best to propose they stop, uncertain which of his two companions would be harder to convince, when the groll seemed to realize for itself Denariel's duress. For it came to an abrupt halt at the far edge of a small clearing, and there waited for them to catch up. They came upon it slowly, cautiously. No sooner had they reached it than the groll began to circle the clearing's edges, sniffing and scratching at earth and brush as if to mark a perimeter.

"He intends that we rest here," Denariel said, confirming Kylac's suspicions.

Kylac did nothing to express his relief. Instead, he surveyed the clearing's jagged floor, comprised of exposed ironshore, and wondered that the groll meant for them—or at least Denariel—to find sleep upon it.

He doubted there would be any questioning the creature, though, and indeed watched a weary Denariel slump promptly against a pitted ridge. So he cast about for a more suitable alternative.

"What o' those bushes there?" he asked, pointing to a tuft of plants with leaves taller and wider than the ordinary man.

"What of them?"

"If'n Her Majesty would permit me, they might serve softer bedding."

Denariel scowled, refusing his offer, but arose and drew a knife with which to take to the task herself. With no objection from their mutant guide, they set to harvesting a pile of the thick, fleshy leaves. The groll, meanwhile, continued to search and stake its claim upon the outskirts of the clearing, presumably to ensure that, should they find sleep, it wouldn't be disturbed.

In its probing, it must have violated the nest of some creature. For there came abruptly a hissing, thrashing, screeching struggle, in which a narrow, lizard-like head lunged at the end of a serpentine neck, again and again, spewing a green ichor amid a wild flapping of hooked, leathery wings.

Intense as it seemed, the fight proved brief. Almost as soon as Kylac had ascertained what was happening, the groll had seized the animal's mouth and pinned its veined wings against its body.

"Wyvern," Denariel said, her voice tight.

Rather than wring the wyvern's neck, the groll aimed it toward the southeast and flung it up into the air. Hissing and squawking, the wyvern wisely took wing, flapping off into the trees.

"He trusts it not to return in the midst of our slumber, then?" Kylac asked.

Denariel snorted, tossing her head in disgust. "His kind doesn't kill so indiscriminately as you."

On that count, Kylac took umbrage. "On the contrary, I give

most o' my adversaries ample choice. Only when I encounter outright monsters or villains do I—"

"You slaughter without feeling," Denariel griped, "without remorse. What is that if not monstrous?"

Kylac watched her return to hacking at leaves. "I'm no stranger to emotion," he admitted, bending back to the work himself. "But I's seen what happens to men ruled by it. I'm not about to let it tarnish my reason or cloud my instinct."

The queen scoffed. "You're a mercenary. A ruffian for hire. Scarcely better than a roadside bandit."

Kylac wondered if she truly felt that way, or if she was merely trying to goad him. "Would that I'd been born a cobbler, to shod the feet o' kings. Or a minstrel, to sing sweet favors from the lips o' maidens. As a sculptor, I might have raised monuments to surpass the gods they honored. As a farmer, to reap harvests so bountiful as to satisfy the hunger of even beggars and urchins." Hefting his blades, he added, "Alas, this is the trade I was born to."

Unimpressed by his arrogance, Denariel just shook her head. "And like any trade or skill, easily set aside, were your own hunger for it not so great."

He supposed there was at least some truth to that, and so left the claim unchallenged. Difficult as it would have been to defy his father's wishes, he'd done so in other ways. So why not this?

Denariel huffed and gathered up her leaves, hauling them over to a smoother patch of ground, where unknown elements had chiseled or worn the ridges and spires of ironshore to blunter nubs. Layering the leaves upon the rock, she soon had a mesh in place to serve as padding through the night—or however long the groll meant to allow them rest.

Kylac did the same, choosing a spot as near to hers as he dared. Even then, the queen cast him a sour glance, as if to suggest he might have positioned himself farther.

By then, the groll was carrying its perimeter higher, into the overhead limbs of trees. As Kylac settled himself down, not really intending to sleep, he marked Denariel's close, fascinated observation of the Ukinh's liquid movements.

"They truly are marvelous creatures," he said.

He watched her clench in response. "Beautiful in ways you cannot see or fathom."

Kylac marveled at the depth of her sentiment. Another lament for her lost beloved, then. He wondered if her feelings for the creature were entirely natural, or if, as Ledron had suggested, they might owe more to the hallucinogenic influence of its oils upon her skin. The latter seemed unlikely, as she hadn't had contact with the creature for months.

"He must have felt the same for you, to sacrifice himself as he did."

Her hatred flared, white-hot amid the thickly laid shadows. "You gave him no choice. Had he not been hobbled by your cursed blade . . ." She trailed off, trembling with fury, choking back tears she wouldn't deign share with him.

Kylac remembered the event somewhat differently. Even wounded, her groll had seemed more than capable of springing aside, evading the maddened jaggeruunt's persistent strikes. Had she fled, as it wished her to, it might have escaped, to reunite with her later.

But he kept the opinion to himself. Knowing he'd caused her enough heartache already. Feeling foolish for having broached the topic to begin with.

"If you are not, in fact, a monster," Denariel said, as soon as she'd composed herself, "you'll not speak of him again." She then drew her cloak more tightly about her, and rolled to her side, turning her back to him and his reflections.

She continued to radiate sorrow and hatred for some time thereafter. Kylac lay wordlessly upon his own pad of leaves there in the noisome darkness. Watching the groll until it had settled into a sentry position high overhead. Making sure even then that it didn't move. Eventually closing his eyes and feigning sleep while Denariel grappled with her demons and whatever memories his painful remarks had unleashed.

Mercifully, the queen soon surrendered to her exhaustion, and fell prey to slumber.

Not long after, with the breath of the Vulture's Hour at his neck, and feeling safer than he had any right to, Kylac yielded to the same.

29

They roused with the lark, the sun's rays already flooding the sky, yet screened by the jungle canopy so that only the residual light reached them. Kylac had actually awakened two hours earlier, with daybreak no more than a red tinge amid the blackness, but had wanted Denariel to sleep longer. The Ukinh, he'd found in its perch. For all he knew, it hadn't slept at all.

At the queen's first stirring, it perked and slithered down from its lookout position. For a moment, it appeared to vanish amid the brush. When returned, it deposited upon the ground a clutch of bulbous roots and a half dozen speckled eggs cupped in an enlarged hand. Denariel nodded and voiced her gratitude to the groll before partaking of both in their raw form. With a dismissive grunt, she left two of the eggs and one of the roots for Kylac.

He promptly declined. "Your Majesty should have her fill."

"I have. The remainder is not to be wasted."

He very nearly received that as a compliment—that food in *his* belly should not be deemed by her a waste. But he stopped short of expressing as much, doubting that she would appreciate any of his clumsy attempts at levity.

"By your leave, Majesty," he said instead, and devoured his portion in short order while the queen drank and stretched and massaged her feet. Meager as the victuals seemed, he found them surprisingly palatable and satisfying. Though, when he too nodded at the groll his appreciation, it only hissed and flared and set forth through the west wall of the clearing, resuming its suspended trek.

"I don't suppose ya know how long or far this jaunt will take us," Kylac said, as Denariel shouldered her few provisions.

"We'll know when we arrive," she replied curtly, and started after.

They traveled until midday without rest, pausing twice to refill waterskins, but elsewise making steady progress. Fortunately, the journey continued to be less than arduous, even for Denariel. The groll's pace was ceaseless, yet maintainable, and its path accommodating, despite the harsh terrain. Kylac marked the many hazards and obstacles bypassed as the leagues gathered in their wake, and estimated them to be traversing ground in a matter of hours that might have cost him days on his own—even had he known his heading. Presuming their destination was indeed the one Denariel sought to reach, he could only be pleased by their progress.

They wasted few breaths on words. Having learned enough to quell his most immediate doubts concerning this venture, Kylac chose to spare the queen the grating revulsion of his voice, and thus spoke only when directly questioned. Denariel had few enough of those, reserved chiefly for the maneuvers employed by General Bahsk in her absence. So Kylac had relayed to her what details he knew of the southerly foray, describing the geographical markers they'd gone by, and detailing the nature of the attacks launched against them by the Grenarr.

The queen's reaction largely surprised him.

"Stubbornness and arrogance aside, I cannot fault the general his decision to sidestep Ollerman's by way of Rendenel."

"Seemed a decent strategy," Kylac agreed, "save that, once again, the Grenarr managed to anticipate it."

"Else were advised beforehand."

"More likely that."

"Yet no mole was uncovered?"

Kylac shrugged. "Not unless Ledron has since brought them to light."

"Bahsk charged *him* with that task?"

"I fear the general issued his final order at Rendenel. Our good captain was to assume command in his stead."

Denariel soured. "A capable guardian he may be, but Ledron is no battlefield commander."

"He had Colonel Garnham to consult with. And Fayne, if'n returned to Indranell as planned."

Sourness gave way to disgust. "The Maul and the Scorpion. Doubtless, he'll be wishing by now that he followed you into the Harrows." She shook her head. "How did Bahsk fall?"

"Found a spear in his throat."

"You witnessed this?"

"I put it there."

Denariel halted and rounded on him in disbelief. "*You* slew him?"

"With fair warning, acknowledged upon our detention."

The queen glanced at the groll, which had paused to look back at them, before returning her fiery glare to Kylac. "In the midst of all that opposes us, you choose to execute our most experienced commander?"

"He made his choice. Mine was to honor my word."

The slope of Denariel's brow sharpened threateningly. Her hands balled into fists. For a moment, he thought she intended to strike him.

"Our guide is departing," he observed.

The queen turned to see that, in fact, the Ukinh had resumed its trek. Showing what little concern it had for their quarrels. Threatening, it seemed, to leave them behind.

Be it idle or genuine, Denariel hissed and muttered unintelligibly before spinning away from him, storming ahead in an effort to catch up.

Kylac permitted her a somewhat larger lead than before, reflecting on how much easier it might have been to lie, or at least omit the full truth of his involvement.

Not with any breath *he* summoned.

The next two hours were spent navigating a narrow, wending course through the heart of a buttonwood swamp. Hemmed in by fetid waters and choking brush, assailed by pungent smells of brackish mold and deadwood decay, Kylac felt the weight of confinement pressing down upon him. Cruel eyes seemed to follow him from every lurking angle, but, as he'd come to expect, not one living creature proved brave or foolish enough to risk an attack. Not in the presence of the groll, which continued to carve an unerring, unchallenged swath through the slime-coated muck and shadowed murk.

With the Falcon's Hour ushering in midafternoon, the swamp thinned at last, emptying into a ravine that cut north and south across their path. Kylac recognized it at once—for the path itself, but more so for the hump of broken hills rising on its far side to the west. Talathandria's Run, Trajan had called it. The Iron Scar. While they hadn't traversed this particular stretch of ground, it was clearly part of the same network that their company had briefly followed during his last trek through the Harrows, when seeking to return Denariel to her father at Avenell.

An auspicious sign, mayhap, to reach a region bearing the name of their quarry. He nearly voiced as much to his companions, but couldn't imagine any response they might care to utter, or that he might care to hear. Until such time as they might find themselves in similar spirits, best to keep his observations and musings to himself.

They followed the ravine north for nearly a quarter mile before edging west along a narrow cleft rising between a pair of jagged cliffs. The slope steepened the higher they climbed, even as it snaked back and forth between folds in the adjoining escarpments. Halfway to the summit, the track became a sliver-thin defile slicing between the two. The momentary relief Kylac had felt at emerging from the swamp was swiftly engulfed by the oppressive weight of the raw stone walls. To question or comment on their path at this juncture, however, might only reveal his discomfort. So again he held his tongue and trusted that their guide would at some point lead them clear.

The defile led to a tunnel, which emptied onto a slope, which they followed to another defile. A labyrinth, their path soon became. A web of ribbon pathways laid amid the clefts and fissures and voids in the mountain rock. Kylac wondered if this was still the most direct route to their destination, or if the groll might be seeking now to confuse them. Either way, he measured his steps and his turns as he went, that he might retrace the fractured string of cuts and slopes and tunnels on his own, should the need arise.

The wildlife here seemed greatly diminished. He crossed paths with insects of every variety. With snakes and lizards. With hard-shelled, scuttling crabs, and fur-coated, lean-limbed rodents. Most had already cleared from his guide's path, and so were glimpsed only hunkered and withdrawn amid the flanking shadows. Kylac took note of their nests and hives and dens regardless. Suspecting that, should he indeed find himself retracing his steps, they might not prove as courteous.

The silence that shrouded him and his reluctant companions prevailed throughout the Falcon's flight and the Kingfisher's. The sun's rays came and went, mostly in slivers, as the afternoon lengthened. It was nearly the Swallow's Hour, just a couple hours before dusk, when they emerged from yet another defile into the shallow bowl of a highland valley. A remarkably verdant valley, marked by a vast meadow of green grasses, flowering brush, and stately trees. Cedar and hemlock and spruce and pine. Or at least cousins to the same. While their forms and colors differed somewhat from the more familiar breeds found on his home isle, he knew them by their scents.

Kylac was momentarily taken aback. To discover a pocket of such relative beauty amid the mostly gnarled, festering tangle of the Harrows surprised him. It shouldn't have. Even the ugliest of oysters could house a pearl. But how long had it been since he'd happened upon a landscape as scenic and serene as this?

His Ukinh guide threaded a path down a rocky slope and waded out into the grasses. Denariel followed. Kylac closed the distance between them. Lush and lovely the grasses might be, full of flitting butterflies and the darting flashes of colorful of birds. But they might conceal any number of skulking predators, as well. Even the calmest of seas held its share of sharks.

It took them more than half of the Swallow's flight to cross the valley floor, but at least they did so unaccosted. Again, Kylac felt the itch of keen interest upon his shoulders, exposing those concealed denizens that marked his movements. One of which he took special notice. For it was not the sharp, fleeting sensation he'd grown accustomed to, but a probing, worming, lingering irritation . . .

And yet, of no discernible cause for distress. It was really only potential threats that concerned him, and here—by virtue of the location, he believed, as much as the presence of the groll—he sensed none.

Which could itself have registered as an alarm, were he seeking ghosts amid the shadows. Up until now, however, the ghosts harbored by this land had shown no fear of the light.

At the west end of the valley, they threaded up and through another slender rift between peaks, emerging within a mountain meadow even lovelier than the last. A smaller, bowl-shaped vale filled with fruit-bearing vegetation and dominated at its center by a shimmering lake. Steep, cave-studded cliffs overlooked the water from all sides, almost hive-like in appearance. A variety of birds circled and glided across the skies, preying upon one another and whatever lived beneath the lake's glistening waters, upon its stony shores, or amid the ocean of surrounding trees. A wilderness still, yet breathtaking to behold.

As they worked their way down amid the lush tangle, Denariel helped herself to a string of berries. When the groll didn't object, Kylac did the same. Drawing a fresh scowl from the queen, he proceeded to eat them. Had she seemed in any way encouraging, he might have been less trusting of them.

Despite the profusion of bright colors and vibrant growth and sweet fragrances, the eyes of this particular vale quickly proved harsher than those of the last, raw and scathing in their interest. Kylac searched the surrounding heights, but glimpsed only blind snatches of stone through the forest canopy. Ashen slopes and jutting crags, broken ledges and chiseled overhangs. Nothing to which he might attribute the dread sensation that had settled over him.

That somewhere above them, from upon the valley rim, their arrival was being observed.

And less than eagerly received.

The Swallow's Hour was giving way to the Wren's when their guide brought them to the southeastern shore of the lake. Placid waters stirred by wind lapped at a pebble-strewn bank. Small gray gnatcatchers flitted about, picking at the rocks before hopping clear and darting off again. Birdsong and other chittering echoes continued to rise upon the valley walls. Even with a clear view of the slopes, however, Kylac saw nothing to warrant the bitter threat he now felt welling up inside him.

At the water's edge, the groll issued a sudden, skyward shriek. Gnatcatchers and other winged creatures scattered. Even those raptors resembling hawks and shrikes turned wing to whatever currents would carry them swiftly away. As the skies emptied, the Ukinh rounded to face Denariel, crouching low. An arm swept out in what might have been a gesture. A growl guttered in its throat. Then it bounded to the south, tracing the shoreline for a half dozen startlingly swift strides, before dashing into the woods. Vanishing amid the foliage with nary a leaf left to quiver in its wake.

"Is this the place, then?" Kylac asked.

"We wait," Denariel confirmed, eyeing the vale's rocky, cave-riddled walls.

"For what?"

The queen frowned as her gaze swept the nearer surroundings. "For *her*, I imagine."

Talathandria. *Imagining* she chose to appear. Left here in the open, they were in plain enough view—from a thousand or more elevated angles. Mayhap that was the purpose of depositing them in this particular location. That this supposed queen of the Ukinha could determine whether to hear them.

Assuming the groll hadn't simply abandoned them to the company of their own lake-cast reflections.

He considered asking how long they might be here—whether they should think to prepare camp, for instance, with dusk little more than an hour distant now—but recalled readily enough the answer Denariel had summoned the last time he'd questioned her along those lines. Even if she knew, she would more likely view it as an opportunity to mock and berate him. Harmless as her barbs might be, he saw no need to grant her the satisfaction.

He watched her lean her self-made spear against a slab of rock, before shedding her satchels and pouches alongside. At which point, her gaze snagged upon something near her feet. Without a word, she eased toward it, bending to collect it from the carpet of shoreline stones. No more than a scrap of deadwood it might have been, small and hook-shaped. Yet she held it cautiously, almost reverently, as if it might seek to bite her.

"What is it?" he asked.

"A claw."

Kylac had already edged around for a closer look. A claw it was. Finger-length, but elsewise unremarkable, until he realized from Denariel's bearing what manner of creature had likely shed it. "Ukinh?"

The queen nodded, more to herself than to him, as if in awe of her find. "I can smell its venom."

So could Kylac, now that he hovered over it. "How is that?" he wondered aloud. From its bleached appearance, the claw wasn't freshly discarded, but had been baking there in the sun for some time. "Is it still potent?"

Denariel nodded, a cold gleam lighting her eyes as she glanced round again at their environs. "A lethal weapon for one who wields it."

"Or *to* that wielder," Kylac observed with a frown, "if mishandled."

Undaunted, the queen stowed the claw in a pocket of her leather tunic. "Difficult enough to prick oneself by accident."

"Why the risk? Does Your Majesty now believe the Ukinha would let her come to harm?"

His sardonic tone brought the lash of her familiar ire. "Of their own will, no. Where the will of Talathandria may lie, I'll not pretend to know. Better prepared, is it not?"

For all the victories scored against her with stauncher arguments, Kylac let this one go. "If'n we're to wait here, I'd sooner not do so with empty stomach. Suppose this Talathandria will object if'n we help ourselves to some o' her fish?"

Denariel scowled, but clearly couldn't say. So Kylac snatched her spear from where she'd set it aside, and carried it down the bank to the water's edge—keeping an eye out for any other stray Ukinh claws that might be hiding underfoot.

He sensed his companion's reflexive protests. But as they went unspoken, he felt no cause to heed them. Leaving her to situate herself as she deemed appropriate, he waded into the lake, watching for flashes of movement amid the ironshore grottos discovered there. A relief, to put the griping queen at his back, distancing himself from her in that small way. While nonetheless maintaining subtle watch of the valley and its movements, alert to the implacable threat that continued to plague him.

It took him only a quarter-mark to spear a pair of brightly striped fish of unknown variety, during which time Denariel had coaxed a small fire to life. He presented them to her without comment, and she received them in kind. That she didn't balk at the offering left him presuming it was safe to eat. Seared over a heated stone, the pinkish meat was easier to stomach than it would have been raw. He thanked her for the effort, but she chose only to grunt wordlessly.

By the time they'd finished, the sun had descended below the valley's rim, scraped by jagged peaks to leave a crimson smear against the gathering darkness. Stars bloomed, brightening steadily. Scores of birds returned to their nests and hollows, while others emerged, ready to hunt. Gimlet eyes peered out at them from the trees of the forest, but only insects dared approach their fire's flames.

Of Talathandria, there remained no sign.

For another two hours, they sat in mutual silence, serenaded by raucous vale song. Denariel stretched and massaged her legs and sought shelter within her private reflections. Kylac considered questions he might extend her, but most centered too closely on the nature and origins of her relationship with the Ukinha. Having no desire to stoke her anger before what might prove to be a precarious parley, he left them unasked.

With the coming of the Starling's Hour, Denariel wrapped herself in her travel cloak and curled up beside the fire. Retiring early, Kylac presumed. Unsurprising, given the demands of her recent journey, and with what little there seemed to be gained in staying awake. Left to assume watch, Kylac did so without remark. *Swift to your slumber, Majesty.*

Within moments, she slept, twitching restively now and again, but well within her dreams. Or nightmares, as seemed more likely. Whichever, she'd earned them, and he knew better than to intercede.

While the stars gleamed in their changeless patterns, a radiant moon tracked slowly across the sky. Small animals of forest and meadow played their games of hide and hunt, predator and prey alike seeking in their own way to greet another dawn. Kylac tended to the fire as needed, keeping its light and its warmth—however unnecessary upon this sultry isle—alive. Elsewise, his vigil proved calm, quiet. The cloud of indistinct menace hovering over him had subsided, as if it too had tired of him and turned away. Amid the storm of recent events, it would seem he'd happened upon a moment's peace.

He closed his eyes for a time, letting them rest while his other senses remained alert. Wondering how many days and nights of this routine yet lay ahead.

Hours later, the sun returned, knifing through rents in the eastern peaks to carve at the night's steadily weakening shroud. Swaths of golden light streaked the lake's suddenly shimmering surface, while a more diffuse illumination filtered through the forest, gradually etching boles and limbs and leaves from matted shadow.

It was the latter that captured and held his attention. For he soon felt the return of the valley's cruel gaze, focused now in approach from the east. With the lake at his back, he studied the emergent intricacies of the vegetation, seeking more meaningful sign.

He sensed them only a moment before they revealed themselves, and so scarcely had time to reach across the low-burning fire to shake Denariel's shoulder. She roused irritably, confused at first by her surroundings, but drawing focus in her hostility toward *him*.

Reading his stance, she turned quickly enough to face the woods, and there see what he had. A pair of grolls, different than the one that had led them here. Eyeing the lakeside trespassers with bodies flared and hulking in unmistakable warning.

Suddenly alert, Denariel gathered herself upon her knees, extending and spreading her arms in a gesture of submission. The grolls hissed, but held their ground. Against every instinct, Kylac remained still, hands aching for his sword hilts.

A moment later, she materialized. The third he'd sensed. Separating from brush and shadow. Slinking down through a thatch of foliage between the two mutants. To regard the intruders with a striking gaze that told Kylac their wait was over.

30

Talathandria's lantern eyes held Kylac fast. Nestled at the heart of her wizened features, the yellow orbs radiated the same menace and displeasure he'd felt upon his arrival at this valley. Whatever her intentions in meeting here, it was clear at once that she had no use for *him*.

That sentiment softened somewhat when she turned her intense appraisal upon Denariel. An outsider, yes, not to be trusted. But there was a glimmer of something more. Hope? Need?

"*Demuun*, Talathandria," Denariel greeted, prostrating herself before the Ukinhan queen. Glaring back at Kylac when he declined to do the same.

"*Gulgari*," the other replied. Part croak, part growl. "I know of you. Denariel."

It struck as odd to have discernible words issue from her cracked lips. For her naked flesh was so mottled and scaly as to resemble a serpent's more than a woman's. While retaining the basic form to which she must have been born, her wild eyes, wispy strands of hair, and that wrinkled, leathery skin served to cast her in a bestial light.

As much mutant as human.

"*Abinama*," Denariel said. "He spoke of me?"

"He spoke of you," Talathandria affirmed, and Kylac realized they must be recalling Denariel's beloved—Abinama by name. "Whelped by an Addaran. Sired by a Grenarrian. A bastard princess."

Denariel tensed. She pushed up to her knees, an edge sharpening her voice. "Made queen, with the passing of my Addaran father."

"*Gulgari*," Talathandria echoed, her own voice like a coarse brush against splintered wood. "Bearing gift, I am told, for the pleasure of my audience."

The pair of grolls, Kylac observed, had yet to blink while fixating upon him. Talathandria's warders, as he was Denariel's. A silent standoff taking place amid the uneasy conversation. The mutants as willing as he to dispense with words and engage in bloodier exchange.

The open threat hovered like a thunderhead over the proceedings, even as the dawning sun continued to burn away shadows and expose the meeting ground—there where the forest fringe abutted the lakeshore. A contrast reflective of his thoughts. For while two Ukinha stood ready to rip his throat out, they stood together, united in cause. Suggesting Denariel's goal might not be as outlandish and unattainable as initially believed.

"For you and the Ukinha," Denariel agreed, and came respectfully now to her feet. "A cessation, I offer. A pledge to bridle my people's willful efforts to extend our boundaries at your expense. Northward they push, these bold settlers. Greedy, arrogant. Season after season, year after year. Pursuing wealth and independence by staking claim to lands beyond those already taken. Hunting the wilds, and those to whom that land truly belongs."

If appreciative, or impressed, or in any way intrigued, the emotions remained trapped among the creases and hollows of Talathandria's shriveled face. "Requiring no blessing from me. Unless gift there is you ask in return."

"An alliance," Denariel admitted hurriedly, as if to voice the request before losing her courage to do so. "If you've not learned of it by now, a great treachery has befallen our people, undertaken and carried out by our longtime rivals, the Grenarr. Having overrun Avenell on the southern shore, they look now to displace us from our northern bastion of Indranell, at the foot of the Gorrethrian Sound. A dire battle we face, if we're to ensure our survival. And so of you and the mighty Ukinha I plead, begging your mercy and your aid, for the strength to avenge my father's death, retake what was stripped from us, and lay claim to my birthright. That we might herald thereafter an era of peaceful coexistence between Addaran and Ukinh."

A simplification, Kylac observed, for all of Denariel's attempt at eloquence. Omitting the truth of her own people's role in the events that had led to their undoing. He wondered immediately if Talathandria could sense it. If not from the dispossessed queen herself, then from he who stood alertly at her shoulder, endeavoring to hold his tongue.

A lengthening silence seemed to validate his concern, while sapping Denariel's already tenuous confidence. Talathandria's leathery visage revealed nothing of her thoughts. But the very lack of visible reaction suggested to Kylac that the Ukinhan queen was unmoved by the noble plea.

Her eventual words, grating and sawing as if from a ravaged throat, confirmed it.

"Gift? A jape, you have brought me. What concern of mine, whether it is Addarans or Grenarr scratching at my borders? Your struggles, one with the other, serve to stall your advance upon my own territory. It has long been among my interests to see this conflict extended, not resolved."

"Save that the Grenarr are dangerously close to *ending* our conflict. Perhaps forever."

"Nonetheless, your promise rings hollow. Suppose you should manage to uphold such decree throughout your reign—whatever its duration. For how long thereafter might your progeny respect your wishes?" The Ukinhan queen hissed while shaking her head. "The Addarans, like most humans, breed too quickly, and will eventually seek to expand their borders as a matter of need. You may as well promise me a dike to hold back the raging ocean."

Denariel seized upon the reference. "Were the Grenarr hobbled, the ocean would be opened to us. We could expand seaward instead of landward."

"Perhaps," Talathandria rasped. "Still I wonder, why should the Grenarr claim to these shores stand subject to yours? They settled here long before you."

Denariel cast Kylac a scowling glance. As if his earlier inquiry along that vein had somehow planted the question in their host's mind. To Talathandria, she responded with surprise. "Noble Majesty, are you not . . . ? Begging pardon, our heritage . . . it is the same."

The Ukinhan queen snorted her derision. "Exiled, was I. Disavowed. Hunted. For you to reclaim me now, in this hour of need?"

"I only meant—"

"My salvation came in giving myself wholly to the Ukinha. If ever I truly was, I am Addaran no longer."

Denariel groped for a response. "I . . . we . . ."

"So I ask again, why should I care as to their fate? Why should *you*? Bearing the blood of both Addaran and Grenarr, why not stand aside and seek place among the victors?"

"Because I seek a family bound not by blood, but by deed."

The Ukinhan queen seemed taken with this response. Not so much in any expression or shift of bearing that Kylac could point to, but in a sudden, inexplicable chill that rippled through him.

Whatever the sentiment, she buried it quickly beneath a fresh, probing suspicion. "And your chosen family, they succor you in this request? An alliance between man and mutant. Creatures so hated, so feared."

The groll to her left snarled.

"I seek in part to save them from themselves," Denariel admitted. "From their own ignorance. Their own foolishness."

"Then they have spurned you, as they once spurned me. You, too, are outcast. And owe them no protection."

Kylac felt the yoke of defeat settling about his companion's shoulders. Stubborn and determined as she might be, she'd expected to find in Talathandria a more sympathetic ear. To be summarily rejected here and now, in what had seemed a desperate, last-gasp endeavor, was swiftly stealing the last of her strength.

It pained him to witness it.

"Yet here we stand," he interjected, drawing another snarl from the one Ukinh, and a growl from its companion. "Brought before ya with your consent, if'n not upon command. With cause, I'll wager. Some object o' *your* desire."

Her scathing attentions raked him but briefly before fixating again on Denariel. "Bold you were in coming to me. Tenacious. You would risk much for this vengeance, this liberation, that you seek."

"Everything," Denariel assured her. "My final breath."

Again that rippling chill, in response to Talathandria's carefully bridled delight. In its wake, Kylac felt as if perched upon a precipice, leaning forward in the moment before a fall.

"Let us speak of mine instead," the Ukinhan queen said. "For I feel its rattle in my lungs, seeking escape."

Denariel frowned. "You . . . you're dying?"

"Of what consequence, a crone as old as I? But to the Ukinha, all. Far more critical to their preservation than war between their feeble enemies is the matter of their procreation. A matter in which I have served them lo these many decades. As consort. As mother. Before I pass, I would see another take my place. A woman of sufficient will and strength to bear the gift of their offspring."

Kylac's flesh tingled at the revelation. *Mother?* But of course. *Ukinha are male,* Denariel had claimed. *They instinctively honor and defend women of any breed.* And why? In part, at least, because a female host was the only way to guarantee the perpetuation of their species.

"You came to me in search of accord," Talathandria pressed. "The one you propose, I cannot accept. But I counter you this. My aid you shall have in retaking your crown, *gulgari*, should you swear to relinquish it thereafter and assume the mantle of steward matron of the Ukinha instead."

Denariel had grown silent, still, dark skin paling at the thought. Kylac fought the urge to speak *for* her, not at all certain what her actual response would be.

"The strength you speak of," she managed finally, "that which you've shown, for more than a century and a half . . . How could one such as I hope to match it?"

Talathandria's lips tightened, a corner of her mouth curling in what might have been a suppressed smile. "You marvel at my longevity. Do not. Copulation with a Ukinh will grant you sustained life as it has me. Surprising, perhaps, given their many lethal aspects. An oversight on the part of their Gorrethrehn creators, I'm sure."

Denariel's frown suggested that the other might have misread her concern. "But to entrust me with what you ask . . . how can you be certain?"

"Certain, I am not. But faith I have in my children. In the prospects they select. Abinama found you worthy. So shall I."

Denariel stiffened, her beloved's name striking like a dagger. "What?"

"Yes, child. Knowing this day would come, he has long been grooming you as my heir. Among candidates put forth by other Ukinha, I admit. But rare are your would-be rivals, and not one of them come to seek me out."

Kylac felt the worming brush of deception buried among her words, but knew far too little of this creature, of her claims, to begin rooting at its source. Accepting as he was, the entire proposal reeked to him of madness and desperation. Hers, Denariel's, and, in blossoming measure, his own.

"A sign not easily ignored," Talathandria continued, and suffered a sudden, wracking cough. "And upon which I would stake my own offer. Should you demonstrate your devotion, I shall summon my scattered brood and lead them as you will. When your enemies are defeated, we shall depart peacefully, my host and I, provided you join us in our return to the wilds."

A promise to save the Addarans if Denariel would agree to save the Ukinha. Heavy as the price might seem, one *could* consider it a fair exchange.

To Kylac, it still screamed of madness.

"What must I do," Denariel asked, "to demonstrate my devotion?"

Another curdling surge of what felt like sinister delight from Talathandria. "Accept the seed of a Ukinh, here and now, that I might measure your willingness to do so."

Making Denariel the first to extend trust in this bargain. "Giving ya what cause to deliver on her request?" Kylac asked. Seeking not so much an answer as to break the rhythm of this discussion, to disrupt its disheartening flow.

The grolls flared, hissing and growling, while Talathandria skewered him with that malevolent gaze. "The *only* cause, as I elsewise have *none*."

But Denariel, too, seemed distraught. "My love is for Abinama. My vow . . . to him alone."

The true source of her consternation, Kylac realized, now that the words had escaped into the dawning air. Her doubts were not so much with whether she could prove adequate in the calling, but with what struck her as the violation of a private oath to her deceased companion.

Challenged now by the pair of them, Talathandria seemed to quickly bleed patience. "Abinama is dead, is he not? Else you could not have ventured this far without him."

Denariel went rigid, as if, even now, to deny it. "We swore to each other—"

"We? No, child. Abinama's aim was to entice you, lure you, to this very moment. You were special to him in no other way. I copulated with him myself many times, though his seed never quickened in me. Your joining with another in no way betrays his memory, as *this* was his ultimate wish for you."

A harsher, more devastating claim, she couldn't have summoned. Truth or manipulation, the words struck Denariel like a volley of flaming arrows. Piercing, burning, consuming. Leaving the taste of ash and charred soul on the wind.

And Talathandria could sense it. Kylac glared at her, at her remorselessness, before deciding he had to say . . . something.

"There are other roads, Your Majesty. We'll journey as ya first proposed, back to Pentania. I's friends there who will aid us. Indebted, they are. Ya needn't do this."

Meager the offer sounded, even to his own ears. A toothless promise, uttered by a voice none wanted to hear. Denariel, mayhap least of all. He felt her chafing, shuddering response. Even if, in that moment, she was too drained, too lost, too heartsick to physically express it.

"If this . . ." she tried and choked up. "If this is what Abi wanted . . ."

"It was," Talathandria assured her, with all the compassion of a serpent strangling its prey. As if realizing as much, she added more tenderly, "If we are in any way the same, you and I, it is in that neither of us truly belonged elsewhere."

A final chord, that struck, within his faltering companion. A note to banish doubts and chase away fears. After a lifetime of being torn, divided, of seeking place and purpose in a world where she would never cleanly fit . . . Why not here?

Her head sagged forward, features crestfallen. But only for a moment, as she armored herself in acceptance. Looking up again, she said simply, "I will do as you ask."

"Your Majesty," Kylac warned, against the onset of dismay, "there are matters here . . . undisclosed."

"Between all of us."

"Majesty—"

"*Empedes morta*," Denariel said, stepping forward with a sudden vigor, cutting short his protest. Words directed not at him, but at their host. A declaration made earlier, Kylac recalled, to the groll that had led them here. While he knew not its meaning, there was no questioning her commitment to it.

Talathandria nodded as if granting a request. As if she, too, understood that, in this, Denariel wouldn't be denied.

"Your father wouldn't want this," said Kylac, grasping.

"He might have deemed it fitting."

"Your mother, then."

"My mother was a woman of duty."

"You're frightened." That caused her to turn and look at him, at least. "Do this because ya believe in it. Not because ya fear it the only way."

"When you are ready, child," Talathandria snarled.

"Bid me farewell, Kronus."

"I'll not leave until I know you're safe."

"You will. While they may yet permit it."

Kylac eyed the eager grolls, but remained motionless, feet rooted to the stones of the lakeshore, arms crossed loosely in front of him.

"She's right. About Abinama. I see it now." Tears welled in her eyes. Eyes brimming with inexplicable need. Whatever the conviction of her words, her face was a wrack of confusion. "Go. Return to Indranell, if you would serve me still. Let them know . . . aid is coming."

Kylac intended no such thing. This turn of events, it all felt wrong. A maelstrom of partial truths and hidden lies. A tempest of emotions too dark, too violent, too thunderous, to see through. He knew only that they were reacting blindly, and that mistakes were being made. Mistakes that couldn't be undone.

"Denariel. Nara. Hear me. Ya shouldn't—"

It was her embrace that cut him short this time. Sudden and fierce and highly unexpected. He reacted quickly enough to withdraw from it, initially, before allowing it to happen. For her to press herself against him, gripping him tightly, urgently. As if he were the last person she might ever chance to hold again.

He mistrusted it all the same. Particularly when the pair of grolls crept abruptly toward him, one on each side. Kylac wrenched free, drawing his swords and twisting forward to shield Denariel. Realizing at once that she didn't likely need a shield. A better course would be to advance on Talathandria. To see how her warders might react with their *steward matron* perched on the edge of a blade.

He never got the chance. As he crouched to make his lunge, feigning a defensive posture to draw the mutants on, he felt a prick in the small of his back. Pain bloomed, a fast-spreading itch giving way to ruthless fire. The grolls halted mid-stride, holding position halfway between him and Talathandria. Behind him . . .

Denariel.

He rounded on her slowly, flush with realization. In her hand, he saw the envenomed claw with which she'd pierced him. Discovered there upon the lakeshore. To be wielded as a weapon should the need arise.

"Much as it would please me to watch them kill you," she said, sniffing back tears with cruel satisfaction, "I staked that claim myself."

Empedes morta. The fire grew hotter, sizzling through his veins. Were the torment not so paralyzing, Kylac might have laughed. At all the chances he'd had to put this doomed cause behind him. To heed Denariel's threats and accept that there could be no reconciliation between them. Wiser as he would have been to forsake her at any of the numerous junctures in the recent past, he'd foolishly remained committed to her.

And this, his reward.

At least he understood now why he'd felt upon this journey like a man condemned. His jaw clenched, forestalling response. His limbs had seized, save for a wracking convulsion. He couldn't even drop his blades, though he could no longer control them. *So this is my end,* he realized, thinking it odd, and rather less glorious than any he might have imagined.

He envisioned his father, frowning upon him in stony disapproval. The image soothed him. So he'd let his guard down. Proving himself less than the iron-hearted killer his father had wanted, and that he'd occasionally feared himself becoming. For all his unfinished business, he could die at peace with that.

The savage pain threw him to the ground, where it ripped and pulled and tore at him, as ravaging as any pack of teeth or talons. He would have preferred a less punishing agony, but mayhap it was warranted. With all the lives he'd taken, he couldn't say he hadn't earned it.

Sky and forest and stony earth danced before his vision as he bucked and writhed uncontrollably, back arching until he thought it must snap. He caught glimpses of the grolls, of Talathandria, of Denariel, standing over him, still holding the instrument of his demise. Amid the throes of his anguish, he wondered if all might unfold as she'd been promised. Hoping that, whatever else, his suffering would provide her a measure of the satisfaction she'd long been seeking.

Amid a spear of sunlight, he thought he saw Briallen, sneering derisively. Another salve amid the torment. Her mockery he would cherish, if he could but visit with her once more.

A fleeting promise. For his gaze returned to the world he knew, snagging upon Talathandria as his body came to a crippling rest. Focusing upon her scaly, wizened face. A final cruelty before the crushing darkness closed round.

The stolen light drawing for him a parting vision of the Ukinhan matron's predatory smile.

31

Death proved warmer than he'd anticipated.

The corpses he'd made study of in his youth were always chill, clammy things. Kept that way, yes, in an effort to preserve them. But he'd observed time and again that, once deprived of an active heartbeat, the mortal body held all the heat of an empty hearth.

On the other side of the shroud, however, within the actual cocoon of death's embrace, he felt cozy, contented. Ensnared by impenetrable blackness, but without the frigid discomfort or utter *lack* of sensation he would have imagined.

Then the blackness began to erode. Eaten away like layers of sand brushed by a gathering wind. The warmth intensified, attended now by a crimson glow. It occurred to him that mayhap he hadn't yet reached his ultimate destination. What he felt now might be but a staging area, an antechamber preceding his descent into the Abyss.

There was indeed a sense of plummeting—or was it rising?—amid the disintegrating darkness before the crimson glow burst into a blinding wash like sunlight. No. Not *like* sunlight. It *was* sunlight. Spearing down through a mottled mesh to brand a fresh vision upon his eyes. Carrying him from his place of infinite repose to . . .

The belly of a chasm. As revealed by a brush-choked sky wedged between a pair of hulking cliffs. The setting's scarred features told him nothing. A place unaccounted for in his fractured memory. Belonging to some description of the afterlife, mayhap. None of which he'd ever been inclined to give much heed to.

The image guttered, blinking in and out of the blackness that had spawned it. It didn't . . . He wasn't . . .

And then he realized. *He* was blinking. Some semblance of his physical form remained intact. Or a mental interpretation of it. Shards, if he could but wrest free of the stubborn strands of this clinging stupor . . .

A face thrust into view. Like the setting, unknown to him. Gnarled and scarred, with a thicket of beard sprouting from a leather hood. Coarse gray hairs knotted or entwined with beads of wood and bone gave it the look of an aged briar bush. A misshapen nose lorded over the ragged tuft, bent by ancient injury. Over *that* lorded a pair of wild eyes, remarkably bright for their lack of color, embedded in hollow sockets. The shelf of a brow cresting it all was spotted with age and lined with craggy furrows.

The furrows deepened. "Huh."

The grunt was the first sound to distinguish itself amid the formless whisper of his aural void, but ushered in a stinging assault of strafing noises—of clicks and squeaks and squeals that struck as vaguely familiar, yet overwhelming when measured against the vanquished silence.

"Thunder's fury," the face murmured, mouth all but buried in that tangle of a beard. "Do you hear me?"

That and more, the voices distinguishing themselves amid the gale. Trilling, chittering, croaking. The rustle of leaf and bough fondled by an idle wind. Jungle sounds. Forest. Or what might pass for either.

"Move, if you can. Or speak?"

The demands made no sense. Dead men didn't move, once their twitching had ceased. They certainly didn't speak, save for what rasping wind might be pressed from their lungs. Serene as it appeared from without, death was proving increasingly vexing within.

And yet, he felt now the pinch and stab of earth beneath him. Of sharp-edged rocks, piercing thorns, probing roots. None of which he should have noticed. Not after the venomous prick from Denariel's—

"Give a nod, if it's all you can muster."

The world shook. A nod. He was nodding. How could that be?

A choking gasp from near at hand. His own throat, struggling to summon a response. To articulate words that might capture and express the horrific nature of this impossible awakening.

"Water," he managed, with a tongue made of leather.

"Mother's mercy," the wild-eyed face replied.

And withdrew. Kylac thought to follow it, but his eyes closed instead. The darkness returned, both blessing and curse. Kylac, yes. His name. In life. In death. Or wherever betwixt the two he'd landed.

A wetness trickled and then splashed over his lips, bringing him to, again. Water. Tepid and brackish, but welcome nonetheless. Invigorating as it penetrated the fissures and canyons carved into his lips, his tongue, his throat. A deluge in the wake of drought. Of the kind that might cause seeds to sprout, or withered roots to return from the—

"Dead," he said, though the word emerged a senseless gargle. He coughed, sputtered. The water retreated. Though he felt halfway to drowning, he yearned for its return.

"You say?"

"I'm not . . ." His parched throat ached and burned with the effort. "Am I not . . . dead?"

"So it seems," Briarbeard huffed, and sat back.

This time, Kylac's gaze followed. To see the waterskin gripped in hands as tanned and leathery as the stranger's face. Tunic and vest and a thin travel cloak were well-worn, marked by rents and patches and stains. Small blades were sheathed about his person in copious quantity, along with tongs and shears. A sling and a flail dangled from one hip, and a coiled whip from the other. The weapons were outnumbered only by pockets and pouches bulging with . . . whatever items he deemed necessary. Sheaves of bark strips, Kylac spied, amid little wooden phials and trinkets of bone. Roots and herbs and powders, less visible, formed a potpourri against the man's own odorous shroud. A staff lay at hand, hooked at the head, leaning against the deadfall upon which he squatted.

A wild woodsman, by every indication with which Kylac was familiar. A ranger. Of the Harrows?

"Ya . . ." Kylac licked the clinging water from his lips. "Ya saved me?"

Briarbeard snorted. "Collected, might be said."

Kylac fought a fresh wave of dizziness as he attempted to right himself. Only to realize that those lingering strands of confusion were actually vines—thin, yet tightly woven—trussing him wrist and ankle.

"Saw what happened," Briarbeard explained, and shook his hooded head. "Alive you may be. But you haven't any right. Strikes a man as me curious."

"Curious," Kylac echoed. Surrendering his struggle against his bonds. Trying to understand. "Ya watched me . . . fall?"

"At the lake. Do you recall?"

"Claw. Ukinh."

Perceiving his difficulties, his inquisitor leaned forward again, sparing him another mouthful of water. "That's right. And after?"

Kylac thought back, shook his head.

"Pair of grolls heaved you over the edge of Frahmen's Stonefall. You took a tumble down the slope of the crevasse."

An event that would seem to account for the numerous unremembered scrapes and bruises now plaguing his body.

"I come down to have a look, discover you've still got a pulse. Naught but a twitch, but more'n any dead man *should* have. So I dragged you here. To observe."

Observe. Observe what? "How long?"

"Yesterday, daybreak." He glanced up. "Afternoon's ebb now."

Near six arcs. A full day's cycle, and half again. "My companion. The woman who . . ."

"The half-breed thought she'd killed you?" Briarbeard eyed him archly, then took a pull of water himself. "What of her?"

"Where . . . What became of her?"

The ranger shrugged. "With the Ukinha. Belongs to them now."

"We needs to . . . Cut me loose."

A click of the ranger's tongue, clearly disapproving. "Not until I have me some answers."

"I must free her."

"Seemed to go willingly enough. Most do. Grolls wouldn't tolerate it any other way."

Kylac tried to follow. "Most. There are others? Women?"

"Mothers."

The word settled like an icy shard in Kylac's stomach, freezing him from within.

"Was that not the purpose agreed upon?"

"It was," Kylac admitted. "Talathandria . . . to take her place."

Briarbeard raised one of his great, bushy brows. "You might have misunderstood."

"Said she was dying."

"Talathandria?" A bark of laughter. "Not how it works, boy. Though softer than the truth, I reckon. Could be part of how she's taken to baiting them."

"A lie?"

Another shrug. "Tell me what was said."

Had he not already? "That she'd see another become matron, mother to the Ukinha. Before she passed. As the only way to ensure their survival."

"And what did your friend venture here seeking?"

"An army," Kylac admitted, desiring to take rein of this discussion, but feeling himself as yet in a poor position to do so. With what little he'd truly discerned about this Harrows ranger, he dared not reveal *too* much. But he needed to reveal *enough*, he sensed, and as eagerly as possible, in an effort to merit trust and speed the matter of his release. "Grenarr have sacked Avenell and threaten to overrun Indranell. She thought mayhap the Ukinha could be united to drive them back."

"That so?" Briarbeard asked, squinting and clenching his jaw as if gnawing on a piece of gravel. "Bold girl. Or foolish."

"Too much o' both," Kylac agreed, looking to hasten past the question of her identity. "Was why she agreed to Talathandria's offer. Accept a groll's seed, win their allegiance, vanquish the Grenarr, and return to the wilds."

"Yet *you* would stop her. Suitor? No," the ranger decided, before Kylac could answer, "more a hired sword, methinks. Paid by someone else to attend her."

"More like that," Kylac agreed.

A shrewd stare, deep and perceptive, gave way to another huff. "You heard a tale, sure. But Talathandria, she ain't dying. Least, doubtful to my eyes. She'll use your friend as a mother, all right, assuming the lass has the strength to serve. If lacking . . . well, not much use for her."

"But—"

"I'll spare you the breath," Briarbeard interjected. As if impatient for reasons of his own. "Ukinha require a female host to breed, yes. Plenty have been so used—even before Talathandria's time. Sometimes competing for the privilege. Precious few, it's had, were able or willing to bring child to term. Many simply lacked the physical constitution. Others, overcome with . . . dismay, sought to kill themselves or the unborn within them."

He leaned forward, fixing Kylac with his half-mad gaze.

"Talathandria was one who had no qualms lying with a Ukinh, and proudly brought forth a child. Coming to learn the act gained her . . . unnatural vitality, she did so again and again, as often as possible, indiscriminately."

So that much, at least, had been true. Insofar as the ranger's corroboration held value. "Then why seek—"

"Eventually, her ability to bear fruit withered. This, decades ago. Stillborn offspring led later to an inability to conceive at all. So she took to ensuring that other women were brought to her and . . . persuaded to give birth. The Ukinha balked, at first, finding it undesirable to seduce or coerce breeding partners in this way. But it soon became clear that their reluctance was a threat to the continuation of their kind. Much as they revere women, they revere the rarity of a Ukinh child more."

Interested as he'd been to better understand the circumstances, Kylac found the narration fast growing tedious. Countering that, every moment the ranger spent in distraction was a moment in which Kylac solidified his bearings, gathered his strength.

More than likely, he was going to need it.

"Can the grolls not manage this themselves?" he asked. "Independently, as before? What purpose does Talathandria truly serve?"

"She aids in the selection process, helping to ascertain the viability of prospective mothers. To limit needless waste of lives, see. Upon screening them, she helps to . . . *convince* them—using whatever story might serve that purpose, it would seem. Most critically, she oversees gestation, where a groll will not, ensuring the whelp is brought to bear. Imprisoning and forcibly nurturing, if need be, both mother and child."

There it was, the crux of his suspicion realized. And the reason he needed to track Denariel down again before it was too late.

"Throughout her reign, Ukinhan populations have grown, thrived. For her efforts, she's rewarded time and again with an act of copulation—despite her barren state. Allowing her to endure."

"And the mothers?" Kylac asked. "Once the child is born?"

"Best as I've seen?" He gestured off into the stony reaches of the chasm's throat. "Frahmen's Stonefall. A carpet of bones, you'll find along that trail. Discarded, so as to pose no threat as rival."

"I's been led to believe the Ukinha nobler creatures than that."

Briarbeard shrugged. "Like any creature, some are kind, some are cruel. To give seed to progeny is in them a powerful instinct. And after several generations of this arrangement, Talathandria is something of a legend, even to them. Honored and obeyed largely beyond question."

"Ya know much," Kylac remarked, "that would seem unknowable to any but the Ukinha."

That earned him another snort. "Harrows have been my home for more years than your life has seen, boy. No living man knows them better than I."

"Then what answers do ya seek o' me?"

"Sniffed that groll venom in ya the moment I approached your carcass. When I discovered it hadn't killed you—least not fully—I resolved to learn why."

"Wish I could tells ya."

"As had I."

Kylac recognized the cold dispassion in Briarbeard's eyes. An appraising stare that reminded him of his father's. "Sageryst," he recalled. "I's tasted it. Harvested from the caverns of Krathen Ungret."

"Would spare you from *ingested* groll venom," the other allowed, before shaking his head. "The mineral did nothing to preserve you here."

"It was an old claw, we found. Old venom."

"Sapping none of its potency."

Confirming Denariel's proclaimed understanding—that the venom was ageless. He couldn't have said why that bothered him, save it meant Denariel had indeed meant to kill him. Not to render him unconscious, or elsewise make it *appear* she'd killed him in an effort to protect him from the grolls. No, her intent must have been as seemed—agony, ending in certain death, delivered by *her* hand.

As harsh and honest as that.

"Has to be some element within your blood itself," Briarbeard mused, "or some vital organ—perhaps interacting with the sageryst—that saved you."

Kylac perked. Not the first, of late, that he'd been accused of harboring unusual blood. Dragon's, if giving ear to the mad ravings of Ithrimir, the Sea Scribe, who'd been so troubled by its imperceptible scent. Hailing somehow from the Sleeper, the Watcher, the Dread Eye of the Deep . . .

"How can ya be certain?" Kylac asked.

The ranger drew a knife sheathed at his shoulder.

"Cutting me loose?"

"Cutting you open. See what you got brewing inside."

He said it matter-of-factly, without any hint of apology, drawing another blade, and a pair of tongs, and laying them out on the fallen trunk beside him. Shedding new light on all those implements tucked and sheathed throughout his tunic. To him, Kylac was no more than a specimen, placed here for his examination.

"A risk you'd be taking," Kylac cautioned. In response to the other's raking scowl, he added, "An aberration ya'll find me, in more ways than one."

Briarbeard grunted. "Determined that much upon sighting you on that groll's heels."

"Oh?" Kylac asked. Stalling now. Buying time for his deadened reflexes to awaken. "And when was it ya chanced across our path?"

"Was you chanced across mine," the ranger replied, rummaging through a pack to produce a small stone mortar. After that came a pouch of some powder, which Briarbeard sniffed at, and another length of vine-woven rope. "Tracking a rare bandercat along the northern rim of Irrish Vale when your little party come along through Tarthu's Cut."

The names told him nothing. "And ya decided to have a peek at our affairs."

Another raking glare. Triggering in Kylac the same sensation felt upon traversing that gateway meadow to the lake-filled valley in which he'd met his end. "As I said, Harrows are my home. Something causes a stir, I make it *my* affair to know about it."

And Kylac had caused quite the stir, he had to admit. "I wondered at the fortuitous timing." Unfortunate, as it now seemed. For if the ranger hadn't nursed him to health, better he might have been to wake on his own, unbound, wherever the grolls had deposited him.

"All of life is chance." Having set down pouch and mortar beside blades and tongs, the ranger began working one end of his vine-rope into a running noose. "It's only a man's will shades a matter blessing or curse."

"Ya must mask your presence well, to creep about this close to a haven o' grolls."

"Even Ukinha can be eluded, tricky as it is. Ain't so much in going undetected as posing no threat. By now, they know me as an observer, not one who intervenes."

"As you're doing here."

"Only after Talathandria departed, your friend leaving you for dead."

That again. His disappointment must have registered in his features, for Briarbeard ceased his work, momentarily, smirking in black amusement.

"Jape of it is, she's the one actually saved you."

"How so?"

"She don't pierce you, those grolls would have torn you to pieces."

As he'd already surmised. If only he could make himself believe her actions had been carried out with that intent. "O' what solace, if'n ya mean to carve me open now?"

"We'll start with a few samples. It don't have to kill you." *But if it should, so be it,* his eyes seemed to say.

The ranger stood. Taller than he'd seemed earlier. With a deft toss, he slung his rope around an overhead branch, bringing the noose down around Kylac's feet. Kylac's heart beat just a little faster, thrumming with excitement. But he held himself near motionless, helpless, mustering no more than a wriggle and a sharp grunt as Briarbeard cinched the noose around his trussed ankles—eyeing him cautiously the entire time. The ranger was himself a creature of the wilderness, well practiced in handling its many denizens. Kylac was likely to get only one chance at freeing himself. Better not to waste it in acting too soon.

"Ya needn't do this," he urged again, as Briarbeard hoisted him by his feet. The branch bowed, but proved heartier than its thickness would suggest. "I intend ya no harm."

The ranger snorted as he tied off his end of the line. "Everything in this world harms, boy. Intended or not. Only way to protect yourself is to gain understanding where you can."

He was left to dangle for a moment upside down, during which time he continued to sag limply, displaying only the barest strength to resist. Briarbeard picked up one of his chosen blades, inspected it, scraped it back and forth against a leather strap, then grunted in satisfaction. Fetching his mortar alongside, he took two strides forward, advancing to within a single pace.

His deceptively smooth movements, coupled with his towering frame, sparked in Kylac a sudden recollection.

"Rashad," it came to him. "Might that be your name?"

The ranger stiffened, telling him it was. "And how might you, an obvious outlander, suppose that?"

Rashad the Mad Wanderer, as the others had referred to him. Or Rashad the Betrayer. To have been beheaded for some treachery against the Addaran crown. "I traveled for a time with your nephew, Trajan."

His tormentor bent low, another raking expression of those tangled brows—so reminiscent of the Tower's that Kylac was embarrassed not to have caught the resemblance earlier—betraying fresh interest. "A boy, nary a whisker upon his cheeks, consorting with Shadowguard?"

"Across the Harrows, no less."

"How fared my nephew, when last you saw him?"

"Courageously. Dead, nonetheless. Within the tunnels o' Krathen Ungret."

Stone-faced as he tried to appear, the ranger flinched. "How?"

"Free me, and I'll tells ya."

Rashad seemed tempted to do just that. A tightened jaw, along with an unblinking stare and a slight tremor in his bearing, betrayed his yearning curiosity. But he gulped down whatever emotion was building inside him. "*Why* you are, more telling than where you've been. On either count, your tongue may deceive, where your viscera will not." His crouch deepened, putting his face level with Kylac's chest. "Just a nick of blood, first. Hold still, I'll make this gentle as I can."

For a *nick of blood*, Kylac might have agreed. But he didn't trust Rashad to stop there, and wasn't inclined to let the Mad Wanderer go probing about his *viscera*. When the ranger leaned in, preceded by his odorous shroud and reaching blade, Kylac summoned his most alarmed expression. "Wait. Please . . ."

Only as the blade kissed the collar of his neck did he lurch aside and buck forward, forehead striking Rashad in the nose. Kylac felt the crunch, taking no joy in it as he held himself upright long enough to pluck a small knife from those sheathed in the Wanderer's vest. A challenge, with hands bound behind him, but not entirely unlike exercises practiced countless times before. As Rashad stepped back to clear his tearing vision, Kylac worked the dull edge of the knife's spine up the small of his back as he descended, bladed edge slicing at the vines binding his wrists.

Rashad lunged, still blinded by the damage to his nose, but striking anyway. Cutting and pulling for added tension, Kylac snapped his wrist tethers just in time to deflect the ranger's thrust and counter with a punch to the throat. While his assailant rasped in search of breath, Kylac curled upward, sawing at the rope from which he hung. Its taut strands parted quickly, enabling him to yank his feet down beneath him as he fell, to catch himself on his toes.

When Rashad came again, Kylac leaned to one side so that the Wanderer barreled past. Still bound at the ankles, he found himself tackled as the other tumbled to the ground, but rolled with the momentum so that he sat upright. Rashad, sprawled prone over his legs, could as easily have been a boar at a feast, so simple was it to press the tip of his stolen blade into the soft flesh behind the ranger's left ear.

Press he did, without driving. Using just enough force to carry the threat.

"It don't has to kill ya," Kylac echoed, then gave a nudge to reassure that it could.

"Festering maggots," Rashad swore. "Just who beyond the Mother's mercy are you?"

"Kronus, I'm called."

"Unbowed," the Wanderer translated, and gave a mad laugh.

"Ya know Old Entien?"

"Fragments. Amid other tongues."

"So hear this in New. I would spare ya, Rashad, having held Trajan as friend and failed him in that calling. Giving thanks to your Fair Mother ya managed to escape the king's justice."

"And why is that?" the ranger huffed, broken nose dripping blood over the dirt and scrub carpeting the chasm floor.

"Because you're going to lead me now in search o' my friend."

Another barking laugh, madder than before. "Kinder it would be to thrust that blade home now." With his own knife still in hand, the Wanderer might yet provoke that outcome—and seemed to be considering it.

"Mayhap. Save, if'n I's heard right, I'd be denying ya what may be the greatest challenge an explorer o' the Harrows has undertaken yet."

"Oh? Pray tell."

"A possible foray into the lair o' Talathandria herself."

32

The rank stench rising from the little wooden bowl was near foul enough to dissuade Kylac from his proposed endeavor before it began.

Rashad seemed not to notice as he hovered over the bowl, mashing and grinding at the paste within. A blend of leaves and root shavings and a powder from the horn of some creature the ranger had called a biringut. Stirred with twelve drops of a milky fluid said to be derived from the bile of a remsquall, whatever that was, produced from one of the ranger's phials. A concoction resulting in what he termed Ynapuleal musk. Having roamed festering swamps and rotting battlefields and the lair of the world's last known dragon, Kylac was yet certain this the most repulsive stink he'd ever encountered.

"How exactly does one devise such an odious mixture?" he asked, coughing against his best effort not to.

The Mad Wanderer kept grinding, but did raise a squinted eye in cutting expression. "Found this particular recipe amid a cache of artifacts left by the Breeders themselves."

"That so?"

"No need to rediscover lessons learnt by others."

Truth enough in that, Kylac supposed. If only he could better perceive what truth could be found in the rest of the ranger's words or deeds. Appearances aside, he wasn't at all convinced that Rashad was with him in this. The Wanderer had balked, initially, at the thought of venturing into Talathandria's private domain. And been steadfast in doing so. Penetrating those confines would almost certainly result in being savaged by whatever grolls—always coming and going—currently attended her. Even should they manage to elude the Ukinha, stealing his former companion or violating Talathandria in any way would ensure the mutants hunted them down. Now or later, Rashad would pay brutally for the crime Kylac intended to commit. As would Kylac. Whatever the nature of his commitment to the young half-breed, no bounty, and no threat, should tempt him to undertake that risk.

"I's no intention o' harming Talathandria," Kylac had vowed in argument, with the ranger still pinned beneath him and his stolen blade. "Only to let my friend know she's been deceived."

"Once in thrall to a Ukinh, few escape it."

"This one has a greater obligation."

At that, the bloodied ranger had snickered. "Surely, her little war will carry on without her."

Prompting Kylac to divulge the truth of Denariel's identity, expressing a measure of surprise that the ranger hadn't discerned it already. Learning in turn that it had been more than three decades since Rashad had concerned himself with Addaran affairs, particularly those of the royal family.

"Desperate she must have been, to journey here herself," the Wanderer had observed slyly. "And not without detractors. Even rival claimants, perhaps?" Yet the ranger hadn't pressed that line, offering instead a grudging acknowledgment of the value that Kylac, at least, placed upon her life. Still not worth it, in any way that a wiser man would measure. "Royals are known to come and go and be replaced as surely as any commoner."

"Ya say the Ukinha are loath to condone any forcible breeding," Kylac had pressed. "By that reckoning, if Denariel were to reconsider, might Talathandria permit her release?"

The hope had earned him a derisive chuckle. "Natural world holds nothing if not possibility. Should persuasion prove your only intent, I suppose you might—just might—be allowed to emerge with life intact."

"And would that make a look inside the matron's warren a more viable temptation to an intrepid ranger as yourself? Or has ya survived in these wilds long as ya has giving rein to fear?"

The simple goad had set Rashad to huffing and blustering. "Think you truly have the stomach for this? Then let us see."

The uneasy consent had been enough for Kylac to withdraw his blade from the other's ear so as to sever his ankle bindings, after which he'd permitted the ranger to rise. Rejecting assistance, Rashad had adjusted his broken nose himself, filling one nostril with a plug of some herbal poultice. Kylac had used that time to question his reluctant companion as to what might be required. While giving ear to the answers, he'd come to sense that mayhap he'd sparked or exposed some other motivation in the ranger, which Rashad kept hidden from him. But as long as they were exploring a path of action, he hadn't wished to delve any further along the latter possibility. Better to set course and *expect* that the Wanderer might seek to betray him somewhere along the way—maintaining his own guard against such treachery.

Offering fair warning, of course, that they would succeed in this, or perish together.

Their first task had been to track down Kylac's borrowed swords—both of which, he'd learned, had been discarded when he was. Rashad had only happened across one, and hadn't found it worth the trouble to collect. But the Wanderer's blades, however numerous, offered insufficient reach to serve Kylac well in combat against a Ukinh. So he'd resolved to seek those carried with him from Rendenel Run, despite Rashad's argument that, if it came to a fight, they were doomed regardless. Finding the first weapon where the ranger had left it, he'd located the other within a crevasse after a quarter-mark's search of the fissure-ridden ground. Notwithstanding his companion's surly disapproval, and inadequate as they seemed for what he intended, he'd been immeasurably reassured by their heft.

From there, he'd followed the Wanderer north and east through a labyrinth of slopes and defiles, to a wooded ravine beyond the rim of Talathandria's lake-filled valley. Rashad had hummed or grumbled to himself near the entirety of that time, to no meaning that

Kylac could discern. Brief pauses had typically been accompanied by birdlike movements of the ranger's head, cocked alertly at one angle or another. Not once had the wild man extended insight as to his thoughts or observations, and not once had Kylac asked. Unless it concerned their mission, he didn't care to probe that tangled ground.

They'd taken a two-hour respite there in the ravine. Necessary, Rashad had insisted, for the musk that would mask their scents wouldn't quicken beneath a waning arc. Only a rising arc—be it sun or moon—would serve. Though Kylac hadn't even feigned understanding at how that could be, and in fact suspected it to be a ploy on the part of the ranger, he'd been reassured already that time was not their most critical factor.

"They'll not have selected a mate," Rashad had claimed. "Not yet."

"How can ya know this?"

"I've seen the strings of suitors a mother draws, and the posture of those to depart unsatisfied. Several cycles always pass in between."

So Kylac had accepted the interval for the benefit it served his mind and limbs, as yet addled and sluggish from his brush with death. He'd tried not to reflect too much on the latter, sensing the question still burned in his companion's mind whenever the ranger chanced to eye him. Bad enough to suffer that scarred, penetrating gaze, without himself rooting inward in search of the unknowable. Fortunately, he didn't suffer the other's curiosity. So he'd proven immune to a venom believed lethal to all. The crucial fact being he was still alive. The reasons could keep for now with blind fortune.

Not even the gods can resist my charm.

A blessing he'd considered it when Rashad had retreated into slumber, taking his insufferable scrutiny with him. Kylac had remained awake nonetheless, vigilant against ruse, alert to any encroachment, worried for Denariel. Even now, after she'd endeavored to kill him. This, to him, constituted the greater mystery. Just what was it he felt he owed the woman?

When the Crow's chase of the Eagle had brought on nightfall, Kylac had roused his companion with a rough shake. The Wanderer had awakened readily, and, to his credit, asked only once if Kylac still intended to do this. When Kylac had confirmed that he did, the ranger had muttered and winced and touched his nose before taking bite of a bulbous root and pulling a long draught from a wineskin—of a fermented fluid that smelled only vaguely like wine. When offered a swig himself, Kylac had politely declined, begging and receiving water instead.

In the near half-mark since, he'd done little more than watch Trajan's infamous uncle mix and mash that odious paste. Trying not to inhale too deeply.

"It's ready," his companion said abruptly, withdrawing pestle and thrusting the little bowl toward him.

Kylac eyed the bowl's contents with skepticism and warning and no small measure of distaste. "Sure this stink won't simply *attract* Ukinha?" *And every other creature within ten leagues?*

"Quickly," Rashad grunted. "Before it loses potency."

"Show me," Kylac urged. Demanded.

The ranger scowled and scoffed, but stuck a pair of fingers into the paste and proceeded to spread it upon the crest of his chest, the nape of his neck, across his brow, and behind each ear. A final dab went to each wrist, after which he offered the bowl again to Kylac. This time, Kylac accepted, smearing himself with small amounts of the Ynapuleal musk in the same manner as his wild companion.

"That it?" he asked, gagging on his own stench.

The Wanderer flashed him a grin of crooked yellow teeth. "Try not to retch. For *that* will bring the mutants running."

Kylac could summon no guarantee. Conceding to the ranger's little game of cruel delight, he ran through a quick series of striking exercises, just to make sure his reflexes hadn't in any way diminished. From his perspective, all felt near to normal.

The ranger just chuckled and shook his bearded head, returning his bowl to his satchel and donning his leather hood. "We trek in silence now. Should I hoot or warble, be still—not a breath. Should I signal halt or crouch? Know that it's too late for either, and we're already dead." He half turned, then looked back with a sneer. "May your descent be a lasting one."

Rancor notwithstanding, the Wanderer wasn't entirely opposed, given how easily he'd succumbed to Kylac's taunts and threats. Or so

Kylac told himself as he trailed Rashad in climbing from the ravine and setting course along a snaking fissure that marred the wooded slope. Heading roughly southwest, in a return toward the heights of Talathandria's valley. His guide had claimed not to know where within the mountainous tunnels the Ukinhan matron made her home. But he did have a notion of where one of the entrances might be, based on his sightings of grolls coming and going, often with various foods or provisions—like ants or bees returning to the nest. He'd witnessed Talathandria herself only from afar, usually down by the lake or among her wild groves of fruit trees. Knowing better, on each occasion, than to attempt to track her.

Regardless, the agreed-upon hope was that the musk they'd applied would successfully mask their scent long enough for them to reach the targeted cave mouth without interference. Should a fight be required . . . well, at least he was armed again.

His palms itched already for the handles of those or some other blades. *His*, were there a god that truly loved him. The night was no louder or quieter than usual. The filtered starlight no brighter or darker. The air no warmer or colder. Yet the jungle seemed to tighten around him with every stride, and his breath to thicken. The excitement and anticipation that generally accompanied him on an excursion like this were present, yet smothered beneath layers of doubt and the specter of fear. Not for himself, but for Denariel, Rashad, whose lives depended on an outcome in which he hadn't but the barest confidence.

His most customary ally gone missing.

Better it might have been were he not also carrying the ghosts of his past. To Denariel and Rashad, it could be said he owed no particular allegiance. But the past failures of which each reminded him—Briallen, Trajan—festered yet like open wounds. Were he to succeed in this, mayhap he would find those particular injuries assuaged.

The very prospect warranted the effort.

Rashad might have been hard-pressed to understand, much less agree, so Kylac kept the musings to himself. The Wanderer appeared as engaged at this juncture as one could expect. Moving beyond the question of cause or the measure of duress and focusing on the simple matter of seeing the task done. Kylac could but hope that task, in the ranger's mind, was the same one he believed they'd agreed to.

They'd scaled a little more than a mile of gnarled, pitted, broken ground before Rashad slowed, drawing into a crouch at the base of a brush-tufted ridge crest. Kylac mimicked his guide's stance, seeing no reason to question it. After a momentary pause, the ranger edged west along the ridge for more than nine hundred paces before turning and creeping north, downslope again. A hundred paces later, the Wanderer tested the wind, then dropped to all fours and crawled slowly along a slithering gully until emerging onto a humpbacked crag of stone.

Kylac followed, right up to the lip of the crag. There, his companion pointed down into the wooded hollow, indicating a black scar in the face of a slope, some thirty paces distant amid the night-cloaked foliage.

A cave mouth. Though essentially indistinguishable from other pocks and fissures Kylac had glimpsed in this region, he presumed this to be the one Rashad had made mention of. A sort of service entrance or rear portal to Talathandria's den, here on the backslope of her valley.

Else the front door, for all they truly knew, with openings on the lake side being more like terraces overlooking a royal gardens. The only way to learn more would be to probe its depths, and see where they might lead.

He looked back to his companion, finding a bitter mien that seemed part warning, and part challenge. Kylac couldn't quite determine whether the ranger was begging him not to enter, or daring him to do so.

His mind was set, either way.

His own expression must have been easier to read, because Rashad snorted and shed his travel cloak before crawling off to one side, slipping down along the crag's northern edge. A small shower of dirt and dead leaves slid down with him, but the ranger seemed unconcerned with the whispering noise wrought by his passage. No cause for delay, then. Kylac slunk after, no heavier or louder than the Wanderer's shadow.

He clung with similar faithfulness to his guide's heels as Rashad rounded the forested slope forming the hollow's near wall. The ranger's wild eyes searched the jungle darkness. Twice, he stopped to sniff the air. Once, he bent to inspect a series of marks in the moist earth. But he continued nonetheless toward the slender rift in the mountain's flesh, with Kylac in close, soundless pursuit. Who reached out with his own senses for any hint of danger . . . to find faint ripples of it all around, everywhere and nowhere.

The nearer they drew to the cave mouth, the more ominous and insistent became the next question concerning this foray. How to see their way? They could light no torch, Rashad had forewarned, lest they wish to proclaim their arrival with fanfare. But Kylac refused to believe that Talathandria would be found dwelling in utter darkness. While the grolls might be comfortable doing so, Kylac had seen the matron's eyes, and they weren't those of a Ukinh. Much as she might wish to be one of them, she wasn't without her human limitations.

Rashad had chosen not to argue, save to mutter something about failing to see death coming. Their tacit understanding on the issue being that either a beacon in some form would present itself within, or they would delve as deep as they could by feel alone.

A somewhat foolish denial, seeming all the more feeble now that the maw of that black breach widened before them. Just a cleft in the rock, really, scarcely allowing two men abreast. Yet, given their purpose, it could have been the maw of a dragon, unhinging now to swallow them whole.

The Mad Wanderer made a warding gesture as he touched its rim, then glared back at Kylac before pressing inside. Knowing no prayers of his own, or whom to send them to, Kylac merely took a final look around the hollow at their backs before plunging after.

33

Wʜᴀᴛ ꜰᴀɪɴᴛ ᴛᴏᴜᴄʜ ᴏꜰ ᴍᴏᴏɴ ᴀɴᴅ sᴛᴀʀs fell across the cave's threshold was swiftly engulfed. Within a half dozen strides, they were blind. Inching ahead with one hand brushing the tunnel wall. The other raised protectively, sweeping from side to side as a screen against hazard. Kylac let his senses shift, surrendering focus on what wasn't there to see, and attuning more to the weight of his surroundings. The bulk of his guide, creeping and shuffling along, heart pumping with excitement and fear. The emptiness of the tunneling void, tempting and teasing them onward. The unfathomable weight of the earth growing around them, piling upon them . . . so timeless and immutable, yet threatening, it seemed, to crush and bury them in an instant.

The first hundred paces felt like a thousand, as Kylac's innate fear of confinement flared within him, demanding he turn about and dart back the way he'd come. Refusing that, he had to fight the urge to dash ahead, to determine more quickly whether they were wasting their time here. As the passing moments mounted, he was reminded of his underwater escape with Ithrimir from Chitral and the Ladrakari, when he'd wanted so badly to draw breath. Impatience here was as it had been there—a false promise. Should he outpace his companion, he might only end up alone, drowning in the coring dark.

So he tamped down his more desperate urges, giving thought and awareness instead to memorizing his path, should the time come to retrace it. To the unspoken attitude of the ranger in front of him, lest the wild man decide abruptly to turn and put a knife in his chest. To the skulking presence, imperceptible as it might be, of any Ukinha set to ward or prowl this lightless corridor. To any of a thousand or more unknown perils or pitfalls to which he might fall victim before this journey was done.

Yet the only sounds were the gentle huff of Rashad's breath, the careful scrape of the Wanderer's boots upon the tunnel floor, the occasional crunch of a loose stone. Kylac heard no rats, no serpents, no insects, and took that as a positive sign. In part because he wished to, knowing he had no real defense in a blackness this impenetrable against the sting of a scorpion like the galamandrytch, or the bite of a beetle like the karatikuus. But in greater part because the absence of such suggested the very real possibility that a greater predator inhabited these underground halls, or at least frequented them regularly . . .

The air, also, was thick, stifling, yet not too stale, or too dank. Suggesting to him other openings, be they tunnels or chimneys, through which winds might blow or breezes might slip. Making it seem more likely that this was not some solitary stream trickling off into a dead end, but a tributary feeding into a larger network of subterranean passages.

More pleasing it would have been if he could smell anything other than his own wretched stink. While inured now, to some extent, to the foulness of the Ynapuleal musk, he sure couldn't sense anything beyond its shroud.

Slow and interminable as their advance seemed, they'd covered fewer than six hundred paces—with nearly twice as many steps—along the curving corridor of rock when they indeed came across a small pool of wan moonlight, gathered at a bend beneath a hole in the ceiling. Just a tease of brightness amid the void, spilled down through a shaft that cored through layers upon layers of rock overhead. Yet a tether in the abyss. A reminder that there was still a world beyond this mountain prison, should they find a means of returning to it.

Past the pool they plunged, with nary a look and not a whisper between them. Neither broaching the possibility of retreat. Having crossed already the threshold of madness, what sense in turning back now?

Consumed again by the suffocating darkness, they proceeded as before, feeling their way along the tunnel wall. Finding niches and depressions in the mountain's flesh, but no branches, no offshoots. A clear blessing, that. For Kylac couldn't begin to guess how they might choose one course over another. And didn't care to burden himself with the potential distraction of turns and directions and the pace counts at which they could be found.

Another fissure resulted in another pool of light filtered from overhead, this one larger than the last. Farther on, another. Kylac wondered if they were natural, or somehow crafted, still seeking indication as to whether they were on track with this incursion, or if Denariel's fate was being decided elsewhere even now, while Rashad had him delving fruitlessly here.

One or the other, how long before he would know?

His patience tested like seldom before, Kylac jolted when the echoes of a bestial cry rippled through the blackness.

He froze, as he felt Rashad do before him. Alarm, followed hard upon by a spike of relief. Neither spoke. But as Kylac recognized the cry as belonging to a Ukinh, he could rest assured that the Wanderer did, too.

The screech was answered by another. Cries that rang not with pain or terror, but with threat, dominance. A challenge had been issued, and that challenge accepted. Rashad had told him it might be so. That there would be more than one groll looking to mate with Denariel, where only one would ultimately do so.

It would seem the competition had already begun.

Whether sensing Kylac's urgency or triggered by his own, Rashad hastened his pace. If the grolls were occupied, now might prove their best chance for finding Denariel before they were discovered. An added risk, hustling through the dark. But, as of yet, the tunnel floor had betrayed no rocks or humps to trip them up, nor pits or cracks to swallow them. Nor should it, if a common passage for entering or exiting the warren. Which seemed likelier now than it had moments earlier.

Before long, he could hear the huffing, snarling echoes that he attributed to grolls in combat. A manifestation, mayhap, of his own yearning. But having fought more than one Ukinh himself, on more than one occasion, he did have a sense of what those ferocious endeavors sounded like. The louder those sounds grew, the more certain he became.

Soon thereafter, the blackness finally retreated, shying from clusters of an unknown mineral studding the halls to either side in strange blooms of crystalline shoots. Natural formations, they might have been, though Kylac suspected elsewise, as he and his guide examined them in passing. The shapes and patterns appeared just a mite too regular for nature's doing, as if planted in the rock by an outside hand. Whatever their origin, they cast a faint amber glow that exposed the tunneling corridor around them with dim, yet steady radiance.

The light, mayhap, that Kylac had suggested they would find.

Like himself, Rashad seemed invigorated. Terrified they could—and mayhap *should*—have been. But the Mad Wanderer clearly bore the same sickness that Kylac had developed over the past few years. The urge to tread where none other dared, to explore the unfathomable, to lay claim to secrets awaiting anyone of intrepid heart and stalwart will.

Though the secrets might perish with them, unshared.

Between the revelation of their surroundings and the savage cries of the embattled grolls drawing them on, their pace doubled yet again. Kylac was duly impressed with his companion's ability to tread lightly. He'd not have guessed it, to look at the thick, rawboned ranger. Though he should have, for the wild man to have survived this long, roaming where he had. In another life, with some additional training, the Wanderer might have made for a capable assassin.

The tunnel snaked and curved, winding from side to side at irregular intervals. Pocket caves opened up now and then to either side, many of them like small, subterranean gardens. Filled with beds of fungi, or blossoms of spiky crystals, or formations of stone like melted tallow bathing in milky, mineral-laden pools. Rashad scarcely gave any of these a second look. Mayhap he'd seen their like before, and thus harbored no great sense of wonder. Mayhap he believed time was running short. Regardless, he seemed to have honed in on the sounds of combat, and carried on as if to reach or bypass them as quickly as possible. Sparing no concern for anything else.

When at last the shrieking, snarling reverberations made it sound as if Ukinha must be fighting all around them, they rounded a bend in the tunnel to find a sprawling cavern, its walls curving away more than a hundred paces to either side, its ceiling lost to darkness. To the south, left of their position, a faint radiance betrayed a broad-mouthed opening on what Kylac would have wagered was the lake-filled valley. To the north, a staggered series of slash-like rents served window to the groll battle, unless its echoes deceived him, illuminated again by moonlight. Other tunnels punctured the far wall, mouths dimly marked by more of the amber crystal blooms, but their inner reaches steeped in mystery.

A hub, of sorts. Or as near to one as he might expect to find here. The cavern itself was dazzling, its walls striped with veins of luminous minerals, and peppered with studs of crystal that shimmered like diamonds. Its floor was broken up by shelves and trenches and hollows, and adorned with intricate formations of rock as wondrous as any carven statuary. Flowers and mushrooms grew in strips and in patches, as did brightly colored grasses and leafy vines resembling ivy. Little of it strictly natural, by his guess, the bulk having more of a harvested, manicured look. Wild, yet lovingly tended. As suitable a den to a matron of the Ukinha as any Kylac could have imagined.

If that's what it was. Given the circumstances, Kylac cared little, save it might mean he was that much closer to finding Denariel.

Rashad seemed of a similar mind, venturing already along the northern wall, nearest the groll fighting. Daring, but the same choice Kylac would have made, in hope of obtaining a better glimpse of that action. By one course or another, they needed to reach the far side, to explore those other caves. Preferably before their own presence was discovered.

They paused at the first of the window breaches, to peer side by side through the slender opening. Beyond lay what Kylac could only call an arena. Another cavern, this one dominated by a broad pit at the center, wherein a pair of grolls were tearing at each other in a ceaseless flurry. Moonlight shone down on them, admitted through an unseen gash in the ceiling. Ukinha ringed the rim of the pit, hunched in observance. Four of them, in all, spaced at each point of the compass. Witnesses. Judges. Combatants themselves. Again, there seemed no knowing without lingering to observe.

Rashad wasn't doing so. Crouching low, he moved on to the next window, and on past to the next. Here, he paused again. Kylac quickly saw why.

Revealed was an elevated corner of the arena cavern that had been obscured before. A jutting ledge upon which Talathandria perched, attended by a pair of grolls. The same pair that had attended her within the valley, Kylac guessed. In the dim light, hard to determine.

Nor did he deem it critical. Vanquished was any remaining question about whether they'd infiltrated the right warren. If the matron was here, so was Denariel.

For the first time, his companion seemed captivated. Talathandria. Likely, this was the closest the Mad Wanderer had come to her. A striking moment, as Kylac recalled, even for him. More so, he suspected, for one who'd been raised within the shadow of her legend.

Yet, he could permit the man only so much wonderment, and so gave the ranger a nudge. Rashad scowled as he withdrew his gaze, but pressed forward again, ducking lower to bypass the final window. Kylac trailed, stealing a final glance with which to search any remaining blind corners. Thinking he might spy Denariel—while at the same time hoping he didn't.

As the latter proved out, he felt both a welcome relief and a hollowing disappointment.

Once past the windows, Rashad drew bead upon the trio of cave mouths arrayed along the western wall. The first, he slipped past with scarcely any hesitation. Wisely, in Kylac's estimation, as its position, along with the whirlwind of sounds from within, suggested it likely led directly to the arena cavern. Making it the last one they might try.

Leaving just two others, neither of any particular distinction. Of roughly the same size, and the same arched shape. Each edged with amber crystals to either side and above, where a keystone might have been. Each choked with darkness beyond a veil of hazy light.

His guide sniffed at the nearest. Discerning what, he couldn't guess. But the Wanderer ducked inside, and Kylac followed, slipping to the opposite tunnel wall, hands dropping to his sword hilts.

The passage proved narrower than any stretch of tunnel they'd followed yet. After a quick jaunt to the right, it straightened for nearly ten paces before bowing to the left—marked by another of the amber crystal blooms. Kylac searched the light, and scoured the darkness, wary of ambush. Trusting that the tension in his limbs and the roiling in his stomach owed only to the tightening confines.

Rashad moved to the near wall, that he might peer carefully around the bend. So Kylac crossed to the far, just two small steps away, but assuming the more visible line of sight. To draw the attention of any sentries away from his guide, or to be better positioned to retaliate should they spy the Wanderer first.

Neither happened. The bend revealed only a continuing corridor. This one, however, appeared to end some dozen paces ahead in a kind of clover formation—three budding cave mouths. The central one was lit overhead by a crystal bloom, revealing a small pool and a wall glittering with minerals beyond. The pair that flanked it, harboring blackness.

Shards, thought Kylac. The more these passages splintered, the longer their search might take. Judging by the echoes of conflict at his back, the grolls were far from finished with each other. Unsurprising, given how quickly a Ukinh's wounds healed, and how evenly matched the mutants had appeared in terms of physical prowess. But even the closest contest between combatants most often ended abruptly. Much as Kylac was willing to call out Talathandria herself, if need be, to determine Denariel's whereabouts, he'd sure hoped to speak with Her Majesty before resorting to such a desperate tactic.

Rashad, too, seemed to hesitate, uncertain whether to proceed or withdraw so as to try the other tunnel. Kylac was tempted to suggest they split up, in an effort to cover more ground, when a cough sounded in the darkness, from the left-hand cave ahead. Unless he'd imagined it. He glanced at his companion, to find his companion glancing at him.

Denariel!

He dashed ahead, unburdened by doubt, no longer fearing ambush. Rashad hastened after, a muttered curse escaping his lips.

The left-hand cave was a pocket of darkness, its mouth only dimly illuminated by the weak light of the tunnel and the pool-filled cave beside it. But as Kylac looked within, he saw at once a familiar form sitting upright at the edge of that veil, peering out from the void. Tethered at the neck by what appeared to be a nettled, vine-woven rope.

Denariel flinched, startled by his abrupt appearance. And flinched again, when Rashad drew up beside him. Her expression was a writhing contortion of conflicting emotions. Shock and relief, denial and hope, fury and shame. Kylac watched her swallow these and more, donning a more familiar mask of irritation and indignation, as she searched for her tongue.

"You've a rare persistence," she managed, her voice hoarse. "Else are simply too foolish to recognize a wager lost."

Incisive and unapologetic. Kylac could have smiled. He would have had her no other way. "Relieved I am to sees ya, Majesty."

"You should be dead," she declared, before glaring suspiciously at Rashad.

The scowling Wanderer glanced back down the corridor as if worried they might have triggered some kind of snare. "This her?" he hissed. "Or some other royal half-breed?"

"Rashad, Her Royal Majesty Denariel."

Her eyes widened, momentarily, in recognition of the Wanderer's name. Then she snorted. A derisive expression that could have meant any number of things. "Come all this way to have your revenge, did you?"

"Revenge?" Kylac echoed.

Her gaze flicked to where his hand gripped a sheathed sword hilt. "You'll have that sooner than an apology, if that's what you're seeking."

Kylac shook his head. "Your Majesty's motivations were clear, as they always has been." That he'd chosen not to see it, to convince himself that her opinion of him had softened in any way, or that she would for one moment alter her stated goals at his urging, was his own foolishness. "I'm here only to warn you o' Talathandria's lie"—he gestured toward the tether around her throat—"and would beg ya consider my aid in making your escape."

Rashad scoffed. "Escape?"

Kylac felt a prickle of annoyance. "That was our purpose."

"Your purpose was to persuade Her Majesty to choose another course, on the chance that Talathandria would allow it." He, too, gestured at the tether. "This would suggest elsewise."

"He's right," Denariel interjected, as if jumping at yet another chance to oppose him. "We'll never flee undetected. If we do, we won't traverse a league before we're caught."

"The Ukinha are occupied," Kylac reminded them. "An exit awaits us no more than sixty paces from here, back in the main cavern."

"Bait for the trap," Rashad grunted.

Denariel nodded, suddenly more sullen than angry. "Even if I should scurry all the way back to Indranell, I would do so defeated, powerless. To what end?"

To wage the next battle, Kylac might have said. To resume the fight on another front, rather than surrender here. He eyed Rashad, who seemed to study her with newfound fascination, then gave rein to impatience. "I came here to free ya," he insisted, and drew a sword.

"You kill her!" Rashad hissed, raising a hand to block him. "If you sever that strand."

Kylac hesitated, but didn't bother to hide his skepticism.

"A vein of stricthyus krahl," the Wanderer explained, pointing at the vine. "Woven within. Its juices would melt her flesh to the bone."

The great banethistle. Kylac needed no reminder as to the plant's devastating effects. He lowered his blade. "What then do ya suggest?"

For a moment, the only response was the snarling echo of the embattled grolls. Denariel merely sulked. But the weight of Rashad's thoughts suggested he was withholding answer. The ranger had anticipated this. Imagined it as the most likely outcome, probably from the outset. A king's portion of the unspoken reasoning that had convinced him to come at all.

The Mad Wanderer squinted deeply, fixing Denariel with a wild, cockeyed gaze. "Does Her Majesty truly care about nothing more than winning sway over a Ukinhan swarm?"

Denariel blinked, frowned, glanced at Kylac as if fearing this to be a ruse of his design. Finally, she nodded. "It is why *I* came."

Rashad's squint deepened. A probe to root out deception. Brimming with his particular strain of madness. "If so, there is but one way."

34

On the chances of escape, Rashad and Denariel proved correct in their assessment.

They'd scarcely emerged from the tunneling passage into the central cavern when the first pair of Ukinha came tearing out of the tunnel beside them—the one Kylac had presumed would lead to the arena cavern. A heartbeat later, two more appeared, the groll quartet fanning out to corral them. Kylac had already stepped forward, swords in hand, to shield his companions, but found himself quickly retreating—as did they—toward the relative shelter of the cave mouth.

Meanwhile, the echoes of combat had ceased. Two more grolls, each bearing dozens of fresh gashes, joined the Ukinhan barricade, increasing its total number to six. There it remained, the individual mutants aligned hip to hip in defensive posture, until the final pair of those Kylac had witnessed earlier stalked near, Talathandria herself sidling up between them.

Kylac couldn't know what, precisely, had given his little company away. If compelled to wager, he'd have set coin on the stringent scent of the acid spilled from Denariel's tethering vine when Rashad had severed it. Not at her neck, but nearer the crack in the stony earth from which they'd discovered it to be growing. A unique, crossbred shoot, the Wanderer had marveled, before placing a clasp upon it and carefully sawing through the lower stalk with a serrated blade. The clasp had served as it did now to stanch the bloodflow from the end still attached to Denariel, but had done nothing to stem the juices spilling from the root onto the cave floor.

Of course, it might as easily have been Denariel's scent, slipping away from her holding place. Or his own, had the Ynapuleal musk lost its potency. Mayhap a ragged breath or a stray footfall had betrayed them. A rogue vibration they'd unleashed in the tunnel bedrock. Or merely an instinct triggered in one of the mutants that had been followed by all. It mattered not, save that the nearby Ukinha had sensed the intruders' presence and responded with due haste.

Now, Talathandria's gaze burned with malevolence. Anger—or mayhap caution—overruled her evident curiosity. "Kill them," she growled.

Kylac wondered if she meant only him and Rashad, or Denariel alongside. He wondered then if he'd be able to slay even one of the assembled grolls before the rest overcame him.

Fortunately, Rashad had anticipated the Ukinhan matron's response, and prepared his companions accordingly. As the grolls crouched or flared or took their first hostile strides, Denariel blurted, "*Rithranykuth!*" The mutants froze at the command. "Challenge, I claim, and these my witnesses. *Darmuth iyk gabrunagun.* As steward matron of the Ukinha."

Kylac felt Denariel's glare against his back. Sensed her scathing desire to let the mutants attack *him*, at least. But Rashad had been adamant. For challenge to be extended, she would require *two* witnesses to stand in support of her, not just one.

Or so the ranger believed, given the Gorrethrehn texts he'd studied. Now to learn whether or not the ageless custom might still be observed. Or if that tradition, like so much else attributed to the Breeders, had perished with their sect.

Judging by the grolls' sudden, snarling hesitation, the declaration was at least recognized. Not unlike the one, Kylac supposed, with which Denariel had sought to spare him—staking claim to his life herself—when he and she had first encountered the Ukinh that had led them to Talathandria's valley. An ancient observance, mayhap, yet unforgotten.

Talathandria must have recognized it, too, given the way she hissed and coiled, seething with bridled rage. She wanted nothing more than to scatter their limbs then and there. To bathe, mayhap, in a stew of their entrails. That she hadn't echoed her initial command told Kylac that she couldn't—or at least feared the potential consequences of doing so.

"*Hitru dun magyth,*" she snarled through her sharpened teeth. A feeble gate straining against the weight of her indignation. "Foolish child. Yet to prove you can bring forth a Ukinhan seed. Failing that, how do you imagine assuming *my* mantle?"

"I couldn't have," Denariel replied snidely, "until you yourself proposed it to me. A falsehood it may have been, but preferable to serving as a disposable pawn."

The Ukinhan matron hunched lower, narrowed gaze hungering for Denariel's throat. Yet she was as keenly aware as Kylac of the expectant stance taken by her cadre of grolls. Seemed that if they were willing to accept the intruder's challenge, she dared not refuse it.

As her eyes raked from Kylac, to Rashad, and back to Denariel, a glimmering madness took spark at the edges of her flickering wrath. "*Indorgaruun naht.* As you will, child."

The twin breaches serving skylight over the arena cavern shone like the eyes of some great deity. Raked in anger. Milky white in their luminescence. Filled with a thousand and more glittering pupils. Seeing everything and nothing while bearing divine witness to the proceedings below.

Only moments before, two grolls had been fighting for the right to lay seed with Denariel. Now, Denariel herself would be fighting. For the right to lie where she chose, while gaining sway over the entire Ukinhan populace.

How the latter might actually play out was something Kylac couldn't quite envision. But there'd been little time to question Rashad's proposal, and none now that the challenge had been extended and accepted. Besides, Denariel herself seemed to see it all clearly enough. Defeat Talathandria, command the Ukinha, dispatch them to flush the Grenarr from Addaran shores. Anything else gave rise to complications she didn't care to consider.

Whatever the eventual cost, she'd expressed already her willingness to pay it.

Nor, in truth, did Kylac care to burden her with his concerns. Just now, she had enough to worry about. This Rithranykuth, as Rashad had explained it, was to be an exercise in supremacy. Ending when Talathandria abdicated her position, or Denariel relinquished her claim upon it.

"And if'n neither will yield?" Kylac had asked.

"Wiser if they don't," the ranger had admitted. "As a merciful victor would have no assurance against future challenge."

Suggesting this contest must end in death, however vague the Wanderer's histories were on the matter. Radiating like a fire at the far edge of the pit, Talathandria's hateful fury left little doubt as to what might happen should she prevail. As for Denariel? Well, there seemed far too much at stake to risk waging this contest more than once.

Begging the question, did the Addaran queen have it in her to kill her rival? Would the attending grolls truly permit it? What would *he* permit, were the outcome to bend instead in Talathandria's favor?

These and myriad other questions must have been gusting through Denariel's head, as well. Kylac could feel her anxiety, even if he she would never admit to it. Understandable, as it was *she* who would be entering the pit.

"This cannot be settled by champions?" Kylac asked now.

Rashad snorted. "Ukinha would deem it cowardly."

"I'll wage my own battle, thank you," Denariel snapped. Sounding confident, even as she failed to hide a tremor of uncertainty. Peering across the pit's surface at her foe, she watched the grolls settle into position—two warding Talathandria, four resuming their observer's stance around its rim.

The remaining pair—those who'd been at each other's throats

only minutes earlier—remained at the intruders' backs.

"What about this?" Kylac asked, taking hold of the length of vine still tethered about Denariel's neck. Louder, that Talathandria might hear, he repeated, "What about this?"

The Ukinh at his shoulder snarled, but looked at Talathandria for direction. Teeth clenched, she gave a grudging nod. The groll nearer Rashad stepped forward, reaching for Denariel's throat. She tensed, as did Kylac, who somehow resisted his urge to draw a blade. Their reflexive fear proved unnecessary. A mere pinch from the mutant appeared to coax the still-living vine into releasing its hold. They watched the thorny strand slacken and uncoil to lie loosely about her shoulders, after which the groll plucked it free and dropped it upon the stony ground at the pit's edge.

A heavy silence descended, sounds of the world beyond muffled by the thick cage of earth.

"They wait for *you* to enter," Rashad mumbled at Denariel.

She drew a steadying breath, then bent toward the pit. The movement drew growls from the Ukinha, and a sneer from Talathandria.

"*Jithre*," the ranger added hastily. "As from the womb."

He'd warned them already that no weapons would be permitted—for good or for ill. It was for this reason, mayhap, that he implied now she was to remove her garments. To demonstrate that she carried into this contest only what nature had bequeathed her.

Rashad frowned at her momentary hesitation. "You must shed your false skins."

Her withering scowl told him she'd taken his meaning already. With sharp, fierce movements, she quickly complied. Tugging free of her boots, her tunic, her breeches. When she stood as naked as Talathandria across from her, she crouched again—this time without complaint—and dropped into the pit.

There she stood, peering up at her opponent, and raised her hands. "Come then, if your crone's limbs can suffer it."

For all her bluster, she looked to Kylac small and frail. Alone within that hole, her ribs and shoulder blades and knobby joints exposing weeks of toil and hardship and inadequate sustenance. He wondered if her mended thumb could withstand this. He wondered when last she might have slept unaccosted by nightmare. He wondered where she would find the necessary strength.

His concerns only flared when Talathandria hissed and sprang down into the pit. Far sprier than her prior posture would have indicated. Faster, more agile, than her withered frame should have permitted. Dust, she should have been, long ago. Yet, in that moment, she indeed seemed more groll than human.

She was on Denariel within two bounding strides. Even standing ready, the young queen scarcely managed to crouch in time to receive her. Overcome by Talathandria's momentum, Denariel toppled backward, borne beneath the other's weight.

A slashing flurry from the enraged, would-be mutant appeared it might end the fight as abruptly as it had begun. Kylac dropped hands to his sword hilts in reflex, and nearly drew them when a tending groll snarled in his ear. He stopped himself not for the threat, but for the understanding that, if Denariel failed to defend herself, he was already too late.

As it happened, the queen managed somehow to fend off the worst of those savage strikes, wresting and wriggling before gathering her feet to her chest and kicking out, driving her assailant to one side.

Breathless, Denariel arose quickly to all fours, a hand going to her throat to ensure she wasn't bleeding out. She was scraped, cut, but nothing vital had been severed.

She'd scarcely caught her breath, however, before Talathandria returned. With the nimble grace of a hunting cat, and the twitching speed of a lizard, the matron tore into her again. This time, Denariel held her feet. Momentarily. Then she was on the pit floor again, grunting and squirming in a desperate struggle for survival.

Kylac glanced at the Ukinha bearing witness. None displayed any emotion, any desire, toward one outcome or another. Or at least, none he could discern. Mayhap they truly would stand by and accept a challenger's victory.

Or mayhap they understood already that the challenger stood no chance.

Even for Kylac, who'd witnessed hand-to-hand contests of near every variety, it was difficult to tell. He could intuit Denariel's capabilities and limitations readily enough. But Talathandria remained a bit of a mystery. Her movements, while mostly humanoid, were just so much faster than they should have been, and groll-like in their variation. Where he might anticipate a strike, the matron would no more than feint. Where he would expect her to dodge, she would counter. Where he'd have blocked, she would evade. Making it confusing to watch, to gain any sense of form or pattern or strategy that might be exposed or turned against her.

More so for Denariel, he imagined, down there in the teeth of the opponent's whirlwind.

Thus far, the queen was proving sufficiently adept at deflecting or avoiding or elsewise weathering the storm—the only reason she still lived. She'd clearly been trained in grappling techniques, and practiced various blocks and holds at some point in her royal upbringing. Yet, her execution was far from polished. He sensed her relying more on instinct than on memory or will. Fair enough. Desperation often served suitable shield. But would it enable her to mount any sort of offensive?

As the moments passed, the pace and intensity of the initial flurry began to wane. While the combatants continued to swat and poke and claw and yank at each other, there was now more grasping, gripping, clinching, clutching. Here, Denariel seemed to fare better, her disadvantage in strength less pronounced than her disadvantage in speed. In truth, she might have been the stronger. She was just having a difficult time bringing that strength to bear, given her crafty opponent's slithering, unpredictable movements.

She'd also suffered, by far, the worst of the opening engagement. Face, limbs, and torso alike were striped with bloody scratches and deep gouges. Her hair, short as it was, was spiked and tufted as if pulled in a hundred different directions. Talathandria's claws had even proven strong enough to leave shallow puncture wounds, chiefly around the abdomen and ribs.

The matron, on the other hand, appeared no more worn or battered than when the contest had started. Surely, she'd been wrenched and bruised, mayhap even scraped and gouged herself. But the injuries didn't mar or enflame her leathery skin the way they had Denariel's.

Nor was her breathing as ragged, or her energy as depleted. If anything, she seemed only now to be warming to the challenge.

The pair saw all of this for themselves as they broke apart in a sudden flourish. Denariel tottered on one knee before rising. Talathandria, crouched and ready, took a moment to circle her like a stalking predator. As queen winced, matron smiled.

"Mistaken, Abinama must have been. A feeble mother, you would have made."

The very mention of her beloved's name stoked an unseen fire in Denariel. Kylac watched it ignite by way of the billowing rage that gripped her. Forgetting her injuries, the queen sprang at her opponent, eager to resume the fight.

But Talathandria simply sidestepped her charge. And then again, when Denariel had gathered herself and launched another. For the next several moments, the mutant led her around the pit, snickering at her failed attempts to reengage. Allowing the foolish upstart to spend her flagging strength in fruitless forays that left her grasping at air, and gasping for breath.

"I warned you, child. Spirit, you've shown. Meriting nothing."

"A lie, it was," Denariel ventured, after another futile rush. "Part of your deception. Abi . . . he *loved* me."

Talathandria's grin was cutting, cruel. "For all that it avails you now."

Denariel growled and came on, trying and failing to anticipate her tormentor's erratic, twisting evasions. All the while, Talathandria's confidence grew, and Kylac wondered if the time had come to intervene.

He flinched when the queen went down. Guessing falsely at the matron's next displacement, she leaned too far to her right and stumbled over her own toes. No sooner had she tasted the thin layer of silt on the pit's floor than Talathandria curled round to pounce.

The observing Ukinha flared in anticipation. Kylac tensed . . . but only until he sensed that familiar spike of furious indignation Denariel harbored, there on her hands and knees. Seasoned by a familiar arrogance. A self-assured sense of superiority so often flaunted to those around her.

Her collapse was a feint.

As her adversary came flying in, the queen's elbow flung back, catching Talathandria in the center of her wizened face. Resulting in an audible crunch, a surprised shriek, and a gout of black blood erupting like the juices of a splattered berry.

In a heartbeat, the rising Denariel hooked her arm around the mutant's retreating neck. Together, they tumbled and rolled, near to Kylac's edge of the pit. Peering down, he watched them struggle. Talathandria flailing and swiping while spitting blood from her face, Denariel writhing and snorting while bearing down on the head caught in her hold. Blinking against the mutant fingers that sought her eyes. Biting at those that probed near her mouth. Straining with every fibrous muscle visible beneath her dark skin to choke the life—or at least the will—from her enemy.

"A legendary reign," Denariel huffed through her exertions. "My honor . . . it is . . . to end it."

For all her desperate refusals and savage thrashing, it was Talathandria who was now losing strength. Her counters slowed, beginning to flounder. Her eyes bulged. Perched so near, Kylac sensed the heat of her fear, rising swiftly toward despair. Again he glanced round at the observing grolls, to see if any meant to intervene, but read no such intent.

He looked back to find those bulging eyes settling upon the strip of vine that had served as Denariel's tether. Lying near Rashad's feet. Loosely coiled at the edge of the pit like a serpent waiting beside a rodent's hole. He thought to kick it away, but the distance would have required a large, sudden movement that might readily spark some manner of retaliation.

So he reassured himself with knowing that it lay beyond Talathandria's present reach, and that weapons of any kind had been forbidden.

Rules. With defeat imminent, the matron gave rein to a more primal instinct. Bucking to one side, she forced Denariel to bend and heft her higher, in order to maintain that strangling hold. The momentary boost in height gave her the reach required to stretch out and seize the vine's head.

Denariel heaved back toward the center of the pit. Talathandria went with her, no longer resisting the chokehold. Focusing her efforts instead on making a loop with the vine and tossing it over her challenger's head.

Drawing the ends tight.

"Is that not a weapon?" Kylac balked.

Rashad frowned. The attending grolls indeed seemed to shrink and look to one another, some in protest, some in confusion. But none made move to interfere.

In the pit, it seemed now a simple matter of who would succumb first to the loss of breath. Despite her early advantage, Denariel was clearly suffering as Talathandria pulled at the ends of her choking vine, sending its thorns and nettles digging into the queen's flesh. Worse, the still-living strand appeared to be cinching and constricting of its own accord, undertaking the instinctive task of the stricthyus krahl strands woven therein.

As Denariel's dusky features purpled, her strength betrayed her, enabling Talathandria to wrest free.

The matron's gasping, sputtering relief blackened almost immediately, consumed by her flaming aggression. With a feral growl, she tugged once more on the opposing lengths of the vine, which held tight as she reached then for the clasp Rashad had left upon its severed tail. As she tore the pinching fastener free, the vine began spilling its acidic blood, to pool there atop the sands of the pit.

Denariel must have gathered quickly what Talathandria intended. For she pulled her hands from where they worked frantically at her own throat to catch her assailant by the forearm, preventing the matron from spraying her with the acidic stream.

Just barely.

As an invisible leash snapped within, Kylac felt a gnarled hand clamp upon his arm. Rashad. The Mad Wanderer knew his yearning, and was advising against it. Worse, the ranger wasn't wrong. Had Kylac not lost his own blades to Sabrynne, he might well have sprung down into the pit anyway, and ended this farce. Balanced the scales against Talathandria, and dealt with the Ukinhan reaction as needed. But his borrowed swords would ultimately serve little use against eight angry grolls, and offer Denariel scant protection against reprisal. And, as earlier, the fight was at a point where already his intervention might come too late. Or disrupt matters in such a way as to work against the very person he desired to save.

Leaving him to wait, and watch, and trust.

For all the value he'd seen trust yield in this world.

Chafing at the rancid taste of his helplessness, Kylac eyed the combatants in their deadlocked pose, pressing and straining against each other. Again he glanced at the Ukinha, yet still they refused to interfere. Or mayhap knew not how. Entranced, they appeared. As their bloodied matron sought to direct the flow of acid over her challenger . . . As the breathless challenger thrust back in desperate resistance . . . As that milky fluid spilled from the vine, steaming as it spread at the combatants' feet . . .

At a final heave from her assailant, Denariel buckled. Simply folded at the elbow, and crumbled at the knees and waist. Forsaking any further struggle. Enabling Talathandria to bring the bleeding vine up overhead.

But she was also lunging forward, ducking under the acid's arc. Yelping as the slender stream grazed her naked back, but committed to her maneuver. Twisting and falling so as to trip the Ukinhan matron at the heels. Dragging her opponent back, wrenched to one side.

Dropping Talathandria into the acidic puddle of her own making.

35

Talathandria wailed as the pooled acid devoured the flesh of her arm and the side of her torso. Pinned beneath Denariel, she really had no chance of escape. All her thrashing only encouraged the acid in its work, splashing it upon her cheek, her chest, her midriff. At the same time, the angle of her fall had led the vine's tail, still gripped in her hand, to spill across her own leg. As she was unable to reposition it, the vine's trickling flow served now to sever the limb just below the knee, steaming as it chewed through meat and bone.

Suffering a spattered drop here or there, Denariel leaned upon her foe, determined to finish this. As determined as Kylac had seen her in the jaggeruunt's cavern, where her precious Abinama had met his end. Enraged beyond reason. Heartsick beyond madness.

Quickly enough, the voracious acid found its way into the Ukinhan matron's lungs, stealing her screams. While the echoes carried about the hard edges of cavern, Talathandria herself could but choke and rasp, eyes flaring with anguish and denial. Still Denariel pressed, staring into those ravaged orbs, gaining strength as her opponent's flagged.

When at last the matron's stubborn convulsions had ceased, Denariel leaned back, rolled aside, and struggled to her knees. Only to topple backward, groping helplessly at the vine still cinched around her neck.

Heedless of any lingering risk, Kylac leapt into the pit. Four of the eight grolls—those perched around the pit's rim as witnesses—did so with him, dropping almost soundlessly alongside. Ignoring them, he reached the fallen Denariel and crouched over her, to have a closer look at the strangling vine and her too-pale face.

"Remove it!" he demanded to the Ukinha hovering over him. Though it appeared the vine had all but bled out, he couldn't well go carving at her throat and risk whatever acidic juices might ooze from that area. "Now!"

He withdrew a step to emphasize the request. Peering into Denariel's desperate eyes, for all the reassurance he could lend her.

The Ukinha at last seemed to come to an agreement. One leaned in, clawed fingers reaching for the vine, pinching the strand as its kinsman had earlier. The vine loosened, relinquishing its hold. With a dexterous yank, the groll slipped it free.

For a moment, Denariel only gaped, and it appeared they might have acted too late. Then she drew a gasping breath, coughed, and gasped again. Kylac bent toward her, but this time, one of the grolls intercepted him with an outstretched arm, snarling. The one beside it did the same, still holding the vine. As it gathered the thorny strand in its palm, its eyes glittered in fierce warning.

That they hadn't attacked him already meant mayhap they wouldn't, barring fresh cause. So Kylac once again restrained himself, satisfied that the immediate threat to Denariel had been removed. Trusting—again—that she would come to no further harm. That, if they neglected to aide in her recovery, the Ukinha would at the least honor their pact to uphold her as their new matron, should she recuperate on her own.

Thus far, they seemed more interested in the steaming, half-eaten carcass of their old one. The four grolls above, like the four below, eyed the twitching remains as if half expecting them to rise up and resume command. Kylac could read little from their feral expressions, their indistinct features rippling with subtle, shapeshifting movements. But he sensed well enough the prickle of ire, the disorientation of surprise, and the sting of dismay, all more human than he might have guessed.

And a curdling embarrassment, he thought, when the groll with the coiled vine flung it down upon Talathandria's corpse and offered a grating hiss. Its kinsmen mimicked the sound. Each then scraped at the stony earth—once with each foot—before rubbing their hands together in a wringing motion.

A communal display of respect, it might have been, or a gesture of condemnation. Mayhap both. But it felt as if they were bidding farewell. Fare riddance.

Whatever their degree of shock and indignation, it failed to subside when their attentions returned to Denariel. As if, even now, they were unconvinced. Of her strength? Her will? Her commitment? Kylac couldn't say, and he cared not. Only that she find it in her to rise, and allay his fears that she may have suffered some lasting damage.

As her ragged breathing settled into a more comfortable rhythm, she managed to prop herself up on one elbow. With her free hand set to idly massaging her damaged throat, she peered past the surrounding grolls, past Kylac, to have a look at her vanquished foe. The young queen's visage, so contorted with pain and fury before, now hung slack. Hollow with realization. With disgust. With shame. She'd done what was needed. And while she wasn't quite sorry for it, she sure couldn't find any satisfaction in it.

Kylac knew well the feeling.

Her gaze found his. For the briefest moment, it was that of a lost waif. Forsaken. Forlorn. Afraid. Her lower lip quivered, and he thought she might weep.

Then, as if recognizing him, that stubborn enmity returned. Her hand fell from her neck, as if it were an admission of weakness. Her eyes darkened, and her brow furrowed into a familiar scowl. Bloodied and winded and battered as she was, she was still Denariel, onetime princess and now queen of Addaranth. And he but a rogue outlander, despised for the persistence of his very presence.

Would she order him killed? Kylac wondered abruptly. While he saw no reason for which the Ukinha might dishonor themselves by unfairly punishing *her*, he imagined they'd be only too eager to dispose of *him*—more fully, this time. Having served his purpose as witness, what need had Denariel to suffer him any longer?

Instead, her gaze slipped back to Talathandria, the edges of her expression flattening, but her eyes still wracked. Mayhap killing him once was sufficient. Mayhap she'd exacted the last of her retribution from the mutant matron. Mayhap she'd simply stomached all she could of murder and vengeance just now.

A shudder rippled through her.

"Her tunic," Kylac said, turning toward Rashad.

The ranger stood in his position at the rim of the pit, peering intently at its heart, as if to memorize every detail of this encounter for a more thorough examination later. At Kylac's command, however, he broke his stare to gather Denariel's garments and toss them below.

Kylac caught them up and carried them toward her. He'd have offered her Rashad's travel cloak, as well, had the ranger not left it behind before entering the warren. She was shivering in earnest now, more likely from the shock of her exertion and injuries than the cavern's tepid breath. Whichever, she required more than the cloak of her own skin to fend off her tremors.

The Ukinha stopped him again before he could reach her, forcing Kylac to tamp his irritation. "She needs warmth," he insisted. "And aid for her wounds."

Cleansing poultices. Cooling compresses. Salves and unguents for her lacerations, and balms for her abrasions. While none of her injuries appeared life-threatening, he'd seen men die of less, once given to infection and rot. Bitten and clawed by one such as Talathandria, Denariel would be foolish to wager elsewise.

"What more has she to prove?" Kylac asked. Of the Ukinha, and then of Rashad.

The Wanderer could only shake his head. They'd entered uncharted waters. Whatever was to happen next, it would unfold without the premonition of history.

Finally, one of the grolls took her garments from him, sniffing at them while pawing through them. As if Kylac or Rashad might have somehow defiled them with their handling. When the mutant at last extended them to her, its manner seemed almost contemptuous.

Denariel eyed the Ukinh plaintively, then sternly, disdaining the garb. The four grolls within the pit continued to observe her closely. The four above continued to eye Kylac and Rashad. Kylac wondered if the Wanderer stood to be punished, too. Was it the Ukinha who would rule on their fates, or Denariel? If the latter, would the grolls abide her decision? As of yet, nothing had been made clear.

None of which altered the most pressing matter at hand. "Your Majesty," Kylac tried again, "let us tend to your injuries."

"My injuries . . . will keep," she replied, rasping through chattering teeth.

"At the least, ya need water, food, rest."

"You are here to tell me . . . what I require?"

"Does Your Majesty seek something else?"

In answer, she attempted to rise, wincing at the endeavor. Kylac moved to assist, but was summarily blocked by the Ukinha, who did nothing themselves to aid her. They simply watched, as if observing some natural oddity. Waiting to see what she intended—what she could manage on her own.

Kylac cringed at the sight of her frail, wobbling effort, her limbs shaking like a newborn foal's. But he felt a strange surge of pride to see her feet take root, and her legs to hold, however tentative their balance.

When at last she'd proven herself stable—or at least in no immediate danger of collapse—she eyed the surrounding grolls and drew a ragged breath. "*Ihm har olnedra, Rithranykuth. Darmuth iyk . . . gabrunagun.* By right, I mean to serve . . . as your steward matron. *Arym oondrecht, pe gamol.*" She paused to catch her breath. "And call upon those present . . . to serve in kind."

Given the seething rancor exhibited by the attending Ukinha, with the acerbic odor still rising from Talathandria's carcass, Kylac doubted the request would prove quite that easy. Yet the nearest grolls were already shrinking as they faced her. Neither bowing nor kneeling, as Ledron and his brood had when swearing fealty to her, but clearly relenting in their stance, as if withdrawing any challenge to her authority.

When Kylac looked, he found those above presenting themselves much the same. If not an oath, then at least an acknowledgment. Their matron was dead, bested, undone in no small measure by her own treachery. In the absence of any obvious alternative, their allegiance now must be to Denariel.

Nonetheless, Kylac remained keenly aware that groll behavior was largely unknown to him. Appearances notwithstanding, a fool he'd be to presume anything. Least of all that which he would *hope* to be true.

"Those who *would* serve me, go now. Convey this witness you have borne. Scatter it like spores in a summer wind. Let it be known to the Ukinha, from those inhabiting the lowest bog, to those dwelling upon the highest summit, that a new matron would honor them, and summons them to her."

Though pleased by the growing strength and confidence in her voice, Kylac was yet concerned by the trembling of her naked limbs, the pallor infusing her dusky face, and the streams of blood still dripping from her lacerated flesh. Making him far less enamored of her intractable singlemindedness—of what seemed an almost fevered focus. What value did her edicts hold if she were to perish before seeing them through?

"*Undreth ahnyu,*" she pressed. "A uniting, I call for. A tideswell against mine enemies, who are now yours. Against those who mean to overwhelm these shores. Who would butcher, enslave, and deceive. *Endrimyr, tor nagu.* That these lands may be cleansed, and a balance restored."

Kylac chanced a glance back at Rashad, to see what the Mad Wanderer might make of these ravings. Was there some precedent for this? Could the Ukinha be persuaded to serve as Denariel intended? Could this great host she imagined assemble without tearing itself apart? If so, could it be bridled, controlled? Or would it slip her reins like a wild horse to set a course and endgame of *its* choosing?

Unsurprisingly, Rashad's face was an inscrutable mask, there amid the mooncast shadows. Intrigued, he might have been. Else horrified. Not altogether different from Kylac himself.

Distant concerns, regardless. Whatever the answers, Kylac didn't sense that the Ukinha would be open to discourse. They would either obey or they wouldn't. And he wasn't much interested in second-guessing Denariel's command, even if he'd believed it possible. All he truly cared about was hastening toward a resolution so that he could see to her health.

"Your Majesty—"

Even that simple interjection drew a savage, hissing response from the gathered grolls. The nearest pair rounded on Kylac with such sudden, intense animosity that he very nearly took to his swords. A mistake, surely, and so he let the weapons be, while somehow holding his ground against his would-be opponents.

"Your wishes are known," he braved, feeling the hot, fetid breath of the nearest grolls upon his cheeks. "If'n these will not obey, let us seek those who shall."

He knew he was overstepping his bounds. He also knew he'd shown patience enough.

For once, it appeared he'd won her agreement.

"Fetch me a challenger," she snarled at the grolls, "if I must prove my claim again. Until then, you've no favor to curry but mine."

The Ukinha looked to one another, flaring or hissing or mewling slightly, softly. Rivals still, for all their cooperation here. Their overriding instinct still to please, that they might win an opportunity to breed.

Or so Kylac presumed. That it was the simplest way for him to make sense of these proceedings didn't necessarily make it true.

Truth or fancy, the four grolls within the pit withdrew. Springing from the pit floor almost in unison, each in its own direction, they paused again to give some indiscernible gesture. Then they turned and darted from the cavern, vanishing through separate cave mouths, at roughly each point of the compass.

It happened so swiftly, so unexpectedly, that even Kylac took a moment to assure himself that they'd actually departed. Unlikely to soon return. Off on their mission, mayhap, or simply deserting. A victory, either way.

That still left the four above—the two who'd escorted Talathandria, and the two erstwhile combatants standing watch even now over Rashad. More than enough to thwart Kylac's wishes, should Denariel continue to refuse them.

"Will Her Majesty permit us now to tend to her?"

He stepped toward her, only to stop again as she recoiled. For a long moment, she regarded him, seeming at war with her own judgment. Impossible as it was to read her thoughts, he understood her and her motives well enough at this point to *guess*, at least, at some of the considerations with which she grappled. Naturally, the urge to have him killed brewed somewhere near the fore. But seasoned here with doubt. A question, mayhap, as to where that might leave her just now—alone with a half-mad ranger and this quartet of Ukinha. The former an outlaw sentenced to death by her own father—or grandfather, as it might have been. The latter of uncertain loyalties, making her standing among them precarious. Vendetta aside, who had yet proven as faithful to her as Kylac?

But that was placing too much emphasis, mayhap, on her limited sense of self-preservation. Her reservations might have only to do, as they had in the past, with his prospective value toward some task still outstanding. The longer she worked to formulate her response, the more fitting that particular possibility struck him.

"It will take time," she admitted finally, "for enough Ukinha to gather here. Days, if not weeks."

"It will indeed. I'd suspect."

"Indranell . . . may already be besieged."

Kylac nodded.

"They should be alerted. Reassured. That aid is to come. Lest they attempt some other desperate maneuver."

"So let us carry word," Kylac agreed. "As soon as your strength is returned."

Denariel shook her head, her gaze drifting up to the grolls at Rashad's back. "I must remain. To unite my warriors. To lead them."

Kylac knew what she was asking, but had no intention of agreeing to it. "So let them rally at Indranell instead. Leave word with one o' your new lieutenants here—"

"They'll not make the march on their own," she said, confident in the assertion. "Nor is there any other I can send with word."

Not a mutant, certainly, as the Addarans would only seek to slay it on sight. "Send the ranger," Kylac proposed.

Her eyes shifted, hooded by a scowl. "And trust him to comply?"

"Mayhap a royal pardon to inspire him?"

Rashad spat. "I'm no herald. And I require no pardon."

"If he would guide you, he would have my gratitude," Denariel replied sternly, speaking still to Kylac. "But it is *you* I would send. You, whom Ledron knows, and may heed. You who may help to safeguard them until my arrival."

Her reasoning was sound. But Kylac hadn't come all this way, endured all that he had—his own death, in a sense—to abandon her now. "Your Majesty—"

"I will hear no protests," she snapped. Imposing as she meant it to sound, the proclamation rang from her trembling form more as a plea. "If you would serve me, this is how you may do so. If not . . . I leave you to whatever purpose the Ukinha may find for you."

An unmistakable threat. One she would be all too happy to fulfill.

Only, she wouldn't. In that moment, it wasn't her warning that spoke to him, but her overwhelming sense of need. She was truly asking this of him because she saw it as the only option. For the good of her Addaran people.

"You have long professed to care for my safety," she said, in answer to his reluctance. "An assumed charge, stolen, from the very beginning. Had you realized it then . . . much that has transpired might have been avoided." She paused, seeming to bite back tears. Of sorrow. Frustration. "Admit it now, and perhaps we can come to some reckoning."

Kylac ached to tell her she was wrong. That she was a rash, haughty, mule-headed girl whose refusal to acknowledge the perils around her wouldn't shield her from them.

But how could he declare as much against the truth behind her words? He himself had questioned, even regretted, the role played in returning her to Addaranth. Mistaken about his purpose from the outset. Blinded by his own aims. Misled, but only because he'd allowed it to happen.

So who was he to balk at her present request? In effect, she was giving him a chance here to atone for that initial misstep. To concede now, as he might have then, that he was *not* her warder. To stop intervening on her behalf, and let her go, in honor of her desire.

Allowing her fate to be one of her own choosing.

The moonlit cavern seemed suddenly a stifling thing, the weight of its walls, and the walls of the pit, closing down around him. The inexorable press of understanding, acceptance, and him helpless to rail against it.

"If'n those are Your Majesty's wishes . . ."

He hesitated, seeking some other answer. Of the observing grolls, a fiercely scowling Rashad, the star-filled rents in the rugged ceiling, the rough sands of the pit floor. There, his gaze snagged upon Talathandria's openmouthed rictus. A grisly sight that infused him now with a peculiar strength. Mayhap because it reminded him of Denariel's—the young woman for whom he so stubbornly feared. Whom he'd failed, time and again.

"What word, precisely, are we to bear?"

36

The winds shifted, bending from the east.

Laden with the scent of smoke.

Kylac looked to Rashad. A bushy scowl told him the ranger had smelled it, too.

Stride for stride, they hastened up the rocky slope. Clambering over juts and crags, skirting jagged fissures, clawing through hedges of stunted brush.

Upon cresting the broken rise, Kylac spied at once the pillars of black smoke that marred the cloudless horizon. Like stalks bowed by their own weight, sprouted from a highland valley beyond the next mountainous ridge.

"Navamere," Rashad grunted, between huffing breaths.

The borderland settlement they'd been seeking. A gateway marking their return to Addaran territory, along the fringe of the Reach. As held by his guide, at least.

"My road ends here, then," the Wanderer added.

A threadbare debate. "Our bargain was to sees I reached Hanninth."

"And you shall. Aim for those sooty spires. Nothing between here and there you can't overcome. Southeast road'll take you to Hanninth. Can't miss it. It's the only one."

Mayhap. If his sour companion wasn't attempting again to deceive him. Twice already, the Wanderer had sought to leave his company. Once by sneaking away in the middle of the night, and once by endeavoring to lead Kylac into a potentially lethal snare. The first had been a short-lived effort doomed within a dozen paces. The second had resulted in the ranger suffering a series of nasty stings, setting him scrambling for one of his herbal concoctions. They'd together pretended it was an accident, but both knew better.

After that, the so-called Betrayer had glumly surrendered to his charge of leading Kylac east to Indranell, as it seemed the only way to shed the irksome rogue for good and all.

"I'd feel better to hear another confirm it," Kylac admitted.

"As I would to bathe in gandoline nectar. But I'll not risk a final breath sullied by man's filth. If you're to kill me, do it here and now, so long as we're rid of each other."

The ranger crossed his arms, glaring in emphasis. Something about treading again on settled ground seemed to genuinely frighten him. A fear that had nothing whatsoever to do, Kylac suspected, with the outlaw's death sentence—or with the marauding Grenarr who'd presumably ranged far enough west to pay this Navamere a visit.

Kylac sighed. "Should I find ya's played me false—"

"Fester, you and your threats. There lies your destination. Mine is behind us."

"You would miss the spectacle?"

"A dead witness is a blind witness. Of which there will be plenty, should your queen unleash her proposed swarm. I aim to bear *living* record of the calamity."

Because those Ukinhan uprisings that had come before would scarcely register as skirmishes compared to what Denariel intended. Or so the Wanderer had it. What few accounts suggested elsewise were but tattered myths and fevered imaginings, of no use in predicting how this storm might actually unfurl.

Either way, Kylac wouldn't begrudge the ranger's desire to maintain a safe distance. After all, Rashad had asked for no part of this quarrel, his role in these events played almost completely under duress.

"And ya'll not be swayed into carrying word back to Her Majesty?"

The Wanderer leveled a hooded, bushy-eyed glare. Though the

idea they'd nurtured into a plan for Addaran salvation had been seeded by Rashad himself, the ranger had made it clear that he'd already had "greater stain on these unnatural proceedings" than any man should. A zealot of the natural world, his oath and creed was to observe only, leaving as scant trace of his existence upon the land as possible.

Clearly, his mind was unchanged on the matter.

Nonetheless, given the stakes, Kylac had felt beholden to try once more.

"How far to Hanninth?"

"Four leagues. Steady pace could put you there by nightfall. At Indranell the moon after that. Should you stop tarrying."

"I'll ask Her Majesty to honor that pardon."

Rashad snorted. Despite Kylac's probing, the Wanderer had confessed nothing on the matter of his exile, refusing to recount in any way the nature of his royal offense. "More likely, I'll find you among the corpses. To finish as we began."

Raising again the lingering question of Kylac's ability to withstand and overcome the Ukinhan venom. A mystery that Kylac himself had been disappointed not to resolve. He'd granted Rashad a blood sample during one of their respites, but had stopped short of surrendering pieces of liver and kidney after his blood alone had told them nothing. His only consolation was that it scarcely mattered, at present. However resistant he might have proven, he doubted Sabrynne Stormweaver or her armies would seek to poison him to death.

"Should it come to that, may ya find the answer to your satisfaction."

Kylac offered the ranger his hand. Rashad snorted again, scowling bitterly, and turned away, stealing a final glance at the distant smoke plumes before starting back down the western slope.

A moment later, Kylac was descending along the *eastern* face, down toward a thickly overgrown ravine below. A thorny tangle that might hide any number of perils, despite his guide's assurances. How often had he seen a tharrowhawk perched outside a dermrat's hole? That he'd all but escaped the Ukinhan Wilds, returning to civilization's threshold, didn't mean he was safe.

Caution aside, it was a liberating feeling, to travel again unfettered. Swifter he could move alone. But what Rashad had lacked in foot speed and stamina, he'd more than accounted for with his intimate knowledge of the hostile territory. Guiding them past obstacles and hazards that might elsewise have waylaid them. Sidestepping unfortunate confrontations such as that with the tree-clinging ornga. Steering them most capably along the shortest possible course—once he'd come to understand that the outlander's skills and instincts granted him little choice.

It was the only reason they'd reached this point as quickly as they had.

Presuming the Wanderer had been truthful upon his departure, the entire return trek would consume a mere five days—no more than his original journey west. Totaling thirteen since Kylac had bid Ledron farewell at Rendenel Run. Not too late, he hoped, to affect the outcome of the Addarans' final stand.

With the clouds of smoke from the next valley darkly hinting elsewise, Kylac hurried to find out.

He reached Indranell before dusk the next day, surpassing Rashad's estimate by outpacing a slow-brightening moon.

He failed to beat the rains.

A powerful deluge, the storm stole color and clarity from the scene of his arrival. Charcoal clouds spilled thick gray curtains across the land, like a veil of web from a spider's hand. The city still stood, but there was no identifying from afar the shadows hunkered upon its battlements. Stalwart Addarans, or conquering Grenarr? Were those watchfires that burned, or pyres of the slain? Was it a living bastion he gazed upon, or merely a ruined husk?

It had struck him unlikely, if not impossible, that the Grenarr forces could have cracked the shell of their remaining prize already. But they'd been underestimating the Great Grendavan's cunning and ruthlessness from the outset. Would she not have a gambit in mind for her final stroke?

The swath of raiding and razing that he'd followed since Navamere had taken similar toll on his confidence. Villages and hamlets and homesteads, all plundered and burned to the ground. Several, from Hanninth in the west, to Severstone east, had been familiar to him. Outposts and settlements he'd passed through in his westward pursuit of Denariel. Untouched at the time, their inhabitants had been foolishly certain they'd remain so. The bright-eyed butcher. The grubby stablehand. The ill-tempered marina woman, Urseth. Corpses now, or wishing they were. And while all signs had suggested it to be the work of smaller parties—scouring patrols no more than fifty strong—who was to say larger companies, alone or in tandem, hadn't enjoyed similar success here?

He curled south in his continuing approach, gaining at last a glimpse of the dark masses encamped upon the highway beyond the city's south gate. A crescent line of Grenarr, just out of bowshot. A regiment to replace that which his small band from Tetherend had encountered and ultimately penetrated eighteen nights past. Re-formed as anticipated, and swollen in number. Not a siege force, but certainly a blockade, meant to deny any passage in or out of the city by way of the Karamoor.

A reassuring sign. For if the Grenarr were still bothering to huddle outside, then they hadn't yet breached the city. Mayhap hadn't even tried. And why should they? With their enemies trapped, why spend in battle what could be won more cheaply through deprivation?

It was a scene more befitting what he'd expected, what he'd *hoped*, to find. Drawing from Kylac a smile of satisfaction. The temptation to continue closer arose within him. Track down a lookout whose tongue he could strip. Slip through the encampment itself, mining for vital rumor as to the Stormweaver's intended endgame. Mayhap kill a commander or two, if only for the ripples of confusion and discord it might sow.

He resisted the urge. There was no knowing what information this group might have been entrusted with—or *misinformation*, as might be. Given Sabrynne's history, one seemed as likely as the next. Surely, Ledron or Fayne or whatever council now controlled Indranell's defenses would have employed spies of their own to glean what they could. Or traded emissaries. Or received offers or demands by any number of means. Better that he reconvene first with the defenders, learn what they already knew—or thought they knew—and *then* decide what additional exploration was required. Mayhap with a more specific objective in mind.

To that end, he redirected northward, clinging to the western tree line, battered by the hammering rains. He'd not known many storms upon these shores to last long—most given only minutes to vent their fury. This one raged and railed accordingly, though already a half-mark old. To the northeast, beyond the city's ramparts, lighting split the sky. Thunder spilled from the seams, rattling the heavens. Causing the earth beneath to shudder.

So much the better. Where caution might ask that he delay his incursion until nightfall, forcing him to wait another hour, he determined that the storm offered cover enough.

At roughly the midriff of the city's meandering western wall, a streambed carried waste from within, wending farther west across a spread of no-man's-land toward lowland vegetable fields abandoned just now. Taking aim, he continued north along a squat, tree-lined ridge for a little more than a hundred paces before detaching himself from the jungle's shelter. After dropping down the face of a short bluff to reach the stream's banks, he started toward the city, feet sliding amid the mud and slime, breathing through his mouth to avoid the worst of the rank odors drummed up by the rains from the stream's fetid surface.

His pace was steady, unhurried. Holding himself in a low crouch, he searched the battlements above for voice or movement that might suggest a lookout's spying eye, while also keen to any scouts the Grenarr might have roving about the stronghold's base. On neither front did he detect threat. Notice from above, now and then, but only in cursory passing. How long had the Addarans been at watch now upon these walls and guard towers? Even with regular rotations, their gazes couldn't be as sharp as they might have been days or weeks ago. Not in these sodden, shrouded conditions. Not against one with his training. And not when their focus was to seek out *clusters* of men that might signify danger. What potential harm did a single invader pose?

He reached the curtain wall unmolested, undetected, where the befouled stream passed beneath the massive stone blocks through a breach grated in rusted iron. Edging north again, he ventured toward a natural rise formed by a jutting mound of stony earth—crowned by a shorter section of battlement. The wall's surface was creased somewhat by the buckled ground, which would further shield him from wandering eyes. Cracks and protrusions and clinging vegetation, while of little aid to the ordinary man, could as well have been stairs and ladder rungs for one such as him. The rains might make a stretch or two interesting, but better *some* degree of challenge, lest he be lulled into boredom.

After eyeing the broken heights in calculating appraisal of the surest, swiftest path, Kylac made one last search of his surroundings. Finding them clear, he reached for the first hold, and began his climb.

THE SENTRIES warding the arched, oaken doors stiffened at Kylac's approach. Less in reaction to him than to Governor Merrinem's chief steward, Yurien, serving usher at his side. A joyless man he'd crossed paths with briefly upon his first visit to this castle. Whose severe features included a sharp chin and a receding, oil-slicked widow's peak dyed a deep onyx. After slinking through the lower city to reach the governor's citadel, Kylac had sought and found the steward for this express purpose—to steer him to Indranell's leaders with minimal resistance and delay.

Thus far, it had worked only too well, with servants and guardsmen at various junctures parting so easily that Kylac had wondered for a time if Yurien was misleading him. The pair before him now, however, displayed no intention of falling aside. Instead, they drew taller, rigid in their stance, tightening grip upon their halberds.

"Flaerik, Jessem," the steward offered in cold greeting. "I bring visitor for His Eminence within."

"They're not to be disturbed," the mutton-bearded Jessem rumbled, scarcely sparing a scowl for Kylac.

"You know this," Flaerik sneered. His own cheeks were beardless, the skin heavily freckled.

"We can send summons after, if you request it," Jessem added helpfully.

A muted crackle echoed in the distance, accompanied by the slightest tremor. Shades of the bombardment upon the city's north face, delivered by the Grenarr ships still clogging the sound. It had commenced a little before dark, as soon as the thunderstorm had abated. Though, from the damage Kylac had paused to witness, the long-expected attack must have been raging intermittently for days now.

More than a week, according to Yurien.

"Mayhap we wait until the Grenarr has ransacked these halls," Kylac suggested, "and burned these doors from their hinges."

"Loose tongue, for an unarmed whelp," said Flaerik.

"Calls himself Kronus," Yurien snapped.

Jessem perked with recognition, suddenly hesitant. But Flaerik only thrust forward like an angry badger. "Call him what you please. Our orders—"

Kylac punched him in the throat. Before he could gasp in response, Kylac had seized his free arm, to wrench it up and around against his back. Pressing his face into the knots of the oaken door, Kylac slipped the longknife from the sentry's own sheath and put its tip to the base of his skull.

Flaerik's halberd fell, clanging against the stone floor.

Jessem, in all that time, had managed only to back into a defensive crouch, halberd leveled in shaking hands.

"His life is yours," Kylac said. "I suggest ya sees to the door."

His cheeks suddenly ashen against the black cinders of his mutton beard, Jessem looked to Yurien.

"Captain Ledron's outlander," Yurien confirmed tartly. "What more harm can he do?" With only slightly more comfort, he added, "They'll be pleased enough to see him."

As Flaerik sputtered, Jessem blinked, and scrambled to open the door.

Kylac tipped his brow to Yurien. "Your queen thanks ya for your aid. And yours," he said to Flaerik. He released the sentry, retaining the knife. "What say I keep this for now, eh? To ward ya from any foolish notions."

He'd left his battered Grenarr blades back in Yurien's office, as a sign of his peaceful intentions. Not bothering to admit that he had no desire to retrieve them. Well as they'd served him, he would do better at this point to replace them.

A glance through the open portal revealed a private feast hall, where gathered a small cluster of men. Heads reached out on craning necks, seeking cause for the interruption. Swiftly spotting Ledron's bald pate among them, Kylac entered, spinning his borrowed longknife playfully in hand.

The chamber, quieted already by the disturbance, was stunned now into silence. Kylac searched the forms and faces for others he knew. Colonel Fayne sat across from Ledron, joined at his bench by the bulbous Captain Jyserra and a pair of lieutenants whose faces were familiar, even if their names weren't. Ledron had with him Colonel Garnham, hauled back from the southern battlefront, along with longtime companions Havrig and Talon—rediscovered, it would appear, from wherever Bahsk had assigned them.

The rest were strangers, most with the soft look and condescending mien of city officials and royal advisors. This included the richly robed man at the head, occupying the only high-backed chair at the table. Governor Merrinem, given the account from Yurien. With some prodding, the chief steward had divulged to Kylac that, upon Ledron's return from the Strebolen, most of the battle-weary soldiers returning with him had come to defer to the captain's command. Or to Garnham's—which, with the colonel's deference, had made their voices one and the same. A shifting of loyalties brought on by their disenchantment with Bahsk, the former general who, despite such certainty in his course, had brought them only defeat.

This in opposition to Fayne, who'd been Bahsk's chief lieutenant. Having experienced no part of the army's bitter losses to the south, Fayne's garrison troops had remained faithful to him, disdaining the thought of saluting a "royal nursemaid." To stave off conflict between their already fractured forces, Ledron had proposed reinstating Merrinem as their governing authority. To stand over both factions and ensure the peace between them.

Merrinem had accepted, if only reluctantly, proceeding to lean heavily, as before, upon his chosen retainers and military commanders. Serving as a figurehead of false unity, while Ledron and Fayne and a small circle of prominent supporters on all sides carried out their squabbles behind closed doors, apart from the agitated, heartsick populace.

Each night, as Yurien had it, they gathered for supper at the governor's table, to deliver their daily reports. On the positions and movement of enemy troops, as witnessed by scouts or lookouts. On self-inflicted crimes and skirmishes within the city's own walls, chiefly between refugees and those set down to monitor and suppress their activities. On the inventory of dwindling food stores, beset by the opposing demands of thieves and hoarders.

On the people's rapidly deteriorating morale, and what might be done about it.

Useless posturing, to hear the governor's chief steward tell it. For there seemed no action to be taken. They were trapped. Whatever proposals were bandied about each night, it was only so that Indranell's so-called leaders could feel some semblance of control. If Kylac had some news, or could offer some hope—any hope—it would doubtless be well received.

Let us see.

"Kronus," Ledron managed in a partial daze. As if fearing he might be addressing an apparition.

"Fair greetings," Kylac offered to all, though none other than Talon seemed pleased at his arrival. "However grim, I daresay I feared worse."

The Head drew back from the table, half rising as if to come and welcome him. "Her Majesty. How fares she?"

"She lives, or did when I left her."

Ledron halted. "You *left* her? Where?"

Another crackling collision rattled the distant ramparts.

"We'll come to Her Majesty," Kylac assured the captain, with a purposeful glance at the others assembled. Tacitly begging the Head's discretion and patience. "I'd know first, how many of ours returned safely?"

Ledron seemed to have misplaced his tongue. Reaching the foot of the table, Kylac looked to Garnham, who answered gruffly. "Who might fight again? Some eight in ten of those set forth. Twenty-four hundred."

A number that matched Yurien's. Serving further confirmation of the steward's account. Kylac nodded. While two in ten was a significant loss, it might have easily been worse. "Plus the thousand here in garrison."

"Nearly all of whom still stand," Fayne boasted.

"I should hope so," Kylac remarked, giving his blade another spin.

"Begging pardon," Merrinem interjected, with a silky voice almost lazy in its cadence. "Are we to know the reason for this intrusion?"

Raised above the others on his chair, the governor was a spindle of a man beneath his satin, sapphire-hued garments. Gold and gems weighed upon his neck and fingers. Even across the table, Kylac smelled the perfumed scents emanating from him as he gestured at last to have the door closed, and saw the powders upon his brow and cheeks, carefully shaven save for a white beard and mustache trimmed closely about his mouth.

"With respect, Your Eminence, I'm come from Her Majesty with a plan for our deliverance. Warranting information on our present outlook."

They needn't learn the plan's full origins. Birthed by Rashad on the heels of Denariel's actions. Refined by rogue and ranger during their return to the city. Knowing it to be cooked up by a notorious madman and infamous outlander might only make it more difficult to swallow. And swallow it they must. For, after much consideration, Kylac was convinced that it offered them their best chance at survival.

If not victory.

Fayne snorted. "Our outlook?"

The colonel's cruel, mocking expression was mirrored by most around the table. By gazes that glimmered with contempt, smirks and scowls alike twisted with derision. A fool he was, to stroll in so brazenly among them. Whatever their desperate need for hope, his couldn't possibly be the answer they'd been seeking.

Kylac stabbed a slice of apple in a near-empty bowl upon the table.

He'd have preferred the duck, but only bony scraps remained. "In the event ya's decided already upon some other course."

"What course?" Ledron asked. "You've seen the ships in the sound, whose strikes now wear at us. To the south, our scouts have it that Grendavan herself is leading some two thousand tar-skins up from Avenell. This on the back of the two thousand who drove us from the Strebolen, who themselves have scattered east and west to pillage and raze our unprotected villages and townships. More than five hundred have gathered again before our southern gates, to be joined by others, I'll wager, when their slaughter is finished."

Since none had objected, Kylac helped himself to another apple slice.

"Yet here we hunker," Garnham spat, "in a stronghold built primarily to resist a sea attack."

"Were it elsewise, we still remain ill equipped to weather a siege," muttered the usually tightlipped Havrig.

Fayne was shaking his head. "So we should abandon our final refuge, they say, to mount another offensive. All but outnumbered now in terms of sword and spear."

"Better now than later, when we're outnumbered for certain," Garnham argued.

"Or half dead from festering within these walls," offered Talon.

"To which others propose we flee east," Fayne snickered, "to the peninsula. To cultivate wild lands once deemed dregs for the tar-skins. Foolishly trusting our enemies to be satisfied with the spoils of our cities."

"With nowhere to regroup, should they decide elsewise," added one of Fayne's supporters.

"They'll run us down," another on his side of the table agreed, "if only *after* we've made those worthless lands inhabitable."

"If we're not picked apart first by creatures along the eastern coast," murmured Jyserra.

"Whatever we seek to do," Ledron snarled, "we can assume our every move will be relayed to our enemies. Just as it must have been in our foray through the canyons. By the treacherous vermin still gnawing at us from within."

By the time they'd taken pause, Kylac had consumed a full apple's worth of slices, along with a pair of stewed carrots and a knob of boiled potato. A meager portion, but, by all appearances, few were eating much better.

Refreshed he felt, nonetheless, to learn that matters were pretty much as he'd discerned them, by way of Yurien's account and his own observations.

"These vermin," he echoed thoughtfully, shaking his knife as he peered around at a circle of irritated, challenging stares. "A persistent plague. One it seems we can do nothing about."

He let his gaze linger upon Ledron, seeking to convey again that there was more to be said, but not within ear of their present company. The seams of the Head's frown deepened. With frustration, but also with understanding, for he offered only stale response. "So what course would Her Majesty propose?"

Kylac leaned in, yoked by an air of regret. "We wait here only to face starvation and sickness, else the blades and flames o' Grendavan's warriors. Our best chance is indeed flight—not eastward, to tamer lands, but west, into the Harrows."

Half of his listeners erupted into protest, their arguments built around words like "daring," "foolhardy," and "desperate."

"That and more," Kylac agreed. "But is it not the one place they may not follow?"

Fayne's smug smile had slipped. Merrinem sat clenching the arms of his chair, knuckles as white as his beard. A reign of fear and anger and confusion.

"If they *do* follow?" a squirming aide asked.

"Then there will be fewer o' them when come against us."

"And fewer of *us*," Fayne reminded the room. "Without walls to shield us. Our last, best bastion is here."

"Not the last," Kylac said. "There are locations that might serve shelter. Should we move quickly enough to claim the ground."

"To what end?" Garnham asked.

"Ah, precisely. To what *end*? The Grenarr seek to eradicate us, as we would them. Neglecting the more sensible question at hand."

"Which is what?" Ledron demanded, his patience drawing thin.

"Terms o' truce." Against their gapes and stares, Kylac explained. "We mean for our enemies to surrender Avenell, and to forgo conquest here, yes? Should we worm free o' this snare and draw them into the wilds, we might lay trap or two to diminish their numbers, evening the scales. Suppose we succeed. Putting aside mutual destruction, what could we offer in exchange for our demands?"

The councilors and soldiers looked to one another, scowling and grunting uncertainly.

"The eastern peninsula?" Kylac threw out as a guess. "As originally agreed?"

That drew another round of protests.

"Treacherous fiends—"

"Wait to stab us in our sleep—"

"Sooner neighbor with the mutants—"

"A moot suggestion," Fayne answered calmly, when the furor had waned. "Even if we were to regain favorable footing, the tar-skins would never adhere to terms of a negotiation, whatever they might claim."

Ledron agreed. "This Grendavan—black-hearted beast that she is—cannot be trusted. As you, of all of us, best know. She must be brought to heel and another set above her, if there is to be any hope of a reconciliation."

A subtle reminder—or mayhap not so subtle—that much of this could be blamed in part on him, for not killing her when he'd had the chance. Kylac nodded in due acknowledgment. "What harm to ask?"

This time, he received mostly jeers. As before, it was Fayne who summarized the prevailing sentiment. "Only someone grown disenchanted with his own head would be foolish enough to put himself before her."

Kylac chuckled. "Here I feared you'd make me draw lots for the privilege."

None laughed with him. Ledron, as he might have guessed, seemed particularly soured by his attempt at mirth. "You would be so senseless?"

"For the chance to avert mass bloodshed? Of a certain. Especially as some may be mine." Ignoring their scoffs, he moved quickly to fend off further objection. "Failing that? I'll set such an affront as to ensure they follow us."

A settling murmur rippled through the chamber.

"And while you're off having your flayed skull fitted to a pike?" Fayne asked.

"Ya takes your people and sneaks west. To regroup and set trap for our adversaries."

"*Where*," Ledron growled, and speared him with an onerous gaze.

Kylac surveyed again the table's leavings. "For that heel o' bread there, I'll tells ya."

37

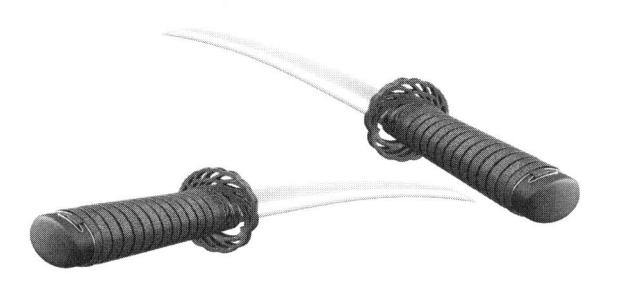

The scouts' reports were wrong.

Gazing down upon the Grenarr encampment, Kylac determined that Sabrynne had mustered considerably more than two thousand warriors. His own wager would have been closer to three. Mayhap even a few hundred more.

It wasn't a tally that told him as much. Arrayed for the night in lines and clusters with no discernible pattern, shrouded in moonlit darkness, screened at the highway's fringes by jungle vegetation, their precise numbers were suitably hidden. But there was no disputing the *weight* of them in his chest, the sheer size and scope and . . . *menace* of their presence. Kylac had long ago learned to measure an adversary by such means—been born with it, really. While owing to instinct more than conventional calculations, he'd found this innate sense to be duly reliable.

Harder it was to gauge where they'd come from. Whether all three thousand had marched up from Avenell together, or whether the reported two thousand had since been bolstered by some of those who'd fought to repel Bahsk at Ollerman's Pass and Rendenel Run. Fortunately, it mattered but little. They were here now from whatever roads, tightly assembled, heading north along the Karamoor with no great secret as to their purpose. Indranell lay a mere ten leagues at

Kylac's back. No more than two days' march, if moving apace. Three if weighed down by siege engines or heavy supply wagons.

He saw no evidence of the latter.

Making it harder, mayhap, to crack the city's shell. But the prospect of a slow death was no more appealing than that of a swift one. *Less*, really. So he hoped Ledron was making good on his promise to see that the city's leaders executed Kylac's proposed plan—the one dreamed up by a half-mad ranger who'd suggested it the best way to not only stem the tide of this war, but to turn it back on their tormentors.

Better sense might have had Kylac himself wagering elsewhere. So many uncertain factors, all or most of which would have to fall in their favor. So he'd been unsurprised by the doubts and challenges the Head had posed upon learning the rest of Kylac's gambit. The portion he'd chosen not to share with Colonel Fayne, Governor Merrinem, and their council, for fear of the spies among them. The portion they wouldn't have believed, and would never have knowingly agreed to.

Madness, had been the Head's own assessment. *Assessing it kindly,* Kylac had agreed. But no more desperate than their circumstances would seem to demand. Shading the maneuver in credibility, and thus limiting suspicion on the part of their enemies. Providing means of pitting Sabrynne's informants against her. Of using these so-called vermin at last to their advantage.

As bait for their trap.

Ledron had continued to rail, of course. But Kylac had had plenty of time to anticipate those protests, and to hone his arguments against them. Given their situation, they couldn't expect anything less than a mad act to save them. Though he'd left it on tentative footing, the Head's bitter, desperate concession had been that the proposal would be carried out.

Nothing he could affect at this juncture, whichever direction the pendulum might have swung since his departure. All he could do was the part he'd agreed to. To seek Sabrynne, or her host's commander, in a last-gasp effort to beg for peace. That some measure of one or both people might be spared. Short of that, to do whatever he could—if anything—to stall their advance. To buy Denariel and her people just a little more time.

He'd set forth diligently, traveling at a comfortable pace all day and most of the night to cover the ten leagues that had brought him here. This after spending the prior night at Indranell recounting for Ledron the culmination of Denariel's quest. And persuading the Blackfist to see it as a victory. And explaining to him how venturing into the tooth of a Ukinhan swarm could in any way *enhance* their chances of survival. And . . .

And doubts be damned. With the Sparrow winging near, he likely had but two full hours before daybreak. Leaving him little time to chart a course for his latest incursion. For with even the shortest Grenarrian standing a head or two taller than himself—with their broad shoulders and scant dress and sable flesh—he'd not likely be able to pass as one of them. Particularly on the move, in daylight. No, if he was to find and treat with the Great Grendavan, now was his best chance.

His eye fell quickly upon the largest tent amid the camp's sprawl, raised at the heart of the mostly slumbering throng. Surrounded by a ring of alert watchmen and flaming braziers. Tricky as it might be to reach her, at least Sabrynne had made herself easy to find.

He was about to duck back into the foliage when something stopped him. A knot in his stomach he knew better than to ignore. What about the Stormweaver had ever been as it appeared? Why should it be so now?

He settled down for another look—a *closer* look. Extending his search. Gaining confidence in his suspicion. Every move she'd made since their dealings had begun had been cloaked in subterfuge and misdirection. Making him a fool to trust the obvious. Assuming the reports that had her leading this horde were correct, where might she have secreted herself?

Somewhere nondescript. Yet still defensible. Far from that gaudy tent, if it were a ruse, yet safely removed from the perimeter, where she might be exposed to ambush. Treading the line between a position of command—standing tall at the head of her people—and safeguarding herself from undue harm.

He took his time, gaze circling out from the center, studying and dismissing various tents and lean-tos and exposed packs of Grenarr warriors. Mentally marking a few as areas of interest, while probing yet for something that would do more to excite his senses. If necessary, he would explore each site displaying promise. But doing so would eat away at his limited time. Better that he be patient and—

His thoughts snagged upon a stretch of ridge along the western flank, about three-quarters to the rear of the camp. Closer to the jungle than he'd imagined Sabrynne might find comfort, but one of the only areas along the highway elevated against attack. More interesting still, it appeared to be the sole stretch of ground that had been stripped bare, trees and brush hacked down and laid low at the roots. Allowing for the three unremarkable tents pitched there, canvas sides painted by the flickering light of a lone watchfire and the shadow of its tending sentry.

Kylac smiled. Why dull their blades or expend the effort to clear ground with the entire highway theirs for the taking? What need for a tent when offered the shelter of trees? Whoever had claimed it had wanted that piece of high ground. And an unobstructed view. And there to reside unseen.

Intrigued as he was, he finished his survey, finding two more sites that might prove worth a look, before slithering south. With each silent stride, he felt more assured, more certain, that he would find her upon that ridge. For the reasons he could define, and for those he couldn't.

Twice he came across roving Grenarr sentries, but the thick vegetation offered such cover that he scarcely had to slow while passing them by. He could have sliced their throats and left them to the worms, but better that he leave them to their rounds, to report as expected. For all the chaos and distraction a good alarm could sow, now wasn't the time.

As he came around in final approach to the targeted ridge, he stepped through a string of snares and past a thickening series of *stationary* sentries. All of which caused his blood to quicken in anticipation. One or the other would have served ample warning against enemy approach. To utilize both here, as nowhere else, gave further promise to his chosen course.

Clever and vigilant as they may have been, they took no notice as he stole around their concealed positions amid the tangle. Darting, creeping, or even crawling as needed. Putting himself finally at the fringe of hastily cleared vegetation marking the ridge.

There he paused. Looking. Listening. Welcoming any indication of who or what lay before him. Wary—for all his confidence—of yet another trap.

When none presented itself, he slipped forward. No more than the shadow of a tree nudged by the wind. Bypassing the first two tents to reach the third, nearest the small overlook. He considered cutting his way inside from the rear. Possessed of his lost blades, he might have done so. With far less trust in his borrowed steel, he chose instead to slink around to the tent's face, within three long-limbed paces of the sentry stood beside the watchfire. Giving the heavily muscled Grenarrian no reason to turn, he ducked through the entry flap.

Darkness awaited him, gathered shadows layered thickly over a mound of furs. Upon those furs, blanketed by a sheer coverlet, lay Sabrynne.

Great Grendavan the Eighth, if indeed all lies concerning that name had been laid bare. Twice deceived already, Kylac could be only so certain. But the Stormweaver was who he'd come for. And now, here before him, asleep on her right side. A small thrill dashed up his spine, attended by a spark of caution. He was, after all, surrounded by some three thousand of her warriors, the nearest within range of her faintest cry. A delicate situation yet, for all his daring and prowess.

He crept toward her, edging around her back. Looking over her stash of weapons for sign of his. Failing to spot them, he turned eye to the rhythmic movement of her chest . . . the sleek outline of her shaven head . . . the shark's fin tattoo upon her throat. The dark setting, silent save for the chittering of the surrounding jungle and crackle of nearby flames, reminded him of the first time he'd taken opportunity to question her. There in her tower quarters of the palace at Avenell. Back when she'd been posing as a mere emissary, a helpless pawn in the schemes of greater men.

In her left hand, she clutched a sheathed dagger, holding it close to her breast. Its hilt was of polished whalebone—alas, not one of his. Kylac crouched, and helped himself to the blade, which but whispered in protest. Sabrynne grunted, then moaned softly. By the time her eyes snapped open, it was to the sensation of her blade's tip pressed against her throat.

"I'd has words with ya, Sabrynne."

Greeting her as he had the last time they'd so met. Sabrynne's eyes glittered with recollection. She blinked, while a slow smile creased her face. Like the kiss of steel, both chilling cold and flaming hot. Flush with genuine amusement.

"The adder," she replied, matching his near-voiceless hiss. "Slithered in from the wilds." A careful swallow. "You've reconsidered my offer, then?"

He found her composure remarkable. While her pulse had quickened, and the muscles in her neck grown taut, her darker emotions of surprise, fear, and anger were well bridled. In no small measure, he suspected, because part of her was duly impressed—if not delighted—to see him again, and in such notable fashion.

"Truthfully, I bring offer o' my own."

"On the edge of a knife. Promising death should I decline?"

"That I should have to repeat it to your successor?" Kylac tsked while shaking his head. "Your answer I'll abide. This is only to ensure we're not interrupted."

Sabrynne arched an eyebrow heavy with skepticism.

"It's death I'd avoid," he insisted. "I's come not as your enemy, but as their envoy."

"At whose bidding? I have it the Pretender found his place in the depths."

A goad. Kylac ignored it. "At my own. As always. To facilitate a quieter resolution to this conflict than the one all seem resigned to."

The Stormweaver scoffed. "Truce?"

"I's eyed this matter from all sides, and for all the salt in the seas cannot fathom where one faction has any greater claim to these lands than another. The Grenarr preceded the Addarans. The Ukinha preceded the Grenarr. Do any deserve to be dispossessed, driven utterly from these shores?"

"Deserve?" she echoed. "If that is the standard, why not all?"

Kylac held his focus. "By my thinking, His Highness Dethaniel had it right from the start. Put aside these old hatreds and lingering enmities. End the ceaseless bloodshed. What hope for any of a peaceful future if'n peace cannot be tendered in the present?"

Sabrynne snickered. "And what should *your* thoughts matter? The thoughts of an outlander. A mercenary. A murderer soaked to his elbows in blood."

Elbows? He'd shed enough to immerse himself. To drown in it. "I's no experience as an arbiter o' land rights," he admitted. "Nor do I believe any lasting peace is possible. I strive only to prevent offense against the weak. Serving a king's daughter, say, and her abducted brother, against their tormentors—*their* people against *yours*." He shook his head. "Save, I come to learn that Dethaniel willfully placed himself in your hands, deceiving his own. And his royal father? A fate that stemmed as much from Addaran betrayal as Grenarr schemes and swords. How, then, am I to lay blame at *your* feet?"

The Stormweaver's brow, until now a mockery of rapt attention, twisted with suspicion. "Would you have me believe your aggrieved princess sees it this way?"

Cleverly seeking answer as to whether Denariel still lived. Kylac saw no reason to deny it. "Her Majesty would have her vengeance, but not at the expense of reclaiming her homeland. She's demonstrated that much already."

"Then it is still *her* you serve."

"No more than I do you. For she means now to end your life as savagely as ya do hers. The blood I would spare flows on both sides."

Sabrynne smirked, then drew a mask of feigned alarm. "Indeed. And what would you have me do to save myself?"

"No more than I's asked o' them. It's the liars and extremists—on both sides—who must be shackled or silenced, if'n the sensible are to prevail. Yours is the ruling voice o' your people. Temper their fury. Call for peace. Ya's proven your might, battered the Addarans to the brink o' defeat. They'll grant your presence on the eastern shores as Dethaniel intended, if'n ya'll but forgo this martial pursuit and return Avenell to Addaran control. Give 'em no cause to finish this fight. Not when ya can ends it here with a single stroke o' mercy."

Mayhap the whisper of his voice undermined his earnestness. Because it felt nearer to an impassioned plea than any he'd uttered before, and his listener had no reaction—scarcely blinked—while waiting for him to finish. When realizing that he *had*, her eyes but narrowed in a discerning squint.

"You'd have me withdraw, when I hold every advantage," she whispered back at him. While the watchfire outside popped and crackled, and the jungle chittered its raucous song. "Now, with centuries of debt set to be collected, I should steer my people from their rightful retribution. Simply slink off into the wilds, chasing scraps like some mangy hound at a lord's table. To labor and toil to tame a land our forefathers long ago settled and had stolen from them already. This is your proposal?"

"Should ya value their lives—"

"No. Posture and dissemble as you will, the landsnakes can but writhe and hiss in their nest. There they shall burn, else venture out to taste our iron, our steel, our sandaled heels."

"And after? The mighty Grenarr, tamers o' the wind, masters o' the seas, to become . . . farmers? Herders? *Landsnakes* themselves?"

Her features flattened, telling him he'd finally brushed a nerve within her. "We will draw from the land what it has to offer. While maintaining our claim to the seas."

"Two very different worlds. Mayhap ya can rule both. Mayhap not. If'n forced to choose, which would ya sooner surrender?"

Her lips sharpened with further argument, but she caught herself and let it go with a cruel smile. "Your arrogance is truly boundless. The only reason you still draw breath is because I willed it. Imprisoning you when I could have killed you. Permitting your escape for *my* purposes. The Pretender rots. I know the landsnakes' movements as soon as they do. So tell me, when did your cunning usurp mine?"

Kylac could have told her precisely when, and where, were he more certain it might actually prove true. Just now, it seemed more practical to let her revel in her superiority. That she didn't imagine he'd suspected her of hidden motives back in Avenell's dungeons, or that there was no adapting to the presence of her informants, suggested her assumptions and resulting manipulations weren't entirely unfailing.

And his aim in coming here had been as much to stoke her anger as it had been to persuade her of peace. To ensure that, when the time came, she would seek to destroy him and those he stood with.

On the small chance that she wasn't already sworn to do so.

She remarked upon his silence with a contemptuous snort. "As I thought. Giving you nothing to barter with. No reason for me to capitulate in any regard. So take my life, if you think it will avail you. But go now, while I still have a mind to be amused by this . . . feeble act of desperation."

"Else ya'll summon your guard?" It was Kylac's turn to smirk. "And watch me slay how many on my way out?"

Her inky eyes smoldered. Much as she wanted to test him, she'd witnessed the cost of doing so. "Should you come before me again, I won't be merciful."

"Should I come before ya again, ya'll no longer have that choice."

He waited, but it seemed she was permitting him final word. Truly, the only one that mattered was that of the stolen blade in his hand. Was he to let her live as promised? Or would he murder her here and now, that he might not have to face her later?

Her very expression was a taunt, an urging, a dare. Fearless, as always. But so was Kylac. Though others might say he would come to regret it, he was nothing if not the embodiment of his spoken word. Whatever the consequences sown by his mercy, he would reap them with a light heart.

"I'll grants ya the rest o' this night to reconsider," he said. "Should ya fail to turn back with the dawn, I set to culling this herd, offering no quarter."

He permitted her one last chance at rebuttal, while taking a final look around for his blades. Suffering a fresh pang at their perceived loss. As she clung to her silence, he backed toward the tent entrance. She eased upright, but made no move against him. Eyeing him like the adder she took *him* for. Smiling a reptilian smile. Telling him she was only too content to play his game, by whatever rules.

"This is yours," he acknowledged, setting her blade at her feet. Then ducked through the opening, and out into the night.

To slip away from the unsuspecting watchman beside the fire.

Melting back into darkness.
 Departing as soundlessly as he'd come.

38

Come daybreak, the Grenarr kept to their northerly heading.

And Kylac kept his word.

He slew eighteen men in the first hour, and a dozen more by midmorning. Not all at once. Most began as solitary, darting strikes, in which he emerged from the jungle flanking the highway just long enough to fell a selected target before retreating again into the foliage. Early on, the one was often multiplied by the number of revenge-minded companions who gave chase. Those who thought to run him down, root him out, strip him of his skin. Amid the lush vegetation, his butchery was only made easier.

Thereafter, they tightened ranks as they marched, distancing themselves from the jungle's fringe, striding shoulder to shoulder, brandishing their weapons at the trees. That just made it necessary, on occasion, for him to take down his victims in small packs, as they were able to react more quickly to his forays. They still couldn't stop him when he decided to withdraw. Not with spears or swords or slings or bows. Not even when they tried to bait or entrap him. His attacks came from all directions, but never at a point where they hoped to lure him.

When both reaching out and hunkering down had failed them, they resorted to setting fire to the jungle woodland. Presumably in an attempt to drive him off or flush him clear. Succeeding only in whipping up curtains of smoke to further veil his attacks. In the hour that the fires burned, he more than doubled his day's tally, slaughtering twoscore. Thereafter, the burning ceased.

By noon, his enemies' collective outrage had become palpable, registering in their twitchy movements and furious gazes, crackling overhead like a brewing lightning storm. All the while, Sabrynne, traveling at the heart of her horde with the one-handed Barkavius and other lieutenants, demonstrated her own resolve by maintaining course and pace. Undaunted, despite her losses. Kylac didn't truly imagine he could kill enough in the time allotted him to change her thinking, or to dissuade her fiercely loyal followers from honoring her command. But there was always a chance that whatever frustration and doubt he could sow among them now might, just might, exact a toll before the end.

In the meantime, his purpose was far simpler. If he couldn't turn them back, he would seek to delay them. To buy time for the proposed exodus of Addarans from Indranell, for Denariel to unite and assemble her army of Ukinha, and for word to be exchanged between the two. At Kylac's urging, Ledron was to have sent trusted messengers west to seek the young queen and bear tidings of their intentions in the form of a sealed writ. To coordinate, if possible, in the execution of the suggested strategy. A perilous undertaking, to be sure, but essential—since Rashad had declined the honor of apprising Her Majesty—if their plan was to meet with success.

Alas, with Sabrynne refusing to be greatly distracted by his attacks, this secondary aim was proving less and less likely. Which still left him his third goal—the one deemed most tenable from the outset. To sow insult. To cultivate their ire. To harry and vex and stoke the flames of vengeance. Ensuring that, if they couldn't punish him, they remained determined to butcher those he stood with.

An objective contradictory, mayhap, to the first two. But if the Grenarr couldn't be deterred, and wouldn't be slowed, then the best he could hope for was to foster in them an unslakable bloodlust. The kind that would demand redress of the most violent kind. For if they were to satisfy themselves with squatting outside Indranell's walls, depriving its remaining citizens, the war was lost. Should they reach the northern stronghold to find it abandoned, and content themselves with the self-imposed exile of their hated adversaries to the dreaded Harrows, the war was lost. With either, more practical approach, the Grenarr would likely entrench themselves too deeply to ever be displaced, relegating the remnants of Denariel's people to a life of bitter savagery amid the isle's unforgiving wilds.

No, better for the Addarans to feign flight, seeking to draw their unsuspecting enemies into his proposed snare. Whether that snare might consume only the Grenarr, or themselves alongside, would be determined by Denariel and her Ukinha. Whether the Addarans might position themselves for the opportunity was contingent upon Ledron and those the Blackfist captain would have had to convince with what portion of the plan they were given to know. Whether the Grenarr might take the bait? That would depend first on whether word of the Addaran retreat was betrayed to the Grenarr as anticipated, and thereafter on whether Sabrynne gave the order to pursue. Insignificant as it might seem amid all that was required, Kylac could see to the latter. By giving such offense that Sabrynne would settle for nothing less than the utter annihilation of those with whom he'd aligned himself.

That much was beholden upon *him*.

He therefore continued his assaults throughout the afternoon and evening, suspending his efforts only long enough to take some occasional rest. To prepare for the night. By sunset, he'd slain more than a hundred men in all.

With the fall of darkness, he began harvesting in earnest.

They'd lit their watchfires, formed an ironclad perimeter around their clustered ranks, and posted lookouts—both roving and stationary—everywhere. But Kylac had begun studying such defenses at Talonar by the age of five, and penetrating them by the age of seven. The Grenarr were vigilant and capable. Sharp-eyed and fearless. It availed them but little. Their size was no match for his speed. Their vastly superior numbers useless against his strike-and-withdraw tactics. He came like lightning and went like smoke. Lunging from the shadows before melting away again. For all their focus and frustration, they couldn't see him, catch him, or hold him any longer than he allowed them to. They'd as easily have sought to spear a ghost, or to cage thunder.

With each engagement, he carried the thrill with him. Not of killing, for he took no enjoyment in such slaughter. Deadly and determined as they held themselves, he saw them as helpless. He was a snake preying upon field mice—the adder, as Sabrynne had long ago named him. But each time he crossed swords, he put his matchless skills to the test. Each time a blade or arrow was aimed at him, he faced the prospect that he'd finally grown too confident, too arrogant, too certain of his invulnerability. He'd been accused of such in the past too often to recall. By his father, his instructors, his fellow students. By enemies and comrades alike. The capricious laws of combat dictated that, one day, those naysayers would be proven correct.

But it wasn't to be this night. As dawn's bloody rays suffused the waning darkness, Kylac found himself alive and without injury. High within the boughs of a tamelfir, gazing down upon the carnage wrought during the moon's cycle. Two hundred dead, not counting those whose wounds had yet to determine their fate. Twice the number he'd killed during the day. Taken together, some tenth of their entire force. At that rate, he might eliminate them all, given a fortnight in which to work.

Alas, they would likely reach Indranell on the morrow, if not by day's end.

Sabrynne and her lieutenants drove them as if the latter were her intent. Leaving the dead to be tended to later, the surviving troops took up a lathering gait. Wending his way through the snarl of jungle flanking the highway, Kylac found himself pressed to keep pace. His attacks became limited to brief periods in which his quarry took rest, some of which he took for himself. Further hampering his efforts were the increasing number of Grenarr who joined them this day—squads and patrols previously dispatched to ransack the surrounding settlements and homesteads. By midmorning, those he'd killed had been replaced. Like that, the gashes in their ranks were healed. Almost as if he'd never wounded them at all.

That he'd reduced the overall number to eventually come against Denariel's people became at that point of little comfort. Sabrynne still had more than enough warriors to besiege Indranell, if the Addarans remained, or to eradicate them if set to hunting them through the wilds. His efforts, however significant, had done little or nothing to alter the eventual outcome. It was still going to come down to whether or not Ledron had been successful in orchestrating the mass exodus, and whether Denariel could summon and control the Ukinha as intended.

In the first hour past midday, the Stormweaver's army came upon a particularly large host of reinforcements at Praxu, the gateway village through which Bahsk had entered the Strebolen on his southerly march. The village structures had been reduced to rubble and cinders, presumably by the six hundred Grenarr encamped among the blackened stones and heaps of ashes. A contingent of those who'd thwarted Bahsk's trek through the canyons, most likely. Here now at their overlord's command, to serve at her pleasure.

Bolstered by their numbers, the Grenarr resumed their running march with fresh energy, fresh pride. Whatever damage Kylac might have inflicted upon their morale seemed fleeting, at best. He'd failed to turn them. Failed to slow them. And failed, it now seemed, even to scratch the heart of their resolve.

He tried not to be overly troubled, reminding himself that, however uncomfortable it might make him, his role in these matters had largely been played out. That which he might truly affect, he had—for good or ill. Like watching the tumble of a die already cast, all that remained for him was to bear witness to the result.

He persisted in culling the enemy's ranks, if only to let his adversaries know they hadn't escaped him. Yet, more and more, he found himself focused on the van, marking the comings and goings of scouts from the northern front. For if word was to arrive from spy or scout that might lead Sabrynne to veer west, it would surely hail from that direction.

With the distance between themselves and Indranell closing, it must surely be soon.

But with each new messenger's report doing nothing to alter the invaders' course, Kylac grew more resigned to the possibility that something had gone wrong. Most likely, the proposed exodus had failed. It *had* been much to ask. Of the Addaran soldiers called upon to sweep aside—again—the hundreds of Grenarr set down to block retreat. Of the terrified citizenry to acknowledge the wisdom of fleeing the relative protection of their walls before becoming entombed by them. Of the token garrison left behind to ensure that the Grenarr didn't claim the city or those stubborn few left behind—from the north or south—entirely unchallenged. Of seeing to all logistics with the desperate haste that would have been required.

Ledron had deemed it plausible, given that similar plans had been explored even before Kylac's return. But the Blackfist might have underestimated Merrinem's or Fayne's resistance to turning west instead of east—or to abandoning the city at all. Unless both had been persuaded, the fruit of his plan might well have rotted on the vine.

Or mayhap he simply hadn't done enough to goad this flock into giving chase. It might be that he needed to set fire to their supply carts, fell one or more of their chief lieutenants, or devise some other, less forgivable slight. None of which struck him as feasible at this juncture, protected as their most prized assets were at the center of the procession. Should he risk such a sortie anyway, and succeed, would it truly make a difference?

The more he pondered his limited options, the less attractive they seemed. Even if he could devise a means to nudge the Stormweaver westward, he dare not be too obvious about it, for fear of arousing suspicion. It was for this reason he hadn't told her himself that the Addarans were fleeing. Such word had to come from one of her own if she was to trust it.

Worried that all he'd done was set spur to a wild horse, Kylac held to his committed course. Reminded with every stride as to why he typically disdained plots and intrigues. For every advantage they might seed grew an unforeseen thorn or weed. Easier he found it, by far, to react to matters more naturally, rather than seek to harness or shape them.

Beset by a growing sense of helplessness, he began to wonder where he'd gone astray. To mentally retrace his steps, reconsider the choices he'd made, and imagine where he might stand if—

But yesterday's decisions were ashes, and he would waste no time reflecting upon them. Understanding how one had fallen into a river did nothing to soothe the torrent's flow.

Accepting as he was, concerns shadowed his every step. Chiefly for Denariel. Had she survived the wounds suffered in her fight against Talathandria? Were the Ukinha assembling as she'd intended? Would they truly accept her command—such fiercely solitary creatures unifying for her desired purpose? As he had no hand in those matters, he tried not to consider them too closely. But his reluctance on that front might also stem from their seeming unlikelihood.

As his doubts edged toward dismay, the onset of midafternoon brought with it the approach of another northern scout. She looked no different than those come before, giving Kylac no reason to believe her arrival portended change. But after shearing through the throng to reach and report to Sabrynne, the Stormweaver unexpectedly called a halt.

Not for rest, Kylac determined. They'd been doing so on the hour, and the last was but a quarter-mark past. Could it be that this was the word for which he'd been waiting? Had the Addarans departed on schedule, Sabrynne would have already heard it. Almost any Grenarr lookout could have observed that much, and cast it into the stream of messages flowing south. Had they been forced to fight through the southern blockade as expected, or fend off pursuit, Sabrynne would surely know *that*, as well. Her captains at Indranell would have sought clarity as to her wishes. Give chase? Maintain their position upon the city's threshold? Lay siege now that the bulk of its defenders had fled? Whatever Sabrynne's response, none need have affected the directive of her own horde, save mayhap to quicken its pace . . . as it had.

But there remained the stolen word Kylac had intended should come only from one of the Stormweaver's secret informants. The part of the plan shared with the entirety of Indranell's council, and with anyone given to act upon it. The name, to begin with, of the frontier location to which the refugees hoped to rally. The Thorncrag. A natural redoubt amid a broken series of plateaus along the Spineway—a rugged northwest track carving into the Reach and the

Harrows beyond. And from there, the more critical plan to trigger a series of rockslides from the shattered slopes of the long, narrow Ebiddan's Breach. Whereby the Addarans might crush and bury a significant portion of their pursuers, laying down barricade against the rest. Forcing the survivors to dig through or clamber over the debris of jagged ironshore boulders and mangled flesh, else backtrack for leagues to reroute along the Mandowyn Trail, a longer, but far friendlier canyon path that looped south before curling north again to the west of the Thorncrag. Giving the Addarans the extra time required—no matter the Grenarr response—to move on and secure their escape.

A plan with merit enough to persuade the Addaran council of potential success. A chance to inflict grievous damage upon their tormentors, while slipping from the noose Indranell had become.

As Kylac had later shared with Ledron, of course, it was also a false plan. Designed to draw Sabrynne's army along the Mandowyn Trail from the start. Should her spies gain word of the council's intent, as anticipated, they would surely warn her of the intended rockslides at Ebiddan's Breach. To avoid those crushing losses and forestall the refugees' eventual departure from the Thorncrag, she would take immediately to the Mandowyn Trail to head them off, would she not?

Ledron had allowed that she might indeed respond as such. *If* she was bent on eradicating them, as all believed. But why should they *seek* to trap themselves at the Thorncrag? It all seemed a rather intricate and perilous subterfuge—leading as they would be almost the entirety of their surviving people—if their only aim was to trade one snare for another. A redoubt at the edge of the Reach, as opposed to their bastion upon the shores of the Gorrethrian Sound.

Because Her Majesty will come, Kylac had insisted. Arriving with her Ukinha at the Stormweaver's back. Pinning the Great Grendavan and her troops between the Addarans entrenched upon the Thorncrag's slopes, and a host of lethal mutants sworn to serve their vengeance-starved matron.

Such was the full stratagem he and Rashad had together conceived, and that he'd eventually persuaded the Head to undertake. Should it fail, the Addaran people would have no choice but to flee into the

Harrows, to scrape out whatever short lives they could amid that savage wilderness—and that if blessed by fortune in their escape. Yet, for all its challenges, all its shortcomings, it had seemed the best means of avoiding a slow, rotting death within Indranell's stone walls. Of countering the Grenarr and retaking the offensive. Of winning an unwinnable war.

Necessitating that Sabrynne steer this horde west—and soon. That Kylac might have indication that the scheme hadn't simply perished in the nest.

After several moments, shouts rippled out through the army's ranks that had them settling down for a more prolonged respite. Tents went up, to shade against the afternoon sun. Perimeter defenses were assembled, and cookfires lit. As if to set camp, here and now, with hours yet to go in the sun's descending arc.

Atop his forested ridge, Kylac settled down alongside, the itch of hope niggling at the nape of his neck. As soon as the command tent was raised, Sabrynne and her lieutenants convened within. Would that he might give ear to the proceedings. But his actions this day had the encampment bristling with the utmost vigilance. Safer it would be to question someone after, to learn what had been decided. The scout, mayhap, though Kylac had decided against such already. Any messenger he detained or killed would serve warning to Sabrynne that the bearer's word might have been compromised. For his own plan to have the chance it needed, the Stormweaver had to believe that *she* held the element of surprise.

So he sat and watched and waited. Drinking from a stolen aleskin, gnawing on purloined strips of salted pork and spinach leaves. Clinging to the huntsman's patience that had served him so well in the past. Trusting that, for all his doubt, it might do so again.

In the end, left to wonder. Which would be his final role? Huntsman? Or prey?

39

The sunset's crimson light fell in a wash across the slopes and shelves of the Thorncrag, painting the people of Addaranth in blood.

It struck Kylac an ill omen. But he refused to acknowledge it as such. Yes, their lives were very much imperiled, clustered upon this barren rock overlooking the borders of the Reach. The remnants of an entire nation, by all practical measures, some tens of thousands of individuals, gathered here at *his* urging. Yet here they were, alive. Arrived, by every indication, without significant casualty. A victory, then. Another piece of his desperate gambit fitted into place.

To avoid raising a stir with his own arrival, he'd made his final ascent along the Thorncrag's south face. Scaling a daunting series of ledges and bluffs beyond the eyes of Addaran lookouts, who might have mistaken him for a Grenarr scout, or asked him to waste time identifying and explaining himself. Now that he'd crested the upper plateau, however, he stole upon the nearest watchman—a lanky-limbed Whitefist with brow and cheeks burned by the sun—and asked the lad where he might find Ledron and the other commanders.

"If you've some grievance, notify your segment's quarter-marshal," the lad replied, after glancing about for some clue as to where Kylac might have come from.

"I bear word from our enemy, the Great Grendavan. Kronus is

my name."

The lad froze, mouth agape. And though it was the reaction he'd been seeking, Kylac found it regrettable. He'd set across the ocean in hopes of *shedding* such notoriety, not merely to don a new, more infamous shade.

"I . . . I'll send for a—"

"Faster to deliver me yourself. The cliff will hold in your absence."

The lad gulped, wide eyes marking the hilts of the Grenarr sabers sheathed at Kylac's back.

"Would ya have me surrender them?"

The Whitefist shook his head. Hurriedly. As if to disavow any such challenge. "Come."

Kylac followed him northeast, cutting across the rugged flats. Treading narrow pathways set down between sprawled companies—segments, the lad had called them—of Addaran refugees. Half-starved and all but stripped of possessions. Most of those he slipped past appeared weary, haggard, heartsick. Others bore strength yet to bicker and quarrel, whether waiting in food lines or hunkered down in their assigned tracts and plots. Here, a father begged additional rations for his pregnant wife. There, a mother defended her boy against accusations of theft. Kylac saw only one altercation come to blows, and that put down swiftly by a clutch of Redfist patrolmen. But it was at once clear to him that he was wading now through a tinderbox beneath a shower of sparks.

And fate or their Fair Mother help them when the flames began to spread.

The younger children seemed better equipped for the hardships, chasing one another across cordoned grounds, or clambering upon jagged humps and other formations sprouted from the dusty stone. Their peals of laughter echoed across the expanse, lending a discordant tone of merriment to the multitude's dull, ocean-like murmur. Oblivious, it would seem, to the dangers stalking them.

No less likely to be butchered for their innocence.

Beyond the civilian encampments, his escort led him back into the militarized perimeter. There were no ropes or ditches or barriers to divide it from the rest of the populace, just a stretch of no-man's-land where stores and armaments had been stockpiled. Redfists and Whitefists eyed their approach, but none seemed overly concerned by it. Most were hunched over shallow bowls of stew, or tearing at shared loaves of stale bread. Others strayed past, alone or in packs, with duties or business of their own. Too many of whom, Kylac noted, looked less like soldiers than civilians in borrowed patches of armor. A *willing* hand deemed an *able* hand.

Hoping to steal a private word with Ledron before meeting with any others, Kylac searched for the Head amid the swirling mix of those at respite and those engaged in activity. Instead, he caught sight of another familiar face—"Worm" Warmund, stirring the contents of a stew kettle. The Whitefist fumbled his ladle when he glanced up to catch Kylac's broad grin.

"Ya knows the fish aren't biting, when a baitworm is tasked as a cook."

"Shards. Talon said you were still running amok. Wasn't certain I believed him."

Kylac clasped the other's hand. "Ledron said the same o' you, when I asked."

Warmund raised an eyebrow. "Did you now?"

Kylac nodded. Prior to heading south to treat with Sabrynne, he'd inquired as to the health of *all* those brought north with Her Majesty's party from the marshland outpost of Tetherend—with particular concern for those rounded up by Bahsk upon striking out on Denariel's westward trail. Sethric, he'd been told, who'd betrayed them to the general, had met his end at Ollerman's Pass, along with "Crawfoot" Laritanis. And Sergeant Penryn, who'd defied Colonel Fayne to stand with Her Majesty, hadn't been seen since Rendenel Run, and was there presumed killed. In addition to Talon, Havrig, and Warmund, Sergeant Trathem remained with them, as did the stewards Hahneth, Egrund, and Aythef, the latter three having been left by Bahsk at Indranell and thereby spared the slaughter in the canyons of the Strebolen.

He'd inquired as to other former companions, as well. Redfists such as Ysander and Jorrand and Moh. Whitefists such as Jaleth and Nadrum and Taeg. But as these were men who'd deserted Denariel and her dying father to depart Tetherend with Fayne, he hadn't borne them the same measure of concern. Some had since perished. Some had survived. Alas for each.

"Too much trouble to greet me yourself before setting off again?" Warmund asked.

"A mite pressed, I fear."

"Aren't we all."

"Slaving over kettles, is it?"

"Just lending hand to Aythef," the Whitefist replied, twisting to peer over his shoulder. "Got him fletching arrows for me in fair trade."

Kylac followed the sailor's gaze. Upon the fringe of a clutch of Seawatch some twenty paces distant, he spied now the onetime royal cook, seated alone, bent over the tail of an arrow. A pile of bare shafts lay at his feet, and a ground quiver full of feathered ones beside him. Even at a distance, and angled in profile, the cook was unmistakable for a body grown hunched and crooked. The intervening weeks would have healed the remainder of those savage injuries to joint and limb suffered at Grenathrok, but only improperly, without harsher treatments. Leaving him a twisted wretch of his former self.

Warmund seemed to sense Kylac's regret. "This endless stirring strains his elbow now. And he deems it a stage of brewing that even a barnacle like me can't bungle too badly." He tried a grim smile. "Truth confessed, I find it calming."

"Ay. That swill seasoned yet?" The voice of a Redfist, approaching with bowl in hand.

Warmund scarcely glanced at the soldier before turning back to Kylac. "Whatever comes of it, I hear tell this is all your doing?"

"*All* would seem unfair due. But I suppose ya'll find none with greater share o' blame."

"Ay! Dock maggot," the Redfist barked, attended now by a pair of companions. "We've rounds to keep."

Warmund scowled, then addressed Kylac's Whitefist escort from the southern bluff. "Narren, you minnow. See these mossy louts lap up more than they spill, would you?"

Narren squirmed with hesitation. "I . . . my post—"

"I'll see him to wherever he's getting, and return to relieve you, eh?"

"Anyone hassles ya," Kylac added, meeting the hungry Redfist's impatient stare, "tell 'em *I'm* brewing the next pot. And that us *outlanders* prefer our swill thick with *red* meat."

While the boorish soldier bristled at the implied threat, one of the newer arrivals behind him frowned in confusion. "Outlander?" he echoed, then blanched. "You . . . you're . . ."

Kylac tipped his brow as he turned away, drawing Warmund with him. He could hear the murmurs now spreading at his back. Reluctant as he'd been to expose himself so brazenly, he hadn't wanted to leave Narren alone there, to suffer those Redfists' barbs. It was only a matter of time before he was recognized anyway. Too many soldiers and sailors and stewards had taken to eyeing him and his Grenarr blades. Wary as he'd been that his coming might spark additional anger or hostilities, be it late or soon, it was an eventuality he had to confront.

"Looking for the captain, then?" Warmund supposed.

"Alone, if possible."

Warmund shook his head. "More likely hounded by jackals. But let's see, eh?" As he looked Kylac over anew, the seams in his leathery face smoothed with relief, his expression reflecting gratitude. "Talon said you'd return to us. Wasn't certain I believed *that*, either."

Kylac clapped the dour sailor's shoulder, and offered a reassuring smirk. Reassured at the same time. Though he hadn't dared to imagine it, there was always the chance his arrival might bring this beleaguered people hope, too.

"Westward trek wasn't too taxing?" he asked after a moment.

Warmund shrugged. "Smoother than most feared. No ambushes, as yet. And only the occasional, light skirmish against our rearguard. Save for a few dogged scouts, the tar-skins seemed almost content to let us go."

As he'd expected. Why should Sabrynne expend her limited blockade forces when her own siege force was en route? A reasonable assumption, but also steeped in optimism. A further relief, then, to confirm the exodus had suffered no great losses.

"Be a lie to say I didn't miss the sea, though," the Whitefist admitted. "Please tell me we didn't crawl all this way only to wither on this dusty rock."

"Could come to that. But I's wagered elsewise."

Forms and faces continued to swim past or fall aside. More and more, Kylac felt their gazes clinging to him like cobwebs, and heard the growing buzz of recognition. Fortunately, it wasn't long before they came upon a squat shelf whereupon Kylac finally spied Ledron, huddled among a circle that very much resembled the city council he'd left behind at Indranell. He found its members turning toward him with squinted gazes, alerted by the rising hum that preceded him.

Warmund caught their shifting attentions, and stopped. "I'll let you to it, then."

"Ya don't care to attend?"

The Whitefist eyed the sentries stationed at the edge of the rise. "I'd best return to my stew, free Narren as promised. I'm on east lookout at the next mark." He started to turn, then hesitated. "Just . . . my family is with us. My wife, my boy . . . and a rawhide sack of bones'll tell you what a shame it is to have borne me." His mien become earnest. "Should I come to harm, will you see *they* don't?"

An untenable challenge it would be, to ward any particular individuals in the coming conflict. Nonetheless, Kylac was compelled to match his former shipmate's imploring gaze. "Not one'll bleed before I do."

Again he clapped the sailor's shoulder, offering a smile before turning away.

The sentries parted as he covered the remaining distance and sprang up the rocky rise. One was the mutton-bearded Jessem, whom Kylac recognized from Indranell. The other . . . was *not* Flaerik, the freckle-faced badger of a Redfist having presumably drawn some other duty, at present.

The command ring was gathered around a stewpot of their own. Kylac approached with hands spread in a gesture of peace. The leaders of the refugee host welcomed him with stern silence. He'd been given to anticipate nothing more.

"Well met," he offered, with a general nod at some familiar faces—Governor Merrinem and his advisors, Colonels Fayne and Garnham, the Blackfist Jyserra, Redfists Havrig and Talon—and a few new to these command proceedings—Simalen, with whom he'd voyaged to and from the Blackmoon Shards, and Sergeant Trathem, met in Avenell's dungeons. Men who'd proven themselves faithful, to one degree or another. Men he might trust.

Or not. Sim, of course, had been among those to depart with Fayne, rather than remain with Denariel, after traveling alongside her to Tetherend. And Trathem . . . so sullen and earnest and desperate and impatient, as if all of this were to him merely an irksome preamble to some greater struggle. The sergeant had served Her Majesty honorably enough, but with what motive? Of the scores whom Kylac had freed from those dungeon bowels, none had clung so steadfastly to his hip who hadn't already known him. Was it truly naught but the Redfist's oath to liege and lands that drove him to attach himself so?

Kylac dismissed the suspicions as quickly as they'd struck him. The matter of Sabrynne's informants had been preying upon his mind of late, likely setting him to chasing ghosts. A distraction he didn't need. It scarcely mattered, the identity of those moles still among them. He'd entrusted only Ledron with the full truth of their strategy here—set down under seal thereafter for delivery to Denariel by the Shadowguard captain's small squad of hand-chosen messengers. As the Head was even less trusting than Kylac, the remainder of their host would have been given to know only what Kylac might choose now to share with them.

"That a shade approaches?" Garnham grumbled, his gruff voice belying a spirited tone.

"Too rosy a pallor for a dead man," Talon added with a jubilant grin.

"What news?" Ledron asked simply.

"We's a day or two, no more, 'fore the Grenarr reach us."

The announcement triggered a chorus of grunted replies.

"Where are they?"

"—scouts have glimpsed no sign."

"—stopped trailing us some time ago."

"—Spineway is all but clear."

And other variations of the same thought. Finally, Merrinem raised his arms to cut through the chatter. "Did you not meet with Grendavan?"

"I fear my overtures were rebuffed."

More murmurs. It was Fayne, this time, who gave them a collective voice. "Where is she, then? If but a day or two out, we ought to have sighted her approach—*if* she's taken the bait you assured us she would."

She hadn't. Not as the colonel understood it. Kylac spared a knowing glance for Ledron before admitting, "She'll not be coming from the east."

An expectant hush.

"Where, then?"

"She advances from the south, edging west along the Mandowyn Trail."

A furor this time, voices erupting with strident intensity.

"Can that be?"

"—that would put her . . ."

"—intends to cut us off."

"—must flee now."

"—never should have left Indranell."

"Enough!" Ledron barked, his own, private understanding ensconced in a grim visage. "You know this? How?"

So Kylac told them. With Ledron serving to silence interruptions, he recounted the meat of his conversation with the Great Grendavan, his attempts to thin her herd throughout the following day, and the enemy's unexpected stand-down that afternoon, now five days past. Upon resuming their march before dawn the next morning, the Grenarr had turned west from the Karamoor along the Spineway. Indicating that they'd received word of the refugee host's exodus and decided to pursue it. Kylac had ceased at that juncture to harry their troops. Leaving Sabrynne to assume . . . whatever she chose. That he'd given up, mayhap, or left her to make report of some kind. Or that he was still out there, marking her movements, to report on them later. As she couldn't do much about him one way or another, he didn't imagine she'd long fretted over his disappearance. She'd had her own scouts and spies to apprise her as to her quarry's movements, and would have held focus on that. Relying on *their* reports to know where the Addarans were going, and what they might know of her reactions to their movements.

In truth, he'd continued to shadow them, farther aback once the sheltering jungle had receded and the gorges and canyon walls of the Spineway had made it harder for him to remain hidden. Harder, but not impossible. After a day's trek, in which Sabrynne overtook and was reinforced by the portion of the blockade force that must have followed the refugees from Indranell, she'd veered south along the Mandowyn Trail. Eschewing the path that would draw her through Ebiddan's Breach. Suggesting she'd been alerted as to the ambush planned for her there. And that, rather than withdraw, she intended presumably to circle around to the west of the Thorncrag—as the refugee council members had themselves now posited—as a means of positioning her troops to sever the Addarans' retreat into the wilds.

He was admittedly *assuming* she'd clung to that course. As soon as she'd ventured south, he'd continued along the shorter Spineway to reach the Thorncrag from the southeast. Thinking it critical that he convey warning.

"Now that it's too late," Fayne observed dryly.

One of Merrinem's advisors cleared his throat. "If we turn back now—"

"Turn back?" Garnham scoffed. "To what? Stuff ourselves right back into the hare's den?"

"We continue west, then," tried another. "Now. Tonight. Be gone before she—"

"Our folk are spent," Sim reminded them all. "Blistered, half-starved, seized with ache. Most gave the whole of their strength to march this far. It was here we promised them rest."

"A luxury we can no longer afford."

"Butchery, should we herd them on now, with the sharks bearing down upon us."

"So we wait instead for them to fall upon us here?"

"Here, we still have a defensible position."

"From the east, if holding the Breach. Approach from the west might as well be carpeted in rose petals."

The latter an exaggeration, sure. But there was no denying the Grenarr would find it easier to assault along the myriad trails and pathways and defiles streaking the Thorncrag's western slopes than they would scaling the ledges and bluffs south, or the steeper cuts and switchbacks through which the Addarans had ascended the eastern rise.

"What other course have we?"

"Are we truly trapped?"

With the tide of despair swelling around him, Kylac regretted being unable to share with them just how much of this was unfurling as he'd planned. While it might serve some reassurance, he and Ledron had steadfastly agreed that they dare not risk letting word of the anticipated Ukinhan reinforcement leak too soon. For fear that it might not reassure anyone, on the one hand. On the other, that it might enable Sabrynne to sidestep their little snare.

"We'll hold here," he urged instead. As if there were nothing to be gained from further debate.

"Will we, now?" Fayne asked. "Because *you* advise it?"

"Because we must."

The handsome colonel shook his head, fallen sunlight reflecting red in his eyes. "So certain. When certain you were a week past the tar-skins would pursue us through Ebiddan's Breach. Until alerted, as they must have been. By some mysterious informant. While you were . . . *where* in all of this? In Grendavan's own tent, you say, where you found no cause to stain your blade with her blood."

Kylac felt the gazes and suspicions of the council members stirring against him. Even Ledron regarded him with a scathing scowl.

"Say it, then," the Head grunted at Fayne. "You fear he's betrayed us?"

The colonel raised his hands in a gesture of feigned innocence. "From all I hear, and what I've witnessed, he's done us scant favor since washing onto our shores. Expending great effort in a cause for which he claims no particular concern. Whose hand would such a weapon better fit? Ours, or our enemy's?"

The earlier murmuring resurfaced. An eddy of grunts and whispers that bespoke a fresh wave of concern. While not aimed directly at Kylac, he felt their ire and mistrust like ants upon his skin.

Ledron let their voices churn and swell before finally giving answer. "Strikes *me* we've done ample damage already among ourselves. Those who stand now upon this rock, we stand as one. Else we've no chance of standing at all. Would any here deny it?" His slowly sweeping glare defied challenge, while seeking to invoke shame among his fellows.

"We'll choose to trust him, or we won't. But I'd sooner each man here reaffirm his own allegiance before questioning that of the man next to him. Agreed?"

"Agreed," said Garnham, his enthusiasm less an endorsement of Kylac than a call for battle.

"Agreed," said Talon.

"Agreed."

"Agreed . . ."

And around the circle the word echoed, cast from man to man, be it grudgingly or heartfelt. Merrinem and his advisors. Soldiers to the left and right. Trathem, Havrig, Sim. Until it was left to Kylac and Fayne, facing each other.

"Agreed," Kylac offered.

Fayne eyed him coolly, without a glimmer of apology. "Beneath a cairn, or atop one such as this, I suppose we all rot the same." Before Ledron could growl in response, he added, "Agreed." And hastily thereafter, "What, then, is to be our battle plan?"

HOURS LATER, Kylac finally had his private word with Ledron.

The Head came upon him as he overlooked a harsh, moonlit wrack of earth spreading for endless leagues to the northwest. A maze of ironshore peaks and valleys, spires and chasms, choked here and there with jungle, that bled away into the vast sweep of the Ukinhan Wilds. Humped and jagged and scarred as that wilderness appeared, Kylac thought he recognized in those moments the rugged majesty attributed to it by admirers such as Rashad, as Denariel. While lacking any of the traditional features with which a bard might cherish a land in song—flowering meadows, rolling hills, sparkling streams—there lived a beauty amid the chaos. Life, where life was at its most violent. Vitality, where death ruled. The Sundered Isle, as she was sometimes called, by Addaran and Grenarrian alike. A landmark of ancient cataclysm, of devastation, and of the gritty, enduring willfulness of nature to persevere.

Alas, all he'd truly hoped to glimpse was some sign that Denariel and her mutant swarm might be on their way.

"Finished your duties already?" he quipped at Ledron's approach.

"Never," the Head grunted.

The tail of the Raven's Hour had midnight fast approaching. Much of the camp had settled into silence. Or as much silence as could be found among forty thousand men, women, and children packed together in slumber. With snores and cries and grunts reverberating among them. Amid crackling watchfires and patrolling sentries. Tents and canopies notwithstanding, beneath an open sky laden with the hum of insects, the windblown echoes of the jungle far below, and the shrieks of nightbirds wheeling on invisible currents high above.

If not silent, then *peaceful*.

Ledron's coming, however, had the feel of an early autumn wind, chill and sharp in chasing the warmth from a summer night. "Have you anything else to report?"

Kylac considered, then shook his head. "Nothing o' consequence. Ya heard it all earlier. With but a different ear than the others, I trust."

Again, the Blackfist grunted, moon and stars adding a ghostly sheen to his bald pate. "Then here's a final piece of news for *you*."

The captain presented from his pocket a small leather tube. A tube Kylac recognized at once. The mere sight of it sparked a shiver of denial. As he accepted it, he forced himself to ask the obvious. "Is this . . ."

"Arrived early this morning. Carried by Rendrik. Lad was feverish, poisoned by harrowroot. Amid the ravings, I gathered his companions were killed. He returned to let me know."

Kylac cracked the tube. Inside, as feared, was a tiny scroll of parchment, still closed with a wax seal. The message that was to have been delivered to Denariel. The word that would have informed her of their gambit here. That would have requested her to join them, Ukinha in tow.

"Finally died an hour ago."

"Why didn't ya speak o' this earlier?"

Ledron snorted. "Because this remains our only choice. I just mean for you to know, we're on our own."

Because Denariel would have no inkling of their plan, which seemed even more desperate and foolhardy than it had from the outset. Silently, Kylac cursed himself. For five days now, he'd been given to revel in his cunning, flush with the pride of success. Having successfully misled Sabrynne, guided her into their trap . . .

He should have known he was in for at least a few more headwinds. He *should* have delivered word of their stratagem himself. But he couldn't have raced to report back to Denariel while observing and shepherding Sabrynne's movements at the same time. He'd had to choose, the one or the other, and had vainly determined that only he could safely meet with and then goad Sabrynne as he had, while a team of seasoned explorers, bearing message from Ledron . . .

In his frustration, he found his thumb idly tracing the delicate ridges of the wax seal. Cliffs and crevasses like those of the landscape that surrounded him. Ravaged, but intact. The sensation gave him a sliver of hope. "At least we know the truth of our ploy here hasn't been exposed."

Ledron scowled at him as if he'd intended it as a jape. "You think this doesn't change matters?"

"Indeed it might. But it might also be she'll come this way regardless."

He and Rashad had discussed the possibility, back when debating the most likely results of this movement or that. If Denariel meant to reinforce her people at Indranell, the Spineway offered the most direct route for a host traveling afoot. Taking the longer, smoother Westway when heading out in search of Talathandria had allowed her to ride for long stretches on stolen mounts, and to scrounge food and water from settlers' stores along the way. But of what advantage would either serve to a swarm of Ukinha? The Spineway was far more barren, and largely uninhabited, but would further serve in that regard by better hiding her host's approach.

If she'd gathered a host to be spied.

"Are we to but pray for that outcome?" the Head asked.

"Is your thought that I should strike forth now and hope Her Majesty is still at home in her valley? Give the word, Captain, and I'll—"

"No. I need your blades. My *people* need your blades." Jaw clenched,

Ledron peered back at the sea of refugees at rest upon the plateau. Of the night's winds, he asked, "What have we done here?"

A breeze gusted past, but carried no answer.

"She will come," Kylac said. Filled with resolve. When, for all he truly knew, she lay back in that valley or somewhere amid the intervening expanse, already dead.

Ledron spun a raking eye upon him, as if to expose the unuttered thought. But the loyal Blackfist wouldn't be the one to give voice to their shared fear. "As I said, this remains our only choice."

Short of endeavoring to return to the snare at Indranell they'd just escaped. Or attempting a dash deeper into the Harrows, only to be run down, in all likelihood, by Sabrynne's army. Better indeed that they stand their ground here, as most with a voice on their makeshift council had ultimately agreed.

"Your people displayed great courage, a worthy resolve, to travel this far," Kylac reminded his companion. "If'n your own faith is spent, what say we strive to honor *theirs*?"

"Theirs?" the Head scoffed. "Bred from a lie."

"An unblossomed truth," Kylac corrected. He'd been quite deliberate in seeding it as such, and in safeguarding the distinction. "When the time is right, all shall see her bloom."

40

The Grenarr assaulted at daybreak.

They'd arrived the evening before—as predicted, just two nights after Kylac's coming. On the heels of the returning spotters sent out along the Mandowyn Trail to mark their approach. Churning to a stop at the foot of the Thorncrag's western slopes. Their thick columns folding and closing against one another to form terraced lines across the great rock's rugged threshold. Some four thousand warriors, all told, setting down with pikes and spears like a layered palisade. Like a series of thorny hedgerows. *Like the jaws of a shark,* Kylac had thought, recalling the look of the creatures up-close. An inescapable trap edged with row upon row of serrated teeth.

There the enemy had rested throughout the night. Eerily quiet. With nary a fire lit among them. Comfortable in the darkness. Their sable flesh just a pool of deeper shadows amid the clefts and fissures of the riven, ironshore ground. They'd presented no emissary, hollered no demands, offered no bargains. The members of the Addaran council had wondered among themselves what this might mean. Was battle truly inevitable? Would Sabrynne seek to storm the plateau? Or would she satisfy herself with starving them there atop their rock? Should they sue once more for peace?

Now, with the sun climbing at the refugees' backs, they had their answer. The enemy was receiving no proposals, save at the head of a spear. Already, the forward lines were splitting again into columns, each threading its way along a separate trail leading up the slope. Spurred by a slow, steady drumbeat. They'd not spent their nighttime hours solely in rest, Kylac determined quickly, but in surveying and scouting the terrain to which they intended to lay claim. Spreading forth now to launch simultaneous attacks along multiple streams of approach. Avoiding, conveniently enough, some of the easier, more obvious pathways where the defenders had spent the last two days building up obstacles and laying down snares.

Suggesting that, even now, Sabrynne had friendly eyes hidden among them.

"Charming plot you've chosen, then, for our people's final resting place," Fayne observed, coming to have a look over Kylac's shoulder.

Much of the Addaran encampment was still mobilizing behind them. Shouts ringing in the morning air, weapons coming to hand, booted feet thumping against the dry, dusty ground. But the army and its commanders had repositioned themselves heavily to the west of the plateau almost as soon as word had been received of Sabrynne's revised strategy. Aligning themselves in response to the shifted battlefront—there to bear the brunt of attack against their citizenry. Beyond bowshot, should the Grenarr take to raining arrows upon them in the night, yet still just a short scamper from the western ridge crest. Though assigned to a trailhead to the southwest, the colonel had come out ahead of his company to see for himself the Grenarr's unfolding tactics. And to remind Kylac once more, it appeared, that he remained suspicious of the outlander's role in all of this.

Fair enough, as Kylac could say the same of him.

"I's yet to encounter the corpse that bemoaned its surroundings. Prideful as they may have been in life."

"Pride inspires greatness," Fayne argued. "Courage. Defiance. What shred we had left to us was taken when we abandoned Indranell."

Kylac didn't have to follow the colonel's glance to take his meaning. East, across the plateau. To the people huddled there. Beyond the soldiers and armaments. Where ordinary citizens bustled about—moving supplies, erecting makeshift barricades, arming and armoring themselves as best they could, with whatever crude materials might serve. But there were others, so many others—chiefly the eldest, the youngest—who could but whimper and cower and fret. Knowing what had come for them, even without seeing it. A specter made worse, mayhap, by their imaginations. Who had to be reassured by friends and fellows that hope remained. That their leaders hadn't herded them all this way only to be butchered by savage tar-skins at the edge of the wilderness. That the Fair Mother Eriyah was merely taking their measure, and would reward them for their faith, their resolve.

Judging by the haze of despair that enveloped them, choked them, few actually believed it.

"I suppose it's on us, then," Kylac said, "to provide that inspiration."

Fayne snorted and shook his head. Peering down again at the black mass snaking its way up from the canyon floor along its splintering streams. "Would that it could still save us."

Kylac bridled a more optimistic retort. He intended to prove the colonel wrong, of course. To hold this ground for as long as necessary. But even he had envisioned this as merely a stalling tactic. A means of delaying the moment in which their enemies had them cornered. Of positioning themselves that much closer to where he intended Denariel should meet them. Of securing for the Addaran queen and now Ukinhan matron those few extra days, hours, that might make all the difference.

On a ground where the Grenarr would be harder-pressed to flee, should the tide shift in such favorable direction.

But the latter owed to a plan that only he and Ledron were privy to. Bolstered by a hope steeped more in desperation than any reasonable logic. The very essence of faith. In trusting that events beyond his control would somehow align with his wishes.

As he disbelieved in the likelihood of such things, he couldn't very well admonish others for the same.

"Whatever their gains this day," he offered instead, "they'll purchase with blood."

The urgent shouts of a favored lieutenant drew Fayne's attention. Their company was ready. The colonel eyed Kylac like rancid meat before turning away. A yoke of despair went with him, harnessed to his shoulders with traces woven of primal fear and a simmering anger. That one of their senior-most commanders should begin this day so disheartened boded ill for the army's morale, Kylac thought. Yet there was no time for speeches or songs, and none who felt like giving them. All knew the stakes, and needed no reminder.

Fight they would, if only for their lack of options.

He watched Fayne's regiment and others trickle downslope along rudimentary pathways. A reflection, initially, of the enemy's movements below. Halfway down, however, the Addarans began to spread out, settling into predetermined positions. Entrenching themselves behind ridges and folds, wedging into cuts and creases, planting their pikes and shields and standards along the rims of fissures and the edges of trails. Stringing a webwork defense across the upper face of the slope, that any Grenarr foolish enough to jiggle its strands would quickly rue the effort.

With Kylac set to serve as the spider.

A name given by his shipmates back on the *Vengeance*, coincidentally enough, when first setting forth for the mysterious Blackmoon Shards. A means of describing his unnatural acrobatics amid the ship's rigging. Used then as an epithet, it would now be more like an invocation. For Ledron had determined not to tether him to any particular location, but rather leave him free to roam. To skitter his way here and there across the slope as he deemed necessary, bringing his blades to bear wherever their defenses required his particular style of reinforcement.

Kylac had consented to the command without objection. As if any could have ordered him elsewise. It was the only sensible use of his talents. He was no foot soldier, to be planted like a stake in the mud—a lone paling in the wall of a palisade. Better that he remain nimble, unfettered. That the decision owed as much or more to the mistrust of men like Fayne as it did to the tactical advantages provided . . . well, he saw no reason to let *that* tarnish the outcome.

So he held there, atop the lip of the plateau, while the soldiers of Addaranth filed and trundled and jostled past. Spotting among the shuffling, scampering, scurrying masses the faces of strangers, of men encountered in passing, and of those he'd come to know. Recalling others, unseen just now, stood somewhere among them. Brave men, and craven. Steadfast, and wavering. Capable, and less so. Would that battle more often distinguished one from the other, he thought. That those who survived would be those most worthy of the privilege.

"Seems you were right," Ledron grumbled, tramping near with Havrig at his shoulder.

"Concerning?"

"Our enemy's impatience."

Kylac nodded. Wishing he'd been wrong. While others had questioned why the tar-skins would risk their lives in attack when they could simply sever further flight, he'd been among those to suspect elsewise. A prolonged siege of the Thorncrag was untenable, given that the Grenarr's access to provisions, in this desolate region, was little better than that of the Addaran refugees. More critically, having treated with her face-to-face, he imagined Sabrynne was past the point of tolerance required to sit here for weeks, foraging where her quarry couldn't, slowly willing them toward surrender.

The time had come to slake her bloodthirst.

Too soon, was Ledron's worry. In his eyes now, as confessed in private conversations earlier. Without any true notion of how long it might take for Denariel to marshal the Ukinha, he couldn't seem to fathom it possible in the mere two weeks they'd afforded her.

"May our resistance give them cause to reconsider." It was the most Kylac could offer. For he, too, had to assume they were on their own. For days yet, if not longer. "We repel them today, they might not be so eager on the morrow."

Ledron shared his typically sour expression and a familiar, surly grunt. "A man as you owes no allegiance. Mine have been wagering as to where you'll be found in the end."

On the side of the Grenarr, some believed. Else fled alone to parts unknown. Kylac had heard the whispers. "A trove to them who say I'm still standing here with ya. A pittance that I'm dead in the attempt. Any other bet? A season in the Abyss."

The words drew a flicker of emotion from the captain's stubbled face. Bolstering his feeble hopes. Precisely what he'd come to hear, Kylac realized. An assurance he desperately desired, yet dared not depend on.

"Fair fighting, Captain."

Ledron nodded and moved on. Havrig followed, with a nod of his own. Working down toward the middle of the slope, where the Head would personally command the troops anchored there. A Blackfist—a royal nursemaid—given authority over a Stonewatch company. An indication of the trust won from his peers. But also an indictment, as a sign of their woeful circumstances.

Strung now in their rows and clusters across the ravaged slopes, the Addarans didn't appear a broken people. More than two thousand strong in their own right, with a thousand more standing in ready reserve, they appeared a spiked iron trap just waiting to be triggered. With Colonels Fayne to the south and Garnham to the north, Ledron's flanks were well warded. Then there was the ground itself, filled with its natural hazards, and further prepared to the defenders' advantage over the past two days. Whatever the numbers or strength of those rising against them, better to be atop the rock than climbing up from below.

The defenders' condition notwithstanding, the Stormweaver was in for a fight.

No better evidenced, mayhap, than by Aythef, whom he'd happened across two nights before—the battered cook struggling with a bundle of spears bound for the west ridge from an eastern stockpile.

"Ya meaning to wield one, too?" Kylac had asked him, while lending hand.

"A chink in our armor, I'd be," the other had muttered ruefully, the words hissing through his broken teeth. "But there's plenty of aid to lend. Conveying orders, sharpening arms, restocking quivers . . . to name but a few."

"None a task any would expect o' *you*, I should think."

"Would you have me go and lie with the infirm?"

"I only mean—"

"I stand for Thane, serving whatever purpose I can. Come agony or death. To honor his vision, his sacrifice."

A fool's vision, Kylac might have ventured, *however tender-hearted.*

"So ask me not to step aside, or slink off to cower amid the rear," the cook had snarled, reassuming the whole of his burden. "For I mean to leave this rock striding in victory, else dragged as a corpse."

Upon which Kylac had let him go, lamenting his own clumsy attempt at providing solace.

The dealing of pain and death seeming so much simpler.

The Grenarr drumbeat quickened, accompanied now by the ominous, mournful wail of seashell horns. A lusty howl escaped the throats of the forward attackers, echoed by those behind them. The roar of an onrushing breaker undaunted by the stony shore.

The Addarans hollered in response. Dozens at first, then hundreds. Summoning their courage. Voicing their indignation. Refusing to be cowed, despite the palpable fear that consumed them.

To their voices, they added a hail of arrows as the enemy came within range. A string of shouts and an ominous thrumming gave rise to the swarm of shafts, launched by archers stationed both below and behind Kylac's position. The sunlight dimmed behind that black cloud, then brightened again as the heads fell. Whistling as one before giving way to the clatter, ping, and crunch of missiles that had missed, been deflected, or—by little more than chance—struck some piece of an advancing Grenarrian.

By the sound of it, there were far too few of the latter.

Amid the smattering of grunts and yelps and stumbling attackers, the enemy's howl intensified. From their rear, the Grenarr loosed their own arrows, to arc over the heads of their advancing pikemen and fall among the rooted defenders. A retaliatory strike that proved, in similar measure, a largely feeble exercise, as shields and bucklers and makeshift scraps of shelter were raised to blunt or deflect. But the counter did serve purpose in holding down those Addaran bowmen positioned upon the slopes—and, to a lesser degree, those farther back atop the plateau. While archers on both sides continued to loose against one another as able, none of the ensuing volleys matched the thickness or intensity of that opening exchange.

The stinging barrage gave way within moments, as all knew it must, to the foot soldiers on either side. From his view at the edge of the plateau, Kylac marked the convergence. The Grenarr worming and grinding their way upslope. The Addarans clinging to the desired ground. The wounded or dead doing nothing to dissuade either side.

Until finally the trap was sprung, its iron teeth slamming together. Screams sharpened as bodies in the middle were pierced and slashed and shredded into bloody gristle. A scale of slaughter Kylac had studied often, but seldom witnessed firsthand. Back on Pentania, he'd visited the Fields of Ravacost on the war-torn border between Menzos and Partha, mostly observing maneuvers from afar. In the battle to retake Kraagen Keep from the hordes of Killangrathor's dragonspawn, he'd stood with Torin, Corathel, and others upon the forefront, experiencing for himself the crushing, chaotic whirlwind of combat between armies. Elsewise, his had always been smaller, more personal engagements. Against overwhelming odds, sure. But usually alone, or with a mere handful of companions. Not hundreds. Not thousands. Not with dozens at a time ripping and thrusting and pummeling and sawing at one another in a single, savage chorus.

Even the skirmishes within the Strebolen—at Ollerman's Pass and Rendenel Run—between these same peoples, paled in comparison to what unfurled now. There, he'd been caged, held back from the front, with a limited, night-shrouded view. By the time he'd been freed, the defenders were already in retreat. Here, he had a clear, overarching vantage. He had the glow of the sun climbing at his back. And he had the Addarans holding fast, refusing to be dislodged from their collective perch.

A recipe for blood. Spilled and sprayed amid a clanging, clamoring tumult. Seasoned with fury and pain, hatred and fear, ecstasy and anguish, all churned together until the cry of one—each drawing its opposing response—was indistinguishable from the wail of the other.

The cacophony rang in Kylac's ears, setting fire to his veins. But he tamped down the urge to react, resisting the impulse that would have him charging down the slope to join the fray. The assignment to which he'd agreed demanded that he wait to gain a sense of the battle's flow. To determine where the defenders were most vulnerable. The terrain, and knowledge of their own strengths and weaknesses, had provided ample clues. But this was the Stormweaver herself confronting them now. All accounts considered, none were convinced she'd made her final play.

So Kylac waited, nerves and muscles dancing beneath his skin, while he watched the mayhem. Marking the surging, splashing, roiling movements along the ragged front line. The ebbs and flows of the Grenarr as they chewed like storm waves upon a pitted coast. The writhing of flotsam caught in the churn. Weighing the initial toll upon each side. Seeking the best point at which to insert himself amid the tumult.

To do more than bear silent witness to this calamity.

For a time, he saw only small penetrations, promptly rejected. A lull tide, for all the thrashing and foaming of its surf. Making the early contest seem a stalemate—with the attackers, if anyone, bearing the brunt of the initial losses. Kylac felt the relief of those Addarans positioned like him higher up the slope, who'd been wondering how well their human levee would hold. Better than they'd dared to imagine, it would seem.

The realization gave rise to a swell of cheers from those defenders not yet actively engaged. A cry meant to salute their compatriots and reassure the civilians warded by their efforts. As the moments passed and the Addarans' confidence grew, their howls took on a jeering tone. Deriding their enemies. Mocking what seemed now an overreaching endeavor. Wiser that the hated tar-skins had let them flee. Instead, the Great Grendavan, in her arrogance, had done nothing more than provide them a chance for retribution.

Their jubilations proved premature.

Kylac sensed the first breaches a moment before he saw them. One to the south, amid Fayne's forward line. Two to the north, amid Garnham's. And the largest nearer the heart of the slope, amid Ledron's. Where strained seams abruptly gave way to spurts of Grenarr warriors, who flooded the gaps. Skirting barricades, edging along fissures, climbing ridges. Gushing inward along whatever vein or nook could be found or forced.

Like the spider, Kylac felt the tug of those incursions. Measured their strength and severity and trickling progress. Garnham's company had all but recovered already, eager units snapping down upon the flanks of the invading lines, or driving them from ledges, or pinning them against jagged rises of stone. As the most seasoned battlefield commander, he'd been given some of the more difficult terrain to defend, along with some of the strongest troops. The same with Fayne to the south, who nonetheless appeared to be having greater difficulty in closing the early gashes. Mayhap because of that weak morale. Mayhap because there were fewer natural obstacles that could be turned to his advantage. The central slope, riven with knobs and folds and crevasses, had been judged less scalable, and thus given to Ledron, with a complement comprised of fewer veterans—scattered in key positions among greener troops. A known liability deemed necessary in the overall strategy. A mistake, it now appeared, as the defenders—collectively startled by the savagery of a Grenarr swarm scarcely deterred by the uninviting ground—shied from the brutal thrust. Wavering as to whether they should seek to withstand the clambering press, or displace already to their fallback positions.

Kylac determined the latter unacceptable, given the tone it could set for the remainder of the battle. He told himself it was this that compelled him, and not a sense of favor toward Ledron, when finally he dashed down the slope in the Blackfist's direction. Slipping along pathways laid down between regiments. Springing from rock formations or across rutted furrows where others stood to impede his progress. Dodging enemy arrows that lanced the air. Set to immerse himself at last in battle's cauldron.

He heard the bellowing of orders to those around him, but spared only passing attention for the commands and the movements they spawned. Letting them fade into the senseless furor of punishing shouts and piercing screams that raged upon the lower slope. Giving feel again to instinct. To the shove and jostle of men around him, growing more pronounced as he neared the front. To the shrieks and wails of the Addarans with whom he'd aligned himself. His brothers now, for all the disparities and mistrust between them. Crying out in need.

He traced those cries to where they rang sharpest, laden with pain and desperation. Drawing him to a black knot of snarling Grenarr, who hacked into his Addaran brothers with pikes and swords. Towering and thick-limbed. Only lightly armored to allow for freer range of movement. Onyx flesh oiled in sweat and rippling with the muscles beneath. Merciless in the application of their longer reach, their swifter speed, their superior strength. Their own, deep-bellied voices raised in a gravelly roar.

41

Into the crest of the enemy wave, Kylac sprang. Swords coming to hand. Arcing and thrusting like the flapping of a bird upon release from its cage. Confusion bloomed in Grenarr eyes—those who were dying or disabled before they realized what had struck them. Awe followed, accompanied by recognition. They'd been told to expect him, and forewarned of his prowess—if they hadn't witnessed it in earlier skirmishes themselves. There was no mistaking him now. The outlander. Kendarrion's asp. He who'd murdered Great Grendavan the Eighth—or thought he had—in the vaulted hall of an Addaran cathedral, amid vows that, for all he'd known, were intended to unite their peoples in peace.

With hungry howls, they surged toward him. Reassured, mayhap, that he was but one man amid the throng. Believing their combined numbers sufficient to corral and butcher him. Driven by a desire to avenge fallen comrades, or by bounties offered by their overlord, or by the sheer momentum of battle.

Whatever their impetus, they died with dreams unrealized. Some, he merely maimed, but his suddenly emboldened Addaran comrades were only too happy to finish the grisly work—to claim kills of their own. Regardless, he roved where he pleased, unslowed, uncontained. Slashing and spinning, worming and dodging, bounding and ducking, as will and instinct took him. Shattering enemy lines and scattering the shards. Leaving bodies heaped and writhing and slumping against their now-uncertain comrades. The result like a funnel cloud touching down upon a stream. Whipping the waters into a foaming frenzy, strewing them with wreckage, filling them with a froth of blood.

Even in the midst of that churn, assailed at every turn by flailing limbs and swinging weapons, Kylac felt free. Liberated at last from plots and schemes and stratagems. From guesses and doubts. From hopes and fears and events over which he had no control. Unshackled at last to do what came most naturally to him. Plying his trade without restraint. While he took no pleasure in killing, a lie it would be to claim he didn't relish an opportunity to test himself against the fray. Offering his life to whoever had the ability or the fortune required to take it. Measuring his skills against others. Daring any and all to prove his better.

Particularly in the defense of those less capable than he. Balancing the scales of conflict.

If life held greater purpose than that, he'd yet to discover it.

Within moments, the wave receded, drained of its strength. Hissing and roiling, it fought to gather and come again. But Kylac's presence had emboldened the allies around him, bringing them forward again with renewed vigor and confidence. Drawing the defenders from their heels, and putting them on their toes. Showing them that the Grenarr bled, too.

"To the south! Kronus! South!"

Ledron. Kylac turned at the cry, to find the Blackfist advancing on his position. Jockeying from the north with a regiment of his own in an effort to seal the breach Kylac had just closed for him. Gesturing wildly now at the fighting over Kylac's shoulder, farther south.

Fayne.

Kylac rounded to see what Ledron had. Almost the entirety of the front line buckling, as Grenarr flooded in behind its soldiers. Redfists scrambling for the next level of barricades farther up the slope. Hewn down from behind for their effort. Cleaved by Grenarr swords. Skewered by Grenarr pikes. Feathered by Grenarr arrows. Fayne himself was urging them to come about, desperately seeking to rally them. Knowing they'd do better to face their enemies than flee. Trying to save as many as he could.

Or mayhap the prideful colonel was simply determined not to be the first of their companies to relinquish ground. It mattered not, his reasons. *His* aim was *their* aim. United in bloody cause. So Kylac raised a blade in acknowledgment to Ledron before spinning in that direction. Raking the Grenarr front while veering southward. Drawing opponents like a flame summoning moths. To touch him meant death. Yet they couldn't seem to resist his allure. If they achieved no other glory in this fight, bringing down the mercenary outlander would make them legends among their peers.

Hastening to reach the slope's southerly expanse, Kylac couldn't stop to engage them all. Rather, he relied on strafing attacks that forced them back a pace or two, giving the Addarans a moment's reprieve—a chance to shore up and resolidify their positions. It would have to be enough. Because if one flank withdrew, it would trigger a retreat all along the front. In most areas, the terraced nature of their limited defenses would allow a breached level only paltry defense against flanking incursions. It was why the bulk of their meager fortifications had been arrayed along the outermost edges—and probably why the Grenarr had driven a wedge straight up the center, where the lines were weaker. Where gullies and trenches that should have slowed them hadn't. Alas, it seemed the enemy had strength to spare, capable of mounting multiple thrusts all along the front, rather than channeling their efforts along one course or another. And if they could sustain that momentum, this was going to be a long day for the defenders.

Or short, rather.

Parrying swords, deflecting spears, ducking arrows, Kylac slashed his way into the melee that the lowermost southern line had become. Slashing throats, piercing eye sockets, cutting nerve tethers or severing crucial tendons. Wasting not a single arc or thrust. If he buried a blade, it was to strike a specific organ—heart or lung or kidney—as fair exchange for the time it would cost him to retrieve his weapon. Just as often, he left it there, taking up a new sword from a fallen foe. In this way, he kept his stolen blades fresh, since they were all he had to work with. Sometimes, he borrowed a weapon for but a single use, sheathing it in the flesh of another. Other times, he turned it on the same man who'd provided it, letting these suffer the sting of their own sabers. Whatever was most expedient, most efficient, in the flash of a particular moment. Actions executed without the burden of emotion, only the calm, calculating precision in which he'd been trained.

More than a score died or fell wounded before him. But the line proved beyond saving—the barricades ripped apart and scattered, the surviving defenders fully committed to reaching the next tier, where waiting compatriots could offer reprieve. Having eyed him there in the throes of his inimitable dance, Fayne had altered orders, commanding the withdrawal. Uncertain, mayhap, as to how he should maneuver his men alongside such chaos. Or unwilling. Leaving Kylac alone to cover the line's retreat.

He did so for several moments. Exposed among the surge of Grenarr. Their press thickening around him. Drawn by the victory, or by the shouts that echoed word of his presence. Ten meager paces, the enemy had won, by overwhelming that first tier. But they'd done so in short order, and there were now fewer than a dozen tiers remaining between them and the crest of the plateau. Where their blades would fall not only upon armored soldiers, but upon the bodies of civilians far less capable of defending themselves. Unless Sabrynne's warriors chose to recognize the distinction, they'd be scythed down like wheat.

With that image in his mind, Kylac held his ground, waiting until convinced Fayne's troops were all safely entrenched behind the next barrier. Serving what distraction he could against those invaders who pressed north now to infiltrate the forward line and force its staggered withdrawal across the remainder of the slope. When convinced the former objective was accomplished, and the latter a point of diminishing success, he finally carved and eddied free of the attackers, skittering away to reach the next line of defense himself.

There, he ignored the awestruck gazes of Addarans who weren't already engaged with the next wave of defense. Stalking past the weary and the wounded. Pressing in among a circle of commanders who huddled around Fayne. Catching the blade of a lieutenant who moved to intercept him and twisting it so that its upthrust tip settled beneath the colonel's chin.

At which point, the huddle froze.

"Be the first to falter again," Kylac said, "and I'll return to assume command o' this company myself."

He weathered Fayne's glare long enough for the colonel to suffer his, then released them to their work and raced north again.

And so it went for the next hour, and the hour kindled from its ashes. The Grenarr pressing almost relentlessly upslope, the forwardmost ranks ebbing only to be spelled by a surge of fresher troops. Climbing as inexorably as a rising king's tide. Traversing ground the defenders hadn't imagined they would even attempt. Using planks and hooked ladders passed from below to span fissures and scale escarpments. Skirting or leaping barricades. Bearing down on the Addarans in hand-to-hand combat like men assailing children. During the Snipe's Hour, the defenders lost another line. During the Pheasant's, they surrendered two more. Neither was relinquished initially by Fayne's company. The first fell to Ledron's, at the center of their host. Though Kylac sought to shore it up, the ground was too broad for him to adequately cover. The next two were compromised to the north. Colonel Garnham fought so doggedly to maintain the first that he was killed in the attempt. The second crumbled much more quickly. Thereafter, Kylac spent much of his time near a Lieutenant Coden, who'd been thrust into Garnham's role when the colonel had fallen, and who seemed traumatized by the truth of it. It wasn't until he, too, was killed, and replaced by yet another lieutenant, that the company seemed to rally and stabilize, loosening Kylac's leash that he might range farther along the slope.

Even so, the truth by then had become undeniable. Even with their defensive advantages, the Addarans were no match for their enemy. The Grenarr were too strong, and too determined. Driven by a sense of self-righteousness. To reclaim what their forebears had lost to treachery and deceit. Not with any final ruses or deceptions of their own, merely an overwhelming force of arms. The rule of might justifying every stretch of ground conquered. This had been their land before it belonged to the Addarans, and would be again.

The defenders, by turn, were clearly demoralized. Exhausted. Stripped of home and possession, most had nothing left to fight for but their lives. And while that could sometimes spur a man to his greatest strength, it just as often robbed him of it. Should they survive, in what capacity? What future was left to them worth clinging to? Endure this horror, and it would only be to face a thousand more.

There were exceptions, of course. Men whose families still lived on the plateau above. Who wouldn't abide the thought of mothers and fathers, wives and husbands, sisters and brothers, daughters and sons, falling prey to these tar-skin animals. But the overall sentiment was one of inevitable defeat, worsening as the morning waxed on. As minor setbacks led to major ones. As weariness and injuries took hold. As their dead were left behind on the lower slopes, to be trampled and defiled by their ruthless oppressors.

As it became ever more likely they might not survive this single day.

Kylac fought elsewise. Without rest, save when the enemy took theirs—generally upon securing a new tier. As if he alone might prevent the Addarans' demise. Fueled by the urgent faces of his soldiering comrades, and the memory of those huddled on the plateau above. Those depending upon him. Whose lives he'd become responsible for the moment he'd persuaded them to follow his plan. Convincing them to forsake their battlements for the open steppe. A slow, wasting death for the *chance*, at least, at reversing their fortunes. Relying on a series of events to play in their favor—most of which *had*. More, in fact, than they knew. And yet, a gallows wager. Unless *all* transpired as intended, death would still find them.

A haunting realization, as a fifth line fell, that the miracle he truly yearned for now was one he couldn't bring to pass. Denariel could be but a league distant, her Ukinhan swarm sprinting and bounding through the canyon trails just beyond the horizon. Or she could only now be setting forth from Talathandria's valley. The Ukinha could have ignored her summons. She could herself be dead. He really had only Rashad's word as to the possibility of the desired outcome, meaning he'd effectively carried out a strategy conceived by a madman—who himself had refused to participate in bringing it to pass.

No, he thought, as he tore into a clutch of Grenarr seeking to clamber up out of a ravine. He also had Denariel's word and stubborn will. She *would* unite the Ukinha, because she'd claimed she would. And of all the roads from the Harrows leading to Indranell, this was the shortest, the most likely. That much, he'd seen mapped out himself. However viable his many doubts, hope hadn't deserted them yet.

But it seemed to him a feeble ally. Fickle. Uncaring. As potent and reliable as this people's Fair Mother Eriyah. He understood better now how Torin, Corathel, and others must have felt in defending Kuuria against the onslaught of Spithaera's dragonspawn. At Morethil, and later at Souaris. Plying their tactics and maneuvers when, all along, their only real hope for survival hinged on Kylac and Allion finding a way to vanquish the mighty Killangrathor. Praying to their own gods, the Ceilhigh, while their cities were devastated and their dead mounted around them.

Was his own fervent desire—for Denariel's coming, here and now—any less wistful than *theirs* had been then?

In fairness, their prayers had ultimately been answered, the dragonspawn turned away from Souaris's half-eaten carcass. As might yet happen here. But that monstrous host had marched first through Morethil, razing the land's capital, the crowning jewel in Emperor Derreg's imperial legacy, in a single day. So which conflict in the Pentanians' effort to stave off eradication would the Thorncrag most closely resemble? The narrow victory at Souaris? Or the calamitous defeat at Morethil?

Because the Addarans wouldn't be given a second chance at this.

When the sixth line succumbed, at the turn of the hour between Finch and Grouse, Kylac felt the onset of desperation. Not yet noon, and already they'd yielded half the slope. More than a thousand of theirs lay dead, with the enemy's losses less than half that. And with each triumph, the Grenarr seemed to double in ferocity, exulting in their success. Even if the Addarans could sustain their rate of defense, the plateau would be breached before nightfall, their people massacred amid the bleeding skies of sunset.

Amid the flash and whirl of his blades, the leaping and skittering of his movements, Kylac wondered what more he might do to stem the tide. He'd been targeting already the enemy commanders, or those he took for such. Those losses hadn't seemed to thwart their gains. He might delve deeper among their masses, seeking out Sabrynne for assassination, but would that slow them, or merely incite them? Truthfully, he doubted the Stormweaver herself could recall this tempest. Her warriors' raging madness was too acute, too widespread, too far flung to be reined in now. Loosed to feed, rare was the pack of hounds willing to stop mid-bite.

Giving him no head to this snake. No overarching task or objective that could end the greater bloodletting. No dragon to be slain. The end would be decided not by some single, glorious stroke, but blow by blow, thrust by thrust, in a brutal contest of attrition.

He happened to see Simalen fall, the familiar Redfist struck in the shoulder by a stray arrow, then pierced from either side by a pair of spears. With harpoon heads, the Grenarr weapons ripped away meaty chunks of flesh as they tore free. Moh, another Kylac knew, took a saber in the back while stooped to help a stumbling companion. The companion was then pinned by a Grenarr boot and pierced through the throat with a splash of blood. Two more souls sent spiraling together into the ever black. Two more bodies laid to rot upon the sunbaked stone.

He watched Olekk and Hamal and Graves join them before the hour was out, become carrion for the scavenging birds circling already overhead. And then Narren, Kylac's original escort upon arrival at the Thorncrag three nights earlier. The Whitefist's young head was near cleaved from his shoulders when he dared hold his ground at the edge of an earthwork while his comrades fled his side. Time and again, Kylac found himself just beyond the reach of someone who needed him. Someone he could have preserved, or at least avenged. But that need was everywhere. And for every man he saved, it seemed a dozen perished.

How many more were men he'd known? Former shipmates or acquaintances who'd seen enough of his acrobatics and bladework to actually believe he'd give them a fighting chance this day?

Burdened with the weight of their misplaced faith, Kylac struggled to lose himself in the battle itself. He would face such reckonings later, should survival demand it. Until then, his only aim was to minimize the toll he'd be asked to pay. To stay keen, focused, dedicated to those who still labored and struggled all around him.

In the back of his mind's eye, he carried with him Briallen's smile. Mocking, as always. But also rueful. Shaded with pity.

With the fall of the seventh line, the terrain undertook a decided shift. Smoothing in the center, while breaking into craggy edges ending now in cliffs. The plan, should they reach this point, had been to transition the more battle-seasoned Fayne in toward the middle, while ushering Ledron southward to assume command of the flank. Now that the moment was upon them, Kylac saw no reason not to execute as intended. Fayne had acquitted himself rather admirably since that initial loss, suggesting that his colonel's clasp had been won with more than those bright eyes and a charming grin. And Ledron, for all his loyalty and determination, had scarcely proven himself the other's equal in inspiring and directing their troops.

The commanders must have agreed, for Kylac came upon them as they neared to crossing paths, reaching Ledron first. A gash over the Blackfist's left eye made it impossible to distinguish his blood from that of friends and foes spattered across his face. His stride carried a hitch not seen before, clearly favoring his right hip. Sergeant Trathem attended him now. Drawn from where, Kylac saw little reason to guess. He greeted them both with sober nods, bridling the urge to ask what had become of the Head's loyal lieutenant, Havrig.

"How fare ya, Captain?" he asked instead.

"Seems they'll not be sated until we're overrun. How long would you wager we can sustain this?"

Kylac's instincts were unclear on the matter. Or mayhap he'd only ceased to listen. "We're relenting too quickly," he admitted.

Ledron's gaze drifted westward, eyes searching the horizon. Kylac's trailed after.

"Three hours," Fayne called as he marched near, flanked by his lieutenants and standard bearer. Blood-spattered himself, but carrying no more than nicks and scrapes to shield and armor.

He couldn't have heard their conversation. Merely guessed at its content. Either way, Ledron felt the need to disagree. "The steepness of the next rise—"

"Flattens beyond," Fayne reminded him. "Three hours," he maintained, "and that if the Mother deigns to warm us with her favor."

A pall of quiet shrouded them, there amid the clanging furor behind the newest front line.

"I'll not accept that," said Ledron.

"Accept it or not, Captain. But we dare wait no longer to signal the civilian retreat."

Their final resort. Winding down the narrow switchbacks by which they'd scaled the Thorncrag to begin with. To flee through the canyons, back toward Indranell. Until chased down from the west, or cut off from the east. Trapped, either way.

"A dead end," Ledron groused. Again his gaze shifted west, while a nearby shriek punctuated his claim.

"Delaying the inevitable," Fayne agreed. "But the only remaining means of buying them more time."

"For what?" Trathem asked, earnest eyes brimming with desperation.

"For whatever draws our captain's gaze westward with such longing."

Ledron spun back abruptly, scowling his mistrust.

"I care not what may be out there," the colonel added hastily, while Kylac privately lauded the soldier's perception. "But if it carries our salvation, we owe our people what chance we can grant them."

The Head fumed, but realized quickly enough the sense in Fayne's words. "Send signal. And let us fight as if the hours left to us count for something."

The colonel gestured to his standard bearer, then looked back to Ledron. "My word, Captain." With a quick glare at Kylac, he added, "I know no other way."

They separated at once, Fayne and his men continuing north, Kylac escorting Ledron and Trathem as they edged south. All while the battling ranks twisted and hollered and heaved against the unrelenting charge of Grenarr. As shouts urged courage and motivation, undercut by the cries of the dying. When sensing a seam between clusters of soldiers bowing to the strain, Kylac took his leave of captain and sergeant and struck forth again, to battle as if with the roiling sea.

The Hawk's Hour marked the arrival of midday. It seemed as

though they'd been battling for weeks. Rare as his acquaintance, Kylac was no stranger to weariness. He felt its brush now. Weighed by losses and the exhaustion of those around him—many of whom had been but waiting for the battle to reach their position. Men who'd nonetheless seen their compatriots slaughtered or driven back, again and again. Men with little reason to hope they might fare any better.

This as the Grenarr seemed strikingly fresh, their stamina just one more attribute by which they measured superior. A benefit of their daily toil upon the seas, mayhap, or another innate gift of their bodies. Kylac couldn't know, and it scarcely mattered. Save to signal a faster-approaching end to this battle than he'd earlier imagined.

Imagined or not, that end pressed callously, irrevocably toward them. As expected, the eighth tier held longer than any before it, the angle of the escarpments and narrowness of the trails cutting across it proving worthy obstacle to the Grenarr ascent. As did the number of boulders the Addarans had prepped to go skidding and tumbling down the slope. But the tier did finally fall, not long after signals and criers had it that Fayne was killed. Kylac had felt the dire casualty like an arrow in the stomach, though he hadn't seen it happen, and only later reconciled the two events as one and the same.

Tiers nine and ten together failed to last as long, so that, only a quarter-mark into the Falcon's Hour, the Addarans found themselves scrabbling for the safety of the eleventh. With only one more behind it. Nearly three-quarters of their overall fighting number dead or crippled. More than a thousand Grenarr slain—some three hundred of which Kylac had himself contributed to—but the remainder advancing stubbornly, in rolling waves to keep their warriors fresh, with nary a reprieve for the beleaguered defenders.

Thus it was, with their inevitable doom on the wind—with just two tiers of defense between their enemies and the plateau above—that Kylac perceived a fresh rhythm amid the tumult. Triggering a cold dread that he was too tired, too belabored, too engrossed to immediately define. It felt at first like a distant avalanche, a crushing weight outpacing the thunder of its roar. Sabrynne's endgame, he thought. Some final trap that he'd expected, and then determined unlikely. Unleashed now, when finally he'd ceased to believe in it.

To catch him off guard, as the Stormweaver was wont to do.

Then he disentangled himself from the knot of Grenarr seeking to penetrate a shallow draw, and climbed a jut of earth to give eye to the forbidding harbinger. An avalanche it was, though much thinner than its ominous weight would portend. A thread spilling from the northwest, down along a winding stretch of canyon belonging to the Spineway. Not black enough to be Grenarr. And coming too quickly. Rising and foaming and eddying like a gushing river, a flash flood, a stream of dead souls come to reclaim their mangled bodies—else drown those who still lived.

Shouts went up, a fresh trumpeting of dismay as lookouts spied the new torrent and sought to give it name. It was their tone that first aroused Kylac's hopes, a chilling dread that waxed in strength, swelling toward unremitting terror. At the crest of the plateau, the nearest lookout cast down his spyglass and fled east, beyond Kylac's view. But the lad's horror spread like fire down the slope, demanding attention, consuming the focus of all not directly engaged upon the front lines. The Grenarr were turning now, too. In response to the defenders. Curious as to what, at this stage, could warrant such a severe, panicked reaction.

By then, Kylac knew. Though he scarcely dared believe it, he'd witnessed this particular fear before. A fear that, from all he'd observed, was reserved for only one creature upon these perilous shores.

Still skeptical that fortune could be so generous after dealing such a stark hand, he held his ground until its name echoed through the ranks. Passed down by those wielding instruments with which to confirm the fast-closing truth. Rippling and rumbling and rattling through the rest like a budding earthquake.

"Groll!" the swell of voices screamed. "Groll!"

42

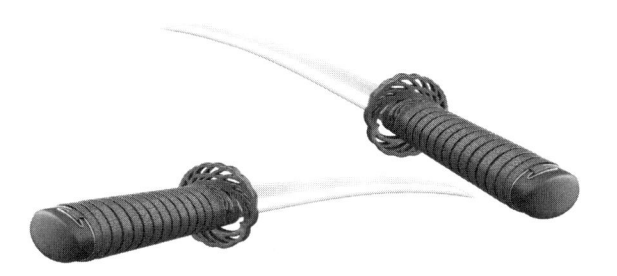

Raised in the Parthan capital of Atharvan, amid the ravaged foothills of the Skullmar Mountains, Kylac had experienced his share of quakes. From minor temblors that felt like nothing more than a passing dizziness, to the stone-buckling surges in which the earth shuddered and rolled like the deck of a ship riding tempest seas. For each, he'd witnessed people's varied reactions. Those gripped by paralysis, who clung to the unstable ground as if seeking to set root within. Those who scrambled about frantically, as if to chance upon an island amid the storm. Those who simply fell to their knees, beseeching some power within the heavens to soothe the fury beneath them.

He saw much the same now, as the Addaran defenders upon the western slopes of the Thorncrag came to realize the truth of the host streaming toward them through the Spineway. Confusion giving way to denial, before surrendering to horror. Soldiers gaped, their weapons falling slack. Soldiers withdrew, shoving and stumbling in a panic. Soldiers swooned, like stringed puppets severed from their crosses.

An army of Ukinha, as Kylac had scarcely dared envision it. Spilling down the canyon trough in a foaming wash. Mottled shades of brown and gray and green. Eerily quiet as they ran and bounded and scrabbled near. Scores of them. Hundreds, even. Voiceless. Relentless. Undeterred by the scale or fury or tumult of the slaughter in progress.

A slaughter diminishing in intensity with every heartbeat that brought the mutants closer . . . closer . . .

"Hold! Hold!" Ledron's voice. A lonely cry amid the gale, striking in its dissonance. A few others took up the echo, bellowing it with their lungs or blasting it with their signal horns. But their obedience was more mechanical than willful, and went mostly unheeded. By any measure, a feeble ribbon set swirl within that cauldron of brewing madness.

Bedlam reigned.

Kylac was among the few to hold his position as the defensive lines crawled upslope like strands of withering ivy. The retreat gained in speed and strength as the Ukinha neared. The Grenarr, however, failed to take advantage, seeing clearly that theirs was the more immediate peril. Turning their backs to the former enemy and receding themselves, downslope, to take defensive posture against the new arrivals. Exposing the mangled bodies and discarded weapons of their trampled foes like the onshore detritus abandoned by a knave's tide. Their own confusion and disbelief was palpable, if more measured. Their response, more controlled. But it was clear that they, too, regarded this unlikely swarm as a hostile action. Whatever its origin, whatever its precise purpose, it could only portend catastrophe.

By that reckoning, they availed themselves admirably, forgoing the dread panic of their adversaries while forming up against the presumed threat. They could have bolted, scattering southward along the Mandowyn. They could have scampered up to higher elevations, seeking refuge amid the terrain or behind the conquered Addaran bulwarks. Instead, they simply shifted ranks, their rear morphing into a second front. Bubbling thickly to the south, Kylac noted, like a serpent coiling protectively.

That's when he saw her. Sabrynne Stormweaver. Great Grendavan the Eighth. With nothing to set her apart from her troops—no trappings, no standards, no special retinue—it was easy to see why he hadn't spotted her before. And why *should* she draw special attention to herself upon the battlefield? Hers was a force given free rein, her aims entrusted to her captains. And they knew she was with them, her fate linked to theirs. What other purpose would lording over them achieve, save to make her more visible to their enemy?

Their reflexive positioning now, however, betrayed her presence near the base of the slope at the southern edge. Her bald head just one of thousands amid the throng, but the only one around which so many others were flocking in a defensive arc, erecting a wall with their bodies between her and the advancing swarm. He could also see her giving orders, barking and gesturing. And though he couldn't begin to distinguish her shouts from those of the general furor, there was something about her motions, her presence, that exuded command.

Then the Ukinha closed, hissing and snarling upon final approach like a tangle of vipers. They gave no other warning, and Kylac found his gaze drawn to the strike their collective cry signaled. For the briefest of moments, it appeared the Grenarr phalanx might hold. Then the grolls were up and over and slithering through, the Grenarr ranks splintering and eroding and collapsing as the mutant venom found and sizzled through their veins, the mutants themselves scarcely slowing as gashes and punctures suffered in the exchange just as quickly began to heal.

The initial charge spawned a massacre as grievously dreadful and one-sided as Kylac could have imagined. He'd seen the damage a single groll could inflict, so startlingly swift and precise and evasive. Denariel had successfully summoned what now appeared three hundred or more. And as the fullness of their numbers came to bear, the Grenarr—mayhap weary, surely unprepared—fell like wheat before the scythe. The tables fully turned, from the butchery he'd envisioned the Grenarr inflicting against the Addaran populace, to . . . this. A bloodbath difficult to describe, save for the sickness it summoned in his stomach, threatening to empty his gorge.

Suddenly, savagely overwhelmed, the Grenarr began backing away, initiating their own retreat. Not south, in the direction from which they'd come, but upslope, scaling the Thorncrag, using their spears and swords and arrows as best they could to stave off pursuit. The strategy—if planned it was, and not just a desperate reflex—surprised Kylac, at first. For it would put their backs to the Addarans, leaving them pinched between enemies and compelled to fight on two fronts. Why, with the Mandowyn open to them?

For any number of reasons, he quickly realized. Surely, Sabrynne understood there was no outpacing the Ukinha—particularly over canyon terrain that would do much less to hamper the mutants' progress than her own. Mayhap she thought the broken slopes would do more to funnel and fend off pursuing attackers. Mayhap she meant to lure the grolls into the midst of the Addarans, whereafter she might hope to slither away. Or mayhap she only intended that, if *her* people were to perish, her pale-skinned enemies would perish alongside.

She couldn't know yet—whatever she might suspect—that her people had been specifically targeted here. Certainly, the Addarans didn't, given the way they'd abandoned their defenses. Only a few dozen remained, peppered lightly about the slope. A handful mobilized by Ledron, the rest a smattering of injured or those simply entranced. Another reason as to why Sabrynne needn't demonstrate particular concern over a landsnake front—it no longer existed. Nor did it seem likely to soon re-form.

Whatever her thinking, her route was chosen, the die cast. With remarkable poise, the Grenarr host shifted again to maintain some semblance of barrier as Sabrynne and those closest to her spurred the departing climb. A slow, steady, disciplined retreat. Even now, far from the frantic dispersal of the landsnakes before them.

Yet, they could maintain that discipline for only so long. The Ukinha assault was like nothing Kylac had ever witnessed. As if the mutants required any other advantages, they worked in tandem to distract and set up blind attacks—one groll drawing an opponent's focus only for another to ravage him from behind. The speed and accuracy with which they bounded and swerved, lashed and lunged, darted and dashed, flared and shrank . . . He could only compare it to a pack of wolves preying upon a herd of sheep—horrifying and mesmerizing at the same time.

Beset by such rabid fury, surrounded by the high-pitched screams of their suffering comrades, the Grenarr ranks soon broke into full flight. In a mad press, they scampered up the slope, rising again over the remains of the prior conflict—so fresh, yet long forgotten. Even the carrion birds, Kylac noted, were winging from the scene, wanting no part of the grolls or their envenomed leavings. Their sharp, indignant cries seeming to mimic those of the men and women trapped below.

Driven by a desperate distress and those long, powerful legs, the Grenarr climbed swiftly. Kylac looked to Ledron, who was looking to him. Stand? Flee?

Kylac shook his head. Neither had any assurance that the Ukinha would stop upon overcoming the Grenarr. Even if it were elsewise, how many of their fighting men could be persuaded to believe it? A disadvantage of their secrecy was that none had any reason to view the mutants as allies. Nor was Kylac fully convinced that anyone should. Indeed, in those fearsome moments, it seemed far more likely that the grolls' bloodlust would carry them past the dark-hued carcasses and on into the pale-skinned ones beyond.

"Go!" he hollered, nodding toward the plateau.

He tarried in his own retreat, giving Ledron and those who could manage it time to stagger on up the slope. Using that time himself to mark the ascent of the scattered knots of Grenarr and the creatures hunting them. Trying to sense or visualize some means by which to stall them. A needless concern, mayhap. But the fewer the Grenarr who reached the top, the less likely it was that the butchery would spill over onto the plateau itself.

It soon became clear that such an outcome was largely beyond his control. He might arrest a few here and there, of course, but the slope was far too wide for him to stem the full breadth of the tide.

Instead, he found a hobbled Redfist limping toward the crest, and lent the man his shoulder—ignoring the mockery in his head that questioned whether he meant to carry the poor soul across the plateau and down the eastern switchbacks, too. *Suffer the weak . . .*

Upon reaching the top, he passed the injured soldier off to a compatriot who was himself nursing a wounded elbow. As they trundled off, Kylac gave eye to the reigning disorder. Encouraged to find that the bulk of the Addaran civilians were far to the east, most of them vanished already into the canyon trails winding down to the Spineway below. With debt to Fayne, for insisting upon their retreat when he had. Buying them the hours needed to vacate the plateau. Still, it would take hours more to negotiate the narrow slopes and treacherous pathways leading to the canyon floor. Where they would be no more safe than they were now, should the Ukinha or the Grenarr pursue them that far.

"Form a line! Form a line!" Kylac shouted. He dashed north along the plateau's western edge, calling out to any who would listen. "The grolls are with *us*! The grolls fight *with* us!"

Most only glanced back at him before doubling their pace. Others, lathered and struggling already, slowed in confusion. A few actually halted and looked to their comrades, as if to question whether they'd heard him correctly.

Kylac continued running until he caught up to Ledron, who himself was urging soldiers to stand their ground—for their families and their countrymen—to a modicum of success.

"What's the aim here?" the Blackfist growled as Kylac reached him.

"Thwart the escape o' those adversaries we can."

"Stealing my people a few more minutes, at best."

"Laying clear demarcation. A line we don't want the Ukinha to cross."

"And if they do?"

"Come, Captain. Would ya sooner live a few moments longer, just to watch your people be massacred?"

Ledron grunted and resumed his calls for reinforcement. At this point, those calls had taken on a life of their own, spread by the nearer of the fleeing Redfists to those farther on. Actually drawing dozens of them back. Seemed many were courageous enough—or confused or weary or desperate enough—to answer the rallying cry. To align themselves with their fellow soldiers along a threadbare front line. To plant themselves as a human shield for those friends and allies who stood a better chance of escape.

Kylac dashed south again, shouting encouragement, praising their mettle. A soldier he wasn't, but he'd heard enough of the prattle with which they girded themselves and bestirred one another to mimic it here. Proclaiming them heroes, one and all. Guardians, noble and selfless. Avowing that this deed would live forever in song. *Should any remain to sing o' this day.*

Sadly, it was chiefly the hobbled and the hopeless who joined them. Men like the Redfist he'd aided up the slope, who with his one-armed companion had staggered back. Mayhap only because they misliked their own chances of escape. Though he chose to believe them motivated by something more.

Not all who chose to stand arrayed themselves upon the plateau's edge. Others were positioning themselves farther back, as if to mark and seal any breaches. Else mayhap only to flee if they didn't like what they saw. Kylac wouldn't disparage them for their reluctance, choosing instead to accept whatever they might be willing to commit.

Over and again, he echoed to those gathered nearer that the Ukinha were with them, with as much sincerity in the belief as he could muster. He didn't know how many accepted it as truth, how many *could*. Most knew them only as ravening monsters. For the creatures to have aligned themselves with the Addaran cause? Well, that would require a level of rational thought that few would have ever had reason to attribute to the beasts.

Mayhap they were merely transfixed by the sight of their enemies' travails. Kylac sensed more than a mite amount of grim, bloodthirsty satisfaction. If their last sight was upon them, why not a vision of the hated tar-skins sprawled about in spine-wrenching agony?

Kylac was more interested in those Grenarr set soon to gain the heights. Trying to judge among those clusters and columns as to which might form the strongest wedges. Which links along the chain of meager defenders were most likely to snap. Which stretch of ridge stood in greatest need of his blades.

At the same time, he found himself searching for Denariel, down amid the Ukinhan swarm. Seeking some sign that she'd traveled with them, and held some rein upon them. That she might, in fact, put an end to the killing before it spread too far.

Failing to find it, he drew his blades, determining to do what he could to bridle this chaos himself.

He was in no position to resist the first wedge of fleeing Grenarr, nor the second. Both struggled only briefly to pierce the Addaran line, pushing through it like a strand of webbing. He was, however, there to set swords to a third and larger regiment, forcing them to stumble and fall back and then veer aside.

But like a boulder in a river, he could do little more than divert the increasing flow, watching it spill away to either flank. Brave Addarans dug in their heels and howled their war cries, but were mostly washed away like pebbles. Though he slew a dozen Grenarr in mere moments, dozens more sprang free, cresting the plateau and continuing eastward, thundering like wild horses across the rocky steppe.

On the slope below, he found Sabrynne's own herd, nearing the crest. Swollen with a thick ring of escorts, ushering her along at its heart. Near the slope's center, but edging northward, toward a break already forged. Kylac felt himself drawn in that direction, though he knew the distance too great for him to overcome in time.

All the same, he committed himself to the attempt. Sprinting along the plateau's edge on the chance that she was delayed, and he might reach her. Unsure what difference her capture would really make, but believing it far better than her escape.

Alas, when he came across the Redfist Ysander engaged in staving off another breaching assault, he was compelled to stop and lend assistance. By the time he'd helped to secure that aim, he looked up to find Sabrynne's pack hewing through the line and guiding her safely onto the plateau.

He was tempted to pursue. Several others already were, hard-pressed as they would be to match a Grenarrian's stride. But it was the pace of the Ukinha that changed his mind. Given to note how quickly they were rising, swarming over the thousand or so Grenarr who hadn't been felled already, Kylac determined it far more critical to stand with those he'd summoned to the front. To demonstrate the courage needed to hold their ground. Right or wrong, to share their fate.

More easily imagined than accomplished. Before them, the Grenarr crumpled in waves. And from the writhing, venom-streaked bodies, sprang the grolls that had killed them. Showing no signs of being sated, no intention of slowing. Mayhap they'd come to end the feuding upon their shores once and for all. By eradicating not just one side, but both. Kylac had been led to understand that the Ukinha wished only to be left alone. Mayhap this was how they meant to ensure it.

Face-to-face with those hissing, snarling, slavering forms, Kylac couldn't fault the defenders as they shied, or froze, or slumped to their knees. A thrill lanced up his own spine, holding him upright. The thrill of standing at the edge of a precipice. Of a plunge into icy waters. Of imminent death.

The Ukinha passed through their line like waters beyond a gate. Leaping overhead or slipping through the gaps in their ranks. A handful at first, then a dozen, then a score. A few soldiers were knocked aside. Others had their weapons dislodged from slack fingers. But none were struck in the process. None given to suffer tooth or claw. Even where a scant few howled in reflexive defiance and managed to raise sword or pike defensively, the grolls simply dodged or deflected the feeble instruments and bounded on their way.

Kylac raised a cheer, to help make real what his Addaran comrades had yet to fully grasp. The Ukinha were in fact here to save them. To slay their oppressors, and their oppressors only. For what purpose, they couldn't yet know. Owing to the grace of Eriyah, it must seem. But their tribulations here were ended. The day suddenly, miraculously, won.

No longer fearing for the front line, Kylac dashed in pursuit of the Ukinha racing now along the plateau. Watching them scrabble and tear and pounce from one area to the next, bringing down the dregs of the fleeing Grenarr. Pity bloomed in his chest. The attackers were routed, annihilated. Their brutality repaid in full. This massacre needn't continue. What remained could only be described as murder.

But the grolls weren't his to leash, their savagery in no way subject to his command. Saddening and sickening as the scene might be, he was merely a spectator now. Mayhap it was only his arrogance that had enabled him to ever imagine elsewise.

And yet, he would do what he could to limit the violence to this day's battle. There were still Grenarr inhabiting Avenell, and those anchored or entrenched outside Indranell. To prevent this or any other shade of butchery from spreading to those locations, a truce would have to be reached. Whatever form that might take, however untenable it might be, the best way to ensure it would be to collar she who spoke for the Grenarr people.

So he ran without looking back, scanning the plateau for sign of Sabrynne's trail. Hers had been the largest contingent, and surely still would be. If he could but reach her before the Ukinha did—while they preyed upon the packs and individuals scattered at her back—mayhap he could apprehend her in time to request that she be spared.

It didn't take him long to spy her. Or her escort, at least. They hadn't ventured as far as he'd feared, running afoul of one of the inner barricades. Erected amid a cluster of rocks and trenches that served to channel passage into a shallow basin beyond. Forcing them to close ranks as they fought to spear and slash their way past. Whoever held the basin seemed to be resisting with the utmost determination. Mayhap knowing who they fought. Mayhap having no choice.

Kylac made for the roiling knot with all haste. Sixty more paces. Fifty. Forty . . .

At thirty, a pair of grolls converged alongside, sniffing and snarling at his flanks before propelling themselves on ahead. Kylac gritted his teeth and fought to stretch his already lengthened stride.

Though the mutants reached the melee before he could, their presence proved a boon. For as they hewed into the rear ranks, Kylac was able to cleave a path of his own almost unchallenged. Accepting a few bruises and lacerations for the privilege, he swerved and spun and sliced his way through the center of the Grenarr brood, listening to the telltale shrieks of those who'd drawn the matchless ferocity of the Ukinha instead.

Down a short slope and into the basin he surged. Where the Grenarr had been ensnared by a troop of Addarans. While outnumbered, the Addarans battled desperately to contain the enemy retinue. Near the eye of that storm, Sabrynne herself was heavily pressed by a raging Redfist. Sergeant Trathem. Who, while gashed and pierced and scarlet-faced, fought less like a man and more like . . . a groll. Ignoring his wounds. Raining blows in a ceaseless, flailing barrage. Grunting and slavering and roaring, "Where is she? Where *is* she?"

Clearly, Kylac had missed some key exchange at the inception of this skirmish. Alas that he could only involve himself in one conflict at a time. Intrigued as he might have been to revisit that unknown beginning, there was little mystery in the ending. After weathering Trathem's reckless assault, Sabrynne parried and twisted and swept his feet out from under him, leaving the sergeant disarmed and choking on the ground, his throat beneath her sandaled heel.

"Where is she?" he rasped, eyes bulging. Mouth groping like a landed fish.

Sabrynne leaned close, sneering down at him. Her lips moved, but the words they formed were lost amid the clangor. She then drove the tip of her sword through his ear, letting him twitch and spasm before wrenching it free.

When she looked up, she saw Kylac advancing, a thin mesh of battling soldiers all that stood between them.

Wisely enough, she used that screen to make her escape.

Not this time.

Kylac slashed, feinted at circling around, and then hacked straight through her rearguard. One warrior was left clutching at the kidney bulging suddenly from his side. The other stumbled when the tendons at the back of his knee abruptly failed him. A third lunged at him, swinging at his head with a heavy, left-handed stroke. Barkavius. The steward of Grenathrok who'd brought Kylac and companions back to Addaranth before severing his own right hand in that terrible display of fealty.

Something stopped Kylac from taking the Grenarrian's remaining hand. He opted instead for a pommel strike to the temple that left his opponent sprawled, senseless.

He disentangled himself from another pair of her devoted warriors, then dashed after her. She was all but alone now, her most loyal lieutenants caught up in securing her escape. She glanced back at him once before increasing her pace, making for another clutch of Grenarr who, in racing by, had spied her and sought now to rally to her side.

In her haste, she appeared to twist her ankle in a shallow rut. Kylac eagerly traversed the remaining ground. Hopping gingerly and then doubling over, she nearly caught him off guard when spinning about and greeting him with a firm, dexterous thrust. Though he recognized the feint in time to evade her strike, his response was a sidelong roll that carried him wide. Increasing again the distance between them. Granting her pack of approaching warriors the time to reach and coalesce around her.

Kylac had just sprung from the stony ground, determined to resume pursuit, when a sharp voice cut through the clamor, shrieking across the flats.

"Grendavan! Where do you run?"

Kylac turned, surprise vying with disbelief, before both were trampled by elation.

Denariel had arrived.

He found her atop a Ukinh, its back swollen and rounded as if to mold itself to her clinging form. Its hips had taken on the shape of stirrups to comfortably cradle her legs, while its shoulders had formed knobs that not only offered grip, but clasped her wrists in turn. While thus burdened, the mutant seemed in no way encumbered as it smoothly loped near.

Sabrynne had seen the pair, too. And while she looked first to maintain her flight, the pair of grolls who appeared ahead of her seemed to persuade her elsewise. Slowing and then stopping, she rounded with a defiant air.

"The bastard princess," she said, seething through her smile. "Fitting . . . that you should join us. What unnatural union . . . have you formed now?"

With an invisible touch, Denariel drew her unlikely mount to a halt. "Another *your* kind forced upon me."

With battle diminishing across the plateau, and an increasing number of grolls coming to circle around them, the Stormweaver did well to hide her fear. "Is that so? Is this to be it, then? Have you come for our final reckoning?"

"I have."

"She's now your prisoner," Kylac said. "Majesty, we may do better to—"

"Silence, rogue. I ask not your council."

The fading sounds of combat enabled the wails and moans of the mortally wounded to swell upon the wind. After hours and hours of ringing tumult, the slowly settling silence seemed all the more ominous.

"Come, then," Sabrynne urged. "Let us reckon. Ruler to ruler."

The grips and knobs in the Ukinh's flesh melted away. Its back shrank as it settled onto its haunches. Denariel slid free. Lightly garbed in an array of pelts and weaves of raw plant fibers.

"Your Majesty," Kylac objected at once. At her glare, he twirled his swords. "She'll have to come through me."

"Stand aside," she said.

"Majesty—"

"This is *my* fight," Denariel spat. "As it was against Talathandria."

"Who nearly killed ya. A shadow o' the fighter this one is."

"You would belittle my victory?"

"Ya don't even have a blade."

"Then hand me yours."

Kylac balked. And then again when he caught the slow spread of Sabrynne's smile.

"Your Majesty, I beg ya—"

"Beg as you must," Denariel replied, striding toward him. "But do it for *your* life, not mine."

She stopped as she reached him, her maddened gaze on Sabrynne as she spoke. "Are you to fancy yourself my warder forever? Do you intend to swear me fealty and cleave hereafter to my side? If not, then favor me now, this once more, and let me prove my own strength."

There was a plaintive tenor to the iron in her tone. Spawning within Kylac a gut-wrenching indecision. He'd doubted her before, when he shouldn't have. Too many times to recount. What was it that made him doubt her now?

Because she wouldn't be the first to refuse his help. And should she suffer for it, should she perish . . . foolishly, senselessly . . . *Never again,* he'd vowed. To himself, and to the ghost of she who'd left him scarred.

She who taunted him even now. Here he was, the only one within view so arrogant as to interfere. A half dozen grolls had gathered round, to wait silently on their matron's will. Scores of Addarans had approached, congregating at various distances, to bear witness to Denariel's command. Sabrynne's clutch of Grenarr, momentarily spared, did their kiros the same courtesy. Men and mutants on either side who stood silent. Not because they lacked valor. Not because their loyalty could be questioned. Simply because they respected their sworn charges enough to abide their decisions.

To let them account for their own lives, secure their own dignity, even where it might relate to their death.

Agonizing against his own movements, he presented one of his sword hilts. "Mark her leg sweep," he said. "And beware her feints."

A tactic Denariel herself had used, he recalled, in the pit against Talathandria. For some reason, the memory gave him hope.

The queen merely nodded as she took the weapon, transfixed still upon Sabrynne. Four strides she took, leaving Kylac behind her, until only a spear's length separated her from her opponent.

"No more shadows in which to hide, Grendavan. No more lies to weave. If you would slay me as you did my brother, my father, I am here. Whenever your courage allows."

So small she looked. So frail. A waif stumbled out of the wilderness. Her dark skin paler than usual. Her limbs leaner. Given her stance, it seemed she could scarcely bear the weight of her borrowed sword.

Sabrynne must have seen much the same—and viewed it with mistrust. For she edged forward only half a step, tentative. Glancing at those around her as if fearing some ruse or snare. Ultimately, she had little choice. And it was *that*, Kylac suspected, which caused her to finally narrow her gaze upon her diminutive adversary with cruel focus.

"Then let us embrace, that this Sundered Isle may be returned to the mutants."

She lunged. As soon as she raised her sword, Denariel lowered hers. Kylac's heart fluttered with reflexive panic. What was she doing?

He saw his confusion reflected in Sabrynne's eyes. Lasting only a heartbeat. Supplanted by terrible understanding as the Ukinh that had delivered Denariel sprang from its crouch. Flying past its erstwhile rider and hurtling into the oncoming Stormweaver. Hissing as it slammed into her. Snarling as it drove her back in a thrashing frenzy, to unleash geysers of blood. Smothering her screams by chewing into her throat, while foreclaws rent her face, and hindclaws shredded the organs that it ripped from her bowels.

All before bearing her to the ground.

43

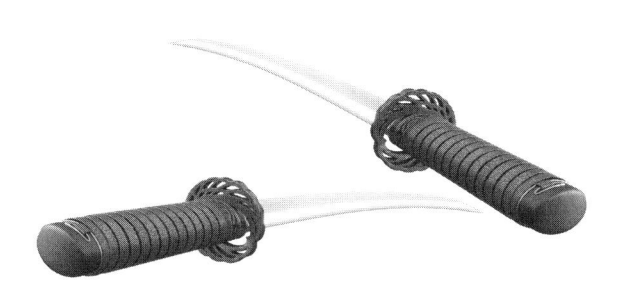

The ukinh's savage assault lasted mere seconds. But when its frenzy abated, little of Sabrynne Stormweaver, Great Grendavan the Eighth, remained recognizable. Her torso shed of its limbs. The flesh pared in ribbons from her bloody skull. The rest of her carcass so thoroughly minced and mangled and scattered as to scarcely resemble anything that might once have been a living, breathing creature.

The groll snorted and snarled at the grisly ruin before leaning back with callous satisfaction. Hide and hairs slathered in its victim's blood, it glanced round as if to discern whether any posed further challenge. Finding only horror and fear and ghastly fascination, it pushed away, returning to Denariel. Kylac winced as it sniffed at her torso before crouching down beside her.

Denariel disregarded the creature, her gaze fixed upon the still-twitching, still-pulsing remains of her adversary. Despite a roiling of emotion, her features were taut, expressionless. Until she chanced to look up and find Kylac staring at her. At which point, she promptly bucked forward, retching violently.

She wasn't alone. As if granted permission by their royal liege, several observers proceeded to empty their stomachs there on the stony ground. Assailed by the smells, Kylac wouldn't have been greatly pressed to let go of *his*. But he tamped down the heaving sensation, unconvinced, for all the resolution Sabrynne's death might bring, that all scores had been settled, the fighting finished.

Indeed, even as most lay dead or cowering, subdued by the mere presence of so many grolls among them, there was now an increasing number of Addaran soldiers flocking to this spot—along with the handful of civilians who'd held back to support them. Most with a caution and hesitation well warranted, yet others with desperate haste. Responding to rumor of Denariel's arrival. Or that the Great Grendavan had been cornered. Or both. Whatever the particular allure, that this stretch of ground was where fates were yet being decided, for those who might care to affect—or at least bear witness to—the outcome.

So it was no surprise when a breathless Ledron came staggering in from the west, emerging from the depression in which Sergeant Trathem had battled to prevent the Stormweaver's escape. Half sprinting, half stumbling, at the head of a small squad of Redfists gamely giving chase.

"Majesty!" he bellowed when he saw her, eyes drawn to her—even at a distance—like a sailor's to the guiding stars. Finding her hunched over, with a blood-drenched groll beside her, propelled him forward in a fresh panic.

The Ukinha nearest Her Majesty growled in response. Kylac thought to sally forth to meet the captain, to impede the Blackfist's frantic progress, but felt it more prudent to avoid any hasty movements that might threaten the still-settling calm. He was about to holler warning instead, when Ledron tripped and went sprawling. By the time the Head had recovered, so had Denariel, rising to reveal herself unharmed. Reassuring her sworn protector so that he and his troops advanced now with greater deference. Raising a fist that seemed to restrain her attending grolls, as an additional precaution.

Turning to glare momentarily at Kylac, as if sensing his desire to intercede.

Her gaze slipped out farther, to sweep the plateau in a broad circle. Assessing the larger conflict, now that her chief rival had been vanquished.

"Gather the survivors," she said, addressing her mutant companion.

The groll tossed back its head and threw up a hacking yelp. Its cry spawned echo among the other Ukinha, across the stony flats, as if to relay her bidding to all.

"Your Majesty," Ledron wheezed upon final, wary approach. Scowling at the blood-soaked mutant beside her. "Are you . . ." His gaze snagged upon the tangle of pulp and bone that had once been Sabrynne. "How fare you?"

She ignored his concern, calling out instead to any Addaran within range of her voice. "Bear word of our triumph. Let our people know they are safe."

Kylac suspected again that this was already happening—though he was less confident "triumph" was the word most heralds and criers would be using. The Grenarr threat was quelled here, yes. But deliverance at the hands of a Ukinhan swarm unrivaled by any other inked in their histories was sure to seed a garden—a jungle—of dread, uncertainty, and suspicion.

He doubted many of those who'd fled east would be halting or returning with any urgent haste.

Nonetheless, a smattering of Addarans turned away to bear message, joined by others and spurred in their departure when Ledron barked, "Her Majesty has spoken!"

Through the veins and gaps left by their withdrawal, others approached—a mob coalescing at a cautious distance. Among the few daring to press to the fore, Kylac spied the misshapen form of Aythef, with Warmund inching along behind him. The former carried a mostly empty quiver, the latter his bow, an arrow still nocked to the string. The royal cook standing to the end—serving whatever purpose—as vowed. Declining to retreat when, given his condition, few would have faulted him for doing so.

Kylac acknowledged them both with a tip of his brow.

Denariel saw them, too. What passed in that moment between her and Aythef, Kylac couldn't quite define. A recognition, of some variety, private and profound. Regarding Prince Dethaniel, he imagined, however obvious the assumption.

While Warmund held back at the edge of the assemblage, Aythef advanced until a far-flung scrap of Sabrynne's entrails squelched beneath his booted foot. It brought him to a halt. A momentary inspection, followed by a straying look at the Stormweaver's splayed carcass, caused him to drop his quiver and vomit.

His sickness garnered no response, for the first of the captive Grenarr were by then being herded near by the Ukinha hissing and seething at their backs. Women, mostly. Almost exclusively. Making it seem no accident. Reminding Kylac of Rashad's claim that the Ukinha revered the females—prospective mothers—of any species. An instinctive veneration they'd honored, even in battle.

Devoted they must be to their new matron, to have so violently slaughtered one at her bidding.

But that wasn't how it had happened, was it? Denariel had summoned no defense, merely placed herself within harm's reach. And a single groll—the one that had carried her here—had intervened, unbidden. Violating its innate admiration, without interference from its kind, because . . .

An icy warmth bloomed in Kylac's chest. Because the mutant wasn't protecting Denariel. It was protecting something—according to Rashad—that the Ukinha revered *more* than women.

The unsettling realization lodged like a thorn in Kylac's gullet, choking off his as-yet-unspoken plea on behalf of the remaining Grenarr.

"Gaze then, upon your overlord," Denariel said to the summoned captives, in a cutting tone that suggested no clemency. "And tell me, who among you would still resist?"

Kylac sensed little of resistance among the remaining enemy. The fresh fires of hatred and defiance still smoldered, but only beneath the smothering ashes of horror and revulsion. The pride of conquest had crumbled, sapped by the instinctive hunger for survival. Not so much for themselves as for those *they* now sought to protect—kinsmen and countrymen back at Indranell, Avenell, who would surely be made to answer for any further challenge extended here.

Their morbid silence seemed to disappoint Denariel. "No? Not one of you? Who delight in physical superiority? Who came here to ravish and pillage and butcher as you have for generations?" She raked them one by one with a raptor's gaze. "For all your strength, all your pride, you would let this atrocity, this insult, go unchallenged?"

"For what purpose?"

The queen rounded on the croaking voice. "What's that? Come, let us see your vile tongue as it wags."

The offending Grenarrian staggered to the fore, a groll's clawed hand gripping his throat. Barkavius. Among the few males to be spared. Mayhap because Kylac had rendered him unconscious in that shallow basin. He wore a dazed look still. Bloodshot eyes swollen with sorrow, and tinged with regret.

"For what purpose would we resist?" he echoed, rumbling voice finding its strength. "Your victory here is absolute. Unquestioned. Mete out your sentences. And we will suffer them with a warrior's dignity."

Denariel's eyes narrowed, gleaming venomously. "Sentences. Like that imposed upon my royal brother, *steward*?"

Then she hadn't forgotten him. He who'd carried out Dethaniel's execution upon the command of Yultus—posing as Grendavan at the time—at the behest of the real Grendavan, Sabrynne.

Barkavius held silent, stone-faced. Making no effort to deny or deflect his guilt. Reacting not at all, save to glance at the familiar faces of Kylac, of Aythef, with . . . Was it loathing? Pity? Remorse? Kylac was unable to decide before the steward returned his gaze to Denariel, hefting his chin bravely.

"Shall I eviscerate you?" the queen asked. "Hang you from a prow? Feed your entrails to a school of flesh-eating fish?" Her attempt at a cruel smile held only pain. "What say you, Aythef?"

The onetime cook seemed not to hear her, fixated as he was upon Sabrynne's ghastly remains. As if to reconcile that shredded, seeping mass with its prior form. Clutching a hand to his mouth to curtail further retching.

"Cook!" Denariel barked, yanking him from his musings.

"Majesty?"

"You were as aggrieved as I by Thane's murder. Perhaps more so. What say you, as to this tar-skin's fate?"

Aythef regarded Barkavius with a whirlwind of sorrow and fury and disgust. As if, with his very gaze, he might twist and rend and obliterate the impassive Grenarrian in much the same way Denariel's Ukinh consort had ravaged Sabrynne. Unexpected it was, then, when finally words spilled meekly from his mouth, in echo of the steward's own. "For what purpose?"

Denariel scowled. "To see his blood spilled. As he spilled Thane's."

Aythef's angst-ridden expression betrayed a roiling desire to do just that. Even as he asked, "Have we not shed blood enough?"

The queen fumed, darkening with disapproval. All around her, Ukinha and Addarans continued to rake the battlefield, inspecting corpses and collecting captives from among the Grenarr dead. If any of her grolls had been slain, they lay down upon the western slopes, where the enemy had fought but briefly to make a stand. Her victory here was, much as Barkavius had described it, indisputable. As crushing and one-sided and overwhelming as any contest could be. A momentous achievement—in the annals of this isle, at least. And yet, it seemed here and now to ring suddenly hollow for her. As if the only glory to be taken from this slaughter ground would be that recognized by others.

She gave Aythef chance to reconsider. "You would have his murderers go unpunished?"

"Were it to bring back His Highness, I would have every last tar-skin bled dry and ground into seasoning," the cook assured her. Before adding wretchedly, "But it won't. And so seems a poor means of honoring a man who only ever sought a better life for all."

True enough, given the deceased prince's professed aims. Taken at his word, Dethaniel's motive had been to end the bloodletting against his people *and* Grendavan's. He'd taken terrible risk in parleying secretly with the enemy, and sacrificed much—his own finger, his sister's happiness—for what he believed to be a greater good. Judge as they might his devious means, few had cause to suggest His Highness had been anything but well-intentioned.

"Thane was naive. And for his goodwill, betrayed. Were *you* slain, would he not seek to avenge you?"

"He'd be better pleased, I feel, were we to look toward the peaceful resolution for which he gave his life."

Kylac found his gaze slipping toward Ledron, Warmund, and

the various Addaran faces around them. Expecting to find outrage, animosity, accusation. Finding instead a common exhaustion that transcended physical fatigue. Once-fiery spirits tempered by the carnage wrought by the Ukinha. Victors unable to celebrate, given their guilt in prevailing where they hadn't any discernible right to do so.

Men made somber, sullen, as if just now realizing how damaging and widespread and self-defeating their part in this generations-old conflict had been.

"Your prince showed great courage," Barkavius allowed. An affront, his voice should have been, and was to some. Stoking the flames of indignation. But a greater number listened urgently, as men often did in the aftermath of a calamity. Hungry for words that might lend clarity to events, provide them meaning. "Would that his noble offer had been met as fairly and fervently as it was extended. That the peace he envisioned had taken root, and come to bloom."

Whatever the atmosphere of soberness and concession, Denariel wasn't yet ready to embrace it. "Obvious words for a man condemned. I suppose next you'll prevail upon me to know you were but following orders. That you would have honored your people's pledge to Thane, if only it had been *your* choice to make."

"It was the will and command of my kiros that your brother perish, yes. But I understand how hollow those words must ring. So let me say it thus. Barkavius Bloodslake I am called. Sole surviving son of Navaritus Tidewrester, Great Grendavan the Seventh. Younger brother of Sabrynne Stormweaver, the one and only Great Grendavan the Eighth. With her passing, chief claimant to the mantle of Great Grendavan the Ninth. Kiros. Overlord of the Grenarr."

He paused to let the words settle, yet pressed ahead before any could respond.

"A life I forfeit to your desire. As just recompense, if you will, for that of your brother. Only, let it seal mercy for my people. Let it buy them a place upon these shores as Dethaniel proposed, or at least safe passage to their vessels, that they may return to the seas. Your hatred, your hunger for retribution, is no less than my sister bore you. But she is dead now. Allowing that you and I may strike a new pact. *I* pleading with *you*, as your brother pleaded with her."

Could it be? Kylac wondered. Before posing as Grendavan, the impersonating Yultus had pretended to be Tormitius, the overlord's chief lieutenant. Back when shackled in the captain's quarters of the *Vengeance* as Ledron's personal captive, the wily Grenarrian had boasted that the Great Grendavan had sons. Offspring who would take up his mantle following his murder in Kendarrion's cathedral. Seeking to convince them that the captured lieutenant himself would provide no value to them as a bargaining chip.

Of the two, Kylac was inclined to believe Barkavius, given the man's solemn earnestness, and that he had yet to catch the steward in a deception. Or mayhap he only *wanted* it to be true, to believe that such a dignified plea was more than a desperate ruse crafted upon the gallows. Either way, a clever turn, to cast Denariel in Sabrynne's shadow. Implying that the Addaran queen must be every bit as cruel as the Stormweaver, should she choose to butcher her conquered adversaries instead of setting them free.

A dangerous revelation, either way. But what else had the Grenarrian to lose?

"Your life, and those of your filthy brood, are mine already," Denariel reminded him. "You beg a great deal with that which holds no value."

"As you say, mighty queen. The terms of victory are yours to set. I only beg you know, my people will abide by any truce. As they would have from the outset, had my kiros not been so bent on reprisals."

Denariel bristled. Unconvinced by the prisoner's polished civility, here and now, where the stench of those Addarans slain by him or his fellow invaders still tainted the wind. Where oaths of fealty and assurances of allegiance would be easy to give, however hard to keep. And how could he claim to speak for an entire people? Heir to the mantle of Grendavan he might be. But he might as easily be looking to shield the true heirs. One or the other, there was nothing to ensure his people would adhere to any promises made on their behalf, or decline to wreak further treachery later.

The queen glared at Aythef, irritated by the very suggestion of an accord. Then at Kylac, as if he'd been the one to seed the notion in the cook's head. As he *would* have, given the chance. He thought to support the idea now, but feared his voice more likely to antagonize her, as it so often did.

Her gaze slid round, taking measure, in search of those who might share or spur her lingering enmity. She found mostly dour, somber faces peering back at her, many of whom shied from her withering scrutiny. Whether belonging to Ledron and his fellow Addarans, or Barkavius and his fellow Grenarr. The Ukinhan visages were harder to read, but Kylac sensed from them no bloodlust, no bestial desire to butcher any more than they already had.

Attacker or defender, victor or vanquished, the taste of battle had gone out of them.

The queen's eyes fell upon her bloody consort, and from there, back to Sabrynne. This time, she appeared to wince, as if struck by a twinge of shame. A fleeting sentiment, so quickly suppressed that it may have been but shadows at play.

Yet, it seemed elsewise when she retraced her circuit, glaring again at Kylac, at Aythef, and finally at Barkavius.

"Captain," she snapped.

"Majesty," Ledron replied crisply.

"Bind and tether these prisoners. Ensure that our wounded are being tended, and squads are assembled to gather our dead." Raising her voice in announcement, she added, "The rest of us leave this sullied ground."

"As you will, my queen."

"As to what the morrow might yield . . ." she muttered, before gnashing her teeth and swallowing her fury. "We shall discuss it on the road to Indranell."

44

Shafts of midday sunlight sliced through the high, arched windows lining the palace throne room. The skies beyond seemed quiet just now, the susurration of wind and murmur of waves and incessant shrieking of seabirds overwhelmed by the fanfare of pipes and horns and drums ushering guests into the vaulted hall. Paired Addaran nobles, resplendent in their new finery, held their noses as they marched behind towering duos of half-naked tar-skin savages. In turn, the Grenarr dignitaries, wrapped in their minimal leather garb, clenched their jaws and jutted their chests as they peered down at the lavishly robed, pale-skinned landsnakes in front of *them*. Interspersed in their arrival, the representatives of each people finally peeled away from one another as they reached their assigned rows amid the congregation. Addarans diverting left, Grenarr right, to stand among their respective parties, divided by the chamber's central aisle.

Where all seemed more comfortable.

Kylac himself stood at the back of the hall, stationed beside the entry doors. Invited by Ledron to attend in a peacekeeping capacity. A suspect request, given that he'd been the one to trigger the violence when last these rival nations had been so gathered. Likely, the captain and his queen had determined it better to know where he'd be, rather than wondering where he might venture if left to his own whims.

None would mistake his for a position of honor amid these proceedings. But then, he wasn't seeking any. Mostly, he'd been keeping from sight. Attentive, yet withdrawn. Relying on Ledron to apprise him of the status of negotiations and logistical matters as the Blackfist deemed necessary. For all his training, Kylac had precious little to offer in the drafting of compacts, the valuation of concessions, or other questions of diplomacy. His interest in seeing this dispute formally resolved had only to do with making certain his swords were no longer required in the bartering.

Thus far, they hadn't been. For the same reason they weren't needed to bridle the rancor and resentment brewing now within this cavernous hall. It was the threat of the Ukinha that kept all appropriately subdued—the two with Denariel atop the dais, and those that roved invisibly among the palace shadows, their whereabouts unknown. Denariel had made it clear that the first to violate the tentative peace would be the first to meet her devoted warders up close.

The bulk of which had been dismissed, given to disperse back into the wilds, as soon as the Addarans had turned toward home. Of the three hundred grolls summoned to the Thorncrag, less than a score had joined the easterly trek along the Spineway into civilized lands. Just enough to ensure Denariel's safety, and to see her will imposed. While horrified by the mutants' continued presence, no Addaran was foolish enough to express as much within the queen's hearing. And by the time they'd reached Indranell, and Barkavius relayed to the Grenarr captains still stationed there—in the sound, and encamped outside the city gates—an account of the devastating events that had made him their kiros, those eighteen grolls had had the same effect as eighteen thousand: an immediate agreement to discuss the terms of Grenarr surrender.

Two days at Indranell had been sufficient for the enemy to relinquish its chokehold upon the city to Denariel's satisfaction. After which, the queen had herded the bulk of her Addaran troops and a swollen contingent of Grenarr captives on south to Avenell. Advance messengers had borne word of their coming, so that the capital, too, lay open to her, yielded without a fight. Many of its former occupants had fled to their vessels. A far greater number had greeted her arrival with backs bowed and knees bent in submission, to beseech her continued mercy.

The queen's entire journey home, then, had taken less than two weeks. Four days south along the Karamoor, after five days east along the Spineway. Leaving behind those reclaiming their homes at Indranell, and, prior to that, those crews tasked with harvesting and returning the remains of the Addaran dead from the Thorncrag. The Grenarr dead had been left to rot. Owing less to any willful disrespect than it did to the taint of their envenomed corpses—and that there were so few of their kinsmen left to tend to them. Whatever objections their people might have, the plateau would be their graveyard, become monument to the terrible conflict that had claimed them.

So it was that, only a fortnight removed from that decisive battle amid the northwest canyons, the leading members of both nations found themselves assembled here, summoned to bear witness to the coronation of the new Addaran ruler. While Denariel and Ledron would have seen the ceremony carried out in private, too many others had advised against it. Given the unusual succession and the weeks of chaos preceding it, the prevailing opinion had been that they dare not forsake the traditional, public spectacle. To do so, Denariel's advisors had argued, could threaten the crown's legitimacy, allowing for objections and challenges from other would-be rulers in the months or years ahead.

Should they desire this peace to be a lasting one, best to do all they could to forestall further infighting.

As the last of the guests reached their places upon the floor, the music gave a final swell, then quieted. A priest stepped forward upon the dais. Far younger than the one who'd presided over the arranged wedding between Denariel and the imposter believed at the time to be Grendavan, in a cathedral not so far from this very hall. Kylac couldn't say what the other's absence might mean, but wouldn't have been surprised were he to learn that the cantankerous old man—so openly spiteful of the Grenarr—had been killed at some point during their occupation of the city.

"Honored citizens," the lad began, voice straining beneath the weight of his nerves. "I bid you welcome."

No choir this time, Kylac observed. And while it could be tradition that excluded them from this particular ceremony, he had to wonder again whether it was *his* actions from before that had led to their omission.

"We stand together, on this momentous occasion. Addaran. Grenarr. Fervent enemies, bound now in blood. Bitter, yet humbled. Burning still with heavy hearts. Aching with fresh wounds. And yet, amid cruelties inflicted, and sorrows suffered, we find the strength to rejoice. To know that after nearly two centuries of hatred and hostility . . ."

They'd signed their treaty the night before. A pact by which the Grenarr were to be spared, given adherence to certain edicts and restrictions to be imposed upon them. General terms had been reached during marches east and south, including territorial boundaries, acceptable trade methods, and codes of conduct. Penalties and punishments for various violations were outlined and agreed upon. By the time they'd reached Avenell, little more had remained but to illuminate and ratify the language of the accord.

A feeble instrument, it had seemed to Kylac. There wasn't parchment enough in all the vaults of the royal palace to soak up the blood spilled over the past decades between these two nations. Yet, a set of scrolls, filled with mere ink and signed by repressed parties, was somehow going to change all that?

An effort it was, he supposed. A symbol of shared commitment. If not to a future any could actually adhere to, then at least to the conviction that all were weary of war.

"In *unity* will we rebuild," the young priest was droning. "In *unity* will we grow. Guided by our faithful leaders. Those who have demonstrated the courage, the foresight, and the self-sacrifice to . . ."

Those who managed to survive, Kylac thought, and who would be charged now with nurturing the tender, delicate truce into something longer-lasting. For the Grenarr, Barkavius Bloodslake. Great Grendavan the Ninth. Granted lordship over the isle's eastern peninsula, to be renamed New Grenah. Where the Grenarr would toil to establish what home they could amid some of the land's less savage terrain. Relying still upon their great ships and knowledge of the sea, but with a more fertile ground upon which to sow seed and set root when compared to the atolls across which their people had so long been scattered. Unmolested by Addaran armies, they might hope to make that inhospitable region habitable. Within a generation or two, for these settlements to flourish.

Crumbs, they might seem. But more than the Grenarr might have hoped for, given the manner in which the war had ended. And all that Denariel was willing to cede to her father's mortal enemies at this time.

She approached now, the young queen herself. Beckoned by the priest. Dressed in a silken gown of simple, yet elegant design. Wearing jewels upon her fingers, and pearls upon her neck. A golden circlet adorned her brow. Useless trappings, she'd fumed, when Egrund had pleaded with her to wear them. Over unnatural garments deemed itchy, rank, with their false dyes. As superficial as the kohl adding depth to her eyes, or the rouge used to soften her cheeks. But this display was not for her, the seneschal had argued. It was for her people. Do them this courtesy, and shed what she would when it was done.

Kylac was surprised she'd acquiesced. But, to Egrund's merit, these "trappings" served the desired effect. Even from his position at the back of the room, Kylac felt the weight of her splendor, her regal majesty. However diminutive her physical stature, in strength, in bearing, she was every inch a queen. A man had but to peer up at her to want to fall to his knees.

Though mayhap that had more to do with the grolls attending her.

The priest eyed the mutants with a palpable anxiety as she drew near. Neither had shifted from its position, but all had heard by now the story of Sabrynne Stormweaver's demise. Kylac saw it in the lad's slow, deliberate movements as he reached for the pillowed crown upon the plinth beside him, and heard it in his tremulous voice as he formally greeted her. The fear that the wrong twitch, the wrong inflection, might see the mutants leap upon him, to ravage him as they had the Great Grendavan.

"We hereby recognize Denariel, daughter of Her Majesty Lytherial, royal heir of His Majesty, King Kendarrion, and would bestow upon you . . ."

Notwithstanding the careful phrasing, Kylac wondered how many

Addarans within the audience might wish to raise objection. As he'd heard it, Denariel had never been particularly well liked by the greater populace. As if the circumstances of her birth were a stain upon her people. That she'd been sired by a Grenarr assailant was, sadly, no great rarity, and might have been forgiven. But, as a member of the royal family, her existence was viewed by many as an affront that could scarcely be tolerated. Kendarrion himself had spared her only for the great love he bore his wife. Kinder it might have been—and a retaliatory blow against their enemies—had he cleansed the royal house of the enemy's taint by returning their dark spawn to the sea.

How much worse would it be now that she'd ascended to the throne?

Any harboring such vile judgment now, however, wisely kept it to themselves. As did any on the *Grenarr* side of the aisle who might snicker or deride or claim consolation in seeing one of *their* blood come to rule. However profane or vindicating Denariel's ascension might seem to either party, none dared violate the sanctity of the ceremony, for fear of the Ukinha—seen or unseen—among them.

"And so we beg you your oath. An oath that would bind you, from now until the end of your days. The oath your royal father took, and his father before him, in this very hall, before this very seat . . ."

Had anyone troubled to ask Kylac's opinion, he might have asked, what could be more fitting? Who better to mend the ancient rift between these warring peoples than one who carried the blood of both? What better symbol might they hope to find for the unity and healing invoked by men like this priest—whether truly yearned for or not—than a ruler of unified lineage?

"Before those assembled in witness, will you take this oath?"

Denariel hefted her chin. "With all my will, and all my heart, I cannot."

A murmur swept the hall, guests turning to one another in confusion. What game was this? Had they heard her correctly? How could she decline the crown? Who else might wear it?

Denariel raised her voice, plowing over the disturbance, as if anxious to deliver her rehearsed response. "While it would honor me beyond measure to assume my royal father's mantle, I have made my oath already. To those who heard our cries, coming to our aid when none other would. Who ensured our survival, and returned to us this palace, this city, this land. To the mighty Ukinha, I am committed, and so mean to fulfill that pledge."

The murmurs swelled, expressions of horror and morbid curiosity and, yes, muted relief. Among the few forewarned of the decision, Kylac himself was unsurprised by the announcement. Even he, however, felt a bittersweet pang that she meant to go through with it. As if, for all his efforts to save her, this result was somehow *his* failing.

The priest raised his arms, begging quiet. The quickness with which the crowd granted it suggested that, however genuine their astonishment, their distress was largely feigned. "Is there one here to whom Her Royal Majesty would abdicate?"

Denariel rounded toward Ledron, who stood with her grolls as her personal shadow. "Should he accept the noble burden, I would bequeath my father's crown to Ledron, captain of the Shadowguard. Who has demonstrated rare loyalty, and unflinching devotion. As he long served my father's royal household, so would he serve our people, as warden king and lord protector of Addaranth."

The grunts and murmurs now were chiefly expressions of approval. A suitable choice, most seemed to agree. Those who didn't—noblemen who might have put forth other candidates or petitioned for the honor themselves—had the decorum and good sense not to vocalize their objections here. Kylac could feel them, though. The simmering jealousies, the indignation, that a man of low birth, a servant of the sword, should be chosen over masters of diplomacy, agriculture, industry, or trade. Men of means, of *worth*. To Kylac, a rankling notion. Just two weeks ago, these same pompous fools would have gladly yielded the last of their ragged possessions not to be murdered or enslaved at the edge of the known wilderness. Yet here they were, their homes and titles and belongings more or less reclaimed, and given already to temptations of wealth and influence and station.

How swiftly they'd forgotten.

Ledron himself had warned Denariel against the ripples her choice might cause, the discord it might sow. His protests had only made her more adamant. Most of the men her father might have selected had been killed, else proven unworthy of his trust. Who better to lead her people than he who'd helped to do so when they needed it most?

"Loath am I to sully such grand titles with my simple name," the Head replied now. "And plead I would with Her Royal Majesty to reconsider." His pause won from Denariel only stony silence. "But disobey her, I will not. If this is her wish, I will see it manifest, and safeguard it with my dying breath."

"Let it be recorded in the annals of our nation," the priest intoned, "that Her Royal Majesty Denariel does hereby abdicate the throne of Addaranth to Captain Ledron, sworn brother of the Shadowguard, and bestow upon him . . ."

So it transpired, as Denariel had willed it, as previously relayed to those in her innermost circle. Suffering this pomp and circumstance to see Ledron crowned, appointed ruler of their people in her stead. To oversee this new age as it unfurled upon the Sundered Isle. An age dedicated to healing, sharing, and mutual forgiveness. With New Grenah to the northeast, the civilized lands of Addaranth to the south, and the rest . . .

The rest governed by the wild creatures of the Harrows, and she who would henceforth watch over them. Denariel, steward matron of the Ukinha. Whose specter would loom long after her departure. Her vow, to Ledron and Barkavius, that she would hold them both to the terms of their accord: to reap what they could of their own lands, and to tread no more in hers. For if any should violate this agreement, she'd warned them darkly, she would hear of it. And respond accordingly.

As it must be, Kylac supposed. For it would seem to answer his earlier question. What better than a shared figurehead to bind these former enemies?

The threat of mutual destruction.

Mere moments later, it was finished. The speeches, the oaths, the prayers, and the transfer of power, as evidenced by the crown around Ledron's shorn head, and the throne upon which he was seated. Warden King Ledron. For all that was wrong with it, it seemed fitting. For all that he didn't want it, a noble calling the Blackfist had earned with deed whatever he lacked in blood.

The music swelled as the guests were paraded before their new liege to pay homage. A remarkably brief ceremony, by the measure of such things. Denariel had vowed to tolerate only so many formalities. And Ledron . . . though he nodded to his subjects with polite resignation, his gaze was disconsolate, and his jaw clenched.

When all respects had been rendered, all acknowledgments given, the warden king and his former queen departed through their archway at the back of the dais. Flanked by a pair of Ukinha. To carry on with matters of the crown, presumably, as it pertained to this new kingdom they'd fashioned.

Thereafter, the audience was dismissed, given to file in orderly fashion toward the exit. While half tempted to give ear to the guests' reactions, Kylac could imagine readily enough what those might be. From enthusiasm—genuine or false—to outright derision, and most everything in between. The bulk of it self-serving, as these survivors struggled to envision what impact this unexpected turn might have upon their own, small lives.

Given that, he saw no need to linger, and thus slipped out at the head of the exodus. For he, too, had more personal business to attend. Unresolved aims to pursue while awaiting some final determination on the matter of his own, undecided fate.

45

His wait proved short.

Only hours after the abdication ceremony, Kylac found himself leaned against a palace parapet, overlooking the departure of Barkavius Bloodslake and his Grenarr contingent. Bound for the harbor ships set to deliver them alongside the remnants of their people upon the northeastern coastline of New Grenah. An embarkation made without ceremony or fanfare. Just a muted procession striking out along city streets still strangely quiet. Marked by a profusion of conflicting emotions from Grenarr and Addaran alike. Pride and shame. Gratitude and resentment. Apology and remorselessness.

Reconciliation and the simmering hunger for vengeance.

Soon after they'd gone, Kylac found himself summoned to an audience chamber. The same in which, upon his first visit to Avenell, he'd seen Denariel reunited with her royal father. Where Ledron's deception about the princess's abduction had been exposed, and the harsh truth of Kylac's unwitting role in bringing Her Highness home from Kuurian shores laid bare.

He stood alone for but a few moments, peering out into the night through the same window from which he'd last exited that chamber—wondering if the setting was intended to hold any particular significance—before Denariel and Ledron entered. A pair of grolls entered on their heels, ominous in their silence, while Havrig and Talon, both elevated from Stonewatch to the order of Shadowguard, stopped just before the threshold, tugging the doors closed behind them.

"Majesty," Kylac greeted with a deft bow to Denariel. And then to Ledron, "Majesty."

The queen glared, eyes stormy, brow furrowed in disapproval, cheeks dark and full. "Your time here is ended, mercenary."

Kylac wondered if she might be playing with him, making use of that long-favored moniker. He decided she wasn't. "And where should it please Her Majesty to send me?"

"To the depths," she snapped, all too predictably. "But I am prevailed upon to consider another destination. One of *your* choosing."

Kylac's gaze strayed to Ledron. Though a stony countenance might try to hide it, there was little chance but that it was the former captain and now warden king who'd given plea on his behalf. "*My* choosing?"

"So long as it carries you *off* this isle," Denariel clarified, "never to return. For I have not my brother's benevolent heart, nor his pacifist aims. For your service to my people," she allowed bitterly, glancing at the floor as she said it, "I do honor his gentler ideals but this once."

She turned her glare upon Ledron, who stepped to a sideboard, producing a key with which he proceeded to unlock one of the cupboard doors. From within, he drew forth a cloth-wrapped bundle lashed with twine. Kylac's heart leapt as the warden king moved to hand it over to Denariel, who nodded instead to deliver it directly to their guest—as if disdaining to sully her own hands.

"Is this . . . ?" Kylac wondered, as he accepted the bundle from Ledron. Smelling the truth already, but scarcely allowing himself to believe it.

But as soon as he felt the bundle in his palms—the familiar heft and balance, the telltale planes and edges—he knew that it was. His blades. Those that Sabrynne had confiscated from him. For which he'd been hunting almost ceaselessly since his return to the palace. What had been done with them, even Barkavius hadn't been able to say, save that, to his knowledge, his sister hadn't kept them for herself. Having hoped to return them to the mercenary, he'd claimed, for use in *her* service. More comfortable with her own weapons—forged and fashioned by her own hand for the sworn purpose of her vengeance. A lie, mayhap, but Kylac had reached instead for the hope it afforded him. That they might still be here, wherever the Stormweaver had stashed them, waiting to be rediscovered.

After hours of relentless search over the course of days, including the whole of that afternoon following Ledron's coronation, he'd all but surrendered the frayed hope of finding them.

Demonstrating once again that victory might be reeled in upon the narrowest of strands.

"How long has Her Majesty had them?"

"One of my Ukinha found and presented them to me," she admitted haughtily, "on the first night of our arrival."

While Kylac had been searching the dungeons and torture chambers beneath the palace, along with other prisons within the city, seeking some sign as to the fate of the Sea Scribe—and others like him—who'd chosen to remain at Avenell rather than attempt escape. Confirming only that the Grenarr had already released any remaining captives, as a sign of good faith, prior to Denariel's imminent return. Finding no evidence or accounts as to whether Ithrimir himself had been among the survivors.

Meaning Denariel had been hiding his weapons from him all that time. Mayhap hoping his hunt for them would keep him occupied, distracted, and therefore less likely to cause harm elsewhere. Mayhap believing that, whatever damage he might cause, it would be lessened without them. Mayhap for no better reason than to take snide pleasure in the fruitlessness of his search.

Even now, she seemed uncomfortable with what amounted to a significant act of generosity. Contrition, even. For she could have kept them, and he might never have known. Or revealed them to him, and *then* kept them, in the hope that he might long suffer the sting of their loss at *her* hands.

"I'm forever in Her Majesty's debt."

"Then bear them hence. Now. Tonight. That I may be on about the business of burying my royal father in a manner more befitting. And remembering my brother beside him, though I've no remains to lay to rest. That I may carry out the last of my affairs here and take my leave without the taint of your presence still festering in my nose."

That she could return to her new home within the Ukinhan Wilds, Kylac thought, and give birth to the mutant seed sprouting within her womb.

Kylac glanced at Ledron. Tempted to refuse. To insist upon staying until able to dissuade Denariel from her chosen course. But how could he justify the effort? Who would possibly argue that he had any right or reason to continue interfering in her life's path?

"It shall please me to honor Her Majesty's wishes."

Denariel soured at the notion of pleasing him. And for a moment seemed on the verge of withdrawing her offer in full.

"Your vessel makes ready as we speak," Ledron interjected, "her hold packed with twelve weeks' provisions. An escort party will deliver you to her. You set sail upon the next king's tide, under wing of the Cardinal."

"A most gracious proposal, Your Majesty. Is this our farewell, then?"

"Fair riddance," Denariel corrected. "Should I see you again, my Ukinha will ensure your suffering is anything but brief."

Kylac studied her, the brash young princess become queen. So steadfast in her feelings toward him. So staunch, so unforgiving, for the pain he'd caused her. Would that he could say he didn't deserve it. Would that he could see in her some spark of joyfulness that he'd helped to preserve. Alas, for all his innate senses and abilities, it seemed his power to better the lives around him remained woefully inadequate.

Offended by his scrutiny, Denariel turned and stalked toward the exit, her grolls flocking soundlessly to her.

"A final question, Majesty," he blurted before he could bridle the thought.

Ledron scowled, head shaking in warning. But, to both men's surprise, she halted, rounding again, brows arched in fierce invitation.

"That ya came upon us when ya did, at the Thorncrag. Was that by chance alone?"

Of all the remaining mysteries or half-answered questions, it was the one he found most troubling. The timing of their salvation. As much as he'd tried to convince himself—before *and* after—that it was possible, it still struck him as a minor miracle the he couldn't quite attribute to happenstance.

"Did you not send the Betrayer to me with word of your strategy?" she asked incisively.

Kylac suppressed the threat of a smirk bred by his relief. The Mad Wanderer. Notwithstanding his express refusal. The true vehicle of the Fair Mother Eriyah's loving grace. "I did. Only didn't know if'n he'd found ya."

"His life I should have taken—and yours—to wager my people so recklessly. Blessed you are, all of you," she added, throwing another glare at Ledron in the bargain, "that I arrived no later than I did."

Kylac acknowledged the truth of it with another bow. By the time he'd straightened, she was at the doors, wrenching one of them open, and marching from the chamber, grolls alongside, without looking back.

Kylac found himself staring at the half-opened portal after she'd gone, listening to her departing footfalls, while awaiting some further sense of closure. Knowing not what he'd expected, but feeling cheated at the actual result.

It was Ledron who finally broke the silence gathered in her royal wake. "Come," he grumbled. "Let us see you to your ship."

"Welcome aboard," a surprisingly sober Taeg tendered, standing by at the head of the gangplank.

Kylac nodded to the gray-maned sailor. "Captain now, is it?"

"If you'll have me."

"Wasn't led to believe I had choice in the matter."

Taeg laughed. "Nor I. But if you have any reservations, I'd sooner hear them now."

Kylac had actually been pleased to learn that the former helmsman and later first mate would be captaining this voyage. Though the Whitefist had seen fit to forsake king and princess at Tetherend, it hadn't been without cause. Nor would his knowledge and skills have been of much benefit had he decided elsewise. It was for this same reason that he'd sought and managed to go mostly unseen throughout the various conflicts to follow. He was no foot soldier, and no great bowman, for that matter. Kylac had seen but glimpses of him at the Thorncrag, aiding chiefly in logistical matters like the storage and movement of provisions—as might a ship's quartermaster. For what little he might have done to acquit himself in battle, however, he'd done nothing to tarnish his reputation as a capable, levelheaded seaman. Which was precisely what Kylac required now.

"A sensible voice ya were on our last voyage," Kylac said, clasping the captain's callused hand. "Ya save a tale or two to pass the time?"

"Did I tell you before about the one-legged fishmonger's wife?"

"Not as I recall."

"Then we've yet to uncork the barrel," Taeg promised with a grin. He looked past Kylac's shoulder to give a wave at the pack of Shadowguard still standing dockside, whose task it had been to deliver him into the captain's possession. Only with the Whitefist's signal did they seem content to turn about and begin their return climb through the city.

"Shall we greet the crew, then?"

Its members formed up at the captain's whistle, dropping from ropes, slithering down the ratlines, or popping up from belowdecks like gophers in a field. Eighteen hands, Kylac counted. Plenty to crew this small, two-masted vessel. He was pleased to find a number of familiar faces among them. Men like Jaleth, Hessel, Stannon, and Vosh. None he might hail as a friend, but men he'd voyaged with before, whose strengths and weaknesses and prejudices and superstitions weren't a mystery to him—or his to them. Of some reassurance as they prepared to sail again into the volatile seas.

Warmund was the last to join the muster, ascending through a deck hatch. His enthusiastic smile stirred in Kylac a measure of surprise. "There you are. Thought maybe you'd decided not to join us."

"Already back to sea?" Kylac asked.

"Taeg offered commission as second mate. Man as me doesn't let that kind of purse slip by."

"What o' your wife, your son?"

"You ever been married? Had yourself any children?"

Kylac shook his head.

"Day comes, you'll learn it's absence breeds fondness."

Others chuckled or grunted or hailed their agreement.

"This here's our boatswain, Garreg," said Taeg. "Our chief steward, Rohlan. Yeomen Stannon and Vosh, you already know. Dommel . . ." And on down the line, calling out his new shipmates by name and position—coxswain, quartermaster, cook, carpenter, and the like.

As the introductions were completed, Kylac realized a key one to be missing.

"No first mate?" He hoped they weren't suggesting he assume the role.

"Wheelhouse," Taeg replied. "Back to it, louts," the captain said to the crew as he drew Warmund and Kylac aft.

Kylac's gaze drifted to larboard as they walked, taking in the night-cloaked slopes and half-ruined remains of Avenell. Wondering why he should feel in any way torn about leaving this land, this Sundered Isle, behind. Already, its capital city twitched with signs of new life. But new life was fragile, causing him to reflect again upon the wary truce set to hold these shores together at the seams. How long might it last? A week? A generation? Inevitably, one or more of the three factions would become greedy and seek to exceed the agreed-upon boundaries. Or an unforgivable slight would be inflicted by one against another. In either instance, all they'd achieved here would likely be undone, fallen victim again to war.

Or mayhap a fourth faction would come from beyond, seeking to claim all. Kylac knew what little sense there was in guessing the many ways in which a peace might be shattered. For now, the bleeding had been stanched, and that was all any man, at any particular time, could hope to ensure. Overcome oppression, make the present one of reason and compromise, and let whatever future could be cultivated in that environment take root.

His roving thoughts drew focus as he reached the wheelhouse, and Kylac heard the angry rustling within. Accompanied by a muttered grumbling he thought he recognized.

"Our first mate," Taeg said sourly.

The gnarled, hunch-shouldered Sea Scribe was stooped over a mound of discarded maps like a predator feasting upon a carcass. Lambskin sheaves filled the cabin, crinkled and torn and cast aside. Empty scroll tubes littered the floor and navigator's table like bones. Amid the scattered heap, the Scribe rooted like a hound for scraps. Bowed by his endeavors and a palpable weight of frustration, it was a moment before he paused, sniffing as if at a foul odor.

He spun abruptly, the wattles at his throat swinging with the movement. He looked no worse than when Kylac had left him—coarse hair spiked in all directions, sallow flesh thin and veined and spotted, sharply raked features peaked toward the center of a piercing expression. His left eye, so bright blue as to be almost iridescent, found Kylac. But only after the right, that solid black orb that looked more like a shark's eye, had fixed upon him.

"Bury me in sand," Ithrimir swore. "Our dragon hatchling, come at last."

"I's been looking for ya," Kylac replied, not quite able to contain his relief. "Feared the Stormweaver might has had ya killed."

"Stormweaver?" The Elementer snorted. "Flotsam, her and all her proud fleet. The Dragon has returned to His rest, but left the oceans in turmoil. The latter, even she could sense. And sought that I might advise her on its shifting patterns."

"Found him wading the tidal flats along the western harbor," said Taeg. "Wish now we'd have left him there."

Unkilled, by virtue of his presumed worth. Freed, when the prisons were emptied. And where had he gone? Straight to the element he knew best.

"These scrawls you brought me are useless," the Scribe growled, gesturing at the clutter around him. "No better than the ones before."

Taeg looked to his second mate.

"Each bore a name or landmark he requested," Warmund assured him.

Ithrimir was unappeased. "Blind and shallow at inception, they'll tell us nothing of a seascape remade by the Dragon's agitations."

"So we start fresh," Warmund proposed. "Clean slate."

The Elementer flashed him that withering glare. "Simple, yes? As walking a yardarm in a hurricane."

"That's why we recruited you," said Taeg, his tone of reminder. "What need have *you* of maps?"

"Precious time, they might have saved us, if pieces there were to be woven together. But none fit as they should."

The captain frowned. "Kronus hasn't even given us our destination."

"Because he doesn't yet know it. I do."

The Scribe looked to Kylac in challenge. Taeg and Warmund looked to him for deliverance.

"And where is that?" Kylac asked.

"Where I am called. Where I have need of you, as you once had need of me." The Elementer's uneven gaze managed to be both demanding and imploring. "But the waves and currents are in thrall to madness, and could carry us anywhere."

Kylac hesitated, inclined to share in his shipmates' discomfort. But where else had he to be? The only destination he'd had cause to consider was Pentania's eastern shore, where he might have hoped to harvest some new blades. Now that he'd regained *his* . . .

Warmund cleared his throat. "Perhaps we'd do better to—"

"So be it," Kylac said. Intrigued by Ithrimir's cryptic words. Moved by his intense certainty. "*Anywhere* it is."